HEROES OF A BROKEN AGE

RAMÓN TERRELL

Cover Art: Martin Maceovic
Cover art by revision: Nick Deligaris

ALSO BY RAMÓN TERRELL

PROLOGUE

"What the hell was that?" Jonstone backed away from the creature, his heart pounding in his chest.

Captain Boyd frantically waved his hand at the stunned soldier. "Get away from it!"

The scream of swords flying from scabbards mingled with those of the dying.

"We can't," the soldier panted. "We can't kill them! We can't even hurt them!" He swallowed and looked into the night sky. The moon lit the darkened city with its cold pale light. It would have been beautiful if not for the carnage filling the streets.

"Secure your nerves, soldier!" the captain ordered.

Jonstone could barely talk around his rapid, shallow breaths. He swallowed, as if that would slow his fluttering heartbeat. "It's not even human. What is it?" The young soldier stood trembling amid the cacophony of battle cries and unearthly bellows, his sword wavering in his shaking hands. The night had been quiet. The city had slept peacefully as it always had. Then the screams had begun, followed by an unearthly laughter that sent chills down his spine. The hairs on the back of the young soldier's neck rose.

Jonstone felt something bump against his foot. "Captain?" He glanced down, and nearly cried out. Captain Boyd's head lay at his feet, the man's empty stare freezing his blood. With mounting terror Jonstone wrenched his eyes from the grisly object and turned around.

A dismembered arm in each hand, the beast looked at him with a red malevolent gaze that spoke of hatred, amusement, and hunger. Its elongated wolf's muzzle yawned open, providing Jonstone a glimpse at several rows of black and yellow teeth like that of a shark.

His mouth fell open in a silent scream, his forgotten sword slipping from his grasp to clatter on the stone street. He'd been in training for over a year, now. He should have been prepared to fight. He wasn't even prepared to run.

Jonstone's own fear held him in its powerful grasp, and the monster inhaled deeply, as if drinking in his terror. He stood before his death. He knew it. He'd thought he didn't fear death, but he was wrong. Standing in front of him and slowly devouring what remained of his captain was a horror like nothing his most frightening nightmares could approach.

It stood considered him for a moment, then turned away. Once it had rounded a corner, the young soldier closed his eyes in thanks to the Gods for his stroke of good fortune. He needed to steady his nerves, pick up his sword, and find any surviving comrades who still fought. Together they might be able to … what? Drive away whatever these things were? Like he'd already just failed to do.

When Jonstone opened his eyes again, he had just enough time to see impossibly wide jaws block out the moonlight as they closed around his face.

T he sound of clanking armor and shuffling boots roused Elizander Dain from his sleep. Something was amiss. The sound of a hesitant knock on the door, followed by the hushed but exasperated demands of his most loyal captain's voice confirmed his suspicions.

A louder, more assured knock sounded at the large double doors, followed by one of them quietly opening. A thin shaft of torchlight streamed across the floor.

"This is madness! His majesty must not be disturbed from his sleep!" It was Milpheus who spoke. Of all Elizander's attendants, Milpheus was the most steadfastly concerned with protocol regarding the King. Elizander smiled through the sound of the man's somewhat annoying nasal voice. His intentions were always in the right place.

"My thanks to you Milpheus," Elizander said, having already donned all but his nightshirt, which he slipped on. I'm already awake. Please allow our good Captain Davros to enter." Milpheus cast Davros a glare. He was little more than half a man, when standing next to the large captain, but if anyone was capable of staring down his nose at you, even when looking up, it was Milpheus. After offering a deep bow to Elizander, the balding hawk-nosed little man shuffled from the room and closed the doors.

"I understand that not every rodent can be exterminated," Captain Davros said in his deep baritone voice, "but the larger ones are much easier to deal with."

Elizander chuckled. "Surely you would not have me cast out one of my most trusted attendants, Davros?"

"He is as unlikable as he is craven, my lord." Ever formal, was Davros. They had been friends since they were scarcely able to walk, but still the captain would not address him in a familiar tone unless Elizander himself spoke otherwise.

"Come, now. There is no one else present. Let us dispense with the formalities, shall we?" Elizander smiled at his gruff friend's nod. "Be easy with Milpheus, old friend. He may be occasionally difficult, but he wishes only to do what is right."

Elizander gave Davros a slap on the back, then frowned. The man was tense. "Another one?"

"Another one," the captain replied. "Found this morning."

"Who was it?" Elizander asked, dropping into a chair by the balcony doors. He indicated for Davros to join him.

"My men are canvassing the city in search of any household missing a middle-aged man."

Elizander took a deep breath. "Were they not able to identify him?"

Davros shook his head. "There wasn't enough left of him. The only reason we knew he was male was because of some of the clothes left with the remains."

"By Holy Jemanah!" Elizander swore. "What does this mean? Is there some animal about? What could possibly be finding its way past every guard post in the city?"

"I know of no animal with such understanding of sentry posts, Zander." Davros shook his head. "It makes no sense."

Elizander looked at his oldest friend. Even in the dim torchlight, the burnished silver chest plate, greaves, and vambraces of his armor positively shimmered. Davros was undoubtedly roused from his sleep with the report of another attack, and had dressed and investigated it himself before coming to report.

"This has to stop." Elizander rested his head in a hand, gazing out the glass doors of the balcony. He ran his other hand through his close cropped gray and black speckled hair. "The people grow nervous and avoid the streets at night, as well they should."

Davros grunted. "Taverns have felt a bite in business. There is also the occasional talk of fleeing to Mairland, though I've instructed my men to 'discreetly' discourage this. At least in public."

Elizander nodded. "Yes. We cannot have such talk traveling through the streets. Not openly, at least."

"Perhaps you should reconsider sending a select group to confirm our, 'standing', with our neighbors."

Elizander was shaking his head before Davros finished speaking. "I'll not spy on our neighbors of Mairland until I am convinced that Lord Mairson plots against me."

"My lord …" Davros sighed. "Zander. It is common knowledge that Lord Mairson's lands are large enough to be a kingdom. It is no secret that he would be more than happy to fashion himself a king and separate from Winsor Kingdom."

"Believe me, old friend," Elizander said, smiling, "I hear the whispers. Lord Mairson would like nothing more than to do as you've said, and end the taxation he incurs from Winsor and form his own province within New Dainland."

Elizander looked out the doors to the sprawling city, and the lush green rolling hills and forests beyond. "This seems a rather barbaric way of bringing his ambitions to fruition. What could he have to gain by sending murderers in secret to attack my people?"

"There is the talk of fleeing Winsor for Mairland," Davros reminded.

Elizander shook his head again. "No. Grisly as these murders have been, it would take something on a much larger scale to send refugees knocking on the gates of Mairland. No. I'm convinced there's something else here, and we must uncover it.

The captain's perpetual frown deepened. "Speaking of the little snake, there's more."

"More?" Elizander stifled the sinking feeling in his stomach.

Davros nodded. "A messenger from Mairland arrived just as I was entering the palace gates. He brings word from Mairson himself and would deliver his message to you immediately. We offered him lodging for the night, but he would not leave without delivering his message."

Now it was Elizander's turn to frown. "And you've kept him waiting all this time?"

"My apologies if I'm out of line, my lord. But I thought not to reward his lack of etiquette with urgency."

Elizander sighed. It was indeed disrespectful to demand an audience at this hour. The circumstances must be dire for Lord Mairson to send word with such urgency. The sinking feeling draped over King Elizander's shoulders like a pall. "Send for the courier."

2

K enyatta opened his eyes, though he lay on his back for a while longer. Endless waves of demons rolled over the lands in his mind's eye, as he recalled the dream from which he'd just escaped. Kita and Seung had been there beside him, as well as the ninja, her samurai brother, and the farstrider.

He wanted to close his eyes again but sat up instead, wary that the dream awaited him if he did. *Not a dream at all, but what, then? Premonition?* Kenyatta climbed out of bed and went to the closet. After donning his tunic and breeches, he resisted the urge to strap on his sword. He was supposed to be working the farmland, after all, not going off to battle. Still, that dream …

Kenyatta stepped outside onto the porch of Mr. and Mrs. Kyung's home and scanned the grounds looking for, what? A demon lurking near the barn? A shadow detaching itself to come for him? He looked over his shoulder at the sound of creaking floorboards to see Mr. Kyung step into the doorway.

"You look like a man looking farther away than those fields," he said. "Time for another visit?"

"Yes, sir," Kenyatta replied. "Seung will come tomorrow."

The older man gave him a playful slap on the arm. "Try not to daydream too hard about her and fall into a creek, eh?"

Kenyatta chuckled. "Yeah man."

Mr. Kyung threw his head back and laughed, then hit him on the arm again. "Ya … MON! You learn my language pretty good. Maybe you teach me more of yours."

"That would be something," Kenyatta replied, reverting back to the common tongue of the land. He wondered what it would sound like, Mr. Kyung speaking the common western tongue in the manner of his people.

Thinking of his beloved and lost homeland of Jamaica darkened his thoughts, but he kept up his smile.

Mr. Kyung's smile faded as he regarded him. "You warrior types carry so much with you that any random thing sparks memories best forgotten." This time he poked Kenyatta in the arm with a bony finger. "You be careful not to let the darkness of the past swallow you."

"I will try." Kenyatta smiled and bowed his head, a few locks falling over his face.

Mr. Kyung turned away. "You make sure you do, young man. Too much life you have left to live, carrying so much weight on your back. He waved a hand at the fields. You've done plenty of work around here to pay for your room and board, but don't let me stop you from doing more."

Kenyatta laughed at that. "Yes sir."

He went around the side of the house toward the barn and grabbed an axe. Mr. Kyung insisted on tending the few animals they had, and since Kenyatta had cut the high grass and any odd errands the kind couple had needed done, he found himself looking for something to do. Winter was still a few months away, so now was the best time to start collecting firewood.

Seung wouldn't approve, of course, but Mr. and Mrs. Kyung had been generous in letting him stay in exchange for working around their property. Elves didn't approve of cutting down trees, but if the Kyung's wanted firewood, Kenyatta would cut firewood.

Elves.

He shook his head at the thought of it. In a world of Cerberus, other monsters out of legend, and even demons, elves had never crossed his mind. What other beings shared this world with humans? And did they share similar feelings toward his species?

Kenyatta thought of what he'd learned of the elves from Seung. More elf than human yet raised among the latter, Seung herself had just begun her education on the other part of her ancestry. One thing she'd made clear; elves didn't particularly care for humans, and even though she was more elf than human, her welcome among them had been tepid at best.

Barely a hundred yards from the barn, Kenyatta felt a comforting presence so familiar and so close, it may as well be a part of himself. He stopped and didn't even try to hold back the big grin across his face. "Watcha wan stalkin' me from behind, sis?"

8

"Not so hard wit me brother daydreamin' 'bout his girliefriend," Taliah answered.

Kenyatta turned to see his older sister standing with a hand on her hip with a knowing smirk on her face. He laughed and dropped his axe, hurrying over to sweep her up in a crushing hug.

"Urgh, get off wit yer stinkin' man-smell!"

Kenyatta made to rub his chin on her and she beat at him till he dropped her. Taliah glared at him through her laughter, and for a time, both just enjoyed the moment.

"You probably guess why I came to find you," Taliah said.

Kenyatta sobered up at the seriousness in her voice. He looked into her eyes and heaved a great sigh. "Yeah man. Last night—"

"You had a dream, and Kita and the others who battled alongside you were there," Taliah finished for him.

All Kenyatta could do was nod.

Taliah returned the gesture. "We don't have a lot of time, Ken. I've already been to see Kita. We're going back to meet him in his home in Cebu, but first we need to collect ya girliefriend." She beaconed him to come stand next to her.

"Wouldn't it have been quicker to just bring him here?" Kenyatta moved to stand behind her, and Taliah closed her eyes.

"Two humans will cause enough uproar. Best not push our luck."

Kenyatta watched from the corner of his eye as his sister's form took on a golden glow that engulfed the world in a flash of light.

* * *

Seung opened her eyes and realized, to her confusion, that she had actually slept. Since the day she had fully taken the reverie for the first time, Seung had come to think of actual human sleep as something of a comatose experience. She couldn't remember the last time she'd fallen into human sleep, yet somehow she'd fallen out of the reverie into it.

She stared at the far wall of her room seeing as though a mural of her recent past had been painted on it. Years of covering her "deformed" ears only to later discover her heritage. Her adventures outside her childhood home of Kyu. The tidal wave, the lava leech, the dragon named Khairon.

Kenyatta.

No doubt the islander had finished his morning rituals and was now helping tend the fields. Perhaps she could visit him a day early and surprise him.

Thinking about Kenyatta drew Seung's wandering mind back to the dream that wasn't a dream. She'd need to talk to DaunyaSai about that—

"Kiluriel!"

Seung blinked at the urgency of Immendiel Mai'lienar's voice. Even though she'd grown accustomed to the *whisper,* it still startled her on occasion to hear words enter her ears and into her mind in such a way.

"What is it?" Seung *whispered* back.

"Come now. I'm above your home. Let no one see you. Hurry!"

Without another word, Seung poked her head out the door. Seeing no one about, she made her way around to the back of her home and jumped, hopping from branch to branch. Never had she imagined she could be capable of such a thing, but it seemed as though her time here in Yathienel had awoken a new language that her body spoke naturally. It was as though it had always been this way. Yathienel was intoxicating!

In short order she found the elven tracker perched on a branch high above. "This must be serious for you to be this high up. What's wrong?"

"Come," was the only response. Seung had no time to speak, for it took all her concentration to keep up with the swift elf as she darted silently from branch to branch with a skill not many in The Wood could equal. In short order they were squatting high in the trees, looking down at two figures staring in the direction of The Wood. Seung's heart skipped a beat when recognized one of them. Kenyatta? And the woman with him could be no one but his sister! Why were they here? *How* were they here? Seung stifled her alarm and tried to remain passive. "All this hurry for two humans?"

Immendiel shook her head impatiently. "There's no time for this, girl. Do not pretend that man is not the one who holds your heart."

He may have held her heart, but right now it was pounding in her chest. "This is a problem, no doubt."

"That is the easy of it," Immendiel replied. "The bigger issue is why he and that woman are right there, looking directly at our home as though they know it's here."

Seung felt her legs weaken under the other elf's suspicious gaze. Not this. Not now. "You have my word that I have not told him where our home lies. I have not spoken to him of the location of Yathienel!"

"And yet, there they stand."

"I know not how or why they're here, but he has told me about his sister. From his words, my guess is that she is a Daunya Master."

"And that would explain their presence?" Immendiel replied.

"It's the only explanation I can think of." Seung fought to slow her rapidly beating heart. "I would never betray Yathienel or The Lady Seiyun. You are my family. Why would I betray you?"

"Why indeed," came the cryptic response.

Seung started to speak several times and stopped. "There is only one way to find out. We can't let them stand down there indefinitely."

Immendiel arched an eyebrow. "Oh?"

Seung frowned at the tracker. "They obviously know what is beyond these bordering woods. The enchantment to befuddle and deter humans seems to have no effect on them. To my eyes, the woman somehow knows, and Kenyatta has told her that they should not enter."

At the mention of the islander's name, Immendiel looked back to the two figures below with narrowed eyes. *"Bresha nosimde mala isala, quyo."* The elf shook her head and dropped from the branch.

Seung's cheeks colored. Despite having never heard the phrase before, she understood it. 'Stupidity is born in the love of the young.' She took a deep breath and followed.

3

General Zhang Da stood over what remained of the corpse. A grisly sight, and one of several that were becoming more frequent. Who or what could have done this to a person? Dismemberment was one thing, but this was something wholly gruesome.

He absently tightened his grip on his spear. The long-shafted weapon ended with a crescent moon-shaped blade on one end, and a straight, sharp end on the other. A deadly heirloom, passed down from his legendary ancestor till finally finding its way into his powerful grasp.

A soldier came beside him and bowed low. "General Zhang Da, no one in the vicinity has seen anything. None have heard a sound."

Zhang Da grunted. Each murder had been the same. Gruesome and savage, and without a single witness. His first thought had been assassins, but he'd quickly dismissed that idea. One sent assassins to murder prominent figures, leaders. And they tended to be quick and efficient. This person, and every one prior, had been regular citizens whose deaths—while tragic— would not have a large scale consequence.

And the brutality.

He clutched his spear even tighter. "Hmph."

The soldier waited silently for instructions. It was times like this when Zhang Da would like more than anything to flee the lives of men and make his own life in the hills, away from the blood and war.

After the End of Technology, China had transitioned into a feudal land once more. The once singular ruling government had shattered, and the shards had landed across the countries and grown into what was now Ba Guo, the Eight Kingdoms.

In comparison to the ancient histories, the conflicts had not lasted nearly as long, for the people had wanted, *demanded*, peace. Before the lands could further descend into the chaos that seemed inevitable, Zhuge Ming, descendant of Zhuge Liang, emerged. Like his revered ancestor, Zhuge Ming had been an unparalleled strategist and had advised Liu Deng, the emperor of the land once again known as Shu Han. Under his guidance, Liu Deng had brought relative peace back to the land of Ba Guo. But now this.

Zhang Da narrowed his eyes at the grisly scene. *Never in our history has anything like this happened. What times come for us?* "Send a messenger to Emperor Liu Xiang," he ordered. "I would speak with him at his pleasure, but convey the urgency of the matter."

"Sir!" the soldier gave a precise bow and departed. Zhang Da inclined his head in return. Unlike his legendary—and often brutal—ancestor, Zhang Da treated his soldiers with kindness. He was firm. Some would even call him hard, but he was fair, and he was respectful of his soldiers.

Zhang Da sighed. The Three Brothers and the legendary strategist. Zhang Da was versed in history, especially the history prior to the Age of Technology. Who would have thought that the hermit Zhuge Liang had actually fathered a child and secured a line that would extend centuries later? And here they all were: Zhang Da, descendant of Zhang Fei. Liu Xiang, descendant of Liu Bei. Guan Xi, descendant of Guan Gong, and Zhuge Xiaoyin, descendant of Zhuge Liang. The descendants of the Three Sworn Brothers and the Strategist, separated by fewer than a hundred miles in any direction. Surely the fates had foreseen troubles to come, for what other reason would the four of them have been born in the same time and proximity? The general thought it more than coincidence that all of them happened to be more versed and practiced in the combat and strategy than any previous generation, save their legendary ancestors.

Zhang Da's own father had been a calligraphy instructor. Not surprising, as his family line had all been possessed of some above average skill at the art. But Zhang Da had immediately taken to the spear. Liu Xiang had taken to the straight swords, Guan Xi was the fiercest warrior in her province, and Zhuge Xiaoyin was a master strategist coveted by all of the kingdoms of Ba Guo.

Immersed in his thoughts, Zhang Da found himself standing before the steps of Shu Han palace. He didn't have to wait long, for it was common knowledge that General Zhang Da and Emperor Liu Xiang were as close as brothers. They would follow the proper protocol, of course, but any word from Da would be met in a timely manner by Xiang. More fodder for whispers about the times to come.

Zhang Da grunted under his breath. Not since the time of the Three Kingdoms, had the families of Zhang, Liu, and Guan, been so close, and superstitious though the general populace might be, most knew the history as well.

A messenger came scurrying down to find the general waiting at the base of the steps. He offered a trembling low bow. "My apologies for your wait, General. I was just given the order to present you—"

"Be at ease," Zhang interrupted. He indicated for the man to escort him. Once inside, the messenger saw him to one of Emperor Xiang's personal attendants, who led him to Xiang's private patio. After his lavish introduction —much to Zhang's exasperation—he stepped out onto the large patio to join his childhood friend. Liu Xiang stood on the patio with his hands clasped behind his back, gazing at the gardens beyond.

"Xiao Fu," the emperor said in his soft voice. "Please bring tea for myself and my honored guest."

"It will be brought directly, your majesty." The attendant bowed low and departed.

Zhang Da waited till the door was closed. "Do you ever tire of the grand titles and reverence?"

"The man or woman who comes to enjoy power should immediately divorce themselves from it, lest their soul be consumed by it." Liu Xiang turned to face the general. His features were somewhat delicate, but with a hint of a hard edge. His hands, as calloused as Zhang's, were thick from a form of strike training known as Heavy Hands. Nearly as tall as Zhang Da himself, the emperor towered over most men, his solid yet slim frame contrasting with Da's more heavily muscled body.

"I doubt your urgency involves a philosophical discussion about the nature of power and the people who wield it," Xiang continued.

Zhang Da started to speak, then stopped at the sound of three gentle knocks on the patio door. A servant entered and arranged a tray of tea, serving two small cups and departing without a sound. The door closed once again, Zhang leveled his gaze on Xiang.

Liu Xiang read the general's face and sighed. "There has been another one."

"Worse than the last," Zhang confirmed. "The attacks are growing more frequent, as you know from my reports. Something is brewing and we must extinguish the fire beneath it before the entire kingdom is engulfed."

"Of course, my friend. But how? I've increased the city guard three times. No matter how many patrols are posted, the attacks still happen. I've ordered all to remain in their homes after dark, and still someone ventures out. The once safe streets of my beloved city are now a fearsome place after sunset."

Zhang Da's features darkened. "Perhaps the accident involving that farm was not so easily forgiven as we thought?"

Liu Xiang frowned at the reminder. "I'd like to think that accidental fire wouldn't have led to this."

"Emperor Qian is slow to forgive and even slower to forget," Zhang replied.

"That fire had been an accident and the drunken soldiers involved were punished accordingly," Liu Xiang said.

"They destroyed acres of land and burned down a farmer's barn." Zhang shrugged. "Qian was incensed."

Liu Xian's brow creased into a deep frown. "If Qian still holds this against me, there is more to this situation. I had the farmer's crops replanted, his home rebuilt, all of his losses replaced. What more could I have done?"

"Nothing, in my mind," Zhang answered. "But we both know the temperament of Qian."

Xian let out a heavy sigh. "Indeed. But I still struggle to believe even Qian would result to acts this extreme."

Zhang grunted. "Perhaps we will not openly suspect him, but we shouldn't rule him out, either."

Xiang nodded. "I struggle to find logic in these attacks, my friend. Rash and temperamental though he may be, I do not believe Qian Hua would respond in such a cowardly way. This reeks of provocation."

"You sound like the lady Zhuge Xiaoyin," Da replied, only half teasing.

Liu Xiang grinned. "I would gladly accept that compliment, were there even a shred of truth to it. We must solve this gruesome riddle before it spreads to the lands of shorter tempers and swift actors. The world needs no more warlords, my friend."

Zhang crossed his arms and looked out beyond the balcony, wading back into the discomfort of his memory. "And bringing our discussion back to the current dilemma?"

"Try to find some semblance of a pattern," Xiang replied. "Anything." He held up a hand, forestalling the coming argument. "I know you have done this already, but we must exhaust every avenue."

Zhang watched him turn away, then stop, as he seemed to come to a decision.

"I'm of a mind that time is closing in on us, Da. You spoke of the Strategist, and indeed she has come to mind frequently since more of these murders have happened. I've a feeling more is at play here than we understand. It's time to enlist her counsel. Send messengers to the lord of the land of Guan that I would speak with Guan Xi. And send messengers to seek out Xiaoyin in the mountains."

Zhang Da raised his eyebrows at that. "You would openly call us all together?" Zhang Da didn't know whether to be excited or alarmed. "Should we not meet in secret, my lord? From all over the eight kingdoms people call us the Three Sworn and the Strategist. The whispers will only grow louder that a trying age is upon us."

"They will, yes. And perhaps the time has arrived that we can no longer deny what we are." Xiang went back to the balcony rail and rested his hands on the smooth worked stone.

"Whether the people know of our meeting or not, they will suspect, and they will wait. It may well be true that the renewed relations between our families are a sign. What that sign is, we don't yet know, but I would not sit and wait, speculating alone while some enemy sews chaos. Call to Guan Xi and Zhuge Xiaoyin, and let the people take comfort, not fear, that there will indeed be a council of The Three Sworn and The Strategist."

4

A lthough he'd long mastered the art of ignoring the sound of Milpheus's scuttling steps beside him, Elizander Dain found that the sliding and scraping penetrated his troubled thoughts. He glanced sidelong at his attendant, who shuffled his burden of rolled up parchments just enough to adjust the spectacles at the tip of his nose.

Dain glanced at the scrolls and was reminded of his education about the Age of Technology when people used flat materials called paper, created from trees. They were apparently more easily stacked and much lighter, but also more fragile. How he wished they had the use of such materials now. How much easier would it have been to manage?

He turned his attention back to the impending meeting with the minister of the Church of Jemanah, and he repressed a snarl. Just the thought of meeting with the opportunistic Brother Dinman dampened Elizander's day. Where something monumental occurred, good or ill, Brother Dinman would be there to proclaim that it was the will of the Jemanahian Gods. The True Gods. Elizander had to step carefully with that one, for he carried in his sleeves the peoples' fears of angering the Gods. No king could stand beside the anger of a God.

Dain was not a man of the cloth, and he didn't pretend to know the will of the Gods, but he did know manipulation when he saw it. The church held power to rival the state, and if it came to blows, the people, his blessed, beloved people would suffer for it. Sure, some would see things for what they were, but homes and families would be divided, and beliefs held against one another. It had happened throughout human history, and Elizander Dain would not see it happen again in his lands.

"My lord? Do you not agree?"

Elizander blinked at the sound of Milpheus's nasal voice. "Hm?"

"The courier, my lord," the attendant said, glancing at him. "Should she be given leave to depart for Mairland?"

"Mmph. If we must," Elizander agreed.

"You've detained the courier as your personal guest for as long as possible before arousing suspicion, my lord," Milpheus said. "I understand your reluctance to let her leave before you understand everything, but if too much time elapses, the situation could become … strained."

"I know, Milpheus. I …" he snapped his fingers. "You are indeed right, of course."

Milpheus eyed him. "Of course."

"How terrible my manners have been," Elizander declared. "I will meet with her at once. Send word to Brother Dinman that, to my regret, I will be late in meeting with him. Some urgent matters have arisen that I must attend to directly."

Milpheus's conspiratorial smirk flashed so quickly it might have never been. "Of course, my lord. You are only one man, and matters of state *must* be attended to. I'm sure our good Brother Dinman would understand. After all, his very church sits on the land of New Dainland, does it not?"

Elizander spared the man a brief smirk of his own. That nasal voice might be a bit annoying, but Milpheus was a capable and loyal attendant who handled matters with efficiency and effectiveness. "I'm sure if our good monk does not understand, you will find a creative way to remind him."

"Of course, my lord." The attendant hurried down a side corridor to a— no doubt—impatiently waiting Brother Dinman. Now accompanied only by his personal guard, Elizander Dain swept through the corridors to the upper levels of the guest quarters. Along the way, he stopped to address a boy trying to look as though he was not loitering near the maid quarters. "You, young man," he called to the boy. "The boy snapped to attention so rigidly Elizander thought his spine might crack. "Easy, son. Don't go so hard on your back or you will end learning the way of a walking cane instead of a sword." The boy relaxed, but only a bit, fear dancing in his eyes. Elizander could practically see his guards' amusement behind him.

"How may I be of service, my lord?" the boy said, dropping to one knee.

"I'm afraid I must interrupt your wait for whatever love interest lurks behind that door," he said, ignoring the boy's flushing cheeks, "and send you to Captain Davros. Have him meet me in the guest quarters, he will know which one."

"It is my honor, my lord!" The boy stood at attention, right fist over his heart, then hurried away.

Dain continued on, taking the steps two at a time until he found the quarters of the Mairland courier. He gave a polite knock and waited.

"Yes?" came the hesitant response. "Come in."

With a boyish smile, Elizander instructed his personal guard to remain outside the door, and entered. Upon seeing the King of Winsor in her room, the courier immediately dropped to one knee, staring at the floor in front of her foot. "My most humble apologies, my lord!" she said. "I'd thought it was a servant, or messenger. Surely the King need not knock in his own kingdom!"

Elizander closed the door behind him. "I find every man and woman, whether farmer, courier, or king, to be deserving of their own privacy. You've traveled quite a distance to my home and are my guest. I fear I have held you here far too long and thought to personally come and see you on your way with well wishes."

"My lord! You do me a great honor! Far more than I deserve, as a simple courier."

"And without a simple courier, how would good Lord Mairson's message have reached me? And how would my message reach him? May I?" Dain indicated a chair, and the courier, nearly horrified at the king having to ask to sit, hurriedly agreed. "And please, rise. Surely that right knee of yours must be getting stiff." Elizander indicated the chair across from him. "Sit with me a moment."

"If it pleases my lord."

"It does," Dain replied. Even standing, she barely stood eye level with Elizander. Short and slight of build; the perfect size for a courier. Her young round face looked to have passed no more than fifteen to seventeen summers. He sat for a time, studying the bright blue eyes that would not meet his. A knock came at the door, and shortly after, Davros entered.

"I don't believe you have had the pleasure of meeting my good Captain Davros Naishere," Elizander said.

She stood and bowed to Davros. "It is an honor, Captain."

Davros responded with a polite nod, then arched an eyebrow at Elizander.

"Please, take your seat," Elizander said to the young lady.

She sat stiffly in her chair, hands gripping either side.

"You're going to break your fingers if you grip that chair any tighter, girl," Davros said.

The courier made a great effort to appear more relaxed. "Have I made some transgression, my lord?"

Elizander figured he'd better get to this quickly before the girl's nerves got the better of her. "Not at all Miss … I don't think I've had the pleasure of your name?"

"Deana, my lord. Deana Willes, daughter to Morland and Milly Willes."

"And a fine daughter Morland and Milly Willes have raised," Elizander replied. "Send them my regards." The girl beamed, and Davros arched his eyebrow even higher. "I wanted to speak with you personally about the events in Mairland. I understand your home has been suffering grisly attacks that have gone unsolved. The murderer or murderers have not been captured."

"Yes, my lord," the girl replied. "Many are afraid to leave their homes at night, and some even fear that their homes are not even safe. Some say that people are being lured out and then killed. No one has seen a thing, and people are afraid." Elizander nodded through the familiar story. "Murders are not uncommon in any city, my lord, but the nature of these killings suggest something very disturbing, and my Lord Mairson thought to send word and warning."

And a set of eyes and ears, no doubt, Elizander thought. "I see. And Lord Mairson sent you with news of these happenings and to inquire about the welfare of Winsor?"

"It is not my place to know my Lord Mairson's reasons for dispatching me here, but that would be my guess, my lord."

Davros looked pointedly at Elizander, who nodded.

"Tell me, young lady," the big man said. Elizander repressed a grin at hearing his friend's baritone voice attempt to soothe. "Have there been many attacks? The report you delivered lacked some detail, and we would share information that can benefit us all. If the city guard is activated, that may drive the murderer from one place to another."

"From Mairland to New Dainland," Deana said, catching on. "No, my lord. The city guard has been increased, but not fully activated. My Lord Mairson wishes to make the murderer wary, but not chase him away. He believes that a more present guard may force the killer or killers to hesitate and eventually make a mistake."

Elizander didn't know if this girl was relaying information Mairson himself had planted, or if she was willingly speaking of the happenings in her homeland. Either way, Mairson thought Dain a fool, or the man himself had lost his senses.

He reached into a pocket and produced a letter bearing the seal of House Dain. "This is my reply, Deana Willes. If Mairland comes to need our aid, Winsor will stand with him."

"My lord is most generous."

Dain stood, the girl rising with him. "We must all be united in this most serious situation. These kinds of attacks have no precedence. Entire civilizations have crumbled under the weight of a fire that grew from just a kindling.

"Take care on your travels, Deana, daughter of Morland and Milly Willes. I'll not have you meeting some ill fate traveling from my kingdom to your home." He made for the door. "I will see that you are well provisioned. Your horse has been well cared for and awaits your return."

That brought a smile to the girl's face. Couriers seemed to love their horses more than people. He supposed it was understandable, given the job both human and animal shared.

"My lord is kind." Deana hesitated. "My ... my lord..." she stammered, just as Davros was reaching for the door.

With his back to her, Elizander stopped and smiled. He turned, planting a polite but curious look on his face. "Yes?"

"Please, my lord," she glanced from one man to the other. "I would speak more, but I fear I shouldn't."

"I assure you, Deana Willes, what you speak here will only be between you, myself, and my most trusted captain, here. What have you?"

"Thank you, my lord." She sat down heavily in her chair, Elizander and Davros reclaiming their own. "There have been many attacks. The city guard has not been fully mobilized, but they are near enough to it. The attacks on the citizens have been vicious but senseless. My Lord Mairson becomes anxious, and looks to the neighboring lands with a suspicious eye." Elizander raised his eyebrows in feigned surprise.

"Has there been any evidence that would suggest any of these neighboring lands to have orchestrated such strange and random killings?"

"None that any of the common people know of, my lord." The girl responded. She wrung her hands and looked at her feet. "Many people do not know what our lord does, or what he suspects. Mostly, they wait and hope he will find the killers, or find a way to stop them."

"But since you, being a courier, are closer to the information in House Mairson, you fear his actions are rash?"

"I'm a simple courier, my lord," Deana replied nervously.

Elizander reached over and placed a hand on her shoulder and gave it a comforting squeeze. "You needn't worry about speaking in confidence with us," Deana. "You have acted wisely."

"Thank you, my lord. I would never, *ever* question my lord Mairson's judgement or his wisdom. It's just that I have family in Windsor, and sometimes my lord Mairson can act ... quickly, about things. I fear there is something more going on. The murders are all happening to common folk. I, I think ..." She hesitated, still looking at her feet.

"What is it, Deana," Davros said. "You may speak candidly."

"You would think me a foolish common girl for what I will say, but I must." She clasped her hands in her lap. "I ... saw something."

Elizander sat a little straighter in his chair. "You saw, something? What something did you see, Deana. This is very important, and why did you not tell Lord Mairson?"

"He would have surely been angered by my wasting his time with this, but my Lord Dain seems so willing to listen and help. No offense to my Lord Mairson."

"Of course," Dain replied, nodding politely. "What did you see?" Next to him, Davros had leaned forward, resting his elbows on his knees, staring intently at the girl. She shrank a bit from that gaze, but continued.

"I ... I saw something squatting over a dead person. It was..." She closed her eyes and took a deep breath. "It was the worst kind of horror I've ever seen. It was eating someone! And it was big, at least eight feet tall. It had spikes on its back and arms as long as a man's body."

"Are you sure you didn't see a large animal after it had attacked a person, girl?" Davros asked.

The girl shook her head emphatically. "I cannot say I have seen every animal in the world, my lord Captain, but whatever that thing was, it stood on two legs and ate with clawed hands. The sounds ..." she gulped, the blood draining from her face. "The tearing and chewing sounds! I couldn't sleep for days, and when I did, the nightmares!" She hugged her knees up to her chest, tears streaming down her cheeks. "My mother and father always taught me to be levelheaded, to see things for what they are and not give in to superstitions and gossip."

She looked up into Elizander's eyes, and her gaze was steady and focused. "My lord, what I saw looked like it came from hell itself. I swear to you now, with Holy Jemanah and all of the Gods as my witnesses, that what I saw was no beast, no monster that roams the wild lands. This thing did not belong here. It smelled wrong. It felt wrong, like the air, the *space* around it was perverted by its presence." Her gaze dropped to the floor in embarrassment. "My lord must think I'm a foolish, superstitious farm girl."

Elizander didn't realize he'd been staring. He glanced at Davros. The captain was composed, but he had known the man long enough to see that he, too, had been caught off guard by the strange account. "I must admit, Deana, that this tale of yours is difficult to accept. But I also will not discredit it out of hand. The murders have been disturbingly gruesome. Perhaps it is some species of monster that we have not previously encountered." He stood, the others rising with him once again.

"As I have said," he told the nervous courier, "this conversation stays within these walls, you have my word. "Rest as long as you need, Deana. Your needs will be met, and when you are ready to return home, your horse will be saddled and ready."

"My lord is most kind. Thank you."

Elizander smiled, Davros nodded, and they left.

"What in the name of the Gods do you make of that?" Davros whispered as they descended the spiraling steps.

"I wish I knew, old friend," Elizander replied.

"Surely you don't believe such a wild tale of a hell beast silently terrorizing the streets?"

"It sounds absurd," Elizander replied. They walked in silence for a time, the personal guard following at a discrete distance. "Tell me this, Davros. Did you see any lie in her eyes? Any hint that she may have been speaking anything but the truth?"

"In her eyes I saw the truth as she knew it," Davros replied. "That, and the terror the memory produced. Whatever she saw, she truly thought it was some sort of spawn of the hells."

Elizander nodded.

Davos shrugged. "Sometimes, when a person sees something frightening, their mind embellishes the event and contaminates the memory. "Could be that she saw a large and unfamiliar animal of some kind, and later her mind conjured images of some demonic creature."

"Yes, but there is one thing that I do find interesting."

"Which is?"

Elizander frowned. "She said that the thing felt wrong. Like the space around it was tainted. What do you make of that?"

The captain shrugged again. "To that, I am at a loss."

"A series of savage, gruesome murders happen here and in Mairland. No killer has been found despite the best efforts of you and your command, and that of Mairland. No witnesses to any of the murders until finally, a courier confesses to seeing what she thinks was a demon, devouring its latest kill. We have no leads, no evidence at all but the extraordinary account from this girl, who is smart enough not to have gone to Lord Mairson with such a tale."

Davros snorted. "That fact alone gives her at least a shred of credibility with me. She would have been lucky not to have been publicly disciplined for wasting his time."

Elizander nodded. "There is an explanation for this, old friend. We simply must find it."

"And unfortunately," Davros replied, "what is simple is rarely easy."

Again, Elizander Dain nodded.

5

"There is nowhere you can hide from me, Iel." Brit smirked at the scrying mirror, though his thoughts lay much farther away. The Ilanyan had moved Takashaniel to another remote location, in the lands of Nomar this time.

He smirked. Time fast approached when he would loose the demonic horde he had gathered and tear down Takashaniel. Once that was done, he would be free to draw upon the endless well of creatures of the abyss to bring under his command.

For now, he was forced to summon the vile things piecemeal, a few at a time and with great effort. And he could only send them so far. Since he was the anchor to which they were tethered to this world, if a fiend ventured too far away they would be forced to return to him, or the connection would fail and the demon would be sent back to the abyss.

He wondered where Zreal had gone. Four years ago he had sent Zreal along with the zitarian, Zshegaza, to battle those five humans fighting for the Tower of Balance. Zshegaza was a cunning one, and Brit suspected she had somehow manipulated Zreal into one of her schemes. It hardly mattered. He would deal with them eventually.

For now, though, Takashaniel.

And Kabriza. That thing had been a pain in Brit's side since first he had summoned it. Unfortunately, it was part of the deal. Grala, lord of the quentranzi, agreed to provide an unending supply of fiends to Brit on the condition that his general, Kabriza, oversee things. It was nonsense, of course.

Demons didn't oversee anything. The existed to wreak havoc and devastation. Brit knew it, Kabriza knew it, and Grala certainly knew it. And they knew he was aware of their intentions. Only a fool would assume loyalty from a demon.

A sense of wrongness slowly permeated the area, like a wave of perversion floating through the air and darkening the space where he stood. "What is it, Kabriza?" Brit said, not bothering to turn and face the newly arrived demon general.

"My lord has a sizable force of quentranzi to command. My lord is the axis upon which we unholy ones exist in this realm. My lord surely must be ready for the attack upon the hated Takashaniel. My lord surely grows impatient to strike a mighty blow and extinguish the beacon of light that the weaklings of this world look to for hope. My lord—"

"Enough, Kabriza," Brit drawled. He could practically see the demon's disgusting grin. If Brit let the baiting and mocking get to him and he lost his hold for even a moment, Kabriza would rend him into an indistinguishable bloody mess. Not that it would be so easy, but still, Brit had no desire to test himself against this fiend, second only to Grala himself. "Have you come here only to tell me of that which I am already aware?"

The quentranzi general moved beside him, a bold act. It was nearly four feet taller than Brit's eight. "What is this day's entertainment, my lord?" the demon rumbled.

Brit didn't bother to acknowledge its proximity. "Not your concern. Have you succeeded in bringing your forces into some semblance of organization?"

"Surely there is no need for such verbal abuse, my great lord," the demon replied. "I seek only to provide companionship and witty conversation in addition to my services as—" the demon gasped and dropped to its knees. After a few heartbeats, it looked up into Brit's eyes and let out a low growl.

"You're pushing your luck, demon," Brit said, still staring at the scrying mirror. "I did not summon you here to offer taunts and disrespect. You *will* obey me or I will send you back to your master in the most painful manner my imagination can conjure. Is there any part of your filthy twisted mind that is unclear about this?"

"Quite clear," Kabriza hissed.

Brit held the demon bent to his will a bit longer, then released it.

Kabriza rose and for a time, both stood silently staring at the scrying mirror and the image of the collecting abysmal hoards. Finally, the demon general turned and stalked from the room. "Your horde of quentranzi await your command," Kabriza said before exiting. "You'll find them more capable than the last. This time, Takashaniel will fall and you may summon a force the size of your choosing. Grala is pleased."

"I'm sure he is," Brit replied. When he said no more, Kabriza growled again and departed. Brit stood watching the mirror. Kabriza would comply for a time, the pain of Brit's will twisting its insides would keep it in line for a while. He needed only keep the powerful fiend in check long enough to destroy Takashaniel, that he may feed on enough of the earth's resources to exert his will over every demon in his service without effort.

Brit's features tightened at that last thought. He didn't have perfect control of the demon general, hence Kabriza's secret summoning of those twin demons to this world without his aid. That was troubling, but not much of a concern. He also knew that Kabriza sought to bring Grala to this world, and Brit could not let that happen. If there was one beast, one fiend in all the abyss Brit did not want to deal with, it was that one. He knew not how powerful Grala was, but he had an idea. He didn't like the prospects of such an encounter.

Brit continued to look into the mirror. Two figures stood at the base of an impressively tall tower that shimmered in the sunlight. A smile crept across his dark face. It was all so futile. They were all dead. They just didn't know it yet.

* * *

"I should not have brought the tower here," Iel said, and not for the first time. He clasped his hands together as he gazed out at the rolling green tree-dotted grasslands without seeing any of it.

"What other place would you have gone?" Mira asked. "No matter your choice, the drek will find us, and the demons will come."

Iel responded with barely audible sigh. She was right, of course. Whether desert or forest or open planes, the drek would have found them, and the land would be sickened once the whole of Brit's demonic force descended. It was just a matter of time.

"Try not to worry yourself too much," Mira said. "The outcome will be as it was four years ago, but this time we will find him."

Iel looked at the young woman; a child, to his eyes, yet she had grown so much since the defense of Takashaniel, those years ago.

"I have connected with the earth again. The wild earth magic will come to our aid once more. When the time comes, the Rizanti will appear. I'm unsure where the centaurs stand, as I have not been able to reach them, and the brunts have also been impossible to contact. My hope is that they are all still alive."

"They are alive, Master Guardian," Mira answered with confidence. "Grimhammer is a strong and capable leader, and Grit and the brunts would not easily fall. I believe we are all separated, but they, as we, endure."

Iel smiled at her. "And so the student becomes the teacher."

Mira's cheeks colored and she looked away. I've learned what you've taught me."

"You make me proud. And the Daunyans have blessed you with incredible abilities. When the time comes, you will be a very capable guardian."

"I still have much to learn," Mira said.

"Not as much as you believe, Mira. You will be ready." Iel closed his eyes for a moment. "Our friend Siti approaches."

As if his words were her introduction, the air in front of them started to shimmer and swirl as individual sparks of energy appeared and coalesced into a female humanoid form.

The transparent blue female stood before them, long hair-like tendrils waving from her delicate head. Her white pupils looked from Iel to Mira and back. The Ilanyan smiled at the palpable kindness radiating from her.

"Guardian Iel, Apprentice Mira, my friends." The magical being's voice radiated a gentle echo like that of a sighing breeze traveling from the depths of glacier. "It has been long since we've spoken."

Iel bowed. "Indeed, Siti, my friend. I only wish we could be here under more desirable circumstances."

"It shall be as it is," Siti replied. "The Rizanti wait, as do I. You know that our time will be limited?"

"Of course, my dear friend," Iel said. "The taint must be held back, and you will meet that challenge even after you have so graciously aided us here."

"It is the will of the Daunyans," Siti replied as she faded from sight.

"A horde of the most powerful demons of the abyss, led by the second most powerful of their kind, summoned by a life sapping drek." Mira shook her head. "Daunyans help us."

Iel once again gazed out into the fields, his thought speeding far beyond them. "They will."

6

Kenyatta didn't know what to make of Seung's uncharacteristically conservative body language. It seemed like a year since they'd last seen each other. He'd wanted to wrap her in a crushing hug the moment she'd come out of the woods. But she'd held out a hand to stop him. It felt like he'd run into a wall of ice.

"How have you come to be here?" Seung asked, and Kenyatta thought he heard a flicker of desperation in her harsh tone. "This place is not for humans."

Since he knew little about why they were here, Kenyatta looked to his sister for help.

"We don't have time to explain," the woman said. "We must speak with the leader of your people. I assure you neither I nor my brother would have sought out your home if it weren't a grave situation."

Seung's look of alarm sent a fresh wave of guilt washing over Kenyatta. "They will not trust me." She looked into Kenyatta's eyes, and he could almost feel her willing him to understand the delicate situation she was in. Her beautiful light brown eyes melted his heart, but the turmoil they now reflected broke it.

"Can you send word?" Taliah asked. "What we have to say affects you all as much as it affects us."

A woman's voice shot from the trees like bolt of lightning and silenced everyone. The elf spoke too quickly for Kenyatta to understand it all, but the intent rang clear enough.

Seung closed her eyes in resignation, as another elven woman emerged from the brush. After a stream of rather harsh—yet still beautifully musical—words, Seung finally translated. "It is because you are important to me that you have not been sent back down the road, befuddled and babbling like infants. You are to leave now."

"I understand your mistrust of us, but I ask anyway that you trust me, elfinestraya," Taliah said. "There are a small number of humans that have held your secret despite the majority of our species' obliviousness. We have kept the promise from ages come and gone. We have remained at the front of the conflict, and we have remained true to the others of The Four." Taliah indicated for Seung to translate.

Kenyatta had never seen Seung this anxious, and that alone drove home for him just how important to her it was that the elves accept her among them. He tried to imagine what that must be like; to find out most of his heritage was something he'd never thought existed, yet was this far older and more powerful species.

Watching her now, he couldn't help wondering that if she was forced to choose human life over elven, where would that leave the two of them? He'd never ask such a thing from her, but the thought of losing Seung after finding her again after two years was a painful thought. She must have seen it in his face, for she leaned ever so subtly toward him. She was restraining herself, he could tell. The elf next to Seung cast her an exasperated look and said something in response. Before she'd finished talking, Seung sprang into his arms, crushing him in a hug. Her body trembled against him, and he could have held her like that forever. The sight of his sister and the elf rolling their eyes shortened the moment.

"What did she say to you?" Kenyatta asked once they'd separated.

"To stop trying to act like an adult and just get it over with."

Kenyatta looked confused. "Adult?"

"I've told you, my love. By their years I am little more than a juvenile."

"You talk less about your people than you believe," Kenyatta replied.

Taliah's dry tone slipped between them like a dusty blanket. "If I may interrupt? We need to move this along."

Seung let go of Kenyatta's hands and faced the woman. "I will speak with Immendiel. No human has ever stepped inside The Wood. *I'm* not even accepted by everyone."

"I understand," Taliah said, "but please assure your companion that the Lady of The Wood will be very interested in what I have to say." Seung relayed the message to the elf named Immendiel, who shook her head through every word. After a few moments of debate, Seung turned back to them. She says we can relay whatever message you have brought, but you cannot enter. We're taking a risk just by meeting with you here."

"We don't have *time* for this," Taliah sighed. "Very well. Tell her that a Chosen of the Daunyans and one of the Children of the Gene seeks an audience."

Seung translated and that got a reaction from the steadfast elf. She looked from one to the other, as though having an inner argument with herself. After a moment, she said something hurriedly to Seung and disappeared into the trees. Moments later, the elf returned, signaling for them to follow. Seung and the elf passed through the brush silently, as Kenyatta and Taliah loudly crunched and swished through the infinite branches and bushes. A few yards ahead, Immendiel spoke and Seung chuckled.

"What did she say?" Kenyatta asked.

"She says the two of you are like an avalanche crashing down a mountain. Every living thing for miles can hear you."

"Really funny, man," Kenyatta replied.

Taliah raised an eyebrow. "Can you tell your friend that the four who are shadowing us need not bother? We are no threat." Seung's mouth fell open, then she recovered and translated. Immendiel turned an equally astonished look on Taliah, followed by a nod of respect.

Kenyatta kept his head straight as he glanced about. "How did you know they were there? I haven't heard or seen a thing."

"I can sense them, Ken," Taliah said. "The Gene of the Daunyans lives within you, but it is a different matter to be a Chosen of the Daunyans. The time is fast coming for you to learn everything, but not yet. Let's first handle this business with Seiyun, then be on our way to Takashaniel."

Kenyatta wasn't sure if he liked the sound of that. For a time, he walked beside his sister, admiring Seung's beautiful elven trousers. Yes, they were nicely made. Surely it was a compliment to recognize and admire good crafts-manship—"

"Wipe your chin, Brother," Taliah said in a disgusted tone. "Or you'll wet your shirt."

Kenyatta pointed innocently. "Have you ever seen clothes made with materials like that? What do they make them with, I wonder?"

Taliah rolled her eyes. "I'm sure your girliefriend's voice could better enlighten you than her backside."

"No, no, I wasn't—"

"Quit diggin' yer hole deeper, man," Taliah interrupted.

Kenyatta threw up his hands. "Fine, forget it," he whispered. Seung glanced over her shoulder and smiled at him. She couldn't have heard them, they'd been whispering, and she was too far ahead. As if in answer, a few strands of her raven hair fell away from a pointed ear as she looked down to hop over a fallen tree. *Guess those ears aren't just for show, then,* he thought, glancing at the tree just behind her after she'd stepped over it. He had *not* looked at her backside again.

An exasperated '*men*' from beside him suggested his sister saw otherwise. Didn't she have anything better to do than watch what he was doing? "Looks like I'll be an aunt sooner than I thought," Taliah muttered.

Kenyatta responded with a nervous chuckle. "She can hear you, you know."

"Yes? What about it?" Taliah stared at him. Kenyatta looked at her, then just shook his head and continued on.

After a moment, he muttered just loud enough for her to hear, "I bet I'll be an uncle before you're an aunt." He smiled in satisfaction when Taliah's lips pressed into a line and she looked away. "Mind your own business, Ken."

"You two finished sparring?" Seung called from ahead. She and Immendiel had stopped.

"We are at the edge of The Wood, Yathienel," the elven tracker announced, which Seung translated. "You must be blindfolded, now."

"Oh," Kenyatta said.

"I trust you, love," Seung said, "but we cannot expect the people of The Wood to share that trust."

"I agree," Taliah said, to all of their surprise. "You cannot shroud your home from the eyes of the Daunyans, but if this would appease your people, let us continue on."

Immendiel said something to Seung who translated, "Do not expect to ever be trusted. The depth of the scars run many centuries deep, and the elves have long memories." Seung looked sad at the admission. "Your reception may be hostile."

"We understand," Taliah said, as Immendiel blindfolded her. Seung gently draped a cloth over Kenyatta's eyes and began to tie it. Several times her delicate fingers brushed his neck. He wanted to kiss those fingers.

"Uksh!" the elven tracker said, then spoke to Seung in tones that suggested disgust. Seung just giggled and whispered in his ear, "Immendiel says we are like children."

"Maybe she needs you to find her a man to boss," Kenyatta whispered over his shoulder. Her hands went rigid for an instant, then she continued, finishing the knot.

"Be careful with your words, love. To say that the Yathieneli are mistrustful of humans is a drastic understatement. Do not to provoke them."

"Understood," Kenyatta said. Seung stood on her tiptoes and kissed him on the cheek. Kenyatta heard another disgusted sound from Immendiel and they started off again.

"Our hidden escorts have decided to close ranks?" Taliah said, after a few moments.

"Yes," Seung replied, again surprised. "They don't know what to expect when we arrive in The Wood."

"All will be fine, Seung," Taliah said. "The news we bring will overshadow any perceived offense. Besides, I would not harm the reputation of my brother's cute little girliefriend."

Kenyatta could hear the smirk in Taliah's voice.

"We're almost there," Seung said. She sounded composed to the point of being stiff. Soon they heard the sounds of many melodious voices whispering nervously around them. Some sounded confused, but more than a few were hostile. After they had walked for some time, Kenyatta and Taliah's blindfolds were finally removed.

When his eyes finally refocused, Kenyatta's lips parted as he took in the splendor of his surroundings. They stood in a great open space, surrounded by unfamiliar trees larger than any he had ever set his eyes upon. Bright blue and green moss coated many, while some had smooth bark and some with a furry look. The smaller plants and shrubs, as well as the moss, glowed an inner light.

Homes were built from shed bark, the wood of fallen trees, or inside the trees themselves. Forest animals milled about the city with the rest of the residents. Seung had described the majesty of Yathienel a few times, but Kenyatta's imagination hadn't done the place justice. These people, these elves, didn't live in the forest, they were part of it.

Beside him, Taliah looked unsurprised. When he thought about it, not much ever seemed to surprise her, but he did see a clear look of appreciation.

"Your home is beautiful," Taliah said, and Kenyatta could only nod in agreement.

Around them, several people muttered in the elven tongue, and he made out Seung's elven name, Kiluriel, along with the often repeated *n'thresha*. He noticed Seung's wounded expression and asked what the word meant. She didn't respond, but Immendiel spoke in a harsh tone to the speakers, who looked embarrassed, and withdrew.

They continued on their way, ignoring the gasps, stares, and glares that lingered on them. A melodic, booming masculine voice halted them. They turned to see a stern-looking male stalking toward them. He stopped before Seung and Immendiel, and Kenyatta noticed just how much bigger he was than any other elf he'd seen so far.

The male spoke quickly in their native tongue, and the two women responded respectfully and calmly, no doubt explaining the situation. After a few moments, he turned to Kenyatta and Taliah. Kenyatta's heart skipped a beat when he realized that he recognized the elf. It was the one Seung said was a Daunya Warrior.

Tinnoviel Nai SaunyaLi stared at them each in turn, his piercing brown eyes taking their measure. "What is meaning of this?" he asked in his broken command of the common western tongue. "You should not come. Humans cannot come to Yathienel."

"It was unavoidable—" Kenyatta tried to explain, but the elf talked over him.

"No excuse good enough! You bring danger to yourselves and all of us." He waved a hand to encompass their surroundings. "To some of our forest friends, the smell of human frightens them away. You bring unrest—"

"Daunya Warrior," Taliah's voice encompassed their immediate space, and the air around them crackled with energy. "It is by the will of the Daunyans that we have found your magnificent home. It was not we who found Yathienel, but the Daunyans who led us to it. Darkness stirs and even the peaceful Elfinestraya will be affected. We must speak with The Lady of Yathienel. Time is not on our side."

Tinnoviel seemed to comprehend most of what she said, but he looked to Seung anyway, who hurried to translate. A worried look flickered across his features but he signaled for them to follow. The Daunya Warrior gave a sharp whistle, and one of the elves that had been shadowing them—a young-looking male—trotted up beside him. Tinnoviel rattled off instructions, and the elf trotted away.

"The Lady Seiyun would already know you are here," Seung said, dropping back to walk with the two siblings, "but a message must still be sent. She would probably prefer to meet with you in private, but given the situation, and that no human feet have touched Yathieneli soil in thousands of years, she will likely see you in the grand hall with all who wish to bear witness."

"Do you think she'll hear reason?" Kenyatta asked.

"She is levelheaded and kind, but I cannot know for sure how she will receive you."

"She will listen," Taliah said. "Too much is at stake for her to do otherwise."

"You seem so sure," Seung said.

"Because it is by the will of the Daunyans that we are here," Taliah replied.

They reached the largest tree either of them had ever seen. From the base of the tree, Kenyatta leaned back to look up, but the top of the tree stood far above the forest canopy. "This is So'orya," Seung explained. "She is the oldest and largest tree in the world."

"Wow!" Kenyatta said.

"Indeed," Taliah breathed, and she looked just as amazed as Kenyatta. Just then, he wished Kita had been with them to see this. He almost laughed at the thought. Two humans seemed bad enough. Three would have caused an uproar.

"You must first ask permission before proceeding," Seung said, gazing up at the magnificent tree. It easily stood taller than any of the remaining sky-reaching buildings that remained from the Age of Technology.

"How do we ask?" Kenyatta said.

"You need only touch her," Seung answered. "Place your palm flat against her trunk."

Kenyatta moved closer to the tree and placed his hand upon it. As soon as he made contact, he was drawn into an awareness that felt as encompassing as the world itself. The presence of the tree dwarfed him so many times over, it felt as if he was in the presence of a God.

The tree entered his mind, searching him, reading him. It was almost more than he could bear, but when he thought he could withstand it no longer, a wash of purifying love cradled him. The warmth and kindness was so pure and potent that he could have lain wrapped in it for the rest of his days. Tears trickled down his cheeks and though he felt the presence releasing him, he wanted to keep the connection for just a little longer. The So'orya left him, and Kenyatta had to lean on the tree for a little longer to refill the emptiness he felt at her departure. Finally, and with great hesitance, he removed his hand and staggered away. He almost fell backwards, but Tinnoviel caught and steadied him.

"So'orya welcomes you to Yathienel, warrior Keyatta," He said, still struggling with Kenyatta's name. She will bear you upon her limbs with love and acceptance."

"You seemed surprised," Kenyatta said.

The elf smirked, apparently the closest he would come to a laugh. "In all my years of life, I never expect to see human touch So'orya. The world changes."

"Does that mean humans can come in here and build a city?" Kenyatta asked. At the look of horror on Tinnoviel's face, he held his hands up. "Whoa, whoa, just joking, man." Kenyatta waved his hands before him in a placating gesture. "Just a joke." After a moment, the elven warrior relaxed, turning back to the tree. Kenyatta squirmed when the elf cast him a sidelong glance.

"Always gotcha mouth moving before ya mind stoppin' ya," Taliah muttered, stepping up to the tree. Beside her, Seung giggled.

"Hey!" Kenyatta threw her a mock wounded look

Instead of just one, Taliah placed both hands on the tree, her eyes closed and her head lowered as if in concentration. Kenyatta frowned, then looked to the others to see that he wasn't the only one surprised. Seung and the others looked equally caught off guard. He heard gasps from behind and realized they had not eluded their unwelcoming entourage.

Taliah's body started to glow from the inside, and a silvery light settled over her. Some of the thinner vines that grew on the tree reached out and gently wrapped about her arms and shoulders in a loving embrace.

Kenyatta, Seung, and all in attendance stood in captivated silence. The vines on the tree extended past her shoulder to drape across her back, and Taliah leaned toward the tree and keeping her hands flat to the trunk, and pressing her body against it.

"What's happening?" Kenyatta whispered. "Why are the vines wrapping around her like that?"

"I ... don't know," Seung whispered back. "I don't think anyone does."

Finally, many moments later, the vines retracted and Taliah stepped away from the tree. She smiled up at it and turned to her brother. "Hers is as close to the love of the Daunyans as you can experience without being in Their presence. We are lucky to have met her, Ken."

Her voice a bit shaky, Immendiel declared it time to move on. Kenyatta tore his gaze from his still glowing sister and the now inanimate vines to stare in disbelief at the many white steps that spiraled around the trunk of the great tree. "Are they expecting us to get there tomorrow?" Kenyatta asked.

"Normally we enjoy ascending the steps of So'orya," Seung replied. "Today, we must take a quicker route."

They ascended the steps until they came to a patio several hundred feet above the ground overlooking the clearing below. Four elves approached and gently grabbed each of their arms. They wore loose fitting white and green robes that hung to their ankles. Looking neither upset, nor unhappy at having to touch the human guests, they each took hold of an object that hung from their necks, and without warning, the group rose into the air.

Kenyatta gritted his teeth, trying not to acknowledge the feeling that his stomach was still on that patio many feet below. The forest foliage passed in a blur as they made their speedy ascent.

When they finally cleared the tree line Kenyatta looked in awe at a landscape carpeted with giant green trees and rolling evergreen hills stretching into the distance. The sun cast a golden light upon the sprawling landscape as it made its western decent, and Kenyatta closed his eyes and basked in the warmth that washed over his face.

And as quickly as they'd begun their ascension, so too came the abruptness of their halt. The four elves deposited their passengers in what looked like a grand living palace. Their robed escorts departed without a word, leaving Immendiel and Tinnoviel to guide them through the halls. As they hurried along, Kenyatta stole glances at the amazing artwork and tapestries that decorated the walls. Everything, even the artwork itself, seemed to be alive, and it wasn't hanging from the walls, but had been worked into them.

At a set of towering double doors Kenyatta guessed was their destination, two elves bearing long-shafted weapons made from the same materials as those Seung and Tinnoviel wielded, stood at attention on either side. At a nod from Tinnoviel, they bowed and opened the doors.

Kenyatta had to remind himself not to let his mouth hang open at the splendor of it all. The grand hall was even more impressive than the hallways. The entire grand hall itself was a work of art that he wasn't sure had been worked by a careful hand, or simply grew to be that way.

Many elves lined both sides of the path in the middle of the grand hall. As the group passed between the throng of onlookers, the stares and glances they received were not altogether unexpected, but they were unnerving all the same. Upon a throne that seemed to grow straight from beneath the floor, sat one of the most beautiful and majestic women Kenyatta had ever seen. An aura of power emanated from her, but he also saw kindness there. As he studied her features, he saw a hint of Seung! Was she a relative? The questions would have to wait, however, for the Lady of The Wood studied them with hard eyes. Kenyatta hoped she was as kind a soul as Taliah had said, because sitting upon her living throne, the queen of the elfinestraya didn't look happy.

7

"Reforge the blade."

Kenjiro's words echoed in Akemi's mind as she considered the challenges to come with *Onisekairu* and *Onihakaisha*. She looked over the barren, rock-strewn hills until her gaze fell over her brother. The samurai sat with his back against a towering oak, honing his blade with a whetstone.

She sat with her back against a tree and closed her eyes. In all her years of hunting demons, *Sekimaru* had served her well. The sword had banished countless demons back to the abyss after being summoned by a foolish human with more arrogance than power.

The Demon Bane and the Demon Destroyer, forged from her old companion. She thought back to that fateful day when *Sekimaru* had grown too hungry, too insistent on defeating their foe. Akemi narrowed her eyes at the memory of Glarus, a particularly nasty demon that had spat a poisonous cloud at her, only for *Sekimaru* to use the cloud as a path into the demon's soul.

Akemi remembered the helplessness she felt at only being able to hold on to the sword as it had devoured the demon and left nothing but a lifeless husk sprawled on the ground that eventually dissolved, not to return to the abyss, but into nothingness.

Even now as she recalled the memory, Akemi still didn't know how the sword had shoved her will aside and devoured the fiend; an act it had not been created to do and was not capable of containing the pure evil it had consumed. Thus corrupted Akemi had been forced to destroy the sword; or so she'd thought.

"Reforge the blade."

Kenjiro's sword was not possessed of sentience, thus he had no experience with such a weapon. Yet his suggestion had been a good one. The moment Akemi had committed herself to the act, it was as if the knowledge of how to do so had always been in her mind. Shatter the blade and release the corruption. But not all of it. Although the only way to truly destroy the corruption was to destroy the blade completely, the ninja demon hunter knew that if she was to hunt again, she would need a weapon possessed of some small part of the beings she fought. Now she held *Onisekairu* and *Onihakaisha*, the two created from the one.

* * *

"It's long past time we leave, Brother." Akemi looked at her brother, who was still busy with his sword.

"I know," Kenjiro responded. "But can you control it? You have only hunted with *Onihakaisha* once."

"There's no choice." Akemi said. "The blade resists when I pull back. There is a hunger there that must be tempered before it can be relied upon. That day will come, but there isn't time for me to tame it now."

"Then hope such a reckoning doesn't come at an inopportune time," Kenjiro said.

Akemi huffed under her breath. "Of course it will be the wrong time. Would you truly expect otherwise?"

The samurai chuckled at that bit of truth. Such moments never arrived bearing convenience. "I feel the Gene. I feel the call of Takashaniel, though it seems to come from a different direction than before."

Akemi thought about that. Nothing was certain when dealing with fiends, and if the guardian felt the need to move the entire tower, something major had either happened or would, soon.

"I suspect others feel it too."

That got Akemi's attention. She turned a questioning look on her brother, then followed his gaze. Not so far away, a figure emerged further up the trail. As he drew closer, Akemi recognized the stature, the body language, the relaxed yet dangerous gait. And, of course, the beautiful face bearing the occasional flippant smirk.

"After four years." She barely noticed her brother's arched eyebrow, for the approaching man interested her almost as much as the hilt of that most amazing sword.

8

Whether it be his determined gait or the dark expression coloring his features, servants were quick to scurry out of the stalking General Zhang Da's path. How? *How*, could there have been yet another killing? And this time it happened not far from the palace. That would have been enough to cause his own outrage, but practically on the heels of the first messenger came a second, bearing a sealed letter from Qian Hua, emperor of Qian, a most temperamental and often irrational man. Zhang Da knew not the contents of the letter, but he could have guessed.

Moments later, the general found himself in Liu Xiang's private quarters. "It seems as though we are seeing quite a bit of each other these days, my friend," the emperor said. "Have you word from ..." he trailed off at the sight of the general's face. "What is it?"

Zhang Da handed the sealed letter to Xiang. After turning the letter in his hands and seeing the seal, he sucked through his teeth and looked up at the general, who nodded. Slowly, deliberately, Liu Xiang broke the seal of House Qian, and began to read:

Emperor Liu Xiang. This letter comes to you on the heels of conflict. I have had murders within my own gates that have gone unsolved, and are, quite frankly, disturbing in nature. Despite my exhaustive efforts, I have been unable to discover the nature of these attacks or their source. Being that we have not been in contact for some time, I felt compelled *to correspond with you about these events. Perhaps you have some insight that I do not? I would speak with you personally on this matter as soon as is possible. I am preparing my departure to your lands in short order, that we might discuss these happenings in a more effective way. Your response will be both appreciated and also met on the road, as I intend to depart shortly after this letter has been sent. Given the time it will take for my arrival in your bountiful lands, I am confident in your being prepared. I regret the abruptness of this message and my not being able to inform you sooner, but there are times when swift action yields the greatest results. I hope this letter finds you well, and I look forward to meeting with you within the next few weeks.*

L*ord Qian Hua*

* * *

Liu Xiang's frown deepened with every word. Once finished, he handed the letter back. Zhang Da's lips moved as he read the letter, his own visage darkening as he reached the end. Finally, he looked up at Xiang, disbelief in his eyes.

"This must be jest," he said read the letter again. "Even Qian would not be so bold. This letter is barely *laced* with respect! His regard for your welfare was an afterthought! I would not have expected such disrespect, even from him!"

Liu Xiang stroked his beard. "He suspects me of silently eroding his authority."

"By sending assassins to kill simple residents?" Zhang Da ground his teeth with every word. "People who have no power or influence?"

"By causing chaos," Liu Xiang replied, in his ever patient voice. "Slowly and deliberately building chaos. The populous becomes concerned that he cannot ensure their safety, and will then turn to another who can protect them."

"Absurd." Zhang Da's body shook with barely contained anger. "Illogical. When was the last time there has been war? When have we ever threatened him in any way?"

Eyes closed, Liu Xiang held up a tired hand through the rant. "Of course it is nonsense, my friend, but we are talking about Hua. Ever has he been a man of action, more than thought."

"Warlord." Da spat. "Always do they look for an excuse."

"And always have they been adept at finding or creating one," Xiang added.

Zhang Da tugged at his thick, long beard. "Do you believe he's behind all this? His restlessness is no secret."

Xiang shook his head. "Simple though this tactic is, and surely within the range of intellect for Hua, I doubt he is behind this. I believe someone knows his mind well and is prodding him from the shadows."

"But if someone knows him well," Zhang Da said, "they may know you just as well. If so, why do the same here? You would not so easily swallow such bait."

"Why, indeed?" Xiang replied, pacing. "But then, why not? Perhaps I would not so easily be baited, but if Qian Hua's actions were as harsh and unreasonable as we know he is capable of, I might rise to the challenge. Or perhaps it simply doesn't matter and the hidden antagonist simply enjoys sowing chaos."

Zhang frowned at that. "The risk doesn't sound equal to the reward."

"But consider that these assassins have been able to elude our best efforts to catch them," Liu Xiang suggested. "They've lured citizens out of their homes despite the imposed curfews. Their confidence is rooted in their ability to commit these horrible killing while at the same time avoiding detection. The end result is conflict between myself and Hua."

"Conflict," Zhang Da echoed. "All of this brings Qian Hua knocking on your door.

Liu Xiang sighed. "And so it does. And so we have none to give him."

"You know as well as I that he won't believe that," Da replied.

Xiang nodded. In times like these he envied the common folk. They needed only work, pay their taxes, and abide by the law. People were free to farm if they had the land, or live in the cities. Xiang kept a tight hold on law in his lands, and through his harshness with crime, the people enjoyed safe and simple lives. He envied their ignorance of the political machinations and posturing that went on in the lives of the rich and powerful that so many of them envied. He chuckled at the irony.

"What is it?" Zhang asked.

Liu looked up. "Nothing, nothing. Send for a scribe. I must attend to the most unpleasant duty of responding to Emperor Qian, who by now is no doubt pushing his entourage at a tiresome pace to reach me while I've had little time to prepare." Xiang stood a little taller as he turned to Zhang Da. "Gather your most trusted men. I will have Xiao Fu gather the head servants and messengers. I want every person who is in charge of workers, every one that we can trust, to be given instructions to prepare for this visit, and to be ready for conflict as well. We must do the former outwardly and in good spirit. The latter, we must do quickly and quietly. I'll not be caught unprepared should our temperamental guest decide on some foolish course of action. Have small bands of our elite soldiers stationed far enough outside the city that, should things go awry, we can send pockets of troops to them to seal off any escape or reinforcements. I didn't want this, but Qian is too volatile to trust."

"Of course, my lord," General Zhang agreed. "That is why Shu Han has lived in peace for so long."

"And it is my hope that peace will continue," Liu Xiang said. "Do you have any word from Guan, or the others?"

The general shook his head. "Not yet. It has only been a week, so they may not have had time yet to respond."

"Let us hope that at the very least, Zhuge Xiaoyin will arrive before our guests. Her council would be most welcome."

"Yes, it would," Zhang agreed.

"Go, my friend," Liu Xiang said. "We must prepare, and quickly.

No sooner had the general departed, than yet another messenger was announced. With a sigh, Xiang nodded. The messenger walked in briskly and dropped to one knee, then handed the sealed letter to the attendant. "My Lord Liu Xiang," the messenger said. "I come from Zhao with news from my Lady Zhao Xiaoyu."

9

B rother Dinman, Minister of the Church of Holy Jemanah sat tapping his slippered foot on the tiled floor. One did not keep a monk of the church waiting in such a manner. Dinman swiped a boney finger down his hawkish nose. The problem with the flock was that they did not respect the church as they should. People feared more the wrath of the self-imposed leaders of the land instead of the wrath of Holy Jemanah Himself. Even the self-styled kings of the lands would one day stand before the judgement of Jemanah.

Brother Dinman adjusted the spectacles sitting on the middle of his long nose and surveyed the waiting room. Such luxuries were decadent and unnecessary. The palace coffers would be better utilized in adding another wing to the church and extending the grounds around it. He would also need to speak with Dain about the use of some of his troops to accompany more groups of brothers to venture farther into the world to help spread the word of Jemanah. The heathens and their many gods must be brought to heel, and quickly. Decadence, lack of dedication, hedonistic lifestyles, and worshiping false imaginary gods were all rampant practices in the city and beyond. This was why Jemanah saw fit to remove technology from the lives of men, so long ago.

He wiped a thin, wrinkled hand over his downturned mouth and looked out the window at the garden beyond. It was a waste! Such resources should be used to strengthen the church, not to plant fragile and non-functional flowers and plants that served little purpose than to show for guests. The flock must be prepared for their judgment when they leave this world and face their *true* lord. All this business with land and palaces and flowers was nonsense; a distraction that led down a path away from salvation and toward damnation. If he led the church, Brother Dinman would have put a stop to such foolishness long ago.

His prim, wrinkled mouth turned down further at the thought of Bishop Marquis. Brother Dinman had shown nothing but dedication and held steadfast to the doctrines of Jemanah to the letter! Never bending. Never swaying. How the majority of the church could have seen the soft and unfocused Marquis as the better candidate instead of Dinman was as ridiculous as it was a disappointment. Oh, Dinman did have supporters, but they were far outnumbered by the other weaklings within the church that wished to have someone coddle them with 'feel good' well wishes and such talk that—as long as they tried to be a good person—everything was fine. Well, if that was the type of bishop the monks of the Church of Jemanah desired, they certainly would *not* have found it in Dinman.

The monk tapped his foot faster on the floor and cast an irritated look out the window. No wonder the people were astray. They were a reflection of their king, who apparently couldn't attend a meeting on time.

* * *

"Is there any word from Lord Mairson?" Elizander asked.

"My Lord," Milpheus breathed. "There has been no word," He broke into a brief trot to keep pace with Elizander and Davros's rapid stride. The attendant caught up and muttered so that only the two men could hear, "if you would rather, I can find a war to wage instead of this meeting with Dinman."

Dain covered his grin with a fist and coughed into it. "Would that we did just that, I fear the man would just stand in the middle of the carnage, tapping that long foot of his."

Brazen as ever, Davros chuckled aloud as Milpheus scurried ahead and waited as the two guards at Dain's private rooms saluted and opened the doors. Milpheus moved inside and announced Elizander's arrival.

"Honored Brother Dinman of the Church of Holy Jemanah, I present King Elizander Dain of Winsor Kingdom!"

Elizander strode into the room and inclined his head to the monk. Ever resistant to change, Brother Dinman wore his traditional dingy brown robes and sandals. Did he ever wash them? The monk sat tapping a bony foot with his arms crossed, studying them all. His spectacles sat perched midway down his buzzard-like nose, his ever down-turned mouth compressed so tightly his chin looked like a wrinkled map below it. Elizander had long ago concluded that this was a permanent expression fixed to the monk's face.

Beside Elizander, Davros's nostrils flared. "You will rise before the King, monk. Show respect for the—"

"Yes *yes*," the monk said, waving an irritable hand but rising nonetheless. "I have not the time nor desire to posture with you, King Elizander." At least he held to proper decorum, if barely. "I suppose I should thank Holy Jemanah Himself that the king has seen fit to meet with me."

Davros stiffened and Elizander settled his friend's temper with a look. "I am here, Brother Dinman. What have you?" The monk stood there, incessantly tapping that bony foot. How Dain would have loved to stomp that foot into the tiles, but that would not do. He stared directly into the monk's eyes and held his gaze until the tapping finally stopped.

"King Elizander," Dinman began in his usual sour tone. "The city has become unsafe. People are being murdered in the moonlit streets and confusion and despair rule the day. The flock has lost its way and Holy Jemanah no longer sees them."

Elizander arched an eyebrow at that. "A somewhat dramatized account, but continue."

The monk glared as he produced a scroll from his sleeve. He slid his spectacles further down his nose as he read.

"You were informed two seasons ago that church attendance was down, and that consequences would be paid, should the flock lose its way. We have thievery and skirmishes, drunkards stumble from bars and fight with each other. Brothels house women of ill repute and are not only tolerated, but allowed to thrive! It is an outrage and blasphemy!"

Davros narrowed his eyes. "Temper your tone, and your tongue, monk, lest you meet with Holy Jemanah sooner than either of you expect." Dain cut a sharp look at the general, who bowed in apology. The threat worked, however, as Dinman did lower his bluster, if only a bit.

"King Elizander Dain. This is your city, your kingdom, and yet you have allowed the flock to manage themselves! Bars and taverns, brothels and gambling houses! It is all blasphemy and flies in the face of the teachings of Holy Jemanah! Surely you must see it. Do the bodies of the nightly slain not trouble you?"

Elizander kept his features placid in spite of the disrespectful question. "I would phrase my questions differently were I you, Brother Dinman. Yes, I am aware of the murders, and yes they trouble me. You may return to your church assured that my best efforts have been brought forth to solve this mystery."

"Mystery, my lord?" Dinman said. "Why, there is no mystery here. Have you not heard me? The flock is misguided. People have lost their way, and devils now rule the streets unchecked, slaughtering civilians."

Elizander could hear Davros grinding his teeth. "I am more aware of the situation than you believe, Brother, and I assure you that the killings are not as numerous as you believe. Still, as I have just said, my best efforts and resources have been brought forth to bring the situation to light and end it."

"The masses turning back to the light of Holy Jemanah is the only action necessary," Dinman pressed. "Have you no desire to see your beloved kingdom saved?"

Elizander suppressed a sigh. "I've not the time for sparring and rhetorical questions, Brother Dinman. As for your concerns, let me address them in kind. The bars and taverns are a social place for people to have food and a drink, should they choose. They are places of music and fun and an option to relieve stress. Always will there be those who indulge too far.

"The brothels are also an option to relieve stress, and provide a place for an unmarried man or woman to know a warm touch or temporary companionship in a safe environment for both parties. Contrary to what you may believe, Brother Dinman, lust does not rule the day in a brothel; not always."

The monk looked thunderstruck. "I see," he said in a very controlled tone. "Well then, perhaps for what you wish of your city, you have things well in hand." He bowed precisely. "As always, the church will remain a shining beacon to those who would seek to cleanse their souls and find salvation in the midst of chaos and sin. Good day to you, King Elizander Dain. May the light of Holy Jemanah shine upon you in these dark times." The monk carefully rolled his scroll and replaced it in its sleeve, then stalked out of the room.

"That was interesting," Davros said as soon as the doors closed behind the fuming monk. "From the way he told it, there are mass killings and drunk and lusting people falling over each other in devil-infested streets." When Elizander didn't respond, Davros looked over to see the other man staring at the floor in front of his feet, his expression thoughtful. "What is it?"

"Perhaps nothing," Dain said after a moment. "Milpheus." The attendant scuttled closer. "What is the talk around the city?"

"People grow concerned about the ever more frequent killings and what they might portend, my lord. Though the chaos that Brother Dinman"—his mouth wrinkled when he said the name—"describes is dramatized to say the least, there is a shadow of truth in that people are fearful."

"My thanks, Milpheus. Have a letter drafted for Bishop Marquis. I would have his ear directly on the matter."

"Of course, my lord." The attendant withdrew.

As soon as they heard the door shut behind them, Davros turned to Elizander. "Now, what is *really* on your mind?"

"I know this will sound foolish, Davros, but did it not strike you as odd that this is the second time we have heard about some devil or demon loose on the streets?"

Davros looked as though he didn't know whether or not to laugh. "Surely you jest. A *devil*? Are we to consult the children's fables and campfire stories to solve this riddle?"

Elizander shook his head. "There is something here that we don't understand, old friend. I no more believe there is a devil loose on the streets of our beautiful city than you do, but there *is* something out there." The King of New Dainland paced back and forth, hands clasped behind his back. "We have murders of such brutality, the bodies of the victims are unrecognizable. And they've increased in frequency." He looked up at the captain. "I believe you used the word, devoured?"

The frowning Davros nodded.

"And this happens in Mairland as well." Elizander clasped his hands behind his back and started pacing again. It always helped to move a bit when trying to think things through. "The attacks appear to have been done by a large animal." He stopped and looked at Davros. "The problem with this, is that an animal has no concept of avoiding the authorities. Some of these attacks have happened very near to where your men have been posted." He patted his hand in the air when Davros flinched. "Peace, general. That was not a rebuke, simply an assessment. My point is, although the attacks appear to be animalistic in nature, there is a cunning involved that would not be present in an animal."

"Whatever the case," Davros said, "he or it, is enjoying itself at our expense." When Elizander turned a questioning look on him, Davros spread his hands. "As much as it grates on me to admit this, whoever it is, mocks us and enjoys our confusion. We're being toyed with, Zander, and I fear that eventually the killer will grow bored and make themselves known, and we will not like it."

"Perhaps not," Elizander said, "but it would simplify things. Better to move against an enemy you can see, than speculate on their identity while they strike at you."

"Possibly." Davros took a long, deep sigh. "There's no sense to the individual murders themselves, but the pattern of them, and the fact that they are occurring in a city governed by a man who would fashion himself your rival? That may be something."

And what of the church? Normally, I would pass that aged carrion crow Dinman out of hand, but my reports show him growing in popularity as of late. It's as though the murders are herding people straight to him. Not the church specifically, mind, but him."

Elizander sighed. "Ever has that man fancied himself a bishop."

"What would our troubles look like if Dinman lived in Mairland instead of New Dainland?" Davros mused. "I find it troubling that people are turning more toward that stinking monk's council with these murders happening."

"It's not unexpected, my friend," Dain said. "Bishop Marquis leads the people to spiritual awareness, but also demands that they think for themselves as individuals and seek answers while coming to the church for guidance. This is all well in times of peace and comfort. But in times of uncertainty and fear, people turn to that which will provide them answers, not guidance. They want to be told what to do. What *exactly* to do."

"'Tis easier to be led in a flock, than to think as an individual," Davros said.

Elizander nodded. "In matters of the spirit, people are most fearful. This talk of devils in the night, coupled with the nature of these murders have left the people afraid, not of law, but of damnation."

"And that," Davros said, "makes Dinman a very dangerous man. He preaches fear—"

"While providing explicit instructions for salvation," Elizander finished. "No speculation, no hints. Just simple, unbending doctrine to follow."

"And what will happen, I wonder, when those who follow the church doctrine to the letter find themselves the next victim?"

"It matters not," Dain replied, walking back to the balcony with Davros in tow. In the distance beyond the beautiful gardens sprawling across the grounds, was a large group of citizens waving their hands and yelling. They were too far away to be understood, but what was clear enough was the skinny, almost fragile-looking figure that stood regally upon a raised dais. The two men glanced at each other. It was Brother Dinman, of course. And as with the previous day, his congregation was a bit larger than before.

10

Malimokuru sat in the shade of a desert palm, eyes closed, breathing slow and deep. Every day he meditated and cultivated the skills he already possessed, in addition to those he'd learned in the year spent living among the amahle. It had been an amazing year. Naiyala, princess of the amahle had beseeched her parents and the Seer to permit the nature reader to live among them, claiming that he had already begun to learn from the Daunya Apprentice, Amata Daunyana, and had shown great promise. After some talk, and Amata's account of their travels together, the king and queen had withdrawn to consult with the Seer.

"In their dawning years, humans bring discord and chaos," the Seer had said. "It is not until their waning years do most find a measure of balance and acceptance. This *abantu* has entered the waning years, yet would become a student. Humility and wisdom lies within." Malimokuru hadn't been particularly appreciative of all that "waning years" talk. "This child will live far longer than is typical of his species. His presence among the amahle portends the start of the new age for *abantu*."

Malimokuru opened his eyes. His closest companion, Nyaka, lounged a few feet away, eyes closed but never fully asleep. The nature reader watched the resting animal. A year ago he and those foolish children and that disgusting guide had come across the little goar cat while traversing the deadly swamp, the *Craig*. Well, they had not actually come across the animal. After surviving an attack by its hungry mother, Malimokuru had spoken to the fallen animal's spirit and agreed to find and care for the cub. To the objections of the others, he had found the little goar cat and taken her with them.

Little. Malimokuru stared at the animal, now a bit larger than a full grown tiger. Malimokuru shook his head. Goar cats reached full size in little more than a year. Nyaka was a runt, among her species. Her mother had been her size once and a half over. What she lacked in size, however, was compensated with speed and dexterity. According to the amahle, the young goar cat was easily the fastest of her kind, and far more agile. Now fully grown, her pelt had changed from its former dim blue color to a smooth, shiny dark blue. Her long tail now sported the thick barbs of an adult, and the nails on her claws were now as long as a large man's finger.

As soon as Malimokuru stood, Nyaka's ears twitched, her tongue flicked in and out, and she squinted her eyes open, rumbling deep in her chest. If unfamiliar with a goar cat, it could be mistaken for a threatening growl. Hardly, was that the case. She rose and stretched her back, digging her sharp claws into the earth.

"Hello, my friend," Malimokuru greeted. "Planning to join me?" He sent friendly thoughts to her, and received a contented response. Though the nature reader mostly communicated with his animal companion via his innate abilities, Nyaka seemed to understand some verbal communication as well. He received images of her hunting in the desert just as she shifted her color to match the light brown sands of the desert before bounding away. Malimokuru smiled in admiration at the amazing animal. As a cub, she could shift her color but not totally control it. Now fully grown, Nyaka could shift her hue at will, camouflaging with her surroundings in little more than a second.

"May the coming of the sun bring you warmth and life, friend Malimokuru."

Malimokuru turned at the sound Naiyala's husky feminine voice. The amahle princess smiled down at him, thin braid-like hair falling over her face.

"May you find warmth and life in the sun's embrace," Malimokuru replied, returning the traditional amahle greeting.

Naiyala inclined her head. The woman stood over a foot taller than Malimokuru, well over seven feet, and not particularly tall by amahle standards.

The nature reader couldn't help but admire the beauty of the woman. Skin as black as polished onyx, he couldn't decide which was more striking in contrast, the bright white teeth showing in her smile, or the white beads that clicked in her waist length hair.

"Is it acceptable among your people, *Umntwana Onomuntu*, to so admire a woman whose age is so little to your own?" Malimokuru could do nothing more than shrug at that, for she often chided him for his poorly concealed admiration of her.

"Depends," he responded. "You'll live longer than me anyway, so what does it matter?" That received a chuckle. Seeing those gleaming white teeth, Malimokuru was reminded of the other nature of the amahle. Like the goar cat, they were able to shift their hue, though not as completely.

Unlike Nyaka, though, amahle skin color could also reflect their state of mind if their feelings were strong enough. Malimokuru shuddered at the memory of having seen the amahle warriors in the thrall of battle rage. With bright red skin, and elongated fangs, they were a terrifying sight. More than once he'd nearly fled upon seeing them. But they were always the same people, gentle with friends, lethal to enemies.

"Come, friend Malimokuru." Naiyala turned and opened a hand toward the village. "Mother and Father wish to speak with you in our home."

Malimokuru raised his eyebrows at that. In the year he'd been living among them, all meetings had taken place outside, or in the village hall. An uneasiness crept into the pit of his stomach.

Naiyala glanced at him. "The warning you feel in your heart is correct. The news is not good." For a time they walked in silence, the clicking of the beads in her hair the only sound in the village.

"I have a feeling I'll be leaving soon," he muttered.

"This concerns you?" Naiyala looked down at him.

Malimokuru took in the sights of the amahle village, the sand, the desert trees and sandstone homes. He smelled cookfires and even the single running stream snaking its way through town. If he left again, would he return? "I'd hoped to spend the rest of my days here. I've grown weary of the world, friend Naiyala. Here," he spread his arms, "it's peaceful and quiet. No one fights, and disagreements are settled peacefully. The year that I have spent among your people is the longest I have ever lived without seeing conflict. You amahle are content with your lives in your beautiful desert home that most humans would consider a harsh environment."

Naiyala turned a puzzled look on him. "What is harsh about these lands?" She looked out past the village and into the surrounding desert landscape. "The sun warms our bodies and the air is warm *in* our bodies. With the coming of dusk, the air cools and when the moon is full, its pale light is too beautiful not to dance under."

Malimokuru nodded. "Most humans would have one thing to say to that. It's too hot."

"Too hot?" Naiyala looked even more confused. "I do not understand."

"No, I wouldn't expect that you could, since you can regulate your body heat to a degree. It's natural for you. Humans can't do this, and if it's too hot, we suffer."

"You seem to thrive among us easily enough, *Umntwana Onomuntu*.".

Malimokuru shrugged. "Humans aren't all the same, Naiyala. Would one of your jungle kin be able to thrive out here as you do? How well would you enjoy life in the jungles? It may not be your preference, but if you and your jungle kin switched places, would you find it uncomfortable?"

Naiyala gave a thoughtful nod at that. "So little time have I spent among *abantu*, I forget you are far more diverse than any other of The Four." The home of the king and queen was much the same as any other solidly built thatch-roofed homes, only larger. The smooth hard surface of the walls were as hard as rock. Malimokuru still had no idea what they were made from. The hardy trees and shrubs that surrounded the home were healthy and thriving in the heat of the desert. Malimokuru had never encountered desert plant life so healthy and happy as those growing here among the amahle. He could feel the contentment radiating from them.

"I guess we should go in," Malimokuru said, resigned.

Naiyala laughed and put a hand on his shoulder. "Come, friend. You will not be banished from our lands. We all must leave so that we may return again."

"Easy to say when you've got the majority of your life ahead of you, young lady."

Naiyala looked at him as though he had spoken nonsense, and opened the door. Malimokuru tried not to gape at the beauty of the place. Amahle were minimalists by nature. Every home he had been invited in—which was all of them—had what was needed, and very little more. The home of the king and queen was no different, but on the walls hung eight of the most impressive paintings he'd ever seen. Seven of the paintings were depictions of each of the Daunyans. Though they were only paintings on a wall, to Malimokuru they seemed to have a presence, like a tiny part of the Daunyans themselves resided within. The eighth painting was perhaps the most powerful of them all. It covered the entire wall, and depicted all seven of the Daunyans together, in various poses and staring back at the viewer. Whomever crafted these works of art must have been touched by the Daunyans while doing so.

On a large handwoven rug sat the king and queen, and also the seer and her apprentices. After greeting each in turn, Naiyala and Malimokuru sat across from them.

"Daughter of the Desert arrives with the nature child," the seer greeted. Although she was several hundred years old, the seer sat erect and strong, only the age lines in her face indicating her advanced years. Malimokuru still found it amazing that these folk lived many centuries when he would be fortunate to reach just one!

"Do not fear your leave-taking *Umntwana Onomuntu*," she continued. "Your life among the amahle is not ended. You will return to live among us as long as you choose. *Inkosi* and *Indlovukazi*," she indicated the king and queen, who smiled, "have spoken it." She looked directly into the nature reader's eyes, and Malimokuru resisted the urge to squirm under her ancient gaze. He was years past a grown man for the Gods' sake.

"Amata Daunyana has spoken of your strength, *Umntwana Onomuntu*, and I see it. You must release that which you are afraid to unleash, and trust in your power to wield it. You love this land and its people, who return your love. The home that you have found among us is precious to you and us all. Times come when we must act to preserve that which we care for." Malimokuru steadied himself. Whatever the task, he would see it done and hopefully live to return.

"You have the mind and calmness of age, but the knowledge and experience of an apprentice, child."

Malimokuru resisted the urge to arch an eyebrow at that. *Haven't been called a child in many years.*

"Change begins, *Umntwana Onomuntu*," the seer went on. "The world will not be divided as it has been, and the veil that blinds the young ones will be lifted. The youngest of The Four, the young ones, will come to know us again. They must not be left to discover the world alone. Still an infant species, they are. You, *Umntwana Onomuntu*, and those you traveled with, and others, will help your people to know and understand the world as you have not before."

He knew what the ancient woman referred to; the destructiveness of his species and the near disastrous response from the others of The Four. "Why does this change come now? For ages my kind have not known of the existence of the amahle, or any others. What's so special about now?"

"The time for avoidance is over," the seer replied. "The others of The Four waited too long, and *abantu* grew too anxious, too diseased and insane. We, the elders of The Four had failed that age. But all happens as it must, and the age of chaos passed. We are at the dawn of a new age. It is not a golden age devoid of strife and conflict, but an age of discovery and mending. The world heals, and with it, so do we all. Your people must know the truth of the world they live in. There is no other way."

"Not all will agree," Naiyala said. "I do not believe any of The Four would agree to this new awareness. It is a dangerous thing."

"Yet inevitable," the seer replied. "Not even the Daunyans move to impede the dawning of one age after another, for they have foreseen it. The unnatural age has ended, the world heals, and The Four must know each other once again."

"What part do I play in this?" Malimokuru asked, still confused.

"The abyss stirs," the seer replied. "The darkness rises and that which holds balance is threatened."

Malimokuru's eyes widened. "My friends mentioned a tower …"

The seer nodded. "Takashaniel, it is named. A dark creature has found a way to create a small breach in the layer between this level of existence and the hells, summoning pure evil to wreak havoc upon the earth. He wishes to exterminate and enslave all *abantu*, and re-create this world for himself. He is a drek, and his name is Brit. His power is formidable, and you, your friends, and *each* of The Four must fight. Should he weaken the Tower of Balance, he will bring forth enough of his hell force to destroy it. If he succeeds, the world will grow dark and poisoned."

"That will never work," Malimokuru said, a wave of anxiety rising in his stomach. "How could he control so many demons powerful enough to accomplish this?"

The seer raised her piercing gaze upward. "He cannot. In his arrogance, the drek believes he can control them all. Already, some slip from his sight, poisoning the lands they travel, causing strife among the oblivious *abantu* civilizations."

"They feed off of our negativity," Malimokuru breathed. "All they need to do is cause chaos and humans will respond."

The ancient amahle nodded gravely. "The time for ignorance has passed, and humans must fight alongside The Four."

"And I have to help by traveling to Takashaniel," Malimokuru said.

The seer stared at him, and the next words she spoke turned his blood to water.

"And the lyrghis wait."

11

T he Lady of Yathienel's stony expression cut into Seung's stomach like a cold knife. "How long have you lived among us?" Her icy tone twisted the knife.

"I have lived here for a year, my Lady," Seung replied. Her heart ached at the cold formality of this confrontation. Her mother's mother had shown her aught but love and kindness, and now she'd betrayed that trust.

"You have learned our customs, traditions, practices, and lifestyles, the queen of Yathienel went on. "You've learned of the measures put in place to protect our people. *Your* people."

Seiyun didn't dare so much as blink. "Yes, my Lady. The people of Yathienel have been kind."

"And in that time, when did you get the impression that a human, not one, but two, would be a welcome addition to our home? When, Kiluriel Sen'Mora, did you ever suspect that we would desire such a thing?"

Seung fought to maintain her composure. "I did not know they had come, my Lady. Not once have I confided the location of our home"—the Lady arched an eyebrow at her, and Seung felt as though her heart had broken apart in her chest "—of Yathienel, my Lady." Was her right to remain among the people of The Wood in question? Would they really cast her out for bringing Kenyatta and his sister?

"Lies from the mouth of *N'thrala!*" someone blurted, using the elven word for human.

"Wrong! It was wrong to trust the filth of *N'thresha!*" another person shouted. Seung flinched at the elven slur directed at the other half of her heritage.

"I will have none of this." Seiyun's calm voice filled the audience chamber like a physical thing crackling with energy. Any rumblings in the audience came to an abrupt end.

Seung stole a glance to the left of Seiyun, where the tranquil DaunyaSai stood. The Daunya Master's presence felt like a lifeline that Seung clung to with a desperation that surprised herself.

Seiyun returned her attention to the young warrior. Beneath her cold, icy gaze Seung saw disappointment, and it cut deeper than any sword could have. "The trust of the Elfinestraya is not easily earned. Your legacy and your actions a year ago have placed you in high regard in the eyes and hearts of the elfinestraya. But you know the history. You know the mistrust and resentment. How could you lead two humans into our home?"

"My Lady, I swear before the Daunyans Themselves that I did no such thing."

"Then you deny any connection with these two?" Seiyun indicated Kenyatta and Taliah, the former standing stoically, the latter looking unconcerned. Kenyatta kept his gaze forward, but Seung could see the pain and guilt in his eyes.

"My Lady, no. The man is Kenyatta, and he is my love …" she stopped short as murmurs rumbled through the assembly hall. Seiyun swept her gaze over the attendees, once again bringing quiet. She indicated for Seung to continue.

Seung took a deep breath. "And the woman is his sister. They come with important news they say you must hear."

"Important to them, perhaps." The Lady leaned forward in her seat. "And how do they know of me, if not from you, Kiluriel? How did they find Yathienel, and how …"

DaunyaSai leaned down to whisper in Seiyun's ear. Her brow creased and she glanced at Taliah. When the Daunya Master finished, she looked directly at Kenyatta and Taliah and spoke in the elven tongue.

"Do you understand the severity of this situation?" DaunyaSai said, interpreting the queen's words.

"We do, my Lady," Taliah responded. Seung thought her heart would stop. The woman's posture suggested equality. How could Kenyatta not have told her about— "It was necessary for us to come, Lady Seiyun," Taliah continued. "Your home is well hidden and protected from the prying and infantile eyes of the youngest of The Four, but nothing is hidden from the

Daunyans." Seiyun's eyes widened, and beside her, DaunyaSai's lips parted. From what Seung knew of the Daunya Master, that was the equivalent of a gasp.

"Who are you, human child?" DaunyaSai said. Around the audience hall, impatient murmurs had begun again. Few elves spoke the common human tongue of Korea. Fewer if any could understand the western tongue.

"My name is Taliah Ihe, and I am sent by the Daunyans."

Seiyun sat back in her seat, her expression unreadable as the Daunya Master translated. "You claim the title of Daunya Master?"

"I claim to do the will of the Daunyans," Taliah replied. "Whatever title my deeds have earned me is not mine to declare."

"How would I know this to be true, young woman?" Seiyun asked through Daunya Sai.

"Your enchantments upon the lands surrounding your home are impressive and effective, Lady Seiyun," Taliah continued, "but the Daunyans granted me passage and have compelled me to seek you out."

To everyone's shock, Taliah took a step forward. "My Lady. Even now, the drek is nearly finished amassing a sizable demonic force to move against the Tower of Balance, Takashaniel." Gasps sounded around the room, for the name of the Tower of Balance, as Seung had been educated, was known to all.

To the astonished onlookers, Taliah waved her hand a circle, and an image as large as herself appeared in the air. "As you can see, the drek has subjugated a major demon. Its name is Kabriza, and it is the general of the quentranzi demon species." The murmurs grew louder until Seiyun—gaze locked on the image—raised a hand. The hall grew silent. The image shifted.

"Four years ago my brother and four others battled a horde of these demons on the very lands of Takashaniel. Fighting alongside the guardian Iel, a force of centaurs led by the mighty Grimhammer, and band of brunts led by the brave Grit, we defeated the horde."

Taliah let the image fade. "Unfortunately, this victory only served to forestall the inevitable. The drek did not join the fight, nor did his demon general. He has eluded us at every turn and now, four years later, the drek has amassed a force larger than the first, and there is a possibility that a number of stray demons roam the lands."

Taliah looked from the Lady of The Wood to DaunyaSai and back. "These are quentranzi, my Lady. Of all species of fiends, they are as cunning as they are destructive. They are a thinking species, and I have no doubt that as the drek uses them, they are using him. Our fear is that when the time is right, they will eliminate him and fully enter this plane. A darkness no human has ever created would result."

Seiyun watched the woman with her unblinking stare, her expression still unreadable. When Kenyatta's sister finished speaking, the elven queen continued staring at her in the ensuing silence. For her part, Taliah Ihe seemed not at all perturbed.

"That is, quite an account you have given," Seiyun said through Daunya-Sai. She consulted privately with the Daunya Master, then rose and addressed the assembled. "My people. You have seen with your eyes and heard with your ears that grave times are upon us. If this proves true, we face a world of darkness and death. We must discover the truth of this matter for ourselves and then we will act. Know that Yathienel and the homes of the elfinestraya will continue to thrive, for we will see it so.

"Return to your homes. Yathienel is only one of many lands in this vast world, and as I pledged one year ago, the people of The Wood will no longer stand by and let our Mother decay. We will discover what we will. We will learn of these events brewing in distant lands, and if we must, we will fight." Cheers sounded throughout the assembly, but Seung didn't miss the down-turned mouths, the frowns, and scowls directed at her and her human companions.

* * *

Seung's relief at the adjournment of that grim assembly came to a quick end when they met in Seiyun's private rooms. For a while no one spoke, waiting out of respect for the Lady of the Wood. A servant brought tea and quickly left, likely sensing the tension in the air. Seiyun regarded them over a few sips before finally breaking the silence. "You take great risk in bringing them here."

Seung fought the urge to lower her eyes. "I know, *Etisah*. But it could not be helped. The news they bring affects Yathienel no less than the rest of the world."

Seiyun arched an eyebrow, half smiling. "Ah child. I have not lived this many centuries and led our people for so long, only to be fooled by my own daughter's daughter. You knew no more of their news than I. Your actions may have been correct, but they were ruled by your heart."

"If I may, my lady Seiyun," DaunyaSai spoke up. "Only by the will of the Daunyans could they have found Yathienel. By that fact alone, were we compelled to hear them."

Seiyun nodded her agreement and looked at the two seated humans, the male studiously drinking his tea, the female sipping hers with every bit the air of a queen. "I regret the less than warm reception we've extended you, but old wounds heal slowly."

"Of course, my Lady," Taliah said. "Only under the most dire circumstances would we have disturbed your home."

"You seem not at all surprised by our existence," Seiyun said. "Perhaps your brother has confided in you?"

A tiny smile crept across Taliah's dark-skinned features. "To the contrary, Lady Seiyun of Yathienel. I have known of the existence of your fair people for most of my life." Kenyatta shot her a surprised look, which she ignored. "Since I was a child, I have seen and heard things that most humans would consider childhood fantasy, or insanity, as an adult. The Daunyans revealed Themselves to me at a rather young, age. It was at times … difficult."

"Touched by the Daunyans," DaunyaSai whispered. "I don't think I have ever heard of such a thing among humans.

"More than merely touched." It was Tinnoviel Nai SaunyaLi who spoke. All eyes turned to him. "She communicated with So'orya."

Seiyun leaned forward in her seat, and DaunyaSai blinked. "You're sure?" the Master asked.

"When she touched So'orya," Tinnoviel explained, "her vines wrapped around her in what was clearly an embrace. I have never seen anything of the sort."

"So'orya's Embrace," DaunyaSai said, his voice thick with wonder. "She is a Daunya Chosen." Seiyun lowered her mug and stared at the woman.

Kenyatta also stared. "What are they talking about?"

Taliah gave him a tap on the leg. "I will explain things later, Ken. I promise." She looked back to the astonished elves. "Yes. It was discovered when I was a child that the Daunyans had made me one of Their Chosen. Since I was five years old, I have lived with a woman who was also a Daunya Chosen."

"And when you are ready, she will ascend and you will take her place," DaunyaSai said, to which Taliah nodded.

Seiyun shifted her gaze between the two humans and her great granddaughter. "I find here, the presence of two Children of the Gene, one of them my own family. Then, a Daunya Chosen finds her way to Yathienel. The world changes and events are in motion." She looked from DaunyaSai to Tinnoviel. "We must speak of this in private." She then turned to Kenyatta, Taliah, and Seung. "Be comfortable until our return."

* * *

As soon as the door closed, Kenyatta looked expectantly at Taliah. His sister glanced at him several times before she spoke. "I couldn't tell you, Ken. It's not something I could discuss, not even with my brother." She ran a hand through her long thick hair. "It's not something I've fully understood, myself, until recently. Every day I learn more of what it means to be a Chosen of the Daunyans."

"Sounds similar to what it's been like with this Children of the Gene thing that everyone keeps talking about," Kenyatta responded. Despite his attempt at understanding, Taliah could still see the hurt in his face.

"I promise you, when our business here is done, there will be time to talk."

Kenyatta held up a hand. "No need to explain. I won't lie and say it doesn't hurt that you kept this from me, but I understand why."

Taliah seemed to think on what she would say next, before finally addressing the others. "The first battle for Takashaniel was a test. The drek believes he's taken our measure, but I don't think he truly understands what he's dealing with either. He may be able to control legions of demons, and even Kabriza, for a time. But that demon general is nothing to take lightly. Brit may have it under control for now, but if Kabriza somehow manages to dispatch him, or bring his master to this plane, we will have a serious problem."

"Its master?" Kenyatta asked.

Taliah nodded. "Grala, the lord of the quentranzi, is the most powerful of their species. If he steps foot upon this world the implications are none you want to think about. The worst possible outcome would be for the drek to somehow lose his hold over Kabriza, and it manages to bring Grala from the abyss. We cannot let that happen."

"I think I do not understand," Seung said. "You're talking about … demons? That is folklore; tales to share around a campfire."

Kenyatta indicated their surroundings. "A little more than a year ago, if someone had told you that you'd be living among elves in a forest, and that more elven blood than human runs through your veins, would you have believed it?"

Seung conceded the point with a nod. "It still seems like a stretch that there are actual demons waiting to come to this world and destroy everything."

"Whether you believe it or not," Taliah said, "they exist and they will bring ruin to this world if the drek succeeds. But there is one barrier Brit must overcome."

Taliah looked past them, into a distant place in her mind's eye. "Takashaniel is the fulcrum upon which balance in this world sits. The problem is that the tower alone cannot keep evil out of the world completely."

She stood and walked to the balcony to gaze out at the great waterfall beyond. "Takashaniel was created as a barrier, for lack of a better term. As long as there are those who have the knowledge and the means, a demon will be summoned to this world from time to time. It has been that way for millennia uncounted. But Takashaniel prevents the world from being overrun with fiends."

"So, how was this drek able to summon a whole horde of the damned things?" Kenyatta asked.

"Brit, has been able to summon so large a force to his side because of the collective consciousness of The Four." Taliah turned her back on the waterfall to looked from Kenyatta to Seung. "You see, when enough negative energy is concentrated in one place, it provides strength to those who feed from it. If there is a large enough concentration of this energy, someone with the right knowledge and ability can exploit it."

"And bring more demons into the world," Seung replied.

Taliah nodded. "Exactly."

Seung frowned. "So, demons are invading the world because humans as a species have produced more negativity, and have had mostly a negative impact on the world?"

"To some extent, yes," Taliah said. "But don't rest so easily on your elven laurels, girliefriend of my brother. While humans did cause many of the problems, it was the potent disdain by the others of The Four that fed the energy. I don't know how well you've studied human history, Seung, but there is more than just the wars and poisoning of the world and destruction. There were also the attempts to heal, the group consciousness towards the greater good. As there were humans who lived deeply in their insanity, there were also those who lived deeply in consciousness, and worked to repair the damage." The elves grew angry, resentful, and distrustful of *all* humans."

Seung stiffened, and Taliah held up a hand to forestall the incoming argument. "I understand the reason for the animosity, but what I am telling you is that such animosity, mostly from the elves, has aided the situation we have now."

"So why did you not share this earlier?" Seung asked. "I see no reason not to."

Taliah responded with a patient smile. "It was difficult enough for your people to digest the presence of two humans in their home. If one of us had the audacity to insinuate that the elves had even a small part to play in the wave of darkness that has penetrated this dimension, do you think my words would have been heard? The Lady Seiyun is wise, as is the Daunya Master with whom she holds counsel. But the population at large cannot be taken for granted. It takes but one mistake for a great cause to fail."

Seung considered the woman's words. "You have a wise sister," she said to Kenyatta. "What happened to you?"

She and Taliah laughed as Kenyatta sputtered over a response. "Jokes," he said, glancing at the two chuckling women. "Always the jokes. So what now? I'm sure we're not leavin' without Kita."

Taliah nodded. "When our business here is done, we will return to Cebu for Kita and then on to Takashaniel. We will speak with Iel about how we will move against the drek." She settled a heavy gaze on both of them. "Our greatest challenges lie ahead."

Kenyatta looked out at the waterfall and the land carpeted with trees beyond. "I may not be a Daunya Chosen, but I can feel things shifting. It's like the world is changing around us."

"This has been coming for centuries, Kenyatta," Taliah said. "This world has seen change from a golden age, to an age of constant change and evolution and strife. The age of chaos has ruled for centuries, and now we are at the dawn of a new age. Discovery."

"I was hoping you were going to say we were headed for a new golden age," Kenyatta said, smirking.

"A new golden age?" Taliah scoffed. "If that were the case, you would not be one of the Heroes and one of the Children of the Gene. Never in the history of the world has there been more than one, let alone *six*."

"Six?" Seung said.

"Heroes?" Kenyatta said at the same time.

Taliah looked from one to the other. "Later. The Lady and the Daunya Master return."

"Your coming has caused quite a situation," The Lady Seiyun remarked. "There are some who've never set eyes upon a human. There are others who had hoped never to do so again." The elven queen looked regretful. "Alas, for all of the long years we live, my people can have selective memories. Your graciousness has not gone unnoticed, Chosen. I have known that a new age was upon us, but as humans must learn to change to survive in this new world, so too will the others of The Four. The passing of the former age has left no one blameless. It is my duty to help the elves in all the lands to remember our responsibility."

"The short time we spent with the amahle has shown me the possibilities for us all, in this new age," Tinnoviel said. "It need not be a golden age for all the peoples of the world to create a better one."

Seiyun nodded her agreement. "And that brings us back to you, Chosen, and you, Warriors of the Gene."

"I do not understand this Gene," Seung said. "What is it?"

"The Gene of the Daunyans," DaunyaSai replied. "It is a rare and powerful thing, and is born in a child when the need for it is greatest."

"The Daunyans prefer not to meddle in the affairs of mortals," Taliah added, "but the abyss always stirs."

"Why don't these Daunyans just destroy the abyss and everything that lives in it?" Kenyatta asked, slicing his hand horizontally through the air. "Just settle it once and for all?"

Taliah shook her head. "You don't understand the origin of the lower realms and their part in the creation of the cycles of the ages. It was the decisions of some of the most powerful among The Four that created the abyss. Through jealousy and anger, fear and hate, these powerful beings were twisted and remade. Words cannot describe the amount of raw power and energy that was corrupted and set loose upon the world. The magnitude of these events created cycles much like the annual seasons we experience, only on a much grander scale."

"And unfortunately," Seiyun interrupted, "we have not the time to discuss it." She turned a look of great respect on Taliah. "My apologies for my abruptness, but while you have a long and dangerous path before you, I must prepare my people for the dawning of this new age. When your work is done, a healing that has been thousands of years in the coming, shall at last begin."

"Of course, Lady Seiyun," Taliah said, bowing her head respectfully.

"And now I must ask," Seiyun continued. "What would you have of me?"

Taliah pursed her lips. "I do not presume what I am about to ask is easy, but I must. If she is willing, I would ask that your daughter's daughter, Seung Kiluriel Sen'Mora, accompany us to do battle in the defense of Takashaniel."

Seiyun's expression spoke of her dislike of the request, but she looked at Seung.

"I would leave with them, *Etisah*," Seung answered. "My love of Yathienel would be shallow indeed if I declined."

Seiyun nodded. "Your love for Yathienel is as deep as any elf I have ever known. But you are fortunate to have lived in the outside world as well. Do not forget your love for it, as many of us have. Fight for the world first, my sweet, and Yathienel will survive."

The sad look in Seiyun's eyes, mother of the mother she'd never known, pulled at Seung's heart. She stood and embraced her still sitting grandmother. Seiyun smiled and returned the hug, patting Seung on the back. "Impulsive child," she scolded affectionately. "Do not join the Daunyans before your time."

"We all join the Daunyans when it is our time," Seung responded.

Seiyun wiped the tears from her eyes. "My daughter's daughter thinks to become my teacher," she said to DaunyaSai.

"Oh, *Etisah*, why do you not just call me your granddaughter?" Seung teased.

Seiyun waved her away. "And have you calling me grandmother? I'll have nothing of the sort." Her mouth turned down in distaste. "Such a horrible human word."

"Of course, *Etisah*," Seung said in mock submissiveness.

Seiyun smiled affectionately, then turned her gaze on the others. "Kiluriel wishes to accompany you, and thus my consent is given. DaunyaSai has selected a group to fight by your side. I believe you are already acquainted with our best tracker, Immendiel Mai'lienar." She indicated the tracker, standing near the balcony. "I also have sent word to DaunyaSai's most promising apprentice, Yurin Kei Daunyana. She, along with our soon to be legendary Daunya Warrior, Tinnoviel Nai SaunyaLi, will also accompany you."

The smirk that crept over Seiyun's features made Seung want to laugh and cry at the same time, for she knew the next name the Lady would speak.

"I have also been informed," Seiyun continued, "in the least affectionate manner as is possible, that one other would not be left behind."

"Tikena Mojin," Seung mumbled. To her own surprise, however, she was only half dreading traveling once again with the tiresome and harsh little elf. Their first adventure together last year had gotten off to a horrible start, but after all they had been through, Seung and Tikena had come to some measure of a truce. It even seemed that during Seung's stay in The Wood over the past year, that the two had formed something of a friendship, though neither would openly admit it.

"I offer you our hospitality for the night," Seiyun declared. "You will be properly provisioned for your departure in the morning."

They thanked the Lady and departed. Seung led Kenyatta and Taliah to a dining room where they could eat in privacy.

"I apologize for this meal being such a segregated arrangement," Seung began, and Taliah shook her head.

"Our arrival was abrupt and disruptive, though unavoidable."

Kenyatta nodded. "No need to create any more problems." As if to punctuate the matter, an elven child who looked to have passed no more than four or five summers peeked around the doorway. Kenyatta smiled and made a face, which earned him a giggle. The little elven girl stepped a little farther into the opening and made a face back at Kenyatta, who laughed and made his eyes cross. The little elven girl giggled again and stuck out her tongue. Just then, the angry voice of an adult sounded from down the hall where the little girl had come from.

A woman who was surely the mother spoke in a sharp tone to the little girl, who flinched. The woman then glared at Kenyatta and Taliah. She gently lifted the little girl and placed her on her hip, then with one last glare, disappeared around the doorway. Kenyatta stared after them for a moment, then turned a helpless look on the others. Seung looked even more wounded than he felt.

They ate in silence for a while, and once finished, spoke about the changing world, and what they could expect in the days to come. After a time, they fell silent again each retreating into their own thoughts to consider what the future may hold. After enduring the covert glances between her brother and Seung, Taliah was relieved to see DaunyaSai enter.

"Ah, Daunya Master," she said, standing. DaunyaSai opened his mouth to speak, then closed it, studying her with a calm and knowing expression. Taliah hooked her elbow with the surprised elf's, and steered him toward the door. "I would have a word with you in private, if I may?"

"Of course, Chosen," the Master said, glancing back at the other two, who seemed not to have noticed the exchange, or that he had even entered the room. "Let us ascend to the top of So'orya while we speak. You will find the view pleasing."

Seung and Kenyatta stared at each long after the other two had departed. Kenyatta found her light brown eyes hypnotizing. He could stare at them for the rest of his life. Seung rested her head in her hands, her round pink lips poking out slightly as she held his gaze. "What to do now, my love?"

"What indeed," Kenyatta said. "I've a few creative things in mind."

"Oh? Tell me."

"I'd rather show you." They stood and left the dining room. As they climbed a pearlescent white spiral staircase, Kenyatta hesitated. "We're not in your home. I wouldn't want to disrespect—" she cut him off with a kiss, then patted his cheek.

"The Lady only offered two rooms, love." Seung smiled, her eyes smoldering. "The elves aren't *that* prudish."

Kenyatta chuckled. "Lead on."

Their room was small, but warm and comfortable, and the window faced the grand waterfall below. Even from this height it was magnificent. For a time, they looked out the window, hand in hand. Finally, Seung turned toward him and ran her hand through his hair. "How long did it take them to grow like this?" She asked, inspecting one of the tightly twisted locks.

"You really want me to explain it now?"

"Not really," she said, head tilted to the side as she continued inspecting the hair in her fingers. She slid her hands down his chest and slipped her delicate fingers underneath his tunic, caressing his torso as she lifted it up and over his head. Her eyes took him in while she ran her hands over the muscles of his stomach and chest. Her fingers were soft and delicate, yet there was strength there as well.

She leaned forward and they shared a brief kiss, then another, until finally she crushed her body to his. Kenyatta was silent as he lifted her lightly woven tunic over her head. They took their time undressing each other, exploring each other.

Kenyatta looked over her shoulder and noticed there was no bed, then remembered that the elves didn't sleep, but took a meditation-like reverie, so Seung had told him.

Where a bed would have been, lay a soft, thick woven rug on the floor. He lowered her onto it, kissing every inch of her body as she held his head in her hands. She pulled him back to eye-level and looked into his dark brown eyes. Her mouth moved, yet no sound came. Though he could have read the words from her lips, he heard them in his mind.

"I love you," she'd said, but not to his ears, but his mind. He flinched at the unexpected experience. Though he couldn't respond in kind, Kenyatta opened his mouth to speak, but she placed her fingers over his lips. "I know."

And as they joined, they felt the arms of Se'lir and Amayilah, the Daunyans of love and creation, encircle them. Their senses were heightened, every caress, every movement, was magnified while they were held in the caress of the Daunyans. Tears of bliss streamed down Seung's face, and she knew, as did Kenyatta, that they were forever joined. The Daunyans of Love and Creation had bonded them.

13

B ehind the gentle, soft spoken exterior of Bishop Marquis, lay a fierce and unbending devotion to Holy Jemanah and the people he shepherded. He sighed, hands clasped behind his back as he gazed out the window of his room at the city below. He liked the view from high above, not out of arrogance, but because he liked to see the city as a whole. Sometimes it was just as affective to see the mood of a city from above, as it was from within. Today the city looked subdued, but also restless. He sighed again.

The people were afraid. The grizzly murders hadn't ceased despite King Elizander's best efforts, and the troublesome Brother Dinman was using the situation to his advantage. Ever had that one mentally fashioned himself leader of the "flock", as he referred to the people. Some of the other brothers in the church had repeatedly expressed concern about the growing popularity of Dinman's fanatical sermons, but what was Marquis to do? If he openly opposed the monk, it would only strengthen the already growing division in the church. Although the majority of the brothers of the Church of Jemanah still supported Bishop Marquis, the last thing the people needed was a divided and fighting clergy.

Marquis knew he needed to do something soon. He left the window and returned to his desk, sliding his reading spectacles up the bridge of his nose. A request had come from the Church of Holly Jemanah in Mairson. Bishop Ardell wished to know of events in New Dainland. As he and Marquis and Elizander himself had known was inevitable, Lord Mairson had begun to openly suspect that Elizander Dain was behind the murders in some way. Of course, Bishop Ardell had tried to—as carefully as possible—assure Mairson that such thoughts were ridiculous, but Lord Mairson was nothing if not unreasonable.

Marquis dipped a feather in a little ink pot at his desk and was beginning to write a response when a gentle knock came at the door. "Come," Marquis said absently as he dipped his pen. He heard the door open, then close. Many minutes passed before he realized the person had not spoken. The realization left no doubt in the bishop's mind the identity of his visitor. Only a member of the Order of Dasha had such patience. The monk could stand there all day if Marquis neglected to speak for so long. That is, if the monk was so inclined. That would never happen, as Marquis was not so foolish.

He looked over his spectacles at the robed figure and raised his eyebrows. "To what do I owe this pleasure, Arief?" the Bishop asked, reminding himself to omit the title of 'Brother'. The monks of the Order of Dasha frowned upon titles of status.

"There is a problem," the deep voice replied.

Marquis resumed his task. "Isn't there always? We have gruesome affairs happening in the city. Lord Mairson casts his gaze here as a possible cause to the happenings in his own city, despite our same situation here. And the killer, whether man or beast, has not been found. Combine this with the increasingly sharp burr in my sandal that is Brother Dinman, and I would say there are plenty of problems of late, my friend." He looked at the silent robed figure, barely able to meet the stony gaze peering back at him from within his cowl. He might have been a statue. "But of course, you did not come here to discuss my problems, or the problems of the city. What have you, then?"

"You are wrong," the monk said. He always spoke this way, direct. In the years Bishop Marquis had known Arief, he could think of no instance when he'd seen the monk show any emotion. He supposed the training that the monks of Dasha underwent would burn the emotions from anyone. He shivered to think about it.

"My business here does involve the city. The killings are by no man or beast from this world."

Marquis sat the feather in the ink pot, confused. "What do you suggest, Arief? If not man or beast from this world, as you put it, then what? Surely the Time of Reckoning is not upon us."

"I leave the religious stories to your brethren, Bishop. I speak in fact alone. What has been killing the people of Winsor is not a person, and not an animal from this world."

74

"Then what is it?" Marquis asked, growing anxious. The more you speak, the less I like it."

"You will like it far less in a moment," Arief replied. "Someone is tampering with the barrier between this world and the abyss. We can feel the veil being tested."

Marquis stared at the monk, hoping he'd misunderstood.

"Someone extremely powerful is dealing with the abyssal. We are sure there is a host of fiends in this world already."

The blood drained from Marquis's face. Not many people knew of the existence—the *true* existence—of the demon realm. Bishop Marquis found himself numbered among the small few who wished they didn't know. "How could such a thing be possible? No one person, no *group* of people could do this."

"I would be inclined to agree," the monk replied. "You know the story of the foolish one from our Order who separated and thought to summon a major demon."

Marquis nodded. "What was left of him was the stuff of nightmares."

"And it took a circle of five to banish it," Arief added, still not a hint of emotion. Marquis wondered if anything could rile the monk. "Whomever has accomplished this much is clearly able to contain them, which means they will continue summon more of the demons until he loses his hold or they figure out a way to eliminate him. It's a matter of time."

Marquis felt a coldness settle in the pit of his stomach. "How would we know if they did manage to kill him?"

"Instead of just one demon killing people one at a time, we will be overrun. Every city, every village, every civilization, ripped apart. A cloak of darkness would descend upon this world like nothing your apocalyptic religious texts could possibly portray."

Bishop Marquis leaned back in his chair and removed his spectacles, running a thick hand through his black and gray speckled hair.

"The Order of Dasha is preparing," Arief continued. "We are too few to stop the wave that is coming, but there are others." He turned to leave.

"Wait," Bishop Marquis said. The monk stopped at the door and half turned. All Marquis could see underneath the cowl of the monk's robes were his eyes, that sometimes seemed to glow. He tried not to think about that. "How do we deal with this thing in the city? Surely I cannot tell King Elizander Dain that there is a demon stalking his streets."

"Do what you must, good Bishop. Whether now, or later, the human populous must *and will* learn the truth of the world and awake from the lie.

Elizander Dain cannot protect his people with ignorance." He paused for a moment, then added, "bring your Brother Dinman under control. He empowers the darkness that descends upon us."

"In the name of Holy Jemanah Himself!" Bishop Marquis breathed.

Arief continued out the door. "Ask your Jemanah to kneel beside you and pray to the Daunyans if you believe it will help."

Marquis sat for a long while in the flickering candlelight of his study. He'd never seen a demon before, but he knew better than to doubt the monk. As the sole ambassador for the Order of Dasha, Arief was capable of things it seemed only Holy Jemanah should be able to accomplish. The Order was smart, in that it stayed hidden. The populous and even the brothers of the Church of Jemanah would be quick to label the monks of Dasha as evil heretics.

He rested his head in his hands. Well, at least he knew what was killing the citizens. The challenge now was how to get the king to understand this without being deemed a fool or having lost his wits. It was times like this when the portly bishop felt every one of his sixty one years. Perhaps it was time to start considering a successor. He slid his hands over his face and massaged his scalp. No. Now wasn't the time for musing over retirement. He needed to speak with King Elizander as soon as possible, though he knew not what he would say. He rose from his desk, thinking to head straight for the king's quarters when there came a knock at the door.

* * *

Marquis didn't bother to hide the weariness in his voice. "Come."

"I knock on the chamber door and a weary man answers in the Bishop's stead?"

King Elizander.

Marquis cleared his voice as he opened the door for the king of Windsor. "Please forgive me, my lord. These times can wear on a man, as I'm sure you understand." He offered the king a seat across from his desk. "How may I be of service?"

"I'm sure you have an idea of why I've come, Bishop," Elizander said.

Marquis made an effort not to slump. "Brother Dinman," he sighed. "Yes, my lord, I am quite aware of his activities of late."

"Then you are also aware that his timing is rather inopportune at the moment, though I would welcome a permanent reprieve from his rather, vigorous, proclamations."

"Trust that I would like nothing better myself, my lord."

"Is this beyond your station?" Elizander inquired.

"If only my intervention could be so simple," Marquis replied. "Irritating and fanatical though he is, Brother Dinman, unfortunately, is no fool. Should I openly denounce his behavior, it would deepen the division in the church."

"I understand your situation, Bishop, but this problem must be handled." Elizander rubbed his smooth chin. "I have enough to concern me with these killings than to be troubled with this. Brother Dinman is a part of the church, and therefore is within your province. I need not tell you that it would not do for me to interfere in matters concerning the Church of Jemanah, Bishop Marquis. It is to you, as bishop of the church, that I must rely upon to see this situation resolved."

Bishop Marquis ran a thick hand through his hair once again and nodded. "Of course, my lord. Never would I ask such a thing as your intervention in matters of the church." He started to say more, then hesitated.

"What is it?" Elizander asked.

"It is ... nothing, my lord. Just a random thought."

"Speak it, good Bishop." Elizander said.

Marquis took a deep breath, inhaling his hopes that the king would not immediately pass him off as insane. "I have ... been informed of the possible identity of the killer."

Elizander Dain gave him a sharp look. "And you've waited till now to share this information?"

The bishop held his hand up to forestall the onslaught. "My lord. It is rather difficult to digest, but disturbing nonetheless." Elizander waved a hand for him to continue. "I would rather look into this matter first before troubling you with the whispered gossip of the city, my lord. I doubt it is worth your time to consider it."

Elizander leaned back in his chair and crossed his arms over his chest. "Let me be the judge of that. What news do you have?"

Marquis looked directly into Elizander's eyes as he spoke. "My lord. As hesitant as I am to speak these words, they come from a reliable source. The one that has been killing the citizens is ... a demon."

Marquis seemed to exhale a breath he'd been holding for some time. Elizander just sat there, staring at Marquis as though waiting for the punch-line of a joke with terrible timing.

The king finally chuckled, but there was no mirth behind it. "You would have me believe that the murders in my city are being committed by a demon? A demon, come crawling from hell to devour the citizens of new

Dainland one person at a time? I'd imagine that if a demon were loose in a city it would slaughter indiscriminately, running through the streets in a crazed frenzy."

Bishop Marquis cleared his throat. "That would depend on the species of demon, my lord. A demon from the upper levels of the abyss would be predisposed to such behavior. The more powerful species are possessed of a higher intelligence..." he trailed off at the warning look from the king.

"Bishop Marquis, I have not come here for a humorous dialogue with you. If you truly have insight into these murders, speak them now, otherwise my visit here is at its end."

"Of course, my lord," Marquis said, bowing his head respectfully. He endured the uncomfortable silence as Dain studied him. He willed the king to see that he was indeed serious.

"Bishop Marquis," Elizander ventured. "You do not strike me as someone who has lost his wits, yet you speak as though you have. What am I to make of this?"

"I cannot say, my lord, as I, too, do not know what to make of this. I assure you there are many scenarios I would have preferred to present to you."

"Yet you believe it? How could you ... *you*, of all people, believe this?"

Marquis spread his hands. "I can only say that this information comes from a very reliable source, my lord. Foolish and fanciful though it sounds."

"And does this reliable source recommend a way to deal with this, ah, demonic problem?"

The bishop stiffened. "My lord, I understand how foolish this all sounds, and I would have discounted it out of hand had it not been for the source of the information."

"Be that as it may, this is not something that I can move on. I cannot lead my men on a demon hunt, lest I risk being taken to the infirmary and having my sanity assessed."

"Of course, my lord," Marquis agreed. "But if I may, I would recommend at least extending your search outside the grounds of the city. Perhaps you may find something."

"You think we may stumble upon this creature?" Elizander said with mild sarcasm.

Again, the bishop spread his hands. "I pray you do not, but we agree that one way or another, this problem must be dealt with."

"If your reliable source is so much more enlightened of the situation than we are, why do they not help?" It was a good point, and Marquis had no answer. "I know not what game this is, or what you know of it, Bishop," Elizander said, and there was no mistaking the warning in his tone, "but I would suggest either you, or this source of yours come forth with more than fanciful enemies for us to hunt down. Between keeping the populace calm, and keeping Mairson placated, I have not the time for religious fiction finding its way into the situation."

More levelheaded than most of his brethren, Marquis wanted to tell Elizander that demons had nothing to do with religion. Instead he chose the wiser response. "Yes, King Elizander. I will do my best to help with these troubles. He waved a hand over the letter from Ardell. "I have been in correspondence with the bishop of Mairland, and he shares our concern about his lord. He has been attempting to reason with the man, but reports indicate his success as, less than we'd hoped for."

Dain nodded, unsurprised. "And does Bishop Ardell share your fears of a supernatural enemy?" Marquis could tell Elizander tried to keep his tone neutral, but a bit of impatience still seeped through.

"I cannot say for sure, but I would suspect not, my lord."

Elizander leaned forward and ran a hand through his dark brown hair. He looked hard at Marquis, assessing him, he knew.

The king finally released him from his vice-like gaze and rose. "I must take my leave, good Bishop. Perhaps I will heed your advice. The killer may stalk the streets and then somehow find a way to flee the city every night. And ... perhaps there is some large animal, an apex predator hunting the streets. I'm sure anyone witnessing such a ghastly sight would think they saw something more."

Marquis felt a swell of gratitude that the king had made an effort to afford him at least that small bit of credibility.

He paused at the door when Marquis spoke up. "I hope your hunt is successful, King Elizander, but I pray it is not."

Elizander Dain turned and looked at him once more. He gave a sharp nod, then stepped out of the office, closing the door quietly behind him.

* * *

Elizander stalked the halls of the palace, his personal guard surrounding him. He disliked such close proximity, but there was nothing for it. Davros was having nothing of his protests, and even Milpheus would not bend on the subject. How surprised he'd been to see the two actually in agreement about something. He quickened his step. The attacks were becoming a nightly occurrence, and tonight he would assemble a party with Davros and patrol the grounds outside the city while a large force scoured the streets within. Either they would catch the killer or killers inside the city, our they would catch them entering or fleeing. One way or another, this ended tonight. A blood-chilling scream rent the air and stopped him in his tracks.

14

Takashaniel called from the west. Akemi had already been discussing it with her brother when the Shinobu had appeared on the road. Somehow, the tower had moved. The dream, the tugging feeling inside, the sudden appearance of the strider. None of it was by chance. Akemi glanced at the farstrider. Some of the sarcastic adventurer still existed in the man beside her, but he seemed haunted; more wary. She'd attempted to speak with him about it, but he'd just responded with that cavalier sarcasm of his.

She thought about the last time they'd spoken, traversing the scarred battlefield in the aftermath of the demon horde attack on Takashaniel. "There's a matter that I must deal with," Shinobu had said. "When it's done, maybe I'll pay you a visit."

"Promise?" Akemi had flirted.

"That depends on whether I have dealt with the matter, or it has dealt with me."

That response left Akemi puzzled. She'd offered to travel with Shinobu and help him with whatever problem he faced, but he'd smiled as he declined. "Only I can deal with this."

At the time, Akemi had thought it simply man foolishness, but seeing him now, she wondered. And what of that sword on his back? She could sense power radiating from it. Having dealt with a sentient blade for most of her life, she knew presence within a weapon when she felt it. The sword resting behind Shinobu's back practically radiated its presence, while Shinobu himself seemed off; as though his thoughts were distant. Though he tried to hide it, Akemi noticed the occasional facial expressions, as though he was reacting to something spoken.

At first she had feared his mind had somehow been damaged, but what she felt from that sword gave her pause. Years ago she'd been told that there were rare objects in the world possessed of such sentience that they could actually communicate telepathically. She'd passed off such a concept as far-fetched at the time. Years later she knew better. She thought of the two swords resting in their scabbards at her lower back.

Akemi allowed her gaze to linger on the strider until he looked back, feeling her eyes on him. He smiled and she returned it. He returned his attention back to the road ahead. Akemi nodded. *Very well.*

"What do you think the world will be like when this is done?"

The sound of Kenjiro's voice wrenched Akemi from her thoughts. "What do you mean? Why would it be any different than it is now? We will fight. And this time, we will hunt down whoever is summoning the demons and we will kill *them* as well."

"You believe that'll be the end of it?" Kenjiro asked.

"Not the absolute end. As long as humans have darkness in their hearts, there will always be the threat of a fiend piercing the barrier into this realm …" she trailed off when her brother shook his head.

"What I meant to ask was, do you really think this conflict will be so neatly contained? How long, before humans are aware of the truth? There is more at stake than a simple battle to stop a horde of demons and the killing of the one who brought them here."

"What are you suggesting, Kenjiro?" Akemi asked.

"It doesn't start or end with this battle, Sister," Kenjiro replied, still looking ahead. "The things we've seen, the beings we've met … how long will the rest of humanity live in ignorance?"

"What does it matter?"

"I don't know if it does, or not. But we're at a turning point. I feel it. Whatever happens when this is done, it will be the start of a revelation to the rest of humanity that there is more to this world than what we've seen or believed. If there are demons and rock people and centaurs, what else?"

"Indeed," Shinobu chimed in. "Trust me, samurai, you have only seen the small of it." Kenjiro looked at him a moment, then returned his gaze forward. Shinobu glanced at *Onihakaisha* and *Onisekairu* strapped to Akemi's back. "You've added a new sword to your collection?"

Akemi shook her head. "No. *Sekimaru* was corrupted. The only way to restore it was for it to be broken and remade." She ran a hand over the hilt of *Onihakaisha*. "As before, the Daunyans had a hand in it. The essence and power of *Sekimaru* was augmented, and the one sword became two. Like twin spirits birthed by the one. The time of *Sekimaru* passed to give way for *Onihakaisha* and *Onisekairu*."

"Can you control them?" the strider asked, looking directly at her. "There is so much aggressive power radiating from those swords."

"They haven't been tested," Akemi admitted. "Not truly. I've not had the time for it."

Shinobu nodded, as though he understood exactly what she meant.

Kenjiro looked ahead at the descending sun. "We have less than an hour before dark." The surrounding landscape had taken on the golden hue of dusk, the shadows of the trees and hills fleeing to the east.

"We should travel till dark," Akemi stated, "then make camp."

"I don't like this," Kenjiro said. "It feels as though we're being driven. Like something is compelling us to move."

"Like something inside is pulling you forward at any cost," Shinobu agreed. "Yes, it's unsettling. Like I cannot rest until we reach the tower."

"You suppose *they* know where we're going?" Akemi asked, jerking her chin in the direction of the path ahead. A mob of twisted, inhuman creatures lumbered toward them.

Kenjiro rested a hand on his sword. "I'm surprised we've made it this far without incident. But what concerns me is why they are being sent."

Akemi nodded. "That drek knows these things pose no real threat, which leads me to wonder what his game is."

"Maybe he hopes one of them will get lucky?" the strider remarked, grinning.

Kenjiro replied, drew his sword. "More likely he wants to delay us."

Akemi felt the eagerness of *Onisekairu* and *Onihakaisha* when she reached back to grip their hilts. The swords practically salivated for the taste of demon essence.

Shinobu's hand hovered over the hilt of his sword. "I'm not so sure delaying us is the goal, here. Does the drek really think a small mob of lower demons such as this," he waved a hand at the approaching creatures, "would hinder us for long?"

"Maybe he's toying with us by sending the most horrible image possible," the samurai said, backing away.

Akemi looked at her brother in confusion, then looked closer at the approaching mob. They weren't demons at all. The creatures staggering toward them were not denizens from the abyss, but corrupted, twisted humans! Mouths too large for their heads hung open in soundless screams. Flesh darkened as though burned clung to their bodies, and milky-white eyes stared straight ahead.

"What in the name of the Daunyans is this?" Shinobu breathed.

"You know what they were," Akemi said. "Twisted and tormented humans. I didn't know the drek could be so creative."

"And now we know why the Ilanyan wishes us to hurry," Kenjiro said.

Akemi drew her swords. "They cannot be saved. The best we can do is release them if their souls are trapped in those corrupted bodies. If they are not, either way, the vessels must be destroyed."

They charged the twisted mob of corrupted humans, suppressing their revulsion as they cut through twisted limbs and bodies, blocking out the sounds of inhuman moaning and gurgling as they felled one after another of the former humans. Within moments, the three warriors had reduced the hapless creatures to a pile of indistinguishable carcasses.

Kenjiro sheathed his sword in disgust. Shinobu wore a similar look of distaste as he stared at the macabre scene.

"We need to burn them," Akemi said, "but be careful not to touch them."

"You think we would?" Shinobu replied.

Akemi struck a pack of tinder and began lighting the bodies afire. Kenjiro and Shinobu followed suit, and soon the air filled with the sickening smell of burning flesh.

They watched the blaze until Akemi declared the bodies burned enough to leave. Kenjiro and Shinobu looked at each other, then at the ninja.

"We need not worry about the land or any animals being corrupted," the ninja demon hunter said. "Nothing will venture close to this patch of ground till the next heavy rain washes away the remaining filth. We burned the bodies before the taint could sap into the earth."

"You don't seem disturbed at all by this," Shinobu observed.

Akemi looked from him to her brother, who was also watching her, a questioning expression on his face as well.

"Have you forgotten my trade?" she asked

"You hunt demons, Akemi," Kenjiro said. "Those were not demons."

"That matters little. I do hunt demons, and demons can be quite creative. They have a habit of toying with humans before and after they kill them. Just as you must shut off your heart when battling a normal human enemy who tries to kill you, so too must you shut off your mind against the thought of what befell the ones we just released."

Akemi sheathed her swords. "They feed from your torment, physical and mental."

After a lengthy moment of studying her face, Shinobu offered a nod appreciation. "There's much yet to learn about you, Ninja."

"Not much of it is pleasing," Akemi responded. "My profession is not a pleasant one, and it takes a toll. Most don't last long."

"But you are different."

"Some would say it's the Gene of the Daunyans," Akemi said, but Shinobu shook his head.

"Who would that "some" say, when most know nothing of it? The Gene augments our physical abilities and perceptions. It does not shield our minds. You know this. The Daunyans selected us because of who and what we are. You told me three years ago that you didn't feel the Gene within you for years."

Akemi shrugged and started down the trail.

"When you are tested, truly tested," Shinobu continued, "it will not be the Gene of the Daunyans that brings you victory any more than a powerful weapon can grant you the skills to use it."

"Such wisdom," Akemi remarked.

Shinobu glared at her in mock annoyance and looked to the horizon. "I have a feeling we will all be tested before this business is done."

"I have a feeling you've already passed your trial, Strider," Akemi said, appraising him. "It's been two years, and you've the look of a man who has been through each of the five hells and come out the other side."

Shinobu continued to stare at the western horizon, cast in a golden glow by the setting sun. "One year," Shinobu said, a wistful tone creeping into his voice. "One year of my life, and I've been shown how blind and naïve our species truly is." He looked at the other two. "The things I've seen in the year since we parted ways are out of legend and nightmares. Our people, humans, have no idea what exists out there, and how fragile we are."

He drew his sword from its sheath and held it before him. The flat blade was a bit wider than a Japanese crafted sword, but the edge looked impossibly sharp. Strange runes adorned the metal, and Akemi had enough experience with the supernatural to know it was of non-human origin.

Akemi started to ask what his point was in holding the sword when it began to change form. As the strider held the sword before him, the blade began to waver as though becoming insubstantial, almost ethereal. Several heartbeats later the blade transformed into what looked like a wavy cloud of light in the shape of a blade.

Seeing the blade of the sword in this state, Akemi thought back to the times she'd battled alongside the strider. "The sword can only maintain a solid state for a short time," she surmised. "That's why you only draw it at the moment it's needed.

"*Zaiku*, its name is." Shinobu looked at the blade with a mixture of appreciation and something else. Wariness? "My life has come close to ending more times than I can count while it has been in my possession." He turned a rather haunted smile on Akemi and Kenjiro.

"What you see is the blade's second form, so to speak. The sheath," Shinobu patted the scabbard strapped to his back, "is what keeps the blade physically linked to this world. I don't pretend to know how it works, but while in the sheath, the blade retains its physical form. The longer the sword is out of its sheath, the less substantial it becomes, but also more powerful."

The strider nodded at Akemi. So, yes, that is why I only draw the sword at the moment I need it. Two, perhaps three blocks or parries and the sword must be replaced to its sheath, but only for an instant. That is the trade-off. If I need more power from the blade, I can keep it out, but there is no way to stop or deflect an attack. Though I must avoid every strike, there is no living thing in this world or any other that can withstand the cut of *Zaiku* in its light form." Shinobu replaced the sword to its sheath.

"And that has been your trial?" Akemi asked. "To master the sword without losing your life?"

Shinobu snorted. "If only it were so easy. I've dealt with quite durable foes from this world and the abyss. But what hunted me when I took up this sword was well beyond anything I've ever encountered from the demon realms."

Akemi and Kenjiro glanced at each other. "What do you mean?" the samurai asked. "If not human or demon, what else exists that would hunt you?"

"A nightmare," the strider replied. "I've avoided speaking of it this long, for even to speak its name would have given me nightmares. I have told none what I am about to tell you."

For a few moments they rode in silence as the golden landscape gradually turned blue, the last rays of the sun lighting the darkening sky. Bird chatter gave way to the song of the night insects and croaking frogs and toads.

"I don't know what hands forged this weapon, but I suspect that whoever created it was rather particular about who could wield it. I don't believe I number among those they had in mind. Once I'd taken up *Zaiku*, a guardian awoke. A thing of terror that pursued me relentlessly since that day." Shinobu gazed into the distance, his eyes giving away the horrors he'd faced. It was the most sober Akemi had ever seen him.

Shinobu took a deep breath and let it out. "The guardian was the Khazira."

15

"Khazira?" Akemi said. As soon as the word left her lips, she felt a sense of dread and had no desire to utter it again.

"I have encountered little that truly struck fear into my heart," Shinobu said, "but that thing was one."

"How long did it track you?" Kenjiro asked.

"That was the strange part," Shinobu said. "When first I took up *Zaiku*, it appeared only moments after. It almost killed me right then. Only through a bit of luck had I managed to elude it. I had been traveling through an underground passageway and had happened upon a chamber I wish I'd never discovered. Back then, even in my obliviousness I doubted human hands could have crafted the place. Against a far wall of the chamber, resting in an alcove, sat the most beautiful sword I'd ever seen. Once I had taken it in my hands, a disembodied voice spoke to me of the consequences of my action. Soon after, the Khazira came."

Shinobu frowned in remembrance of that fateful day. "This sword has the ability to shift into a dimension called the spectral realm, which was how I eluded the Khazira."

He ran a hand over his face and around the back of his neck. "It chased me from this dimension to the spectral and back until I finally gave it the slip. For a year there'd been nothing, and I began to think I'd escaped it entirely. I was wrong."

"It still hunts you?" Kenjiro asked.

They found a knoll in the middle of a patch of woods and set camp for the night. Luck was with them, as the cool dusk air did not carry with it the smell of rain, but only a comforting breeze.

"I'll not lie to you," Shinobu said, and Akemi could tell he was picking his words. "I'm not sure the thing can be destroyed, but I dealt it enough injury that it hasn't pursued me for some time."

Akemi glanced at Kenjiro and knew what he was thinking. She turned back to the strider. "Let us hope this monster is a permanent part of your past."

"Indeed," Shinobu agreed. But whether or not it is truly destroyed, you need not worry. It has no quarrel with you, only the possessor of the sword. It would come only for me."

"Our thanks for your concern, Strider," Kenjiro said, "but three years ago we named you friend. We share each other's fate, for good or ill. Let's just hope this beast is a memory and no more."

Shinobu bowed his head in thanks.

"That little confrontation back there has me concerned," Akemi said, once the men had returned with firewood.

"Concerned?" Kenjiro shook his head. "We fought a group of demonized human beings and you are merely concerned. I should not be surprised."

"Nothing," she said, "but a demon can turn a human into such a thing."

"So the drek is having humans turned into monsters. Is that a surprise?"

"Yes" Akemi replied. "What gain would there be in having humans turned into monsters? You saw how they moved. Their limbs were twisted and their minds destroyed. No army could be created out of that."

"Perhaps to dishearten us?" Shinobu offered, but she shook her head.

"He would be a fool would think such a thing. We are not oblivious humans living in villages and cities, blind to the truth. We have battled his force before."

Kenjiro tore a strip from his skewer of roasting meat and took a bite. "What are you suggesting? The drek is no fool. There is a reason for this."

"Or perhaps," Akemi replied, "he doesn't have as tight a hold on his minions as he believes. The last thing the drek wants is for the human population to become aware of him and what he's doing until he's ready. Capturing and twisting humans into monsters wouldn't serve his goal."

"You believe there are strays doing this without his knowledge?" Kenjiro asked. "There have always been demons that find a way into this dimension from time to time. It is not wholly unusual."

"But it takes a certain intellect," Akemi said. "Most of the demons that pierce the barrier are lower fiends possessed only of enough cunning to skulk the barriers until they find a way to sneak through. Usually via a foolish human that knows too much for their own good."

"A summoning," Kenjiro said.

Akemi nodded. "Sometimes a powerful and foolish person with access to too much of the wrong knowledge and tools manages to catch the attention of a more powerful fiend. The result is almost always a death more hideous than your imagination could conjure."

Akemi closed her eyes. The crackling campfire provided a soothing melody while breaking the chill of the moonlit night. Cicadas and amphibians serenaded each other over the soft whistle of the breezy woods.

"Sometimes," she continued, "something even worse happens. A merging."

"A *merging*?" Shinobu echoed. He looked at Kenjiro to see a worried look on the samurai's face. Since he'd known the man, Shinobu couldn't remember seeing much emotion from him.

"Sometimes, through subtlety, a demon can trick a human into believing it is something that it is not, and merge with them. More often than not, however, it is when a human that is evil to the core of their being, summons a powerful demon. In their arrogance they believe they are powerful enough to contain the fiend, and they make a deal.

"In exchange for access to this world, the demon can merge with the one who summoned it. The human is now far more powerful than ever, and the demon not only has access to this plane of existence, but also cannot be banished in the same manner. They gain the human's intellect, making it smarter and better able to understand the earth plane." She looked at the two sitting opposite the fire.

"I'm sure I need not tell you how dangerous a situation like that could be."

"You speak from experience," the strider said, only half asking.

Akemi nodded. "Only once, have I encountered such an abomination. A *seaph*. Stronger than a human, resistant to most forms of earthly injury, and can think like a human. The worst traits in each come together to create a beast that is more difficult to kill than most demons." She sat staring absently into the campfire, the flames reflecting in her light brown eyes. "Pray you never meet one."

Kenjiro, being the older brother to a Ninja Demon Hunter, already knew of the existence of *seaphs*. Never had Akemi come so close to death than when she'd battled one of the dangerous things. "I suppose we should prepare ourselves for the possibility of encountering one?"

"Prepare for it and hope against it," came the reply.

"Well," Shinobu said, "this all makes for a great bedtime story. Sleep should come much easier now." He smirked at Akemi, who couldn't help but chuckle. "Perhaps I'll keep first watch?"

"I would rather," she said, standing. "Night is the best cover, and I've a sense for them."

"As you wish," the strider said, untying his bedroll. "I sleep light anyway, so help will be timely, eh samurai?" Kenjiro simply shook his head and untied his bedroll, laying atop it with his sword beside him. Shinobu shrugged and did the same.

Akemi watched them for a few moments before climbing a nearby tree, leaping from branch to branch. She didn't climb to the top, but only high enough to have a clear vantage point. Kenjiro had never been as good as she at climbing and leaping the branches. He'd always fallen if he tried to keep up. She smiled at the memories of a household with two children, one training as a samurai, and one a ninja. Their parents had been proud of them both, but there had been an underlying favoritism for Kenjiro's path. She did not begrudge her parents. The samurai were noble and honorable, embodying all that a person, warrior or general citizen, admired in their homeland.

The path of the ninja was not so glorious. Spies and assassins, ninjas were hired to kill without being identified. As time passed, the ninja warrior began to evolve and sects emerged. Few of the human populous knew or believed that demons truly existed, so it seemed that ninjas were well suited for dealing with the fiends. Japanese stories and folklore commonly spoke of the ninja hunting and battling demons that came to this world.

Akemi huffed in bitter amusement. Her family hadn't understood even the beginning of her training. A simple ninja would not survive long as a demon hunter. The strider did not understand when she'd said that most ninjas didn't last long as demon hunters. Only one type of demon hunter that she had ever known of could survive as a lone hunter.

She closed her eyes, allowing the crisp night air to caress her face and neck. She opened them again, sighing. It had taken years for the family to adjust with the two of them training in opposite paths in the same home. Her parents had been proud when Kenjiro had finally become a samurai. They had also been proud when Akemi had earned the rank of Master Ninja, a title few achieved. She could have led her sect if she'd chosen. Despite her accomplishment, her parents saw Kenjiro's achievements as more "honorable".

Master Ninja. Her parents had been proud, to be sure, but they hadn't known the truth; nor would they ever. The sect to which she'd belonged was far more dangerous than a village of Master Ninjas. At times, she wondered what their parents would have thought if they'd known …

She snapped from her musings and froze. Her intuition burned within her that something was amiss. Crouched over a dozen feet above the ground, she scanned the perimeter of the campsite. Nothing moved, nothing looked out of place. But the cicadas had gone quiet. The insects and frogs, every form of nightlife in the woods had fled and a palpable tension descended on the campsite.

She reached a hand behind her back and felt the hilt of *Onihakaisha*. She felt the sword pleading with her to draw it forth, that fodder was near and it was time to feed. *Only when it is time,* she said to the sword through her mind.

The force of her will kept the hungry weapon in check, and it quieted. She need not feel for *Onisekairu*. The more aggressive of the two, it was no doubt spoiling for a fight. She'd not yet experienced the two swords at the same time. *Onihakaisha* would feed on a vanquished demon until it was too weak to sustain itself in this dimension, finally receding back to the abyss. *Onisekairu*, however, would utterly destroy the essence of the fiend in a whirlwind of primal hunger for destruction, burning the abysmal creature's essence into oblivion. She felt confident she could withstand the onslaught of the two swords feeding at the same time, but didn't discount her lingering doubt.

Ever so slowly, a creeping sense of wrongness permeated the surroundings. It was as though a perversion of all that was right infected the area. The feeling intensified until she could feel it on her skin. The hairs on the back of her neck stood on end, and she clenched her teeth, hand still gripping the hilt of *Onihakaisha*. The sword practically begged her to draw it forth. *Your time comes soon, but you* will *obey me.* Her thoughts subdued the sword again but it was needless, for their conversation had barely ceased when she saw them.

16

* * *

Liu Xiang rubbed his temples as he read the letter, then re read it. He didn't know if he was pleased or disturbed with this news. Apparently, Empress Zhao Xiaoyu's scouts had spied Hua's entourage and warned her that the warlord was en route before his forward messengers reached her city to announce his arrival.

Liu Xiang would have kissed the empress had she stood before him. Ever was she a blessed neighbor, and well did she know the mind of Qian Hua. For years, Empress Zhao Xiaoyu had been dodging the advances of Hua. The warlord had been suing for a union between the two of them, claiming their unity would strengthen their kingdoms and enrich both lands and their people.

No fool, Xiaoyu, understood the underlying intent. The truth was that Qian Hua had been spoiling for a fight. Unsatisfied with his holdings, he coveted the rich and bountiful lands of Shu Han. No fool himself, Hua knew that initiating conflict with Xiang would likely result in defeat at worst, or a victory with a weakened military at best, leaving him vulnerable to reprisal.

A union between Qian and Zhao would give him more than the means to take Shu Han and give Guan Xi pause. Liu Xiang smiled at the letter, written in the empress's own beautiful flowing script. Zhao Xiaoyu knew Qian's game. Her lands would be absorbed by the insatiable warlord and a trend of violence and war would begin. Xiaoyu had effectively fended off Qian's advances for years without offending the man, and Liu Xiang sometimes wondered if Xiaoyu had been receiving council from Zhuge Xiaoyin herself. The few who knew of the existence of Zhuge Xiaoyin would never have believed she remained in contact with anyone. As her ancestor had been, she was largely a recluse, preferring life in the quiet and tranquil mountains to the bustling and obnoxious cities with their overgrown populations. It seemed this post technological age was perfectly suited for the descendant of the legendary strategist.

Empress Zhao Xiaoyu was one of the few who knew the truth of the Three Sworn and the Strategist. While it was common knowledge that Liu Xiang, Guan Xi, and Zhang Da were sworn siblings just as their ancestors had been, their dealings with Zhuge Xiaoyin were unknown to most, and merely speculation to few. Liu Xiang had not yet determined what all this meant, but he knew that fate hadn't drawn them together and given him a powerful and intelligent ally in Empress Xiaoyu for no reason.

Liu Xiang placed the letter on his desk and rose, crossing the room to pour a cup of green tea. For a while he closed his eyes and enjoyed the aroma as the steam drifted up and over his face.

"Xiao Fu," he said. The attendant arrived immediately and bowed. "Send word to General Zhang Da. I would speak with him."

"As my lord wishes," the attendant said. He bowed again and departed.

"This is not how it's supposed to be," the emperor thought aloud. He took a long sip and went back to his seat. "We are not supposed to collect in huge civilizations and fight with one another. When will men learn that we must coexist?"

"The words of a man who thinks of the benefit of his people, and not his station," a woman's quiet voice replied. "If I didn't know better, I would say you were something more than an emperor."

Xiang smiled at the welcomed sound of Zhuge Xiaoyin's voice. He turned to see the strategist standing near the balcony doors and could only speculate how she'd managed to scale the wall of the building to reach his balcony. "I'm beginning to think you either disdain doors, or enjoy surprising me and embarrassing my guards."

Xiaoyin responded with a slanted smile. "Privacy comes with its own risks, but I suspect if someone had come calling for your death, they would meet with more than a helpless ruler, Emperor Liu Xiang."

Liu Xiang crossed the room and lifted his dear friend from the ground in a crushing hug. "Your timing is most welcome. Trouble brews and an ambitious neighbor comes knocking."

"Qian Hua," came the muffled reply. Xiang sat her back down and she made and exaggerated gasp, to which the emperor chuckled. "He remains in Zhao still," Xiaoyin went on. "*Charming* the Empress."

"As always, he seeks a militaristic advantage," Xiang said.

Zhuge Xiaoyin nodded. "And what he lacks in patience, he makes up for with persistence. He will continue to pursue the matter until either the empress outright refuses him, or finally agrees."

"He must know that she would never agree to such a union," Xiang said, pouring tea and offering it to his guest. "Why would he continue to pursue a matter that has only ever resulted in failure? He is no fool. He must know that Xiaoyu doesn't want Zhao to be absorbed by Qian, which is precisely what would happen if ever they were to marry, regardless of his promises."

Xiaoyin accepted the little ceramic cup of tea with both hands and a nod of thanks. "But he also knows that the country has lived in relative peace for generations. Only small skirmishes here and there that have been quelled swiftly. He knows that the populace enjoys life absent the threat of war. They would no doubt apply pressure to their rulers to maintain this lifestyle."

"And Qian is aware of his reputation," Liu Xiang said. "People would fear his reaction if his desires aren't met." He turned and looked out upon the gardens to temper his anger. "The qualities of a tyrant."

"The qualities of a warlord," Zhuge Xiaoyin replied. "In his mind, those who would go to such pains to avoid conflict are simply afraid. Only a coward runs from battle."

Liu Xiang clasped his hands behind his back to avoid slamming them on the table. "I've half a mind to give him the war he's wanted for so long. Ever has his gaze lingered on Shu Han. Never has the vastness of Qian been enough. Perhaps I should give him his war as one last gift before I end his rule and cleanse the world of his entire line."

"That sounds like action taken in anger from a decision made in anger. Would a pugnacious Warlord Qian be replaced by a tainted Emperor Liu Xiang?"

Xiang mentally flinched at the disapproval in her tone. "I understand your point of view, my friend, but what good does a warlord serve this world? Men almost broke the world, and despite the strife and death, we have been given a second chance. Men like this Qian Hua cannot be allowed to poison the world again."

"Unfortunately, it is the way of it until we have further evolved as a species. To dispose of Qian," Xiaoyin continued, "using his own prescribed methods would only serve to clear the path for another as bad or worse. The karmic cycle is undeniable. You know this."

Xiang did know, and that was what irritated him even more. While Qian would like nothing more than an excuse to wage war, absorb Zhao and take Shu Han, Liu Xiang and Zhao Xiaoyu the closest neighboring lands wanted peace. If it came to war, ultimately, only Qian Hua's will would be served, even if the result were his death. The thought disgusted Xiang the more he thought about it. A gentle hand rested on his shoulder and he turned to look down into his friend's tranquil brown eyes. Those eyes seemed to read into his very thoughts. He smiled and turned away.

"Stay centered, my friend," Zhuge Xiaoyin said. "With Guan Xi and Zhang Da, together we will find a solution to this challenge."

Xiang's eyebrows raised, but then he closed his eyes and chuckled. Of course she knew he'd sent for them. She was Zhuge Xiaoyin.

"Your attendant returns with General Zhang Da."

"Perhaps you should disappear until I have sent Xiao Fu away ..." he turned back and blinked. She was already gone. He chuckled again. Unlike her revered ancestor, Xiaoyin was more than just a strategist.

17

"Come," Liu Xiang said when he heard the three knocks at his door. Xiao Fu entered and announced General Zhang Da, who looked to be struggling not to roll his eyes. Liu Xiang nodded his thanks and dismissed the attendant.

The general stepped in and executed a precise bow. "Does word travel so quickly?" he asked once the doors were closed.

"Word?" Xiang replied. When Zhang Da sighed, he knew, and a great weight settled onto his shoulders. "Not another one. This cannot continue."

"I've stationed my best soldiers throughout the city," Zhang Da said. "They patrol in greater numbers throughout the night. Whoever this is, I wish I could enlist their skills. We've had no leads at all. And these killings make no sense."

Zhang Da clasped his long beard in his fist and gave it a tug. "Citizens. Average citizens who hold no position of authority." My only thought is that this is to send a message. Maybe the killer attempts to put you on edge." He shook his head. "Nothing about this makes sense."

"Yet the results have been straightforward."

Faster than Xiang's eyes could follow, Zhang Da's spear was at the ready and he stood between himself and the direction of the voice. He relaxed when the graceful form of Zhuge Xiaoyin appeared. "Well well," the general said. "The Mystic herself has arrived before anyone else! He strode forward and lifted the tiny woman off the floor in a tight embrace.

"That is quite enough, my inappropriate friend!" Xiaoyin said, but she giggled in spite of herself. "It won't do for us to carry on like this."

"Bah! There's no one else here, and it's good see you after so long!"

"Indeed," Liu Xiang agreed. "I cannot name the feeling, but when we are all together, it is as though there is nothing we cannot accomplish."

"And there are only three of us here so far!" Zhang Da declared, causing Xiang to put a finger to his lips. "When we're all assembled," Da continued in a quieter voice, "we will make sense of this together!"

"There may be more sense to this already than you've realized," Xiaoyin replied. "The killer or killers have eluded you at every turn, which has you in a fluster. The same is happening in Qian, causing Hua to mobilize and grow more aggressive in his courting of Empress Zhao before he comes knocking on your door. We all know that Qian will fail in Zhao and come here, most certainly irritated. He will attempt to question you about the murders in his lands without outright accusing you of having some hand in it.

"When he receives no enlightening information his suspicions will be confirmed in his own mind and he will withdraw, either conferring with his spies, or leaving more within your city. One way or another, Qian will find a way to bend this situation into a cause for conflict in the hope of his finally capturing Shu Han and securing Zhao."

Liu Xiang could see Zhang Da's ire rising with every word, and he put a comforting hand on the general's shoulder. Although he practiced a great deal more control than his explosive ancestor, the man could still have a volcano of a temper. "All of this sounds exactly like Qian," Xiang said, "but how would he secure Zhao during a campaign here? Surely he knows Zhao will ally with us against him."

"Empress Zhao has done well in sidestepping his advances," Zhuge Xiaoyin replied, "but Qian Hua knows that Zhao is an ally of Shu Han. He is a warlord. He would plan for such a possibility."

Xiang and Da joined Xiaoyin as she crossed the room to the balcony where she stood silent for a while, staring out at the gardens below.

"Qian Hua thinks himself a dragon," Zhang Da said. "The axis upon which all of the other kingdoms should revolve." The general looked as though he wanted to spit. "His self-delusions would ruin the world."

"Emperor Qian is what he is," Zhuge Xiaoyin said. "We are fortunate in that we understand his nature."

"He spoils for a fight," Da said disdainfully, "and masks it with aspirations to unite the kingdoms for the good of the people. The very people who have already enjoyed peace for generations."

"So long as his vision is achieved, I believe Qian cares little of his perception," Xiaoyin said.

A dark grin appeared on the general's face. "Perhaps when he sees all of us together, along with the legendary Zhuge Xiaoyin, his vision may cloud."

Xiaoyin shook her head. "I cannot be seen here." She looked at Liu Xiang. "This is an advantage. He can suspect what he will, but he can only speculate on what he cannot see for himself. Empress Zhao has never outright confirmed her alliance with you, claiming the desire only for peace through neutrality.

"This is not a lie, though it's hardly a stretch to know where her alliance lies. If Qian sees me here, he will know that I advise you. He has always thought ill of me and been distrustful of my practices. This wouldn't help your interactions with him. Whatever he may suspect, let it not be confirmed. Best that he not think of me at all."

"I count myself lucky to be in the presence of both wisdom and youth in the same vessel," Zhang Da said. "Such is a rare thing."

The young woman smiled, a flash of girlish charm that came and went. "Someone must keep you men from breaking the world."

"Will you remain here?" Liu Xiang asked.

"I leave at nightfall," Xiaoyin answered, "but I will not be far. I would have a look at Qian's entourage and gauge its mood. I don't believe he comes here for outright conflict, but I do think intimidation is his goal. I wouldn't be surprised to see some of his best warriors among his ranks."

"And no doubt, some "friendly" competitions and sparring," Xiang added, catching the hint.

"To take our measure," Zhang Da surmised.

"Likely," Xiaoyin said. "If I'm able, I will return to you before he arrives." She thought for a moment. "And when Guan Xi arrives, have her remain unseen as well. The less you look like you're preparing for something, the better. Her presence could be just what Qian Hua is looking for."

Liu Xiang inclined his head. "Your wisdom is most welcome and appreciated, Strategist."

"There is more to one's life than strategy, my friend," came the reply. "Insight is a valuable thing."

"And what further insight would you share with us this day?" Zhang Da asked, smiling.

Without hesitation Xiaoyin said, "The Creators of the Dao are here to be known by us. Find Them."

* * *

The tendrils of darkness stretched across the land of Shu Han until the full body of night blanketed the world. Tiny forms of nightlife sang to each other, only to be dominated by the incessant buzzing of the cicadas. The moon hovered bright and big in the sky, illuminating the city in a pale light that held no warmth, but had a mystical beauty all its own.

On nights like this, Zhang Da found himself most at peace and able to think clearly. He stood next to Liu Xiang on the highest balcony of palace, overlooking the city. Beneath the calm exterior, he knew his childhood friend was concerned about the coming of Qian Hua.

"He'll not do anything foolish," Da said, breaking the long silence.

"That doesn't concern me," Xiang replied. "In truth, it is not Qian Hua himself that concerns me so, but what he is. I'm not sure Hua truly recognizes the evil in his actions. He doesn't realize that his bloodlust and insatiable appetite for power and holdings benefit few beyond himself. His ambitions would destroy the people he claims to protect."

"There are some who view rule under a warlord as security," Zhang Da said. "A rule with an iron fist whose enemies balk at the thought of challenging him. The corrupt leading the blind."

"The corrupt leading the blind and corruptible," Xiang amended, and Zhang Da nodded.

They frowned out at the moonlit city for a time, each wrapped in their own thoughts, when something caught Zhang Da's attention. He leaned forward.

Xiang followed Da's gaze but saw nothing. "What is it?"

"I don't know, but I thought I saw a large shadow in that alley down there." He pointed toward a distant street. "It disappeared before I could get a good look—"

A scream pierced the silence and both men went rigid. A large shadow appeared again, further away, then disappeared again. Zhang Da had a white knuckled grip on his spear.

Liu Xian hurried to his bedside and snatched up his sword. "What in the name of the creators—"

Another scream shattered the silent night, followed by another, then a third. A chill went down the emperor's spine. From their vantage point, they could see the groups of city watch moving in the general direction of the screams, but it seemed as though the attacker knew where they were and kept ahead, or in some cases, behind them. Each scream had been where the watch had been only moments ago, or just moments ahead of where they would be.

"We're being toyed with," Zhang Da said.

"And Hua's coming is no coincidence," Xiang said darkly.

"You think he has a hand in this?"

Liu Xiang shook his head. "Not at all."

Zhang Da looked at the emperor in confusion for a moment before the realization dawned. "But how would he react if we cannot catch this killer before he gets here—"

"And a similar fate befalls one of his own in our city," Liu Xiang finished. The two men looked at each other, then back at the city. Not a single candle-light had flickered to life in any house. The people had smartly kept their homes dark and quiet, though it was uncertain what good it would do.

"We've got to stop this," Zhang Da said.

Xiang nodded. "Quickly."

"How will you do that, emperor?" a voice whispered from behind.

18

"A beautiful morning, hmm?" Taliah cast Kenyatta and Seung a devious glance. "A truly glorious morning." Kenyatta glared at her while Seung looked confused.

Taliah looked to the bright blue sky and the clouds drifting on their lazy path above The Wood. "Truly amazing. It just feels as though the Daunyans are with us! In fact, to some of us it must feel as though *Se'lir* and *Amayilah* Themselves cradle us in their warm and loving embrace of creation."

"Ya mind tellin' me whatcha goin' on about?" Kenyatta asked in level tone.

Taliah cast him an innocent look. "Whatever do you mean, brother? I'm just in awe of the awesome power of," she paused then finished, "um ... *creation*." Kenyatta frowned at her then glanced at Seung, who apparently had caught on, as her cheeks were coloring.

"Don't worry," Taliah said, winking at Seung. "*Amayilah* will send them only when the time is right." The flush in Seung's cheeks deepened as she studied the ground directly in front of her feet. "The Daunyans use their Children of the Gene hard, but they reward in equal measure. As I'm sure you now know, those heightened senses of yours are not restricted to the battle-field, hmm?"

"You gonna keep chirping—"

Taliah nodded her chin toward the trees before Kenyatta could gain any momentum. "Our companions arrive."

DaunyaSai, followed by Tinnoviel Nai SaunyaLi, Immendiel Mai'lienar,

Yurin Kei Daunyana, and Tikena Mojin appeared on a gravel path, talking amongst themselves as they made their way to the waiting trio.

"What's she talking about?" Kenyatta whispered. "This *Amayilah* sending someone?"

Seung glanced at him, her eyes darting up before quickly returning to the place in front of her feet. "*Amayilah* is the Goddess of Creation," she whispered sheepishly. Beyond all possibility, her cheeks darkened even further.

"Goddess of Creation?" Kenyatta repeated, confused. He blinked several times as comprehension dawned on him, then looked at his smirking sister, then back at Seung. How?"

"Come on, Ken," Taliah said, exasperated. "As if anyone couldn't see it in the way you two pretend to merely like each other." She waggled her fingers at them. Your individual spirit energies are all wrapped up together, I can barely distinguish you It could be no clearer unless *Se'lir* Herself appeared between you." She looked at Kenyatta. "*Se'lir* is the Daunyan ... the Goddess, of love. I really must fully educate you on the Gods, Ken. Humans are largely ignorant of them. I can't allow my own brother remain so."

Once the elves reached the waiting trio and introductions were made, the elven Daunya Master led Taliah aside to converse in private while the others made ready for their departure.

Yurin arched a suspicious eyebrow at Kenyatta and Seung, her gaze lingering on Seung for several uncomfortable heartbeats before she finally looked away. Kenyatta found the mysterious elf unsettling. The irises of her dark brown eyes were surrounded by a yellow ring, and there was a palpable energy that surrounded her. Being so close in proximity to the elf was almost unbearable.

The one named Tinnoviel nodded in greeting, as well as the tracker, Immendiel. Last, came the tiny and hostile one, Tikena Mojin. Kenyatta moved to shake her hand, only to have the little creature recoil in disgust. "Ah, no, but thank you." She looked at his hand as though it were coated in dung. Although they'd met a year ago in the lands of Askata, the elf had been rather aloof. Seung had informed him of how Tikena was one of the least tolerant elves of humans as a species, and thought of them as little more than a filthy and destructive nuisance.

"Yeah man, yeah man," he said, nodding at her as though he understood perfectly. The little elf frowned, then spun on her heel and went to speak with Yurin. "I thought you were exaggerating 'bout dat one," Kenyatta remarked.

Seung shook her head. "She was not as polite to me when first we met."

Kenyatta stole glances at her as she chuckled at the surly Tikena. When they'd first met, she'd worn her hair close to the sides of her head in an almost protective manner. He'd thought it strange at the time but figured it was one of the many things about Seung that were so different from her people. Her human people.

The more he learned about Seung, the more Kenyatta came to admire her. A child with no memory of her parents and not knowing who and what she truly was, had grown to become the leader of her village's warrior class.

She noticed him looking at her and frowned. "What?"

"Nothing. Just, nothing." He smiled and she rolled her eyes. He poked her in the ribs with a finger.

"Ugh! Will you stop it?" she snapped, trying not to giggle. Someone cleared their throat, and Seung looked sheepishly at her elven companions. Yurin, Tikena, and Immendiel stared at them, eyes half lidded with blank expressions on their faces while Tinnoviel pointedly checked the contents of his travel pack. One by one, the three elven women turned away, shaking their heads and hoisting their packs.

"Will you stop acting the child?" she whispered at him.

"Where's the fun in that?" Kenyatta whispered back.

"You embarrass me. For over a year I have worked to earn respect. By elven years, I am little more than juvenile to begin with."

"There will be plenty of time for seriousness," Kenyatta said, an uncharacteristic edge to his tone that caught her attention. "The world changes and the abyss stirs. Before I go to fight and possibly die battling the darkness, I would have my legacy be one of laughter and joy and love. I find that laughter helps to pierce the shadow within us all." He gave her an affectionate rub on the back, then went to retrieve his travel pack, passing a returning DaunyaSai and Taliah.

"The Lady Seiyun wished to be here to see you off in person," the Daunya Master said, "but her obligations would not permit it. She sends word that she wishes you well and may the Daunyans give you strength for your trials ahead. I add my well wishes to hers. May the Daunyans watch over you and see you safely returned." He smiled at everyone, his gaze lingering on Seung and Kenyatta. He gave them a knowing smile, then departed.

"What was that about?" Kenyatta asked, nodding his chin in the direction of the departing Master.

Seung shrugged. "From what your sister said, I would guess that he can see our intertwined spirit energies as well, just as Yurin can see it."

"Hence the look," Kenyatta said.

"Yes."

"Just don't let that hostile little sprite find out," Kenyatta said, glancing at Tikena off to the side, waiting impatiently for everyone else. A horrified look came and went across Seung's face, and she nodded her agreement.

"Time is not on our side," Taliah said, stepping into the center of the group.

"When is it ever?" Tikena muttered under her breath, drawing a sharp look from Tinnoviel.

Taliah smiled at her. "True words. Our destination lies many miles to the west. I will use a form of travel called plane skimming, or *skimming*, for short. We will be able to step through a different plane of existence and then back to our own, but traveling a much farther distance than by conventional means."

She looked at the assembled group. "In moments, we will number eight. I can easily manage myself and one or two others. With so large a group as this, I will need all of you to focus with me. I will create what is called a mind connect, in which all of our minds will link, giving us a collective focus and keeping us together as we step from one plane to another. Should someone break the connection, they would be separated from the group, either remaining in this world, or lost in another. Does everyone understand?" Everyone nodded.

Taliah searched every face until satisfied everyone understood the gravity of the situation. "Fortunately for us Yurin Kei Daunyana, whom I am told is DaunyaSai's most advanced apprentice, accompanies us. This will make it easier." She looked at the apprentice. "I will need you to buffer the mind link, solidify it, and make focus easier for everyone to stay connected." The apprentice nodded.

Taliah said nothing for several heartbeats, then lowered her head. A blue light began to glow from inside her body and gradually moved to outline her form. It disconnected from her body and flowed outward until it enveloped the startled group.

Kenyatta focused on connecting with his sister's mind when he felt Yurin Kei Daunyana's presence. He went rigid at the shock of the connection, but gradually opened himself to her. As if by the click of a lock, he felt his mind snap into place, aligned completely with his sister's as well as the elven apprentice.

"We're ready," Taliah said. "Now that now that our minds have reached this level of familiarity, it will come easier next time. Now, step with me."

As one, the group took a step forward, then another. As they walked, their surroundings began to waver, then shift as though they were walking through a giant bubble. The shifting intensified until an entirely new landscape surrounded them. The shock of the change caused the connection to shudder, but with the aid of Yurin, the startled group—and thus, the connection —recovered.

Kenyatta opened his eyes to see what looked to be a twisted version of their own world. It was like looking through a mirror and seeing a distorted reflection.

"This is the spectral plane," Kenyatta nearly jumped at the sound of his sister's voice in his mind. The lack of reaction from the elves reminded him of what Seung had told him of their ability to speak into each other's minds. The *whisper*, she'd called it.

"It is a warped version of our world, as you can see," she continued.

A greenish glow permeated the place, as did an ever-present mist floating throughout. Pale blue light came from no particular source, as though floating in the air. The effect gave the environment a haunted appearance which made the group uneasy. Kenyatta had *skimmed* with Taliah before, but he'd never been here. He wondered what led to her choice of worlds to *skim*, or if it was a choice at all.

"Does anything live here?" Tinnoviel's voice asked in their minds.

"Yes," Taliah answered. *"And we are as distinguishable as an anomaly to the denizens of this dimension as they would be in ours."*

"Who are they?" Seung asked.

"Nothing human," Taliah answered. *"And many are unfriendly."*

The group traveled in wary silence, instinctually wanting to remain unnoticed. They passed by a lake, but instead of water, a thick waving vapor floated in its place. Tinnoviel knelt by the substance, eyeing it. He looked up at Taliah.

"In the spectral realm, water is nearly as insubstantial as air," she answered. *"If you were to leap in, your descent would be slower. If you were to jump while inside of it, you would float longer and higher. Take care, however. If you fall in and cannot get out, you would be trapped, just as if you'd fallen in a hole too tall and steep for you to climb out of."*

They continued on, passing trees and plants that looked as they did in the physical plane, but a bit less substantial. Structures were often larger and shaped differently, a wall that was six feet tall in the physical plane, was taller and uneven, one side taller than the other, or leaning in one direction or another. Buildings leaned in impossible angles, and even the ground seemed off.

"If this world is a reflection of our own," Tikena's mind asked, *"how*

would our path be shorter?" Kenyatta could feel the grudge in her tone, as though the diminutive elf had to tear the question from her mind to ask a human about something of which she had no knowledge.

"And excellent question, Tikena," Taliah responded. *"We are nearly upon your answer."* Within moments of the exchange, they came to a swirling cone of energy spiraling into the hazy blue-green sky.

"This is a vortex," Taliah explained. *"It can transport us to distant locations. It can even take us back to the physical plane. Now, step into it with me, and hold the connection."*

Kenyatta clenched his jaw as he focused on holding his connection with Taliah. It felt as if he stood at the center of a tempest, yet the winds were not substantial enough to move them. It was an odd sensation that was hard for the mind to settle upon; both confusing and exhilarating.

After a moment, they were moving. This time, it felt as though their bodies were being stretched into thin long strands that were miles in length. Kenyatta could feel the minds of the others, struggling to hold the connection while not panicking. As abruptly as they'd been hurled into the vortex, the experience ended. Everyone lay sprawled on the ground, save Yurin, who was down to one knee, and Taliah, who stood unaffected.

"A bit of warning next time, Chosen?" Tinnoviel remarked, rising to his feet.

"My apologies," Taliah responded. *"There was not much I could say to prepare you. Still, you did well. All of you. We have reached our destination."*

They looked around. The bent and warped surroundings were the same, only on a different landscape. In the distance, however, stood a tower higher than any structure any of the group had ever seen; any except Kenyatta and Taliah. It was Takashaniel, the Tower of Balance. *"Focus on holding the connection,"* Taliah said, *"We will return to our dimension."*

Seconds later, that same sensation of passing through one bubbling world to the next occurred and they found themselves standing in an open grassy field of rolling hills. In the distance, Takashaniel, which reflected every color in the spectrum, shimmered as a beacon of power and stability.

Though he had seen it before, Kenyatta still stared in as much awe as those who were seeing for the first time. Takashaniel; the magnificent structure said to have been made by mortal hands aided by the power of the Daunyans.

Upon reaching the tower, Kenyatta recognized the woman descending the steps to greet them. She had the same long silky black hair and sincere, light brown eyes as he remembered when first they'd met. "Mira! Good to see you again."

Mira clasped her hands over her heart and offered a warm smile. "Hello, Kenyatta! It seems a lifetime has passed since you were last here. Kenyatta rushed over and lifted her from the ground in a big hug.

"Your coming is most welcome," Mira said, smiling at the others. "Iel has been on edge for some time."

"What about Kita?" Kenyatta asked, looking from Mira to Taliah. "I thought we were supposed to get him on the way here."

"That was an option," Taliah said. "But I decided it would be easier to get all of you here in one trip, then get Kita." She turned away. "I'll be back with him shortly so that Iel can enlighten everyone together of the situation."

As Taliah stepped from their dimension to another, Mira led Kenyatta and the elves into Takashaniel.

They looked around at the glowing, multicolored walls, some transparent, some solid. The godly energy of the Daunyans filled the tower, passing around and through the awestruck party.

"Be welcome, elves of The Four," a soft voice declared. "May the essence of Takashaniel comfort and restore you."

Mira smiled and stepped aside as the group looked upon the caretaker of the Takashaniel. His gray and black marble-colored skin reflected the very walls of the tower, as though made of the stone itself. He looked on them with purple eyes that glowed with welcome above his smile.

"I am Iel, friends, and it is my honor to welcome you to the Tower of Balance. The Tower of the Daunyans."

19

"Dammit!", Elizander swore as he raced through the halls, his personal guard close in step. The murderers where becoming far too bold in the past several days. He skidded to a stop at the sight of Milpheus's ashen face.

"M ... m ... my lord!" he stammered, dry washing his shaking hands. "Another attack, my lord!"

"My hearing is still acute, Milpheus," Elizander snapped, then immediately regretted it. The attendant was reacting in shock and had come to help. He softened his tone. "Have you any news?"

"Captain Davros has sent men to the gates in hopes of catching them trying to exit the city."

"Thank you. Please, see to the servants and the household."

"What of you, my lord?"

"I will join the captain and we will put an end to this, tonight." Milpheus clearly didn't like that answer, but he read the determination in Elizander's face and stepped aside with a bow.

"Everyone who is not a soldier is to remain in their quarters," Dain called over his shoulder. "Until word has come that tonight's business is done, *everyone* remains inside."

* * *

"On my back and flanks," Elizander said when his personal guard attempted to surround." He sensed the hesitance of his men and women to leave even one opening, but they obeyed.

Not long into his search, a soldier came galloping toward them on horseback, the swift clip clip clop, of its shod hooves echoed across the cobblestone streets. The soldier drew reign and dismounted, falling to one knee before the king.

"Rise and report, soldier," Elizander ordered. He knew his tone was sharper than warranted, but there was no time for formality. "What news have you?"

The soldier snapped to attention and saluted. "My lord, we've been combing the streets since the moment we heard the screams."

"How many?" Elizander asked.

"There have been five, my lord."

"Five!" Elizander nearly shouted. He turned to the nearest personal guard. "My horse! NOW!" The guard bowed quickly and withdrew.

"My lord," the soldier continued. "Captain Davros sent a contingent to the gates, but—"

"That is not where the killers will be caught, he believes," Elizander finished. "Of course not. Only a fool would commit these murders then try to walk right out the front gates. It is a necessary step. I would believe the captain has positioned more men outside the perimeter of the city while more within the city attempt to find and flush them out."

"Yes, my lord," the soldier responded, bowing. "Captain Davros awaits your majesty at the southwestern wall."

"Take me to him," Elizander said, grabbing the proffered reins from the returned soldier. He swung into the saddle. More clip-clopping echoed through the courtyard, as stable hands hurried to the royal guard, their mounts in tow.

Once mounted, Dain and the royal guard raced through the streets following the soldier. In moments they were outside the city gates and following the outer wall until they finally met with Davros and his men, positioned just behind the tree line. The southwestern part of Winsor was the least traveled and the mostly likely place for someone to make an escape.

"What news?" Elizander asked as he and the royal guard drew reign.

"We are unsure, my lord," Davros said. The failing light cast angry shadows across the captain's face.

"What do you mean, you're unsure?"

"My men have been quick to respond. Every time we heard an attack, we were there within minutes, only to see the remains of the victim freshly painting the walls and ground, or spread across the street. I can't imagine anything human could do this, and so quickly."

The words of the bishop whispered in the back of his mind, and Elizander felt his pulse quicken. *No,* he thought. *It's not possible. It's just some animal we've never seen before.* Absurd as he felt, he found himself hoping it was some strange animal and not a fairy tale nightmare come to life in his kingdom.

"Whatever it is, it's always just ahead of us," Davros continued. "Seems to show up and attack at a place we've just left. I positioned men on the rooftops but they've see nothing."

Dain had never seen Davros so close to being flustered as he was now.

"What is going on?" Dain said to no one in particular. None of this made sense.

His mount's sudden, shuffling snapped him from his thoughts and he tightened his grip on the reins. His soldier's horses all whickered and danced about, the whites of their eyes a shining sign of their fear.

"I've a feeling we're about to find out," Davros said, looking this way and that. Soldiers cursed, drawing weapons and restraining their anxious mounts when without warning, a hulking shadowy figure leaped over the wall. It hit the ground with a heavy thud and charged straight toward them.

"What in the name of Jemanah?" Davros swore.

Elizander Dain had a similar oath caught in his throat. The horses reared, some dislodging their riders, others bolting before the riders could bring them under control. Elizander pulled the reins to one side, clearing the way just as the thing, whatever it was, streaked past them. He saw that Davros had done the same in the opposite direction. Sadly, four of the royal guard had not gotten their mounts under control in time and the thing ran straight into them, sweeping a long arm outward and literally dashing men and horses aside as though they were children's toys.

Elizander looked in disbelief. The lucky had been dislodged from their saddles and thrown aside. Others were still astride their falling mounts and were crushed as the falling animals rolled over them.

Elizander nodded to Davros, who then ordered a few of his men to tend to the wounded before he and the rest of the force wheeled their mounts and gave chase.

As the cool night air assaulted his face, Elizander felt a rush of adrenaline pumping through his veins. *This ends now. Whatever that animal was, it dies tonight!* From the corner of his eye, he saw Davros passing between the trees to his left. The trail was easy to follow. The beast left scratched and scarred trees and trampled shrubs in its wake.

Glancing at the other soldiers, Dain silently praised his captain, for several spear wielders rode with them. Judging from the size of the thing, any weapon with range would be needed …

Something large crashed into one of the soldiers to his right, taking the screaming horse and rider down. Elizander's mount snorted and surged forward. He gave the horse its head, not knowing whether to stop and turn, or keep running. How had it gotten behind them? Was there more than one?

"My lord!" he heard Davros call. "DO NOT STOP!"

Dain glanced over his shoulder to see something larger than he and his horse combined, racing behind them. The sight of the hulking four-legged creature sent a quiver of fear down his back, and Elizander urged his mount on. He needn't have bothered, for the horse knew it was racing for its life, and flew through the trees, neck extended, ears pinned back.

Dain could hear the grunting of whatever it was that pursued them. Was it growing tired? He heard the scream of yet another of the soldiers that denied that possibility. How could something, anything, keep up with fully running horses, dispatch the riders, and still keep pace with them? The bishop's words pressed to the front of his mind once again, and he was finding it harder to deny. No animal could have been in front of them and somehow doubled back to chase them that quickly.

The remaining royal guard closed ranks around him just as an unearthly roar rent the otherwise quiet night. Elizander forced himself to peer over his shoulder to see that the two spearmen at the rear had managed to impale the beast before it could tackle them. He was just about to give the order to turn and finish the beast—for surely it was mortally wounded after taking two spears in the chest—when the thing came tearing up the path behind them again!

The beast leapt toward them, and Elizander thought it the end of them all. Once again, his brave spearmen impaled the monster. This time, however, it landed and snapped the spears as if they were little more than twigs, then leaped again, crashing into the spearmen and hurling men and mounts into the air as though they weighed nothing.

Astride his running mount, the rush of air caused Elizander's eyes to tear. To his relief, Davros was still at his side. Only four remained of the ten royal guard. Would any of them survive this night? One of the horses close behind was tackled to the ground so hard, it caused Dain's own mount to stumble. Elizander leaped from the saddle just before his horse went down. He hit the ground rolling, absorbing most of the impact. Dazed, he scrambled to his feet to see his horse dash into the woods. "MY LORD!" he heard the captain shout. "Elizander! Run!"

The king looked up just in time to see the monster tearing down the path toward him, one of the two remaining spearmen close in pursuit. The soldier leaped from his horse and drove the spear through the monster's back and into the ground. The monster was halted and tumbled, and the solder was launched off its back. He hit the ground hard, but to his credit, he staggered to his feet and drew his sword.

The beast slowly rose up on two feet and stalked toward the soldier. It towered over the man at what must have been nine feet tall. Its gray, leathery skin closed around the imbedded spear, and it wrapped a long-fingered claw around the shaft and yanked it free. Before Elizander's shocked eyes, the wound closed completely.

Beneath eyes that looked to stretch from the front of its face around the side of its head, there appeared to be no mouth. An instant later, however, a film of some sort split, and a grotesquely wide maw opened to reveal a snaking tongue and two rows of jagged teeth.

The last spearman came thundering down the path, tip leveled at the hulking beast. "Run, Elizander!" he heard Davros call again, drawing up beside him. Dain drew his sword. He knew he should run, but he couldn't leave his men to die.

"Dammit!" Davros swore. "You're the king! You must flee!"

"That thing can outrun our horses!" Dain shot back. "It would kill us one by one. We may survive if we stand together!" He heard the captain swear yet another oath as he ripped his sword from its sheath.

As he passed, the spearman impaled the monster, driving the shaft halfway through its body. The hideous beast barely registered the injury, for it continued to slowly stalk toward them, each step a heavy thud that made the ground vibrate beneath their feet. "We can't fight it," Davros said, and Elizander knew it to be the truth. The captain was no coward, nor was he a fool. This beast was beyond them.

"It seems we die tonight, old friend," he said.

"It will be my honor," Davros replied.

"RUN MY LORD!" they heard, and an instant later, several soldiers crashed into the beast from the side, a tumbling mass of men and horses bearing the monster to the ground.

Dain felt a firm hand grip his shoulder. "My lord, we must!" Davros's eyes were pleading. "They sacrifice for you. Let their lives not be wasted!"

Elizander ground his teeth, but nodded. They swept the remaining soldier away, the three fleeing into the cover of the woods. The spearman who had impaled the beast on his last pass was now behind them. Dain glanced over his shoulder just in time to see the monster burst from under the new attackers, a shower of blood and limbs flying in every direction. *By holy Jemanah Himself!* Elizander thought.

"My lord!" the horseman called. "I will bear you back to the pala YAAAAAA!" his screams filled the night air, then cut off. Dain saw it all and wished he hadn't. The monster yanked the soldier from his horse with such force, his feet were lifted over his head. The fallen soldier's horse continued to run with them, the whites of its terrified eyes practically shining in the night.

The three remaining men, Elizander, Davros, and the last soldier ran for their lives, not daring to look back. They heard the triple thud of the monster's footfalls as it pursued. Elizander stumbled as he was suddenly splashed with blood, the force nearly causing him to fall. The last soldier. He was killed so fast he hadn't even time to scream.

"Enough!" the king yelled. "We die fighting!" He stopped and spun, drawing his sword in one motion. Davros stopped with him and drew his weapon as well. The beast also stopped, and now stalked deliberately toward them.

"Come, hell spawn!" Elizander shouted. "Let us be done with this." The response came as a sound that could only be described as a half growl half hiss.

It crouched as it continued to creep forward, holding its thick arms out at its sides. Despite the raging fear radiating through his body at the sight of the hulking monstrosity, Elizander Dain stood tall. "And this is how it ends."

"It has been an honor, my friend," Davros said. The captain raised his sword and bellowed, charging the beast with the King of Winsor close behind. The monster swatted Davros into the brush as though he were a doll. It brought the same arm back and, before Elizander could strike, gripped his body with one clawed hand, lifting him from the ground. The king thought he knew fear, but he hadn't. Now, face to face with this hideous monster, he knew that this was indeed a demon from hell, and that his death was upon him. He silently prayed to Holy Jemanah for a swift death.

It slowly tightened its grip, and he could feel his ribs shifting. It became more and more difficult to draw breath, and colored dots appeared in his narrowing vision. He growled through his teeth when one of his ribs cracked, and that cost him more precious air. The demon raised its other claw, and Elizander closed his eyes … and he fell to the ground.

Grunting from the pain in his side, he sat up and looked at the staggering demon. Tiny pinpricks of light were shining from inside its body where some wound had been inflicted.

"You have been baited and toyed with, King Elizander Dain." The speaker stood on the limb of a tree, several feet above the head of the still recovering demon. The robed figure's features were hidden within a black cowl.

"Look upon this beast of the abyss and finally know the truth." The speaker may well have been a statue, standing perfectly still upon the branch. The fiend rose and turned toward the robed figure, but before it could strike, the black-robed man drew a strange looking whip from his sleeve. As he let it fall, Dain saw three loose strands ended with small hooks.

The demon lunged, and the monk leaped over its head, launching the whip. It wrapped around the monster's neck and when he landed, he snapped his arm back. The demon stumbled but remained upright, grabbing hold of the whip and pulling. The man leaped with the pull, flying toward the demon, and Elizander knew he was dead.

To his disbelief, the monk somehow avoided the slashing claw in midair and grabbed its shoulder, slinging himself around and onto its back. He'd never let go of the whip, and now it was wrapped around the monster's neck and under one arm. The man drew the slack and pulled. The whip tore at the monster's thick hide and for the second time that night, the monster showed pain.

"Return to Ooragh, hell spawn," the man growled. With startling strength, he yanked the whip free, the hooks tearing gray flesh from around the demon's neck and the left side of its chest as the whip came around its body. He leapt from its back as it stumbled forward. He then drew the whip over his shoulder, leaning back with the motion, and struck repeatedly.

Everywhere the weapon struck, damage was done to the fiend, and black blood oozed from the many wounds inflicted. Every time the demon tried to rise, the man struck it down. Finally, its flesh flayed from its body, the demon sank to the ground.

To Elizander's continued amazement, the thing still struggled to rise, albeit the effort was a feeble one.

"The Zzrt are especially stubborn and difficult to kill," the man said, approaching the creature.

"The what?" Elizander said, while thinking, *usually difficult to kill? Usually?*

"Zzrt, King Elizander Dain," the man repeated. "A higher class of demon, although this one was somewhat weak." He waved his right hand over the beast, then his left, chanting in a language the king had never heard. When the man was done, the demon erupted in blue fire. He held out a hand over the screeching fiend and its corporeal form evaporated into mist, drawing toward the man's hand, held out like a claw.

He whipped his right hand in an arc behind him and the air started to ripple. A red wave appeared, and the man whipped his left hand across it, trailing the mist that was the fallen demon in front of it. A few heartbeats later and the thing was gone, presumably sent back to the hell it had come from.

Elizander started to speak, but the man quickly moved to where the demon had been. He waved his hands slowly back and forth over the area, chanting in that strange language again. Tiny blue flames sprang from the ground. The flames roared to life and rose nearly as tall as the robed figure, then died away. "If they bleed upon ground," the man said, rising, "it must be cleansed, lest it poison the earth."

The many questions that sprang to the king's mind were lost to pain and exhaustion. He did manage one question. "Who are you?" He instinctually backed away when the man approached. He winced at the pain in his side and simply stood. If this mysterious person had meant him harm, there was little Elizander could do about it. Besides, he'd just gone to the trouble of saving him from a demon.

"I am an ally," the man answered. "And the time has finally come that we must talk."

20

F rom his vantage point, high in the hills surrounding Takashaniel, Brit could only nod in appreciation. The Ilanyan had chosen this new location well. There was no cover for over a mile in any direction, and the tower sat atop a hill, affording a view of the surrounding fields as well as sitting in a more defensible position.

It mattered little. Demons were not humans. They did not fear death, no matter how many of their number perished, and some could cover great distances with incredible speed. Hills or no hills.

A breeze stirred his long orange hair, causing it to dance like flames about his head. Some of those humans Iel had enlisted before had arrived. The Ilanyan knew he was coming.

The drek didn't mind admitting to himself that the humans were formidable. He didn't know from where they'd come, or why they were possessed of such abilities that were far beyond anything typical of their fragile species, but he wasn't concerned by it. How many were they? Five? Six? It would take more than a handful of humans, no matter how powerful, to withstand the tide that rising against them.

He cast his reddish gaze about the surrounding hills and the thick forests beyond. He cared not for the world itself, only what he could use of it. He was not entirely unlike the demons he summoned, in that he fed from the essence of other living things.

How long could he live on this world, leeching its rich life force? Could the world continuously repair itself, providing a limitless source of nourishment? The possibilities were enticing. Of course, there was a cost. The very demons he summoned to destroy Takashaniel existed only for chaos and destruction. Their presence in this dimension was a twisted perversion of nature that corrupted all that they came in contact with.

Brit wasn't concerned by this either. What damage the fiends inflicted might be repaired once they had served their purpose and he'd banished the filthy things back to the abyss. They were simply tools to be used and discarded once they'd fulfilled their purpose.

He looked to the east where he could feel those twins Kabriza had summoned. He'd have to watch them. More importantly, he would need to keep a close watch on the quentranzi general. Kabriza was a crafty one, and if Brit let his guard slip … well, he wouldn't. He had Kabriza firm in hand, and by extension, the tremendous horde he'd summoned over these many months.

That Brit couldn't scry their movements, however, was a concern he needed to address. Somehow those two were shrouded from his gaze. It would have been easier if he had his lackey at his disposal.

That stray thought turned Brit's mind to Zreal and Zshegaza. He was still unsure what had befallen those two. It had been two years since the first battle and he'd heard nothing of the duo. It seemed unlikely that both of them had been killed in the subsequent routing of the demonic forces. Knowing what he did about Zshegaza, Brit suspected she and his servant decided on a different life path.

He shrugged the thought away. They were either dead or neglected to return to him, in which case he would deal with them when this business with Takashaniel was finished.

Brit smiled at the thought and turned away, ripping a hole in the air before him and stepping through. He thought about how fun it would be to watch how Iel dealt with the thing he'd found hibernating beneath the ground right in the center of the field behind the tower. He would have to wake it soon.

M alimokuru sat his horse in silence, Naiyala and Amata Daunyana by his side as they waited while Sakhile and Ayanda scouted ahead. Thinking of Ayanda reminded Malimokuru of Jabulani, the elder hunter. Jabu, as he was known by his friends.

Thinking of his friend drew a sigh out of Malimokuru. The elder hunter had died battling a lava leech; a monstrosity of an animal that they had encountered within the mountain range known as The Sentinels.

For many days they'd traveled together, the nature reader, those two foolish boys Kenyatta and Kita, and the four amahle they had encountered in the desert province of Phoenix. The death of the Elder Hunter had saddened the three humans, but the amahle were a different people. At the moment the warrior had been killed, the remaining amahle had gone into a rage that had been quite frightening.

After the battle had ended, however, they'd returned home, and Naiyala, Amata, and Sakhile had all taken turns, telling Jabulani's story. They spoke of his first hunt against some large animal Malimokuru had never heard of, but that had threatened their village. They told of the many hunts throughout Jabu's long life. They spoke of his life from as early as any could remember, concluding with his final hunt with the three *abantu* and the battle under The Sentinels.

Ayanda was a young hunter, second to Jabulani. He wore his hair in the manner all amahle hunters did, shaved on the sides of the head, while thickly braided in the middle with sharp barbs woven within. His hair fell to the middle of his back, but lacked the bladed tips, as Naiyala and Amata possessed. Malimokuru wondered if only certain individuals wore those lethal tips, or if there was a significance to it other than an unexpected weapon.

The nature reader thought again of Jabulani and smiled to himself. At his age, death was not such a faraway concept. How many people dear to him had he said goodbye to throughout his life? More than he could remember. Malimokuru gripped the reigns as his horse started prancing sideways. He looked sharply at Nyaka to his right, the goar cat hopping sideways toward the horse, then back again. Every time she came near, Malimokuru's horse would whicker and shuffle about, nervously rolling his eyes as he watched the goar cat. It didn't take a nature reader to see that the Nyaka was having fun with the nervous horse. Predators were intelligent, but Nyaka proved to have a startling level of intellect.

"Stop tryin' to give me horse a heart attack, girl," he chastised her. "Or I'll be ridin' your back instead." Nyaka responded with a playful, high-pitched bark. Malimokuru shivered at the thought of playing with the lethal animal. The large dark blue goar cat was not a great deal smaller than his horse.

Nyaka stood from paw to shoulder just under five feet tall. Her legs beneath the knees were thin and lean, whereas above the knees was thick corded muscle that flexed with every step. Several rows of teeth complimented her long muzzle. Those things were sharp enough to slice through things Malimokuru didn't care to think about.

She looked at him with comprehending bright blue eyes, her mouth hanging open as though in a wide smile; a smile wide and deep enough to take a man's head clean in one bite. He shivered again. Nyaka had been cute when he'd first found her, deep in the deadly swamp-ridden woods known as The Craig. Through unfortunate circumstances they'd had to kill her mother or be eaten. The vulnerable cub would surely have died, so Malimokuru had taken Nyaka and raised her. That cub was now frightening. Her barbed tail—a sign of adulthood—flicked back and forth, another indication she was feeling playful.

Malimokuru glanced at her paws, each the size of his head, and thought about the retractable claws that he'd seen snatch out the throat of a Krindra. Nyaka communicated to him images of the thrill of the hunt and the fulfillment of fresh meat. His stomach churned. "I wish you wouldn't share so much detail, man," he said. "Just go do what you do, and I'll see you when you find us again."

He could have sworn the little bark she responded with as she bounded away was more like a chuckle. As she moved farther away, her color shifted to match the sandy brown surroundings of the desert, and within a few heartbeats she disappeared into the landscape.

"She goes for the hunt, friend Malimokuru," Naiyala said as she matched the walking horse with her long strides. She grinned at him. "Always can I tell when she speaks to you of the hunt. The color in your face fades."

"The image of her not so gently removing the entrails from some unfortunate animal isn't very enticing to my mind," Malimokuru grumbled, and the amahle princess laughed, reaching over and slapping his leg. Malimokuru could taste the bile in his throat at the thought of the goar cat tearing another animal apart. "How does it not bother you?"

"Life is as it is," Naiyala answered. "Animals eat the way they were created to, as do we all."

Malimokuru nodded at that. "I suppose. And that reminds me of something I've been meaning to ask. Why is it that you have hunters and elder hunters, but you do not eat animals?"

"Survival, *Umntwana Onomuntu*," Naiyala answered, calling Malimokuru by his title in her language. "There are large and dangerous beasts in the world, and when our scouts determine that they mean to come to our home to hunt, we must prevent it."

"Animals don't typically hunt the two legged," Malimokuru replied.

"Have you not seen things more dangerous than you imagined?" Naiyala countered. "Have you not seen with your own eyes that there is more in this world than you once thought?"

Malimokuru conceded the point with a nod.

"You will see more," the woman went on. "The world changes, friend Malimokuru. There are things that have lain dormant, hibernating for ages come and gone. With the world less strangled than it was, the sleeping will awaken, and changes will happen, and all the lands will be more different than you can imagine."

"Somehow, that gives me little comfort," Malimokuru replied.

Naiyala shrugged. "Life is as it is."

"And *abantu* will learn to live in this new world or perish." It was Amata Daunyana who spoke. Malimokuru had forgotten the seer's apprentice was still there, so silent was she.

"True enough," he replied. He thought of the brief time he'd spent among the elfinestrayan people before parting ways to travel with the amahle. "Do you think of humans as a plague like the elves do?"

She turned her pale green gaze on him. "No more a plague than a child in need of disciplining. Your people are young and foolish, like children with too many tools with which to build, but not the sense to use them responsibly. But, all will be as it will, *Umntwana Onomuntu. Abantu* will learn. They've no choice."

As if appearing out of the sands surrounding them, Sakhile and Ayanda came trotting back to the group. Malimokuru shook his head. Sometimes he wondered if these people were akin to goar cats, for they shared the same innate camouflage abilities. Naiyala and Amata tossed the new arrivals their packs, which they shouldered. When blending to their surroundings, amahle wore as little as possible, since their skin could shift colors whereas clothing could not.

"The way is clear, *Inkosazana*," Ayanda said, falling in stride with the two women and the mounted nature reader.

"What's on the other side of those hills?" Malimokuru asked.

"Open plains, *Umntwana Onomuntu*," the hunter said. "The land opens and stretches for several leagues before we find green fields again."

"That is what makes me uneasy," Sakhile said. "I have passed through these desert lands many times. I have crossed the plains that we will soon reach, but something bothers me about it today. It feels as though something lies in wait."

"You believe something waits for us ahead?" Naiyala asked.

"It is a feeling, *Inkosazana*. More than that, I cannot say."

Naiyala thought for a moment, then deferred to Amata. "What is your feeling, Daunyana?"

"We will see what we will," came the reply.

An hour later the group reached the hills overlooking the open plains beyond. Aside from the occasional shrubs or skeletal trees that dotted the cracked landscape, little in the form of life inhabited the parched, sunburned land.

Malimokuru whistled through his teeth. "I'm not much liking the sight of that, even if there isn't any danger. That's a long time in the middle of nowhere with the sun hanging on our heads. Maybe we should wait till night-fall, when the sun isn't so hot."

Ayanda shook his head. "If something awaits our passage, it may be a bad thing for you."

"I hadn't thought of that," Malimokuru said, then he frowned. "Bad for me? Why would this be bad for me and not all of us?"

"Because you cannot see in the dark, friend Malimokuru," Sakhile answered with a smile. It always unnerved the nature reader when these people smiled. That almost polished onyx black skin contrasting frighteningly with the bright white teeth. The effect was especially disturbing at night, though he was sure they did it just to toy with him. Amahle humor!

"Still," Naiyala said, "it may be a good idea to pass through at night. Whatever is there may not see us, or at least not see well in the dark."

"And if it does?" Malimokuru said, feeling more vulnerable by the second.

"Then we will be forced to deal with it," the princess replied.

"*Umntwana Onomuntu* could wait here until it is done, if there is something down there," Ayanda suggested.

"Nonsense, boy!" Malimokuru snapped, which brought an amused expression from the others. "Okay, I'm old." He glared at them, daring anyone to expound on his admission.

"That doesn't mean I'm useless. I'm not going to hide on this hill shaking like a coward while you four deal with whatever is down there. And what would I look like if you go down there only to find out there's nothing to fear. Twice the coward, I think! I go, and if it comes to it, I'll be fightin' in the dark with you. I can take care of myself. Might even teach you children something." Malimokuru was sure they were suppressing laughter. All but the apprentice, anyway. Ever focused, was that one.

"There is something down there," Amata said as though she had not heard any of the conversation. "I do not know what it is, but I know it's there."

Malimokuru concentrated on the barren land below and nodded. "Yeah man. Nothing goes near that stretch of land. Not even the smallest animal. Even the carrion crows above fly higher when they pass over. Something's there, and we're not going to like it."

"We will camp here," Naiyala decided. "And cross the plain in the cover of darkness."

Not long after they had set up camp in the shade of a few desert palm trees, the sands took on the shape of a large four-legged animal lumbering its way toward them. Eyes lidded and belly full, Nyaka flopped beside Malimokuru, tongue flicking in and out like a snake. The nature reader sat leaning against the tree, stroking the coarse fur of the six-hundred-pound animal. She rumbled deep in her chest as she fell asleep.

"Never would I have believed my eyes would tell me that *abantu* could make friends with *Umzingeli Unwabu*," Ayanda said.

"Well, every day is a lesson," Malimokuru replied. "Two years ago I never would have believed I'd meet eight-foot-tall chameleon folk living in the desert." Malimokuru looked back to the valley below and frowned. "Why don't we just go around the valley? It's out of the way, but at least we would avoid whatever is down there."

"Because it matters not, friend Malimokuru," Amata Daunyana said, seating herself cross-legged between the two. What is down there is meant for us. I see this. If we were to try and avoid it, it would either attack us anyway, or continue to lie in wait and then fall upon another who would travel through this place. We know it is here, we cannot leave it for another."

Malimokuru grumbled under his breath. More amahle thinking. He couldn't argue with the logic, but he didn't have to like it either.

* * *

A gentle hand on his shoulder roused Malimokuru from his nap. He sat up and rubbed his eyes. The pale light of the waning moon shined brightly upon the landscape. He leaned against the tree and let the majestic power of the desert wash over him. He looked around into the semi-dark night, searching for his companions.

"Well, let's see you," he whispered. As one, the four amahle practically materialized around him. "Always showing off," he muttered. How nice would it be if he could hide himself in plain sight. Maybe then he might feel safer about all this business. On his other side, Nyaka rumbled in her chest, nudging him with that long lethal muzzle of hers. He rubbed her head.

"We must be on our way, friend Malimokuru," Ayanda said. Over the hunter's shoulder, he saw Amata Daunyana standing at the edge of the hill, eyes closed and her hands resting at her side.

Malimokuru collected his gear and joined her. He looked out at the moonlit valley below, a gaping maw waiting to snap its jaws shut upon their entrance.

The apprentice nodded. "Evil twists nature, *Umntwana Onomuntu*. What lies in wait is of this world, but has been poisoned by things not from this world. Before this night is done, you will come to fully understand the importance of what we are about."

Sakhile brought Malimokuru's horse and handed over the reins. Malimokuru felt a pang of guilt, leading the animal into certain danger. He placed a comforting hand on the horse's soft nose and closed his eyes. He sent feelings of love and appreciation for the animal bearing him this far, and thanked it.

He communicated danger to the animal, and projected the warning toward the valley they were about to cross. To the best of his ability, he explained that the horse could make its own way if it chose to. To his gratitude and misgiving, his loyal companion sent images of remaining with them, bearing him as far as he needed to go.

Malimokuru swung into the saddle and gave the horse a pat on the neck. "I will strive to be worthy of your friendship."

He looked at the others, patiently waiting for him. They could think what they would about his age, but he was still in good shape. Even without those blast-it-all long legs of theirs.

"Are you ready, friend Malimokuru?" Naiyala asked, placing a hand on his shoulder. Astride his mount, he was about her height, yet still shorter than some of the other amahle.

"I'm ready, friend Naiyala," he responded.

"I do not know what waits for us," Amata Daunyana said to Naiyala, "but it is twisted and angry."

"Then we must deliver it from its torment," Naiyala replied.

"All fine and good," the nature reader muttered. "Let's just not get *ourselves* delivered." The comment was received with quiet laughter, and even the Seer's Apprentice responded with a flicker of a grin.

Malimokuru was glad to have Naiyala and Amata Daunyana at his side as they followed the scouts into the valley. His hand drifted to his pouch of sands for reassurance. "You know, whatever is out here is probably going to wait till we are right in the middle of this valley before springing on us."

"That would make the most sense," Ayanda replied, spear in hand as he scanned the surrounds.

Malimokuru pointed ahead. "It would make sense for it to come out of the tree line up ahead, don't you think?"

"Something stirs," Amata said.

They cast about, searching the valley for some form of disturbance, but nothing seemed to be amiss.

Malimokuru gasped. He felt it. Fear, rage, pain, and confusion all massive and all wrapped tightly in a cloak of evil. "What in the name of ..."

The ground burst open in an explosion of dirt and rock. Malimokuru's horse reared and bolted, and for a moment all he could do was hold on to the terrified animal. He looked over his shoulder to see a huge, twisted monster like nothing he'd ever set eyes upon.

He pushed down his fear and pulled on the reigns. The horse grunted and shook its head in protest, but Malimokuru managed to steer it in an arc so that he might come around behind the monster. Soon enough, he had his mount racing toward the monster's back.

I'm too old for this.

* * *

The amahle leapt backward away from the exploding ground, gliding through the shower of debris. Midair, they brandished their weapons, landing in a crouch as the twisted monstrosity climbed its way out of the ground.

On its back, tentacles as long as Naiyala was tall writhed and twitched as if feeling the air for something to grab hold of. Two sets of slitted red eyes glared at the four warriors and a mouth large enough to swallow them all whole opened to reveal rows upon rows of teeth as long as Naiyala's legs. With every step, it ripped the ground, claws slicing into the earth. It clawed the ground and screamed, the piercing sound flying in the faces of the amahle warriors, who braced themselves through the onslaught.

The ground shook to the rhythm of the charging monster, chunks of rock and soil flying with each pounding stomp. The amahle waited as one, crouched in the path of a beast easily five times as large as an elephant.

Naiyala snarled and bared her elongating fangs. At her sides, the other amahle began their shift as well. Their skin became as red as the battle rage that burned within. Naiyala hissed, and the amahle warriors charged.

The monster screeched again, but so deep were the amahle in their battle rage that it had no effect. Spears held in clawed hands, they raced across the valley until they were but a few yards from the beast. One after the other, they leaped high into the air.

Naiyala landed on the monster's back, stabbed her spear deep into its flesh, then leaped off. After her, Sakhile did the same, and after him, Ayanda, followed by Amata. One after the other they struck the same spot.

The beast roared and spun. As it turned, Naiyala—still airborne—threw herself into a forward flip. Upside down and in line with one of its eyes, she drove her spear into one of the glowing red orbs.

So fast were the amahle, that the other three struck before the monster could react. The four warriors hit the ground and turned to face the partially blinded beast. It flailed in agony, lashing out with claws and tail until it spotted the bright red warriors with its sole remaining eye.

The amahle charged again and fanned out at its sides. They raced past its forelegs, Naiyala and Ayanda stabbing the back ankles while the trailing two struck the front.

It lifted a giant claw and stomped the ground. The earth trembled beneath their feet, but so too did blood gush from the gaping wounds of its ankle. The beast's leg partially gave out under the sudden pain just as the four warriors met together under its midsection.

As one, they leapt straight up and stabbed their spears into its belly. Once they landed, they jumped straight up again, repeating the attack. The monster stumbled about, trying to move away, but the amahle warriors were too fast. Once, twice, a third and fourth time they stuck, each driving their spear deep into the soft flesh.

After the final attack, they landed and leapt away, each in a different direction. The monster wailed and curled in on itself, trying to protect its wounded belly. In the dark of the night, the four red warriors glowed, and their equally red eyes bore into their adversary as they prepared to strike again.

The monster stumbled forward, then fell into thrashing frenzy. Seeing Naiyala hesitate, the amahle fell back to her side.

When the monster stumbled sideways and turned, they saw Nyaka on its tail. The goar cat must have shifted to blend with the night. Now she clawed her way up its tail and onto its back. It thrashed and even reared up on its hind legs, but it made no difference. Nyaka sank her claws deeply into its back, thick corded leg muscles holding her in place until the beast fell back to all-fours. She hopped onto its neck, bit down, and began ripping and tearing.

The monster screeched and turned, throwing blood and saliva in every direction as it tried in vain to shake the troublesome goar cat free. But, the jaws of a goar cat were strong indeed. Nyaka held on, enduring the shaking and bucking of the massive beast as it shook the ground with every stomp.

Covered in blood, Nyaka once again pumped her front and rear legs, shredding the thick hide and tentacles while her unbreakable bite held her in place.

Naiyala let out an open-mouthed hiss and the amahle lifted their spears into the air. Ayanda dropped his weapon and drew his bow. He reached over his shoulder and nocked an arrow. Once, twice, thrice, he fired. His arm was fast and his aim was true. The arrows found their mark in the last good eye of the beast. It reared on its hind legs again, and the other three amahle launched their spears into its exposed neck. Again, Ayanda fired, the arrows also finding their marks near the embedded spears.

The amahle charged again, Naiyala, Sakhile, and Ayanda veering to either side of the monster. Amata Daunyana's eyes flared bright, and she stopped before the rearing monster.

* * *

M alimokuru cringed and pulled his horse to a stop. He had no intention of getting near that savagery. He trusted and had come to love his friends, but he still found them terrifying when in their battle rage. He also doubted he would be needed, as they were doing considerable damage without him.

He knew which sands he wanted to use, but considering the sheer size of the thing, he wasn't sure it would be enough. Then he saw Nyaka leap onto its tail and make her way to its neck where she began ravaging it.

Malimokuru almost felt sorry for the monster, for surely the pain must be unbearable. "The company I keep," he muttered, hopping off the horse and creeping forward. His horse would fight him against every step closer to the thing anyway, and he couldn't blame it.

He dug into the pouch, quietly saying the words of an incantation. He could feel the energy warming in his hand. The amahle were charging again, only this time, three of them darted to the sides and Amata Daunyana stopped in front of the rearing monster. Her body swayed and her arms waved in various patterns, as though she were in dance.

Despite the circumstances, Malimokuru found himself captivated by the beauty of the dance. He could feel the power radiating from her, even at this distance. Amata's hue shifted from red to silver, and the nature reader froze at the sight. The amount of power flowing from the apprentice should have come from a body the size of the monster advancing on her.

Malimokuru glanced down at his hand and repeated the incantation in reverse, withdrawing the power from the sands and letting it slip through his fingers back into the pouch. He looked back to the scene just in time to see Nyaka give a mighty leap from the monster's back. It was a long way down and she hit the ground hard, rolling in a spray of dirt. She sprang to her feet and bounded away, and Malimokuru let out a breath he didn't know he'd been holding.

* * *

A mata Daunyana danced first to the Daunya of Spirit. She felt the presence of Omalah as His golden light filling her. She then shifted her dance and became more aggressive. Her gestures and movements grew harsh and direct, her steps more like stomps whereas before they flowed like water. The dark blue light of Boraka laced over that of Omalah.

With the power of the Gods of Spirit and Destruction flowing through her silver body, Amata Daunyana finished the dance with a mighty stomp that sent waves of power rippling through the air. She thrust her right hand toward the sky, and her left toward the ground. Her skyward hand glowed bright with the light of Omalah, her lower hand with the light of Boraka.

"The vessel in which the taint is hosted be destroyed by the fist of Boraka. The spirit which has been diseased be purified by the hand of Omalah." She brought her hands together, planted her feet, and thrust her palms out to either side of her body. Blue and golden flaming light flared to life in her hands.

The power arced outward and slammed into the sides of the beast. The monster shuddered under the onslaught. The sound of its screech tore at the air as the destructive power of Boraka burned away its body till nothing but ashes remained. The gentle light of Omalah, however, held the ethereal shape of the beast.

Before their eyes, the form changed, and the golden outline became more substantial. In moments, the hideous monster was replaced by an equally large, but very different animal. Its presence was no longer angry and twisted and confused, but at peace.

It stood shimmering in the golden light until Amata stopped and lowered her hands. The hues of the amahle shifted back to their normal faint purple color as the battle rage subsided. "Your body has been destroyed," Amata Daunyana said, "but your spirit is liberated, Seitadon. Go. Be at peace." The image of the animal drifted away in tiny golden particles spreading through the air. They settled gently into the ground where they glowed briefly, then absorbed into the earth.

Having mounted his horse again, Malimokuru, trotted up to the gathered amahle and Nyaka. "Someone want to tell me what that was? Before it disappeared, I got a sense of connection to the earth, like it was as much a part of the earth as it was its own self."

"That is because it was an earth elemental, friend Malimokuru," Amata Daunyana replied.

Malimokuru raised his eyebrows at that. "An earth elemental? They actually exist?"

The apprentice gave him a tolerating look, as one would a child having learned something new. "Perhaps there is still much you will discover about this world, *abantu*."

"Still taking some getting used to, you understand," he replied. "Nothing in our history has ever mentioned anything about all this."

"That is not true, friend Malimokuru," Naiyala said. "Some of your ancient human people have left behind art that shows a greater knowledge about the world than *abantu* of this age. Ever have my people been confused as to how you could grow less knowledgeable about the world you live in as time progresses forward."

"Sometimes I wonder the same thing," the nature reader said.

Sakhile pointed at the other end of the valley. In the distance stood rolling hills carpeted with sand and desert flora, dusted by the occasional breeze-swept sand cloud. "We should set camp in the trees on the other side of the hills."

"Did that elemental back there have anything to do with what we're going to deal with?" Malimokuru asked Amata as they traversed the wide-open landscape.

The apprentice nodded. "The spawns of the origins of evil are being set loose upon this world *Umntwana Onomuntu*. What we are seeing now is only the beginning. If we fail, things will become much worse."

Ayanda froze and hissed through his bared teeth, causing everyone to stop and scan the area.

Malimokuru squinted in the pale moonlight at the trees ahead. Inhuman figures slinked about the hills and started to close the distance. The nature reader slipped a hand into his sand pouch. Things were already getting much worse.

22

Taliah's warm fingers entwined with his own, Kita could only once again stand in awe of the majesty of Takashaniel. Just the sight of the magnificent tower, glimmering in every color of the spectrum, was enough to lift his spirts, no matter how dark of a day he might have. The structure reached so high into the heavens that the top could not be seen through the puffy white clouds drifting across the sky. Takashaniel radiated tranquility.

"It seems a shame that people don't know it exists," he murmured.

"Does it?" Taliah replied.

Kita shrugged. "Maybe if people knew this existed, we might not have made such a mess of things."

"Come," Taliah said, evading the conversation. "The others wait for us inside." When she noticed Kita looking at her, she sighed. "Love. I have been given glimpses into the history of the world. I've seen how things were before and during the Age of Technology. We were off to a good start. But it all changed. It has been talked about enough among us all, yet not enough to most. You don't know what almost happened." She looked up at the tower with regretful eyes. "The world was nearly a different place."

"You mean how we almost destroyed it?"

Taliah looked back at him. "That was one possibility, but remember that there are others that had no intention of perishing alongside us."

Kita went silent as he pondered the unsaid implications, and the ominous undertone to her words.

"I guess all that's left to do is move forward with the lessons we've learned from our past."

"That is the hope, but not the history," Taliah replied.

Once they had ascended the steps to the front of the tower, Kita turned and looked back at the surrounding grassy field and let out a heavy breath. "I know this is a different place, but I can still see in my mind the battle we fought. It seems like so long ago, and ironic that we will fight here again, in this different place that seems so much the same."

He admired the rolling grassy hills and the trees beyond. Elk roamed these hills. Bears, large cats, birds, small animals. "A shame. The world is a beautiful place. Even the unpopulated cities that are little more than overgrown ruins are made beautiful again. Nature strives to make things right, and this drek brings demons to destroy it again."

"Demons need energy to feed off of in order to remain in this dimension," Taliah said. "Come, they're waiting on us."

They entered to find Kenyatta, Seung, and four elves seated on floor cushions along with Iel and his student, Mira. It seemed so long ago since he'd last seen the Ilanyan guardian and his most capable student.

Looking over the seated group, Kita recognized three of the elves, Tinnoviel Nai SaunyaLi, an incredible warrior, and Tikena Mojin, the tiny and rather unfriendly one. The third who sat facing them was the unforgettable Yurin Kei Daunyana. The woman studied him and Taliah with haunting yellow-ringed brown eyes that were just as unreadable as he remembered.

The fourth elf was a slender woman with long black hair that hung freely down to the middle of her back. She looked at him with a hard but not unfriendly crystalline gaze.

Iel stood and smiled at them. "And now we're all here." He indicated two unoccupied cushions. "Please join us."

"May I?" Kita asked, indicating the cushion beside the unfamiliar elf. She tipped her head in response and waved an open hand over it.

"I'm Kita. Pleasure to meet you." After a brief translation from Seung, the elf tipped her head again with a polite smile.

"Immendiel Mai'lienar," the woman replied, to which Kita mentally stumbled over for awhile.

"You haven't missed much, man," Kenyatta said. "We've mostly been passing time till you arrived, so as not to cover the same thing twice." Seung translated the islander's words to the elves.

"Good thing he explained that," Tikena muttered in the human western tongue.

Seung shot Tikena a warning look that the little elf pretended not to see.

"What'd she say?" Kenyatta whispered to Seung, who just waved off the inquiry.

"Unfortunately," Iel began, "time is not in our favor, so I must limit the pleasantries and cut straight to the heart of the situation. I managed to buy us some time by moving Takashaniel to the location in which it now sits. It was my hope that Brit would be hard put to find it again, but the drek is resourceful. It took him but a few months to find it again, and I expect he will attack soon."

"Can you not simply relocate the tower again?" Tinnoviel asked, and Seung translated.

"That is possible, but it would take time, and it would matter little, since he'd find it again. I'll not pretend to know the full scope of his abilities, but he is powerful. The fact that he's been able to penetrate the barrier between this plane and the abyss as far as he has is proof. We must stop him soon before he loses control of the horde he's summoned."

"You think it could come to that?" Kita asked.

"He overestimates his ability to control all of them," Iel answered. "Small cracks are appearing in the dam, and it is a matter of time before it bursts. He has found a way to penetrate the barrier, but he grows too ambitious."

"If he's been able to do this," Tinnoviel asked, "why has he not attacked sooner?"

"It has taken him years just to figure out a way to do it," Iel answered. "And it's taken just as long to prepare himself to manage the task, and to summon the fiends. He can only summon so many demons at once. The force that he's amassed has taken some time to build."

Iel looked at the four elves. "Three years ago these two warriors," he indicated Kenyatta and Kita, "along with three others aided me in the defense of Takashaniel against a horde of demons. Most were lower-level fiends, but a good number of them had been quentranzi."

Tinnoviel blinked, while Tikena and Immendiel sucked in a breath. A frown flickered across Yurin's brow.

"Quentranzi?" the elven tracker responded. "Five humans fought a force of quentranzi?"

"We weren't the only ones," Kenyatta said. "There was a clan of centaurs and brunts that fought with us."

"Not to mention those things you summoned, Iel," Kita added.

"Yes," Iel agreed. "Siti will return to aid us as long as is possible, and the

Rizanti will return to our side as well. As for the brunts and Grimhammer's clan, I do not know."

"How do you know this Brit has found you again? Yurin Kei Daunyana asked." Though he'd heard it throughout their trip at sea together, Kita still thought he might never grow accustomed to the melodious voices the elves possessed, as though they were speaking in song. He even found the male elf's deeper voice pleasing to the ear.

"I sense the presence of nearby fiends recently," Iel said. "It's a small thing, which leads me to believe it is a lesser demon, more of what a human would typically be capable of summoning. They are used as familiars or messengers.

"One thing to keep in mind is that whenever there is negative energy of any kind, it is at the very least, possible, for them to enter this world. Thoughts are in many ways more powerful than actions." He glanced at the little elf as he said this. Tinnoviel chuckled quietly and Yurin spared the now scowling Tikena a glance.

"The drek has lost some control over his general, Kabriza," Mira added. "In the kingdom of Winsor, we've discovered the presence of a small number of them. The region is already descending into conflict, with neighboring lands eyeing each other with suspicion."

"I went there to learn what I could," Iel said. "People are being killed in the most grisly manner, and the authorities have no leads as to who the killers are. I found seven of the creatures and dispatched four. The others were elusive and I cannot remain away from Takashaniel for long, lest Brit discover my absence and exploit it."

"Around the same time," Mira continued, "several kingdoms in the land of Ba Guo have had similar occurrences. The problem is spreading, and is not limited to any region. Demons cannot venture too far from the one who summons it, unless that individual dies. In this case, however, the drek has made a dangerous mistake. In summoning the quentranzi general, Kabriza, he has introduced an irritant to this plane, one that is powerful enough to sustain one of its own kind over great distances. Kabriza does not need Brit to sustain itself here. It is the most powerful demon of its species second only to Grala, the lord of the quentranzi.

"So, what you're saying," Seung spread her hands, "is that these demons are spreading without the drek's knowledge?"

Mira nodded. "In each of these kingdoms, their neighbors are experiencing the same problems. In Ba Guo, the kingdom of Qian is ruled by a warlord who is as aggressive as he is ambitious. For years he has sought an excuse to expand his reach. His greed and desire for conflict has attracted the demons.

"In New Dainland, the ruler of Mairland is irrational and incorrigible. Thus have they found him an easy target." Mira fixed the guests with a sobering gaze. "The implications, should either or both kingdoms converge on the other, would be disastrous. The raw fear, anger, and bloodlust that would result in such conflicts would strengthen the entire mass of demons Brit has summoned, making them more dangerous not only to us, but to him as well."

"And if they kill him," Yurin said, catching on, "they would have free range of this world."

"And be a stronger threat to Takashaniel," Kenyatta finished.

"If Takashaniel were to fall," Mira said, "there would be nothing stopping Kabriza from ripping a large enough hole in the barrier between this world and the abyss to bring as many fiends as it desires."

"There is a bigger problem." Iel said. "If Brit were to fall, Kabriza could rip a pathway through the veil for his master, Grala. Should that monster ever set foot in this dimension …" he shook his head. "It must not happen."

"And so this comes back around to us," Tinnoviel said. "You need us to prevent these wars from happening by hunting down and eliminating the demons hiding there. It sounds like the situation is nearly out of control already."

"We've had some luck," Iel replied. "New Dainland and Ba Guo are the only two places the demons have ventured outside Brit's influence. Whether it is the range Kabriza is able to afford them or other factors, we don't know. We must take advantage of this and stop it before they spread further."

A frown creased Tinnoviel's brow as he mulled over the information. "We understand and will aid you. However, I'll not frivolously endanger the four of us by entering either of these cities."

"In spite of all that has happened, you believe you would still be in danger?"

The elven warrior cast Mira a polite smile. "Past experiences indicate as much."

Beside him, Tikena scowled at the floor in front of her. Seung looked at the troubled elf with remorse, though she was careful to hide it. Years ago, Tikena's parents had been killed in their attempt to appeal to the leaders of a human civilization after the End of Technology. They had tried to explain the occurrence and how their people had a part in it and why. They were met with suspicion and anger, and later imprisoned and executed.

Seung had to fight down her resentment at just the memory. In that light, she couldn't really blame the often hostile elf for her dislike of humans.

"I'll not ask that of you," Iel said, jarring Seung from thoughts of Tikena's past. "Your aid here would be most valuable, if you're willing to give it."

"You have it," Tinnoviel said.

Iel smiled. "For the entirety of your stay, may you find comfort and peace." He turned to face Kenyatta and Kita. "What of you, children of the gene?"

The two men shared a look. "As before, we stand with you," Kita said.

Iel inclined his head in thanks. "And what of you, friend Seung Yoon? Your strong elven features would mark you as surely your companions. I would not ask you to enter any human city for that same reason."

"My whole life I've lived among humans and blended in," Seung replied. "I will go to New Dainland as well."

"Hopefully we can conclude this business quickly," Taliah said, "and I can get them back. I'd feel much easier about this if we are all here and prepared for the drek's coming."

"As will I," Iel agreed.

"What of the strider, the ninja, and her brother?" Taliah asked. "I can find them where they are and brief them of the situation before bringing them here."

"A good idea," the Ilanyan agreed. "This would save time."

"We should split our efforts," Taliah suggested. "Things are happening faster as the days pass. The drek will move on us soon and he knows nothing of the trouble brewing in New Dainland and Ba Guo. If we try to deal with this one by one, we'll find ourselves out of time. I should take these three," she indicated Kenyatta, Kita, and Seung, "straight to New Dainland.

"From there, I would find the other three who would be better suited to deal with the problems in Ba Guo. Since we are not dealing with an entire force of fiends, but perhaps one or two, it shouldn't take long and we can be back to assist in the preparations and stand with you when Brit finally comes."

"A good plan," Iel said. "Both groups are equal to the task before them."

"I will speak with the Elden," Tinnoviel said, drawing everyone's attention. "These lands are not wholly familiar to me, but I do know that the city of the Elden lies in the forests near here. They are more reclusive than we of Yathienel, but perhaps this common cause will draw them from their homeland." Seung saw Immendiel cast the Daunya Warrior a cautious look. It was there and gone so fast, she almost missed it.

Seung remembered hearing about the Elden elves. They were very much a reclusive people, preferring to live in their thick jungle homes away from the affairs of the wider world. She thought of them with a pang of regret, for it reminded her of Tinnoviel's childhood friend, the Elden ranger Alurien MerTana. The orphaned Alurien had been adopted by The Lady Seiyun and the people of The Wood, and had grown up as one of them. Despite the differences in culture, Seiyun had been adamant that Alurien learn his Elden Heritage.

The loss of Alurien in the depths of The Sentinels mountains had been like the loss of a brother to Tinnoviel. He bore the pain of it in his eyes still. Seung wondered why Immendiel was wary of visiting these jungle elves. Would they be angry that one of their own had fallen?

"Your effort would be appreciated, Daunya Warrior," Iel replied. "And that concludes our meeting. I am happy to offer you the hospitality of Takashaniel. You will find that the more you explore, the more invigorated you will feel." He stood, the others rising with him.

"Please, be at home, and experience as much as there is to offer. You will find that communing with the Daunyans is easier here because of the nature of Takashaniel. There are places to take the reverie, for those of you who do so." He looked to the elves when he spoke, and they nodded their appreciation.

"Before you partake of the offerings of this creation of the Daunyans, however, I would recommend that you accompany Mira to infuse your weapons." Seung frowned, but when she looked at Kenyatta, he and Kita seemed to understand what the Ilanyan had meant.

"I leave you with Mira, and will see you at dawn."

Kenyatta stared blankly at the passing floors as the transparent platform took them to the upper levels of the tower. "Anyone find it coincidental that the word 'dawn' sounds a lot like the name of the Gods?"

Mira nodded. "The word has an ancient origin. Humans from a land known as Mu knew of the Daunyans, and gave the beauty of the coming of the sun each day a piece of Their namesake. To these people, little could compare to the coming of the new day, and the rejuvenating energy brought by the sun. Thus, they named this daily event 'dawn'."

"What would they have named this *event* if they lived in the Rainlands?" the ever-sour Tikena asked. "Don't always see the sun every day, there."

"And yet the sun's light penetrates the thickest of rain clouds," Mira said. "Even in the darkest of cloudy days, one still knows that a new day has come." Tikena muttered under her breath about the term undoubtedly having elven origin as they reached the tenth floor of the tower.

Kita looked down at the transparent platform beneath them and his face paled. Each level of the tower was transparent, and one could literally see through every floor beneath their feet to the bottom. His legs started to feel wobbly. "I forgot how disturbing it is being this far up and seeing everything below."

The platform finally stopped and Mira led them to a circular room with transparent walls glowing in the many soft colors of the spectrum. As they approached the door, it opened of its own accord and they stepped through. As the last person entered, the colors of the walls solidified until they were no longer transparent.

"Here, we will enter the process of infusing your weapons," Mira said. "Aside from Kenyatta and Kita, does anyone else have experience in battling demons?" When no one indicated they had, she continued. "Since they are not from this dimension, and far more durable than anything native to this plane, demons cannot be killed by a weapon created by materials originating from this world. I have only seen two exceptions to this. One was crafted specifically for battling demons and is unique in that regard. The other has a mysterious origin, and I suspect it may not be from this dimension, either. Your weapons, though strong and beautifully crafted, must be infused with Daunyanic energy, which is lethal to an abysmal creature."

"I sense the Gene of the Daunyans within you," she said to Seung. "When the time comes, your body and spirit will react. Your physical abilities will be limited only by your imagination."

My imagination? Seung recalled the stories Kenyatta had told her over the last year. It had all sounded outlandish at the time, but given her own recent adventures—including her own heritage—she couldn't dismiss it. What could it mean for her, that she carried this Godly gene inside?

"I will need you to place your weapons on the floor, here." Mira indicated the center of the room. "Please arrange them in a circle, tips pointing inward."

Seung didn't know what she had expected of the process, but sitting in a meditative state outside the ring of weapons hadn't come to mind.

For a time, she sat in the bliss of her own center, existing and nothing more. Then, a feeling of euphoria entered her being. It was gradual at first, then, as if waiting for her to open the door, it rushed in.

The euphoric energy washed over Seung, filling every pore, every hair follicle. Seung resisted the urge to gasp as she felt the presence grow and permeate her body. The energy grew more intense, surging through her being until she felt as if she could no longer contain it.

Seung opened her eyes and saw the same awe on her companion's faces. The tempest of raw energy flowed through the room. Seung focused through the blizzard of Daunyanic energy that swirled around them; through them.

Despite the overwhelming sensations, however, it was all inward. Nothing stirred in the quiet room; not a strand of hair, nor lace of a boot. The tempest they felt was not perceptible by the physical senses.

Daunyanic energy swirled throughout the room, then funneled into the weapons on the floor. Seung felt it as clearly as if she'd seen it with her own eyes.

Taliah moved forward and stood between the seated Tinnoviel and Yurin Kei Daunyana. She placed her palms together and closed her eyes. After several moments, she turned her palms outward, thumbs and forefingers touching. "Se'lir." A few moments passed and she spoke again. "Boraka."

Seung sensed two distinct energies at that moment, as if the presence of two beings had entered the room. In that moment she felt as tiny as a grain of sand lying before all of creation. She felt as fragile as a blade of grass in the presence of this power. It filled her to the point she thought she would burst. A gentle warmth filled her in that moment; a smile, from creation itself.

Like the waves of the ocean receding from the beach, the power pulled away, and with it, the euphoria that filled her entire existence. Seung let out a long trembling sigh, emptiness replacing her exhilaration.

"I would give anything to experience that again," Immendiel whispered. "Was that the Daunyans we felt?"

Mira nodded. "It was. Whenever one connects with the power of the Daunyans, no matter how little or great, there is a feeling of completeness beyond description."

A sudden spark of warmth flared in Seung's core. It was a small thing at first, but she felt it instantly. The warmth expanded in waves, growing with each pulsation until it had completely filled her body. Without thinking, she closed her eyes and opened herself to it.

When Seung opened her eyes again, she gasped. The colors of Takashaniel were brighter and more vibrant than they were before. As she looked from one person to the next, she saw that each of her friends glowed with a palpable inner radiance. Tikena and Immendiel glowed brightly, Kenyatta and Kita glowed brighter, and Yurin Kei Daunyana glowed brighter still. Tinnoviel glowed as brightly as the Daunya Apprentice.

Seung looked down at herself. She glowed as bright as Kenyatta and Kita!

Across the room, Taliah glowed so bright it hurt her eyes to look upon her. The woman looked at her with an approving smile.

"You see it," Taliah said. "You are experiencing the Gene for the first time, Seung Kiluriel MerTana Yoon. You are one of the Children of the Gene, blessed by the Daunyans before your birth, to protect this world against the abyss.

"All of you have been touched by the Daunyans this day, and are forever changed. The feeling you experience now will fade, but some of the Daunyanic Essence that flowed through you will remain. Now, take up your weapons."

The six warriors rose and reclaimed their weapons. "Never have I felt such a thing," Tinnoviel said, his voice filled with awe. "I have channeled a small bit of Boraka's power, but never have I felt what permeates my very being."

"I will return for you tomorrow," Taliah said, addressing Kenyatta, Kita, and Seung. "Please excuse me."

"I also must attend to some of my errands," Mira said, following Taliah to the door. "Should you have any needs, you have but to notify any of the attendants that reside here."

"That was amazing," Tikena whispered. "The feeling resonates in me still."

"As it does in me," Immendiel agreed, "though it is fading." She looked at Seung, and her eyes held a degree of respect that had never been there before. "This is how it feels to be a Child of the Gene, Kiluriel?"

Seung shrugged. "This is new to me, too. I feel more alive than I've ever felt, and capable of things I would never have imagined possible."

"The power only comes when there is need," Kenyatta said. "It'll fade in time, but when you need it, it'll fill you like an ocean."

Seung inspected *Vyirayoi*. Power coursed through the weapon like the blood flowing through her veins. She had never fought a demon before, but in that moment, Seung felt that the bite of her weapon would bring down any fiend.

"It's going to be long days from this point forward," Kita said. "I'm going to have a look around before I get some rest."

Kenyatta smirked at him. "Yeah man. Have a "look around" and tell my sister I'll see her tomorrow."

"The odd humor of humans," Immendiel said, watching the two humans shoving and laughing at each other as Kita left the room.

"I think it's just that those two are odd," Seung said, drawing a round of chuckling.

Kenyatta glanced at the laughing elves. "I'm gonna learn that talk eventually," he muttered.

"Don't be so paranoid, love. It's not always about you."

"Care to translate?"

"Aw." Seung pinched his cheek and he grunted, swatting away her hand with a mock snarl.

"This is such a beautiful structure." Immendiel walked along the colorful walls, leaning in close to inspect the soft-colored pulsations. As she studied the wall it grew hazy, then to the tracker's astonishment, it became transparent and they were afforded a view of the surrounding lands. "By the Daunyans! Everything about this place is beautiful. A shame the taint of the abyss will touch these lands soon."

"As it will touch every land hence," Tinnoviel replied, "should we fail."

It was a dark thought, but one that every member of the group knew was true. Grim looks passed between them all, and though Seung hadn't translated the exchange for Kenyatta, she saw that he caught the feeling of what was said. As they stood before the wall gazing at the landscape beyond, the sun made its gradual arc across the sky.

Seung moved closer to Kenyatta. His warm energy mingled with her own, and for a time she allowed herself to enjoy it. This could be the beginning of their adventures together, or the end.

23

Liu Xiang and Zhang Da turned and drew their weapons in the same motion. Two figures stood shrouded in the shadows. Zhang Da planted his feet and leveled his spear. The two figures seemed unmoved.

"Identify yourselves," Liu Xiang demanded.

"What would you know from me, Emperor?"

"Are you hard of hear?" Zhang Da said. He inched forward to stand just ahead of Liu.

"Identify yourselves and tell me what part you play in this?" Liu ordered.

"What makes you think we have a part in any of this?" one of the figures asked.

"You're playing a dangerous game with my patience," Zhang Da growled. "Speak or be put to the question!"

"Peace, General." One of the figures stepped closer. "We come to help—"

The man had made a mistake. He'd come too close. No sooner had the thought come to Liu's mind than Zhang Da exploded into action.

The general thrust the spear forward attempting to drive the intruder back. The intruder sidestepped the maneuver with alarming ease.

Growling, Da drew the spear back and thrust it forward again with a twist of his wrist. The tip of the spear shot forward in a circular motion. Instead of backstepping to avoid the waving spear tip his opponent ducked beneath. As Zhang Da retracted, the man straightened but made no move to attack.

Liu Xiang watched with growing concern. That one exchange had left

Zhang Da vulnerable for one fatal moment. He kept an eye on the second intruder, who'd made no move to attack. What was going on?

Zhang Da brought the spear around in an arc, whipping the tip from the side. At the last moment, he stopped the motion, causing the shaft to bend, and the spear tip to stab sideways. Again, the shrouded figure easily avoided the attack, leaning back as the spear jabbed harmlessly in front of his face. Quick as the strike of a snake, Zhang Da retracted yet again and thrust forward, attempting to catch his opponent off balance.

What happened next had Liu Xiang staring in stunned amazement. As Zhang Da's spear thrust forward, the man sidestepped again, avoiding the spear tip by mere inches. He brought a straightened arm arcing down, tucking the spear under that arm. He continued the maneuver and kept the spear tucked under each arm as he spun along the shaft and closed the distance.

Liu Xiang barely had time to register what had happened. The man had not only avoided Zhang Da's attack, but kept the general from retracting his spear. Now he stood directly in front of the startled Zhang.

The general delivered a sideways chop to the neck. The man leaped away, tucking his knees to his chest, arms extended as though he were flying backward. Again, he landed and waited.

Liu Xiang's eyes widened. He'd seen that type of maneuver before, during a visit to one of five temples legendary for their warrior monks. "Stop, General!" He ignored Da's incredulous glance and sheathed his swords. "Do the monks of Shaolin come to antagonize us in the midst of a crisis?"

He moved to stand beside Zhang, who still had his spear leveled at the monk. The general was one of the best warriors in all of Shu Han. Xiang had never seen his friend so easily bested in a fight. He watched as the general grudgingly relaxed, stabbing the butt of the spear into the ground. He scowled, but gave a stiff bow.

"I apologize, warrior," the monk said. "I stepped forth to enter the light, not to provoke confrontation. May I do so now?"

Zhang Da looked to Liu Xiang, who nodded. He gave the monk a curt nod. The warrior monk stepped forward and lowered his hood. Pale moonlight washed over his shaved, dotted head, and Xiang knew it to be true. During the Age of Technology, the way of the warrior monk had been somewhat of a novelty to outsiders. It wasn't until after the End of Technology that the monks of Shaolin returned to the practices preceding the Age of Technology.

"I am Shi Xing Long." The monk pressed his palms together and bowed.

"This is Shi Xiao Ren." He indicated the monk beside him, who echoed Xing Long's gesture.

"May we assume you are here to shed light on our situation, monk?" Zhang Da asked, straight to the point as always.

"We are not positive about the source, General," Xing Long replied. "But it feels wrong."

Zhang Da frowned. "You come here to tell us it feels wrong? If the birds and animals could speak, if the *insects* that hop on the ground could speak, they would tell us that much."

"I should phrase it another way. The wrongness is a wrongness to nature itself. A perversion of nature floats in the air like a noxious cloud. Since the attacks started, so too, arrived the taint."

Liu Xiang turned to look upon his beloved Shu Han. The screams had stopped and the night patrol seemed to have gotten the matter in hand. A tense quiet settled over the nervous city. "While I appreciate your description of the problem from your perspective it does little to shed light on the situation. No matter the feel of it, the attacks must be stopped, yet we have not found the *how* of it. Have you any insight, Shi Xing Long of Shaolin?"

The monk was quiet for a moment. "I have suspicions, but they are not what I can share without proof, Emperor Liu Xiang."

"I would hear what you have to say regardless of proof. I must explore every avenue."

"What I speak of deals in matters of the mystical," Shi Xing Long replied. "The secular mind requires proof of these things. I cannot yet reveal our suspicions until we are sure."

"Then, we return to the question," the ever hotblooded Zhang Da snapped. "Why are you here?"

"To warn you that what plagues your city is an irritant in the Dao Itself."

"An irritant in the Dao?" Xiang looked at Zhang Da, who wore and equally baffled expression. "What do you mean, an irritant? What do you suggest?"

"The monks of Shaolin stand with you, descendant of Liu Bei, and descendant of Zhang Fei. You, all of you, as the descendants of the Three Sworn and the Strategist, have come together after centuries. The time of a new age is upon us. An age both beautiful and more dangerous than any time in our known history. You will be tested, and the Order of Shaolin will stand with you."

"I don't know whether to thank you or hold you by your ankles and shake it out of you," Zhang Da said, exasperated. "What are you talking about?"

The monk returned to the shadows beside his companion. Together, they stepped back further and disappeared into the night. Zhang Da stood with his mouth hanging open.

"I've never known a monk of Shaolin to operate in such mystery, Liu Xiang said after Da had hurriedly ushered him back into his rooms and closed and locked the doors.

"You've never known a monk of Shaolin at all."

"Well, we know *of* them. The stories are mostly consistent. When a mystic speaks, one listens carefully."

"Mostly because they never speak in straight lines and you must concentrate, lest you go as crazy as they are," the pragmatic general said.

Liu Xiang chuckled at his impatient friend. Though as fierce as his legendary ancestor, Zhang Da had learned from mistakes of his forebear. He practiced kindness and compassion to his men that in turn earned their loyalty. He had respect and admiration from his soldiers, instead of the fear and resentment that Zhang Fei's men were said to have held for him.

"I think you are in need of a pilgrimage to Huashan, my friend," Liu Xiang said, referring to the legendary mountain that was home to Daoist monks for millennia and more.

"I would sooner be doing something productive, my lord," Da replied.

"Take heart, old friend. We will get to the heart of this. Sooner or later the ones responsible will make a mistake and we'll have them."

"Then let us hope they make a mistake soon. Qian will be here within the week."

Xiang couldn't deny the problems that would likely arise when the warlord set foot in the palace of Shu Han. "I've a feeling all of this has been an orchestrated dance culminating to the disaster they would set upon us at the expense of Shu Han and Qian. What puzzles me, though, is who stands to gain from our conflict? What outside player is hiding in the shadows waiting to benefit?"

"None come to mind besides the man who'll be on our doorstep in but a week," Zhang Da replied.

"The benefactor is not always the direct instigator. Foolish and hot tempered he may be, but I cannot conjure the image of Qian Hua orchestrating the grisly murders of random citizens in his city and ours. How much gain would there be in creating an excuse to come here under the pretense of discussing it?" He spread his hands.

"Qian comes here with soldiers, no doubt, and has one of them murdered within my city to create a cause for him to then leave and then return with a sizable force to assault us?" Liu shook his head. "He may be conniving, devious, and opportunistic, but one thing Qian Hua is not and never has been, is stupid.

Zhang Da stroked his ample beard. "Xiaoyin has been able to anticipate the possible motivations and actions of Qian, but she hasn't offered any insight on who may be the cause of our problems."

They stood in silence in the candlelit room for a time, each wrapped in his own thoughts. Liu Xiang patted his friend on the shoulder. "There will be no epiphanies to be had in an exhausted mind. We will put the matter to rest for the night.

Zhang grunted. "What bothers me most of all is that this could end in a battle fought for the benefit and entertainment of a hidden player. I don't like the idea of being a piece on someone's chessboard."

Those last words lingered in Liu Xiang's mind long after the general had gone.

24

This must be a joke. Akemi drew her blades and whistled. At her signal, Kenjiro and the Shinobu were on their feet, weapons in hand. Misshapen forms resembling humans converged on the two back-to-back warriors.

"What is this?" Shinobu crouched, hand hovering over the hilt of his sword.

"What does it look like?" Kenjiro replied, holding his sword before him.

From her perch, Akemi stared in disbelief. *Zombies? This isn't possible.* She shook her head in revulsion as one former human, carrying a tree branch approached Kenjiro. She watched as the circle closed in upon the two warriors beneath her. She wasn't worried about them. Kenjiro and Shinobu were more than a match for these lumbering enemies. What interested her was the cause of all this.

"Care to join us?" Shinobu yelled.

Kenjiro shook his head. "Don't bother. She's a ninja. When the best opportunity to strike comes, she'll show up."

"They look like humans," Shinobu said. "What could twist people into something so grotesque? How could their forms be so bent and warped?"

A twisted creature got too close and lunged for Kenjiro. With a flick of his sword, the samurai severed the reaching arm. "You've fought demons, before, have you not?"

"This is different." In one motion Shinobu drew his sword and struck, severing the head of the nearest creature. The sword was back in its sheath before the head hit the ground.

"They tend to do things like this until they're found and banished, or destroyed," Kenjiro replied. He deflected a sloppy swing of a shortsword and cut down the attacker.

"Hence the need for demon hunters like your beautiful sister." Shinobu said, cleaving straight through a swinging sword and the attacker in one blow. His back to the Kenjiro, Shinobu smirked. He could feel the samurai's warning glare on his back. His smile vanished, when a hulking form leapt over the advancing former humans, and slashed a clawed hand at him.

"Watch your back!" he yelled as he dove aside, cutting down two advancing enemies with a quick left-right cut before spinning around to face this new and more mobile threat."

Kenjiro's instincts took over, and he spun and raised his sword, correctly anticipating the strider not being there and a new attacker in his place. The airborne creature was unable to stop its descent, and the horizontally ascending sword cleaved straight through flesh and bone, severing the limb.

He followed up the defensive maneuver by bringing his sword around and down, cutting the creature down with a horizontal swipe that laid it low. "That was no zombie."

"Must you call them that?" Akemi said from above as she descended on two more leaping monsters. "Zombies don't exist." She cut them across the back as she descended, then crisscrossed her blades several times, cutting her enemies down before they could fully turn to offer any offense.

"What do you call them, then?" Kenjiro asked, easily felling another stumbling foe.

"Anything else." Akemi wrinkled her nose in disgust as she cut down four twisted forms, her hands a blur of precision. "My life's story as a demon hunter isn't interesting enough, so the fates toss in zombies to give it a nice, trite appeal."

"My sympathies to your sullied ego," Kenjiro said as he cut down yet another in a seemingly endless wave of misshapen creatures.

"Siblings," Shinobu muttered. With a zigzagging cut of his otherworldly sword, he left several enemies motionless on the ground. "You suppose they want to eat us?"

"Ugh. Must you?" Akemi felled several lumbering creatures and backed away as more replaced them.

Shinobu smirked. "I speak it as I see it."

And so it went; the twisted former humans advancing on the three warriors to be cut down until finally, none were left but the three warriors surrounded by a macabre scene of death, or rather as Shinobu wondered, undeath.

"First time I've fought so many foes and not been at least tired," Shinobu said.

They waited, scanning the nighttime woods for any additional threat but none appeared.

"Fortunately, the trees are still damp from the rain," Akemi remarked as she set fire to the corpses. "I am loathe to scorch the trees, but it would be far worse if these things were to rapidly decompose into the ground if not burned."

"Burning or not," Shinobu said, "the ashes will settle and the remains will seep into the soil."

"No. This is evil that has animated a corpse and tainted it. There is not much left of the bodies, which is why they are so disfigured. Fire will cause them to practically evaporate. What's left that was made of this world will remain. What doesn't belong will be burned away and banished back from where it came."

"Simple fire can do this?" Shinobu asked, thinking of their past encounters from three years ago.

"The more powerful the evil, the more powerful the tools needed to defeat it. I've never encountered something like this, but from my experience, these are animated corpses. Only lesser demons can animate a vessel from this plane. Once the vessel is destroyed, they have no means to remain in this dimension." She looked over her shoulder at the dead creatures that had been more dangerous. "We should make haste."

"What do you know?" Kenjiro asked.

Akemi gestured for him to join her, nodding at one of the downed monsters.

Shinobu stopped what he was doing when Kenjiro swore an oath. "What is it?"

"This," the demon hunter said, "is a fledgling *seaph*."

* * *

They traveled the open fields and rolling hills in silence for a time, reflecting on their recent encounter with the demon-possessed human corpses and the fledgling *seaphs*, as Akemi had called them.

"What escapes me," Shinobu said, breaking the silence, "is why bother with zombies when they can just create an army of *seaphs*? Seems to me it would accomplish whatever they're doing much quicker."

"There lies a large part of the problem," Akemi replied. "The presence of *seaphs* along with the demon-possessed suggests that Brit has nothing to do with it. He may have no knowledge of this. Demons are not as organized in mind or action as a human or the drek. They act on impulse and revel in chaos and destruction. They're not here for any specific agenda other than to kill and destroy, and cause as much havoc as possible. To a demon, negativity is a source of nourishment. They've somehow been able to pull lesser fiends through the barrier between our two worlds and imprison them within the bodies of dead humans."

Tendrils of the eastern sun's light snaked across the land, piercing the night to bring about the golden dawn.

Akemi shaded her eyes as she peered into the distance. Given last night's events, it was a welcome sight. "The inhabited corpses aren't a major problem. Even the least skilled fighter could defend against the clumsy things. What concerns me aside from Brit's lack of control over the fiends, is that a *seaph* can only be created by the union of a lesser demon and a willing host. No matter how strong, an evil entity cannot enter a host without consent."

"Which means," Shinobu said, "there are people who not only know about the existence of demons, but are uniting with them on purpose."

"Enticed by the promise of power and immortality," Akemi said. "These individuals are already corrupt in heart, so it would take little effort for a low-level fiend to tempt a human to join with it."

"So that, back there," the strider jabbed a thumb over his shoulder, "is what we can expect in the days to come unless we stop this?"

"No. That is an *idea* of what will come. It takes little time for a *seaph* to reach maturity. Once it does, it will be far more formidable than those back there." Akemi turned her piercing dark brown eyes on the farstrider. "This is going to get much worse before it gets better."

The normally easygoing strider looked into the distance, his features uncharacteristically hard. "How long does it take one of these *seaphs* to reach maturity?"

"About seven days."

"Of course," he replied, raising a hand and letting it drop to his side. "This would have been much too easy otherwise."

On Akemi's other side, Kenjiro grunted.

"If there's any positive to be found in this," Akemi said, ignoring her brother, "it's that these occurrences have just started. Brit's influence on his demons must have begun to slip recently, otherwise we would have encountered this before now. That makes me think there is still time to put a stop to it before the world is overrun."

Shinobu raised his eyebrows. "You think it could get to that?"

"It would take some time, but if we fail to hunt them all down, yes, it could happen. If that fool drek manages to destroy or even weaken Takashaniel enough, it could happen even faster."

"The world is a large place," Shinobu said. "How can we possibly find them all?"

"We can't. There's always another fiend to slay. As long as there is evil in the world there will always be a narrow slit in the barrier for them to slip through. We need to kill the drek. But before we do that, we need to eliminate the quentranzi he thinks he is using to summon more fiends to serve him. When they've been dealt with, the horde to which they're tethered will be banished back to the abyss."

"Our problem seems straightforward, then," Shinobu said. "We kill those two, our problems are solved."

Akemi shook her head. "You still don't understand. Any native of the abyss remains here subject to the summoner's will or a condition."

Shinobu frowned in thought. "But, it's inhabiting a vessel native to this plane it's not subject to the same conditions."

Akemi nodded. "Regardless of the outcome, the drek has brought changes to this world that may forever remain a reality."

"One thing at a time, then," Shinobu said. "We still have no idea where the drek is, where his demon general is, or for that matter, where Takashaniel lies. I feel the pull of the Tower as strongly as you two, but how far away is it?"

"I'm sure *she* has the answer to that," Kenjiro said.

Shinobu and Akemi followed the samurai's gaze. A lone figure stood atop a mound in the distance ahead. The sun cast a golden silhouette around her, like a halo.

Despite the distance, Akemi knew they'd met her before, after the first battle at Takashaniel. She had a brother who was as carefree as a child, yet as deadly a warrior as herself or her companions.

Taliah slid aside several thick locks of raven hair and smiled. "It's time."

"A long time it's been," Akemi said, reverting to the common tongue of the western lands. "Though we barely spoke when last we met."

"Indeed," the woman said. To their surprise, she spoke in their native tongue.

"I am relieved you speak our language," Kenjiro said. "Better that I do not have to stumble through yours."

"What brings you to us this fine chilled spring day?" Shinobu asked. "We were just enjoying a nice brisk stroll through the fields, getting into adventures with zombies and all other manner of nasties choosing to join us on our merry trail!"

Taliah tilted her head at him. "Did you just say, zombies?" She glanced at Akemi as the ninja shook her head in disgust.

"Yes," Kenjiro answered, casting a sidelong glance at the farstrider. "Unpleasant business, to be sure."

Akemi sighed. "They were not *zombies*. They were former humans, the bodies of dead humans animated by lesser evil from the upper hell levels."

"A dead body," Shinobu remarked, his voice laced with sarcasm "animated and walking. Demon possessed or not, sounds like a zombie to me." Akemi glared at him. Shinobu sniggered.

"It's like talking to my brother," Taliah muttered, reverting back to the western tongue and running a hand through her hair. "You're moving in the right direction, which means you feel the call of Takashaniel. Time is against us, so we must be quick. I will transport you in the same manner as how I've come to you now."

"To Takashaniel," Kenjiro said.

"Not yet. Things are in motion and Brit will move soon. There is more at work than his own plans." She arched an eyebrow at the lack of surprise between the trio. "What do you know?"

And so they exchanged stories, the trio of warriors relating the events of their past few days, and Taliah giving her account of what was discussed at Takashaniel.

"The dream that was not a dream," Kenjiro murmured. "It seems we've all shared a version of it. The time comes again, that we must battle for this tower; this Takashaniel."

Taliah nodded. "You already know the implications, should Takashaniel fall. What you've told me is also troubling. The presence of demon-inhabited dead is not as concerning to me as your encounter with these fledgling *seaphs*. You're sure about their nature?"

Akemi nodded. "For half my life I've hunted demons; I know them well. Those corpses were inhabited by abysmal entities, and the things with them were fledgling *seaphs*. What I'm unsure of is whether it was the *seaphs* or something else driving those former humans."

"You think that's possible?" Kenjiro asked.

"It makes sense. It would take a powerful demon to compel a lesser into this world without the knowledge of the one with whom they are *tethered*. That makes me believe we're dealing with at least one extremely powerful quentranzi. The presence of *seaphs* alongside the inhabited humans suggest they're planning something. Quentranzi are one of the few species of demon that are possessed of a higher intelligence. *Seaphs*, although not nearly as powerful as quentranzi, are smarter, and difficult to kill."

"Then we have even less time," Taliah said.

"So where is it you plan to take us, if not Takashaniel?" Kenjiro asked.

"Ba Guo."

"Ba Guo?" the three echoed in unison.

"You would take us to the land of Eight Kingdoms?" Shinobu replied. "What happens in these lands that we must attend to?"

"Potential disaster," Taliah replied. "Grisly murders have been happening in Shu Han. Emperor Liu Xiang has not been able to deduce the cause, but it it's easy to figure out for those with the eyes to see."

"Demons," Akemi said.

"It's going to be an interesting time explaining what's going on unless we can provide proof," Shinobu said. "And every demon we've ever defeated is either sent back to the abyss or utterly destroyed."

"We may have help," Taliah said. "The monks of Songshan will be more receptive to what we have to say."

"Songshan?" Kenjiro said. "The Order of Shaolin? They haven't rebuilt the temple since the final time it was destroyed. You're saying it still exists?"

"It does," Taliah replied. "Eradication under the fist of more than one suspicious ruling party has taught them the better part of … discretion. Few know they've endure in any real numbers since they retreated farther into the mountains. To find their temple, one must traverse the harsh terrain of the mountains. Few who travel to learn their ways return to the common world. Those who do mingle under a secular guise."

"I've a feeling this will change soon," Akemi said.

"Likely it will," Taliah agreed. "The drek has forced changes upon us all, many that are undesirable. I will take you to speak with the monks of Shaolin first. From there, we can decide on how to approach Liu Xiang. He is a sensible ruler, and is likely to consider what we have to say."

"Nothing short of throwing a demon at his feet would convince him," Akemi said. "The human populace has no knowledge of the abyss, much less its spawn. To most people, they are stories and legends; folklore and nothing more."

"That's where you come in, demon hunter," Taliah said. "You've a sense for their presence, do you not? With help from Shaolin, we can open Liu Xiang's eyes to the truth."

"Why is this more important than moving straight for Takashaniel?" Shinobu asked. "We kill the head, the serpent dies."

"These killings are happening in another land close to Shu Han as well, one ruled by a warlord named Qian Hua. He is a volatile man whose hand is quicker than his reason. These killings could cause a war between the two lands that would envelop the neighboring Zhao. At first, we were unsure what the demons were planning by antagonizing Qian. We thought maybe they were prodding the warlord for the simple fun of causing chaos. But after your account of the demon-possessed bodies you fought, and the potential problem of these *seaphs*, I have a better understanding."

Kenjiro narrowed his eyes. "By causing a battle between the two emperors—"

"The numerous dead can be reanimated with lesser demons and controlled by the *seaphs*," Akemi finished.

Taliah nodded. "And this is not an isolated problem. The same is happening in New Dainland."

"And all the while our oblivious friend, Brit, is moving to destroy the one barrier that prevents this world from becoming an extension of the abyss." Shinobu shook his head. "Unbelievable."

"He believes he is powerful enough to hold them in check," Taliah said. "What he does not believe, however, is that his demon general, Kabriza, is cunning enough to do exactly what it is doing without his knowledge. The irony of this situation is that we must preserve the drek's life long enough to banish Kabriza. If Brit dies first, Kabriza will have full autonomy."

"Sounds like a problem," Shinobu said.

They spoke of the plans laid out at Takashaniel, and the three warriors inquired about Kita and Kenyatta. Taliah informed them of the duo's involvement, as well as their new companions.

"Elves." Shinobu laughed. "I'm sure I shouldn't be surprised."

"Given the things we've seen over the course of these past three years," Akemi said, "it shouldn't be a surprise. Still, in myth …"

"And you say they stumbled upon the lair of a dragon?" Kenjiro shook his head. "I wish I could have been there."

"From the story they told me," Taliah said, "it was a near disaster. Khairon The Blue nearly slaughtered them all."

"If the lore holds true," Shinobu said, "the dragons of the west are more volatile than those of the east."

"And that is fodder for another lengthy discussion," Taliah said. "I should get you to Ba Guo now.

Shinobu hesitated. "I'd like to help, but I don't want to drop in the middle of someone else's war."

"It hasn't gotten to war yet, and it doesn't matter either way. We're fighting on three fronts, but we can stop two wars from happening if we're quick."

"And if we are not?" Kenjiro asked, though they all knew the answer.

"Then we do what we must," Taliah replied.

"Ironic," Shinobu said. "An army of demons is trying to break into our world and may succeed because humans are too busy fighting themselves to know any better."

Akemi closed her eyes and let her head fall back, the sun warm on her face. "I'm tired of this endless dance." She opened her eyes to see Kenjiro staring at her. "Over fifteen years I have hunted demons. I've seen this time and again. They can't come here of their own accord, no matter how powerful they are. They must be summoned. Summoned! You know what this means."

"So long as there is evil in this world the demon realm will have a link to it." The air in front of Taliah rippled. "Cast your weariness aside, for now. We go to Ba Guo."

Akemi's hands drifted to the hilts of her two hungry swords. She was indeed weary of the endless cycle of humans summoning demons, but she was a demon hunter. She loved battling fiends as much as she loathed their existence. The thirst for demon blood buzzed through the swords. *Soon. You will have the blood you hunger for.*

* * *

As alien as the experience was, the trio hadn't the time to marvel at Taliah's method of transportation. They'd touched down in earshot of a large force on the march.

Being the most agile among the trees, Akemi found a sizable one and leapt branch to branch till she had a panoramic view of the land. She watched the scene below long enough to absorb the details, then descended to the others.

"I speculate a force near to three hundred soldiers on the move in the direction of Shu Han. I couldn't determine the mood of the procession, but either way it doesn't look good."

"The hours pass like minutes," Taliah said. "Time slips through our fingers."

"Do we stay to the plan and continue on to Songshan?" Shinobu asked. "Or do we head to Shu Han ahead of this army?"

"I cannot imagine an emperor as capable as I've heard Liu Xiang to be, caught off guard by this," Kenjiro said.

"And if this is a war party?" Akemi asked.

"Then best if we're there for the eventual appearance of the fiends behind this," Taliah replied. "Since conventional weapons cannot kill them, our help would be needed."

But as the group listened to the approaching force, they wondered how they would make a difference against the evil that would no doubt be scattered within the ranks of both armies.

They set out, hoping they were not wading into the middle of a war.

2 6

E lizander Dain awoke from a sleep fit for the dead. For a while he lay on
his back, feeling the warmth of the gently crackling fireplace. Slowly,
grudgingly, he opened his eyes. Through the window he could see the cold
heavy rain of spring outside. The gray sky cried steady tears upon the lands of
New Dainland, washing away the impurities inherent in the life of a large
city.

His groggy thoughts flowed through the mud of his mind, and he gave
himself a mental shake. He raised a hand to rub his head and immediately
regretted it. A fresh wave of pain washed up his left side and made his head
spin. He tensed, gritting his teeth, then slowly lowered his arm back to his
side.

"Our beloved king returns to the land of the living."

Milpheus

The attendant appeared at Elizander's bedside. "You must be careful with
those ribs, my lord. The bonesetter corrected three of them and wrapped your
side. Praise to Holy Jemanah that you only cracked two. Please do not undo
his fine work."

"I don't think I have enough strength to lace my boots, much less do
anything else to damage myself further. Help me sit up." When Milpheus
hesitated, he added, "I'll not spend the day on my back, especially while
speaking."

With Milpheus's aid, Elizander sat upright, the attendant having stacked pillows behind his back. He took a slow, deep breath to test his ribs and winced.

Milpheus brought him a steaming mug of herbal tea, which he gratefully accepted. The warm drink soothed his insides and helped him to relax. For a time he sat in silence, eyes closed and listening to the crackle of the fireplace. When he opened his eyes again, Milpheus was still standing patiently at his bedside. Had he dozed off?

"You've been through quite an ordeal, my lord. You really must take better care. Your kingdom depends on your personal discretion. And speaking of your kingdom," Milpheus cleared his throat. "Perhaps you should consider finding a queen and securing your line of succession."

Elizander waved it all away. He had no time for any of that. The memory of how his ribs had come to be damaged was returning. "How long have I slept?"

"Two days, my lord."

"I've slept for two days? Why didn't anyone wake me?" Milpheus's patient expression calmed Elizander. What would have been the point? What would he have done? He could barely keep his eyes open even after two days of sleep.

As though seeing that Elizander had come to that conclusion, Milpheus nodded. "While I consider the harrowing tale of your brush with death three nights ago to be, creative, he was correct that you would need a couple days of rest."

Elizander frowned. "He?"

"A rather unapproachable monk."

"You found this monk unlikable?" When he received no response, Elizander turned his head to look at Milpheus. "If my foggy mind serves me, a monk saved my life."

"We all have our shining moments," came the dry response. Elizander could only wonder what a conversation between those two had been like. Suddenly, his thoughts went to Davros. Again, Milpheus seemed to read his mind. "I gather the alarmed expression is for your loyal captain? He came away from the ordeal a trifle better than you, my lord. He sustained a concussion and a few black and blue bruises, but little else. He has come to check in on you frequently."

As if on cue, there was a knock at the door.

Milpheus wrinkled his lips. "Speak of the undesirable and it will darken your doorstep."

"Admit him," Elizander said, repressing what would no doubt be painful laughter. He never understood why those two so disliked each other.

Milpheus opened the door, admitting a battered looking Captain Davros. He walked with a subtle limp, and had a bandage wrapped around his head. Despite his obvious injuries, the captain still moved with a sure step.

"My Lord Elizander Dain," Milpheus announced crisply. "I present Captain Davros Naishere."

"Greetings, my lord," Davros boomed. "It's good to see you among the living again." He limped over and clasped hands with the king, taking care for his damaged ribs. Elizander smiled, grateful to be in the presence of his longtime friend.

"Milpheus, would you be so kind ..." he trailed off as the captain shook his head.

"It feels as though a slimy film forms on my tongue as I speak these words," Davros said, "but the attendant should remain. He has been thoroughly briefed."

Elizander's eyebrows rose. "Oh?" He looked at Milpheus, who nodded.

"It was deemed necessary, my lord," the attendant said.

"By whom?"

"By myself, Lord Elizander Dain of Winsor Kingdom," answered a quiet voice from the corner of the room. Davros swore an oath, drawing his sword. Milpheus gasped and took a step back. Elizander started to rise, winced, and fell back onto his pillows, taking careful, deep breaths.

"Be at ease, Captain Davros Naishere." A robed man stepped into Elizander's line of sight. "I am an ally."

"Allies do not sneak into the royal bedchamber of the king." Davros exclaimed, advancing on the monk. "Allies do not skulk the shadows unknown to those with whom they claim allegiance!"

"Please stay your hand, captain," the monk said, and Elizander couldn't tell if he was pleading or advising.

Finally having recovered from the sharp wave of pain in his side, Elizander spoke. "Please, Captain Davros. Stand down." Davros stared hard at the intruder, and Elizander thought he might not obey the order. After a few tense moments, however, he sheathed his sword but remained on the same side of the bed as the hooded figure.

"It was necessary for my presence near you to remain unknown, including yourself, Lord Elizander Dain," the monk said.

Elizander held up a hand. "Let us shorten it to just our names."

"If that is your wish, my lord."

Dain nodded, leaning back into his pillows. By Jemanah was he tired!

"Discretion," the monk continued, "has outweighed protocol. Many among my Order have mingled close and from afar for generations. It wasn't until the last several years that we have had to keep a closer watch. I was specifically selected as your guardian."

"My guardian?" Elizander glanced at Davros, who looked on the verge of drawing his sword again. "Do you mean to say that you have been watching over me without my knowledge?"

"I have shadowed your movements for four years." He seemed not at all uncomfortable admitting this.

Davros had a white-knuckled grip on the hilt of his sword. "What Order is this?"

"The Order of Dasha," Captain Davros.

"You have us at a disadvantage, monk of the Order of Dasha," Elizander said. "You know us, be we know not even your name."

The monk nodded, his eyes seeming to recede farther into the shadow of his cowl, if that were possible. "I am Arief, of the Mahlab sect of Dasha."

"Mahlab," Elizander repeated, thinking the monk was quite far from his home in the land that was once known as the Middle East. "You've come some distance to be my guardian angel."

"I am hardly an Arisha of Daunya," Arief answered as though Elizander had spoken literally.

"A what?" Davros asked.

Arief's discomforting gaze remained focused on Elizander. "An Arisha, Captain. The Daunya Children, as they are known. There is no earthly term to precisely describe them."

"Might you enlighten us as to what a Daunya is?" Davros asked, rolling his eyes.

"Perhaps another time," the monk replied.

"Yes, indeed," Elizander said. "How and why have you come to be so close to me without my knowledge or that of my personal guard?"

Arief inclined his head. "Be assured that your soldiers are well trained. You are well protected, my lord."

"Answer the question," Davros said. His frown deepened until his brow cast a shadow over his eyes.

"Of course. As you learned three days ago, there are things your men cannot protect you against."

Elizander absently placed a hand to his head. "The details of that night are still hazy."

"Hence the necessity of my revelation this day. The Order of Dasha has existed long before the Age of Technology. We were formed out of the necessity to buffer the efforts of many who would help to maintain balance in this world, lest the denizens of the abyss gain a foothold.

"Within the scope of creation there are multiple dimensions; planes of existence. Each dimension vibrates on either a higher or lower level, and has its own attributes. Here, on what we think of as the physical plane, things appear solid, like the floor upon which we stand. From this reality, if we were to gaze upon another dimension, it would seem insubstantial or ethereal.

"The higher dimensions are where celestial beings reside. Among them are the departed humans and animals. There is far more to this, but I've not the time."

Elizander and Davros stole glances at each other during the statuesque monk's fantastical story.

"Please allow me to finish. You can assess my mental stability in private if you wish."

Elizander nodded politely. "Right. Continue."

Arief nodded. "The spirits of those who have lived on this world ascend to the higher planes, native to our true existence. It is there that all knowledge is available to us and that we truly understand ourselves within the scope of creation.

"The Arishas are the only beings that reside on the higher planes that sometimes exercise more than an indirect influence in our lives. These are powerful beings who answer only to The Daunyans; also known as The Seven. They are the Gods to which all of creation is connected. It is to Them that we all pray, whether we realize it or not."

"You say these Daunyans are responsible for all life," Davros said, "yet these atrocities happen?"

"Men make choices of their own will, Captain," Arief replied. "And that leads us to the crux of the matter. On the lower planes of existence, those that vibrate at the slowest rate, are the abysmal realms. You would refer to them as The Hells, or Demon Realm. As you might guess, demons, devils, and all other manner of evil are native to that dimension. There are five levels to the abyss. The higher the level, the lower the class of demon, with the most powerful residing on the fifth and lowest level."

"Why would the Gods, these Daunyans, create such a thing?" Elizander asked, trying to mask his disbelief.

"They did not," the monk replied. "Though the abysmal realm is home to extremely powerful beings, they are still nothing in comparison to the Daunyans. But they were not wrought by the Daunyans, but by the spirits of powerful humans who had turned from the light. It is this reason why we humans have been forced to deal with the evil, and why the Daunyans have not simply eradicated it. As long as evil exists among us, the lower vibrating abysmal realm will endure. The Daunyans will always help us, but it is within ourselves that we must hold Their light. Within Their light, evil cannot exist.

"From time to time, a human wielding more power and knowledge than they should, is tempted away from the light and summons denizens from the abyss. It starts with a lowly creature, such as an imp. Then, as their confidence grows, the summoner brings larger and more powerful creatures to this world until they reach a demon that is beyond them. Their subsequent death frees this demon from its summoner; its *tether*, and it has free reign in this world."

"And what?" Davros said. "You hunt them down?"

"There are those among us who do. We serve as more than demon hunters, but that is one function." The monk turned his gaze back to Elizander. "Four years ago, we became aware of the resonance of larger than normal demonic presence in this world. There hasn't been this much raw evil since the times during the Age of Technology. Shortly after this discovery, we learned that a small resonance had appeared here, in New Dainland. We were unsure what this meant, so I was dispatched to find out. My initial fear was that you had been taken over by an evil entity, hence my need to remain unknown. Once I learned the truth, I remained to watch over you."

"And if you deemed me 'taken over'?" Elizander asked.

"We need not explore the obvious, my Lord King Elizander," Arief replied, reverting to formality. "One of the functions of my Order is to battle evil. Therefore you already know the answer to your seeded question."

"Pick your next words with extra care, monk." Davros had moved just a little closer to Arief while placing himself partially between the monk and Elizander.

That this monk who claimed to be his guardian could have just as easily been his assassin was sobering. Elizander felt a chill in the pit of his stomach at the notion.

"I haven't been able to determine the exact number," Arief continued, unperturbed by Davros's threat, "but I know that there are at least seven mid-level demons and one major demon present in the lands surrounding your city."

"Pfft!" Davros rolled his eyes. "We lack a campfire to enhance this tale."

"Did your impact with those two trees loosen your memory, Captain

Davros?" There was an air of danger in Arief's tone that gave even the fear-less captain pause. "Do you remember what it looked like? Do you believe it was an animal you'd never seen before, or an animal at all?" The monk grew more menacing with each word, though he had not moved. "Did you not feel the wrongness about it, as though raw evil twisted the space around it? Even someone less in tune should have perceived this."

Though it clearly pained him, Davros nodded, if somewhat grudgingly.

Elizander found he couldn't dismiss the feeling he'd had, either. He'd gotten a clear view of the beast and it had indeed felt wrong; like it didn't belong in this world.

"I understand that what I say is beyond the boundaries of believability, but the simple truth is that there is evil gathering against you for reasons we do not know. Left unchecked, they will have your lands engulfed in chaos and yourself, removed, or worse."

The cold lump in Elizander's gut spread. "The very concept is more than I would allow myself to consider, but I cannot deny what you say."

"Come, my lord," Davros said. "A demon? Truly there is a better explana-tion than a demon running around, no matter how wrong the thing felt."

"Do you not remember the beast?" Elizander replied. "Could you explain what it was?"

"Perhaps it was a diseased animal, or some beast of the wilds undis-covered."

Arief's hooded gaze shifted to Davros. "It was an animal that has eluded you all these weeks? An animal murdering random citizens while the same happens in Mairland, a land that is governed by a man who happens to be rash of nature, taking little thought in his actions? How many animals have you seen decay into mist when they're killed?"

Elizander held up a hand. "Whatever the nature of this beast, your point is well made, monk. How do we proceed from here?"

The question had barely left his lips when there came a heavy knock at the door. Elizander looked back to Arief, but he was gone. *How?* Davros, having also looked to the door, searched the room for the disappeared monk. He wore a similarly perplexed expression.

With an effort, Elizander climbed out of the bed and carefully straight-ened, holding a hand to his ribcage. It felt as though a wave of fire washed up his side.

"I'd know that knock anywhere," Milpheus sighed, and Davros sighed just as heavily.

"Ever has Dinman been a pain," Davros growled.

"Indeed," Milpheus agreed. He reached for the door and as he turned the knob, the door opened to admit Brother Dinman of the Church of Holy Jemanah. The move brushed on outrage, but the man expertly timed the intrusion with the turning of the knob. Milpheus shuffled back, glaring balefully at the priest's back.

"My apologies for interrupting your rest, my lord," Dinman said. His tone spoke nothing of apology or humility. "I felt it was of the utmost importance that I speak with you immediately.

"Is there some emergency that requires my attention, Brother Dinman?" Elizander asked with mechanical courtesy.

"Nothing that cannot be dealt with, my lord."

"Then the purpose for this visit is?" Milpheus asked.

"Not to be discussed with an attendant," came the dismissive retort. He stood silent, head held high as though waiting. The silence stretched until finally Elizander spoke.

"Please feel free to deliver your message, Brother Dinman. As you can see, I am still in recovery."

The priest glanced several times at Milpheus. Once it was apparent that Elizander had no intention of sending the attendant away, he huffed.

"Very well … my lord. The flock is unnerved by your recent brush with death. There is panic and uncertainty in the city. Though we at the Church of Holy Jemanah do what we can, we are not able to provide aid autonomously."

"Nor is there need for you to do so," Elizander said, frowning.

"It is my wish that the church be able to lead the flock in your absence while you recover, my lord. Such daily issues need not disrupt your recovery."

"I am heartened by your concern for the ease of my recovery, Brother Dinman, but you need not trouble yourself. Despite my condition, I am still functional in my station. Just as I have confidence in your abilities within your own." Elizander took careful note of the barely suppressed fury behind the mask of calmness and the stiff bow of obeisance.

"Of course, my lord," the priest replied.

"If there is a great deal of concern about my well-being, I will see to it that these fears are put to rest. Please send my regards to Bishop Marquis, with whom I am sure you have consulted, for his loyal concern for my recovery. All will continue as it has been. We have eliminated one of the killers and are on watch for others. I believe we have quelled the attacks at least for now."

The priest smiled politely as Elizander spoke, and bowed stiffly once again. "A relief it is that you are strong and able, my lord," Dinman said. "We pray for your swift recovery."

"More like he's praying for your sudden demise," Davros rumbled when the door closed behind Dinman. "I'm sure I don't have to tell you to watch that one. He only lacks a forked tongue to reveal his true nature."

Elizander nodded absently. Dinman was up to something. He would need to have another talk with Bishop Marquis. The last thing he needed was trouble from that avenue to compound things.

"Brother Dinman has always been skilled at picking less than opportune times to show up," Elizander said, easing himself back into bed. "I feel I could fight a battle and still have more energy than one session in his presence."

"I could keep an eye on him," Milpheus suggested. "My contacts see and hear everything. I can have them sharpen their focus upon the priest's activities." Davros raised his eyebrows and he tipped his head in appreciation.

Elizander tried not to look relieved. "That would be a most welcome help, Milpheus."

"Then allow me to see to the matter immediately, my lord."

Elizander nodded, and the attendant took his leave. For a few moments the two men silently scrutinized the shadows in the room. Changing his mind about the bed, Elizander gingerly swung one leg over the side, then the other. He held a hand up to forestall Davros's aid, and slowly stood.

"Well, what do you make of all this, old friend?" Elizander carefully made his way to one of the chairs around the hearth. Indicating the captain take the other seat, he lowered himself into it.

"I can't say that any of this business bodes well. While my sensibilities deny what that thing was, my eyes and instincts say otherwise."

"My feelings are the same," Elizander agreed. "My rational mind wants to reason that my memory recalls a demonic beast from a fear and panicked moment, yet I know what I saw. I know how big it was and what it felt like when it held me in one large hand, slowly crushing the life from me."

Davros grunted. "I could see the evil in its eyes. A bear couldn't have swatted me that far away. I only survived because I was in full armor."

"That creepy monk informed me that conventionally crafted weapons won't work on those things unless they are infused with power of some sort." Davros snarled as he said the last bit.

"I saw him dispatch the thing with my own eyes, and with little effort." Elizander sighed, basking in the warmth of the crackling fire. *I could sit here forever.* "That thing killed all of our men and would have had us as well, had Arief not come."

"If anyone else told me this, I wouldn't believe it. How could one man have taken that thing down?"

"I don't know," Elizander replied. "But if we have such dangerous enemies in our midst, I don't mind having equally dangerous allies."

"He makes me uneasy," Davros said in a low voice, scanning the shadows again.

"And I as well," Elizander agreed. "I plan to have another talk with our shadowy friend when next he appears. I would know more of this Order of Dasha."

M alimokuru scrambled out of the saddle and reached for his pouch. Twisted, grotesque figures lurched from the darkness, some holding weapons, some dragging elongated hands on the ground. As they closed the distance, he saw that they were human ... or at least they had been. The off-colored skin and misshapen, twisted limbs and milky eyes spoke of something sinister at play.

"What in the name of the Daunyans?" he swore, taking in the macabre scene. "Are my eyes tellin' me that we're lookin' at the dead walking? I'm gettin' too old for this."

"They are abomination, *Umntwana Onomuntu*," Amata Daunyana said, her voice deepening, her tone dangerous. "They are your dead, re-inhabited by the weakest of creatures from the dark world."

"They don't look too coordinated," Malimokuru observed. "What cause could this serve?"

"There is more to this than we know." Naiyala readied her spear.

"And our answers await us at the Tower of Balance," Amata said.

"Then let us be done with this business," Naiyala growled. As she spoke, more of the repulsive things came milling out of the trees.

"No," Sakhile said. "This is a delay." The others looked at him questioningly, and then Ayanda caught the tracker's meaning.

"He's right," the hunter said. "It would be a boon to our enemy if they did kill us, but that's not their intention." The first line of twisted figures reached them, lunging forward with a startling burst of speed.

Sakhile swatted one of the things aside and more lunged forward. "They know these things are no threat. Whatever the dark ones are doing, they must be close to their goal if they try delaying us like this."

Naiyala picked up one of the demon-ridden corpses by the head and hurled it into the nearest cluster, scattering them to the ground. Amata called to Boraka. A soft glow of yellow formed around her body. The glow erupted to flames and flew into a group of the lumbering corpses.

Sakhile and Ayanda, moved in opposite directions, dispatching several at a time.

Malimokuru shouted an incantation as he threw a handful of sands at creatures before him. The sands lit into tiny flares of light that cut into tainted flesh. Unable to feel pain, the creatures stumbled but continued their advance.

To his right Amata Daunyana blasted another group with fire. The former humans moaned and fell over, quickly burning away.

"Fire." Malimokuru reached into his pouch as a nearby corpse lunged at him. There was a surprising amount of weight behind the blow. Malimokuru rolled with the impact and came up to one knee. He opened his fist and blew the sands from his palm.

The sand flew into the creature's face, and the hiss of its burning ragged flesh made Malimokuru's stomach churn. The demon-inhabited corpse showed no sign of pain, however, but simply fell to its knees and burned away. The creature was close enough for him to hear a tiny scream escape the corpse's mouth. Green mist seeped from the mouth of the corpse and evaporated. Malimokuru snarled in disgust. "Go back to whichever hell you come from."

He climbed to his feet and he saw the amahle batting the corpses away as though they were of no consequence. Malimokuru gripped as large a handful of sands as he could hold, ran to the fore, and a whipped his hand in an arc.

The sands spread through the air over the ambling corpses. He yelled the triggering incantation, and a fiery mist settled over the approaching former humans. Those that could, staggered onward while the rest simply dropped to the ground and burned.

Only a few remained, and he would have been happy to let the others finish, but then a screech rent the air. Another group of former humans emerged from the trees. Unlike the demon-inhabited corpses, these were more mobile. They came leaping from the woods, covering ground much faster. Malimokuru's heart skipped a beat. They moved like human-sized frogs, leaping instead of running. "This isn't going to be as easy."

The amahle must have agreed. Their dark blue skin shifted red as they entered the battle rage. With a hiss and a thrust of their spears, the towering warriors leaped forward to meet the new threat.

It was a terrifying sight, and Malimokuru, capable though he was, kept his distance. Fearsome though these new monsters were, they stood no chance against the larger, stronger, and faster amahle.

One of the animal-like humanoids leaped at least half a dozen feet into the air. Sakhile leaped higher still, gliding over it and impaling it with his spear as he passed. He arched his back and swung the screeching thing over his head and smashed it to the ground when he landed.

Ayanda and Naiyala tore into any of the humanoid creatures that managed to slip inside the reach of their spears. Amata Daunyana's bright red body lit with the yellow fire of Boraka. She cast the flames away from her body and burned all that came near.

She raked her claws across the face of the closest monster. It fell screaming and writhing on the ground. These weren't animated corpses like the others, but they weren't altogether human either. A chill ran through Malimokuru. These things had been human once, but they weren't dead like those zombie creatures they'd just fought. Were they living humans, twisted in some way? Was that possible?

His thoughts were cut short as one of the leaping humanoids cleared the fight and came tearing straight for him. Malimokuru swallowed his fear and set his feet, clutching at a handful of sand. His lips moved as he mouthed the incantation. The monster leaped as Malimokuru launched the sands and threw himself aside.

Thousands of the tiny acidic particles flew through its body, burning it from the inside out. It crashed to the ground, thrashing and clawing at the air until it lay still, acrid smoke seeping from its mouth, eyes, and ears.

He returned his attention to the greater fight and saw that it was over. Five sets of eyes and teeth smiled at him, glowing frighteningly in the darkness. Malimokuru repressed a quiver.

The amahle laughed at his discomfort, as always. Even the usually solemn Amata chuckled. Amahle humor!

"You handle yourself well for an elder, friend Malimokuru," Naiyala said. "Be assured that we would not let harm come to you."

"Yet you let one of dem tings through?"

"Strength is found in resistance," Sakhile said, watching as Amata walked the battleground, burning away the fallen demon-inhabited corpses. "You must fight if you are to be ready for the real fight.

Malimokuru understood the logic, but he didn't have to like it. "Just warn me next time, ya?"

"We camp for the night, but away from this battleground" Naiyala said after the laughter subsided. "And tomorrow, we move as swift as your animal companion can manage."

"I sense the taint released by the fallen dead ones," Amata said. "Do you see here?" She pointed at a patch of ground blackened by one of the rapidly decaying corpses. "This poison must not be allowed to seep into the ground, or it will cause sickness to the land and any who come into contact with it. She prayed to Omalah, passing her onyx hand over the tainted area. The black patch gradually lightened until the taint was gone.

Watching the Amata Daunyana work, Malimokuru was starting to understand the need for haste.

"I am curious what these things are," Ayanda said, standing over the corpse of one of the hideous, leaping creatures. He stood a bit back, prodding it with his spear.

Amata Daunyana came to squat over the corpse. "This was a living body, cohabited by a human spirit and a weaker dark one."

"How is that possible?" Malimokuru asked. "No spirit can possess a person unless they consent ..." he trailed off, and the apprentice nodded. "Impossible. There are people who would welcome becoming this?" He knew his incredulity was naïve, however. A studier of history, Malimokuru knew that the promise of power never failed to corrupt the corruptible.

"Two will keep watch," Naiyala said once they found a suitable campsite amidst a gathering of pines.

"I will set wards to alert us to any threat," Amata Daunyana said. "They will provide minor protection as well; enough for us to react."

Just then, Nyaka practically materialized from the night and came trotting towards them. In all the chaos, Malimokuru had forgotten about the goar cat. He sent his thoughts to her, asking about her activities during their attack.

He received images of fleeing darkness, of escaping huge jaws of gaping blackness that would swallow her whole. His eyes widened. After a moment, he understood. The goar cat was fearless when it came to creatures of this world, but she balked at an encounter with the denizens of the abyss. Malimokuru didn't blame. He sent thoughts of comfort and companionship to his loyal companion.

Nyaka moved closer to settle beside him, but Malimokuru urged her to sleep on the opposite side of the campsite from his horse, the poor animal having suffered enough stress for the day. He received a response that felt like amusement from the goar cat. He sighed yet again, and settled down to sleep.

"Their pace is leisurely," Akemi called down from her perch high in the trees. She watched for a while longer, then made her way back down. "They make an effort to appear unthreatening, but only a fool would believe it."

"What would it matter?" Shinobu replied. "It isn't as if Liu Xiang will challenge the point and risk creating an incident."

Kenjiro nodded. "Likely he will be prepared to welcome or resist them, whichever becomes necessary."

"We need to speak to Liu Xiang before that party arrives," Akemi said. "He's on the verge of a twofold disaster."

"Short of dropping a demon at his feet," Kenjiro said. "I don't see how we can convince him of the nature of his true enemy."

"Akemi and I are able to sense them," Taliah said. "If the creature lingers near, we may be able to lead the emperor to it."

They struck out ahead of the approaching Qian force and soon Wuhan came into view. Even from their distance an hour away, the sprawling coastal city stood tall and proud. Huge buildings reaching to the heavens were still present, though many were grown over by ivy and other slithering plant life.

As the group drew closer, it became clear that some these overgrown buildings were used as high-vantage guard posts. Where time had rotted sections that had been glass or metal, stonework and wood had been used to reinforce buildings where possible. As with most cities, shorter buildings had been completely torn down, the parts salvaged and repurposed for other structures.

The care and pride taken into the appearance of the newly envisioned Wuhan was a testament to its leader and industrious, creative population.

"Impressive," Akemi remarked, gazing up at the towering structures.

"I would one day travel the world just to see how every land has recreated itself since the End," Shinobu said. "To see the echoes of the past reflected in the rebuilding of what once was." His gaze fell to the entrance ahead. "You think they'll let us in?"

Four sentries stood guard, each with a sword strapped to their hip and a spear in hand. When the group approached, two of the guards moved in front of the gate, crossing their spears to block the way. They spoke in the common tongue of Ba Guo; not threatening, but obvious by their tone that they would know the business of the visitors.

"I may be of use here," Shinobu said, stepping forward. As he spoke, he gestured to himself, and to each of the party in turn. The sentries gave no indication one way or another how they were receiving this information. When they looked upon Kenjiro, approval was plain on their features. Akemi, they regarded with suspicion, and Taliah with interest.

When their gaze fell upon her, the Daunya Chosen smiled, her eyes sparkling. In that moment, a sense of calm blanketed the group. The tension ebbed, and everyone relaxed. Now, when the strider spoke, the guards nodded and were more agreeable, speaking in friendly tones. One of the guards pointed further in the city, and the two stepped back and bowed. The group returned the greeting and continued through.

"What did you say to them?" Akemi asked while glancing suspiciously at Taliah.

"That we had traveled a great distance to visit Wuhan. They mentioned that it was a dangerous time and that we would be better served to leave. They seemed not to like it when I suggested we might be of service, but then the whole mood changed and they relaxed. I felt it too. I don't know what happened." Akemi eyed Taliah again, and Kenjiro glanced from his sister to the other woman. The Daunya Chosen looked forward, as though unaware of the ninja's lingering gaze.

"He said there were many sights to see, here in Wuhan. The center of the city is where the emperor resides, though he was adamant about the possibility of us being denied an audience."

"I don't see us having a problem," Kenjiro said. The stare of many passersby lingered on the samurai. Resplendent in his beautiful Yoroi and

Hakama, he walked with an air of dignity that was difficult not to notice. "With such a sizable force converging on him, the emperor will at the very least be curious about four strangers happening into his city with information about his problems."

They reached a place the guard had named Central Square. Tall brick walls encircled the red stone pavilion where finely dressed people milled about. Barely visible beyond the walls sat a large pagoda beneath a weeping willow.

Shinobu led them in that direction where they encountered another pair of guards. After several minutes of back and forth discussion, the guard dispatched a low ranking youth looking to have passed no more than seventeen years.

"He sent the boy off to make the emperor aware of our arrival," Shinobu said. "They're suspicious, but the presence of our samurai friend, here, lends us a bit of credibility."

"No subtle aid this time?" Akemi asked, glancing at Taliah.

"An overused tool loses its effectiveness."

"Fair enough."

And so they waited, admiring the expert craftsmanship that had gone into maintaining the post technology city. Men and women jogged by pulling passenger-laden rickshaws while robed academics strolled by, casting the occasional curious glance at the unlikely group of foreigners.

Having spent a great deal of her life in the kingdom of Ghana, Taliah had found life there more busy than her native Jamaica. She'd seen nothing like this. Where her people crafted beautiful homes and tools from the land directly, the people here, much like in the western lands of Nomar, crafted things from the former Age of Technology, and a heavy use of steel and brick wherever possible.

The young guard finally returned with a small contingent of soldiers in tow. He bowed to his superior and relaying his message. After listening to the report, the guard turned back to the waiting foreigners. He addressed them equally, and after he finished, Shinobu translated.

"He says that Emperor Liu Xiang is interested in our presence here, and grants us an audience." The young guard stepped in front of them, indicating they should follow.

The inner grounds were actually a courtyard housing lovingly manicured gardens of bright-colored vegetation.

"The emperor has an eye for the gardens of our homeland, Akemi remarked, nodding at the red maples and bonsai trees with their thick, curved trunks.

Before they were halfway across the courtyard, the guard stopped and spoke to Shinobu. "He says we are required to deposit our weapons there." He pointed at a rack against a far wall, unnoticeable unless you knew what you were looking for.

The group carefully arranged their weapons on the rack. Akemi took the greatest amount of time to remove the many shurikens visible and hidden about her person. She offered the anxious young guard a smile, his nervousness no doubt the result of the reputation her profession as much as her concealed weapons.

Kenjiro narrowed his eyes at his sister and slowly shook his head. "Ninja."

The guard looked pointedly at Taliah, who smiled and, spread her arms. Shinobu spoke, no doubt explaining that the Daunya Chosen carried no weapons.

After giving her a once-over, the guard gave a sharp nod and led them back to the main path.

They came to the steps of the palace, where stood a man in intricately embroidered dark blue robes. At over six feet tall, he was half a head taller than most of his personal guard.

Kenjiro arched an eyebrow at the voluminous robes that swished about the emperor's every step. "Those robes conceal more than his size," the samurai remarked. "Look at the cut of the sleeves and skirts, and the length. Emperor or not, that man is a warrior."

The steady, sure steps of the emperor were complimented by a man a few steps behind him and to the right. Even larger of build, this fierce-looking warrior stood a few inches taller. Somewhat similar to the emperor, the man wore a loose flowing robe with one sleeve, leaving the other heavily muscled arm exposed along with part of the chest.

Over his thick broad shoulder, rested a wavy steel-tipped spear with a thick and heavy shaft. Akemi couldn't imagine trying to wield such a weapon, but this imposing man looked as though he could handle it with ease. He might not have been the largest man she had ever met, but he looked as though he could overpower an ox.

A few steps back and to the left of the emperor was a woman close to Akemi's stature. She looked to have passed perhaps fewer than twenty years, but as they drew closer, Akemi saw a wisdom in her light brown eyes that extended beyond her age.

The woman studied them quickly and precisely, taking everything in. Akemi had no doubt that by the time the two groups reached each other, the young lady—an advisor, she would guess—had taken their measure.

Finally, a few steps behind the woman, was a monk wrapped in an orange robe that hung several inches above his sandaled feet. He was slight of build, no more than perhaps five and a half feet. His shaved head sported nine red circles. The eyes in that serene face bespoke an almost palpable power that made him likely the most dangerous of the four.

"It seems in his wisdom, my old teacher was correct in forcing me to study the Japanese language," the emperor said, speaking their tongue perfectly. "Though I fear I may not speak her tongue," he continued, gesturing toward Taliah.

"We may all speak comfortably, this day," Taliah replied in the language of Japan, bowing respectfully.

The emperor's eyebrows rose and he laughed softly. "Well then. Things will be easier indeed. I am Emperor Liu Xiang of Shu Han." He indicated the man to his left. "This unnecessarily stern man is General Zhang Da." The man executed a precise bow. "This," Liu Xiang continued, "is my trusted advisor Zhuge Xiaoyin." The young lady's thin pink lips stretched into a smile as she curtsied. "And this," the emperor continued, "is Shi Xing Long." The introduction of the monk seemed abridged. Akemi took note of the silent robed figure. She had not been an avid student of world history, but her memory hinted at some significance of a monk wanting his Order to remain anonymous. Could luck be with them and this man was a monk of Shaolin?

After the introductions were exchanged, the emperor turned, indicating they walk with him through the garden. "I fear time is against me at present, so you must excuse my bluntness. What brings you to Shu Han? I find the appearance of a samurai, a ninja, and a, farstrider," he said the last word uncertainly, "more than coincidence. And what of you," he asked, indicating Taliah. "Though people still travel the world, I see few visitors from such faraway lands as yourself."

"Emperor Liu Xiang," Taliah said. "Thank you for meeting with us. Time is indeed against us all, so I will be quick to the point. As I'm sure you're aware, there is a sizable force moving in the direction of your city that should arrive by tomorrow."

The emperor's face was unreadable, as were his companions. The general seemed to harden, just a bit.

"We come with news that will help you, though it may be difficult for you to accept what we have to say."

"You seem to know quite a bit about the goings on in a land not your own," the emperor remarked.

"The scope of this problem reaches far beyond your borders, or even your country." Taliah answered.

"Oh?" Liu Xiang raised his eyebrows. "How far might this problem reach?"

"Across the world, Emperor."

Liu Xiang responded with a polite smile. "I see That is quite large in scope, don't you think? What have you seen that could affect the entire world? I will admit that our impending visitor is an abrupt surprise, but I've seen no evidence of any fancied conquests stretching around the world."

He was being careful, and Akemi didn't blame him. She glanced at Zhuge Xiaoyin. The woman's placid features gave nothing away, despite the fact that she was looking directly at Akemi. The two locked gazes for a heartbeat and Xiaoyin's focus returned to the conversation.

"Might we speak in a more secure environment, Emperor?" Taliah said, glancing around. There may be ears listening where they shouldn't."

"I assure you these grounds are secure, my mysterious visitors," Xiang replied.

"Very well." Taliah told them of the drek and his plans to attack Takashaniel. She told them of his demon general and how they believe it was one of its minions that was responsible for the murders in both Shu Han and Qian, and that they were prodding Qian Hua into action.

"So," Liu Xiang said, frowning a bit. "You would have me believe that at least one demon is loose in my city as well as that of Qian Hua, and that they are sowing seeds of distrust in his mind so that he might move against me? For the sake of this interesting conversation, let us ignore the unbelievable element to this and say that it is true. What potential gain can be had from inciting such chaos? I'll not name myself an expert in the psychology of demons, but there should be more to gain than simply reveling in the madness."

Taliah nodded. "Creatures from the abysmal realms feed on negativity of any kind. The stronger the negativity, the more they have to consume. A battle of the scale that could happen between your two forces would provide an intoxicating amount of negative energy, and numerous vessels for their weaker kind."

"Vessels?"

"At present, they are able to rip a small tear in the barrier between our two dimensions for their weaker kind to enter and animate the corpses of the deceased."

Liu Xiang studied them all for several moments after Taliah had stopped speaking. "Your eyes tell me that you have already considered the possibility that I would dismiss you out of hand as a band of traveling storytellers that may have lost their wits along the way. But not a one of you looks like any storyteller of a sort I've ever seen. Not a one of you looks as though your minds are as fragile as your tale would have me believe. So what am I to make of this? I have a neighboring warlord who will come knocking on my gates tomorrow to discuss recent events in both our cities. Preceding him, is the most unlikely combination of visitors bringing tales of demons and zombies. What would you believe, in my place?"

Akemi felt a tingle of energy. It was so slight she could have easily missed it had she not the benefit of a lifetime of training. Taliah's eyes flicked over to Akemi, then back to Xiang. It was a quick exchange, but Akemi thought there was something to it. Had the Daunya Chosen also felt it?

I would require proof, before I would believe anything," Taliah answered the emperor.

"And as you say, I will require proof of this unbelievable tale."

He knew more than he was letting on. He may not believe it entirely, but someone had already told him something of a similar nature. The general looked too practical and straightforward. She then glanced at the young sharp-eyed woman. It was possible. No. Hers was a calculating mind.

Akemi suspected that the reason the emperor had not had them cast out was because he'd received no signal from that one. Taliah was sure this Zhuge Xiaoyin could read a lie on the face of a stone.

That left the monk. She looked at him and he returned her gaze with a slight bow. Akemi had the feeling that Taliah had just validated what the monk had been trying to tell the emperor before their arrival. It made sense. There were a small number of organizations that understood the world beyond this one.

Taliah turned to Akemi and nodded.

"Thought you'd never ask. Xiang's personal guard could only begin to draw their weapons by the time Akemi let fly her three hidden shurikens. Less than a couple dozen feet to Liu Xiang's side, the shurikens punched into what looked like nothing but open air.

A pained growl split the tense silence and a crouched figured material-ized. General Zhang Da, was on top of it in an instant, spear leveled at the now steaming creature. It tried to rise but fell over, its life force seeping through the wounds inflicted by the imbedded shurikens.

Liu Xiang gasped. At his side, Zhuge Xiaoyin had a hand over her mouth. The monk, though caught by surprise, was more composed than the others. Yes, that one knew of the existence of demons on some level. How far did his knowledge stretch, and was it academic or experience?

"You need not bother, general," Akemi said. "It is returning to its home in the first hell."

When the creature had fully dissolved, General Zhang Da relaxed, but only a bit. The man looked as though he wasn't sure whether to be thankful or outraged that the ninja still had hidden weapons, despite having dispatched a possible assassin in their midst.

"That was a skulker," Akemi stated. "They are weak and mostly serve as spies for more powerful demons, or to a human that is equipped to manage them. They can slip through a tiny rip in the barrier between this world and theirs, and hide almost within an area that I can only describe as a seam between the two worlds. That is why you could not see it."

"How long was that thing there?" Zhang Da demanded.

"I noticed it about halfway through your conversation," Akemi admitted.

"And you waited till now to act?" The general turned to face the much smaller ninja, towering over her by at over a foot.

"You needed proof," she replied, not the least bit threatened. "Your proof happened to present itself, though the timing was a bit off." The general's face hardened, the muscles in his jaw tensing. Akemi put a hand on her hip. "General Zhang Da. Do you truly believe that we would allow your emperor's life to be in danger even for a moment? Please calm yourself. If at any time I felt there was a danger, I would have dealt with it immediately."

"Peace, General," Liu Xiang said.

With some visible effort, Zhang Da relaxed. Their interaction suggested a long friendship. There was a familiarity that reminded Taliah of Kenyatta and Kita's brother-like friendship. "She speaks the truth," the Chosen said. "Skulkers are primarily spies and occasionally assassins. Their value lies in their invisibility."

The monk looked askance at Liu Xiang. After a nod from the emperor, he spoke. "How did you know it was there?"

"I have hunted demons for most of my life," Akemi answered, once Shinobu had translated. "I can sense them."

"I am able to sense and see them," Taliah said. "The moment it appeared I knew it was here."

Akemi blinked. Interesting.

"You are a Daunya Master?" the monk guessed. Taliah shook her head. "No, but I am blessed with skills that serve The Seven."

"Humble words to be expected from a Daunya Chosen," the monk correctly surmised. "Only once have I met a Daunya Master, and not since before the Age of Technology has anyone seen a Daunya Chosen." He bowed respectfully. "It is an honor."

"What I am is what has been bestowed upon me by the Daunyans," Taliah replied. "We serve the same Gods, only with different functions." She bowed to him. "It is my honor to meet you, warrior monk of Shaolin."

Though subtle, his facial expression confirmed what Taliah had told them. Their temple having been destroyed many times over history, the monks of Shaolin had become a secretive lot, choosing anonymity when dealing with the general populous.

"Fear not," Taliah assured him. "Whenever Shaolin chooses to make its presence known again, it will not be from myself or my companions."

Shi Xing Long inclined his head in thanks. "Many wish for that time never to arrive, though some among us believe that time is coming soon. The presence of that," he indicated the area where the three shurikens lay on the ground, "says as much. The world changes and our survival is in question."

"I've seen it with my own eyes," Liu Xiang said, shaking his head, "but it still seems impossible. My logic tells me that my eyes have deceived me."

"Then my eyes lie as well, my lord" Zhang Da said. "I saw the same as you." He looked to Akemi and Taliah. "Something akin to that thing is what's been causing our problems?"

"Something many times worse," Akemi said, and Taliah nodded.

"The thing that stalks your streets is capable of killing everyone here and leaving your city a graveyard. Conventionally crafted weapons from this world do little more than cause temporary injury, and it would take a great deal of skill to injure what we suspect is here."

"I believe there may be at least three major demons from the lower levels of the abyss," Taliah added. "It is possible they command weaker fiends."

Zhang Da frowned. "Why would they not simply go on a killing rampage since we could not stop them?"

"If left to their own devices," Taliah replied, "that is what they'd have done. The reason they haven't is why we believe there is an extremely powerful demon holding their leashes."

"And so you come to assist us." Liu Xiang cast another wary glance at the place the skulker had been. "I cannot deny this as truth, given what I've just witnessed. But I still struggle to understand the depth of this situation beyond the obvious desire for death and destruction that one would deem typical of these ... once fictitious monsters."

"They were never fictitious, emperor," Akemi said. "We have hunted them in secret for centuries. I'm starting to believe that keeping humans ignorant of this was probably a mistake. Nothing can remain secret forever."

"But sadly, timing is sometimes more important than the information itself," Liu Xiang said.

"Given this new information," Zhuge Xiaoyin said, "I would wager Warlord Qian Hua is receiving quiet whispers of conquest and power that lie on the other side of a forcefully taken Wuhan. Knowing the nature of Qian Hua, I would suspect these hell monsters will find him more easily persuaded than you, Emperor."

Liu Xiang's visage tightened. "And unfortunately, there may be nothing we can do to avoid a confrontation. Hua is difficult to deal with under the best of circumstances. If there is some hidden player fanning the flames of his ambition, we must be prepared."

"You must be prepared to face the living and the dead," Taliah said. "If this comes to pass, you face the possibility of fighting his forces as well as his and *your* slain soldiers as well."

Clouds passed in front of the sun and cast the garden in shadow. A chilly breeze slithered across the walkway, whispering ominous promises in their ears. For a while, the company stood in silence while Liu Xiang digested this most unusual situation.

The emperor rose out of his contemplation when a woman appeared in the entrance to the garden.

Liu Xiang, Zhuge Xiaoyin, and even the stern Zhang Da brightened at the sight of the robed and hooded woman staring at them from the entrance. She drew her hood back as she approached, revealing silky black hair that slipped over her shoulders and fell to her shoulders. Her smile was as fierce as her burning brown eyes, her every step solid and sure.

She held a long-shafted weapon with an impressive wide flat blade that gradually curved upward, coming to a sharp point. On the back half of the flat blade was another sharp tip, a red tassel attached. Akemi squinted at the weapon. She'd heard of such a weapon, wielded by one of the mightiest warriors in Ba Guo's history.

Feminine and hard as iron at the same time, the woman's voice boomed across the distance like an ocean wave. "Xuande! It's good to see you!"

"Could it really be?" Liu Xiang's face looked like a struggle between formality and elation.

"It appears our sister has finally arrived." The ever stern General Zhang Da's face lit with a broad smile that he hid by inclining his head.

"Greetings, Sister Guan Xi!" Zhuge Xiaoyin said.

Even Xiaoyin, with her formal curtsy and smooth features, seemed barely able to contain her joy.

"Greetings little sister Kongming," Guan Xi replied. "And brothers Xuande and Yide," she said, referring to Liu Xiang and Zhang Da respectively.

"Kongming, Xuande, and Yide?" Akemi caught Kenjiro's eye while Shinobu struggled to keep up and translate the exchange. Through all of it, the names Guan Xi had spoken struck a chord.

"I don't believe it," Kenjiro said. "Can it be true that we stand here with the descendants of the Three Sworn and the Strategist?

"How many centuries have passed?" Akemi said. "And now legend is reborn. "This is as clear a sign as can be."

"I fear I am at a disadvantage," Taliah said, glancing between one group and the other.

"Do you know the ancient history of Ba Guo?" Akemi asked. "When it was ruled by the Three Kingdoms?"

Taliah shook her head. "I only know some small bit of the history."

"In times before the Age of Technology there were three kingdoms that ruled this land. It was a time of conflict and many battles were fought. Three men rose to prominence during that time. Liu Bei, Zhang Fei, and Guan Gong. They became friends, and as time passed, swore to each other as brothers. They became known as the Three Brothers, or, Three Sworn Brothers." Akemi nodded toward the emperor.

"Liu Bei was known for his compassion and love for his people. He was of humble birth and rose to power to become the beloved emperor of his lands."

She then nodded at the general. "Zhang Fei was also a good man, but was known for his fiery temper and ruthlessness. Though his prowess in battle was legendary, his judgment was sometimes sullied when he indulged too far in the drink. He was known to have treated his own men with brutality. Those who would have been loyal to him became wary of his violent moods." Akemi cast a long, appraising look at the newly arrived Guan Xi.

"And here we have the descendant of the legendary Guan Gong, also known as Guan Yu, depending on where you are." She looked at Taliah. "There are many statues and paintings of him.

"He was a large man with a long thick black beard that he either held in his hand or had folded in a box fastened to his midsection. Guan Gong's military prowess is legendary. Even we in Japan know well of him. The weapon he wielded was invented by him and bore his namesake. The Guandao."

"When the Three Sworn were together, it was as if nothing could stop them. Then, when Liu Bei faced great difficulty, he came to see a recluse who was a genius military strategist. His name was Zhuge Liang. Together, the Three Brothers and the Strategist could move heaven and earth itself."

Kenjiro moved beside his sister, the lot of them forgotten while the reunited friends talked. "What's interesting is how these four even exist." He leaned toward Akemi, still not taking his eyes from the group. "Zhang Fei and Guan Gong both died with their sons. Zhuge Liang was a recluse who shunned general society. Only Liu Bei could have possibly had an heir."

Akemi reached up and patted her brother on the shoulder. "During times of war, important figures in history have always seen the prudence in keeping the existence of their successors hidden, when necessary. It's plausible that every one of those men had at least one child that no one but those closest to them knew about. It is a testament to their discretion that the secrets had held for so long."

"How do you know so much about this?" Taliah asked.

Akemi shrugged. "I've a thirst for knowledge of the ancient warrior class. All have attributes in common. Whether it is our legendary

Miyamoto Musashi, the Three Sworn Brothers, or Shaka of the Zulu nation from the continent where you spent most of your life. Every one of them did what was needed and excelled beyond the boundaries of normal humanity. I have little doubt that most of the warriors from human history have a successor that walks the lands, regardless of the stories passed down through time."

Taliah smiled in appreciation of the ninja's knowledge. "You speak the truth. King Shaka's line was supposed to have died out long ago, but there is at least one that is known to live in this age."

"Forgive my rudeness," Liu Xiang interrupted with a smile. "It has been long since last we've seen each other."

Akemi returned his smile. "And so the descendants of the Three Brothers and the Strategist are reunited."

"You know the history!" Guan Xi replied heartily, every bit as big as her ancestor, in presence, if not in stature.

"There are some whose legends cannot be contained within the boundaries of their homelands," Akemi said.

Zhang Da nodded. "Warriors know and study warriors." His voice boomed with energy, and in that moment he seemed even more like his mighty ancestor, if more controlled."

"How do you think Warlord Qian will react?" Taliah asked, "upon learning that the descendants of such legendary figures are reunited on the eve of his arrival?" The question draped a blanket of sobriety over the gaiety of the moment.

"I see the spark of a strategist in you," Xiaoyin remarked.

"And only a spark it is, by comparison to Zhuge Xiaoyin," Taliah replied. "Which is why I would ask leave to speak with you in private if Emperor Liu Xiang would be so gracious."

"It shall be arranged," Liu Xiang said. "For now, we will dine together in proper welcome to our guests, and our returned sister!" He shared a look with Zhang Da, and the general barked an order at one of his guards. After a moment of conversing in their native tongue, the guard departed for the gate. A few moments later, three guards came holding each of the three warriors' weapons wrapped in cloths.

"Though I cannot allow you to openly wear your weapons inside the grounds, they will never be far from your presence," the emperor said. The level of respect and the measure of trust he was showing them was not lost on the group.

Zhang Da leveled his heavy gaze on Akemi. He offered a curt nod, which she returned. The general had not forgotten her deception, but he appreciated her actions.

"I would recommend a small affair," Zhuge Xiaoyin said. "The populous may not know of our presence but I would still recommend discretion."

"If the warlord has spies here, he will see it as plotting if we do not," Zhang Da countered.

"Yet if we make it broadly known that we are reunited, the people will take it as a sign. With Qian's coming, the sudden appearance of Guan Xi and myself will create whispers of a sign of things to come. They will associate it with the arrival of Warlord Qian, and his spies would interpret it in the same manner.

"For now at least, Qian must be diplomatic. He doesn't have enough allies to openly move on Shu Han, and he cannot avoid conflict with Shu Han's allies without the pretense of provocation. Qian cannot move against you, Emperor, if we deny him a reason."

"Why not eliminate him and be done with it?" Zhang Da whispered. "We have the strength and no one would deny that he has been provoking you for years. It's common knowledge that his greedy vision has extended all the way to Shu Han and beyond. He would conquer us if he could, then sweep right past us."

"We could," Liu Xiang agreed. "But how much better would that make us than Qian himself? *And* his successor is an unknown variable that could be far worse."

Zhang Da grunted in surrender, and Guan Xi gave him a slap on the back.

Liu Xiang turned to the visitors. "Allow Shu Han to more properly welcome you. Given today's events, I would have you in the palace for the duration of your stay. Explore the city as you wish, and upon your return there will be servants to escort you to your private rooms. Return with your appetite, for tonight you will feast with us." With General Zhang Da and General Guan Xi in tow, Liu Xiang took his leave.

30

Hours beyond the forest surrounding Takashaniel, the elves marched in silence, each was wrapped within their own thoughts of what was to come, and what part they would play. The smell of flowers and damp earth beneath their feet, the vines, and moss-covered trees, their entire surroundings symbolized that once again, the world was threatened by darkness, and once again, the elves must play a part in stemming the tide, while remaining shrouded from the human world.

Tikena had argued that they should no longer remain hidden. "If the world of N'thresha are to benefit from our sacrifice," she had said, "let them know who we are. Now that they no longer have their weapons to kill the world, they should know their place in it. I say they should know that they are not the owners of this world, but they share it with many others. Strip them of their arrogance and humble them. Let them see!"

So angry, that one, yet Tinnoviel couldn't blame Tikena, given the tragedy that had befallen her family. Nor could he deny the firm ground upon which her argument stood. Maybe it was time for humans to learn the truth. He pushed those musings aside. At the moment, his larger concern was how to convince the Elden to help. Approaching them would be like approaching an entire population of elves of like mind to Tikena; resentful and mistrusting of humans. He was not looking forward to it.

"You are concerned that the Elden will not help us."

Yurin's voice snapped Tinnoviel from his thoughts. "You know them as much as I. Do you think this will be easy?"

"How many of your life's accomplishments have been easy?"

Tinnoviel looked at the Daunya Apprentice, gliding through the foliage as if it was a clear path. "None that I can think of."

In response, Yurin simply nodded. That was often how a conversation went with the sober apprentice, but just as often that was all that was needed. *DaunyaSai chose well with that one,* he thought.

The terrain began to descend, the forest canopy opening while the vegetation actually grew thicker. Eventually they reached the rim of a canyon, the forest continuing down into its depths. They peered down into the yawning bowl of vegetation, each no doubt wondering what lay at the bottom.

"What now? Tikena asked.

"We wait," Tinnoviel said.

"For how long?"

"Not long at all, little cousin," came an answer from within the trees.

No sooner had the words been spoken than the elves formed up into a defensive circle. They scanned the surroundings but the speaker was nowhere to be found.

Tinnoviel relaxed. Only an Elden could so completely conceal themselves in the trees. "I am Tinnoviel Nai SaunyaLi. We come to speak with our Elden cousins about matters important to us all."

"Your tone carries an ominous weight," the hidden speaker replied. The voice came from behind. Tinnoviel looked over his shoulder. Surely the speaker wasn't behind them.

He smirked. This was a variation of the *whisper.* While his people were able to speak directly into the ears of the intended recipient, the Elden were able to send their voice in the direction of their choosing. "Do you intend to continue this conversation in concealment, or will you speak with us openly?"

After a few moments of silence, a heavily tattooed elf appeared from the trees on the very path they had just taken. Deep green markings spiraled around his body and seemed to glow against his pale skin. His black hair was tied back and hung loosely about his shoulders.

"You have traveled across the ocean and far across the lands and through the forests to find us, cousin. What ill news do you darken our home with?"

Tinnoviel had expected this, but the bluntness was still startling. "You assume we bring ill news?"

The Elden waved an impatient hand. "No games. Would you truly have us believe you've traveled so far to say hello? Or have you come to invite us to your home to share bread?"

Tinnoviel felt a pang of guilt and bowed respectfully. "You are right, and it is true. I wish it were otherwise, but it is true that we visit upon our Elden cousins with ill tidings."

The stern elf gave a sharp nod. "It must have been long since the last time you've come to visit us. Otherwise you would have remembered our distaste for speaking in curves."

Tinnoviel chuckled at the truth of it. The Elden were a straight-forward people, preferring bluntness and openness over the verbal posturing that they found both frustrating and duplicitous. The easiest way to lose the trust of an Elden was to use subtlety.

"This is Tikena Mojin, Immendiel Mai'lienar, and Yurin Kei Daunyana." Tinnoviel indicated each in turn.

The Elden raised his eyebrows. "A Daunya Warrior and a Daunya Apprentice visit the land of the Elden? What plague has befallen the land that we would receive such guests?"

"We're not exactly helpless either, you know!" Tikena snapped. Next to her, Immendiel tried to hide her smirk. The Elden smiled in amusement at the young elf and bowed his head respectfully.

"We hope to explain the purpose of our arrival in one breath, for all to hear." Tinnoviel looked at the trees over the other's shoulder. "And you have us at quite the disadvantage. I've given you our names, yet we know not yours.

"I am Eqyar Umayi." He gave a bird-like whistle and three similarly tattooed elves emerged from the trees. "This is Bram Leamar," Eqyar said, indicating a rather solidly built elf with light blue markings that spiraled his arms and legs. "This is Uluyama Melima," he said, indicating a female elf, slight of build, but with fierce green eyes. Dark green tattoos, similar to Eqyar's flowed over her limbs.

"And this is Neart Oyauna," Eqyar said, indicating the third elf on his right. Pale green markings like ivy vines wrapped about his tall slender form.

"Well met," Tinnoviel said with a bow. "We come seeking audience with Queen Mayana. There are events in motion that the Elden must be made aware of."

Eqyar's eyebrows rose. "Your errand is so urgent that you have not the time to stay and visit with us?"

"I wish it were otherwise," Tinnoviel replied. "There are happenings that will affect the world from our lands to yours and beyond."

"My ears tell me you come seeking help, Daunya Warrior," Eqyar said.

"And to have come this far, you must need a lot of it. I feel we will not like what you have to tell us."

Tinnoviel spread his hands. "Indeed, Eqyar Umayi. I believe you will like nothing that I have to say." Beside him, Tikena and Immendiel tensed, while Yurin remained passive.

Eqyar studied Tinnoviel for several tense moments, then nodded. "We will take you to Queen Mayana."

They passed through the thickly wooded forest, picking their way unobtrusively as only an elf could. Good though the Elfinestrayans were, the Elden were ever better at traversing the forest.

Tikena quickened her pace and came up beside their guide. "I've never been to the city of the Elden."

Uluyama glanced at her as she hopped over a fallen tree. "Not many have. We prefer our home to the outside world, and we have all that we need here. There is little need for us to venture out of the forest."

"Do you not ever have a desire to see the outside world?"

"I have never considered it," Uluyama said. "We have food, shelter, love, and family, here. All whom we share the forest with live in harmony. Why would we venture out where the plague of humans taint the world?"

Tinnoviel watched as Tikena's own hesitation to agree seemed to surprise even herself. Little more than a year ago she would have readily agreed with Uluyama's sentiment. He smiled to himself. The *haloren*, Kiluriel.

Despite her great effort to dislike her, Tikena had come to like the brave and good-hearted Kiluriel. Of course, Tikena would never openly admit such a thing, of course; Kiluriel was part human, after all. Still, Tikena liked the woman. She even liked her amusing human companion and his friend.

"Do you disagree?" the Uluyama asked, reading the hesitance on her face.

"I think the less time I spend around them, the better, though—" Tikena's mouth twisted as though she'd tasted something sour, "I admit, some of them aren't so bad."

Uluyama cast her a dubious look. "As you say. I heard the stories. They are an evil that should be swept from the world. There was a time it would have been done, but the leaders of the world decided against it. I've never understood our hesitance. They no longer have their big weapons to kill the world, and few of them are able to properly defend themselves. They could have been wiped from the land in little time if all of The Three had combined our efforts to exterminate them."

"The Three?" Tikena frowned. "Don't you mean The Four?"

Uluyama's green braids swished as she shook her head. "The Elden only acknowledge The Three. We do not see how the Daunyans could have willingly created such vile creatures to cohabit this world. Do the Elfinestraya not think the same?"

Tinnoviel discretely listened to the conversation, hoping his dear companion had grown as much as she seemed, during their last adventure.

"Not exactly," Tikena said. "Lady Seiyun would have us avoid contact with them, but she does not believe they are evil or should be swept from the land."

Uluyama frowned. "You agree?"

"I ... don't know."

They came to a stop and Uluyama chirped. After a series of responses, they continued.

Tinnoviel picked out several Elden shadowing them on each side.

"Do not be wary, Uluyama said. "They allow you to see them as a courtesy and a welcome."

Tikena looked at the other in admiration. "You blend so perfectly with the forest."

"Do your people not do the same?"

"We do, but not like you."

Uluyama nodded. "I always see because I know how to look. Your eyes do not know how to look, so you do not see. None can blend into the forest better than Elden."

Once again, Tinnoviel saw the subtle hesitation in Tikena's features. Was she thinking of the amahle, who were able to change the hue of their skin like a chameleon to blend to their surroundings? He nodded with pride. Tinnoviel had known Tikena her whole life, and the girl had indeed grown over the last year. Likely she was coming to the same realization, speaking with a girl whose outlook was so much like her own, not long ago.

"We are here," Uluyama. The vegetation started to thin, and they saw more watchers crouched high in the trees.

Of their four escorts, only Eqyar remained. With a brief look at Tikena in parting, Uluyama departed with the others.

Word must have traveled swiftly, for they didn't have long to wait. A woman in a gown adorned with feathers and tiny colorful stones arrived. Her long green hair fell to her ankles, nearly enveloping her legs as though it was a second gown. Her stern gray-eyed gazed took in every member of the visiting party. If the Elfinestrayans had deep angular features, this woman, like her Elden people, had features as sharp as a knife.

All knelt before her, and the visitors followed their lead. The queen's thin, pointed eyebrows drew down toward the bridge of her nose as she regarded them.

"Distant cousins from Yathienel. Be welcome and be at home. Though you are visitors, you are also family." Once she had spoken, all the assembled rose. "And family is expected to be forthcoming with each other." The queen's stern visage never changed as she spoke. Tinnoviel hoped this wasn't an indication of how things would proceed.

"It has been too many years since last our peoples have visited each other. The blood of the Elden, our son Alurien MerTana has fallen, and now four visitors from the land he called home have arrived to his true homeland."

Tinnoviel stepped to the front of the group, and dropped to one knee before the queen. He remained silent until Mayana indicated he stand. "Speak, Warrior of the Daunyans."

"Queen Mayana of the Elden, and our family," Tinnoviel began. "Part of me died the day my friend, my brother, Alurien MerTana was taken from this world. You know the story, but I feel compelled to say again. He lived a life of honor and was held in the highest regard among the Elfinestraya. He died valiantly while battling a lava leech." There was a collective murmur of approval from the assembly. Formidable and raging monsters, lava leeches were few, but among the most dangerous creatures known to the world. "He was given an honorable burial at the base of The Sentinels, within which he had fallen." There was another, less approving murmur.

"Why would you leave his body in such a place?" Mayana demanded. "The messenger you sent did not tell us this."

"Before the business that brings us here was discovered, my Lady Seiyun had already arranged for us to travel here, to tell you the story in full. Alurien deserved no less. Events have happened that delayed our coming."

The queen waved a hand. "We will visit this business of yours soon enough. Who decided to leave our son's body in the cold lands. Who would presume to do this?"

Tinnoviel didn't flinch in the face of the queen's disapproval. "My lady, it was Khairon the Blue, of the Blue Daunyarka."

At the mention of the blue dragon's name, the assembly gasped, and the murmuring began anew. The queen silenced the chatter with an upraised hand. There was a flicker of amazement in her eyes. "From the Age of Legends come the Daunyarka. In all my years, only once have I witnessed the magnificence of the Guardians of the Daunyans.

"It was Khairon, Queen Mayana, who erected a statue of ice over the grave of Alurien MerTana, alongside our beloved Nuviel Titika and a mighty amahle Elder Hunter, honoring and immortalizing them for all time."

"You traveled alongside the Tall Ones? The queen looked from Tinnoviel to his companions and back. "You fought beside the amahle?"

"Briefly, my lady. The lava leech would have wipe out our party had not the Tall Ones arrived."

Mayana was silent as she digested all that she'd heard. Tinnoviel watched the many fond and troubled thoughts pass across her face.

"Dear Elfinestrayan cousins, the forest of the Elden is your home outside of your homeland. Be welcome and be comfortable. It saddens our hearts to hear of the loss of your Nuviel Titika, and the amahle Elder Hunter. Tonight we will dine in their honor."

Tinnoviel bowed.

"But first," Mayana continued, "we will speak of this business that brings you here."

That was the way of it with the Elden. All business discussed openly for all who wished to hear it. And so he related their venture to Takashaniel with the Daunya Chosen, and their meeting with Iel. He spoke of the Ilanyan's warning of the impending demonic attack and how the outcome would affect the world over. He was quick to add that the amahle had agreed to fight, though more conservative about the role the people of Yathienel would play.

"An army of demons of the lowest levels of the abyss are too much even for a Daunya Warrior, an Apprentice, and even a force of amahle," the queen remarked. "Who else aids you in this war?"

Tinnoviel took a deep breath. "Five humans and Kiluriel Sen'Mora," he answered, and waited through the expected uproar. The assembly rumbled at the news, and the queen's hand shot into the air once again, bringing immediate silence.

"You would have us aid you in a battle against one evil alongside another? Fight alongside one enemy to expel the other?"

"My lady," Tinnoviel ventured carefully, "I have seen with my own eyes that not all humans are as you see them ..."

"They are a plague that nearly killed the world and all who live upon it," Queen Mayana spoke right over him. "Whatever few that you claim are attempting to right the wrongs are far outnumbered. They would dig a ditch to stop a flood. If not for The Three, they would have destroyed themselves and all of us with them. It is not known how they escaped from the abyss to inhabit our beautiful earth, but to the abyss they should be returned."

The four visitors gazed warily at the rumbling assembly, some standing on the ground, many in the trees. Tinnoviel knew it was a near fool's errand to seek the help of these elves who were not only the most reclusive, but also the most mistrustful of humans. Still, he had to try.

"They do what is right, my lady. We've decided to help them."

"Their hatred brought the demons into existence, let them destroy each other."

And they feed on the hate of all, including yours. "Queen Mayana, if Takashaniel is destroyed, our world will be overrun. There will be no safety, no place to live where they cannot find us. If we do not unite against this evil, it will matter not from whom it was originally spawned. All will be engulfed in its darkness."

Anger radiated from the queen. Tinnoviel hoped he had not misspoken. "Ever have we been forced to clean their mess. We have been forced to live with the disasters they have brought upon our homes and this is but another. You would have me sacrifice Elden lives to aid them?"

"To aid the world, Queen Mayana," Tinnoviel said, bowing again. "This is a cause that affects the world beyond our homelands. We cannot ignore it."

Mayana responded with a predatory smile. "Lady Seiyun would send a force of her people, as she asks me to do, and the amahle also agree to fight." She held up five fingers. "And the aid from humans number five. Such a humble force, would you not agree, Daunya Warrior?"

Tinnoviel opened his mouth to speak, but the queen held up a finger to forestall him. "Of course the mass of human population do not know of the existence of their own creations. Is it not time for their ignorance to be lifted? Should not more of them rise to this challenge?"

"I do believe that the time is upon them," Tinnoviel replied, thinking of New Dainland and Ba Guo. "Their time of ignorance is passing. But as the veil lifts from their eyes, we must—"

"Then, I ask a final question. What difference could five humans I presume are warriors of some competent skill, make against this threat?"

"They are Children of the Gene," my lady.

The silence was palpable.

Mayana's fierce gaze was directed at Tinnoviel, but it passed right through him. "How could this be possible? Why would the Daunyans choose to bless an evil taint with Their power?" Now she did look at him. "How do you expect me to believe this?"

"I know not the will of the Daunyans, but I do know from my own eyes and the depths of my spirit that those five humans, and our Kiluriel, are blessed with the Gene of the Daunyans. And there is another." Tinnoviel paused for effect. This was what he hoped would sway them. "There is a sixth human, sister to one of the warriors. She is a Chosen." The crowd gasped. The queen's lips parted. She held her composure, but her eyes spoke the truth. She was shaken by the news.

"A Daunya Chosen. The Daunyans would select a ... *human*, as one of Their Chosen. Not in three hundred years have I seen a Daunya Chosen walk upon the earth. You are sure of this?" Tinnoviel nodded. "You are a Daunya Warrior and do not lie, Tinnoviel Nai SaunyaLi. I find this impossible to believe, but it comes from you, so I believe it. I promise only that I will think on it. I understand your urgency on the matter but this is all I will give you for now. Eqyar. I entrust our visitors to you, that they will find comfort before we dine tonight."

"An honor, my lady," the scout replied, bowing low.

"You will have what you need to rest and be clean from your journey. Be at peace during your stay, Tinnoviel Nai SaunyaLi, Yurin Kei Daunyana, Immendiel Mai'lienar, and Tikena Mojin." Without another word, the queen of the Elden left, her personal guard following close behind. Little by little, the assembled crowd disbursed until only the four visitors and Eqyar remained. Without a word, the scout signaled for them to follow.

"I'm not sure if that went well or not," Tikena said to Immendiel as they followed Eqyar through the forest.

"I suspect if it went badly, we wouldn't still be here," Immendiel responded. "I won't pretend to be optimistic about our chances but at least he managed to get her to consider it, which is more than I'd expected."

"You think there's still a chance she will refuse?"

A tiny frown creased Immendiel's brow. "Look into your own heart and answer that question, Tikena Mojin."

K*im would have marveled at this place.* Seung stood in admiration of the surrounding landscape of Takashaniel of the majestic landscape surrounding Takashaniel. She wondered if it was because of the tower that the flora enveloping the flowing hills and grasslands glowed with such an inner radiance.

She also wondered how her village was doing, and that brought her thoughts back to her friend, her brother, Kim. He would have wanted to stand beside her in the battle to come. He hadn't been happy to see her leave again after she had returned from her long journey only to leave again after a few weeks. She'd felt guilty having to lie to her people about seeking adventure and seeing the world. It wasn't completely untrue, but she obviously could not tell them the truth of her lineage.

"I love Kyu, but miss our home, Kiluriel," her Aunt Meilura had said. "Now that you've begun your journey to discovery your true identity, I can return."

A raindrop fell on her nose, then another. More drops fell, at first in little pitter patters here and there, then the clouds opened and emptied on the land below. In minutes she was soaked, but the air was warm, damp, and fresh.

A childish smile crept over her lips as she felt the rain streaming down her face. She started jogging for the trees. The rain intensified until she was running through a wall of showers, her clothes clinging to her body like a second skin.

Under the sanctuary of the trees, she leaned her head back and enjoyed the raindrops on her face. She ran her hands over her head, slicking her soaked black hair away from her face. The forest was silent save for the rain. Walking through the woods, she cupped her hands together and collected fresh water for a drink.

Before she realized how far she'd gone, Seung found herself standing atop a hill overlooking the surrounding woods. She turned and looked back the way she'd come. Though she couldn't clearly see the way back to the tower, she instinctively knew which direction the structure stood.

As a child she'd found it impossible to become lost in a forest. Her friends had come to rely on her when they went deep into the woods to play. Perhaps it was her elven blood? She smiled again as she debated roaming farther into the woods or returning to the tower. She turned to roam a little further when the smile evaporated from her face. She couldn't say how, but she knew she was no longer alone.

Seung let her head fall back and closed her eyes, pretending to enjoy the rain on her face while actually listening. There. In one motion she spun and drew the dagger strapped to her leg.

As soon as she saw her watcher, she dropped into a defensive crouch and skittered away, putting some distance between them. The thing standing before her was even taller than the towering people with the midnight-colored skin.

Angry orange hair fell behind its shoulders like flames growing from its scalp. It wore a long black cloak that hung just above its ankles. While Seung was soaked through, the rain spattered an inch from its dry body. Unfriendly reddish-blue eyes glared down at her.

Seung took a breath and blew it out in a steady stream through pursed lips. She tightened her grip on the dagger, which felt woefully inadequate.

"Enjoying a little romp in the forest, girl?" the thing said. Its voice made the air crackle with energy. "Are you yet another one of these Children of the Gene, Iel is so adept at digging up to delay me?"

Seung narrowed her eyes. This was the one Iel called a drek. Brit, his name was. The muscles in her legs bunched as she crouched into a defensive stance.

"Oh, now that's rude, girl. Have you not learned better? Is this how you welcome a visitor?"

"Spare me your nonsense, drek. You're here to destroy what I'm here to defend."

Brit shrugged. "I'll concede that point." He looked around at their surroundings, clearly bored. "Why go to all this trouble? Iel has no doubt told you what I plan to do and how, yet he is blind to many of the things I do. Surely you must know that you prepare to battle for a lost cause. Six humans, an Ilanyan, and his apprentice."

"Even if he manages to rally the ever illusive centaurs and brunts to his side again, can you make yourself believe such a small force can stop the wave that will overtake you? I command an army of demons larger than your small human mind can imagine. The first battle was but a taste. Why volunteer to suffer?"

Seung looked at him as though he were insane. "And, your alternative? Should we cower in fear as demons roam the land, twisting and destroying everything? Should we allow you to wipe us out and all that we love?"

The drek chuckled through her response. "You do not understand, girl."

Seung clenched her jaw. If he called her 'girl' one more time, she would be on him before the word finished leaving his lips.

"If you were to cease this foolish plan of stopping me, by the time I have drained this world, you and your kind would have long since died away. Why worry about it? How long does a human live? You would be lucky to reach near to a century. By the time this world is dead, you would have lived countless lives. If you were to step aside, I would banish every demon away and be done with them."

"And you would just simply let Takashaniel remain standing?"

"The tower matters little. It exists to maintain balance in a nonphysical nature. It keeps demons from crashing into this world in a raving bloodlust. But lately, I find it to be less effective than it was intended, don't you?"

Seung held her dagger in a white-knuckled grip. How she wished she'd brought *Vyirayoi*. "Do you think I believe anything you've said? We agree to just step aside for you to slowly feed off of the world's energy until it's drained dry? And in return, you banish every demon you've brought to this world. You must think me a fool."

"It doesn't matter what you think or believe, or what you perceive my intentions to be. You step aside, you live your short lives relatively unaffected. If you fight, you die now, and in unimaginable torment. One option will take me less time, and will be far less desirable for you than the other. Either way, you will die and I will have this world."

"You're getting on my nerves."

Brit laughed. "You are a tart one aren't you, girl—"

Seung slashed the dagger at his legs. The drek easily avoided her. She pressed the attack, but her adversary sidestepped her backhanded swipe. She leapt and turned midair with a slash at his throat.

Brit leaned away from the attack. "You'll have to do better than that."

Seung reversed her grip as she drew a second dagger from behind her lower back. She worked the weapons in a blinding combination that would have left a lesser foe helpless and quickly dead.

The drek smiled as he backed away. "Poor girl. Perhaps if I were a demon, that Gene burning inside your frail body would be of some use?" She darted to the side, slashing at his midsection as she went. And missed. How could someone this big be so fast?

Seung leaped backward, turning as she moved. She brought her right dagger around in a right hook in line for his face. Brit swatted her aside with little more than a casual backhand.

The stinging blow sent Seung spinning head over heels. She gritted her teeth as she hit the ground and barely kept the air from being blasted from her lungs. She ignored the tiny sparks of pain burning in her shoulder and rolled with the impact. She came back upright, planted her feet, and launched herself back him.

Again, the drek reacted impossibly fast. He stopped her midair with a palm to her midsection. As soon as she hit the ground he grabbed her by the throat.

He lifted her off the ground as though she were less than a child. His vice-like grip threatened to break her neck and she dropped her daggers and held on to his wrist to support some of her weight. Black splotches appeared in her narrowing vision.

"I wonder what would happen if a demon was here." Brit lifted her until she was at eye-level. "Would your fabulous Gene activate only when you were close to it, only to go dormant when you were close to me? Or would it simply activate in your little body and remain so as long as there was a demon present?" He held her closer to his face. "What do you think, little one?"

His voice sounded far away. Tiny rivulets of water streamed from Seung's soaked hair into her mouth as she fought for each breath. If he wanted to, he could have crushed every bone in her neck with little effort.

"You are a warrior. A warrior deals death to others, but must be prepared to meet death themselves. Are you prepared? Have you made peace with all that you will never accomplish after I've mangled your tiny little body?"

Seung managed to suck in two quick sips of air, just enough to stay conscious.

Brit's red-blue eyes narrowed over his smug grin. "With all of the taint and destruction your kind have wrought upon this world, how could you think of questioning what I do? Have you not done the same for centuries? I have no more love for this world than your kind, but the difference is that I speak openly.

"I do not pretend to understand what stopped your iron tools and metal structures from working, but it made things much easier for me."

He doesn't know about the elves or the amahle. The thought came as if through a pool of mud. Just as she started to black out she hit the ground in a heap, coughing and wheezing for sweet fresh air. She turned onto her side, still gasping and coughing while air passed through her bruised windpipe and filled her lungs. From the corner of her eye she saw the drek turn. As he did, she saw the shaft of an arrow as large around as her arm imbedded in his shoulder. Another struck him with an audible thud.

Brit's body jerked from the impact. He growled and yanked the arrows free. Two small streams of blood ran down his arm and chest. Seung frowned. There should have been far more blood than that.

"Apparently my question about the centaurs has been answered."

Seung saw the truth of his statement when Four centaurs emerged from the trees, bows drawn and leveled at the drek.

"You wish to have your battle now?" one of the half equine half human beings said. His voice was a deep growl. Two more centaurs stepped up to the base of the hill, arrows trained up at the cornered drek.

"Come now, hybrid. Do you honestly believe your arrows can do anything to me? Do you think you can kill me with airborne sticks attached with pointy tips?" The centaurs stood their ground and said nothing more.

"I admit that while the thought of slaughtering six centaurs and a human is enticing, you are right. Now is not the time." He looked down at Seung, who was still on the ground. "Say a prayer of thanks to whatever Gods you pray to. Tomorrow is not promised. That is the way of things, is it not?"

"Any closer to her and we will see how well you pull an arrow from your eye," the centaur warned.

"Impatient," Brit remarked. "Very well. I will see you again soon. Tell the keeper of your herd that time grows short."

One of the centaurs roared and loosed an arrow, but the drek had already stepped through a rip in the air and was gone. The arrow instead zipped through the air and embedded itself into a tree.

"Cloudfoot!" the speaker scolded.

Seung shook off her shock at being surrounded by mythical creatures and looked at the centaur apparently named Cloudfoot. He bowed his head, inclining his body in a posture of deference. "My apologies, Warsong."

The cinnamon-colored Warsong approached Seung and stopped several feet away. "How did you come to be here, human woman?"

Seung struggled to rise but her legs wobbled beneath. The centaur was quick, to her side and held her steady. "You have wandered too far into the forest and become lost. How is it you've survived this long?" The others had gathered around now. The rain lightened to a heavy mist and without the threat of the drek, the damp smells of wet earth and vegetation returned.

Seung took a deep breath and filled her lungs with the sweet smells around her. She was suddenly exhausted and all she could do was let her head hang. Several strands of hair slid from the side of her head to reveal a pointed ear.

The centaurs rumbled in shock.

"She's an elf!" one of them said.

"She doesn't look like any elf I've ever seen," said another.

"She is only part elf." Warsong lifted her chin with a callused, but gentle hand. "More elf than human, though she looks enough human to have fooled us. I didn't know such coupling still happened."

"That explains the reason she's so far into the forest," Cloudfoot said, which earned him another reproachful look from Warsong. He bowed his head again and withdrew silently to stand at the back of the group.

"She cannot be Elden," one of the others said, to a round of laughter. "That would be as likely as me taking a horse as my mate." More laughter.

Ever stern, Warsong didn't join in the laughter. "Impossible. She must be from a different land."

Another centaur moved to stand beside Warsong. He was larger and more muscularly built. He bowed his head in deference. "The Elden are closest. We should take her there."

"They might kill her on sight," Warsong said, never taking his eyes off of Seung. "You know how they feel about humans. A half breed, even one that is more elf than human, would not be met with kindness."

"To the guardian?" the larger one asked.

"Yes," Warsong replied. "He will know what to do with her." He lifted Seung in strong arms and started down the hill. They had barely begun to move when she finally gave way to exhaustion, and darkness took her.

* * *

S eung woke from the oblivion of dreamless sleep to a warm hand holding hers in a gentle grip. She knew that hand, and offered a weak smile.

"Ya wan tell me where in tha five layers of all the hells ya been wanderen' to have a clan of centaurs come carryin' ya back?"

"Mmm." She rested her other hand atop his and gave it a squeeze. They stayed like that for a while, and she lay with her eyes closed, tired but content.

"I met our mysterious enemy." Her the words came out in a croak. She swallowed and instantly regretted it.

"So I heard," Kenyatta replied, his accent fading along with his concern.

It was just as well. Her head hurt too much to try comprehending his islander talk, cute as she found it. "I just went for a walk—"

"In the middle of a downpour?"

"Great time for a walk in the forest."

"Elf," was his only reply. She opened her mouth to say more, but he silenced her with an upraised hand. "Save it and tell everyone at the same time. If you can walk, there's a few concerned friends who want to see you."

He took her to a covered space beside the tower, shielded from the rain. Where she'd basked in being out in the rain not long ago, now Seung found herself wishing she could remain inside in front of a fire with a mug of tea.

"Centaurs won't enter any structure," Kenyatta said, reading her expression. I don't know if it's a fear of enclosures or something else, but you'll not find one inside anything that has a wall."

One of the centaurs waved as they approached. "Glad to see you among the living again, little elf," Warsong, greeted. The rest of the clan smiled at her.

"If not for you, I would not be." Seung placed a hand on his muscly arm. "Thank you."

"They told me you met Brit in the forest," Iel said, concern creasing his marble-colored features.

"Yes."

"But he is—"

"Beyond anything I was capable of," Seung interrupted. "Even if I had *Vyirayoi* with me, I doubt I'd have defeated him. As sure as I am that I am standing here with you, I am equally sure I would have died if our centaur friends had not come." And then she related the rest of the encounter, and what she'd gleaned from the conversation.

"So he believes there are only humans, brunts, and centaurs living in this world," Iel said once she finished. "If we're able to convince the elves to help us, that could be an advantage." Seung wanted to say that the Elfinestraya would help, but she wasn't entirely sure. From what she'd learned from Tinnoviel, the people of The Wood, though not as harsh in their feelings as the Elden, were still loathe to include themselves in any situation that involved the world of humans.

"We'll have all we need to get the job done," Kenyatta said, as though reading her mind.

Kita placed a comforting hand on her shoulder. "We've got strong friends. You still haven't met the other three we battled beside. And the amahle stand with us. Brit will have a harder time of it than he thinks."

Seung didn't know whether it was true or not. She could still feel the pain in her throat from her strangulation by the drek. He'd held her several feet off the ground with one hand. The effort been so casual Seung might have been an infant instead of a fully grown woman. She never imagined anyone could be so strong.

A few yards away, a space in the air rippled, and Taliah stepped onto the field.

The Daunya Chosen took in each member of the group silently before she finally spoke. "My greetings, centaurs." She looked at Iel and Kenyatta, and finally Seung. Her brow creased with concern when her eyes fell upon Seung. "What's happened?"

B rit glared at the blasted wasteland surrounding his home. He'd enjoyed its uninviting appearance for many years, but it was no longer nourishing. He would need to be more discreet in the future. The human girl and those hybrid creatures were no threat to him, but if the Ilanyan had shown up, that confrontation could have ended differently.

He'd toyed with the girl too long, not suspecting the centaurs to be patrolling the forest so far from their home. They hadn't been there a few days ago. He looked at his shoulder and chest, where the arrows had struck. They'd done little damage but that didn't excuse his carelessness.

"Has your invulnerability been challenged, *tether*?" a grating voice asked from behind.

How he hated being called *tether*, but apparently that's how demons referred to those who summoned them to the earth plane. It was logical, given he was their link to this world, but that fact did little to curb his irritation. "Begone."

"Arzeth leaves so the *tether* can lick his wounds in private," the demon teased. "Maybe the *tether* is not as strong—"

Brit lashed out with one of his large hands and ripped out Arzeth's throat. The demon's last words ended in a gurgle as it fell twitching on the ground while its throat began to heal.

A few moments of blissful quiet came to an end when it finally recovered and stood again. It turned its baleful glare on Brit. "Arzeth apologizes, mighty *teth—*" Brit snatched out its throat again. Once more, the demon collapsed to the ground. Brit held his hand over the twitching body. He curled his fingers and incinerated the fiend with a blast of green fire.

He snarled at the noxious fog that was the demon evaporating back to the abyss. Had he been less careless, he would have done the same to that human girl and been done with it.

"Arzeth's mouth has finally ended his stay here in the beautiful light of the lovely earth realm." On Brit's other side, Kabriza's rumbling voice was like a group of boulders grinding in its throat.

"There is another whose voice puts their stay here in jeopardy."

"Oh?"

"Indeed," Brit responded, turning his back to the fiend. Though it would take considerably more effort to defeat Kabriza than Arzeth, Brit was confident he could, if it came to it. "You've done as I ordered?"

"The elemental is ready, and the Large Ones are waiting."

What Kabriza called the "Large Ones", were a species of quentranzi that stood over four hundred feet tall. The first time he'd attacked Takashaniel, he'd managed to send a smaller one of those things. This time, with Kabriza's help, he had four. He smiled to himself. It was time to finish this. He had his demonic forces well in hand, and had managed to bring a huge force of the fiends to this dimension despite the presence of Takashaniel.

And now he had the measure of Iel's frail little humans. Even if they decimated his forces, he was confident he could deal with them all before they had a chance to organize any kind of defense against him. Brit could think of no reason why that tower would be anything more than a memory in just a handful of days.

"Ready your forces. The sooner we topple that annoying tower, the sooner you can have your feast upon this world's inhabitants as promised."

"And the sooner you can begin feeding on this world all by yourself," Kabriza added. "Drek, how powerful will you truly become, once you've devoured the life essence of an entire world."

"More powerful than your twisted mind can imagine," Brit replied. "It will take a millennium and more for me to drain this world, but once it is done, I will see my kind once again, if any still live."

"And subjugate them all," Kabriza added. "Your kind and mine have much in common."

Brit half turned, eyeing the greater fiend. "In some ways, yes. Perhaps this is why I am well suited to keep you and your vermin well in hand."

"Of course," Kabriza said, a bit more quietly. "Who better?" An electric spark lit the room and it was gone.

Brit smiled.

* * *

"This news bothers me," Taliah said. They sat on floor cushions in a warm room high in the tower, overlooking the land for as far as the eye could see. The centaurs had departed a while ago, Warsong promising to relate the day's events to Grimhammer, the leader of their clan.

"I don't know how he came this close without my being aware of it." Iel said. "I should have felt his presence."

"Apparently he's found a way around that," Taliah said. She looked at Seung. "And you're very lucky."

Still gazing absently into her tea, Seung could only nod.

Taliah leaned over and placed a comforting hand on the other woman's knee. "You've glimpsed your death and walked away from it. You will be ready next time. Make him pay for his mistake."

"I'll not pretend that he hasn't shaken me, but I will make him pay."

"He'll be food for the carrion crows before you even get there." A shadow passed across Kenyatta's normally jovial features.

"You okay?" Taliah asked, a bit of concern in her voice.

"I'm fine," Kenyatta replied. He made an effort at brightening his features. "What now?"

"Now, we rest. Tomorrow, I take you to New Dainland where you we will speak with King Elizander Dain about the troubles plaguing his land. As with emperor Liu Xiang, I have a feeling the king is on the brink of conflict with his neighbor, and hasn't figured out the cause."

"Not anymore," Iel interrupted, and Taliah cast him a surprised look. "He laid a trap for what he thought were the persons responsible for the attacks. It ended near to disaster in a confrontation with a Zzrt."

Taliah sucked in a breath. "Is he still live?"

"Yes, and he was extremely lucky. A monk of the Order of Dasha saved him and his captain."

"The Order of Dasha?" Kita said. "Never heard of it."

"That's because you aren't of the Order of Dasha," Taliah replied. "They're one of a very small number of human factions that are aware of the world in its entirety. They have worked in secrecy for centuries, keeping the human population protected and wholly ignorant of the existence of not only the demon realm, but also of those with whom we share this world."

"Can you tell me why that was considered a good idea?" Kenyatta asked.

It was Seung who answered. "Humans are mistrustful and hateful of each other. How do you think they would have reacted to the elves, or the amahle?"

"I guess that's true," Kita admitted. "But it looks like the time for ignorance is coming to an end."

"And without the world-killing tools and weapons of the past," Seung said. "We don't have to hide anymore for fear of being completely wiped away."

"We?" Kenyatta said. "The more time that passes the more you seem to relate more to your elven heritage than your human."

"You have not lived my life, love," Seung replied. "I've lived most of it in puzzlement of why I looked and felt and even in some ways, thought, differently. When first you saw me, did I not look different from any other human being you'd ever met?"

"Different, but beautiful," Kenyatta agreed.

Kita smirked, and Taliah rolled her eyes.

"I spent my whole life hiding what was different about me," Seung said. "Then I discovered a new world and society and culture that I never knew existed. A part of me that I didn't know existed had awakened. I've seen the other side of things and I cannot blame the elves for how they feel."

"Sadly, this is true," Taliah spread her hands. "But past scars must be healed if we are to survive."

"Tinnoviel Nai SaunyaLi, and his group are visiting the Elden now," Iel said. "I doubt the likelihood for success, but he's determined to try."

"Then, everyone is doing what they can." Taliah stood and looked to Seung, Kita, and Kenyatta. "I should also warn you that I suspect Brit's demon general has pawns of its own. When I found the ninja and her brother and the strider, they had already killed two groups of demon animated corpses and three *seaphs*.

"A *seaph* is the result of the joining of a human and a lower-level demon. This joining grants the human power and strength far beyond what is natural, and grants the demon entry to this world without the necessity of a *tether*; a being native to this world to summon it."

"That doesn't sound so bad," Kita said. "We've fought major demons. Lower-level fiends shouldn't be a problem."

"That is true for a fledgling *seaph*. But it's their intelligence that makes them dangerous. Most demons, no matter how powerful, possess a rather base intellect. Their thoughts are primal in nature, with only a small number of them possessed of any type of cunning. Quentranzi are the only known species capable of such thought. A *seaph*, however, has the intellect of a human mind, a stronger human body, and some abilities inherent in those from the abyss."

"A smart demon that can move among humans," Kenyatta replied dryly.

"As time passes, the demon essence gradually absorbs the host from the inside out. Eventually, you have a demon in a twisted human body. They may not be as powerful as a quentranzi, but they're more intelligent and familiar with this world due to their human vessel. They can control the demon-ridden corpses of humans as well."

"So we may never find them all?" Kita asked. "Since they look human?"

"That is a possibility we might have to accept. By the time they start to change, the damage will have been done."

"Lovely," Kita said.

"You should rest and prepare yourselves," Taliah said. "There's a lot to do."

"There's more?" Iel asked once the others were gone.

Taliah nodded. "We found *skulkers*."

That gave Iel pause. "What is the demon general planning? I have trouble believing Brit could be so ignorant of this."

"How could he know?" Taliah said. "His arrogance clouds his vision. By summoning the second most powerful quentranzi in the abyss, he granted it access to this world and all of the evil and corruption in it. Kabriza is dependent on Brit as its *tether*, but it is not dependent on him to summon its own kind into this world, even if in small numbers. What bothers me more is that this is being done in spite of the presence of Takashaniel."

"This tower was crafted by mortal hands infused with the power of the Daunyans," Iel explained. "Mortals can only channel so much of the power of the Gods, and so, magnificent though Takashaniel is, its power is but a flicker of the Daunyans. But trust this, Chosen. Without the tower, this world would have been overrun long before Brit began his scheming."

"And if he achieves this foolish plan of his," Taliah said, "he and all of us with him are doomed."

Iel turned back to the grassy fields, still glistening from the rain. "If that happens, all will wish humans had succeeded in destroying the world."

33

L iu Xiang stood within the concealment of one of the four battlements that connected the wall around the front of Wuhan. As he watched the approaching warlord and his entourage, a sigh escaped him. This was an aggressive military force Qian was trying to disguise as an escort for safety. The army marched in unison, their thunderous footfalls heard even from Xiang's vantage point a mile away.

"I'm sure we need not speak the obvious."

Liu Xiang glanced to his left at the sound of the strider's voice. "No." He looked back to the approaching force. "Qian is brash and often unreasonable, but this is brazen even for him."

On his other side, Zhang Da bristled. "This is a thinly veiled threat, my lord."

"This does indeed make little sense," Zhuge Xiaoyin said. "He doesn't seem to care enough to even give the appearance of coming to talk."

"Could be that his spies have already created some infraction to justify all this," Zhang Da suggested. "Perhaps some concocted proof of your supposed duplicity."

"That's quite the cynical perspective," Liu Xiang replied.

Da waved his hand out at the scene before them. The military force was no more than half an hour from reaching the gates. "Such a large force will tax our resources and our city, my lord. It looks as though Qian Hua has not taken these things into consideration before burdening you with his presence. Or perhaps he has."

"Either way, we will be as ready as we can. You've prepared your men?"

"Our forces are ready, and we sent runners out to inform the populous of the impending incursion. The message was worded neutral, but the warning should be clear. If he has spies here, there is nothing overt for them to use against you."

Liu Xiang pursed his lips. It was no secret that Zhang Da had no affection for Qian Hua. If left to his own devices, Da would have found a way to eliminate the troublesome man long ago. Despite the fact that more than a few provinces considered Hua an irritant, such brash action as removing him without proper cause could eventually lead to chaos and lawlessness.

"I would add that you need not allow his entire force to enter," Xiaoyin suggested. "It wouldn't be unreasonable for you to require the bulk of his force to remain outside the gates, as they would crowd and overburden the city."

Liu Xiang nodded. "It was his choice to bring so large a force. Let him look after their needs." He turned away. "We prepare for his arrival."

Guan Xi patted Xiang on the shoulder as he passed. "Let him come! He will leave in peace or in pieces. Either way, Shu Han will be the better for it."

Zhang Da huffed. "The world would be better for the latter option." Guan Xi laughed.

"That one has liquid fire for blood," Kenjiro remarked, looking at Guan.

"Why not ask her out for a cup of tea?" Akemi suggested.

"I think she would better respond to a mug of beer," Shinobu said.

"Perhaps I may."

Akemi nearly choked on her own shock. "Can it be that beneath the sour exterior, my brother actually may have a bit of sweetness?"

"Can it be that one day my little sister will close her mouth for longer than a few seconds?"

"You suggesting I grow a stone jaw like you?"

"Only if it closes tight."

A snort drew their attention to the departing Shinobu. "I enjoy watching you two, but we'd better catch up with them."

Akemi took one last look at the approaching force. It took no warrior's instinct to see the wrongness in this. She had a feeling that on the visitor's rack, *Onihakaisha* and *Onisekairu* were quickening in anticipation.

* * *

L iu Xiang and General Zhang Da rode out with an honor guard to meet the approaching warlord. Despite being surrounded by his best men, his greatest warrior sitting to his left, and archers on their "normal" patrols, Liu Xiang nevertheless felt exposed.

The force came to a halt, and Qian Hua, followed by his own general rode ahead. Xiang had thought to receive the warlord in his grand audience chamber, assuming a position of superiority as was his right. Zhuge Xiaoyin had suggested against it, arguing that he could immediately take the man's measure and decide how much or little of his force Xiang would allow into Wuhan.

"Finally!" Qian exclaimed. "Liu Xiang finally meets with the Lord of Qian. Too long it has been since we have visited upon one another."

Beside Liu Xiang, Da stiffened. It was outright disrespectful that Qian had omitted Xiang's title while speaking of his own, lesser station. Liu Xiang knew that while he may choose to ignore the slight, his loyal friend and general wouldn't. "Warlord Qian Hua. Always are you welcome to Shu Han and to the city of Wuhan."

Qian waved a hand. "Yes of course, my thanks. I do hope that my letter and abrupt visit to your good city did not cause you much inconvenience. I believe both our respective situations demanded immediate action."

"Of course," Xiang said noncommittally.

"And it is good to see the ever gruff Zhang Da as well! I see the spear of Fei has not yet gone brittle through the ages."

"And it never will," Da replied. As he inclined his head, he caught sight of Qian's general. The world may well have ceased to exist in that moment as the two locked gazes, the unspoken challenge like a silent bellow between them.

"I see you are becoming acquainted with my own General Qian Ning," Hua said. His words were kind, his tone arrogant. Even Qian's posture radiated imperiousness.

Most disturbing, however, were his eyes. There was something behind the eyes of the man that weren't quite right. It was as though a malevolence lurked just beneath the exterior. In that moment, Liu Xiang knew that this would end badly, as Zhang Da had foretold. This man was as far from trustworthy as was possible, and for Xiang to allow the entirety of Qian's force into his beloved city would be to invite a serpent into his house.

"I'm sure you would rather take comfort within the city—" Liu Xiang said.

"That would be pleasing, for sure."

Xiang thought he saw the man's eyes actually glint. "I regret that I cannot accommodate your entire force, however," Xiang continued. "Impressive though they are, they are simply too numerous."

Hua made an effort to hide his disappointment. "There are many among my men who would look upon the splendor of Wuhan for the first time."

I'm sure they would. "That is regrettable. Had I known you would arrive in such numbers I would have better prepared."

"One cannot be too safe in such dangerous times. Can your fine city accommodate a smaller number of us?"

"I think we can comfortably house you and thirty of your men. The rest will be free to camp outside the city, as there is plenty to forage. Should they require more, Wuhan will assist."

Qian looked as though he wanted to argue, but thought against it. "Most gracious of you, Emperor." Xiang refrained from bristling at the mockery in Hua's tone. Something was definitely wrong. The warlord had never been the most desirable of company, but this was especially rude, even for him.

Beside Xiang, Zhang Da did an admirable job of restraining himself. If Liu Xiang gave even the slightest indication he desired it, Da would cut Qian Hua down without hesitation. "Ride with me and be welcome to Wuhan."

They rode through the gates, Zhang Da to his right, and Qian to his left, the warlord's son and general on *his* left. After Qian had exchanged a few words with Ning, the man wheeled his horse about and galloped back.

"The men will be disappointed but thirty of my best will be pleased. All know better than to voice their displeasure, however." He glanced sidelong at Xiang. "A man must rule with a hand as hard as the steel on his hip if we are to keep the people in check. Otherwise we have situations like that which brings me here."

"Of course," Liu Xiang replied. Upon re-entering Wuhan, Xiang felt as though he had released a breath he'd been holding for a lifetime. From the corner of his eye, Xiang noted Qian Hua's eyes darting this way and that. On occasion his gaze would linger on a particular building or street.

"You look about as though you come to Wuhan for the first time," General Zhang said.

"I simply marvel at how things so rapidly change in the world and how well the people of Wuhan and their lord manage these changes."

"I am sure Warlord Qian has handled these changes just as well," Liu Xiang replied, and Qian puffed up with pride. Something may be different about the man, but his overdeveloped ego was still intact.

All through the streets, people recognized their beloved emperor and bowed as the procession passed. Some even called in friendly greeting.

"You disapprove, Lord Qian?" Xiang asked.

"I find it unusual that the people are on such familiar terms with their ruler," Hua answered. "The people should have a healthy amount of fear of their governing body."

Xiang's eyebrows rose. "You would command respect through fear?"

Hua shook his head. "Their respect is born through their fear. I demand obedience, not admiration."

Xiang bit back his disgust. As his ancestor had been, Xiang adored and cherished every person in his kingdom. It warmed his heart to see the genuine smiles of his people. It was an honor that parents were comfortable enough with their emperor that they brought their children to meet him.

He strived to maintain a good and healthy lifestyle for his people, and worked hard to earn and keep their respect and love. His rule was firm, but it was also fair and just. Liu Xiang never sought their admiration, but the people's love and thriving made his rule worthwhile. He could not imagine ruling a kingdom in such a way as Qian Hua.

"You do not approve."

Xiang looked at the man. "We have very different ways of governing our lands. You rule with an iron hand, I with an open one."

The warlord threw his head back and laughed. "Pray you do not find that open hand stripped of any gold it once held, my friend."

"If the people need it more and I have the means, it's theirs to have."

"As you say."

They came to the stables and dismounted, handing their reigns to the stable hands and making for the palace. At the courtyard, they were met by a beautiful Japanese woman in a stunning silk gown. Liu Xiang clenched his teeth together, lest his mouth fall open.

The woman looked directly into his eyes and he recognized that it was the ninja, Akemi. He also saw the warning in her eyes. Did she have those two terrifying swords hidden somewhere within her flowing gown. She curtsied, her hand brushing one of the beautifully tied folds of her gown, and Xiang thought perhaps she had.

"What have we here?" Qian Hua said. "Surely you hadn't enough time to send all the way to Japan for a Geisha to entertain me!" His narrowed eyes glinted with lust.

"Warlord Qian Hua, I introduce you to my visitor from Japan, Akemi Miyamoto." Akemi smiled and curtsied once more.

In that moment, Liu Xiang couldn't have been more glad the ninja was on his side. Behind that lovely smile lay the fangs of a viper.

* * *

Akemi studied Warlord Qian Hua and didn't like what she saw in his eyes. His whole presence was off-putting. From a distance, the man's swagger suggested the city already belonged to him. As they drew closer, *Onihakaisha* and *Onisekairu* quickened from within the folds of her gown. She could feel the challenge of the Demon Destroyer, and the hunger of the Demon Bane.

She brushed the hilt of *Onihakaisha*, hiding the movement with a curtsy. The more volatile of the two swords calmed. She had already suspected him, but the swords strapped to her lower back erased any doubt. This Warlord Qian had sold his soul, and he had done it some time ago.

The man was a fully formed *seaph*. She couldn't help but appreciate how he'd managed to undergo the transformation without those closest to him discovering. Unless they, too, had been subverted. She glanced at some of the soldiers under his command. No. She didn't feel the taint within the warlord's small entourage.

Hua strode up to her, his air of superiority and narcissism practically coming off him in waves. After Liu Xiang's introduction, and Hua's following insult, they resumed their path to the palace, Akemi falling in step behind.

She couldn't tell if he had felt the presence of her swords. If he had, he'd concealed it well. *Seaphs,* though far more durable than any normal human, feared weapons like hers. She had picked up on no such fear from Qian Hua. Either he was unperceptive or incredibly foolish.

"So how will you entertain us tonight, little geisha?" Qian asked, favoring her with a lecherous grin. "I must admit my curiosity regarding the subtle skills of the famous whores of the geisha houses."

Xiang frowned. "Lord Qian, you give offense to my guest—" he trailed off at the touch of Akemi's hand on the back of his arm.

"No offense has been taken, my good Lord Liu Xiang. She turned her attention to Hua.

"There are many skills I have been trained to perform, my lord. You will find my company quite interesting, I promise. Lust glimmered in the man's eyes. She hoped this would be as easy as she'd anticipated. If she could get the warlord alone for just a moment, she could deal with him quickly.

Of course there would be the problem of explaining his death to the entire armed force at Emperor Liu Xiang's doorstep, but that was for later.

He radiated malevolent power, a very wrong power that would be nearly imperceivable to the others, who would feel it only as an uneasiness or wrong feeling. If they were more perceptive, they would feel that something was not quite right about him. Akemi could almost see the evil radiating from the man. She could feel it, taste it.

As they walked through the palace, Qian spoke grandly of his conquests, and how he planned to unify the tribes that lived up to this point, autonomously in the mountains.

"They must be brought to heel." The warlord clenched his fist. "Only when all men have been brought under the banner of Qian can the lands know true order." He glanced at Xiang and Zhang Da. "I refer to those who live within my lands, of course."

"I'm sure that is exactly what you meant," Liu Xiang responded. When Qian turned to admire a passing maid, he and Zhang Da shared a look.

They rounded a corner and a man dressed in a tunic and breeches of fine silk passed them. When he reached Akemi, Kenjiro raised an eyebrow. Akemi nodded ever so slightly, and the samurai's jaw clenched. It was a subtle exchange that took less than a heartbeat.

They reached the open hall and were met by a group of attendants. "Lord Qian," Xiang said. "I give you into the care of my most capable attendants so that you may freshen up for the banquette tonight in your honor. Should you wish it, I will arrange an escort for you to tour the palace grounds for fresh air, if the weather permits.

"Most kind of you," Hua replied. "I would very much like to take refreshment. As for company, I require no more than your girl here." He indicated Akemi with a lazy hand. "If you can find the will to separate yourself from her."

Xiang glanced at Akemi and she gave him a subtle nod. "That can be arranged," he replied.

"Then it is settled. Come, geisha. I would have you now rather than later. Actually, I will have you now *and* later."

Liu Xiang cleared his throat. "I must delay your meeting with Akemi for but a short time. I have some things to discuss with her first."

"What could an emperor possibly have to discuss with a performing whore?" Qian asked, incredulous. "Oh, I forget. The emperor with a heart larger than the chest that carries it. "Come!" He jerked his head at the attendants that scurried to lead him to his room, his boots thudding with each heavy step.

Once they had rounded the corner and his footfalls had faded in the distance, the others resumed walking. Liu Xiang was taking no chances, putting as much distance from the man as possible.

"Would you have me remove his head now or in front of his army before or after we have decimated it?" Zhang Da asked.

"I'm sure nothing would please you more, my friend."

"I lost count how many offenses he's given since the moment we met. His pompousness is astounding."

"You would have a harder time of removing his head than you think, mighty General Zhang," Akemi said.

Zhang let out a hearty guffaw. "I've had Qian's measure for years now. I can have him to his knees in short order."

"If that was Warlord Qian Hua, I would not doubt you."

"What do you mean?" Xiang asked. They entered his private rooms and the personal guard closed the doors behind them, leaving the trio alone.

"That was Warlord Qian in body only. He is no longer the man you knew, though I suspect he may not have been any more likable than the demon's interpretation of him."

"Demon?" Zhang Da chuckled. "I will admit he is probably as close to a demon as you will meet in a man, but I saw no demon, just a blustering fool of a ruler."

Xiang rubbed his chin. "He is different from when last we met with him. And there is something about his eyes that I don't like. As though there is something lurking just behind them."

Akemi nodded. "He is a *seaph*, and far more dangerous than Qian Hua ever could have been."

"A what?" Da frowned. And so Akemi gave them a brief explanation. When she was done, they stood in silence for a while until finally Liu Xiang spoke.

"How should we deal with him?"

"I can go to his room and eliminate him now," Akemi said. The general looked at her doubtfully, then seemed to change his mind at the set of her features.

"You believe you can?" Xiang asked. "On the basis of your own account, these *seaphs* are very dangerous."

Akemi felt the insatiable hunger of her swords radiating from her back. "I've dealt with worse."

34

It took an effort not to scowl as Akemi shuffled quickly along the halls of the palace. Unfortunately she would have to keep up this geisha act a while longer, for Liu Xiang would not permit her to kill the warlord just yet. She had argued that it would eliminate the larger problem and cripple the army camped outside the city.

The emperor had countered that without proof of Qian's corruption, it would look like an assassination. Whether Qian's son was a *seaph* or not his outrage wouldn't be questioned, and the situation would rapidly deteriorate. Though it grated on her, Akemi couldn't deny the logic.

She also had to admit—if only to herself—that she wanted to put an end to the warlord for his ignorance. Geisha? Whore? Only an uneducated outsider would think such a thing. Not to mention she was not dressed like a geisha! She was actually wearing a silk gown given to her by Liu Xiang himself! She couldn't wait to slide *Onihakaisha* between the *seaph's* ribs and send him to oblivion.

Unfortunately that would have to wait. She had to leave her two swords in the care of Shinobu, who was patrolling the tree line around the perimeter of the army's encampment. She would have liked to have her weapons handy, but couldn't take the chance. If Qian caught on to the nature of the swords and figured out what she was, things could take a bad turn. She took solace in the feeling of the blade she had strapped across her lower back, and the two in her hair.

She reached Qian's visiting quarters and knocked. A nervous looking servant opened it hesitantly and then looked into Akemi's eyes, almost pitying. She could only imagine what this girl had to endure while the warlord took his pleasure while awaiting her.

Taking a deep breath and swallowing her distaste, Akemi entered. The girl scurried out the door as she closed it and turned to face Qian. He lounged in a chair in the corner of the room, his lecherous stare sliding up and down her body like a grinning oil slick.

"There you are, little flower," he said in her native tongue. "Come, have a seat right here." He patted his lap. Akemi strode across the room and took a seat in a chair several paces from him. Akemi never took her eyes off of the man. She could feel the malevolence wafting from him like a noxious cloud. He was a walking toxin.

Akemi feigned being impressed. There was no language demons capable of speech could not utter. "You speak my language."

He shrugged. "There is much that I know. So, little flower," Qian looked at his lap, then at her. "Are we to start with playing games or will we be done with the nonsense. I have business."

"I'm sure you do, my lord" She attached the last bit almost grudgingly.

He narrowed an eye at her. "You don't seem much like a geisha."

"How many have you met?"

"None, I admit. But you seem the opposite of what I would imagine one to be."

Akemi shrugged a shoulder. "Perhaps you do not know enough about them."

"Aha! Them! So you aren't a geisha after all."

"I never claimed to be, lord Qian. My heritage and a silk gown are not the criteria. You assumed. I did not correct you."

"Such a firm tongue," Qian said softly, eyeing her with lidded eyes. "You cause a stir in me. Why not come a little closer?" He patted his lap again.

"Why would I sit on your lap, Lord Qian?"

"You would sit here because I have told you to do so." His face grew serious. "I say again that I've not the time or inclination of playing your little games, geisha. I would have my pleasure and be done so that I may attend to important matters."

"You've the sound of a man with ambition on the mind," Akemi deflected.

The warlord nodded. "Too many things must be done and there is not the time for weakling, squeamish lords to take hesitant steps where a firm foot is required. The lands must be ruled, not coddled. I suspect Liu has been clinging too tightly to the robes of Zhao Xiaoyu, for he rules like a woman."

He seemed to catch himself, looking back in Akemi's direction. "But what matter is this of yours, little flower, hmm? You are merely a visitor here, and not subject to the goings on in Ba Guo."

"I've an interest in the goings on in Ba Guo, and a mind for conversation. I find the thoughts of Warlord Qian Hua quite fascinating."

"Is that so," Hua said. "Perhaps Liu Xiang would know my private thoughts. Perhaps the pretty face of a geisha could stir my tongue as well as my loins, hmm?"

"Perhaps that is true. You would do well to be alert for such a circumstance, should one arise." Qian's face darkened and Akemi smiled. "I have already told you, lord Qian. I am not a geisha and I am hardly a spy." Ironically, both statements were true. "I am a visitor here as are you. I simply happened upon your path—"

Qian cut her off. "I will say again that I've no mind for foolishness!" He stood, removing his belt and tunic. His bare chest was lined with thick hard muscle. "You will pleasure me and you will scamper back to your emperor when I am finished with you. Now get over here."

Akemi slowly, deliberately, rose from her seat, locking eyes with the warlord. In the space of a heartbeat, he seemed to hesitate. He was struggling to place her.

"I apologize if I have given offense or have misled you, lord Qian. If it pleases you, I could acquire the location of the nearest brothel where you may take your pleasure there. As for myself," She smiled. "I fear you would not find me very good intimate company."

"I will be the judge of your qualities, geisha," he said, lunging for her. He caught her arm and pulled her close, or tried to. He looked down at her unmoved arm, then back at her face, eyes wide with disbelief. "A strong little flower," Qian hissed. He pulled again with more strength, and this time she allowed herself to be moved.

Being this close to the demonic stench was stifling. "This is inappropriate, my lord."

"Worry not. We will cross well into more inappropriate territory soon enough. He grabbed her shoulders and attempted to push her to her knees. Her hands snapped up and grabbed his wrists. Before he could get a measure of her strength, she twisted out of his grasp, giving a small yelp as she did. The attempt at sounding frail was flimsy even to her ears.

An evil smiled crossed his face. "Perhaps Liu Xiang sends an assassin to my room then?"

"Of course not!" Akemi tried to sound shocked. "I feel as though I should leave now, lord Qian."

"I don't think so," he said. Akemi glanced at his chest and arms. The muscle beneath his hardening skin was shifting, like snakes slithering under a blanket.

Like a tiny flame as hot as an inferno, the Gene of the Daunyans quickened inside Akemi. She backed away and angled toward the door. Her vision and hearing became more acute. It felt as if every muscle in her body came alive.

"If you lie on the bed like a good little flower, I won't be long. Since you have already wasted my time, if you struggle," he shrugged, "well, you need not be conscious, or even alive."

Akemi watched as his skin continued to harden. Despite the enhanced abilities granted her by the gene, she had no weapons. Once Qian's skin was fully hardened, he would have an undisputed edge should she resist. If his skin formed into the armor she suspected it could, nothing short of her two swords—far from her grasp—would penetrate it. She needed to get out of the room.

"I must decline, my lord." Akemi made for the door, and as she suspected, he'd anticipated it. Before he could react, she reversed her movement, sprinting across the room and leaping out of the open window. The chill night air rushed across her face as she plummeted headfirst towards the ground far below.

Several floors down she reached out for a balcony guardrail. Just as she grabbed hold of the rail, she used the momentum to swing her body up. With strength augmented by the Gene of the Daunyans burning inside, Akemi swung her body up and over the rail to land in a crouch on the balcony.

She leaned over the side and looked up. Qian was leaning over his balcony, glaring hatefully down at her. For a moment it looked as though he would leap down after her. She had no doubt he could plummet the five stories with more damage to the ground than himself. No, he needed to keep his human guise, just as she needed to keep up her own pretense. He favored her with an evil, chilling smile, nodded, and disappeared back into his room.

There was something about a human inhabited by a demon that Akemi found more unsettling than encountering a demon itself.

Akemi began climbing down. Once she reached the ground, she walked as quickly as she could while appearing inconspicuous. Some of the thirty soldiers Liu Xiang had allowed in the city walked the halls as though inspecting them. A few gazes lingered on her as she passed, including the occasional knowing chuckle and lewd remark. After several minutes she finally reached Xiang's private rooms.

"Emperor Xiang?" She asked in her minimal use of the native tongue of the land. One of the guards rattled off a response before finally shaking his head at the lost look in her eyes. She did, however, hear the name Qian ...

The doors burst open and Qian and his son came stomping out of the room, his personal guard in tow. How had he beaten her here?

General Ning spotted her as she stepped aside and said something in a harsh tone. The two personal guards rounded on her, leveling their weapons. She backed away, looking from one guard to the other. The one on the left was the less experienced of the two, she could see it in his eyes and the way he held himself. He would attack first to prove himself. She would disarm and kill him, then work the other guard between herself and the father and son.

Before the confrontation could play out, Liu Xiang, followed by Zhang Da strode from the room. The emperor barked a single command, power and authority carrying his voice through the halls. After a few tense moments, Qian Hua signaled to Ning, who commanded his guards to stand down. With another of those evil smiles, the warlord turned his back on them and continued on.

"Would I be wrong to guess that he claimed you sent an assassin to his room," Akemi asked dryly.

The emperor's nostrils flared, but the ninja held up a hand. "Before you throttle me, lord Liu Xiang, know that I attempted no such thing. He advanced on me and I escaped through a window. I can only guess that he surmised I was not a simple toy sent by you, so he found the convenient excuse he sought."

"He claimed you tried to assault him," the general replied. "That you attempted to seduce him to glean information on his intentions, and when that failed, you attacked him."

Akemi almost laughed. "I will admit I am interested in his intentions here, but I assure you I could not have seduced him if I had been inclined. The evil he is emitting is enough to smother me." The two men looked at her, confused. "I am very sensitive to it," she said. "It's what makes me a good demon hunter. When he tried to force me, I thwarted his attempts as discreetly as I could without giving myself away."

"He didn't believe his own words any more than I did," Zhang Da said to the emperor. "You knew that he was looking for an excuse, my lord. I don't believe this could have ended any other way. If he was truly here to help figure out this supposed problem plaguing our two cities, would he have been so insistent on having a woman attend him now? I believe he would have had his pleasure with her and then killed her, claiming she was an assassin and creating the same situation he already has." He pointed at Akemi. "She was simply the first opportunity he saw, and having her alone was the perfect situation."

"And I was a fool to have allowed it," Liu Xiang scolded himself.

"It was either me or someone else, emperor," Akemi said. "You already knew this was coming to a fight as well as Qian."

Further down the hall, Shinobu rounded the same corner Qian and his men had gone. "Need I report the mood of your departing guests?"

"We are well aware," Liu Xiang said.

"He had the look of a man who was trying to look grim but was secretly elated. I overheard him speaking to his general. He said something about return fire."

"It is a strategy he intends to employ." Zhuge Xiaoyin stepped from around a corner. "He will take his army and leave immediately, only to return in the middle of the night and rain flaming arrows upon us. He will then charge in and take Wuhan with brutal force."

Shinobu glanced around the corner from where she had come. "Where did you come from?"

"You get used to it if you remain long enough," Zhang Da said.

"That is unethical. There has been no talk of this and he has not even declared war." Xiang's visage darkened. "This is treacherous, even for him."

"It is cowardice," Zhang Da added.

"It is the fastest way to take the city before any allies can be made aware," Xiaoyin said.

"And it's also what a *seaph* in a warlord's body would do." Akemi said. "I'll not pretend to understand how men thought that the atrocities of war should have rules to them, but there is no honor and no rules when dealing with abysmal creatures."

"I'm still having a difficult time accepting the fact that demons exist and that we are about to do battle with one." Zhang Da hefted his large spear. "But if battle one we must, we will send it back to the hell it came from." Kenjiro came stalking from the same direction Shinobu had just come, the familiar grim set to his jaw.

"Da. You have scouts concealed in the woods. Perhaps reinforce them and send them further out.

"Fewer numbers are less easily detected, my lord. I can send them farther out and replace them at their former posts. My best rangers can hunt down and eliminate any scouts they find while we prepare our forces."

"There is a possibility that he will have reinforcements already on the move," Zhuge Xiaoyin said. "We don't want your men trapped between them." She looked to the emperor. "Empress Zhao is an ally, my lord."

Liu Xiang nodded. "Send for a runner," he said to one of his personal guard, who executed a precise bow and left. "I will send word of Qian's duplicity. If she moves quickly, her forces can be here within a day."

"I will accompany your messenger, my lord," Xiaoyin said. "I can better brief her of the situation and assist in finding the best possible advantage."

"Do you believe this empress will enter a conflict that doesn't involve her?" Akemi asked.

Xiaoyin nodded. "Empress Zhao knows well that a conflict with Shu Han involves the land of Zhao. If Shu Han falls to Qian, Zhao will be next. He will try to force her hand in marriage and absorb her lands into his own. Even before Qian Hua was occupied by this demon, he has long considered Zhao a tantalizing asset."

The creases in Liu Xiang's forehead deepened. "I agree. She will act quickly. I am loathe to let you leave my side, Kongming, but I have the most capable general Zhang and Guan at my side." He looked at Akemi, Shinobu and Kenjiro. "And three warriors who will lend me their blades?"

Shinobu bowed. "I had hoped you wouldn't exclude us, Emperor."

Akemi did her best to stifle her impatience. "I would reiterate, Emperor, that I can be gone in moments and eliminate him after nightfall. Save the trouble of time, bloodshed, and resources."

"Spoken like a ninja," Zhang Da said. "Would that we could handle it in such a manner, I would send you out immediately. Unfortunately, he is no doubt already at the center of his force and will remain there until he is ready to invade us."

"And the problem is?"

Liu Xiang, Zhang Da, and even Zhuge Xiaoyin turned puzzled looks on her. "Are you so confident that you believe you can enter his camp, dispatch him, then leave without being detected?" Xiang asked.

Akemi smiled.

"Perhaps we let her try?" Da said, casting a dubious look the ninja's way.

Liu Xiang shook his head. "I don't doubt your skills, Ninja, but I'm not a man given to risks of such high stakes. You will have your chance at him since, as you say, our weapons will have no effect.

In response, Akemi smiled. "Inform your men to have plenty of fire ready."

M alimokuru missed his horse. He kicked a cluster of gravel and watched the pebbles bouncing and spinning toward the floor of the canyon. The horse would never have been able to safely descend the steep, gravelly slope. Luckily he his friends were kind, and knew the land. The amahle had been happy to divert their path to find a herd of wild horses. He felt better knowing he'd released his mount into their care.

Naiyala came to stand beside him, gazing out at the yawning canyon below.

"It's a beautiful world we live in," he answered. On his other side, Nyaka lay curled up beside a boulder. Occasionally her forked tongue would flick in and out and her ears swiveled in the direction of any foreign sound.

"It is," the princess said. "And getting more beautiful every day. Soon, our Mother will be healed and whole again."

"Assuming She is not overrun with demons."

Naiyala chuckled and he looked up at her. She smiled, her onyx black face was positively radiant. If he wasn't such an old man, he would have found himself in her thrall, no matter she wasn't human. His face must have betrayed his thoughts, for her skin lightened to a dark brown color, still several shades darker than his own. He knew that look, for amahle blushed in reverse.

"Yeah all right, you read my mind, gyal," he said, reverting to his native accent. "Yer cute. Beautiful, even. But I'm an old badger well past my foolish years. I was jyas admirin' you, is all." He waved a dismissive hand.

Naiyala's smiled deepened and she put a long-fingered hand on his shoulder and gave it a squeeze. "I am sure you were a ... what word is it? Hand done man?"

Nyaka stirred at Malimokuru's bark of laughter. Behind him, the others looked questioningly at them. "Sorry. No, it's handsome, not hand done." He wiped tears from his eyes, his shoulders still bouncing.

Naiyala shared in his mirth. "Ah, hand some, then. It is sometimes hard to remember your tongue. Humans have so many different languages around the world. It can be difficult for us to remember. Amahle all speak the same tongue the world over."

"Sounds convenient," Malimokuru remarked, turning back to the canyon. Naiyala followed his gaze, and Ayanda and Amata came to join them. For a time they stood in silence, admiring the view. Then they heard a low growl followed by a hiss. Nyaka crept slowly beside the nature reader, her hackles raised. Her barbed tail flicked left and right and her bright blue eyes narrowed. Another hiss.

"Not again." Malimokuru threw his hands up. "I don't see anything. What is it now?"

"Sakhile approaches, and swiftly," Ayanda said.

A few moments later, the scout scrambled over the side of the rocky bluff. "Do you see it?" he asked.

"See what?" Naiyala glanced from the scout to the still hissing goar cat. She followed the animal's gaze to one of the far cliffs and spotted a lone winged figure.

"There!" Ayanda said, pointing to the opposite hill of the valley. "Another one."

"They were the ones watching us when we battled the dark ones a year ago," Sakhile said. "I'm sure of this."

Malimokuru felt a chill shoot through his body as he looked from one winged creature to the other. They stood as still as statues and were easy to miss. "I think they're waiting for us to cross through the canyon." He was starting to hate canyons.

"We have no choice," Sakhile said. "It will come to a fight whether we go through or around. If I am to fight, I would rather it be without a cliff nearby."

"We will cross and deal with them when they come." Naiyala looked to Amata Daunyana. "You're sure?"

The Daunya Apprentice inclined her head. "The enchantments I've placed on your weapons is sufficient, *Inkosazana*."

Nyaka had gone quiet, and as the party started away, she crouched low to the ground and her color shifted. She blended into the brown landscape as though her body were bending the light around it.

"Do you think they've seen us?" Malimokuru asked.

Sakhile grunted. "They've probably been shadowing us for a while. Likely they've decided to reveal themselves."

Malimokuru thought that was a calm way of putting it. He turned his attention again to the distant figures, seemingly waiting on them. How had two demons simply shown up in this world, and why had they taken an interest in him and his friends?

Those two fool boys are involved in this. I know it. After traveling with Kenyatta and Kita for the time he had, Malimokuru was almost certain it had something to do with them, though he didn't know why. He began picking his way down the loose rocky slope. "Probably up to their nostrils in some kinda trouble."

"You spoke?" Naiyala looked up at him from below.

"Just thinking aloud."

"Thinking about fools?" Ayanda said, from much further down the slope. "You spoke of fools, friend Malimokuru."

Malimokuru sighed. Just how far could these people hear and see, anyway? "Ya man. Don't worry about it." Funny he said that, because looking at those waiting demons, all he could do was worry.

* * *

K abriza straightened over the carcass of a demon it had been devouring. Occasionally, one of the lesser fiends felt they could challenge the quentranzi general. Boldness such as this was always met with brutality and satiated hunger. The twins had made contact through their link. The fool drek was not as all-knowing as he believed. Brit knew of the existence of the twins, but he thought he still had control over them through Kabriza. Fool. Kabriza was a quentranzi, not some minor imp or demon from one of the upper levels of the hells.

Apparently, the twins had encountered a small group of amahle traveling with an old human. The demon general found this odd, but the human was inconsequential. The presence of amahle traveling great distances with purpose did draw his attention, however. Kabriza rumbled a hideous chuckle in its belly at the thought of its oblivious "master".

How stupid the drek was in not knowing of the presence of more than just humans in this world. Humans made a boisterous show of their presence, but those they shared the world with were much more subtle and possessed of creative abilities to remain undetected. Of course, no living thing could hide from the demon realm. Ever have they crossed in and out of this dimension in some fashion or another. Kabriza's summoner, no matter how powerful, had made a convenient mistake; he had assumed that humans were his only concern. He would learn otherwise.

Tiny red flames danced from the demon's narrowed eyes. Kabriza didn't need Brit's plan to succeed in order to bring the demon realm to earth. All that was needed was Takashaniel destroyed. Tiny fires danced in Kabriza's eyes as it sent a telepathic response to the twins, Greash and Zkora. *"Tear them apart."* Excited bloodlust came in response.

The quentranzi severed the connection and looked down on its victim. With a motion from a clawed yellow hand, the half-eaten demon burst into flames and was gone, leaving only a patch of scorched ground where it once lay. Kabriza wondered how the flesh of a drek would taste.

G reash studied its prey as they reached the base of the cliff. Kabriza's response couldn't have been clearer or more satisfying.

They would take two each and leave the little human for last. Greash thought it amusing that the mortal amahle would allow a fragile old flea to accompany them, but it mattered not. After discovering the little band a year ago and keeping watch on them ever since, Greash and Zkora would finally have their fun before returning to play in the human lands.

Through their bond, Greash felt Zkora's excitement. The demon studied the group more closely. The amahle fleas were shedding nearly all of their clothes. Greash curled its upper lip, baring a long thick fang. The more garb they shed, the less of it Greash would need to rip off while devouring them alive.

Greash glanced at Zkora, as still as a statue and waiting just as patiently. Once the little group of ants passed into the middle of the canyon, Greash sent Zkora a signal through their connection. Time for blood.

* * *

M alimokuru shouldered his pack after stuffing the sparse clothing of Naiyala and the others inside. Those cursed winged things were still watching them, like the gargoyle statues that haunted tall buildings in the cities he'd been to. *But* those *gargoyles stay put.*

He glanced around, wondering where Nyaka had gone. The goar cat was not given to fright, so he could only assume she was finding an advantageous position to attack from. He hoped she wouldn't do anything foolish.

Malimokuru tried to shake off the ominous feeling the dull brown landscape invoked. The occasional crosswind sighed through the passes like a melodious dirge foretelling a grim future.

As the minutes passed, dark clouds crept in from the north shadowing the landscape and bringing a chill to the air. A raindrop spattered on his forehead. He looked up to see a ceiling of dark storm clouds gathering, no doubt preparing to empty their contents on his head.

"What a relief," Malimokuru held out a hand as the raindrops came more frequently. "I was afraid this would be easy."

"Are you so powerful, friend Malimokuru?" Ayanda asked, "that you would fear battling two dark ones would be easy?"

Malimokuru sighed at the genuine curiosity in the youngest amahle's expression. "It was sarcasm, boy." When he received a confused look, he tried to explain. "I know this isn't going to be easy, I was just … I wasn't joking, exactly, but … never mind. I'll try to explain when I'm not afraid I'm going to die." Ayanda looked even more confused, but let it go with a shrug.

A spiderweb of lightning scarred the dark sky, and an instant after, thunder rumbled. Malimokuru hunched against the increasing rain and wind. "Our bad luck would have to get really creative to make this worse."

By the time they reached the middle of the canyon the storm had arrived in earnest, and they were soaked through. Malimokuru was sure he saw crouching shadows. With every illuminating crackle of lightning he spotted something—or many somethings—keeping pace with them along walls and sparse foliage littering the canyon floor.

A bolt of lightning struck the ground, little more than a hundred feet in front of them. The power of the impact lifted Malimokuru off the ground and the next thing he knew, he was on his back, shaking and temporarily blinded by the sudden flash of light. The amahle held their ground, growling as they braced themselves against the onslaught of wind and rain and rocky debris.

Malimokuru sniffed the air with increasing dread. A lightning storm and they were soaked and in the middle of a what might as well be a bowl.

Several more flashes and the sound of electricity buzzed in sync with the flickering spear of lightning that continuously pounded the ground. The air buzzed with electricity. Malimokuru felt the tiny hairs on his arms stand on end as the lightning bolt continuously struck the ground ahead. Then it stopped.

In place of the last bolt stood a two-legged figure with arms as thick around as his body. Its legs, however, were thin and as long as Malimokuru was tall. Electricity streaked up and down its body. It flexed claws big enough to hold any one of the amahle in its grasp.

Sparks lit from its claws and showered from its fang-ridden mouth like foam, lighting its narrow head.

Malimokuru scrambled to his feet and the amahle warriors positioned themselves around him. Ayanda and Sakhile had arrows nocked, and Naiyala had a throwing spear in each hand. Another handy thing about the tall folk was that they did not favor one hand over the other, and couldn't understand when Malimokuru said he was right-handed. "But you have two hands," Naiyala had once said.

He took a deep breath and exhaled to clear his thoughts. The beast—obviously having a liking for electricity—hadn't moved. For the span of several heartbeats, nothing happened. Electricity sparked and danced on the monster's body. The constant buzzing in Malimokuru's ears was deafening.

"Sakhile," Naiyala said. "You and I will take the *rage*. Amata and Ayanda, you will blend. With silent nods, the warriors heeded her instructions. As they moved, their hue shifted until they were barely visible. Another flash of lightning, another clap of thunder.

Naiyala snarled, revealing the two sets of elongating fangs. Her onyx black skin shifted until it was as red as the blood Malimokuru hoped would remain in his body after this fight was done.

He unconsciously backed away. He would never grow accustomed to the amahles' frightening transformation.

He returned his attention to the waiting demon. He had already mentally prepared himself with the incantations he believed would be effective, and had his pouch of sands ready. He reached a hand in, grasping a handful as he waited for whatever was to happen.

The two red amahle closed the distance, and as if they had crossed some imaginary boundary, the demon opened its hands, palms facing skyward, and drew in a bolt of electricity from the sky.

Just before the bolt reached the demon, it split in two and went into each hand. Malimokuru shielded his eyes from the dazzling light and instinctively dropped to the ground. His instincts saved him, for those same two bolts whipped through the air and would have slammed into him, had he still been standing. Despite not being hit, he felt the electricity coursing through his teeth, and his heartbeat was thrown off.

Naiyala and Sakhile had leapt over the blast, the latter letting fly an arrow that shot through the air and into the demon's shoulder. A growl was the only indication the missile had found its mark.

Right behind him, Naiyala hurled one of her spears. Her aim was just as true, and her spear found its mark in the center of its belly. The spear punched through its midsection and out of its back. The demon staggered, buzzing in what sounded like pain.

The two amahle warriors landed, hissing. Sakhile shot another arrow, his shot landing mere inches beside the first. He let fly a third and fourth, all landing near the previous. Naiyala launched her second spear, striking the fiend this time in the chest.

The demon staggered under the onslaught, and fell back a few steps, looking as if it were about to fall. A moment later, however, it straightened and narrowed its red eyes. Sparks of electricity coursed all over its body and several brilliant flashes of electrical light lit the darkened canyon. The arrows and spears imbedded in its body caught fire and disintegrated. The wounds began to close, and within a few heartbeats, it looked as if it had never been harmed.

It opened its mouth, showers of sparks bubbling out like foam. It raised a clawed hand, and arcs of lightning shot from each talon, racing through the air to slam into the two warriors. They were thrown back, past the crouching nature reader and hit the ground rolling and twitching while tendrils of smoke slithered from their bodies.

Once the spasms passed, Naiyala and Sakhile rose, their eyes glowing with rage. Malimokuru's mouth fell open at the sheer durability of the amahle. If he'd been struck by that electricity, he would have been burned to ashes on the spot, if not blown apart.

Reassured that his friends were okay, he drew his hand from the pouch and threw a handful of sand at the beast, yelling an incantation. Every grain of sand froze and elongated, slamming into the demon in a shower of razor-like shards. The demon grunted and shielded its face with its arms.

Malimokuru took a mental note of the reaction. He'd expected as much. Now, the question was could he generate enough power to do any real damage to the thing.

The thought hadn't finished in his mind before another rain of icy shards fell upon the demon and knocked it to the ground. It was quick to its feet, however, and sent an arc of electricity in the direction the shards had come from. It was a blind retort that yielded no result. It roared as one after another, six arrows struck its lower back. When it spun to face the new threat, another blast of icy shards hit it from behind.

While it was struggling to recover, Malimokuru sent a handful of sand spreading in the air and yelled another incantation. The sand clung together like an icy net and draped over the fiend.

The water mixed with electricity sent the monster into an agonized frenzy. It retaliated with a shockwave from its body that threw all five of combatants into the air. Malimokuru landed and rolled, sliding to a stop. His bones felt like they'd creaked from the impact, but he wasn't that old! No, he wasn't!

He groaned as he lifted himself up onto his elbows and squinted into the rain. There was something he didn't understand. The thing manipulated electricity, but it was raining, and electricity and water were a deadly mix. Why was it not affected by the rain, but by the ice shards? He had no time to contemplate it, for the demon pointed a clawed hand in his direction.

Malimokuru frantically rolled aside just as an arc of lightning blasted into the ground, charging a puddle of water and sending jolts of electricity through him. The jolt lifted him into the air. He never felt himself hit the ground, so busy was he convulsing.

Amata Daunyana called to Boraka and threw a wave of ice at the demon. Despite its body being jerked this way and that by the assault, the demon managed to hurl a bolt of lightning at her.

Ayanda let fly several more arrows even as the grunting Amata flew past him. The arrows, though enchanted by the Daunya Apprentice, were not enough to finish the beast, however. With a flap of its wings, it quickly closed the distance and slammed its shoulder into him. At the moment of impact, the fiend released a blast of electricity.

Ayanda flew back and crashed into a boulder. He gritted his fanged teeth against the convulsions.

Naiyala released the rage and shifted her hue to blend with the darkness. She sprinted in a round-about path to the demon. She reached into her sack of short spears and drew another. As she came around to its side, she darted in close and speared it in its left side. Before it could respond, she speared it three more times as she moved around to its back. It tried to turn and face her, but she was nearly impossible to see.

Sakhile followed the princess's lead and blended with the darkness. He sprinted toward the beast and let fly arrow after arrow. The demon, now assaulted from both amahle let out a screech of rage, and released another shockwave. As before, the blast scattered the attackers.

Naiyala landed in a puddle of water, which betrayed her position. The fiend sent an arc of electricity speeding into her. With the other hand, the demon blasted the still recovering Ayanda. The bolt launched him over the boulder.

Amata Daunyana hopped to her feet and leapt high into the air, drew her hands over her head, and whipped them downward. Every raindrop around her merged, froze, and changed direction. The ice shards zipped across the distance and punched into the demon's body.

The shards were too thick and too large to evaporate from the heat its body gave off. The water mixed with the electricity caused it a fair amount of damage.

Malimokuru nodded to himself. The raindrops evaporated before touching the thing, but the ice shards were cold enough that they penetrated the wave of heat its body emitted.

Amata landed and whipped her hands across her body, crisscrossing her arms. Again, every drop of rain around her sped into the demon, freezing into ice needles as they traveled.

That gave Malimokuru an idea. He reached into his pouch and drew as much sand as he could hold. He trotted toward the stunned fiend and threw the sands in a spreading motion, yelling an incantation. The sand grains combined and re-formed into a blanket of water that fell over the demon. Sparks and crackles lit the darkened area, and its inhumanly screech rent the air. The demon fell over onto its side, convulsing until it finally lay still, wisps of smoke wafting from its body. Malimokuru wrinkled his nose at the nauseating smell of burning demon flesh.

Ayanda crawled from behind the boulder, the others likewise gathering themselves.

Malimokuru wiped his face. By now, the rain had intensified into a deluge.

Sakhile looked around. The water was starting to rise. "The canyon is going to flood at this rate."

The truth of his words were easy to see. The low areas of the canyon were already filling with water.

The felled demon's body sparked once, then again, then once more, and then it was on its feet before anyone could react. It grabbed Sakhile by the neck and lifted him from the ground. The scout grabbed and scratched, but the demon had him in an iron grip.

Naiyala moved in fast and impaled the fiend in the stomach and through its back. With a growl of effort, she lifted the demon from its feet and swung it over her head, slamming it to the ground behind her. The monster never let go of Sakhile, and continued to squeeze the breath out of him. Naiyala's enchanted spear had done some damage, however, for the fiend was weakening.

"Sakhile!" she shouted, tossing him a spear.

The scout snatched the weapon out of the air and ran it through the demon's neck. It gurgled and finally let go. Upside down in midair, Ayanda glided over the demon's head, bow drawn, and let fly arrow after arrow as he arced over the fiend and landed on the other side of it. Naiyala launched another spear that took it in the back of the head.

Amata Daunyana, standing next to a large puddle of water, whipped her hands in an upward motion, sending the water rushing at the demon. As it flew, it formed into a long slender spear of ice that stabbed into its back, coming out through the abdomen.

Malimokuru reached into his pouch and whipped a small handful of sand over the beast, once again speaking the words that changed every granule into tiny ice needles.

The combined assault brought the demon to its knees. Naiyala rushed in as it struggled to stand. She grabbed one of the spears imbedded in the huge torso, and yanked it free. The amahle princess spun the spear over her head and whipped it sideways to slam in the side of the demon's head. The beast was again thrown from its feet.

Before it hit the ground, Naiyala was in the air, descending upon it. The princess roared as she drove the spear through its body and into the ground. She grabbed the other spear that had been pushed from its body when it hit, and drove it through the chest.

The sound the fiend made would have broken the nature reader's heart, had the beast not been the most unholy of creatures. It lay pinned to the earth, struggling to pull the two spears free. Ayanda knocked another arrow and drew, but Sakhile's upraised hand stopped him.

Amata Daunyan approached the fallen demon. She closed her eyes briefly, then opened them and focused her gaze on it. With an outstretched hand, fingers curled like claws, she spoke a word Malimokuru didn't recognize. The word crackled with energy, and wave of power erupted from the apprentice and pounded into the fiend. Its wailing faded along with its body, as the wave of light energy dissolved it into nothingness.

"That was not the light of Boraka," Malimokuru said, moving closer.

"It was the light of Se'lir. The quickest way to destroy a demon is with the love of Se'lir's light."

"You waited till now because you wanted a dramatic finale?" Malimokuru asked, his voice burning with sarcasm.

"To focus her light, one must first find at least a small measure of love within, to project without." Amata turned her piercing eyes on him. "How easy would you accomplish such a thing in the midst of battle, *abantu*?"

Malimokuru nodded and raised his hand in apology, again reminded that amahle did not always understand friendly sarcasm, or sarcasm at all, sometimes.

"We must leave now!" Sakhile yelled over the downpour. "This canyon is going to flood."

"It's already starting!" Ayanda pointed behind them in the direction they'd come. Water had collected and was now running along the ground, filling cracks and crevices. The group resumed their trek across the valley, jogging against the punishing wall of rain.

Malimokuru thanked the Gods that he had always been a healthy and active man. Though he was well into his sixties, he was still hale and able to keep a speedy pace for a fit human of half his age. He knew that his four friends were moving at what was a very slow pace to allow him to keep up. Malimokuru had seen with his own eyes that they could run down a horse, whether in a full sprint, or long distance.

He lowered his head and pushed on, squinting against the sheets of rain that had long since soaked through his clothes. *At least it's still warm.*

Malimokuru looked ahead at the rim of the valley and his heart sank. Those two winged things had not moved. In the chaos of battle he hadn't realized that the demon they'd just fought wasn't one of those two.

He'd just allowed himself to wonder if they might actually be statues, when they leapt from their positions, high into the air, and landed a short distance ahead. The ground vibrated with a heavy thud upon their landing. The two identical demons straightened. They looked large even from this distance, and Malimokuru judged them to be closer to ten feet tall than nine. It was difficult to make out any distinct features, but one thing was certain; they had no intention of letting the party pass.

37

The rocks and boulders and the valley wall passed in a blur as Naiyala and Sakhile sprinted toward the winged fiends. At the last instant, Naiyala crossed behind the slightly faster scout, who crossed in front of her. They lunged forward, each attacking the demon opposite them. This unexpected maneuver gained them a bit of surprise, and they were able to score a few blows before regrouping for another strike.

The fiends, caught off guard, grunted but seemed otherwise unaffected by the initial attack. The talons on their hands and feet elongated as they lunged forward. The fiery amahle dodged the attacks, baring their fangs as they countered with their spears. Naiyala impaled her enemy, withdrew the spear and impaled it again, once twice, a third time before the winged fiend could react.

It screeched as the enchanted weapon left burning wounds in its body. It slashed at her and she leapt away. With a snarl, it spread its wings and went after her, tackling the princess and carrying her higher into the air before arcing downward. With a thunderous report, they crashed into the earth.

* * *

After an impact that would have shattered the body of a human, the amahle female was hurt, but alive. Greash stood over her and drew his arm back, aiming razor sharp talons for a killing blow. Before his stroke fell, a blur of teeth and claws slammed into him with bone-jarring force. He went down in a tangle of wings and limbs, but was quick to his feet, looking for this new threat.

A lance of dark purple light blasted him in the chest and threw him into a cluster of boulders. Greash gnashed his teeth, trying to shrug off agonizing fire burning inside him. Another blast came and Greash recovered at the last moment. He spread his wings and leapt over it.

The demon opened his fanged mouth and roared an unearthly shockwave in the direction of the purple blast. He snarled in triumph when he saw a splash not far from where his attack hit.

Greash landed and felt over the barely visible prone figure until he found its neck. He grabbed hold and lifted the little pest off the ground. Greash squeezed until he heard a gasp, and the weak creature finally came into focus. It was a female with dull gray skin. She clutched his wrist, but her strength was already fading.

"Prepare for eternity."

He laughed as he squeezed, but his laughter faded when he felt warmth, then a burning sensation creep up his arm. Just as he realized what was happening, his arm felt as though it was being melted. With a furious bark, he dropped the amahle witch.

She gasped when hit the ground. Greash salivated as he raised his foot, ready to drive the talons on his toes straight through her skull. Once again, something slammed into him. Teeth and claws tore into his scaly armored flesh, sending spikes of pain through his body.

The attacker came into focus and Greash saw that it was the four-legged creature he'd seen following his quarry. He grabbed hold of it and hurled it off him. Greash looked down at his torn torso and growled. Despite the wounds already closing, it still hurt. He would rip that animal apart! He lifted his head just in time to see a wide set of jaws closing over his face.

* * *

Zkora's arms were riddled with slashes and holes where the little red nuisance was feathering him with arrow after stinging arrow. The wounds healed, but not nearly as quick as they were inflicted. And it *hurt*. Someone must have enchanted the weapon with Daunyanic power. If this little pest managed a well-aimed shot, he could be seriously wounded.

Zkora lashed out, and the amahle ducked as expected. He lifted his knee, scoring a glancing blow on his adversary's chin. The little red fleas were fast, he had to admit. Just as he moved in for the attack, five deep pinpricks of pain lit in his back. He turned in a circle, reaching futilely for the source. It was as though ice and fire were burning him at the same time. Something struck him in the side of the neck, and a fresh wave of agony lit like an icy inferno.

Zkora knelt and clutched the shaft of an arrow. Gritting his jagged teeth, he yanked the bolt free, tearing a substantial amount of flesh from his neck in the process. He threw his head back and howled in anguish.

An amahle rushed him again and impaled him through the chest, the force of the stab pushing him down. He could feel his essence being burned away as the enchanted weapon did its work inside him.

Rage built up inside. Zkora forced the red pest back until he was standing again. With a murderous snarl, he yanked the spear free and hurled it and the wielder over his shoulder. He heard another arrow whizzing toward him and at the last moment, slapped the bolt aside. He panted, pushing away the pain while he waited for his body to heal.

Through the roaring deluge, Zkora heard a soft footfall, then another. He tucked his head in, hiding the smile on his face while the tissue in his neck continued to knit. The amahle was smart, however, and didn't come within reach.

Fine. Zkora knelt and punched his hand into the ground. His arm merged with the earth and a dozen feet away, a large hand reached out of the ground and grabbed the elusive flea and pulled him under.

Zkora stood and yanked his arm out of the ground, clutching the now dull gray colored amahle in one hand. It hissed at him but was clearly weakening.

"What have we here?" Zkora grinned, revealing a row of sharp teeth and fangs. "A fragile little animal hides and attacks from behind." He lifted the amahle by the ankle until they were face to face, though the other was upside down.

"I've never tasted amahle flesh, though I hear it is quite tough. Perhaps I will need to tenderize you." He punched the little gray weakling in the stomach, blasting the wind from him. "I will rip your heart from your chest now, and when I have finished with your companions, I will return to finish your carcass."

The defiant little animal stabbed him in the leg with an arrow Zkora hadn't realized he held. Despite the fiery pain racing through his leg, the fiend lunged forward to bite out his victim's throat.

He stopped short when he felt little grains of sand cling to his body. He heard someone yell a phrase, and then his back was ablaze.

Zkora let the amahle go and screamed at the sky. Another blanket of that cursed sand hit him, followed by more intense burning.

Zkora saw the old human Greash had thought harmless. It was a mistake to ignore the little speck of a creature, but Zkora would correct that oversight now. He took a step toward the human, then stopped. Something caught the corner of his vision and he looked into the dark, rain filled sky just in time to see another amahle descending on him.

* * *

An instant before Sakhile was about to drive his spear into the demon's side, it looked up and saw him. With shocking speed it swatted his spear aside and struck him a solid palm to the chest. The wind flew from Sakhile's lungs with a single gasp.

He flew backwards, skidding and bouncing across the wet ground. Sakhile rolled onto his hands and knees, coughing and wheezing. The water was up to his wrists, now, and steadily rising. He looked up just in time to see the fiend whip out one of its wings and bat their human friend aside. Finishing the motion, it crouched and launched itself into the air.

Sakhile felt the ground vibrate as the demon landed beside him. He felt sharp talons bite into his leg as it yanked his feet from under him and lifted him up.

Everything passed in a blur As Sakhile went up in an arc, and back down. He shielded his head with his arms just before colliding with the ground. He ears rang from the impact and his vision blurred. Through his dizziness, he felt himself rising again. The rain pelted his face as he rose again in an arc. Sakhile barely had the presence of mind to cover his head again before he was slammed into the ground a second time.

He moaned, but even his own voice felt far away. Sakhile lay limp on the soaked earth, the demon's rasping breath grating over him as it clutched his throbbing leg.

"I know you amahle vermin are tough, but how much can you endure?" The demon lifted him again.

* * *

S akhile clenched his teeth together, partly to deny the pain, and partly to keep them from clicking together as the demon shook him. He reached over his shoulder, thinking to grab an arrow and drive it into the monster's midsection. The quiver was empty. In a final burst of strength, the scout curled his body upward and grabbed the demon's wrist. He sank his elongated fangs into its forearm.

It cursed and its grip loosened enough for Sakhile to yank his foot free. He spat the foul blood from his mouth with a curse. He had little time remaining before the enraged fiend gutted him on the spot. Sakhile kicked both his feet into its face with enough force to propel himself away.

He hit the ground hard and lay there, still trying to catch his breath. The pain in his shoulders and back was still fresh from the beating he'd just taken.

Malimokuru rushed to his side. "You alright, bwoy?"

With an effort, Sakhile propped himself up with an elbow. "I will survive, friend Malimokuru." He looked over his shoulder at the angry demon stalking toward them.

Sakhile watched Malimokuru slip his hand into a pouch at his waist. Once the demon was within range, he whipped his hand out.

The demon grinned and swiped a clawed hand outward, blowing the sands aside. It followed up with a swipe that sent a wave of fire slamming into them.

Sakhile howled, rolling in the mud and water, his skin singed. Malimokuru also rolled on the ground. They were lucky it was raining and water was beginning to rise. That last thought was alarming, for the water level in the valley was now ankle deep. Sakhile struggled to his feet and lunged at the fiend, only to be swatted aside as though he were a child.

The demon bared its fangs in a wider grin. "Your magic dust will not save you, human germ."

"You call me a germ?" Malimokuru retorted. "Walkin' filth wan call me a germ. Ya bom got much nerve talkin' at me with all tha stink ya trailin' behind you!"

"You speak a strange tongue, human. Maybe it will be clearer if I rip it out."

Malimokuru took a step back and slipped a hand into his pouch. The demon laughed and in the blink of an eye, it closed the distance between them and swatted him aside with a bone-jarring backhand that sent him flying. The world spun as Malimokuru flipped through the air. He hit the ground and heard something snap, and a wave of pain lanced through his shoulder just before he slipped into unconsciousness.

* * *

Sakhile struggled to rise as he watched the winged demon, laughing as it casually walked over to the unconscious Malimokuru. His strength would not come, but still he struggled to rise nonetheless. It didn't matter. Even if he could find his feet, Sakhile would not be able to reach the monster in time before it killed his human friend.

He watched as it lifted a foot armed with talons on each of its three toes. He growled under his breath, struggling to his feet, and stumbled forward. He knew he would be too late, but he had to try.

The fiend's back arched and it stumbled to the side. Sakhile's puzzlement was replaced with excitement, when Nyaka's large form shifted into focus.

The goar cat pounced onto the demon and savaged its back, gripping with its foreclaws while raking the rear. She tore right through the tough scale armor and into the vulnerable flesh underneath. The monster struggle to rise, all the while wailing in rage and agony.

Over eight hundred pounds of heavily muscled goar cat held it pinned to the ground, however, and continued to tear into its back. The demon tucked in a wing and thrust it sideways, finally dislodging the animal. Nyaka turned midair and landed on her feet. She sprang right back at the fiend as soon as she touched the ground.

The demon was quick back to its feet as though the deep gouges in its back were inconsequential. It spread its wings and arms, standing wide, waiting.

Nyaka skidded to a stop and stared at the waiting fiend. The demon tilted its head. "A smart one, are you?" Nyaka growled as she circled her target. The demon turned with her. "Perhaps you need some motivation." It started backing toward the unconscious nature reader.

Nyaka barked and hissed, lowering her body and stalking in closer. The muscles in her legs bunched as she crept ever closer. "That's it, animal. Come closer." Again the goar cat stopped as if waiting. "Very well," the demon said, moving again toward the human.

It had taken two steps when a spear took it from behind, passing through it's back and out of its chest. It let out an unearthly screech and spun toward its attacker with startling speed. It swung its arm down and pounded the surprised Ayanda to the ground. Still roaring, it picked him up and slammed him to the ground again, then a third time, then it lifted him and reared its arm back, then screeched again and dropped the unconscious Ayanda.

Nyaka bit down with enough force to crunch into the bone, then released and hopped back. She circled the demon, her wide perpetually grinning maw in an open snarl as she circled her enemy.

* * *

kora's ruined arm hung at his side as he turned to keep the cursed goar cat in sight. The limb was already mending, albeit painfully. And slowly. He needed to get that enchanted spear out of his body while he had the strength. Zkora could feel the cursed Daunyanic power sapping his life force. Every time he raised his hand to pull it free, the animal lunged at him. It was like the blasted animal knew what was happening.

Zkora stole a glance to his left to see the unthinkable. Greash was down to one knee, barely fending off two red amahle creatures. One was attempting to drive her spear into his throat, while the other was bombarding him with the power of Boraka, the purple light of the Daunya of Destruction glowing disgustingly through her body. And what had happened to his head? It looked like something massive had crushed it!

Zkora returned his gaze to the hissing goar cat. "I'm going to gut you slowly, animal—" As soon as the words left his mouth, the beast charged him. He waited, a hungry grin spreading across his face. His grin fell away when the goar cat faded from sight.

The demon squinted. He tried to listen, but the roar of the pounding rain was too loud to make out any distinct sounds.

Thinking the animal would have circled around to attack from behind, he spun, whipping a wing out as he did. The expected impact didn't happen, but after he had turned, the animal slammed into his back and sent him sprawling to the ground.

Zkora gnashed his teeth through the pain of talons ripping through his back. How could he have been outsmarted by an unthinking animal? It had waited for him to turn and then done what he'd expected and attacked from the back, only he had stupidly shown his—still healing—back to the wretched animal!

By the time Zkora had gotten to his knees, the goar cat had already jumped off. "Enough of this.". He tried to turn and lunge at the animal, but fell over. It was then, that the pain in his lower leg hit him. He looked back to see part of his leg ravaged and broken.

Taking his sight from the dangerous animal cost him. When he turned to see his leg, a thick barbed tail took him in the eyes. The power behind the blow snapped Zkora's head back and knocked him onto his side, the spear in his stomach preventing him from falling flat.

Blinded and enraged, the demon opened his mouth to shout his rage. An arrow took him in the mouth, and another in the throat.

Rage turned to desperation as the demon pulled at the shafts. The pain was like fire in his mouth and neck. He finally yanked the bolts free and a spear took him in the chest, then another in the midsection. All of these cursed weapons were enchanted with Daunyanic power!

Zkora spat a mouthful of black blood. He could heal himself if he could just get these enchanted shafts out of his body.

The goar cat slammed into him again and bit into the side of his neck. Powerful jaws crushed his neck just below the arrow shaft and it was gone again. It was like the blasted animal knew not to snap the bolt free!

Zkora choked on his own blood as he struggled to rise. He managed to snap the spear in his midsection and throat, and yanked the arrow out of his mouth. He spread his wings and hopped to his feet, crouching for a mighty leap.

Just as he began to rise into the air, an arrow passed through the membrane in his left wing, and in the same instant, that cursed goar cat had leaped with him, biting into his leg and grabbing hold with its claws.

Zkora screeched in frustration as the world spun and the ground rushed to meet him.

* * *

Greash struggled to heal his crushed head and torn wing. He could have easily overpowered the one that fought to drive the spear through his neck, but the witch burned him from behind with the power of the hated Boraka.

It was only by a stroke of luck that the witch had not the strength to channel enough of the Destroyer's power through her. If she'd been but a little stronger, Greash would have been burned from the world and sent back to the abyss; or simply obliterated.

The tip of the Daunya enchanted spear inched ever closer to his throat, and the assault from behind was steadily weakening him.

With a desperate burst of energy, the demon gave a great heave. He slung the female aside, and followed the motion through by extending his wing out.

He caught the witch fully and sent her sprawling. The fiery onslaught ceased, but it cost him.

His left wing touched the amahle woman while she was filled with the power of the destructive God. Greash screamed his agony at the heavens, his partially melted wing twitching at his side. A wound inflicted by a God would never heal. His wing was ruined!

Slowly, deliberately, the demon rose to his feet, the bones in his head cracking and reforming as they mended together. He turned his baleful glare on the amahle woman. "I will carefully dismember you, witch, before sending you to your Gods in pieces—"

A spear punched through his back and came out of his chest. He arched his back, howling as he spun around. The amahle held on to the spear and was still behind him. He grabbed the shaft and pulled it through, screeching at the burn, but pulling the woman close enough for him to reach behind his back and grab hold of her arm.

He yanked her around to face him, grabbed her by the body and lifted her high into the air. Snarling, he slammed her through the ankle-length water and into the soft wet ground. With a splash, he lifted her and slammed her again, then a third time.

Greash smiled as he held her under the water. To her credit, the fragile little pest kicked and scratched his arms, but her efforts were beginning to slow. Greash heard an echoing wail, followed by a ground shaking thud. He looked up to see his brother Zkora, rolling in a tangle of wings and bright blue fur as he fought to extricate himself from that troublesome animal.

A sharp pain in his side brought Greash's attention back to his own fight. He released the woman and clutched at the enchanted arrow that she had stabbed into his side.

Another painful blast of Daunyanic power slammed into him. The weight behind that blow was heavier than before, and sent him splashing to the ground.

Greash sloshed to his feet and bellowed through the pain as he yanked the arrow from his side. He crouched low and roared at the amahle witch. His voice sent a shockwave through the knee-deep water. The force of the shockwave combined with the water slammed into the troublesome woman and washed her far enough away that he need not worry about her until he finished off the defiant one at his feet.

When he looked down, however, the other female was gone. He didn't bother to look about. These pests could blend to their surroundings like no other vermin in this world, save the annoying animal Zkora fought. He concentrated his hearing through the roar of the downpour. After several moments passed and no attack came, he ventured a look in the distance. Zkora had injured the two stubborn amahle, but the feeble old human and his pet were taking a toll.

Greash realized his mistake. He and Zkora had watched this group fight the skelion, confident in the demon's bioelectrical abilities to make short work of them.

Not only had he and Zkora been wrong, but they had not felt or seen the witch use any power granted by Boraka. They'd known that he and Zkora were watching, and she must have held back, not channeling the God power, but simply manipulating the elements around her. Clever.

Greash growled deep in his throat. He and Zkora had attacked, and they had been ready with weapons infused by Godly power and a witch at their side. He'd underestimated them.

He crouched and spread his wings. Greash winced at the painful retort from his injury, but fortunately his left wing wasn't completely ruined. He might still be able to fly. With a mighty leap, Greash beat his wings and launched himself into the air. He'd barely begun his ascent when a white hot pain burned through his back and blasted out of his abdomen.

Greash didn't have to look down to know that the chameleon bitch had waited till he tried to fly, leapt with him and drove one of her cursed spears through his back! The pain was unbearable and his strength fled. His assent stopped, and all Greash could do was watch the rapid approach of the ground below.

* * *

Naiyala held on to the spear that she'd driven into the demon's back. Once again she let the battle rage take her. She reached down her thigh and drew a curved knife with a serrated edge. She clenched her teeth, baring her elongated fangs, and drove the knife to the hilt between the demon's shoulder blades. Its agonized wail fueled her rage. She yanked the knife free and stabbed again and again, riding the demon as it plummeted to the ground.

After at least a dozen strokes, she drew the blade back and stabbed it through the back of the neck. At the last possible instant when the spiraling fiend was right-side-up, she leaped from its back as it crashed in a magnificent splash.

Naiyala also landed with a splash in water that was ankle-deep not long ago. Tall though she was, the water was past her knees now.

She looked around for the others. The other demon had managed to free itself from Nyaka and trudged through the water to its twin. It lifted the other and yanked out the imbedded weapons. The winged monster draped its twin over its shoulder, crouched, the leapt into the air with a beat of its leathery wings. The dark sky and showering rain obscured her vision, and in seconds they had disappeared.

Naiyala's chest heaved as she took a deep, relieved breath. Her body ached in more places than she cared to consider, but time was short. She sloshed through the steadily rising water till she found Amata Daunyana, leaning against a rock. "Can you walk?"

"Yes, but some of my ribs are broken."

Naiyala sucked in her breath, but the apprentice waved away her concern. I have called upon the Daunyans to aid my healing. I believe I can climb."

Naiyala looked at their surroundings. It looked as though the small canyon was fast becoming a lake. As gently as she could manage, she slipped under the other woman's arm and supported her as they made for the nearest canyon wall. She spared a glance over her shoulder and saw that the others had gathered themselves up and were moving toward them. They looked no better off than she and Amata, though oddly enough, Malimokuru looked to be in the best shape of all, haggard though he was.

"I can climb without assistance," Amata Daunyana said, and her voice sounded a bit stronger. Together, they climbed side-by-side up the boulder-ridden wall, thankful not only that the large rocks provided easy handholds, but they remained embedded despite the wetness of the canyon wall. Through pain and exhaustion they climbed and rested.

They came to the final fifteen feet and stopped. The wall was steep and slippery, and there was no way to climb it. It was an easy jump, but Amata's injuries hadn't completely mended yet.

Amata saw the concern in her face and jerked her chin toward the cliff edge. "I will make it with your help. You go first."

With a nod, Naiyala leapt the final distance. Fresh hot pain shot through her injured back with the effort. As soon as she landed, Naiyala turned and lay on her stomach. She looked over the edge and reached her hand down.

Amata looked up at her, and for the span of a few heartbeats, they held each other's gaze. Amata broke eye contact and took a few deep breaths. She looked up again, her eyes asking if Naiyala was ready. "I am here and I see you!" Naiyala shouted over the deluge.

Amata gathered herself and took one last deep breath. She jumped, a high-pitched yelp escaping her lip as she stretched her body to its limit.

Naiyala strained to her limit and caught Amata's hand. Before Amata's momentum stopped, Naiyala pulled with all her strength and swung the other woman over the edge. There was no way for the apprentice to land softly, and Naiyala heard the expected thud and the pained grunt that followed. She rushed to Amata's side and tried to inspect her wounds.

Amata waved her away. "I am fine. See to the others, *Inkosazana*."

Without a word, Naiyala rushed to the rim of the canyon and looked over the edge. She was just in time to see Ayanda shoot up over the side to land gracefully on the safe high ground. He spun and moved back to the edge, much as she had done, and dropped to his stomach.

Naiyala rushed beside him. "Do you need help?"

"Only if you can get them to stop arguing," the young hunter said.

Naiyala peeked over the edge. The corner of her mouth twitched at the sight of friend Malimokuru, gesturing emphatically in their direction. She couldn't hear his words, but from the way his head darted and bobbed, she guessed he was more than a little hesitant about what Sakhile was suggesting. "He will toss him?"

"I do not believe a human can jump such a distance." Despite the situation, Naiyala chuckled. She returned her attention to the arguing pair and shouted down to them. When she had their attention, she pointed past them, huge chunks of the muddy valley wall were dislodging and falling away.

The pair stopped arguing. Malimokuru heaved a sigh and nodded to Sakhile, who looked up at Ayanda and Naiyala, who nodded. After a little more arguing and positioning, they finally moved into place and Sakhile set his feet. He clasped his fingers in front of him and squatted into position.

Malimokuru looked up at Naiyala and Ayanda. Even in the dark, rainy space between them she saw the anxiety in his face. He grabbed Sakhile's shoulders and put a foot in his cupped hands.

After a few practice bounces, he pushed off, and Sakhile added his own strength. The poor old human came shooting up toward them, screaming and flailing his arms and legs the whole way. Ayanda managed to grab hold of one of his waving arms and lifted him over. The hunter deposited Malimokuru on the ground as gently as he could. A few moments later, Sakhile came flying over the rim and landed in a roll, groaning and holding his injured shoulder.

"A broken down group we are," Ayanda said.

"An alive group we are," the shaken Malimokuru replied.

"There is shelter in those trees." Sakhile pointed past them to a patch of woods about a half mile away.

"Anything that will ease the pounding this rain is puttin' on my head is welcome," Malimokuru said.

The battered group dragged themselves toward the woods.

"I regret we weren't able to finish the battle decisively," Ayanda said.

"I've a feeling that will happen next time," Malimokuru replied. "One way or another."

"You think they will find us again?"

Malimokuru looked at the young hunter as though he were a nice naïve boy. "Count on it."

"We will be ready."

"Oh yes," the old man replied. "Oh yes."

"Why does it seem like everywhere we shortcut with you, we gotta travel through the demon realm to get there?"

Taliah threw Kenyatta an impatient look. "Unfortunately, demons make it their business to have access to every part of this dimension. They are able to do this because evil exists in our world."

"There is good, too," Kita said as they crept up a grassless hill overlooking barren and blasted lands beyond. "Why are there not as many passages through the heavens?"

Several braids fell over Taliah's face when she shook her head. "You don't understand. It's about vibration. The heavens, as you call them, are vibrating at a rate so fast that normal humans cannot consciously perceive it. That's why ascended loved ones are difficult for us to see from our existence in this plane. The faster the vibration, the lighter and more energetic and pure a spirit is.

"Contrast that with the demon realm. It vibrates at the slowest rate possible while the physical, or earth plane, exists in between the two.

"It is the powerful negative energy, here, that makes the demon realm so accessible."

They crested the hill and immediately dropped to the dry cracked ground. A demon easily double the size of an elephant wandered by. The beast was a dull brown and gray color, and though it looked slow of wit, the muscles that flexed beneath its ragged skin were big and hard.

"What was that?" Seung whispered. She stared wide-eyed after the lumbering behemoth, her hand absently straying toward the shaft of *Vyirayoi*.

"There are too many species of demon to name without making a study of them," Taliah answered, rising once the beast was far enough away.

"Intense negative energy is the main building block of the abysmal realm as we know it. It began with negative thoughts from the earliest humans. Anger, greed, jealousy. These things were the start, but it was not until evil spawned from these emotions that the abysmal realm and the denizens first came to be."

"So, you're saying that negative energy spawned from human conflict and ultimately started the creation of the hells and its inhabitants?" Kita shook his head. "How can that be possible?"

"You have the general idea, but not the entire grasp of it. There is a realm where all negative thoughts were once held."

Seung frowned. "How do you contain a thought?"

"Everything is made of energy," Taliah explained. They hid again as another hulking demon passed by, this one the two brothers were familiar with.

"That was a Zzrt," Kita whispered. "We're in the highest level of the hells are we not? This is where the weaker demons exist. That," he pointed after the departing fiend, "is a species of quentranzi. What's it doing here?"

"That's unusual," Taliah said. "I'll have to discuss it with Iel when I return."

"Please continue," Seung said, still staring after the Zzrt who was now almost out of sight. The red sky was covered by a ceiling of ominous brown clouds. An occasional bolt of black lightning scarred the sky, and winged horrors with long spindly limbs and clawed hands glided lazily overhead. Whatever they were, they looked big even from that distance.

"All things are made of energy," Taliah continued. Even our thoughts. How do you think all of creation came to be? How do you think Daunya Masters are able to channel the power of the Gods? They must first visualize it, then attune to it. It all starts with intent, and the mind leads the body. Energy is never destroyed; it only changes form."

"So, when a demon is utterly destroyed ..." Kenyatta said.

"It is not really destroyed, but simply transformed, and more easily absorbed by the loving light of the Daunyans, in which no evil can exist."

Kenyatta thought about a certain demon-hunting ninja with a sword that did more than "transform" a demon.

The charred remains of a patch of woodlands clawed its way toward the sky. Perched on the black branches, silver birds watched them with an unsettling intelligence in their crimson eyes.

"To answer your question, Seung," Taliah continued. You contain thoughts in your mind all the time. In humanity's infancy, negative energy in the form of thoughts and actions were contained in a dimension that is largely neutral and where such energy could be fed back into the light.

"As time passed, the potency of the energy, grew stronger. Given the nature of this plane, the negative energy gained advantage. The dimension that contained the negativity was and is still known by its ancient name, Neirvan.

"As the populations of The Four grew, conflicts began to happen most frequently among humans, I'm sorry to say. Because of this, the realm of Neirvan housed more and increasingly powerful negative energies. The energies began to take shape and develop awareness.

"The actions of humans, and the animosity of the others of the Four toward them exacerbated the problem. It grew so bad that Dreaph, guardian of Neirvan, found trouble containing the rapidly evolving malevolent energies.

"For a time he was able to keep the evil contained, forcing it to lower and lower levels of Neirvan until finally, the evil evolved into what we know of as demons.

"Overwhelmed but crafty, Dreaph was able to sense that some of these demons had a flicker of light in them. Grasping on to this hope, Dreaph managed to drain some of the evil from them and infuse them with light energy. These newly transformed creatures were the first of his forces created from the very evil he battled. Together they held the demons back and sealed away the five lowest levels of Neirvan, and destroyed the other three between what we know of as the five hells and the Neirvan as it exists now."

"This Dreaph," Kita said. "He destroyed three levels of a dimension?" Kita glanced at Kenyatta, who looked just as mystified.

"The guardian of Neirvan is not one given to chances," Taliah answered. "Extreme though his actions were, it is now impossible for demons to access Neirvan directly."

"Interesting," Kita said. "And with five hell realms to inhabit, demons started to spread?"

"The hellish realms themselves spawned the demons we know of today," Taliah replied. "Through all of time Dreaph keeps watch, and his small force stands with him."

"What are these creatures that stand with him?" Seung asked.

"They are the lyrghis. And they are neither good nor evil, but powerful and dangerous. I have heard accounts of humans who have attained a level of skill in which they were able to summon one to their side."

"Somehow I feel like that's not a good idea," Kita said, glancing at the sky as a group of Bachatttas flew overhead.

"Haven't seen the likes of those pesky things in a few years," Kenyatta remarked, following Kita's gaze. "Almost makes me wish I had a bow and arrow."

"What would you do with it?" Kita asked, still watching the winged creatures recede into the distance. "You couldn't hit a target the size of that Zzrt if it stood still for you."

"How do you know?"

"You don't even *own* a bow! Do you just talk to hear your voice; like a parrot?"

Kenyatta shoved Kita, who shoved him back. Taliah rolled her eyes and looked at Seung, who chuckled. "Now you know why I moved so far away," Taliah said to the other woman.

"They're cute," Seung said.

"You haven't spent enough time with them."

"What would happen if someone were to summon a lyrghis, but couldn't control it?" Seung asked, returning to the subject.

"None can control them," Taliah answered. "The summoner must have the will to lead a lyrghis. As to what would happen if the summoner was not strong enough, I don't know. I don't imagine it would be good."

"Best to leave stuff like that alone," Kenyatta said, and no one disagreed.

"How much farther do we have to go in this place?" Kita asked. The barren and blasted landscape was filled with every manner of undesirable creature that scurried, stalked, crawled, or flew. They'd seen trees grab up wolf-sized animals that wandered too close. They'd seen large monsters catch and devour smaller ones, and vice versa.

"Not much longer." Taliah said. "This route has taken us out of the way, but it is also farther away from a nest of winged demons you don't want to think about. Ever heard of a harpy?"

Kenyatta let his head hang back in exasperation. "Are you really telling me that harpies, exist? *Harpies?*"

"I'm telling you that there is a species of demon here that are exactly what human stories depicting harpies are based on." Taliah pointed to a vortex several hundred feet away. "That will transport us to the lands a few miles outside New Dainland."

"Then let's move it double time and be gone from here," Kita said.

"Walk quickly but do not run," Taliah warned. "We don't want any attention on us—" A massive red hand burst out of the ground. They stopped and backed away, Kenyatta drawing his swords as Kita and Seung brought their weapons to bear.

A huge red-skinned demon climbed out of the torn ground. Horns as thick as Kita's body curled down beside its jaws. Its thick muscled torso was covered in tiny black spikes and its long thick legs bent as it lowered itself to look down at the four diminutive humans.

"Come closer, little humans," it said. Its deep yet quiet voice sent a shiver down Kenyatta's spine. Another demon burst out of the ground beside them. This one was not as large, but it was tall and slender, covered with orange scales. It had horns as well, protruding from its forehead and curling back over its head.

"They think to travel to the fool King Dain," the demon said. Seung flinched at the sound of its raspy voice. She turned at the sound of yet another demon entering through a ball of fire that simply appeared, then broke apart when the fiery blue fiend stepped out.

"Little human fodder." A lava-like substance spilled from its mouth as it spoke. Thick substance plopped to the ground with a loud sizzle. "Barely enough to sate my appetite if I ate you all at once. There is nothing you can do to save a king who is already dead."

"These are quentranzi," Taliah said quietly to the others. "We need to find out why they're lurking here in Beezrah, the first hell."

"She wishes to take them back to the mortal realm," the fiend on their right cackled.

Kenyatta gritted his teeth. It sounded like metal tearing through metal.

"Let her try," the first demon replied. "How much power from your Gods can you channel through that fragile little body of yours?"

"Enough to burn you away," Taliah said, signaling for the others to gather closer.

"Which one do you want?" Kita asked Kenyatta.

"The one on the right."

"I've got the left."

"And what of me?" Seung asked. She tightened her grip on *Vyirayoi*. "Am I supposed to hide and watch?"

"You will all wait until I give you the signal," Taliah interrupted, "then you will run for the vortex."

"You speak like you won't be joining us," Kenyatta said.

"Of course I'll be joining you. There are only three—"

Four more demons of various sizes and shapes—all quentranzi—materialized around them.

"Okay, perhaps not."

"We're not leaving you here by yourself, so don't ask," Kenyatta said.

"You may not want to believe this, Ken, but these demons are not like the ones you faced over three years ago. They may well be beyond you."

"Impossible," Kenyatta said, hoping his words were true.

"We feast on them now," a demon said.

"Let them talk, first," another said. "Savor their fear.".

"Believe what you will," Taliah said to Kenyatta. A soft blue glow appeared around her body as though seeping from her pores. "Nonetheless, I will hold them while you reach the vortex." One of the fiends from behind approached, and Taliah turned and incinerated it with a wave of white light.

Three more took its place. "This was a trap I was not expecting."

His sister's even tone sent a chill through Kenyatta. He only heard it when she was angry and focused.

"They've known our plans for some time," she continued. "I will know how, and I will find out from one of them."

Kenyatta wanted to argue, but he dared not speak. Another demon, the biggest yet, appeared and exhaled a foul orange fire from its mouth into the vortex. The spiral twisted out of control, then changed into the same orange color.

"What did that thing do? Kenyatta ducked a whipping tail and countered with swipe of his sword as it passed overhead. Sparks flew from the impact but it dealt little damage.

"It corrupted the vortex," Taliah growled. "Enter it now and you would most likely be transported to the lowest level of the hells. I can't be certain, so don't go near it."

"Then what now?" Kita asked as he struck a nearby demon with his staff. It stumbled away, laughing.

Seung whirled *Vyirayoi* and struck a nearby demon in the leg. She skittered back out of reach before it caught her in the face with a snapping pincer. "Our weapons have no effect."

"This is their world." Taliah burned away another fiend. "They're stronger, here." She spun on her heel and sent the purple light of Boraka intertwined with the white light of Se'lir spiraling into the largest demons. The combined power lifted them into the air. They disintegrated before they hit the ground.

Taliah whipped her hand in front of the four warriors and the space around shifted. Rippling white light fell around them like a dome.

"You will not arrive in New Dainland, but you will not be too great a distance from it, I hope. It's the best I can manage without a vortex."

"Well then come on!" Kenyatta shouted." He could already feel himself being pulled away. A demon lunged at them but passed harmlessly through. Taliah blasted it apart. "You can't stay here by yourself! Taliah come on! We're not leaving—"

"Please, Kenyatta. Stop with the theatrics. I'll see you soon, but I need answers." She ducked the stab of a spear-tipped tail. The fiend curled its tail back and stabbed again.

Taliah made a casual gesture with one hand that burned the monster across the chest. It fell onto its side and a grotesque scream tore from its throat. "I'll have answers from one of these things and then I'll come to you." She dispatched two more demons before another three burst from the ground to confront her. The last thing they saw was Taliah surrounded by no less than thirty quentranzi. Kenyatta hollered and ran towards her.

He stopped and took in the new surroundings. With an effort he tried to slow his heartbeat, which was hammering in his chest.

Light shown from an opening high above, dimly lighting a place of stone from all around and underfoot.

"We're in a cave," Seung said.

"I don't see a way out," Kita replied. "There's only that pathway that leads into the dark."

Kenyatta stared off into the darkness ahead. A cold determination settled inside him. He started toward the tunnel. At the edge of the light he stopped and looked over his shoulder. "You coming?"

"You got night vision or something?" Kita asked.

"Doesn't matter. We'll find something that burns and light it."

"We don't know what's down there."

Seung's voice almost melted the ice inside him. Almost. "Doesn't matter. Whatever is down there will stay away and live, or not."

Kenyatta could feel the eyes of his companions on his back as he waded into the darkness. He held his swords in a white-knuckled grip. If he loosened his grip even for a moment, he feared so too would he lose his grip on the rage simmering inside.

They tore of bits of clothing and wrapped them around a few long pieces of wood they found scattered on the ground. Using spark and tinder, they lit their makeshift torches and descended into the darkness.

Brit did this. The muscles in Kenyatta's jaw started to ache from clenching his teeth. Logically he knew that Taliah was more likely to have survived that encounter than the three of them. But she was alone in the demon realm, surrounded by a force of quentranzi.

He took a deep breath and used his torch to illuminate the walls of the tunnel. They were smooth as though worked by expert hands.

Kenyatta narrowed his eyes as he peered into the darkness ahead. Someone had been tunneling down here.

39

The darkness was so thick it swallowed the meager light of their torches little more than an arm's length away.

Kita squinted into the blackness ahead. "I don't like this. We can't see in any direction. If something comes up on us, we wouldn't know until it's too late."

"Then we'll have to keep our ears open and trust our intuition." Kenyatta's voice was cold and matter-of-fact.

Kita switched places with Seung, moving to the middle of the group. He placed a gentle hand on his friend's shoulder. "You alright?"

Kenyatta heaved a sigh. "Not really. I can feel through our bond that she still lives, but did you see how many demons surrounded her before she sent us away? And I doubt there weren't more coming. If our weapons had been effective, we would still have been hard pressed to deal with that."

"She'll be fine," Kita said, not sure if he were trying to convince Kenyatta or himself. "She's tough. You said yourself that you don't truly know what she is capable of."

"Yeah man. But I can't feel too good about my sister surrounded by demons we couldn't kill, and in the demon realm, no doubt."

Speaking of which, we need to figure out what Brit's doing to have quentranzi roaming the first hell. I don't know much about the abyss, but it sounds like bad news to me."

"Food for thought once we find fresh air again," Kenyatta said, his tone carrying an air of finality.

Kita gave his friend's shoulder a final pat, then fell back. He and Seung shared a look as he moved past.

Good fortune was with them, as no threat presented itself and they were able to travel unmolested on a rocky path angling ever downward.

"Hold!" Seung whispered. "The tunnel comes to an end ahead. The space opens up."

"How do you know that?" Kenyatta asked, half turning to look at her.

"Have you seen these ears?" Seung replied, leaning her head toward him.

Kita smiled when he heard Kenyatta chuckle. When Ken was in a rare dark mood, little could break him out of it. He watched Seung elbow him in the ribs, forcing a bit more laughter. They were good for each other.

"If we didn't have these torches I could grasp our environment better," Seung went on. "I can't explain it."

Kenyatta shrugged. "If you can feel your way through here better than us, take the lead."

"It wasn't so much what I heard," Seung said as she moved out ahead. "But that the sound is no longer closed in. Until now, the crunching of gravel under our feet bounced off the walls. It was closed in. Now, the sound travels away from us. We're coming to a big opening."

They moved at a slower pace, picking their steps with more care. After another fifty feet, Seung pulled them to a stop, then closed her eyes.

She picked up a stone and tossed it low to the ground. It bounced a few times then ... nothing. "Long drop in front of us. Hopefully there's a path around it."

They crept forward and, as Seung had indicated, the path ended about a dozen feet beyond the mouth of the tunnel.

"By the Daunyans," she breathed. A village could easily fit in here."

"I don't like the look of that." Kita pointed at the pathways that criss-crossed the yawning black pit that dominated the area.

Kenyatta inspected one of the many sconces casing their dull light along the wall of the massive circular chamber. "Who built this? And why the pit?"

"I don't suppose those torches lit themselves," Kita said. "What do we make of this?"

"These pathways are maintained," Seung added. "They're not as rocky as the tunnel we just traveled."

Kenyatta eyed the place and scratched his head. "A bigger question is who could or would want to live down here? We've traveled at least a mile, steadily moving downward. We're under a mountain."

"You think we're under a mountain?" Seung sounded as if she could barely breathe.

"Makes sense," Kenyatta said absently, staring at the stalactites hanging like fangs high above. "I've been through a number of caves in my time, but this is different."

"Not another mountain. I'd hoped never to see the inside of another mountain for the rest of my life."

Kenyatta's brow creased with concern. "You okay?"

"I'm fine."

She wasn't, but Kenyatta wasn't about to press her. "Look there." He pointed toward the far end of the chasm. "There's another tunnel down there."

"And over there." Kita pointed to the right.

Kenyatta looked from one path to the other, analyzing them all as if a solution would present itself. "I wouldn't mind a map right now."

"Let's just chose and get moving," Seung said. "We're not provisioned for a lengthy stay inside a mountain."

"I don't know for sure, but I don't think it will come to that." Kenyatta started down the path that encircled the pit. "Taliah sent us here in desperation because she didn't have time to think where to send us. I do know that she is never without her wits on any situation. If she sent us here, it's because she's at least familiar with the location and she knew we'd have a good chance of making it out. I'm guessing we're in New Dainland."

"Or rather, under one of its mountains," Seung said dryly.

The flickering light cast by the torches created a grim ambience to the large open space. The twisted, stretching shadows of the stalactites danced in the light like devious caricatures of their physical counterparts. "I guess we should feel fortunate that nothing has found us," Seung said.

"I don't want to imagine what lives down here," Kenyatta said.

Kita wiped the back of his hand over his brow. The farther down they descended, the more stale and thick the air became. "Whatever might live here, I would just as soon leave it undisturbed."

Seung nodded. "I've not the heart for another lava leach, or basilisk, or whatever surprises from the world of legend might be lurking in this hole."

Kenyatta pointed at the diverging paths. "Which one?"

"Maybe the far side of the pit," Kita offered. Kenyatta shrugged, and Seung offered a noncommittal grunt. "The far side it is," he said with artificial cheer.

"Who could live here?" Seung wondered aloud as they made their way down the circuitous pathway. "We are far below the surface."

Kenyatta shrugged again. "Judging from the smoothness of the tunnel, these pathways, and the sconces, they must be human-like, at the least."

"But why? The darkness and still, stale air and being surrounded by rock is oppressive. I can't wait to be out."

"Hopefully one of these tunnels will start to head upwards," Kenyatta said. "And soon. My head is starting to sweat."

"I think I've got a blade in my pack if you want to shave off those locks," Kita suggested.

"Come near me with it."

They came to the tunnel on the far side of the pit and peered inside. To their relief the tunnel was lit with more wall sconces, different in design than the ones they'd left behind.

"I don't think I like this." Seung peered into the dimly lit corridor. "Intelligent or not, I can only think evil things would want to live down in this darkness."

"We don't know for sure they're evil," Kenyatta replied. "Whoever they are, you can't judge them because they live under a mountain."

"What good has ever come of our encounters beneath the surface of the world? Back in the Rainlands, we traveled under the mountain range you passed over, and were attacked by dog-sized scorpions, only to escape them by stumbling into a *flesh forge*."

Kenyatta saw her wince at just mentioning that. Likely Seung had just thrust herself back into the memory of her friend, Nuviel Titika, taken from them by the evil of the Scorpion Lord, to then be saved by Nakiya, the Daunya Child.

She'd told him of her gentle and kindhearted friend, now dancing with Nakiya among the Daunyans. He rested a hand on her shoulder and gave it a squeeze.

Seung placed her hand on top of his, but her face was still hard as she relived the memories. "What of our confrontation underneath the Sentinels? Those mountains housed not only the lava leech that took your Jabulani, and our Alurien MerTana, but a Daunyarka lives there. A *dragon*. It was by luck that you traveled with Darius or we would have died before we could convince Khairon that we were not enemies."

"That's true, but you've just proved the point. Rash though Khairon was, he turned out not to be evil, but blinded by his mistrust."

"I'm sure that would have sounded good on our epitaphs," Seung muttered.

The tunnel opened into a rotunda. Five floor-to-ceiling pillars stood equidistant in a square. Two additional pillars stood close together in the middle of the other five.

* * *

"What in the name of Se'lir?" Seung breathed. She leaned closer to marvel at one of the many intricately chiseled walls. Although the hard lines and edges of the runes and artistic images clashed with her elven sensibilities, they were undeniably beautiful. In a sturdy, hard kind of way.

"These images have been crafted to perfection," Kita said, his voice filled with awe as he ran a hand over the depiction of a rather short, stout warrior with a huge beard hoisting an impressive axe over his head.

"Funny you should mention Se'lir," Kenyatta said. "Based on what you've told me, isn't this her right here?"

Seung looked at the middle pillar in front of Kenyatta. "It is," she gasped. "But how? Where are we?"

"Every one of these pillars has an image of these Daunyans you've spoken about," Kita said as he inspected another pillar.

Seung moved from one pillar to the next, her face lighting up with each discovery. "Of course! Each pillar is crafted in the image of one of The Seven! Se'lir, Quel'yar, Nakiya, Boraka, and Oberon. Their pillars surround Amayilah and Omalah, the Daunyans of Creation and Spirit."

"Well, if these are the Daunyans, we can rule out the possibility that humans live here," Kita said. "Humankind still doesn't know of the existence of these Gods."

"It's still possible," Seung replied. "There are small factions that have kept the knowledge of the true Gods. This could be a lair, or place of meeting."

"Mmm. I doubt it," Kenyatta said. "I can't imagine any human thinking it necessary to tunnel this far into the earth for any reason."

"Oh no?" Seung raised an eyebrow. "Haven't been studying your history, I see." She ran a hand over the lifelike image of Oberon, set within the pillar. "Do you not know of the need for underground dwellings that were built beneath the surface when the possibility of men killing the earth was very real?

271

"Humans had crafted weapons that would not only scorch the world, but poison the air for decades; a century. They built underground dwellings to escape whatever fate they would have faced in breathing the contaminated air."

"I know the history," Kenyatta replied soberly. "But I doubt they would have gone to the trouble of crafting such masterful art as this." He spread his hands to encompass the room. "And no human who knew of the existence of the Daunyans would have been a part of the events that almost killed the world."

"No," Seung Agreed. "They would have created all this to escape mankind's fate."

"This is amazing work," Kita said, still marveling at the hand carved mural on the wall. "Whoever did this, I'd sure like to meet—"

"Shush!" Seung stared at the floor for a moment, then spoke again, though no sound came from her lips. *"Do you hear that?"*

When no response came, she turned to see a confused Kenyatta and a startled Kita. She gave him an apologetic look. She'd forgotten she'd never spoken to him using the *whisper*. *"My apologies, Kita. I will explain this later. Do you hear that sound?"*

Lacking the necessary vocal anatomy to respond in kind, Kita shook his head.

"It's coming from that way." Seung pointed to the left tunnel of the three on the opposite end of the rotunda.

"I don't hear anything," Kenyatta audibly whispered. "I think those beautiful ears of yours hear better than ours, love."

Seung rolled her eyes, though her cheeks did color a bit. "Let's go see who's down there."

"Or we could avoid whoever it is and continue on," Kita suggested.

"They pray to the Daunyans," Seung said. "I doubt they're enemies."

"Praying to the right God doesn't always mean right action."

"You're both right," Kenyatta said. "But I agree with checking it out. We could creep around in the dark for who knows how long, or we could take a chance and maybe meet someone who can show us the way out."

* * *

"I still don't hear anything," Kita whispered in the gradually encroaching darkness. "Argh." He rubbed the back of his head. "Why is it so low down here?" The trio nearly had to bend themselves in half to navigate the low-ceilinged tunnel.

"You will hear," Seung replied as she led the way ever downward. "It's getting louder."

"I think I hear something now," Kenyatta said just as Seung called for a halt.

Kita dropped to one knee and touched the ground. "You guys feel that? Vibrations."

"Yeah man," Kenyatta replied. Like from a drum."

"So, what then?" Seung asked. "A band comes all the way down here to make music?"

"Only one way to find out."

"I hope they're playing by torchlight," Kita said. "We're about to turn another corner and the light from that room will be gone."

They rounded yet another corner to see the flickering glow of torchlight at the end of the path, a few dozen feet ahead.

Kenyatta and Kita signaled to Seung that they now heard it; the rhythmic pounding of what were undoubtedly large drums. They moved to the corner and peeked around.

Kita's mouth fell open as he gaped at the scene before him. "What in the name of the Gods?"

40

Liu Xiang pushed down his irritation at having to wait on Qian Hua's messenger. He never had the mind for such formalities and would much rather have met the man in his own private study, or even out in the throng walking and speaking freely.

He sighed. It could never be this way, at least, not with Qian. If he met on such familiar terms with a simple messenger, the man would report back, and Qian would interpret it as a sign of weakness and ill breeding.

No. He must adhere to the proper formalities and look down upon the man who was no doubt coming to issue his ruler's demand for Xiang's immediate surrender of not only himself, but his beloved Shu Han. Xiang bristled with indignation at the very thought of it.

To his right, General Zhang Da stood erect and radiating a fury Xiang could not approach. "Why does the fool persist with this nonsense?" Zhang's deep voice boomed through the attendance hall. "He intends to take Shu Han. Why go through all the trouble of pretending to come here in peace, then claiming that one of your guests attempted to assassinate him? It makes no sense."

To Xiang's left, Guan Xi harrumphed. "You expect logic from that one? Ever has he been an itch that needed to be scratched."

Xiang shook his head. "We've spoken about this. Illogical he may be, but Qian has never played his hand until now. No matter how shallow it seems, he now has a justifiable motive for attacking Wuhan.

"If you'd wanted to assassinate him, why would you have allowed him to leave?" Zhang Da said.

"We can question the unusual wit of Qian till twilight," Guan Xi said. "It doesn't change the situation, and in this case, the truth would hardly matter if he succeeds. I suspect the posturing was little more than a way to get himself and his men into the city to have a look around. Once he has Wuhan, he can craft whatever story he wishes. Who would contradict him?"

"General Guan is right." Akemi strode into the hall between her samurai brother and the strider. "As long as he gave the appearance of coming here in good spirit, the truth matters little. I wouldn't be surprised if his reinforcements are closer than you think, and that he left another force in Zhao to ensure that no aid comes from the empress."

Zhang Da's frown deepened. "You suggest he has Empress Zhao under siege as well?"

"He may have her under siege by way of having his men there under some façade, forcing the empress to entertain them. Either way, she may well have "guests" she can't slip by." Akemi looked from the emperor to his two generals and grinned.

Guan Xi arched an eyebrow at her." You find something amusing, Ninja?"

That one had fire in her eyes. Where Zhang Da was carefully controlled fury, Guan Xi was calm and civil with a hidden passion that drove her blade into her enemies. Akemi could feel it wafting off of the woman. She'd have made a great demon hunter. "Not amusing, but exhilarating that I battle alongside legends reborn."

"I would have you here when the messenger arrives," Xiang stated. "Once this business is done we will need to move quickly." No sooner had the words left his mouth than one of his attendants came through the door to announce the messenger, who shoved the attendant aside as he entered. Liu Xiang stifled indignant fury at the open disrespect. The messenger was flanked by four guards. Xiang gave a barely perceptible nod to his own guards who closed the doors, two remaining within."

"I have no time or patience for your town crier to speak my appearance, Liu. I'm here to deliver my terms and be gone from this pla—"

His last word was severed as abruptly as his head, which toppled to the floor. Everyone in the room stood frozen in shock. Akemi had leapt from the dais and passed beside the messenger to slide to a stop behind him. One of her blades was stained with the man's blood.

Liu Xiang stared at the ninja. How could a human being be so fast?"

There was a collective gasp, then the four soldiers accompanying the messenger reached for their weapons and were immediately surrounded by the two guards and Kenjiro and Shinobu. Slowly, they removed their hands from their weapons.

"What is the meaning of this?" Liu Xiang was on his feet, barely containing his fury. "Who gave you leave to murder a messenger in my own court—"

"My apologies, Emperor," Akemi interrupted. "But what remained of that messenger was beyond redemption."

"What ..." Liu Xiang sputtered, but Guan Xi placed a hand on his shoulder and pointed to the headless corpse. Liu Xiang's eyes widened in horror as he watched a translucent, vaporous creature seep out of the neck. It threw its head back and its mouth opened in a silent scream as it evaporated into nothingness.

"What did I just see?" Xiang tore his gaze away from the grisly remains and looked at Akemi. "What was that?"

"The death of a *seaph*," the ninja replied. "If he had been permitted to leave, you would have been infested with demon inhabited corpses shortly after."

"And what of them?" Zhang Da asked, stalking toward the soldiers. They shrank away from the general, looking from him to the corpse.

"They are human."

Liu Xiang addressed his guards. "Take them to the dungeons," Liu Xiang ordered his guards. "And not a word of this to anyone but the other two who will accompany you. I will have them aware of the situation."

Qian's shaken soldiers were rounded up, relieved of their weapons, and hustled out of the hall.

"Send for my sword and armor!" Xiang turned to Akemi. "It appears I owe you an apology and my thanks, Ninja Demon Huntress."

"Your apology is not needed, and your gratitude is appreciated, Emperor. But we must act quickly. If Qian sent one juvenile *seaph* into your midst, his attack is imminent."

Moments later, four attendants rushed into the audience hall and began fitting the emperor into his armor. Moments later, Shi Xing Long and his companion were announced. They arrived in loose-fitting orange pants, their shins wrapped with black, crisscrossed strips of cloth. On their torsos, they wore a simple vest of light cloth tied at the waist with a black sash.

Liu Xiang nodded to them. "I would ask the purpose for your visit, good monks, though my heart hopes for a specific answer."

"We come to fight alongside the emperor of Shu Han," Shi Xing Long replied.

"How many do you number?"

"Myself and my protégé, my lord."

Liu Xiang felt his surge of hope fade. "Only two of you?"

"My lord." The monks bowed deep. "I believe you will find us helpful."

"Helpful?" Zhang Da guffawed. "I—"

Guan Xi looked past Liu Xiang and made eye-contact with Da before he could get a full head of steam. He quieted, but his features remained tight.

The doors to the hall opened to admit one of the two remaining guards. "My lord. It's starting."

41

From atop the battlements they watched Qian's advancing force, which was far larger than it had been when he'd first arrived.

Liu Xiang's mind went to the soldiers he'd dispatched to scout for the coming force.

As though reading his thoughts, General Qian Ning rode to the front of the army and stopped just outside of bow range.

"Liu Xiang!" he shouted. "You lost these in the woods! We found them for you!" He tossed a wool sack out in front of him to land with a thud on the ground. With a smug grin, he turned and rode back to the battle line.

After the general had gone, a soldier was sent out to retrieve the sack. Moments later, the expected report came. The sack contained the heads of six of his men. Liu Xiang felt several emotions at once; sadness at the death of his men, elation that not all of them had been caught and killed, and anger that they had been treated in so dishonorable a fashion.

"My lord?" Zhang Da asked, in a strangled voice, clearly struggling to contain his fury.

"Any word from Xiaoyin?"

"None," Da replied. "But it's hardly unexpected. "The last thing we need is for one of Empress Xiaoyu's messengers to be caught moving in this direction."

Liu Xiang nodded. His friend was right, but he wished he knew if Zhuge Xiaoyin had made it safely to Zhao. If the ninja was correct and Qian had a force there, she could be caught.

A lone figure rode into the clearing. Xiang frowned in confusion. Qian Hua seemed to have grown in the past two days, and there was a sense of wrongness about him that the emperor couldn't place.

Xiang beckoned Akemi to his side. "What am I looking at?"

"What you see," Akemi said, "is the body of Warlord Qian Hua, now fully inhabited by the lower-class demon he originally agreed to share his body with. It has gradually consumed him over time. Now it alone inhabits Qian's body while retaining his memories and intellect. What you see below is no longer Qian Hua."

Liu Xiang fought to contain his revulsion. "And of course, no one else knows this, so for the sake of appearance—"

"You are battling Warlord Qian, whom I have apparently attempted to assassinate."

"Of course." Xiang ran hand over his face and looked up at the sky. Clouds were drifting in from the north and the smell of rain was in the air.

"Xiang!" the *seaph* warlord bellowed. "Your cowardly actions have stripped you of the honor of your title and the influence of your station. You have murdered my messenger and his escort. Step forth from your gates like a man, and your city will be spared. Resist me and I will crush you without mercy."

Liu Xiang wondered how this thing knew the messenger had been slain. "Spare me your theatrics! I don't know what you've become, but I suspect your men would distance themselves from you should they see what you truly are."

The warlord narrowed his eyes and a flicker of red passed across his pupils. Even from atop the walls, they saw it. "In the name of the Gods," Zhang Da breathed. "It is true, then."

Akemi rolled her eyes. "Yes yes, it's all true, General. We must get on with this. Your good warlord down there draws this out because he has time, and because the longer a *seaph* is allowed to mature, the stronger its fledglings become. We must strike now."

Kenjiro moved beside Zhang Da. "Akemi knows demons better than anyone. We must act quickly. What you see is only the beginning of what's out there."

"When night comes," Akemi added, "you'll like this business even less, I assure you."

"So be it." Zhang Da turned to Liu Xiang, who nodded. He turned back to Kenjiro "I want you with me. You, Strider. You have a place with Xiao Fu, my Second." Shinobu inclined his head. "Ninja. I suspect you have your own way of doing things, given the nature of your station. I wish you luck and good hunting. Bring the bastard down. We'll see you on the field."

Akemi nodded and winked at him, then Kenjiro, and headed in the opposite direction as Shinobu.

"Where's she going?" Guan Xi asked as she watched the ninja go. "There's nothing but trees to that side of the walls."

"My whole life I have fought beside my sister and still I cannot explain her methods. Just trust that you will find her wherever that thing is." Kenjiro pointed at the warlord, who casually turned his horse around and walked back to the battle line.

"She's going to have a time of it trying to wade through that force to get to him."

"Anyone who tries to stop her will die. My only concern is this warlord. I've never encountered a *seaph* before, but from the stories Akemi has told me, they are nasty creatures when fully developed."

"Duly noted," Liu Xiang replied. "General Zhang Da. Deploy your forces at the rear of the city. By the time they come around from the west, the battle will have commenced. Have the archers and crossbowmen ready."

"Yes, my lord." The general dispatched a soldier to relay his orders.

"And so it begins," Liu Xiang lamented. "Generations of peace without bloodshed, and it all ends today."

* * *

Xiao Fu was a man of small physical stature, yet he exuded the confidence of a seasoned commander. Shinobu took in the state of Xiao Fu's company; some two hundred soldiers. They were spoiling for a fight. "Your men are eager."

"You don't know Qian," Xiao Fu replied.

They watched the advancing regimen led by Zhang Da, the grim general's face as hard as stone. "Ever has that man been a mosquito, buzzing around to find a vulnerable spot to bite. His brazenness is an offense to Shu Han. For years General Zhang has longed to put this rabid dog down. Only political posturing has prevented it till now."

As the captain spoke, Qian and Zhang's forces met. The sound of battle cries, clanging steel, and dying soldiers filled their ears. Shinobu felt a chill settle in the pit of his stomach. If what Akemi said was true, the bodies of the dying would fight again. He reached over his shoulder and felt the reassuring presence of the hilt of his sword.

"Easy, warrior," Xiao Fu said, misunderstanding the strider's gesture. "You'll get your chance soon enough. There's plenty for us all."

"More than you realize," Shinobu muttered under his breath.

Atop his powerful warhorse, Zhang Da rode across their line of sight. Few in his path were quick enough to escape the swing and stab of his spear. The sheer power of the man was startling.

Two men grabbed hold of Zhang's spear and tried to wrench it from his grasp. The general pulled back with such force that one of the men lost his grip and fell.

With a great roar, Zhang Da lifted the other unlucky soldier and hosted him over his head. Shinobu could only nod in admiration.

Xiao Fu grinned. "You admire the prowess of our mighty general."

"How could I not?"

General Zhang swatted two men away, then speared a third. He yanked his weapon free, then reversed the attack to impale yet another soldier creeping up from behind. His horse reared and clubbed an enemy soldier in the head with iron shod hooves. The man crumbled to the ground.

As soon as his horse reared, Zhang whipped his spear in an arc behind him, slashing several enemies at once.

Shinobu whistled through his teeth. The movement between horse and rider was perfect; the benefit of years of training and battle together.

"Draw swords!" From astride his mount, Xiao Fu looked down at Shinobu. "Are you ready, foreigner?"

Shinobu ran his fingers along the hilt of his sword again. He knew better than to draw the weapon so soon. *"The abyss swirls, my companion,"* the sword spoke into his mind. He visibly flinched, drawing a questioning look from Xiao Fu which he ignored. Though he'd carried the mysterious weapon for some years, now. It rarely spoke, which made the rare occasions it did, startling. *"Denizens of the demon realm wait eagerly to inhabit these who so willingly provide them vessels."*

"How do you know this?" Shinobu asked. The only response he received was amusement. How could an inanimate object actually have awareness? He shook his head and focused back on the battle.

"Are you well?" Xiao Fu asked.

Shinobu glanced up at the captain, who looked back at him with uncertainty. "I'm fine. Just a few thoughts."

Xiao Fu grunted and returned his attention to the battlefield. "It's time."

"See you when it's done," Shinobu said.

"That is my hope, strange warrior." Xiao Fu thrust his sword toward the battlefield. With a great bellow, the two hundred-strong force charged. Shinobu moved with them, keeping his body lower to the ground. As soon as the opportunity presented itself, he veered away from the regimen. Striders did not fight in large masses of bodies, but alone or spaced from each other.

Shinobu cut a path of death a comfortable distance from Xiao Fu's immediate force, then went about his work.

A spearman thrust his weapon for Shinobu's abdomen. He spun to the side and grabbed the weapon with his left hand. He continued his turn, drew his sword in one motion, and cut the man down. He had replaced the sword to its sheath before the soldier hit the ground.

Two more approached and he turned to meet them, hand hovering over the hilt. "This one thinks he's good enough not to draw his—" the man's words ended in a gurgle. Shinobu whipped his sword out in an arc across his throat and replaced it before the soldier's hands rose to clasp the mortal wound.

The second soldier backed away, fear bright in his eyes. The tip of a sword thrust through his abdomen and he fell to the ground. One of Xiao Fu's men gave Shinobu a grim nod and turned away.

"Killing demons is far more satisfying," Shinobu muttered to himself. It was then that he realized no one else came to challenge him. *Odd.*

He turned at the sound of heavy footfalls and craned his head back as he took in the full size of a new enemy.

* * *

Astride his horse, Zhang Da was a force of destruction amidst the Qian soldiers. Inspired by the general's courage, Zhang's forces pressed Qian ever harder. Liu Xiang felt his own spirit surge when near the fearless general. With every strike, every thrust, every roar of defiance, Da more resembled his ancestor. In moments, Liu Xiang saw in his friend the spirit of the mighty Zhang Fei. Woe to his enemies.

A soldier arrived beside Xiang's mount and executed a precise bow. "My lord. Captain Xiao Fu has taken the field even as we push Qian's forces further back. At the rate the battle progresses, we'll have Qian in hand within the day."

Liu Xiang studied the battlefield. It seemed true enough. "What is your name, soldier?" he asked without taking his eyes from the battle.

"Cao Wei, my lord."

Xiang nodded. Cao Wei. He wondered if this young soldier was of any relation to the intelligent but traitorous Cao Cao, who had proven to be the greatest and most dangerous enemy of the Three Brothers. How ironic it would be, if Cao Cao's own descendant now fought alongside Liu Bei's, as Cao himself once had before his betrayal. The coincidence seemed too great, but then, Xiang had learned many times that the Gods were not without a sense of humor.

"Learn this lesson well, Cao Wei. The tide of a battle can turn quickly. This snake has two heads. Until both have been severed, the snake is still able to strike a deadly blow. Your report is noted."

Cao Wei bowed deeply. "I will remember your lesson, my lord."

Xiang stared after the departing soldier. He hoped the boy would survive for his own sake of course, but it might be interesting to learn about Cao Wei's lineage.

A horn sounded from north east of their position, wrenching Xiang's attention back to the battle. The horn sounded again, and a contingent of what he guessed to be about hundred men streamed over the hillside, swords and spears held high. Though he'd expected Qian to have reinforcements, it was still a troubling sight.

Liu Xiang drew his sword, and his regiment drew with him. With a roar from deep in his belly, Xiang thrust his sword forward and urged his mount into motion.

The roar of countless hooves thundering onto the field was deafening. Time seemed to slow to a crawl the instant before Liu Xiang's force met the enemy. The moment lingered for an eternity and a heartbeat at once, then time caught up, and the forces collided in a chaotic medley of death.

* * *

Zhang Da fought at the head of his force and cut a bloody path Qian's ranks. He worked his way to the right, then arced forward, fighting his way to Qian's flank as Guan Xi moved at the forward position. He had started out side by side with Guan, then left her to push ahead while he pushed from the side. Now they had formed an L-shaped thrust to drive Qian's forces tighter in on themselves. They had begun to give ground toward the east when Xiao Fu took the field. They had Qian effectively boxed in from three sides. It was early in the fight and all seemed to be going well, which sounded a warning in the seasoned general's mind.

As if his thoughts were made manifest, a horn sounded and a force of at least five hundred soldiers poured over the north eastern hill at the back of

Xiao Fu's regiment. To his credit, Captain Xiao Fu pivoted quickly to meet this new threat. He wouldn't hold, though, for he now fought on two fronts, pressed in between Qian's forces.

Zhang Da considered breaking off to aid Xiao Fu when the Liu Xiang arrived. The emperor's force was like a wall that slammed straight into the thick of Qian's ambush.

Several Qian soldiers broke through Da's ranks and charged him. Zhang Da spun his horse about and whipped his spear in a blinding arc. He took one soldier across the throat, instantly taking him out of the fight. The shaft of his spear bent, as Da quickly reversed the motion and snapped it back. The side of the iron spearhead smacked the second soldier in the side of the head. Zhang had already stabbed the third Qian soldier even as his previous victim crumbled to the ground.

The metallic smell of blood and the thickness of sweat—both man and beast—filled his nostrils, and he took it in, swimming in his own personal sea of revulsion.

Across the battlefield Guan Xi worked her way toward Liu Xiang, but her forces were pressed by Qian's swelling numbers.

From the corner of his eye, Zhang noted Kenjiro. The samurai was surrounded, and Da thought he was surely doomed. But the warrior displayed an inhuman skill, dispatching any who came too near. He held his impressive, bloodstained sword in one hand and a short blade—a *tanto,* Zhang thought it was called—in the other. Kenjiro dodged and countered, thrust and parried. The samurai was a whirlwind of death that quickly had his adversaries on their heels.

"Worry not, Zhang," a voice yelled over the din of battle. "The samurai you've been hiding will die alongside the rest of you."

Zhang Da turned to face Qian's general, and son, Qian Ning. Both Qian and Liu soldiers alike drew back to clear a path for the large, armored man. "You know not who or what you fight for, General," Zhang Da said. "Your father has crossed a line."

"No! He smells weakness! Your emperor has grown soft; decadent and ill-suited to rule."

Zhang Da whirled his spear over his head, and tucked it under his arm. "Only a tyrant rules by the tip of a sword. All of the kingdoms of Ba Guo know this."

Ning leveled his spear at Zhang Da. "All of the kingdoms of Ba Guo will fall in line or know the hand of a true ruler." The general dismounted, and Zhang followed suit. This was a personal battle long in the coming.

"The kingdoms of Ba Guo would resist your father to a man and woman. You would have to kill every soul upon these lands."

"If that is what is necessary, so shall it be done!"

Zhang let his disgust show on his face. That this man would suggest such a thing was madness. If he was not demon possessed, he was of like mind. "You and your father are rabid dogs that must be put down."

Qian Ning sneered. "Then come, Zhang Da, descendent of the fabled Zhang Fei. I will send you to your ancestor!"

* * *

Guan Xi whirled her legendary weapon with graceful yet efficient skill. Her Guandao—the ancient weapon named after her mighty ancestor—was nearly the same hundred ten pounds it weighed centuries ago. Restored throughout the ages, and finally come into her capable grasp, the weapon was every bit as formidable as it had been in the ages past.

A soldier charged in, thrusting his blade at her abdomen. She spun the long-shafted weapon and turned his sword away. Keeping with the momentum, she bent forward and ducked a sweeping sword aimed at her neck. She brought the Guandao up and over her back, now spinning horizontally. Using the strength in her forearms and wrists, she kept the weapon spinning even as it disemboweled a rear attacker.

Still bent forward, Guan Xi moved with the momentum of the heavy weapon. She spun it over her back, then swept it around her side and beheaded the man in front of her.

Guan Xi kept the weapon moving, whirling it vertically and horizontally as she walked through the mass of fighting soldiers. She turned and skipped, swayed and spun, all the while her perfectly weighted weapon lay low enemy after enemy.

From the corner of her eye, she saw Xuande battling a new force that had taken the field. She turned her efforts in that direction, thinking to work her way to him. Guan Xi had waited for the three of them to battle alongside each other as their ancestors had done. She had not wished for war, but the blood in her veins ran hot. What would it be like to battle alongside her sworn brothers now, as Guan Yu, Liu Bei, and Zhang Fei had done?

Two soldiers emerged from the fighting. They wasted no time in their attack, one slashing high while the other stabbed low. Guan Xi bent backward, dodging the swinging blade while spinning her weapon and turning aside the stab. She planted her feet, stopped the spinning shaft, and thrusted it up. The maneuver forced the second attacker's sword tip above her head.

She turned the shaft of her Guandao and forced the man's sword down, simultaneously parrying a stab from the first attacker. They hopped back, then lunged in again.

"I didn't know Qian had skilled men in his army," Guan Xi taunted. No reply came other than a continued and coordinated offensive. "You two are no fun!" She blocked a blade coming at her right, while receiving a glancing cut to the shoulder.

She ignored the burn and whirled her Guandao to drive them back. She moved in a rhythmic pace with the spin of the blade. Despite the weapon being nearly as heavy as she was, a lifetime of training made the weapon as much a part of her body as any other limb.

Guan forced them into a defensive posture. She kept the weapon spinning, changing the cadence of her movements in relation to the weapon's angle. She slowed, then sped up, preventing her adversaries from having a chance to find an opening.

The soldiers moved with her on either side and seemed as though they could read each other's thoughts. The man on her right feinted a stab for her ribs, drew back a swiped at her leg. But that was also a feint. He stopped short, drew back, and stabbed high.

He was so quick that Guan Xi had almost missed it. She was just fast enough to deflect the tip of the sword down from her neck, but suffered a superficial cut along the top of her shoulder. She leaned to her right, narrowly avoiding a swipe at her left ribcage. She skipped over a swipe at her ankle and spun the Guandao around to slam into her underarm. The momentum combined with the weight of the weapon spun her sideways as she dropped into a crouch.

Her opponents moved around her, their steps as light as a cat, their eyes equally measuring. Guan Xi looked from one to the other. She'd heard of these two before.

"The Twins of Qian," she said with a wicked smile. "Hua must have more respect for Liu Xiang than he lets on if he brought you two."

Of course, the twins said nothing. They never spoke. Every kingdom in Ba Guo knew of the Twins of Qian. They were two of the most formidable warriors in all of Ba Guo, and had somehow come into the service of the warlord. Identical in appearance, opposites in fighting style. One favored more straightforward attacks; thrusts, stabs, quick vertical swipes. The other favored more rounded attacks; arcing cuts, horizontal and sweeping motions. Alone, they were formidable. Together they were a deadly force.

Guan Xi shrugged with satisfaction. "I'm flattered that I've caught your attention."

The twins attacked. General Guan met them.

42

Milpheus stepped as quickly as he dared without attracting any unwanted attention. It was rare when anything riled him up, but what he saw today was disturbing. For years Elizander had humored the troublesome Brother Dinman in spite of Milpheus's warnings. Ever had the insufferable monk beat his drum about Elizander, *King* Elizander, was not ruling the "flock" with as firm a hand as he should; that when Holy Jemanah returned, the king and his people would be subjected to harsh judgment. Only through constant vigilance against the sins of man, and utter devotion to the church would the lives of his people be saved.

For the most part, Elizander tolerated the monk's incessant preaching, only occasionally setting the pushy Dinman back in his place when he'd gone too far.

Milpheus snarled. Bishop Marquis was showing more than a little weakness in allowing one of his brethren to become such a wildcard. King Elizander had remained adamant about not interfering with the affairs of the church, only stepping in when absolutely necessary. Such a stance would have been proper, if the church had a stronger leader.

On his way back from delivering a message to Bishop Marquis from King Elizander, Milpheus had seen that a separation of the church was the least of their concerns. Passing through the gardens in the quiet of night, Milpheus overheard voices speaking quietly. Ever suspicious, he'd followed the sounds of the voices until he came to a hiding place in a wall of shrubbery surrounding the rose gardens on the remote side of the city.

Disgust swirled in Milpheus's stomach at the memory of what he'd over-heard. There had been talk of the need for Bishop Marquis to step down, or to form a separate church for the *true* followers of Jemanah. The recent attacks apparently were proof of Jemanah's displeasure. King Elizander needing to come to heel. Jemanah and *only* Jemanah was the true ruler of the people. And conveniently, the church delivered His message.

Milpheus had to resist the urge to spit. The implications of this line of reasoning couldn't be any clearer.

Hearing his footsteps echo through the halls reminded Milpheus of how long it had been since the palace had been truly at ease. Ever since Elizander and the hotheaded Captain Davros had nearly gotten themselves killed by a demon—Milpheus still had trouble making himself believe such a thing—there had been no more killings.

Of course, the monk who had saved Elizander had suggested this was no more than a temporary reprieve. That may be so, but it was comforting to have the city back to normal, if only for a short while until they got the situation—and that venomous Dinman—in hand.

He came to the double doors of King Elizander's rooms where six of his personal guard stood. Elizander had argued against the added security, claiming it gave the look of a fearful and paranoid king. In the end, Milpheus and Davros had teamed against him, which had surprised all three of them, and the extra guards were put in place.

"I must speak with king Elizander."

"The hour is late," one of the guards, a young man looking to have seen perhaps twenty summers.

"Yes yes." Milpheus waved a hand dismissively. "I'm aware the hour is late, the king has retired, and I can visit him on the morrow. I've been saying those words since long before you were born, boy. I am King Elizander's personal attendant. I wouldn't visit upon him at this hour if it weren't urgent.

The boy looked as if he would refuse, but one of the other guards Milpheus knew to be a veteran of thirty years in service to the crown, nodded. The youth's face tightened, but he stepped aside.

The young soldier had barely gotten out of the way when Milpheus blew past him. Boys playing at being soldiers, that's what most of them were. Milpheus decided he would have to have a talk with Captain Davros about being more discriminative in his choice of personal guards.

Milpheus found the king standing on his patio, hands clasped behind his back, staring out over the moonlit city. The pale orb in the sky had entered its waning phase, but managed to cast a bit of its magical light upon Windsor.

"Good evening old friend. What brings you at this hour?"

"Humph. Old friend yourself," Milpheus snapped. "Before you were born, when youngsters had manners, it was unheard of for a person to refer to their elder as 'old'."

"Peace, Milpheus," Elizander said with a chuckle. "A term of endearment, nothing more. I refer to our good Captain Davros in much the same way."

Milpheus snorted. "That giant boar will be fortunate if he reaches 'old' status."

"What brings you here?" Elizander tried again. "I don't plan to retire for a few hours yet. Perhaps a game of *Houses*?"

Milpheus was touched by the king's genuine desire to spend friendly time with him. He was every bit his parents' child. "We really must find you a queen, my lord. Though I would enjoy a game of *Houses*, you would be better served in the company of one who would provide you with more fulfilling company than I … and perhaps an heir or two."

"We've traveled that path plenty of times. I appreciate your concern and I assure you I've given it thought. Perhaps when this matter settles and things have reverted to a reasonable calm, I'll give it more serious consideration. For now, leave it as it is."

Milpheus bowed and didn't try to hide his predatory grin. That drew an eye-roll from the ensnared young king. "Very well, my lord. We shall revisit this matter soon. And as it stands, there is indeed another matter that we must discuss. It involves a certain Brother Dinman."

Elizander sighed. "Unless he has committed some crime that lies outside the jurisdiction of the church, I'd like to occupy my thoughts elsewhere."

Milpheus shook his head. "We can ignore him no longer, my lord. On the way from delivering your message to Bishop Marquis, I overheard Brother Dinman …"

"Spied on Brother Dinman, you mean."

"… speaking with a sizable congregation about the state of affairs of Windsor and its leadership within and without the church."

"His complaints about the bishop and me are nothing new, Milpheus."

"They are gaining support, my lord." I took no formal count, but I place his congregation tonight around fifty to sixty people."

"Notable but not so large a group."

"Late into the night and at the farthest edge of the city? My king, he could not host a larger group because it would require louder speech and for now, discretion is a valuable tool. He speaks openly of not only the weakness of Bishop Marquis, but also of the crown's inability to keep the wellbeing of the people in hand. He suggests the kingdom fall under the rulership of the church entirely. He would supplant Bishop Marquis and *you* in one stroke."

Elizander's relaxed features tightened. "You heard him say this?"

"In so many words, yes."

"The severity of what you suggest will require more than the mere suggestion of it. I cannot act on speculation."

"Trust me, my lord. There is little to speculate. His intent is quite clear. Did you not tell me yourself that you saw him speaking to a large congregation not long ago? When you saw it, was your first thought that he was spreading the word of Holy Jemanah and praising the leadership of King Elizander and Bishop Marquis? Could you speak such words without it sounding like a mockery in your own ears?"

Elizander chopped the air with his hand. "Enough."

Milpheus closed his mouth and swallowed the rest of his words.

Elizander sighed. "There is a strong ring of truth to your words. But I cannot silence him because I don't agree with his message. I do not have proof, I'll look as weak and desperate as he speaks of me."

"Then we have something of a conundrum."

"I could send him away," Elizander suggested. "Give him a task that would take him far from here."

"You would do nothing more than plant a poisonous seed far away that would grow large enough to return and contaminate your garden here," Milpheus countered. "Of course, if he were to meet with some unfortunate end—"

"I'll have none of that!" Elizander snapped. His voice was stern, but his lips trembled with suppressed mirth. "Have you and Davros come together for yet another common goal? I would expect such a suggestion to come from him."

"And would the suggestion gain greater consideration if it came from the chapped lips of your good captain?"

"Hardly!"

"Then we must think hard and we must think quickly."

Elizander nodded. "It seems I have myth-turned-reality stalking my people from one end, and a troublesome weed infecting my garden on the other. The timing couldn't be more inauspicious."

"If trouble came at the perfect time, it wouldn't be troublesome, my lord. And the auspiciousness of its timing, or lack thereof, is dependent on the position of the individual. These times that may be troublesome for you, would prove convenient for one who would use fear as momentum to propel them toward their goal."

Elizander leaned on the rail of the balcony. "I wonder how our good Brother Dinman would react if he knew that there was an actual demon behind these attacks."

"Oh, I can tell you," Milpheus said in mock cheer. "He would declare it Holy Jemanah's displeasure at yours and the bishop's straying from the righteous path. There is selfishness and fanaticism in the eyes of that man. I truly believe that if Jemanah Himself returned tomorrow, Dinman would find a way to exploit it. There is more ambition in the heart of that one than holy righteousness."

"You need not convince me of that," Elizander said. "I see much the same when I look into his eyes ..." He tilted his head when Milpheus's face brightened. "What is it?"

"Dinman is ambitious, yes?"

"Of course. Have we not been discussing this the whole time?"

"And, he wishes to take leadership of the entire kingdom. Whether or not he believes it, he preaches that the attacks are a message of Holy Jemanah's displeasure." Elizander nodded impatiently, signaling Milpheus to get on with it. "Dinman has managed to grow a congregation founded in fear and the belief that he could do a better job."

Elizander's mouth twitched with distaste. "I assume there is a reason you're telling me this other than to make me annoyed before bed?"

Milpheus's smile broadened. "I believe we've found the solution to your problem, my lord."

B rother Dinman strode briskly through the halls of Windsor Palace, his mind racing. He couldn't remember the last time either the inept "Bishop" Marquis, or the soft-hearted "King" Elizander had called upon him. The fact that they had both had summoned him at once had the monk suspicious.

Perhaps they had found out about his late-night gatherings and decided to be done with him. Would they send him away; imprison him? They dared not. It would only further serve his goals. Such a pathetic play on their part would only prove that they were desperate to keep their tenuous hold on the people. Brother Dinman would expose them for what they truly were, one way or another.

But he hadn't expected them to move so soon. Dinman was no fool. He knew that eventually it would come to a confrontation between himself and the king and bishop. He had just hoped for more time to build momentum and the sympathies of more of the flock. Things rarely went exactly as one planned, no matter the circumstance. Fine. Let them reveal their hand.

A small group of monks strode toward him, talking and laughing at some inane subject matter, no doubt. As they neared each other, the monks' chatter quieted to whispers, then finally died as they passed. A good distance away, they resumed their conversation.

That was fine with Dinman. Too often these days, the brothers of the church were overly concerned with befriending and coddling the flock, and not bringing them to heel and preparing them for the return of Holy Jemanah.

The people didn't need priestly friends, they needed doctrine. They needed stern, stoic leadership to prepare them for the transition when the Savior returned.

Brother Dinman smiled to himself. When he gained control of the church and dealt with that child upon the throne, the kingdom would flourish under his leadership.

A monk in dark brown wool robes rounded the corner and a smile slithered across Dinman's face. "Greetings, Brother Tardein."

The other monk nodded to him. "Brother Dinman." He had a crisp, cold way of speaking. Most in the church felt Brother Tardein was harsh and unfriendly. Dinman, on the other hand, knew better. Tardein had been trained in the old ways. Back before the church had gone soft and digressed into coddling its devotees and the greater flock it managed. Becoming a monk of the Church of Jemanah was a rigorous training of the mind, body, and spirit. Though his training had been tough, even Dinman had not undergone the harsh conditioning that Tardein had endured.

"You are well, Brother?"

Tardein stared at Dinman, unblinking. "Spare the tiny talk for one who would have either the time or the inclination to entertain it. What do you want?"

"I have been called to attend upon Bishop Marquis and King Elizander."

"And you've pulled me from my business to inform me of this?"

Dinman nodded. "Do you not believe the church has been soft for some time now, Brother?" As hoped, Dinman received the wrinkled, affirmative downturned grin from the morose monk. "Is it not true that the Brothers of the church are too lax in their devotions, and have strayed from the teachings of Holy Jemanah?"

"Too long has the church been out of touch with the needs of the people, and too long has the church and its followers strayed from the righteous path." Brother Tardein's gaze intensified. "And too long have you known my feelings about the state of the church to decide now to address it with me. So I ask you once again, Brother Dinman. What are you after?"

Dinman tucked his hands in the sleeves of his robes. "What I do is always for the benefit of the church and the followers of Holy Jemanah. I would restore the church to its former strength and see that infidels be cleansed by the light of Holy Jemanah, or banished from the land."

"You speak as though from a position rivaling both the bishop and the king, Brother Dinman. You have held counsel with them? What have they to say of your grand vision?"

"I plan to bring that very question to light," Dinman said. He spread an arm outward to encompass the hall. "Have a look for yourself. Our leaders, the leaders of this grand city and the lands beyond are living in decadence, debauchery, allowing the flock to recede into sin and heathenism. The word of Holy Jemanah has been sullied by outside pagan influences that our king and bishop have allowed to flourish, like the weeds in the crops upon which we must feed."

"I can appreciate your point without the dramatics," Tardein replied.

"I would bring these issues to the king and bishop, yet again. Alone, I can accomplish little, but combined with the influence of one such as yourself, Brother Tardein, we can affect change that will save our great city from the chaos in which it descends."

"I am unsure I have witnessed the chaos you speak of, Brother."

"No?" Dinman widened his eyes and raised his eyebrows high. "Why ... what of these attacks over the past months, Brother? What of the gruesome deaths that have been visited upon our once great and holy city? The people have strayed, but that is to be expected of the flock. It is the job of those who have devoted our lives to shepherding the masses and spreading the message of Holy Jemanah, who are most accountable. Holy Jemanah is angry, and these unholy, dare I say, demonic, attacks on the people are proof enough of the Savior's displeasure. Do you not agree, Brother Tardein?"

"There is truth in what you say," Tardein replied cautiously. "You still haven't spoken your business, and I am not of a mind to repeat myself again."

"I need you and any who would stand with me to pull the shroud from Bishop Marquis's eyes and wake our king from his slumber of blind indifference."

"You speak dangerous words, Brother."

Dinman spread his hands. "I only speak what you yourself have thought for years, do I not?"

"My thoughts are my own. What you suggest has a ring of ambition to it that I find disconcerting."

"I work for the welfare of the church and its followers."

Brother Tardein studied Dinman for a moment. "Perhaps." He shuffled around Dinman and continued on his way.

Dinman smiled to himself. One never knew for sure where the old monk stood on any matter until he spoke his mind fully. Still, Dinman was positive he'd at least sown some seeds in the mind of the stern Tardein.

He considered the end of their conversation as he continued to the audience hall and gave himself a mental check. Tardein was right. He must take greater care with his words. His congregation was growing, and so too was his influence. And his confidence.

Dinman mustn't let his progress make him reckless. *Discretion*, he told himself. He would quietly grow his influence, and very soon Elizander and Marquis would not be able to so easily dismiss him.

After far too long a walk in the insufferably large and overindulgent palace, Dinman arrived at the doors to the audience hall. One of the guards opened the door to allow the page to enter and announce him. Dinman eyed the guards with disapproval. He didn't know who had attacked and killed so many of the king's men, and nearly the king himself, but it was still a waste of resources to have so many to guard a door, especially when he knew there would be more guards within the hall itself.

Perhaps if the king was more focused on adhering to the tenants of Holy Jemanah instead of his popularity among the flock, such excessive security would be unnecessary. The love of the people was irrelevant. They must fear and respect their ruler, and the will of Holy Jemanah from whom the king's power originated.

One of the doors opened to admit him. As he strode inside, Brother Dinman saw that every eye was focused on him. A streak of fear went down his spine, yet he held his head high as he strode forward with confidence. As expected, the king sat on his throne, regal and self-satisfied as he basked in the luxury and influence of his inherited station. The glittering crown of gold that sat atop his head was enough to make Dinman nauseous. Such bold arrogance was inexcusable.

Beside the king, weak Bishop Marquis stood resplendent in the magnificent white and gold robes of his station, though the rotund man did little justice to the title. His ample belly and multiple chins were screaming proof that he enjoyed his station far too much. Dinman mentally scowled. There was so much to be done. So much to change.

"Brother Dinman arrives at last," Bishop Marquis said, spreading his thick arms wide in greeting.

"One must not keep the king of New Dainland, or the bishop of Windsor waiting," Dinman replied, attempting to bury the contempt in his voice. Judging by the way Marquis flinched, he must not have hidden it very well.

"I'm sure you are curious as to the reason of your summons," Marquis continued.

Dinman spread his arms. "I must admit that a summons from the Bishop *and* King of Windsor does have me curious."

"As you and all of the assembled are aware," King Elizander began, "the attacks on the beloved citizens of Windsor have ceased."

"It has so far, my lord," Dinman allowed. "By all accounts, life has begun to return to what it was since before the attacks."

"Indeed it has. I am a man of practicality, Brother Dinman. Being of practical mind leads me to believe these attacks have only been temporarily stopped." Restless murmurs rumbled through the assembly until the king raised a hand for silence. "I have discussed the matter at length with Bishop Marquis."

"I am sure you have gleaned a great deal of insight," Dinman replied neutrally. Marquis narrowed his eyes.

Elizander let out a small huff that could have been mistaken for a snicker. "Before we explore that avenue, I would have your thoughts on the matter."

Dinman froze. In the few heartbeats that passed, the monk felt a chill settle in the pit of his stomach. He wasn't a trusting man, and now he felt as though he had just stepped into fox den. He must tread carefully. "What matter my thoughts, my lord? I am but one of many servants of the Church of Jemanah."

"You are one of the most active brothers of the church, my son," Marquis said warmly. You have devoted yourself tirelessly to spreading the word of Holy Jemanah to the masses. People come from every part of New Dainland to listen to you speak. Though I've not had the time to gain inspiration from your words myself, your fervor in spreading the wisdom of Holy Jemanah is undeniable."

Dinman didn't know what to think of this. The bishop knew about his meetings, yet approved of them? Was this a trap? Dinman had never known Marquis to be possessed of any sort of cunning. Superstitious, maybe. But not cunning.

On the other hand, the king, soft though he was, did possess at least a degree of wit; enough for Dinman to be wary of the man. Perhaps Dain knew of Dinman's secret meetings and sought to get him to incriminate himself.

"All of my work is for the good of the church and the people of Windsor, and by extension, the great city of New Dainland."

"Let us cut to the heart of the matter," Elizander said. "The attacks had been happening for weeks with no sign of stopping. Our best efforts nearly ended in disaster."

Dinman stole a glance at the murmuring crowd. Word had spread about a supposed encounter between Elizander and his team, and the assailants.

"It was only several days before that time," Marquis said, "that I became aware of your efforts, Brother Dinman. Since that time, the attacks have ceased. Holy Jemanah is kind."

Dinman frowned. "Indeed. Holy Jemanah is kind to His followers." *What were they after?*

"Brother Dinman, the bishop continued. "It is obvious to any with eyes that it was your tireless efforts in delivering the word and power of Holy Jemanah that has made the difference here. Because of your actions, the attacks have ceased. By beseeching Holy Jemanah for aid, you have spread His word and will, and in doing so, strengthened the people against the evil that has plagued our city."

"You give me far more credit than I deserve, Bishop Marquis," Dinman replied, his chin rising with every word.

"Nonsense," the bishop chided. "You've proven how much of an asset you are to the church and all of Windsor. Accept what you've earned."

Now we come to it, Dinman thought. "And pray, what is it that I have earned, Bishop Marquis?" the monk asked.

"Why, a stronger role in the church, of course. And thus, New Dainland will have a stronger defense against the unholy beasts that would devour us in their darkness. Surely there must be some devilry at work, given the gruesomeness of the killings and our inability to stop them till your faithful intervention.

Bishop Maquis and Elizander Dain shared a look. The sleeves of Marquis's voluminous robes hung loose as he spread his arms. "For your tireless service to the Crown, the Church of Holy Jemanah, and the people of Windsor, I name you Holy Arbitrator."

"Holy Arbitrator?" Dinman's mouth hung open. "Father Bishop, such a title does not exist."

"Further proof of the necessity for change," the bishop replied. "There has been a lacking in the church, a rift between our congregation and our Savior, Holy Jemanah, that none knew till you stepped in to bridge."

Dinman felt a growing excitement replace his anxiety. "What does this title afford me, Father Bishop?"

"Autonomy. You have freedom to do what needs to be done to help ensure the spiritual safety of our great city. You are my right hand, Holy Arbitrator Dinman."

"The crown is in full support of the church in bestowing this title upon you," Elizander said. And all of the power and responsibility that comes with it.

Dinman's mind whirled at the possibilities. "I believe you have been visited upon by wisdom, my king."

"All that is left is your acceptance of your knew role as Holy Arbitrator, Brother," Bishop Marquis said.

A tiny smile crept across Dinman's face and he quickly suppressed it. Oh how the man so publicly spun the rope that formed the noose he was so willingly wrapping around not only his own neck, but that of his beloved king as well. "Nothing makes me happier than to better serve the church, the people of Windsor, and most of all, Holy Jemanah Himself, to whom we all owe our lives and salvation."

"Indeed," the king said. "Then so it shall be."

"From this day forth," Marquis announced. "In concurrence with King Elizander Dain, I, Bishop Marquis De Lanceon and by extension, the Church of Holy Jemanah, grant you, Brother Dinman Squarchile the title of Holy Arbitrator." The room echoed with polite applause.

Dinman kept his head and his gaze straight, flushing with anger and embarrassment at the assembly's lack of enthusiasm. So be it. Every one of these infidels would come to heel. Elizander and Marquis had unwittingly accelerated his influence in the church.

"I humbly accept the role granted me, and will do my best to see the will of Holy Jemanah done. It is a great responsibility to shepherd the flock, but I will see it done."

"Then so shall it be," the king said. "I hereby conclude this business and congratulate you, Holy Arbitrator."

The din of conversation filled the air as the assembled filed out of the hall. Bishop Marquis stepped down from the dais and stopped before Dinman. He inclined his head with a smile.

Dinman returned the gesture. "You humble me, Bishop."

"It is that very humility that has granted you your station, Arbitrator," Marquis said. Dinman couldn't help but smile at the sound of his new title. It had a powerful ring to it.

"Accompany us to my private study," Marquis continued. "We must formally record today's business in the official logbook."

"Of course, Bishop," Dinman said. It took an effort not to rub his hands together.

* * *

Elizander sat in a chair in the corner of the candlelit room, his worm-like attendant at his side. Dinman opted to remain standing. Seated at his desk, Bishop Marquis penned the formal document appointing the monk to his new position. Once finished, the three of them reviewed the document and signed it. Marquis then handed it to a scribe who took it to his desk in the next room to begin making a copy.

"A great responsibility you've undertaken, this day," King Elizander said. "New Dainland is lucky to have such a devout brother of the church."

"The mantle of responsibility must be taken up with a firm grasp, my lord, lest our society degenerate to the chaos of times past."

"Indeed," the king replied. That one word made Dinman just a bit uncomfortable for some reason.

"Of course, I will need the freedom to see to matters without immediately seeking approval, Dinman ventured. I would always defer to the bishop, of course, but I must be able to attend to matters as needed, if I am to ensure that the will of Holy Jemanah is served."

Elizander raised his eyebrows. "You would act first and consult after?" He looked at Father Bishop.

The fat man nodded his head, his second chin wiggling. "I admit that I would prefer you discuss your actions with me first, Arbitrator Dinman, but if you feel it necessary to act swiftly for the need of the people, it is understandable."

"And I will need leave to serve the people with a firmer hand than the one which has coddled them these many years, Father," Dinman continued, gaining confidence. "If we are to ensure the will of Holy Jemanah is done, the flock must be better prepared for His return."

"I would not trouble the lives of my people," the king said. "I believe my rule has been firm and fair, and New Dainland thrives."

"And yet, the need for my appointed title has arisen, my lord." The king's face darkened, and Dinman softened his tone. "I speak not in doubt of your rulership, but that none but Holy Jemanah are perfect. Sometimes we must make changes whether large or small."

The king looked as if he were going to protest, then simply nodded. Beside him, the little man, Milpheus remained passive. Dinman wondered if he was even listening to the conversation. Of course he was, the monk decided. The little spider heard everything.

After several tense moments, Elizander nodded. "Very well. I am confident that you will do what must to be done. Good luck and congratulations, Holy Arbitrator Dinman."

Dinman nodded and turned to leave. He stopped at the door and looked over his shoulder. Three sets of eyes stared at him, waiting. "Of course, I would need a new set of robes to distinguish my station, Bishop Marquis."

"Of course," Marquis replied. "Shall I see it done, or would you like to attend to it personally?"

"I would like to see to the matter myself if it pleases you. I am sure you have more important matters demanding your attention."

The bishop nodded.

Dinman left the fools to their business.

* * *

T he three men sat in silence, staring at the door Dinman had departed through. After completing three copies of the official document, the scribe delivered them to Bishop Marquis, bowed to Elizander, and took his leave. Marquis saw him to the door, peeking outside the room in both directions before shutting it.

"If his chin rose any higher, we would need to place mirrors on the ceiling so that he might still see us."

Elizander chuckled. "That one is ambitious."

"Dangerously so," Milpheus added. "There is plotting in the eyes of that man."

"Such a man could be more dangerous than any demon."

Marquis looked incredulous. "Both would lead the people to ruin."

Elizander continued to stare at the door to the bishop's chamber. One can be openly fought. The other must be handled with care."

Milpheus rubbed his bare chin. "Your friends are here?"

"Yes," Marquis replied. "Though I admit I do not like gambling in the midst of so many people."

"Nor do I," Elizander agreed.

"I'm afraid it is a necessary course of action," Milpheus said. "He's dangerously close to posing a threat."

"This business is being … monitored?"

Milpheus bowed, and when he straightened, he wore a grin from ear to ear. "Indeed, my lord."

44

J *ing jing jing jing jing jing doom jing jing jing doom jing jing jing doom*
jing jing jing doom jing jing jing doom jing jing jing doom jing da da da
doom doom, doom doom da da da da, da doom doom, doom doom, da
da da da da doom doom, doom doom da da

The three warriors crouched around the corner just outside the torchlight watching in disbelief at the scene before them. Twenty to thirty workers, half armed with picks and half with iron hammers—both of which looked as heavy as the stone pillars they'd left behind—pounded and chiseled into the mountain to the rhythm of deep bass drums and the jingle of chimes.

They looked at each other, each seeing the shock on the other's face. These industrious workers seemed unconcerned about bringing the ceiling down upon them with all that vibration. More amazing was that they could work at all in the thick stale hot air down there.

Kenyatta held his hand horizontal in front of him, just under five feet high. Despite his confused frown, the side of his mouth twitched.

"You have got to be kidding me," Kita whispered. "We've stumbled on a group of *Dwarves?*"

"They've got a nice beat going," Kenyatta remarked, earning a glare from his friend. He shrugged. "Well, they do."

"So none of this," he waved his hand at the scene around the bend, "is shocking to you at all?"

"What's more shocking to me is that we didn't guess this earlier," Kenyatta replied. "Now that I see them, I think how obvious it should have been.

All this talk about The Four; humans, amahle, elves. Seems like the obvious last group would be dwarves."

"I thought it was the brunts," Kita said, peeking around the corner again. "They certainly aren't human."

"Well maybe they're a distant relative or something."

Seung wrinkled her nose. "Why would anybody want to live under a mountain?"

"Ain't that a right thoughty question you've presented there, lass."

They spun as one, drawing their weapons. "What's this?" the speaker said in mock surprise. "I told ye, boys. There ain't no manners left in the world. Ye get three tall folk come skulkin' 'round in our tunnels, spy on us while we work, then draw on us unprovoked." With muscled arms thicker than Kenyatta's legs, the speaker hefted an intimidating axe and rested it on his right shoulder.

"I ... you startled us," Kita stammered. They lowered their weapons, eyeing the one dwarf to the next. They were outnumbered two to one, not counting the workers around the corner. "We mean no trouble. We're simply lost."

The resulting roar of laughter flowed through the tunnels, and the music around the corner stopped.

"Here that, boys?" These folk're lost down here in our tunnels. Imagine that! Hey, Corban. Go let the king know he's fer havin' visitors soon."

Beside the speaker, a dwarf much smaller in stature pounded a fist to his chest. "Aye!" He jogged back down the tunnel.

Seung rolled her eyes.

"What's that, lass? Ye got no ear for our humor?"

"I've got not time for your nonsense," came the tart reply.

Kenyatta gritted his teeth. "Jyas joking, man. "Her jyas got a mouth for jokes sometimes, ya know." The dwarves frowned, glancing at each other in confusion.

"He said she was just joking," Kita translated.

Kenyatta blinked. "The way dem talk, and they got nerve not to understand me?"

"Why is it your accent only comes out when your nervous or angry, or when you're reminded of your homeland?" Seung asked.

Kenyatta opened, then closed his mouth. "I ... don't do that."

"Maybe save yer blabberin' for later," the dwarf said.

Seung opened her mouth to speak, but Kenyatta touched her arm. "Please don't make these people angry," he whispered into her ear. "I don't much want to deal with the business end of one of those axes."

Seung glared at him, then at the dwarves. Then, she turned her glare on the workers shuffling around the bend. "Whatever."

The lead dwarf tilted his head. "Ye don't find yer situation a little strained?"

"The only thing strained is my nose." Seung gave the dwarf a once-over.

The dwarf narrowed his eyes at her, and Kita and Kenyatta tensed. After a long and uncomfortable moment, the leader burst into a deep belly laugh, the others joining him.

Kita and Kenyatta shared a nervous glance and joined in.

"Ye got a right spicy lass there, eh laddy?" the dwarf said, winking at Kenyatta.

"I have?"

"Suren ye two be sharin' more'n a mug of ale, or I'm a rock eatin' grongolian."

"We should take 'em to King Shatterhammer," the dwarf on the leader's left side said.

"Ah right, right. Almost fergot. And almost fergot to find out what *yer* business is down here."

Kita opened his mouth to speak, but the dwarf held up a startlingly large —and thick—hand. "Not fer me ears to be hearin' afore me king's ears be hearin'. I'll kindly be askin' ye to place yer fine—if poorly—crafted weapons on the ground. Ole Bordok there'll take care of 'em fer ye without a doubt."

The dwarf jerked his chin to a grizzled one-eyed dwarf that barely stood as high as Kita's shoulder.

"Name's Bordok. Bordok Stonesplitter." The dwarf walked up stuck out a hand.

Kenyatta tentatively took it and fought back tears as the bones in his hand were nearly ground to dust, and his arm threatening to be shaken from its socket. When the dwarf finally—mercifully—let go, he went to Kita who clenched his jaw as he suffered the same greeting.

The dwarf then turned to Seung. "Ain't proper like, shakin' a lass's hand." He placed his hand on his beard and bowed.

Seung's mouth crinkled. "Um, nice to meet you as well, Bordok Stonesplitter." She dipped into a curtsy.

The burly dwarf collected their weapons with an air of respect.

"No need to be nervous about all this," the leader said. "Long as ye tell the truth and ye ain't fer causin' problems, ye'll be gettin' yer weapons back and on yer way."

"Not much choice but to take your word on that," Kita said.

"Nope. But we're good for it. The only thing a dwarf's got beside his beard is his word."

"Aye!" the others responded in unison.

"And where're me manners?"

"Perhaps lost in your beard?" Seung offered. Another roar of laughter.

"Aye lass," the dwarf said, wiping tears from his eyes. "Fer a dainty one like yerself, ye got a good bit o' spice in ye?" He leaned around her and offered an exaggerated wink at Kenyatta. Seung opened and closed her mouth several times while Kenyatta struggled not to laugh. "Looks like she's not fer words on that one!" Another roar of laughter.

Seung shot a glance at Kenyatta, who studiously examined the ceiling of the tunnel.

"As I was sayin', I fergot me manners. Name's Felk Boulderbasher." He offered an incline of his head in lieu of a handshake.

Kenyatta sighed in relief before he caught himself, drawing a snicker from Kita.

"Watch it, boy," Felk warned. "Ye don't be comin' in another man's house'n makin' fun with his name."

"My apologies, Felk Boulderbasher. I wasn't—"

Felk held up a hand. "Quit flappin' yer lips and c'mon."

The procession started back the way the three companions had come.

"Speakin' of names," Felk said over his shoulder. "Ye ain't offered yers yet."

"Kenyatta Ihe."

"Kita Sepata."

"Seung Yoon."

The dwarf smirked. "Might be fer laughin' at all of them strange names meself, but I won't."

They re-entered the rotunda and turned left, taking the tunnel the companions had bypassed earlier. Sometime later, they came to the largest set of stone doors they had ever seen; easily twenty feet tall.

"I have a question," Kita asked, after Felk had sent one of his men in to announce their arrival. "For what reason do you need such tall doors?"

Felk looked taken aback. "Suren yer jokin'. Ye can't be havin' small doors fer large rooms!"

"But why large rooms?" Kita ventured, carefully. "You all are so … compact, that it seems unnecessary."

Now it was Felk's turn to roll his eyes. "And I'm sure never has a human built something larger'n what they needed?" He spread his thickly muscled arms and leaned back, gazing at the beautifully chiseled art that adorned the walls and even the ceilings above. "What better way to express yer love fer yer home, than to fancy it up big and nice!"

Kita smiled. "Fair enough."

"Although I prefer the beauty of the forests above," Seung said, "your people have a masterful talent with the stone."

Felk squinted at her. "Ye've the look and sound of one of them fairy folk live in the forests, dancin' round with fireflies 'n talkin to deers and the like." The dwarf tucked his elbows to his side and bent his arms, flapping his hands and wiggling his fingers.

Both Kenyatta and Kita choked back their laughter. Seung's nostrils flared, but she bit back what was surely a venomous retort.

"Hmm." Felk rubbed his chin. "Maybe not all fairy. Ye've got the look of human to you, but I ain't never heared of anything like that afore."

"Surprising," Seung replied dryly.

One of the doors opened again and Corbin stepped out. "The king'll see ye now."

The audience hall was larger than any they'd ever seen. The walls and ceilings—lit by what must have been dozens of torches—were crafted by expert hands. The procession stopped, and their gaze fell upon a large throne upon which sat a dwarf who was bigger than any they had yet met, but far too small for his seat.

"I present you to King Dakra Shatterhammer!" Felk declared. "Me king," he said, dropping to one knee. The others, Kita, Kenyatta, and Seung included, followed suit. "We've done good work this day and found visitors along the way."

The dwarf king placed his hands on the armrests of his throne and leaned forward. "How many times I telled ye to quit rhymin' at me!"

45

Dakra Shatterhammer's saws moved sideways as he gnashed. "I telled ye once, I've telled ye a hunnerd times already! Quit rhymin' at me! I ain't no sweetbun-arsed human needin' entertainment with rhymes 'n caps with jinglin' bells hangin' off it!"

"S ... sweetbun-arsed?" Kenyatta silently heaved as he held back the laughter. Kita elbowed him in the ribs.

"Rhymes and caps with jingling bells?" Kenyatta continued, this time in the ear of the nearest dwarf, which happened to be Corban. "Is he joking, or does he not realize that they don't do that anymore?"

The young dwarf grunted at him. "Hmph. King don't get out much. Can't remember if'n he's even been outta Iron Forge in me own lifetime, short though it's been."

Kenyatta was about to ask Corban's age, when the king spoke again.

"I'm supposin' that one there with the twisty hair got somethin' interestin' to share with more'n just the boy, hmm?" Kenyatta absently rubbed one of his shoulder-length locks between a thumb and forefinger. "Well?" the king demanded. "Speak laddy. We gots plenty 'o time, but the likes of yerself only got, what? Thirty, forty years left to ye, maybe?" There was a rumbling of laughter.

"My apologies, King Shatterhammer," Kenyatta said formally. "I—"

"Fer the love 'o steel and iron, get up off yer knee already; the lot 'o ye!"

They stood, and Kenyatta continued. "As I was saying—"

"What's the name, laddy? The NAME!"

"I … er … Kenyatta, King Shatterhammer—"

"And what lands ye be comin' from, gived ye such a sun-browned hide? Never seen such a thing. Ye must be burnt somethin' painful to be so dark."

Seung covered her mouth, but her shoulders bounced with repressed mirth. Kenyatta glanced back at her, then at Kita, who shooed him with a hand. "Go on. You heard the question. How'd you get that tan, island boy?"

"You only a few shades lighter than me, bwoy," Kenyatta muttered, facing the king again. "I'm not tanned by the sun. I'm born with skin like this."

"Bah but yer for thinkin' ole Dakra Shatterhammer a fool! Ain't nobody born with a hide like that."

"He speaks the truth, me king," Corban said. "If'n its okay that I'm sayin' so. Been to the open lands enough times to see a few things. There's places where folk are born in many shades."

"Sounds excitin'," the king said, skeptically. "I'll get ye to tell me about it some time."

"Yes me king. There's many grand and unusual stuff out there in the larger—"

"I didn't say tell me now, ye danged goat! I said later!"

"Of course, me king." Corban stepped back and cleared his throat.

King Shatterhammer turned his bright blue eyes back on the newcomers. "So. Looks like we got us a motley crew come crawlin' through our tunnels. What bringed ye here? What're ye about?"

Kenyatta couldn't begin to think of how to relate their story. They seemed reclusive, so how much would these people know of the surface world? How could he possibly tell them about skimming plains with his sister and her having to transport them here in an emergency.

"Ye thinkin' mighty hard, laddy," Dakra remarked, his voice taking on a warning tone. "Only a man thinkin' of a good lie have to wait so long to answer a question."

"Not at all, King Shatterhammer," Kenyatta spoke up. "It's just that our tale is so remarkable that we fear you may not believe it."

"Well, s'pose ye tell it and let me be the judge. Ain't promisin' I'll believe ye, but I'm promisin' to listen."

Kenyatta felt Seung's comforting hand on his left shoulder, then Kita's hand on his right.

They took turns telling their story in full, omitting no details. Although there was no sun to show how much time passed, several torches had to be replaced in the wall sconces during their telling.

The king listened in silence, occasionally leaning forward with a hand on his knee, the other stroking his beard, but never once interrupting. When the story finally concluded with their arrival at Iron Forge, Dakra leaned back in his seat.

"That's quite a story. Can't deny it's on the bright side of extraordinary. Some feller summonin' demons, fightin' strange monsters. Can't believe ye actually met up with a clan of grongolians and still got yer skin. Ye even met up with a lava leech and yer standin' here afterward." Around the throne room were rumbles of appreciation.

"And yer tellin' me ye met a Daunyarka … a dragon. By Boraka's bloody axe! I can't see ye lyin' about that, if only because I can't figger a human knowin' about any of the things ye told us about. And ye survived it all. Great warriors ye must be."

"We've had a lot of help and a lot of luck," Kenyatta said.

"Bah! We all have help and luck. Ne'er met someone didn't benefit from a little luck now and then. Luck don't come often enough to see ye outta some of the muck ye three done fell into. Heh. Still can't believe ye met up with some brunt fellers. Imagine that."

"Are the brunts different from you?" Kita asked.

King Dakra looked at him as though it should have been obvious. "O' course! Ye got eyes in yer noggin don't ye? Still, they's related to us all the same. Kinda like how ye all's humans, but look and sound different dependin' on where ye come from. Can't say we're as diverse as ye human folk, but there's a bit o' difference fer sure."

"Will you help us return to the surface?" Seung asked.

The king studied her. "The lass here likes to take the direct route to things." He nodded in approval. "Good quality in a woman." He scrutinized her a bit more, then grinned. "Though she could do with a few whiskers at the chin. Ne'er could figger out how men could stand a woman without even a little stubble."

Seung's face twisted in horror. Kenyatta and Kita snorted.

"Mmm. Yup. I s'pose I could help ye. Don't normally take a liking to ye human folk." He looked at Seung. "And ain't ne'er met an elf I didn't think was just plain strange. Still, I believe ye told me the truth, and ye feel right to me. And if yer tale be even half the truth, ye doin' the world a great service. It burns me arse that I'm makin' it so easy on ye, but I'll help ye out of our home and back to the open lands."

"King Shatterhammer," Seung said. "Since, as you said, we are doing the world a great service, perhaps the dwarves of Clan Shatterhammer could take their place alongside the others of The Four and battle this great evil with us."

Dakra stared at her for a long moment, never blinking. "And why, young lass, would I be considerin' that?"

Seung spread her hands. "As you just said, our errand is a service to the world, Clan Shatterhammer included."

"Ye might be right about that, but wasn't Clan Shatterhammer that brought all these problems. Why would I risk the neck of a single dwarf for the problems of men? They made their mess. Let 'em clean it up themselves."

"Men know not even of the existence of The Four, though they are one of us. They have no knowledge of the Daunyans, Daunyarka, or demons. We who fight, fight in small numbers against many."

"Then best be gettin' on yer way," Dakra replied. "Ye may be able to spread the word quick enough to get some more help."

"King Shatterhammer. You know as well as I that even if every human in the world knew of the greater danger that faces them, they would be ill prepared in time to make a difference. They would just die." Dakra looked indifferent. Seung took a different approach. "The others of The Four stand with—"

"Bah, I've heared enough about this! Ye want yer necks intact, ye got 'em. Ye need a way out, ye got one. I got nothin' fer humans and their problems. They broke the world, let 'em fix it." He nodded to Felk. "Get 'em fresh water and provisions and get 'em outta here."

As Felk's command gathered together and ushered the three companions out of the throne room, Seung made one last play. "You know I'm part elf. Would you send me to the world above to brag how we of the forest were willing to do battle while the dwarves of Shatterhammer were not?" They reached the huge double doors and were being herded out when they heard the king's voice.

"Halt!" They stopped and turned to see Dakra, having left his throne, stomping toward them. He walked right up to Seung and stopped, hands on his hips, and leaned back to look up at her. It would have been a comical sight, if not for the obvious fact that he could break every bone in her body with little effort.

"Ye think to play on ole King Dakra's pride, do ye?"

"Absolutely," Seung admitted.

Kenyatta's eyes nearly dropped out their sockets. He glanced at Kita, who promptly closed his gaping mouth.

Hands clasped behind his back, Dakra paced back and forth for several moments, grumbling to himself. "Felk! Get over here!"

Felk hurried forward. "What have ye, me king?"

"I'm not tellin' ye or nobody else to fight. But I'm offerin' ye a chance to give the dwarves a say in the histry books. I'm not fer liking to put our necks out for human problems, but I'm *really* not fer liking us sittin' down here while a bunch of tree huggin' fairy folk take all the credit. It's yer choice. What say ye?"

Felk thought for only a heartbeat. "How many can I take with me?"

Dakra scratched his chin. "Don't care how much danger they say it is. I'm not riskin' too many necks. Ye can take twenty warriors who'll volunteer." Felk gave a sharp nod and Dakra clapped him on the shoulder. "Just make sure yer comin' back, ye ole boar. Ye still got a couple hunnerd years left in ye at least. I'll need 'em here."

"Me and me axe are comin' back, and that's not fer doubtin'." Felk clapped the king on the shoulder, and with a nod and a grunt between them, gave each other a friendly shove. Felk turned and ushered the visitors out of the throne room.

* * *

Seung could hardly believe their good fortune. The situation had gone from being hopelessly lost under a mountain to not only acquiring an escort out, but with a force—albeit a small one—of warriors to help. Her grandmother, Lady Seiyun had committed no more than the elves she'd traveled with to Takashaniel, claiming that she would need to meet with the council before she could decide whether the elfinestraya would fully make a stand with them.

This dwarf king Dakra had listened to their tale and judged them true, and had committed to stand with them. The fact that it was only twenty dwarves was irrelevant to the fact that he had chosen to help. It was quite an insight and quite a contrast for the young *haloren* to ponder between these folk and her own elven people.

She looked to her left at Felk, axe gripped in his thick hand, stomping alongside her. "A question, Felk Boulderbasher," Seung said.

"Hmm?"

"How is it that your people so easily speak the western human common tongue?"

"Can't trade if ye can't talk," Felk answered.

"You trade with them?"

Felk looked at her as one would a naïve child. "I'm guessin' yer people can do it all yerselves," he said, voice thick with sarcasm, "but somebody's always better at doin' somethin' than yerself." They rounded a corner and took a dimly lit tunnel that went uphill for a stretch, then down. "Not too much in the way of vegetables growin' under a mountain. Not that we eat too many of 'em."

"That would explain the stink," Seung muttered under her breath.

"What's that, lass?"

"Nothing, nothing." Behind her, Kenyatta shook his head, still looking at the very sharp axe gripped in Felk's bone crushing hand.

"How do you disguise yourselves?" she continued. "There are small humans, but they look and are built nothing like you."

Felk shrugged. "Ain't hard. And that's two questions."

"I'm a poor counter. So, if I may ask, why is King Shatterhammer's throne so large? It seems two of him could fit in it."

"Reminds every king that the station is bigger than he is."

"Interesting philosophy."

"Hmph."

They stopped at a heavy-looking stone door that Felk pushed open with one hand and entered. As they followed him in, Kita gave the door a casual tug. It didn't budge. Then, with two hands, he tugged on the stone door again, this time only managing to move it a few inches.

"Hey!" Felk snapped. "What're ye about over there? Ain't no doors where ye come from?"

"Ah, no," Kita replied eyeing the thick door in disbelief. "I mean yes, we have doors. Just admiring the craftsmanship."

That seemed to settle the dwarf down a bit. "Plenty of other things to admire than a basic stone door. Didn't know you human folk was so easy to impress."

After the rest of the procession filed through, he jabbed a finger at the ground in front of him. "Wait here. We won't be long." He turned to walk away, then turned back. "And fer dang blasted sake, if ye gotta touch stuff, be careful. Ye say yer warriors, and me king's fer believin' ye." He gave them all an appraising look. "Got me own doubts, but if King Shatterhammer's fer believin' ye, that's enough for me." Felk led the others farther in the chamber, leaving two dwarves to watch them.

Kenyatta leaned over to Kita. "What were you doing with that door?"

"You saw me tug on it," Kita answered. "It took a considerable amount of strength for me to budge it. I'm not the strongest man in the world, but that thing is heavy. I'd give it a few hundred pounds easily."

Kenyatta's mouth fell open. "Strong suckers aren't they?"

"They are," Seung said. "But how much of a difference can twenty of them make in the face of a horde of demons?"

"More of a difference than without them." Kita replied. "Every number counts." At Seung's noncommittal shrug, Kita huffed, raised his hand. "You didn't get the handshake."

"Yeah man," Kenyatta agreed, flexing his fingers. "I could feel my pulse in my hand afterward."

Some time passed before Felk and his men finally returned. The dwarven warriors were resplendent in shimmering onyx black armor with a golden crest depicting a hammer and axe crossed, with a chisel down the center emblazoned above the left breast.

"Wow." Kita took in the runes chiseled into the helm and arms of Felk's armor. The smooth lines and curves spoke of an attention to detail he'd never seen before.

Strapped to Felk's waist was a one-sided axe with a thick, pick-style point back of the head. The shield strapped to his back was a silver burnished affair that reflected every light in the room.

"Alright boys," Felk declared. "Got twelve of ye here. That leaves room fer another eight." He jerked his chin in the direction of the three companions. "Gonna take these three 'n head on up to the surface. I need one of ye to go find Gruff Strongarm. I'm sure he'll want in on the action. Tell him to bring ten dwarves with him. Two of 'em need to be spellcasters.

"If'n we're to be battlin' demonkind, as the leggy ones here say, we'll need to put a little heat on our axes; Get Boraka to puff a little spice into 'em." He pointed at a dwarf with a sandy colored beard. "You there, Jegra. Take me message and get you to Gruff. We're not fer travelin' too fast. Them tall ones aren't used to the air down here. Can't have 'em layin' down on me."

"Aye," Jegra grunted, then stomped off.

"We've traveled underground before," Kita said indignantly, "or did you already forget our adventure under the Sentinels?"

Felk waved him away. "Ye try and keep a dwarf's pace down here and ye'll lay down out fer sure. Now come on. We're leavin'."

"If I remember correctly," Kenyatta said, "King Dakra said you were allowed only twenty warriors, and we've got twelve here. You just sent for ten more."

"Nope," Felk replied. "We're allowed twenty *warriors*. I sent for ten dwarves. Two of 'em are spellcasters. The other eight will be warriors." He eyed Kenyatta. "Numbers not yer thing? I thought ye looked like a smart feller."

All Kenyatta could do was laugh.

"How long will it take us to reach the surface?" Seung asked.

Kenyatta tried to hide the concern on his face just as Seung tried to hide her longing for the surface. This environment would be oppressive to a human. He couldn't imagine how it would affect an elf.

"'Bout half a day's travel, maybe a little more."

Seung's shoulders slumped. "Oh."

Felk laughed. "Buck up, lass. Ye'll be back outside with yer trees and flowers and pixie dust in no time. We'll get ye there."

"Thanks," Seung grumbled.

S everal hours following their fight with the twin demons, the battered and weary band came upon a humble-sized farm.

Despite being soaked, and now baked by the returned sun, Malimokuru's spirits rose at the welcome sight.

The farmers must have known the rain was coming, for the fields looked and smelled freshly cut. Livestock and fowl socialized under the cover of shelters in a barn nearly twice the size of the house beside it.

A barrel-chested man with forearms like clubs raked the stable with two younger men who must have been his sons. Malimokuru smiled inwardly. Nothing like a family farm.

"We will wait for you in the woods," Naiyala said.

Malimokuru nodded, and they started away. By now, the man and his sons had noticed them and had stopped to watch.

They had the look of folk who lived their whole lives working in the heat and cold of the fields. Though fair-skinned by heritage, they were nonetheless, sun-darkened from years of toiling under the fiery orb creeping toward the western horizon.

"Good day to you," Malimokuru said. He stopped a respectful distance away. "I hope not to intrude upon you, but I been traveling a long distance and hoped for some human contact and maybe any local news ya wan share wit me."

The farmer nodded toward the departing amahle. "Your tall friends over there not good enough human contact for you?"

"I must admit that they are good people and good friends, but they are mostly a reclusive lot. They don't care much for company as I do."

The farmer pointed a dirt-caked finger in the direction Malimokuru and the amahle were headed. "There's a city, Arland, 'bout four hours from here if you're walkin'."

"I confess, I do know of the place, but I find cities less personable than good family folk."

"Now listen here, traveler. I don't mean to be rude, and you seem like a good fellow to my eyes and ears, but if you'll pardon my rudeness," he gave Malimokuru a once-over, "you don't look like a man from these parts, and you seem a little farther along in years to be traveling so far."

"I don't know where you come from, but there ain't no city or town for at least a day in the direction you came from, and you got another four hours till you reach Arland.

"You stop off here asking to break bread while leaving your friends up the road. I might be a little suspicious. We don't much get visitors out this far, except traders from the city. And you don't look like no trader from any city I've seen anywhere near here. Don't sound like one either. You speak right enough, but there's a little twinge of the unfamiliar in your words."

Thinking of how his accent did indeed slip in an out at random, Malimokuru laughed and spread his hands. "I'm actually from very far away …" he trailed off at the sight of a woman he guessed to be the farmer's wife, stomping down the porch.

"What's going on here, Hank? You gonna keep our guest standing out in the sun or you gonna offer him some sweet tea?"

"Can't just be trusting everybody who comes off the road. There's all types roaming around—"

"And how often all them types give us a stop-by?" his wife countered. She shouldered her way between Hank and his larger son. "Besides. If this man thought to try something, I'm sure you and the boys could manage."

She turned to Malimokuru. "You've a foreign look about you, but I'm sure foreign folk get hungry all the same?"

"I … well, yes." Malimokuru glanced at the husband and sons. "But there's no lie in your husband's words, ma'am. I don't mean to intrude—"

"Of course. You're welcome to a meal and drink if you're hungry, Mr …"

"Malimokuru Oyame, ma'am." He watched her chew on that, then added, "you can jyas call me Mali."

She smiled. "Dyrna, Mr. Mali." She looked at her husband and sons. "I'm sure you boys have worked up as big an appetite as our friend, here." She looked back to Malimokuru. "Would you like to join us?"

"I don't mean to cause any fuss—".

"Nonsense. You're no fuss at all. Hank is just the suspicious type."

"Where're you from, Mr. Mali?" Hank asked while Dyrna poured five mugs of water. "As I said outside, we don't get visitors out this far too often."

"I'm from the island of Jamaica." Malimokuru gazed out the window at the infinite green and brown fields stretching into the distance. "Though, it no longer exists."

"Don't know much about Jamaica. Where is it, and why do you say it doesn't exist?"

Malimokuru wasn't surprised by the lack of knowledge of his homeland. Ever since travel had reverted back to the times before the height of technology, common folk traveled less, and not as far. Several generations was all it took for distant lands to fall into obscurity.

"Jamaica was a tropical island. It was washed over by a huge tidal wave. Many people escaped, but many did not. I was among the lucky."

"Sorry to hear about the loss of your home."

The sound of Hank's voice jarred Malimokuru from his daydream back to the present. He blinked and smiled politely.

"Ain't nothing worse than to lose your home," Hank added.

"Well, enough about that. I didn't come to darken your doorstep with tales of foreign disasters."

"Mmm. Fair enough. "What is it you come here for, eh? You said you wanted some company and news, was it?"

"If you've any to share." Malimokuru took a long draw of sweet, cool water. "It's been a long, soggy, and frequently cold journey. I like to know what awaits me on the road ahead whenever possible. I've lost track of the days, but it's been well over two weeks my companions and I have been on the trails."

"And where are these trails leading you?" Hank inquired.

"Can't say for sure, but probably another three or four days northeast."

"Never been too far up north and east. Weather's harsh up there, especially this time of year. Tends to storm violently, from what I hear."

That deflated Malimokuru quite a bit. More harsh weather was not what he'd had in mind. Then again, he'd had none of this fool business in mind. "Nevertheless, I must continue on."

"Do what you got to do," Hank replied. "As I said, I got nothing for you up northeast, but I can tell you that Arland is the last major city you'll pass through for another two weeks on foot."

Dyrna sat down between her husband and the nature reader. "The last people passing through spoke of strange things happening there. Folks disappearing in the night. Unearthly animal sounds carrying in the air, and beasts never seen before. I heard one man say it was demons walkin' the earth, and that there's nothing a person can do to defend against them."

Hank rolled his eyes. "Dyrna. Do you seriously believe all that? Demons? Really now. There ain't no demons walking around anywhere and there certainly ain't no weird sounds carrying in the air. I think that trader you're talking about was just pulling at your fanciful imagination. Ain't no more demons walking the world than there are angels."

"How do you know?" Dyrna shot back. "You the last word on good and evil? I tell you," she turned back to Malimokuru. "I've seen some people I know was evil to the core, like they was some kind of mean-spirited thing making itself look like a human being. If there's not demons walking the earth, there's something akin to it out there."

Hank sighed. "All we need is a campfire and we'll have the full effect for our guest."

Malimokuru hid his shock. Was this demon situation already out of control, like some plague spreading across the world faster than they could stop it? "You wouldn't happen to know the name of that trader you spoke with, would you?"

Hank laughed. "Come now, good sir. You don't believe any of this—"

"Jon Pierson," Dyrna blurted. "Can't say I can ever forget a man like that. Mountain of a man, he was. Closer to seven feet tall than six. And he had this voice as deep as any I've ever heard, and a slightly red tinge to his skin. If ever a man could lift a house and drop it on your head, I got the feeling that Mr. Pierson could do it."

Hank actually nodded in agreement. "He was polite and traded fair with us, but I never felt comfortable around him. It was like fishing in a river next to a grizzly bear. It has its fish and you've got yours, but all it would take is one swipe ..."

Malimokuru felt his insides go cold. Red-tinged skin. Nearly seven feet tall with a booming deep voice. Overwhelmingly powerful presence. He shook his head. It couldn't be possible.

"You alright, friend?" Hank asked.

Malimokuru looked up to see Hank and Dyrna eyeing him. "Uh, yes. Just a lot to chew on, what you've given me. Er, what direction was this man heading in?"

"Same as you, friend," Hank replied. "Said he was for Arland to sell off the rest of his wares. Said he wouldn't have much need to trade after he reached the place."

Malimokuru was certain he knew why that was. He glanced out the window and saw that the sun had past midway in the sky. "You're great and generous hosts, Hank and Dyrna. Time has passed more quickly than I thought." He stood, Hank and Dyrna rising with him.

"You sure you can't stay a while longer," Dyrna asked hopefully. "We don't often get visitors out this way, and I'm sure you've got a handful of stories to share."

"If time permitted, I would have loved to share what few interesting adventures my humble life has accumulated, but I must be going. I was hoping I could come to a mutually agreeable price for refilling my water and provisions, and perhaps if you have a horse you'd be willing to part with as well."

Hank thought on that. "We've got Millie. We keep our larger quarter horses for herding and farm work, but Millie is a riding horse and little else. Not much use for a single purpose horse around here when we can use the quarters for farming and transport. She's a good girl and will take care of you if you do the same."

"Hey Pa!" The smaller of the two sons came jogging up the porch and into the kitchen. "Pa!"

"What is it, Devin? What's got you all riled up?"

"I just saw some animal stalking around the farm. Biggest thing I ever seen!"

"What are you talking about?"

"On four legs it looked to stand almost as tall as a man's shoulders, and it had this long barbed tail. It didn't get too close, but I know what I saw. It was some blue-like color!"

Uh oh. Malimokuru glanced around nervously. Nyaka must have gotten impatient. He opened his mind and immediately connected with the goar cat. As he expected, he received feelings of impatience and then, curiosity directed at the animals around the farm. If he didn't get away from there quickly, this good family might lose some of their livestock.

"Probably a big coyote or a wolf or something," Hank said. "It's hot and bright outside."

"I know what I saw. Wolves and coyotes don't come around this close in the daylight, and that thing was *big*. Like nothing I ever seen. And it ain't no bear, either.

"Well in that case," Malimokuru said, thinking fast, "I'd better have a look at that horse and get going before it gets dark and it turns out to be something that hunts in the night."

"Smart man," Hank agreed, though he did throw an exasperated look at his son.

* * *

T rue to their word, the amahle joined Malimokuru a mile down the road from the farm. Nyaka had joined him as soon as the farm was out of sight. It took considerable effort to bring his new mount under control, as the animal was wisely nervous around the fearsome goar cat. Occasionally he would have to send calming thoughts to the animal to reassure it.

"How was your visit on the farm, friend Malimokuru?" Nyaka asked once they'd rejoined him.

"Informative," he replied. When she gave him an expectant look, he continued. "Demons roam the land, people disappear in the night, and an old 'friend' might be waiting for us in Arland."

47

The eastern horizon glowed blue with the promise of dawn. It was during that time, when life began to stir, that Malimokuru found himself in an inn near the edge of town sitting on a porch across from a man who he believed was a friend, but never found himself comfortable around. On either side of them, disguised in their cloths and head wrappings were his amahle friends, who looked only a bit less uncomfortable.

"You seem ill at ease, my young friend," Darius said. He sipped his tea, eyeing Malimokuru over the top of his mug.

Malimokuru could never be sure if the man was teasing or serious. He also hadn't been young in decades, yet to a man like Darius, he was little more than a child. "You seem comfortable enough for both of us."

Darius chuckled. It was a deep, rumbling sound that made Malimokuru's chest cavity vibrate. "I cannot deny my pleasure at having this little reunion with you, my friends."

Malimokuru raised his eyebrows. "I thought a reunion involved parties who attended by choice." Naiyala placed a hand on Malimokuru's shoulder and gave him a cautionary squeeze.

Darius frowned. "Your words are harsh. After so much we have overcome together, I thought we would have formed a mutual bond; a camaraderie born of mutual struggles and triumphs." He waved an open hand to encompass Naiyala and the others. You seem to have found comfort in the company of your amahle companions, no?"

"Well, yes."

"And even the fearsome goar cat claims your friendship," Darius continued. "To my eyes, it looks as though all of you have formed a powerful bond. What have I done to exclude myself from this honor?"

Malimokuru stared at him. He was hesitant to believe it, but Darius seemed sincere. "Yeah man. You're right, of course. You've been a good friend to us, and have helped us at great risk to yourself while asking for little in return."

"And yet you are not at ease in my presence."

Malimokuru sighed. He didn't want to offend Darius and, not because he could dispatch the five of them in short order, but because the man seemed to genuinely desire their friendship. "It's not that I dislike you, Darius. It's just hard to relax around you."

Darius arched an eyebrow. "Do explain."

"You see? That right there" Malimokuru pointed at his eyebrow. "It's like sitting across from a predator; like you're the lion and I'm the gazelle ... no, not even a gazelle. A mouse."

Darius laughed in surprise during Malimokuru's mini rant. "You feel that way in my presence? All of you?" He looked from one face to the next in sincere curiosity.

"You really don't know, do you?" Malimokuru asked.

Darius considered the question before he answered. "I admit that I'm not unaware of what you say. However, I had thought that battling elementals, an ice master, and a lava leech together would have formed a friendly bond."

"You forgot the dragon," Malimokuru added, only half joking.

"Mmm. Perhaps. Khairon is not of my tribe, so I suppose that confrontation would count, wouldn't it?"

Malimokuru's mouth dropped open. "You have to ask? He almost slaughtered ..." he trailed off and thought about that time not so long ago. Darius hadn't said it, but if not for his aid, every one of them wouldn't be here today. The lava leech would have wiped out Naiyala and her warriors as well as the elves.

And even if they'd survived that, there was the matter of the dragon. Darius alone had been the reason mighty Khairon The Blue hadn't slaughtered them.

"We owe you more than we can say." Malimokuru nodded through every word he spoke, as if urging himself to speak them. "Please do not mistake our uneasiness for dislike ... my friend. You exude a presence that can be overwhelming at times."

He paused. "Well, *most* of the time." He leaned forward and extended his hand, which Darius took in his own. "I would gladly call you friend, Darius. Please forgive my hesitance and lack of gratitude for all that you've contributed to our success and survival."

"We see you, friend Darius," Naiyala said, inclining her head. Amata, Sakhile, and Ayanda followed suit.

Darius half smiled. Malimokuru guessed it was as close to elation that he was capable of.

"Your words are kind, my friends. You have opened yourselves to me with great effort, so I will do the same. What you experience in my presence is part of the reason I lead a solitary life. Humans find my company difficult to endure, though they don't know why. Such is the way of life for a drojan."

"The people of The Dragon Tribe," Darius clarified upon Malimokuru's uncomprehending expression. "The true name of our species is the drojan, just as the true name of the dragons is the Daunyarka. We share the blood of the dragons."

"How is that possible?" Malimokuru asked.

"We don't readily share our history with outsiders, but perhaps one day I will. For now, there is no time. When last we met, I had compelled your friends to me and imposed my presence upon your party. It was a necessity."

"How could you have known who they were?"

Darius's chuckle made the air around them vibrate. "Children of the Gene are impossible to miss for those with the eyes to see them and the intuition to feel them. I knew of their presence before they set foot in Phoenix.

"Though I've only lived little more than a dozen human lifetimes, I have lain eyes upon a Child of the Gene once before. When one of them is born, monumental change comes in their wake. Now, the Daunyans have seen fit to deliver three in one age, though I believe the young woman with elf blood is oblivious to the Gene within her. It is a remarkable precedent."

Malimokuru's eyebrows rose. "The young lady? Seung? You're sure about that?" Darius responded only with a patient smile."

Now it was Malimokuru's turn to grin. "If you think that's remarkable, what would you say to six of them?"

Darius leaned forward. "Six? You toy with me, nature reader."

Malimokuru shook his head. "Kita and Kenyatta shared this with me at the beginning of our travels. There are three other Children of the Gene that they fought beside a year before we met. At the time, I hadn't understood what that meant."

"It means," Darius said, standing, "that there is even greater change coming, and we'll have to battle through hell to see it done."

"We are leaving?" Naiyala asked.

"Yes. The wheels are turning, and the players are in motion. Demons are appearing in lands around the world, and it will get worse. I suspect your Ilanyan friend is preparing the defense of Takashaniel."

"You know about that?"

Darius nodded. "Surviving a long time in this world takes more than the ability to live many years. Daunyarka, drojan, The Four; all know of the Tower of Balance. Humans have simply forgotten and allowed the place to slip into legend, then obscurity."

Malimokuru stood as well. "I guess that means we get moving."

"Yes," Darius agreed. "The tear between this world and the abyss will be ripped asunder if Takashaniel falls."

"Are there more of your kind that could help stop this?

A shadow passed across the Darius's face. He left the patio, Malimokuru and the others in tow. After he turned in the key to his room, they walked down a quiet street, the amahle keeping their hoods in place to obscure their features. Just when Malimokuru thought he hadn't intended to answer the question, Darius spoke.

"Your question assumes that all of my kind are goodly folk. Or sympathetic, for that matter." They rounded a corner and crossed a street filled with hawkers and shoppers, buildings that had been gutted and used for purposes that ranged from shops of various businesses, to stables or livestock stores.

Malimokuru didn't know what the city of Arland was like during the Age of Technology, but it had not only survived the cataclysms of the End of Technology, but thrived.

"Drojans care little for the affairs of The Four. We mostly live in solitude, or sometimes in pairs, and rarely commingle with other species."

"But in this case," Malimokuru replied, "if the world is overrun with demons, everybody suffers."

"If the scenario you present comes to pass, my friend, it might or might not mark the world's ultimate descent into permanent darkness. There are forces of nature you cannot fathom. Not even your ancient legends truly grasp them."

"Still, the world would be hell for a very long time," Malimokuru said. Darius responded with noncommittal grunt.

They came to the stable that housed Malimokuru's and Darius's horses. After securing their mounts, they walked out of the city gates and then quickened their pace, the four amahle easily pacing the cantering horses. About a mile outside Arland, Nyaka appeared, shadowing them from a comfortable distance for the wary horses. Malimokuru had finally coaxed her to repress her amusement and stop tormenting the animals.

"Just as there are different types of humans or amahle," Darius said, "there are different types of drojans, and also different types of Daunyarka. Some are more friendly than others, and some are wholly unfriendly."

"Unfriendly?" Malimokuru echoed.

"They are the emotions of nature, friend Malimokuru." It was Amata Daunyana who'd spoken as she jogged beside his galloping horse. "Some are kindhearted, some are standoffish, and some are aggressive. All are nature personified."

"The Daunya Apprentice speaks truly," Darius said. "Daunyarka were the first creation of Amayilah, the Daunya of Creation, yet they are known as Boraka's Guardians. They have stood with Him through eternity."

"Ya man," Malimokuru replied. "So they're protectors. Wouldn't stand to reason that they'd fight with us? And I think we've lost the original question."

"Be still and listen, friend. The lives of the drojan are intertwined with that of the Daunyarka."

To their relief, the road angled farther north than east, keeping the glaring eastern sun out of their eyes. Malimokuru kept a wary eye out for the winged demons but fortunately had seen no sign of them.

"Those Daunyarka who came fully into this world were subjected to all that the earth has experienced. Just as different humans have certain attributes that are unique unto them, so too do all other species, including Daunyarka. As a result, so too do we, the drojan; the creations of the dragons."

"Creations?" Malimokuru was not sure how to feel about this revelation. He looked at Naiyala, who wore an equally shocked expression.

"I have heard of the people of The Tribe," Amata Daunyana said. "Born of the blood of Daunyarka and the Mother upon which we live."

"I'm not sure I understand this," Malimokuru said.

"Of course not," Darius replied. "What I speak of precedes the existence of your species by more years than you can comprehend. My people were created by the blood of the dragons and the raw elemental power of the earth itself."

"So you were not actually born from a dragon," Malimokuru ventured. "But from the magical essence of a dragon mingling with that of the earth?"

Darius looked impressed. "You've grasped the concept of it, though simplistic ..."

"Would mean that you would inherit the attributes of the specific dragon from which you are descended?"

Darius tipped his head. "Bravo. We of The Tribe are direct descendants of Daunyarka. Everything they are, we are, but to a smaller degree."

"And that was why you were able to repel Khairon's attack back in the Sentinels?" Malimokuru frowned in confusion at Darius's responding grin.

"I repelled an attack by an amused Daunyarka that was having more fun than he'd had in centuries. Make no mistake my human friend. Khairon is no lava leech. Had he truly wanted to kill all who had entered his lair, he could have done so. If it came to a true fight between us, I could probably have died with the satisfaction of inflicting a few wounds that would have pained him for a time."

Malimokuru shivered at the thought of anything that was capable of killing this man. But then, he'd been carried hundreds of miles by the great blue dragon and felt his presence. It was like being in the gentle grasp of a living mountain. "So again, bringing the subject back around to my original question?"

"Drojans are as likely to involve ourselves in the affairs of the world as our dragon ancestors, which is to say, not at all. And I should add that you do not want to see the full force of the rage and power of a dragon."

They slowed their horses to a canter, then to a trot, finally bringing the horses to a stop and dismounting to continue on foot. Naiyala and her clan slowed to walk beside them, only mildly winded while the exhausted horses' nostrils flared.

"You intend to fight with us, friend Darius?" Naiyala asked as they climbed up a grassy knoll. The rested at the top, taking in the panoramic view of the wetlands that stretched before them.

Malimokuru sighed. "Why does it have to be swamplands?"

"I do intend to fight beside you, *Inkosazana*," Darius answered. "Though I wish I could say that my intentions were wholly benevolent. The truth is that while I do wish to avoid this world falling to a dark fate, I also enjoy the excitement. I have been inactive for more years than I can remember. I have reached a point where death would be preferable to a millennium of boredom."

"Whatever your motivation, we welcome your aid, friend Darius," Naiyala replied.

"Does no one else find the prospect of traversing swampland unnerving?" Malimokuru asked, still scanning the landscape.

"An unfortunate necessity," Darius replied. "It is directly between us and our destination. Take heart. We are closer than it appears. If Takashaniel was not shrouded from view, you would be able to see its glory from here."

"I don't doubt it, but we left an undecided confrontation with two resilient demons behind us. I have a feeling we'll see them again."

"You've left enemies at your back?" Darius asked.

"More like they left us at theirs." Malimokuru couldn't help sparing a glance at the trail behind them.

Darius shrugged. "We will deal with them when the time comes."

The weary Malimokuru shook his head and said a silent prayer to the Daunyans that Darius had decided to befriend them.

Tinnoviel's heart hammered in his chest as he gazed upon the magnificent Takashaniel from atop one of the surrounding hills. How could Queen Mayana of the Elden have refused to send aid?

In spite of every warning, the recounts of himself and every member of his party of their past battles, despite all his pleas, she'd refused. "*N'thresha* created this problem," she'd said when they spoke in private. "Let them solve it themselves. I admire your kindness and willingness to fight alongside them, but I do not share it. The Daunyans have seen fit to bless six humans with Their power, and make one Their Chosen. Let that be enough."

That had ended the argument and the Elden queen had offered them her indefinite hospitality, but had made it clear that the matter was settled. To not give a show of disrespect in lieu of her decision, they remained for another full day before departing, explaining that they had to return to assist with preparations.

Despite her refusal to unite with the defenders, Mayana had graciously seen to it they were fully provisioned and ready for their return to the tower. "I pray to Amayilah Herself that you do not lose your lives solving human problems, Tinnoviel Nai SaunyaLi," she'd said. Deep down, in a not so small part of his mind, Tinnoviel shared her sentiment.

A tiny fist punched him lightly in the arm. "You did your best, TinTin," Tikena said, smiling up at him. "We'll just have to do it all ourselves."

Tinnoviel rested a hand on her shoulder and smiled. Her head barely reached his elbow, but she had the spirit of a tiger. "Indeed we will, little one."

* * *

"My Yathieneli friends," Iel opened his arms in greeting. "How did you fair with your Elden cousins?" His smile faded when he saw the answering somber expressions. "I see. Take heart, my friends. I confess that I held little hope for your success. Of the elven people, only the Myzelli are as reclusive and mistrustful of humans as the Elden. Sadly, your results with them would have been the same."

"They believe they can expel the demon threat, should it find them," Tinnoviel said, an edge of irritation in his voice. "I don't believe they fully grasp the situation."

"The matter is settled," Iel said. "We will do what we must. I've been visited by a clan of centaurs, who helped defend against the first attack. They will fight with us again."

"Centaurs," Tinnoviel said with a rueful smile. "I cannot remember when last I saw one. I suppose the last age saw all of us retreating into seclusion, even from each other."

"You've been the guardian of Takashaniel for years uncounted," Yurin said. "You know better than any how severe the tear is that bridges the two dimensions. How has the drek managed to rip a hole open between the two worlds and summon such a large force of demons despite the integrity of the tower?"

Iel started to walk, the others falling into step with him. "It was a stroke of luck. The nature of the drek is the ability to gradually leach energy. It's how they sustain themselves indefinitely. They aren't a numerous species, thank the Daunyans, but they are migratory by necessity.

Over time, the drek began to take less care in controlling their population and began to set up permanent civilizations. The constant leeching of their surroundings meant that there were virtually no deaths among their population, yet they began to procreate at a faster rate.

Not long after, their mortality rate reversed, whether due to lack of sustenance or genocide, I don't know.

"Being one of the most powerful of his kind, Brit was tasked with finding another part of this world for his species to inhabit."

A herd of whitetail deer trotted across the open field, several stopping to smell the air. They looked in the party's direction, then continued on.

"Brit is capable of traveling in a similar manner as the Daunya Chosen, but instead of shifting the space around himself to step through, much like one would step through a giant bubble, Brit rips a hole in the space and creates a bridge to his destination, leaving the area weakened and unstable. Over time, the damaged space repairs itself, but if it were say, continually held open ..."

"Then it would weaken enough to allow him to summon demons faster than Takashaniel could balance the forces and expel them," Yurin finished. "His leeching nature made this possible."

Iel nodded. "You see the problem. In being able to bypass the natural laws of this world, he's been able to sidestep the influence of Takashaniel long enough to create and maintain a wound, if you will, in the barrier between this world and the abyss.

"Of course, Takashaniel would eventually balance the intrusion by either expelling a number of the demons, or infusing more children with the Gene of the Daunyans."

"I thought the Daunyans infused Their power in the host," Yurin said.

Iel shook his head. "Takashaniel was built in the physical realm by mortal hands, but it is a living, sentient being created by the Daunyans. It exists in the light dimension, but has a different function than its physical manifestation in this world."

"That is interesting," Yurin replied.

Tinnoviel arched an eyebrow at her. It was the first time he'd ever seen her surprised by anything.

Iel stopped walking. "We are not alone."

Immendiel drew her weapon as the elves formed a defensive circle. "What is it?"

"It's very subtle," Iel said. I don't sense enough power from it to be much of a threat, but there is something here and it means us no good."

"A weak enemy that is difficult to spot," Tinnoviel said. "This sounds like a spy."

Iel nodded. "I believe you're right. And in this vast expanse, there is virtually no way to find it. They are able to blend with their surroundings by bending the light around them. *Skulkers*."

"Now that I focus, I feel something more," Yurin said as she stared absently ahead. "There is a sickness in the land that is difficult to pinpoint, but is large and malevolent."

"A taint," Iel confirmed. "I can't sense it as you do, but I feel the wrongness."

"Perhaps our enemy has found a way to sicken the land around Takashaniel," Yurin said.

"Impossible. There is no safer land than here."

"Something is here," Yurin insisted. "If it isn't on these grounds than perhaps it's underneath."

"If what you say is true," Iel said, "a demon would not survive long this close to Takashaniel and so far from its summoner."

"Then it must be a creature native to this world," Yurin said. "Tainted by the abyss."

"How do we find it?" Tikena asked, scanning the landscape as though she might spot the danger at any moment.

"It would take more time than we have available to us," Yurin said.

If Iel heard them, he gave no indication. He stared absently at the ground for long time, and all the elves could do was wait.

He closed his eyes. "Our enemy plays a smart game. I don't know how he's done it, but I believe Brit has found a way to corrupt a sleeping earth elemental."

Tinnoviel felt his heart drop into his stomach. Behind him, Tikena groaned and Immendiel muttered an oath.

"We cannot locate an earth elemental in time to cleanse it," Yurin said, stoic as usual. "The best we can do is plan for its appearance when the drek unleashes it on us. I need time to prepare."

"All of Takashaniel is at your disposal," Iel said. "This will be the final conflict, friends."

"We will be ready," Tinnoviel said, placing a hand on the guardian's shoulder.

Iel stared into the distance, his normally kind features hardened. "As will he."

A kemi forced herself to ignore her distaste of conventional warfare as she moved from place to place, dispatching Qian soldiers on the way toward her targets. Such a manner of battle was inefficient. Better to find the most influential figures and eliminate them one by one, or if they were foolish enough to venture too close together, she might dispatch more than one at a time.

From somewhere behind, she heard the roar of Liu Xiang's mighty general as he clashed with Qian's son, General Ning. She didn't spare them a second thought, for the *seaph* was far more important.

Akemi scanned the battlefield and saw Qian—or what had been Qian—astride his horse, far removed from the actual fighting. She narrowed her eyes. There was no cowardice in Hua's position. He wasn't afraid to fight, nor did he care about the lives of his men.

They were tools, to him. He'd let his forces tire out Xiang's, and when the time came to strike, he and his surrounding force would be fresh while his adversaries were spent. It mattered not how many of Qian's soldiers died so long as they served their purpose.

As if to punctuate her thoughts, another contingent charged the field and flanked Liu Xiang. Kenjiro fought in that skirmish. For every man one of Liu's soldiers cut down, her brother felled three.

A soft *shing* penetrated the noise of battle. Akemi turned her attention to the right and saw Shinobu crossing blades with quite possibly the largest man on the battlefield.

Halfway between six and seven feet tall, the beast of a man swung a weapon that looked like a large pillar. His body was easily twice as wide as the Shinobu's, and it looked as though he was made of layer upon layer of muscle. Whether he managed to hit the strider with that pillar, or got a hand on him, it would be a quick death.

She couldn't worry about Shinobu, for Hua had again caught her attention. Three of his lieutenants had fanned out and begun to form a pincer to force their way through and close in around Liu Xiang. Qian himself had moved forward, but at a much slower pace.

Akemi checked her gear, making sure the finger-length shurikens strapped to her forearms and the sides of her shins were tightly secured. She reached into a pouch at her side and drew three four-point star shaped shurikens, each held between her fingers.

The lieutenant closest to her led his force in an arc, closing the distance between them.

Akemi kept low to the ground, using her height and speed to her advantage. Any Qian soldier that noticed her died quickly and silently.

Once within range, she darted between several embattled warriors until she got an opening. She leapt toward a Qian soldier's back while at the same time, hurling the three shurikens at the mounted soldier.

She didn't need to see the projectiles hit their mark, for the cries of alarm from the surrounding men confirmed that she'd hit her mark.

Akemi landed atop the soldier battling one of Liu Xiang's men. She stabbed and slit his throat as she rode him down. When the dead soldier hit the ground, she rolled forward and kept moving.

She made her way to the second lieutenant, guarded by his own contingent. This time, her approach was noted, and the commanding soldier pointed his sword at her, barking orders in the native tongue of the land. The four nearest soldiers trained their weapons on her.

The ninja never slowed. She crisscrossed her arms in front of her midsection, then whipped her hands out. A storm of four-point shurikens flew into the lieutenant's guards. The men hadn't expected such an unorthodox attack. They fell, clutching bleeding faces and throats. Before most of them hit the ground, Akemi was already gliding toward the lieutenant. She crossed her arms again and grabbed two shurikens at each forearm.

Akemi let fly, but this lieutenant was more prepared. He managed to deflect three of the blades, suffering a wound in his right shoulder from the fourth. To his credit, the man ignored the pain and leveled his sword at the helplessly gliding woman. Akemi was anything but helpless.

After she'd thrown the shurikens, Akemi continued the motion. She swung her arms around and grabbed the hilts of *Onisekairu* and *Onihakaisha*. At the last instant, she drew one of her swords and slashed downward, forcing his sword beneath her.

She used the momentum to roll over his shoulder. As she passed, she drew the other sword in a reverse grip and stabbed backward. Her aim was true, and *Onihakaisha* found his upper back. Akemi reversed her grip again and pulled the sword free as she landed in a crouch beside the horse.

Two spearmen converged on her even as the lieutenant slumped in the saddle. The soldiers twisted their wrists with each thrust of the spear. A red sash attached to the spearhead flapped at her face with each thrust.

A distracting attachment. *Clever.* She dodged and parried to stay one step ahead, but the spears were like angry cobras. Several times a spear tip would wiggle around her parry and score a cut on her arm, her shoulder, her hip.

Several vicious exchanges had Akemi backpedaling to get a better measure of her adversaries. As they circled each other, Akemi spared a glance to the west and saw the sun speeding toward the horizon. If she couldn't eliminate Qian before sundown, this fight would take an undesirable turn.

At any moment, demon-inhabited corpses from both sides would rise against them. It was simply a matter of when the *seaph* decided to raise them.

She returned her attention to the two spear wielding soldiers and lowered into a crouch. The man on her left always attacked first, closely followed by the other. As she'd predicted, the soldier on her left thrust his spear.

Akemi held her ground and at the last second, parried the attack and forced the spear toward the second. Before the first man could retract, she changed her grip on her right-hand sword from reverse to a forward grip and chopped down. Just as the head of the spear was severed, she whipped her left sword around with blinding speed toward the first man's neck.

Whether it was the grisly sight itself, or the thump of his partner's head hitting the ground, the second soldier retreated several steps. He stole a glance at the severed head, then back at Akemi. He swallowed.

Akemi lowered into a crouch and circled him. In a slow and deliberate motion, she reversed her grip on her right-hand sword. Now the flat of both blades rested against her forearms, one held across her chest, the other behind her back. She winked. "Don't be shy. We all must die sometime."

The soldier snarled and thrust his spear forward and quickly retracted, then moved his hands to the middle of the shaft. He spun it vertically speeding wheel while whipping it to the left and right of his body.

Akemi thought to laugh at the showmanship, but had to leap aside as he repositioned his hands and brought the spear tip racing down toward her head. Narrowly avoiding the attack, she came back to her feet and ducked just as he swung the spear horizontally toward her head. She barely had time to register the whoosh of air as the spear passed over, for it came in again at her feet.

Thinking quickly, she avoided the sweep by leaping forward instead of up. As she'd expected, the soldier had anticipated her to jump either up or back to avoid his sweep, and had begun an upward swing. Before he realized his mistake, she was already inside his reach, and *Onisekairu* found his throat. The spear fell from his hands as he dropped to his knees, clasping his throat as blood streamed through his fingers.

Akemi turned to see that the last lieutenant pressing Liu Xiang from the left flank. She had to hope the emperor was equal to the threat, because her target was the warlord.

Through the screeches and clangs of steel, the war cries and dying screams, and the coppery smell of blood, Akemi scanned the battlefield until finally locating the warlord. He sat his horse, scanning the battle with little concern, his face fixed with an inhuman grin.

She started weaving her way toward him, a shadow unnoticed by all but the few unfortunate who registered her presence. Slashing a hamstring or stabbing between shoulder blades as she passed, Akemi provided what aid she could to her allies as she worked her way to Qian. His personal guard noted her advance and formed a defensive ring around him, those closest coming together to block the way.

Never slowing, Akemi sheathed both her swords and whipped her arms around to crisscross in front of her midsection. As before, she let fly a barrage of four point shurikens. These soldiers were more skilled than the bulk of Qian's forces. The front men parried some of the projectiles, while many still found their marks.

Two men fell, clutching eyes and throats, while three others shrugged away their injuries. They had no chance. Before the first shurikens had found their marks, the ninja had already reached into her pouch and let fly a second volley, further decimating Qian's guards.

Qian smirked at her as if she'd done something amusing. He drew his broadsword and pointed it at her. He barked an order in a voice that didn't sound like his own.

He's gone completely. Akemi watched as the remaining guards tried to surround her. Another cursed spearman stepped into the ranks as well.

In a similar fashion as the previous spearmen, but with far more skill, he thrust the spearhead toward her and twisted his wrist.

Akemi leaped above the weapon in a forward flip, bringing her swords down across his chest, cutting a **V** from his shoulders to his waist. She was already past him as he fell, switching to a forward grip with her left sword. The two remaining guards managed to fend off her attacks long enough to press back. From the corner of her eye, Akemi saw Qian's horse bearing down on her, the warlord's spear tip aimed at her back.

* * *

"G etting tired of this dance yet, boy?" Zhang Da asked. In truth, the other general was not much younger than he was, but the insult was enough.

"It's past time I skewered you like the pig you are." Ning lunged and stabbed for his face. Da took a step back then thrust his spear forward and twisted his wrist. The spearhead came spinning forward in a circular motion, whipping around the sword and scoring a deep cut in the seam of Ning's armor, at the elbow. Ning retreated and studied Zhang through narrowed eyes.

Zhang Da smiled wickedly. The fight had almost ended right there. Ning had thought his weapon the same as any other spear, and had nearly paid for the assumption with his life. Not only was Zhang Da's spear larger and heavier, but also had a longer, thicker shaft and a longer, thicker head.

Ning feinted a thrust that Zhang saw for what it was. When he failed to react, Ning came in hard, parrying Zhang's defensive thrust and stepping inside his reach. Ning tried to take off his head with a backhanded swipe. Zhang ducked the attack and released the spear with his right hand, twisting his body toward Ning with an outward thrust of his palm into the other man's chest.

He immediately retreated a few steps, regaining his posture. The strike caused Ning to stagger back, but he laughed. "Was that supposed to hurt?"

"Not really."

Ning tilted his head, then laughed again. "Save the mystical monk magic tricks for some other fool, Da. It ill suits even you!"

"Some other fool. Then you finally admit to being a fool?" Now it was Zhang's turn to laugh.

Ning's nostrils flared. "I'll be sure to preserve that smile on your head as it rots on a pike, in the middle of your beloved city."

"You've got the situation mixed, boy."

Ning bellowed and came at him again. Zhang picked off his attacks one by one and countered. Back and forth they went, each scoring tiny nicks or glancing cuts, and each time, Zhang Da dealing a bit more damage to the warlord's son.

They clashed again, Qian Ning stabbing for Zhang's chest. He stopped short and swiped low, then high.

Zhang Da grinned. Ning thought him unable to recognize the feint and react in time to the true attack.

A lesser man might have fallen, but General Zhang Da was the descendent of the mighty Zhang Fei. He whipped the butt of his spear around to turn aside the low swipe while following the motion through. He continued the turn and snapped the butt of his spear into the side of Ning's head. As the other man stumbled sideways, Zhang continued his turn, and delivered a spinning sideways kick to the ribs.

Somehow, the man kept his feet, but Zhang wasn't finished. As soon as his foot touched the ground, Zhang spun his spearhead around and slammed it into the side of his opponent's head with crushing force.

Zhang swung his spear around in the opposite direction to catch Qian Ning in the face even as he staggered to the side.

Da stepped back and twisted his wrist as he thrust his spear forward. Somehow, Ning had just enough presence of mind to offer a parry. There wasn't enough strength behind it and the spearhead slipped through and punched into his side. Zhang pulled the spear free and backed off. Ning regained his footing and lifted his sword to a defensive position. The move was slow and labored.

His sword slipped from his grasp and Ning staggered forward and dropped to his knees. He struggled to stand again, confusion twisting his features.

Zhang kept an eye on the surrounding Qian soldiers, but all watched in shock as the man fumbled with his sword, blood trickling from the corner of his mouth. He fell again, but growled and forced himself up to one knee.

Ning's frown deepened. He stared on the ground in front of him, concentrating on taking one breath after the other. His shoulders rose and fell, and he blinked several times. The look on his face told that he knew the truth of his fate. He slowly, lifted his gaze to look Da in the eyes.

Da held the man's gaze for several heartbeats and it seemed time itself came to a stop. Ning's head shook, and for an instant it looked like he gave Zhang a nod; one warrior to another. His gaze hollowed as the life left his eyes, and General Qian Ning succumbed to death.

* * *

Sweat trickled from Gaun Xi's brow as she powered the shaft of her weapon up to stop the descending chop of a sword. She turned aside, twisting her weapon to force the sword sideways to block a horizontal swipe at her head. The thin, corded muscles in her arms flexed as she twisted the weapon back around and angled it forward in an upward cut at the first attacker. He was forced to release the sword and hop back.

Before she could gain an advantage, however, the second twin stepped in sideways in an almost sitting crouch, and whipped the blade of his sword upward, forcing her to similarly hop back.

He used his free hand to grab the sword and toss it to his brother. It was all done in a single fluid movement that Guan couldn't help but admire. She offered an appreciative nod.

"You're good, but I don't have time for this. You fight on the wrong side. Can you not see what's happening?" One of the twins, circled in one direction while the other moved in the opposite. "So be it."

The twin in front of her swung his sword in a sideways cut at her midsection. Xi rotated her weapon as she turned her body. She knocked the sword back and forced the stabbing sword of the second twin up.

She followed the attack through, completing the spin as she stepped forward. The spear tipped end of Xi's Guandao came down on the forearm of the twin in front of her as he instinctively raised his arm to deflect the blow. Despite the sound of breaking bone, he merely flinched.

The second twin sprang forward with a flurry of attacks. The tip of his sword was a blur that forced Xi to backpedal as she fought to keep from being sliced or skewered.

The first twin tucked his arm close to his chest and raised his sword. He bared his teeth and joined his brother. Guan Xi had to work hard to keep her adversaries from cutting her to ribbons. Despite his injury, the first twin was still dangerously fast.

They maneuvered her between them again, and Guan Xi fell into her rhythm. She kept her Guandao moving, deflecting and parrying. She skipped over the swipe of a sword at her leg, spinning her weapon above her head and then down. When he dodged, she used the momentum and weight of the weapon to create more speed as she whipped her foot around to snap into the side of his head.

The twin turned with the blow to absorb most of the impact. He followed up with a horizontal cut that forced Guan Xi to duck.

While bent over, Xi released one hand from the shaft of her weapon and spun it over her back. The resulting retreat of her adversaries bought her enough time to recover.

Guan had managed to maneuver the warriors in front of her again. When she straightened, she kept moving with the turn of the heavy weapon, readying her offense. A horrifying sight caught her attention and she stopped short and slammed the shaft into her underarm.

A misshappen soldier shambled his way toward them. At first glance he might have looked injured and limping, but as he drew closer, the truth became clear. Guan Xi's eyes widened, and she shouted a warning to her adversaries.

It would have been a ridiculous distraction tactic, but they must have seen the truth in her eyes.

As one, they turned and leapt aside as the pale, twisted soldier clumsily slashed downward at them. The first twin stabbed the twisted soldier in the arm. Before the dropped sword hit the ground, the second twin beheaded him. The faint sound of a wail drifted in the air and a sickly vapor seeped out of the open wound. The two men watched in horror, then turned back to Guan Xi.

Equally horrified, she pointed the tip of her weapon at the fallen soldier. "This is what you fight alongside! This is what your leader plans! If you don't believe me, look at his uniform!"

The truth was undeniable. The fallen soldier wore a Qian uniform. The twins cast her a skeptical look, but had no time to consider it. Several more demon-ridden corpses bearing the uniforms of both Qian and Liu advanced on them.

"They are your true foe," Guan said when she saw their indecision. "I will fight with you if you if you will fight with me."

Two sets of hard eyes looked into hers. The two warriors nodded and positioned themselves on either side of Guan Xi. She cast her reservations of being flanked by what were her enemies just moments ago, and focused on their true foe.

* * *

Shinobu dove aside once again to avoid being flattened by the ridiculous weapon his hulking adversary wielded. How could anyone wield such a thing?

"No sword or spear for you, eh?" he remarked in the tongue of Ba Guo. "A stone pillar makes far more sense."

The giant of a man gave the pillar resting on his shoulder a little tap. "Don't worry about my choice of weapon, little one. After you've felt its weight upon you, nothing will matter."

Shinobu didn't doubt for a second the truth of that statement, should he falter. "I'm afraid that will never happen, my huge friend. The giant's casual shrug said that he'd heard similar from past victims.

He lunged forward and ducked as he swung the pillar down. The man was fast for his size, not to mention wielding a weapon that likely weighed more than Shinobu himself!

The strider leapt backwards just in time to get out of the way. As soon as he landed, Shinobu dove into a sideways roll. He felt the ground vibrate when the pillar crashed into the ground beside him.

His adversary dragged the pillar through the soil as he lifted it. Shinobu turned his head away to keep the showering of dirt and grass out of his eyes.

Shinobu's instincts screamed at him to keep moving. He rolled to his feet and dove into another somersault, the crashing pillar right behind him. When he got his feet under him once more, Shinobu leapt and turned in the air. He drew his sword from over his shoulder and slashed at his enemy.

Up came the pillar. If Shinobu had wielded any normal sword, the impact would have severely damaged or even shattered the blade. *Zaiku* was anything but normal. The blade bit into the pillar and left a deep gash. The sword was back in its sheath before his feet touched the ground.

The giant man laughed. "I'm impressed your sword is still in one piece. It'll fetch a pretty price." He rubbed his chin. Or perhaps I'll keep it as a souvenir to commemorate our battle, yes?

"I'd hoped to avoid this." Shinobu slid *Zaiku* from its sheath and held it at his side.

"What do you hope to do with that little twig?"

Shinobu said nothing, for his enemy's wasn't the only voice that spoke to him. The magnificent blade at his side longed for the release of its true power. The man indecipherable symbols etched into the blue-silver blade began to pulsate. "You will find out soon enough." He scanned the surrounding embattled soldiers. "You ever find it odd that duels such ours rarely go unhindered?"

"No, I don't wonder. It is because these weaklings," he waved a heavily muscled arm to encompass the mass of bodies, "know better than to interfere in a struggle between two real warriors. If one of Qian's men intervenes, I'll put him down, myself." He tilted his head. "Your sword appears to be fading away."

Shinobu grinned. It was a good attempt to hide his shock, but the strider saw it in his eyes. "Indeed."

He didn't need to look at the blade, for the longer *Zaiku* remained free of its sheath, the more insubstantial—and thus, powerful—it would become. "I think your man Qian wouldn't like you cutting down his men."

"To hell with what he doesn't like," came the response.

Which hell? Shinobu thought, but kept that thought to himself.

The giant lunged in and thrust the flat end of the pillar forward. Shinobu backstepped and sliced downward. The ethereal blade split part of the top of the pillar. A large chunk of the weapon broke off and hit the ground with a heavy thud.

Shinobu unleashed a barrage of attacks with the spectral blade, slicing off pieces of the pillar whenever it made contact.

The ferocity of Shinobu's sudden offense, and the power of *Zaiku* reduced the mighty weapon to a cluster of chunks lying on the ground.

The giant warrior took a defensive stance. The way he looked from Shinobu to the spectral blade, however, betrayed his determination. "You have an amazing sword, warrior. Will it be as effective against steel?"

"Steel?" Shinobu's heart sank as he watched his adversary reach over his shoulder and draw what was without a doubt the largest, thickest curved broadsword he had ever seen. One cut with that thing and his strength behind it could cleave a man in half. "How long did it take the smithy to create that thing?"

"Six months. He started to advance, then stopped and frowned.

Shinobu matched his expression. "What now? Have you used that ridiculous chunk of rock for so long you forgot how to use a sword?"

"No, fool. I'm confused about what's creeping up behind you."

Shinobu rolled his eyes. "We've devolved to insulting each other's intelligence, now …"

The slightest sound of an unusual, shambling gait found his ears and his instincts took control. Shinobu spun and lopped off the head of a soldier wearing a Liu uniform just as it attempted to cut him down. A faint scream floated on the air and a wicked vapor drifted out of the wound. Shinobu looked on in horror as a grotesque inhuman face floated in front of him. Its mouth stretched open in a silent scream as it dissipated.

Shinobu nearly forgot the other man, and turned to see him equally horrified,

"What was that?"

"It's starting," Shinobu said by way of an answer. "Your warlord commands the dead."

The warrior glared at him. "You think me an idiot? "He pointed at the decapitated soldier. "That man wears the uniform of Liu."

"And what of those?" Shinobu said, pointing at more twisted dead soldiers bearing uniforms from both sides shuffling toward them.

"If Warlord Qian commanded them as you say, they would attack you, not me." Despite his words, the big man went into a defensive stance, eyeing the advancing ghouls.

"You place too much faith in the faithless, mighty warrior, Shinobu replied. "Qian does not need a living army when he can raise the dead of his allies and enemies. Eventually there would be no living left to oppose him."

"What are you insinuating?" Wei tightened his grip on his sword as a knot of twisted soldiers lumbered toward them. "Be quick with your words!"

"I'm saying that if you and I die, Qian will simply pull a weaker fiend from the demon realm and shove it into our lifeless bodies. He'll reanimate us into one of those." Shinobu pointed at the advancing demon-ridden corpses.

The indecision on Wei's face was telling. It sounded ridiculous, but the evidence advancing on them was irrefutable. "Like hell he will!" With single swing of his broadsword, the mighty warrior cleaved through flesh and bone, dividing two approaching bodies into four.

"No one deserves such a fate." Shinobu cut down the nearest former human, then the one behind it. "We fight together, then?"

The man nodded. "I don't know if your words are true, but I know what my eyes see. We fight together, for now. And my name is Wei, so you can stop calling me giant warrior." He laid low another three demon-ridden corpses with a mighty swing of his sword.

"As you say. My name is Shinobu."

"Then fight with me, Shinobu, and we will see what we see when this is done."

Side by side they blazed a violent trail through the growing mass of demon inhabited bodies. To the west, the sun began its ominous descent toward the horizon. Shinobu's sense of dread grew when he saw that more and more of the fallen were rising again to fight the living on both sides.

"Must we kill every dead soldier again?" Wei growled, felling another former human that jabbed a spear at him.

"You'll not like my answer," Shinobu replied.

"Speak."

"The only way to stop this is to cut down Qian."

Shinobu heard Wei's responding grunt and glanced at the man. He received a skeptical sidelong glance in return.

"We'll see soon enough if your words are true," Wei said as he cut down three more enemies. "If they are, I'll cut the bastard down myself."

Someone is already on that task, Shinobu thought, then his mind clicked on something. He looked harder at the hulking man beside him. Seven feet tall if he was an inch, and made of solid muscle head to toe.

And speaking of his head, it was shaven clean. The way the man grabbed a lumbering former human by the arm and hoisted him over his shoulder with one hand, Shinobu had heard of such a man before, in Ba Guo's ancient history. A giant of a man, loyal to a man who had betrayed the three kingdoms.

Wei. Shinobu cut down a lunging former human, then the one behind it. "You said your name is Wei?"

5 0

"You've given me quite the surprise, woman," Qian said, guiding his nervous horse in a circle around the crouching ninja. "I had not expected a capable warrior resided in that delicious little body of yours."

"Why not dismount and see how capable a warrior this delicious little body houses," Akemi replied sweetly.

"I would love to, but I have a kingdom to establish with the stilling of the heart of that weakling Xiang."

"You and I know that you desire nothing of the sort. You would raise every dead soldier on this field to bring more of your kind to into this world." The *seaph* frowned at her in surprise and she responded with a narrowed-eyed grin. "Yes, *seaph*. I know what you are. How do you think your men will react when they discover the truth of their ruler? What do you think they will do?"

The thing that had been Qian chopped his hand through the air. "It's of no consequence. In little time this entire field will be an army of my creation, and your empty vessel will serve as an excellent host. Perhaps I will honor you as my second in command."

Akemi's grin broadened. She'd hunted demons for too long to be shaken by the threat. "Do you know what these are, *seaph*?" She raised her swords. "Can you feel them?" She sensed the spike of anxiety in the demon inhabiting Qian Hua's body.

"You do feel them, don't you? I will introduce you to them personally.

One would devour you whole, the other would simply obliterate you. Which would you prefer?"

A trace of something inhuman laced Qian's laughter. "You would have me believe a human could wield such power? I will send you to a hell where you will be torn asunder and reformed, every moment of every day for eternity. You will beg for the same oblivion you claim those toys of yours can deliver upon me. You know not what you confront, little girl."

Akemi's smile never faltered. It was nervous. Despite its bluster, the *seaph* felt the power of her swords. It was all she could do to contain them herself, especially *Onihakaisha*. It was practically demanding to be unleashed on this hybrid monster.

She felt a warm surge of power within her body. The Gene. Her sight grew sharper, her hearing more acute. She was keenly aware of every muscle in her body, and their augmented strength and speed. The fiend had awoken the Gene within her.

"I am here, demon," she replied in a deep, almost seductive voice. "You have but to come to me."

The *seaph* launched its spear and she turned aside. With her augmented senses, Akemi watched the missile pass as though it were a feather drifting to toward the ground.

"You hurt my feelings, demon. Do you not wish to come down from there and embrace me?" She spread her arms, each shimmering sword held in a reverse grip. "Come. Dance with me."

The *seaph* rammed his heels into his horse's sides and the poor animal lunged forward. Akemi rolled aside as Qian took a swipe at her head. He turned his mount and charged again, and again, Akemi easily avoided his attack.

"Play this as long as you like, woman. Time is on my si—aaaarrrrrggghh-hh!" Blood flowed between his fingers as he clutched the shuriken embedded in his left eye. A guttural sound rumbled from his gritted teeth as he struggled to yank the Daunya-blessed blade free. "You have no idea the torment that awaits you."

Akemi rolled her eyes. "I could have destroyed you while you were tending to your poor little eye. I could have cut you down from that horse several times now. I haven't. Would you know why?"

"You are delusional, but I will humor you."

She ignored the *seaph's* attempt to retain its pride. "Take your weakling demon spawn and return to the abyss, and I will allow it." The demon-inhabited Qian looked at her incredulously. She shrugged "If you refuse, I will destroy you."

"You think highly of your skills—"

"You are a demon from the first level of the abyss, the weakest. I have hunted fiends that would devour you simply because you crossed their path. I offer you one last chance, leave and take your minions. If you refuse, I will not send you back to the abyss; I will obliterate you."

The *seaph* snarled and kicked his horse into action. Akemi lowered into a crouch and waited as the terrified animal bore down on her. When it was several running strides away, she leaped forward, farther and faster than any human should have been capable of. As she glided toward Qian, the demon warlord tried to skewer her in midair.

Akemi swept Onihakaisha down and forced his sword low. She used the momentum of the swing to roll her body sideways and crash into his head.

The horse reared, furthering Qian's fall, and the animal was already in flight before the warlord hit the ground.

Akemi rolled her swords around in her hands as she waited for the *seaph* to recover. She stole a glance at her surroundings, but she needn't worry about an attack from any Qian soldiers. Those who were still human looked on in horror at the green mist wafting from the warlord's remaining eye.

Qian slowly turned to face her, hands flexing as though needing something to crush. The sun had completely dipped below the horizon, and night had fallen. Soldiers on both sides still fought, although the battle was increasingly changing from Qian against Liu, to the living against the demon-ridden dead. A greater, more grotesque enemy had forced the two sides to unite against it.

"I don't see any more dead rising, little demon," Akemi taunted. "I'm guessing you can't summon them while concentrating on me?" Her face brightened. "You've actually done the emperor a favor. Once I've destroyed you, Qian's forces will have seen you for what you truly are. I'm sure their loyalty will need a new home. And now, having played your hand in full, you've created a more united force that is aware of your existence. In one night you've made my job so much easier by practically defeating yourself. I'm almost tempted to spare you just for that." She smiled brightly.

Nothing of the Qian-*seaph's* roar sounded human this time. He charged, sword held high. Though he wielded only one weapon against her two, the fiend was surprisingly fast, and the ninja had to work to fend him off.

"Impressive," Akemi admitted, ducking a sweep at her head. She saw an opening and swiped *Onisekairu* at its head, which Qian easily ducked. Then she brought *Onihakaisha* in for a low swipe. Qian reacted quicker than she'd expected, and threw his hips backwards to avoid the passing blade. As he straightened, he brought his sword around in a vertical chop.

Akemi lifted both swords up over her head in a crisscrossed block. The *seaph* was stronger than she'd anticipated. The power behind Qian's stroke drove her down to her knee.

She saw a booted foot coming for her face, but could not break away in time. She managed to skirt aside just enough to avoid being kicked in the face. Once, twice, a third time, the *seaph* kicked her in the abdomen. The heavy blows took the wind out of her lungs, but still she held Qian's sword at bay.

"You're a tough one," the warlord said. When no response came, he laughed. "What? No response. No smart-mouthed quip? Where is the superior humor, little female?"

"I'm … just saving it … for when I'm winning … the fight."

Qian drew his foot back again. This time, Akemi waited till the last instant, then rolled aside and let her arms drop. The sudden release of resistance caused him to stumble and she used the moment to catch her breath.

In her left hand, *Onisekairu* buzzed with hunger, while *Onihakaisha* was a raging tempest in her right. "There will be more before this whole business is done," she whispered to the swords. "But one of you will go unsatisfied this night."

She hadn't expected her words to have any effect, but to her surprise, the demands of the blades lessened. *So, you do hear me,* she thought. Again she was surprised when her mind received a mental feeling of what could only be described as agreement.

Akemi heard the sounds of bones cracking and skin stretching. She returned her attention to Qian to see the *seaph* rising to his full height; a height that far exceeded what he'd been just moments ago. Akemi's eyebrows rose along with the height of the former human warlord.

Now over eight feet tall, Qian favored her with a wicked grin. He ripped off his armor to reveal hardening skin. His flesh creased and wrinkled until his body looked to be made of stone.

"We've played enough," the *seaph* said, and there was no hint of anything human in its voice.

With the full form of the *seaph* revealed, the hunger of her swords renewed. Akemi tightened her grip on her swords. She'd only fought with them a few times, and neither battle had been with any powerful adversary.

This monster had aroused her swords, and she couldn't be sure which was the greater threat.

* * *

Though sorely pressed on their right flank, Liu Xiang's men fought valiantly against the forces of Qian. To his amazement, one of his soldiers had reported that the ninja had single-handedly eliminated two of the three lieutenants that sought to trap his forces in a pincer maneuver.

From astride his mount, Liu Xiang had also been able to see the samurai at the head of his left flank, cutting his way through the Qian forces. If he never fought again after this day, Kenjiro had already done the legacy of the samurai proud. Warriors such as these were only born in times of great need.

After the last light of the sun abandoned the land, Liu Xiang began to think the battle might not see dawn until another messenger arrived. The soldier clearly thought the emperor would not believe his account of dead men rising to fight again, but Xiang knew better. He had already been warned by his guests of this possibility.

Though his men fought fearlessly despite the horror of confronting their former comrades as well as fallen enemies, it seemed there could be no victory. Every fallen soldier was raised again to fight once more. If he didn't figure something out quickly, the battlefield would soon consist of nothing but dead bodies inhabited by demonic entities.

In the midst of those dark thoughts, something happened that gave the emperor a glimmer of hope. Little by little, his and Qian's forces had begun to unite against the dead soldiers. "Perhaps we will survive this day after all," he said to himself. A roar of defiance drowned out the din of battle, and Liu Xiang saw the mighty General Zhang Da battling tirelessly against numerous dead soldiers. He was working his way toward Xiang, but there were too many enemies.

He was just about to send a contingent to aid the general, when he spotted Guan Xi—alongside the infamous Twins of Qian—working their way toward him. Xiang shook his head. "This day grows stranger by the moment."

As the hours passed and the battle raged into the night, the tide seemed to turn in Xiang's favor. Though things looked hopeful, the emperor knew better. Things could change in an instant.

What he saw was heartening, however. The last of the demon-inhabited were being cut down and no more of the recent dead were rising. Zhang Da made it to his side, and soon after, Guan Xi and the Twins of Qian. He glanced at the two men and gave a firm nod. The responded with a respectful bow. Xiang dared to hope this tentative alliance could become lasting, but for now he'd take what he could get.

"We've turned the tide, my lord," Zhang Da reported. "But attention seems to be focused further afield."

Xiang nodded absently as he strained to see in the dim light. "Let us see for ourselves."

They waded through the throngs of soldiers, tending their own and each other's wounds and trying to make sense of the macabre turn of events. Here and there, the occasional ring of steel on steel could be heard.

Huge torches had finally been lit on the city walls, casting a weak but welcome light across some of the battlefield. As they drew closer, Xiang from his higher vantage point saw the dark silhouette of a figure who towered over all present.

The unnaturally tall figure looked like Warlord Qian—or rather, a grotesque version—but the guttural sound that came from his mouth sounded monstrous. He wore no armor to protect his torso, but his skin looked to have hardened into a rock-like texture.

Liu Xiang couldn't believe what he was seeing. One of the warlord's eyes emitted a green glow that looked like a tiny flame.

The Qian Hua demon moved with such speed and dexterity that Xiang had to admit to himself that he was glad it wasn't him fighting the creature. The combatants clashed again and Xiang saw that the other combatant was the ninja demon hunter.

As emperor, Liu Xiang had learned early in his career to be able to read a person and take their measure. He'd thought he had a good read on not only Akemi, but her brother and the farstrider. Seeing the duel ahead, he realized that it was impossible *not* to underestimate them.

"Looks like this fight has drawn everyone's attention, my lord," Guan Xi remarked. "She fights well ... for a slithery ninja, that is."

Xiang smiled to himself. Guan Xi rarely complimented anyone's battle prowess. "Where is the samurai? I would think he'd want to aid his sister against so monstrous a foe."

"The samurai watches the battle from the other side of the ring," Guan answered. "I suspect he wishes not to replace Warlord Qian, for I am sure that's what would happen if he were to interfere"

"Of course," Xiang replied. "Your foolish unspoken warrior's code."

Guan Xi laughed. "Well there is an unspoken code, Xuande, but I suspect in this case, it is simple pride and satisfaction. Ninja care little for honorable face to face combat. They kill in the most simple and efficient manner possible. I believe our little shadow assassin would not wish to be robbed of the gratification in overcoming her foe."

The ring of steel on steel reached a new crescendo as sparks exploded from the colliding blades and danced in the air around the combatants. Xiang tore his gaze away from the magnificent duel to take in the scene. He almost laughed at the unlikeliness of two opposing forces standing side by side to watch the spectacle. Could he use this mutually horrifying night to advantage?

"Good men who discover they have followed a corrupt ruler may yet be swayed, my lord."

Liu Xiang looked down to his right to see Zhang Da watching the duel. The general glanced up at him, and though it was too dark to see for sure, Xiang thought he saw him give a little wink.

Xiang returned his attention to the spectacle before them. "Perhaps, old friend."

* * *

Akemi rolled and leapt, feinted and counterattacked. She blocked weak attacks and parried stronger ones. This Qian demon was a more worthy adversary than she'd expected. The demon had fully absorbed Qian and assimilated every memory, skill, and ability of the warlord. Had this been a normal human fight, it would be much the same experience she was having now. The man, demon-ridden or not, was good. Very good.

"What's on your mind, little geisha?"

"I'm thinking." They clashed again. Qian chopped his sword down and Akemi parried with *Onihakaisha*. She slashed *Onisekairu* across his chest, scoring a gash in the rocky flesh.

Other than bits of rock—or whatever it was—falling away, the *seaph* showed no sign of having felt it at all. "About what?"

"What business is it of yours?" Akemi sliced him across the arm and received a backhanded punch to the midsection that sent her rolling backward. She kept rolling to absorb the impact and put some distance between them. As soon as her feet came under her, she leapt forward.

The sudden reversal surprised the advancing *seaph*. Before he could react she dealt him a well-placed slash across the neck as she glided by. A line of blood flowed from the wound.

Akemi took a deep breath to steady her patience. That blow should have taken his head.

"I'd wager you're thinking of ways to dispatch me," Qian replied. "For that reason alone it is very much my business."

"You have a point," Akemi said. "If you must know …" she grunted from the strain of using both her swords to deflect a diagonal overhead chop. He was strong! "I'm trying … to fight while suppressing my sense of *smell*. Is that hard skin or crusty muck raked from a stable coating your body? You *stink*, Warlord Qian."

The *seaph* snarled and stabbed for her face. When she sidestepped, he whipped his sword to the right. Akemi ducked the follow-up and cut a deep slice across his arm.

"I will devour you, body and soul, vermin." Despite the bleeding wound across his forearm, Qian chopped his sword down again and Akemi easily sidestepped. The blade practically sliced the air open in front of her on its descent, where it cut deep into the ground.

"Mistake!" Akemi announced cheerfully. She darted forward and, changing to a forward grip with both swords, brought them down on Qian's exposed arm with all her strength.

With a resounding crack, the lower half of Qian Hua's sword arm hit the ground with a heavy thump.

The *seaph* dropped to a knee and screeched. It spun around and slashed out with its remaining clawed hand, but the attack was clumsy and slow. Akemi hopped out of reach and slashed *Onisekairu* across its hand.

She turned her other wrist, angling the tip of *Onihakaisha* at the kneeling monster's heart. With speed augmented by the power of the Daunyans, Akemi drove the *Demon Destroyer* into Qian Hua's chest.

As soon as the blade pierced the armored skin and tasted the demonic essence within, it plunged itself further in.

The sudden reaction of the blade startled Akemi, and before she could react, *Onihakaisha* had driven itself in to the hilt.

It seemed all of time had stopped. The demon within Qian's body was pinned, the watching soldiers entranced by the sight, and Akemi held fast.

Qian's body shuddered, then fell into convulsions. He let out a tiny scream that turned into a deafening wail.

Akemi fought against the instinct to release the ravenous sword and endured the tempest of raw energy swirling around her. Her hair whipped across her face and for a moment she thought she might be swept away in the swirling storm of power.

It took all of her will to keep from being drawn into the sword, for now it was a contest of wills. While *Onihakaisha* drew the demon from Qian's body and ripped it apart, so too did it try to dominate its wielder. Should she falter now, the sword would use Akemi to facilitate the feeding of its insatiable hunger.

She closed her eyes. The sword was in a state similar to bloodlust. It savored every bit of the destruction of the *seaph*. If *Onihakaisha* had a voice, it would have laughed maniacally. In her left hand, *Onisekairu* quickened of its own volition. Akemi couldn't spare the energy to be wary of the sword, but she needn't have worried. To her surprise, she felt the *Demon Bane* feeding on the raw energy that swirled around them!

To Akemi, who held on for her very existence, it seemed a lifetime passed until finally the struggle ended. She slumped to her knees but dared not release the imbedded *Onihakaisha*.

Akemi wanted nothing more than to sleep. She forced herself to keep her eyes open but before she realized it, she fell into darkness. In her semiconscious state she heard muffled voices, then felt herself being lifted and carried away.

"Damned crazy woman still hasn't let go of those cursed swords."

She felt gentle yet familiar hands grab hers and guide one of her swords into the sheath at her back. The same was done for the other, and then, finally, she felt safe to release them. She forced her eyes open to see that Kenjiro held her in his arms. His concerned smile made her respond in kind.

Shinobu's face appeared over her, concern etched on his features. "How are you, insane woman?"

Akemi produced a trembling smile. "Sleepy." Her eyes grew heavy, and the world faded away.

Having set out immediately after reaching the surface, the band of dwarves, two humans, and a *haloren* crossed lands vast and unfamiliar. The dwarves, however, seemed to know exactly where they were. The band marched at a steady clip and never once slowed to get the lay of the land.

"Where are we?" Kita asked.

"'Bout half a day's march west of the human city of Winsor," Felk answered. "Figgered ye were in somethin' of a hurry from what ye told me king, so we're movin' quick. Should reach Winsor a few hours after dawn."

"We appreciate it," Kita replied.

"If I'm fer understandin' ye correct, yer plannin' to try and convince the king of New Dainland that he's got a demon problem that's only gonna spread unless he can deal with it?"

Kenyatta nodded. "That's it."

"I'm sure ye'll have a great time of it," Felk said, his voice thick with sarcasm. "Ye human folk're pretty blind to what's around ye."

"It's hard to believe something exists that you've never seen and has only existed in legend," Kita argued.

"Oh?" Felk raised his eyebrows. "So yer tellin' me that humans have seen the Gods afore?"

"Afore?" Kenyatta snickered under his breath to Seung. "Did he really say afore?"

Seung's lips crinkled.

"People need to believe in a higher being," Kita explained, "something bigger than ourselves."

Felk snorted. "Don't make much sense what ye just said, and I ain't fer seein' much difference. Ye got stories about the Gods that reach back thousands of years and more that eventually turned into stories about a single God." Felk shook his head in disgust. "Don't know how that happened. I ask ye, how'd ye forget about the other *six* Gods? How in all the hells could ye have possibly forgotten about six Gods?"

He shook his head again. "Eh, never mind that fer later. Gettin' back to me point. Ye even got stories and legends about us dwarves. Though I don't much like the singing part. Don't know who gave ye the idea that we like singin' so durned much."

"I wish I could tell you, Felk," Kita laughed. "Never in my wildest dreams could I have imagined I'd be having this conversation with an actual dwarf."

"Bah, ye human folk're strange, ye are! Walkin' round the world not knowin' who yer sharin' it with."

"What really burns me arse," another dwarf chimed in, "is why yer kind are so enthralled with them fairy folk." Kita offered a sideways smile to the robed dwarf. Paigra Stormshield was one of the two dwarven spellcasters that had chosen to accompany them.

He was clothed in red and black robes made of thick burlap materials that were actually interwoven with tiny links of chain mail made of a metal he had never seen before. Kita found himself wanting a robe like that for himself. "What's so enticing about a bunch of skinny folk bouncin' round in the trees chirpin' at each other?"

Seung arched an eyebrow. "Chirping? Our language shares nothing with our bird friends, though we can communicate with them, in some manner."

The dwarven spellcaster smirked. "Heh. We'll just leave that one up to a matter of interpretation, lass."

"I suppose our language would sound like chirping to a bunch of stumplike people whose language sounds like boulders gargling and burping at one another."

Paigra and Felk's mouths dropped open and they looked at each other, then at Seung.

"Ha!" Felk jabbed Kenyatta in the ribs, causing him to bend sideways in an attempt to soften the impact. "Me pride's wantin' to draw me axe, but the rest of me admires that fiery tongue! I'm tellin' ye," he tried to jab Kenyatta again but this time he discretely stepped sideways. "If that one ever grows a beard of any kind, or even just some whiskers, I'm fer stealin' her from ye!"

Kenyatta glanced at Seung and smiled deviously. "Felk Boulderbasher. If she ever grows a beard, she's yours."

"Is that so?" Seung replied icily. "My appearance is what forms our bond? I'll be sure to keep that in mind." She quickened her step.

Kenyatta threw up his hands and went to catch up. "C'mon gyal! Ya know I'm jyas jokin'! Ya know I'm not all about dat, now! Ya soul what matters most to me."

"Uh huh."

Kita and Felk glanced at each other, and another round of laughter ensued.

* * *

Warmth came with the rising of the sun in the east, and though they had to shade their eyes against the bright burning orb in the sky, it was a welcome sight. According to Marik, who knew the land best, they were only a few hours from Winsor. To the relief of all, the terrain looked to be sprinkled with little more than the occasional cluster of hillocks and rock-strewn fields.

"How're we to get to this tower?" Felk bit into a hunk of dried meat and proceeded to dine as audibly as seemed possible. "Yer story told us yer not havin' much time on yer side.

"Stands to reason," Felk continued, "that we should've just jumped on the nearest boat and headed straight there. I'm not makin' light of King Dain's problems and all, but seems like the bigger problem lies that way." He stabbed a thumb over his shoulder.

"Disaster is hovering over Winsor." Kenyatta discreetly picked a leaf from a nearby tree and flicked the half-masticated debris from his arm. "If the problem is allowed to escalate, it'll grow out of control quickly and the entire city could be overrun. And my sister can transport us faster than any ship."

"Oh?" Felk tore off another chunk. "She a spellcaster of some sort?"

"You could say that."

"Hmph." Paigra said, "That outta be somethin' to see; a human spellcaster. I know there're more'n a few of 'em in the world, but they all live in secret. A shame. Becoming a spellcaster ain't nothin' easy. We celebrate when somebody attains such a Daunya-blessed honor."

"With everything we've seen in these past several years," Kenyatta said,

"I think things like that will probably change. If we're going to survive in this new world, we'll have to accept things we didn't before, and change the way we think."

"Won't happen overnight, young laddy," Paigra said. "Folks is stubborn. Don't even wanna think about how long it would take our kind to accept such a drastic change to what we know. After ye lived a few hunnerd years, ye tend to settle in yer ways."

"The elves don't suffer such self-imposed limitations," Seung declared, somewhat haughtily.

Felk smirked at her. "Ye need to stop breathin' so much of them fairy sprinkles, little lass. Yer kin ain't no less stubborn than ours. How quick were ye to convince yer queen to aid yer cause? How large a force is she sendin' to ye? Me guess is not much more'n ye see right here." Felk waved a hand to encompass their little procession. "The truth is that nobody's gonna send a large force of their own people where there's human foolishness involved." He patted the air with his hands when Kita and Kenyatta started to argue.

"I know, I know. We've been round that rock afore. I'm not suggestin' it's right thinkin', but ye got to understand where we're standin' too. We got long memories, and it takes some doing to gain trust that was lost thousands of years ago. So what're ye plannin' fer when we get to Winsor?"

"Find some fairy sprinkles to inhale," came Seung's casual reply.

* * *

The sun had burned away the last of the spring morning chill when they finally reached the Winsor borderlands.

"Here's where it gets a little prickly," Felk said. "I'm not really fer riskin' our necks goin' into that place. No offense, but some of ye leggy folk got a habit of reactin' harsh to things ye don't understand."

"I thought you were able to disguise yourselves as small humans?" Kita said.

"Aye, our spellcasters can do that. But I imagine a band of armed short people would draw as much attention as us in our real skins." Felk stroked his beard. "Tell ye what. I'll send one of me spellcasters with ye. That way, he can communicate quickly back here in case there's some emergency."

"I can live with that," Kita replied.

"Gonna have to, because that's the way of it."

Kita opened and closed his mouth. "Um, sure. Okay, well I guess we should move on, then."

"Right. Hey Merk!"

A somewhat shorter dwarf shouldered his way from the back of the group. "Aye."

Felk nodded and turned back to the three companions. "Merk Iamfeld, here, is goin' in with ye. Any problems, he can communicate with Paigra more quickly than runnin' back."

"I guess there's nothing left than to head in," Kita said. "I hope we're not too late."

"Stuff's happened already," Paigra stated, as though discussing the weather. "Been scannin' the surroundings since we got here. 'Bout a mile off that way," he pointed north of Winsor. "I can feel some leftover resonance."

"Resonance?" Kenyatta asked.

"Aye. Think of it like a residue that lingers in the air. It don't go away too fast, and if ye know what yer about, ye can sense it up to a week after a demon's gone, unless they did more damage to the land, then it's there longer."

"We already knew things had started," Seung said.

"No, but there's a pretty good amount of deaths lingerin' around the resonance," Paigra replied. "I can feel it from here."

"Then let's find out the extent the damage this thing, or things, have done."

Paigra nodded and gave Merk a hard slap on the back. "Mind yerself, laddy. I don't feel anything lingerin' about, but that don't mean ain't nothin' there."

"Aye." Merk shouldered his pack and gave a firm nod. He walked up to Kenyatta, Kita, and Seung, and looked up at them.

After a rather uncomfortable moment, Kita cleared his throat. "Um, you ready, then?"

"That's why I'm standin' here," came the gruff reply.

The motley trio attracted more than a few glances as they wove their way through the various streets. At Merk's insistence, they stopped at a blacksmith's shop. Kenyatta perused the impressive merchandise, thinking that if he hadn't the weapons he did, there might have been a few choice items he'd have bought.

"Stuff's made of decent materials, I guess," Merk commented. The dwarf had used what he'd called a simple spell to shroud himself with an appearance that was similar to his own stature, making it easy for him to appear more like a small human. "Ain't too strong though. Wouldn't hold up too strong to a heavy weapon. This shield here would crumble under a good hammer blow; leave the wearer with a broken arm."

"I don't think many human fighters use hammers in battle, Mr. Iamfeld," Kita replied.

"Hmph." The dwarf stomped off to inspect some axes on the far wall, muttering about being prepared for anything.

"See something you like, young sirs and milady?" A thin, muscly man stepped into the display room. He wiped his hands on his dirty apron and waved a hand to encompass the shop.

"Just having a look," Kita said. "You have diverse stock."

"Gotta have the best around here these days," the blacksmith responded. "What with the attacks and all. Of course, since the king and bishop named a high-ranking monk with the title of Holy Arbitrator, people been walking around feeling safe again." He snorted. "No need for you all to worry about it. I can tell you're not from here, anyway. No need troubling yourselves."

"I'd rather hear any news you'd offer," Kenyatta said. "What's happening in this fine city?"

"Eh, probably shouldn't be talking about it, but I'll not have my conscience on my back if something happened to you and I didn't warn you. For months now, people been coming up missing. Well," the blacksmith shuddered, "not necessarily *missing*, but, well, very messily dead."

"Messily?" Kita repeated.

"Let's put it this way, young sir. People been found in the worse condition you ever want to find a person. Unless you're putting together a puzzle and don't care what the parts are made out of, you might be traumatized at what the city law enforcement's been finding after dark."

"Sounds awful," Kita replied. "And the king and bishop believe that promoting a high-ranking monk to this new position—"

"Holy Arbitrator."

"Yes, that. They think it will help?"

The blacksmith glanced over his shoulder at a few patrons being helped by his apprentice, then leaned closer and lowered his voice. "I'm a God fearin' man, just like any other of the goodly folk here. I know Holy Jemanah works His ways, but I'm not thinking a practical minded man like King Elizander would be going for such a thing. Anybody who's been paying attention knows that there's been rumblings in the church."

"Rumblings," Kita said.

"Yup. King Elizander Dain and Bishop Marquis have been doing the best they can about these murders, but it's been really mysterious. Not even his best man, Captain Davros, has been able to crack it. Of course, when things like this happen, rumors and superstitions start to surface."

"Some people have been saying it's Mairson from Mairland that's been causing the trouble. Others have been saying it's demons roaming the streets at night that's been leaving people scattered all over the walls."

He rolled his eyes. "Both are ridiculous. That Mairson may be an impetuous and unreasonable man most of the time, but he ain't got the stomach for the type of conflict that would happen if the king found out he was behind it. And demons? Pfft. People are just too superstitious. Ain't no more demons running around here than there are fairies."

A few feet away Seung arched a sharp—and very elven-like—eyebrow.

"What do you suspect?" Kita asked the blacksmith.

"Don't know for sure. One thing I can't deny is that this whole business is a mystery. One night, the king himself and Captain Davros and a contingent of his men went out in force to catch the killers once and for all."

Kita glanced at Kenyatta and Seung. "What happened?"

"The killers wiped out the entire contingent except for the king and captain, and they made it back in pretty bad shape. I think it was a stroke of luck that they survived. It was just like before. All of the dead soldiers had been ripped apart. I'd say maybe it was a bear or some other large animal, since there's all kinds of beasts that showing up in the world that's never been seen before."

"Have there been any attacks since then?" Kita asked.

"That's the thing. Shortly after the last incident, they named that trouble-making monk Holy Arbitrator and, much as I hate to admit it, the attacks haven't happened since. They're claiming that Holy Jemanah's will has been met and He will see no more attacks on the city as long as things remain that way."

More likely the demon was slain and retaliation hasn't happened yet, Kita thought.

"If you ask me," the talkative blacksmith continued, "it's a lot of poli-ticking and capitalizing going on. I don't know where these killers are or where they came from, but somebody's taking advantage of the situation."

"We should get moving," Kenyatta said, glancing outside the shop at the waning daylight.

"Of course, of course," the blacksmith replied, now looking worried he'd said too much. "Now mind you, I'm a loyal man. I don't mean saying the king is trying to take advantage or manipulate anybody. It's just that there's a lot of things happening in the shadows—"

Kita held up a hand. "Peace, good sir. We're not inquisitors or any manner of spy. We are travelers who've learned to survive by knowing the happen-ings of the places we visit. You need not fear us repeating what was said, here. Our thanks for your insight."

The blacksmith visibly relaxed. "Of course, of course, young man. And if you don't mind my saying so," he glanced at Merk, hefting an axe and trying not to look sour in the face, "you four are quite strange company."

"One never knows where you'll meet friends," Kita replied.

* * *

"There's talk of demons after all," Kenyatta said after they had exited the shop. "I wonder if people truly believe it."

"It's almost funny," Seung said. Kenyatta noticed that she had arranged her long, raven hair to hang over her ears again. "These people don't know how right they are."

"They'll know soon enough," Kita said.

"Yeah man," Kenyatta looked around the vendor square and wondered just how many people did believe the truth, whether through their religious beliefs or personal experience. After all, who would talk about such an encounter? "The world's changing too fast for people to be as oblivious as they've been all these years."

"I wouldn't mind being far away from any major civilization when the great revelation does happen. People tend to panic."

"I think people will respond more calmly if things are presented to them the right way," Kenyatta replied.

Seung smirked. "That'll be interesting. Who would volunteer to be the ambassador for that presentation? I wouldn't do it, and I can think of no full-blooded elf that would agree to such a thing."

"How about you, Mr. Iamfeld?" Kita asked the dwarf spellcaster, who'd been walking in silence during their conversation.

"It'd take a demand from Boraka Himself to coax me into such foolishness. Humans wanna know fer sure if we exist, let 'em come talk to us, and in very, *very* small numbers."

Kenyatta laughed. "I cyan't say I blame you, good sir."

"Why the heck ye talk like that?" Merk asked, looking up at the stunned islander.

Kenyatta frowned. "Like what?"

"Most of the time, ye talk so I can understand. Then sometimes ye start talkin' all strange like. Makes me have to concentrate real hard to follow."

Kenyatta shrugged. "To me, I don't sound unusual. Maybe I sound strange to you just as you sound different to me."

"Hmph."

The grounds of New Dainland Palace came into view as they traversed the many streets and alleys of the sprawling city. Brown-robed monks wove their way through the throngs, going about their daily business, and sometimes stopping to offer assistance whenever the need presented itself.

A pair of the robed figures turned a corner and started down the street in their direction. As the men drew closer, they could see that one of the monks was a young man who looked to have seen no more than twenty years. The frowning older man next to him likely had seen triple as many years.

Kita smiled and inclined his head. "Greetings."

"Greetings to you as well," the young monk replied. "May Holy Jemanah's blessed light shine upon you now and always." He tilted his head, studying the group. The older monk had silently continued on, as though hoping his young companion would move follow. Seeing that was not the case, he turned and stalked back.

"I'm sure these people have business to be about, Brother Pryke," he said tartly.

Kita and Kenyatta bowed to the older monk—Merk rather stiffly—and Seung inclined her head.

"We wouldn't want to waylay you, good monk," Kita said. "We're just admiring your magnificent city."

"Not at all," the younger monk said. "I am brother Pryke Deilar, and this is brother Tardein. We are of the Church of Holy Jemanah." The enthusiastic young man spoke of the church with a verbal flourish that was undeniably charming. "Whereabouts have you come from?"

"We've traveled from across the sea to arrive in New Dainland, Brother Pryke," Kita answered. "We've heard so many accounts of how inspiring New Dainland is and thought to see it for ourselves."

"You are quite the … diverse … little party," Brother Tardein said, an air of skepticism clear in his voice. "A man from the Caribbean islands, a man and woman from the Asian lands and," he looked down at Merk and his frown deepened, "a man with the affliction of 'smallism'." Merk's lower jaw moved left to right as he ground his teeth.

"Yes, our group is a unique one," Kenyatta interjected before the dwarf could utter a scathing reply. "Life tends to place a person in circumstances that create all sorts of scenarios. Our friendship happens to be one such result."

Brother Tardein's gaze rose to meet Kenyatta's. "Indeed they do, young man." His eyes fell upon the hilt of the sword on Kenyatta's back. "Or should I say, young warriors?"

"I'm afraid so," Kita replied. "It is a dangerous world now."

"It has always been a dangerous world, young man. There are some who would argue that the world is safer now than it has been for centuries."

"There's a truth that bears repeat'n," Merk muttered under his breath.

Tardein's attention returned to the dwarf. "And what of you, sir? We have many afflicted who come to New Dainland seeking the blessings of Holy

Jemanah. While I am doubtful your situation could be cured and your proper height granted, perhaps a brother of the church might ease the discomfort that plagues you."

"I'll keep that in mind," Merk rumbled.

"If it's no trouble," Kita deflected, "is there any interesting news of late?"

Brother Pryke brightened. "Why, yes there is! As a matter of fact, New Dainland is now the first city to name a monk of the Church of Jemanah as Holy Arbitrator. It is a great honor that has been bestowed upon our very own Brother Dinman."

"Holy Arbitrator?" Kenyatta said. "I've never heard of such a title."

"It did not exist before now," Pryke chirped. "It was a necessary action that our good and wise Bishop Marquis took in response to the city's recent troubles. Under the added leadership of our new Holy Arbitrator, we've not seen any of the problems that had plagued New Dainland for the past several months."

"Troubles?" Kita said. "What sort of troubles would prompt a bishop to create a new title and function for one of his brethren to help deal with?"

"I fear we have tarried and must be on our way," brother Tardein interrupted. "I am confident that you needn't worry about anything more than a pleasant stay here. May the light of Holy Jemanah shine upon you." He continued on.

"If you wish to hear the words of the Holy Arbitrator in person," Brother Pryke whispered hurriedly, "and receive your blessings for the day, visit the Round Gardens northeast of here. I have not had the pleasure myself, but perhaps you may find inspiration—"

"BROTHER PRYKE," Tardein called from further down the street. With a quick bow, the young monk hurried away.

"Anyone have insight on that most unusual encounter?" Seung asked, still staring in the direction the monks had gone.

"Looked to me like an old piece of fruit that's been soured by age was placed next to a younger piece of fruit in hopes of sweetening it." Kenyatta smiled. "I think if enough time passes between those two, the opposite is likely to happen.

"That older monk, Tardein, was an unfriendly one," Kita said.

"Nah, a suspicious one," Merk corrected. "We best be careful how and where we step. I don't like the smell of this business. Men ruled by superstition and organizations rarely have any kind of useful insight to the will of the Gods. I admit I ain't been a spellcaster more'n fifty years, but it's long enough to know that big titles and grand proclamations don't do nothin' but test a God's sense of humor. People like them," he jabbed a thumb in the direction the monks had gone, "see the source of their problems resting on the shoulders of that what's different."

"I think we should go listen in on this speech being given by this Holy Arbitrator," Kenyatta said. "It's a hunch, but I have a feeling we might find something useful."

"Time isn't on our side," Seung argued.

"No, but from what that monk told us, the gardens aren't far off and we might learn something to help us when we deliver our outlandish tale to the king."

Seung looked like she wanted to argue further, but conceded. "You have a point. I still cannot think of any way we can convince this man of our sanity once we deliver our message, much less get him to believe us."

Kita nodded at Merk. "If all else fails, we can enlist a little demonstration from our spellcaster here."

Merk snorted. "Not likely, boy. I cast a simple spell and they'll either believe ye, or declare us evil and kill us all. I already told ye once; beware the superstitious and the fearful."

"You really think they'd react so harshly?" Kita asked. "I would think someone with the responsibilities as heavy as that of a king would be more levelheaded than that."

The dwarf gave him a look that suggested he was naïve. "Study yer histry, laddy. It's filled with folk that have been imprisoned and killed to death for simply suggestin' things that went against the popular beliefs of the time. The only way I'm doin' me casting thing is to speak to Paigra to get the others here, or to get us outta here in a hurry. That's the only thing I'm fer doin'. The rest is up to yerselves."

"They will come to believe our tale eventually," Seung said as they continued on their way. "They may not have discovered who's killing people yet but they will."

"Well, that's one way of looking at it," Kita said sarcastically. "But it'd be nice to avoid that avenue if possible."

"Of course," Seung said. "I'm not being callous about this, just practical. As desirable as it would be to avoid any more deaths, people are what they are. Without proof no one will believe us, and I couldn't blame them. I can think of no time in human recorded history when a person has come in contact with a demon. Not long ago I would have questioned your wits if you'd come to me with such stories."

They rounded another corner and came to a path leading straight toward an impressive garden. It seemed that every manner of flower and plant grew in the place, stifling the busy sounds of the streets in its tranquility.

"Beautiful," Seung breathed.

"Hmph. I'd prefer the sculpted boulders of Boulderhead Spire, but this ain't half bad."

"Boulderhead Spire?" Kita repeated, chuckling.

Merk nodded. "Yeah. Big climb up the rocky side of Mount Croughton. Long climb up, but worth it. The boulders in that valley once ye reach the top are like nothin' ye ever laid eyes on."

"Boulderhead?" Kita asked again, frowning, smiling, and shaking his head at the same time.

"Yes! Boulderhead! What of it? Ye got a problem with it?"

Kita held up his hands in a surrendering gesture. "Peace, Merk Iamfeld. I'm not mocking you. It's just that the names your people give to places are unusual to us."

"Us?" Kenyatta said. "Don't include me in this."

Kita glared at the back of his friend's head, then turned back to Merk. "I apologize if I've offended you."

"Don't worry about it, laddy." He gave Kita a slap on the back that made his heart skip a beat. "Truth is, we oftentimes name places after important folk. Boulderhead Spire is named after Borndas Boulderhead, of the Boulderhead Clan. Now there was a feller could fight! Strong as a mammoth, he was!" Kenyatta almost stumbled upon hearing the spellcaster describe someone as "strong". Every dwarf they'd encountered was easily twice as strong as any man he'd ever met!

"Back in the ancient days, when animals still grew big, he took down one of them giant cats ye'd call a saber tooth. Thing nearly killed him to death, but he managed to muscle it down long enough to get a blade in its neck. Fed his family fer weeks on the meat, and warmed 'em with the pelt."

Kita's mouth fell open. "Your people were around back then?"

"Of course, laddy! We all were, all of The Four were around back then. Of course, little missy's fairy folk would like to believe they was the first to touch this world, but it ain't so. The first ones to walk the lands was actually the dragons, but they's different from us, I guess you could say. After them, the rest of us came."

"It would be great to hear the history of The Four in your words, Mr. Merk Iamfeld," Seung replied sincerely, "but we've found the congregation brother Pryke spoke of."

Standing behind a podium overlooking a large body of people was a man dressed in silken robes of brown and red. He spoke with grand gestures, waving his hands and arms, the voluminous sleeves of his robes accentuating his movements.

"I'll not be placin' meself in the middle of that," the dwarf said.

"Nor will any of us, I think," Seung replied.

"This has the look of a cult," Kenyatta said, scanning the faces of the onlookers.

"I can't bring myself to believe that a king could be so foolish as to allow something like this to go unnoticed in his own city," Seung said. "There must be more to this than we see."

"Yes, there is," Kenyatta said evenly. "It's not unheard of for a king such as Elizander to rule with a firm but fair hand, allowing the people to speak and express themselves freely so long as they don't pose a threat." He nodded toward the speaker, who was undoubtedly this Holy Arbitrator Dinman. "You get a man who has his own designs in mind and seeks to build a following, but does it in such a way as to not get himself into trouble."

"And if the king silences him," Kita added, catching on, "he proves the speaker right, and makes himself look like a tyrant in the process."

"So the king must handle the fox with care, lest he reach into the den and is bitten by the pack." Seung narrowed her eyes at the dramatic monk.

"Why would the king and bishop create a title of some measure of power, then appoint it to a man like this?" Kita asked. "I can't make sense of it."

"There is some maneuvering going on here," Seung said. "But does this concern us?"

The group froze after hearing what Dinman said next.

"... I tell you now, ladies and gentlemen. There are unholy things in this world. There are people that stalk these very streets that mean us harm, and some of them have brought the unholy with them! In ages long passed, there have been those who would use evil as a means of creating havoc and destruction upon mankind!

"Sometimes, the right person is able to strike a deal and convince the devil to loosen his leash on the lapdogs who serve him! I tell you that it is these people who cause our troubles!"

He waved his arm in a sweeping gesture. "Think, my flock! You've heard, and some of you have even seen what happened to the unfortunate people who have met with death at the bloodthirsty fangs of one of the devil's lapdogs. Who other than they could commit such savagery?"

The crowd shouted in agreement. Some shook their fists in the air. "I tell you, good people of Winsor," Dinman continued. Holy Jemanah is displeased! Why else would He allow such atrocities to befall us?

"And can we blame Him? We, who have shirked our duties to Him. We, who have lived in gluttony and decadent sin. Evil cannot thrive where the light of Holy Jemanah shines, and we have allowed that light to dim so that now, evil lurks in the shadows, waiting to snatch us away into its infinite darkness and pull us down to kneel before its cursed master."

"I tell you that we must redouble our efforts! We must sharpen our devotions and do away with nonsense. Our devotion to Holy Jemanah is all that matters in these tiny lives that we lead. Only those who have devoted their lives to Holy Jemanah will be spared these horrors and be preserved when He returns!"

The monk fell silent and studied the crowd. Everyone stood in rapt attention, hanging on his every word. "There is a dispute between humanity and our Savior, and it falls to me, your Holy Arbitrator, to settle it by guiding you back to the light and preparing you for salvation ..."

"I've heard enough," Seung said. "Such harsh words from a spiritual teacher. The monks of my homeland would be disheartened to hear this."

"I think the monks from many different lands would be disheartened to hear this," Kenyatta agreed.

"And *I* think," Merk said, staring a short distance to the right of the ranting monk, "that this King Elizander ain't as stupid as we think. Look."

They followed the dwarf's gaze.

"I don't see anything," Kita said.

"Ain't surprisin'. It's because he don't want to be seen."

"Who doesn't want to be seen?" Seung asked.

"The hooded monk in the extra dark robes standin' still as a statue in the shadows of the nearby trees, not ten feet away from the loudmouth."

"I don't see anything at all," Kenyatta said.

"It's because he's usin' what's called a *shroud*," Merk replied. "Simple spell. Causes ye to wrap yerself in the shadow of an object as if it were a blanket. With one of them spells, ye could stand right next to a person and they wouldn't know ye was there unless ye breathed on their neck."

"Interesting," Seung said, still staring at the shadowed area as though she could see the hidden figure.

"I think we should be going," Kita said. "We need to gain an audience with the king and get our business done. Whatever political issues are going on, it doesn't concern us."

Merk never stopped looking at the shaded area beside Dinman, but he nodded. "Let's get this done and be gone outta here."

* * *

Holy Arbitrator Dinman saw the four strangers discreetly enter and exit the grounds where he gave his speech. They never fully stepped into the open, but remained somewhat hidden in the hallways leading to the garden. Normally, the monk would not have thought twice about foreigners, for there were always people passing through from distant lands. Those four, however, were more than a little odd.

* * *

A dozen paces to Dinman's side, Arief also took note of the departing group. He found them even more interesting than Dinman, whom he'd been watching for days—unbeknownst to the boisterous monk, of course. The dwarf was particularly interesting. He was wrapped in a spell of transfiguration, but Arief saw right through it. What would prompt a dwarf to travel with two men and a woman that looked as though she could pass for an elf? As a member of the Order of Dasha, Arief had directly taken part in keeping certain parts of the world obscure from the human population. Recent events were leading him to believe this role would soon be redundant.

As he watched the three warriors and the dwarven spellcaster, the Dasha monk wondered if the humans knew the truth of their companion. They looked competent enough, but that mattered little if the dwarven spellcaster didn't want them to know his true identity. Things were getting interesting, and Arief could feel to his core that all of these events were connected, and he would not leave New Dainland until he found out how.

53

The gates of New Dainland Palace were as impressive as they were well guarded. The ivy-covered stone walls were topped with head-sized knobs carved with spiraling flower vines that looked as though they grew from the stone spheres. The black iron fence stood ten feet high and the tips of each bar were crafted to look like arrowheads.

Behind the barred fences were thick square pillars of stonework spaced a foot apart for the entire length on both sides.

Two guards stood at the entrance to the closed gate, and evenly spaced guards stood post along the perimeter.

Upon nearing the gate, the party was met with crossed halberds.

"No entry at this time."

"It's imperative that we be granted an audience with King Elizander Dain," Kita said.

The guard who'd spoken turned his icy blue glare on Kita. The man's face was a veritable map of scars, tracing back to many hard-fought battles. "State your business."

"Our message is for the king's ears. We're not at liberty to discuss it with anyone but him."

"Impossible. You seek audience with the King of Winsor under secrecy. You will not be granted entrance. Withdraw."

"Bah but what'd ye expect, coming to the gates like that!" Merk scolded as he stepped forward and gave a subtle wave of his hand, keeping the movement small so as not to alert the other guards. "What me young," he glanced at Kita disapprovingly, "and quite frankly foolish companion here meant to say was that we need to speak with yer king about important business that is of concern to him. Ain't nothin' else ye need be knowin' but that."

The once alert guards' eyes glazed over, but their posture remained alert. The officer who'd spoken nodded and lifted his halberd, his partner following suit. "You may enter."

Once they were a safe distance away and well into the courtyard, Kita caught up with the swift walking dwarf. "What did you do to them?"

"Simple *compulsion*, laddy. Nothin' brain-damagin', if that's yer worry."

"Sounds like a dangerous tool."

"So's a hammer."

There were more guards posted throughout the carefully landscaped courtyard. Though their presence was noted, the trio went unchallenged.

"Now that we're here," Seung asked. "How are we going to get an audience?" They turned down a walkway lined with sculpted columns lined with ivy spiraling their lengths.

"I think we're about to find out," Merk said from behind. His voice sounded strained and he'd stopped walking.

"Taking a break?" Kenyatta said. "I think we can discuss this while we walk. Merk?"

"Not likely," Seung said, looking as strained and alarmed as Merk.

"What?" Kenyatta said. He turned toward her, or tried to. His body was frozen where he stood.

"Your concern is not with the king, but with convincing me you are not here with malicious intent." The voice was quiet, powerful, and left no room to interpret the implications, should they fail to do just what was demanded.

Merk swore a muffled curse. "Dang it all! How'd I not feel him?"

"Surely you know better, master dwarf. There are ways of avoiding detection. I feel that you are experienced enough to be capable of such a thing, were you not so careless." A robed and hooded man stepped from behind a column several feet to Merk's right side. "Or did you feel it unlikely to encounter one such as myself in a human city?"

"Ain't an unusual assumption," the dwarf replied.

"Yet one that could shorten your considerable lifespan."

"Noted."

A trio of ladies dressed in finely embroidered gowns turned down the corridor. They passed within inches of each of the four companions, completely unaware of their presence. Kita, Kenyatta, and Seung looked after them, confused until Merk muttered, "*shroud.*" The others glanced at their feet. Each of them were standing in the shadow of one of the huge columns that spiraled high above their heads.

"Very good, master dwarf. And now I ask you, using your dwarven candor, why are you here?" After a moment, Kita opened his mouth to speak, but the monk's upraised hand forestalled him. "I can see the lie forming on your lips, warrior. I'll not force the truth from you because it is unnecessary. I will, however, caution you to think carefully about the words you speak to me. Doubt if you like, but I *will* hear the lie as soon as you utter it."

"Best tell him, laddy," Merk said.

"We're here to warn the king about the killings in New Dainland," Kita said. "We know who they are, or rather, what they are."

The monk tilted his head. "What do you know of it? You're foreigners; that much is clear. The three of you, one of which whose elven features I cannot dismiss, come here in the company of a dwarf who is in the guise of a small human. "What could you know of the goings on in New Dainland?"

"We know of the demons murdering citizens," Kenyatta said.

The monk stood in silence for several moments, wrapped in a stillness that even statues could only aspire to.

The force restraining them fell away with the same abruptness as it had bound them.

"Come." The monk started down the corridor.

The companions looked at each other. What choice did they have?

"Mind if I ask who you are?" Kenyatta asked.

"Yes," the monk answered.

"Who are you?" Seung asked defiantly.

"Someone with not much patience," came the response.

"You've an interesting way of treating allies."

"I'm unaccustomed to allies who compel guards to grant them entry to the king's palace. That is usually the method of an enemy."

"How else would we have been able to speak your king?" Seung replied. "I doubt those guards know the truth of this situation, and time isn't on our side."

"How would you have gained an audience with the king had I not inter-cepted you? Would your spellcaster have simply compelled every guard to stand aside until you kicked open the king's door?"

Seung opened her mouth to argue, then pressed her lips together and conceded the point with a nod.

"Your audience with Kind Elizander is born of my appreciation for your dilemma," the monk went on. "That, and my own interest in how you know what you do.

A skinny man holding a ledger shuffled rounded a corner ahead and hurried to meet them. He stopped a few feet in front of the party and gave them a once-over. His appraisal complete, he turned to the monk. "One of your, ahem, colleagues *entered* my study to inform me that you are seeking immediate audience with the king, and that you have four individuals of interest in tow."

"You've rushed here to inform me of my message to you." The monk's dry tone was a statement, not a question.

"I've rushed here to find out what business this is. I cannot simply tell the king he will have visitors just because you say it is so. I'm confident you are aware—"

"I am quite aware, attendant. But the gravity of the situation demanded swifter action."

The attendant grumbled but fell in step with them. "And who are these people?" When no response came, he sighed. "Your message has been delivered and the king has been informed. I've done this on your strong, if recent, reputation here. In lieu of that, I would appreciate a bit of information so that I do not enter into this situation looking the uninformed fool."

"These four come to New Dainland with information about the demon attacks."

The blood drained from the attendant's composed face. "How would they know this?"

The monk was silent for a moment. "I am confident your question was posed in earshot of our guests."

The attendant narrowed his eyes at the robed figure before falling back a step to pace with the others. "My apologies for ignoring your presence and for our 'friend' Arief's personality. My name is Milpheus Catbowe, First Attendant to his majesty King Elizander Dain."

"A pleasure, Mr. Catbowe," Kenyatta said, proud of himself for keeping a straight face as he pronounced the man's name.

The attendant flinched. "Please, call me Milpheus."

"You got it, Milpheus." Kenyatta introduced himself and his friends. "The situation is about to get worse ..." he trailed off in confusion when he saw alarm and excitement flash across the man's visage.

"Spare the rest of your news for the king," Milpheus replied in a low voice. "I won't have this spoken of in the open."

Their tour of the palace was a series of open and enclosed corridors that were bathed in the thick rays of sunlight that shined around the pillars, or decorated by amazing handwoven tapestries and watercolor paintings. Liveried servants bearing a giant oak insignia upon the left breast moved about their business with alacrity, stealing glances at the unusual group as they navigated the endless halls.

After what seemed an indeterminable amount of time, they finally reached a set of doors flanked by two sets of guards. While Milpheus spoke with one of the guards and entered, Kenyatta leaned over to Kita and whispered, "amazing that this place is so big, and these doors still don't stand as tall as the one's in that dwarven hall."

A few moments later Milpheus returned. "You may enter."

Seated upon a throne with a back made in the likeness of a giant shield, was a man of average size, with sandy brown hair close-cropped on the sides and a bit longer on top. His bright green gaze settled on them like a heavy pall as they approached the throne.

Milpheus knelt, the others following his lead. "My lord King Elizander Dain, Servant of the Shield Throne, I present to you, Kita Sepata, of the Philippine Islands, Kenyatta Ihe, of the Jamaican Islands, Seung Yoon, of the Korean Island, and Merk Iamfeld of … Clan Shatterhammer."

A tiny frown flickered across the king's brow and he leaned forward. "Clan Shatterhammer? Please excuse my ignorance, Master Iamfeld, but what is Clan Shatterhammer?"

"Clan of me kin, blood and bone. For ages come and gone we work the stone." The dwarf looked into the king's eyes as he spoke the words. "Clan Shatterhammer used to trade with yer ancestor's ancestor's ancestor's ancestors, young laddy."

"Oh?" Elizander leaned back again. "I am well learned in my family's history, Master Iamfeld, and I can assure you there is no mention of a Clan Shatterhammer."

"It's because ye humans tend to leave yer memories behind after a few years. Just a few generations and ye forget even those who you traded with for centuries."

Now the king looked truly perplexed. "Humans?" He turned his gaze to Milpheus, then to Arief who stood to the side, still and silent. "Whom have you brought to me and what game is this?"

"It is time for the shroud to be lifted from the eyes of the human collective, King Elizander Dain," Arief declared in his usual low voice. "Show him, Master dwarf."

"Show me what?" Elizander demanded, just as the image of the small man began to waver and blur until a slightly taller and much stockier robed dwarf stood in its place.

With an effort, the king held his composure, but he looked as though he would have backed right through the throne if it were possible. "What is this? What lie do my eyes tell me?"

"You share the world with more than your own kind, King Elizander," Seung said, rising and pulling her hair back.

Elizander's eyes widened even further at the sight of her slightly pointed ears. He managed to tear his eyes away from her to see an equally stunned look on Milpheus's face. "Am I truly to believe that I am in the presence a dwarf and an elf?" He looked to Arief. "Childhood stories come to life before my eyes?"

The monk nodded. "As I told you days before, King Elizander. It has been the task of my order to maintain the shroud of ignorance over the eyes of the human populace. The time has arrived when the shroud must be lifted and humankind understand their place in the world with those who have remained hidden from them for centuries."

Elizander stood and stepped down from the throne and approached the group, alternating his gaze from Seung to Merk. "Forgive me, but might I look closer, that I may know for my own sake that they are real?" Seung hesitated a moment, then remembered what it was like when she had discovered her people for the first time. Her face softened and she nodded.

"I am not a full-blooded elf," she said, "though most of the blood that runs in my veins is elven."

The king's smile might have belonged to a child discovering the wonder of the forest for the first time. He nodded turned to Merk.

"Alright now, I'll be shakin' yer hand if ye like, but I ain't fer ye closely lookin' about me person."

Elizander laughed. "Of course, Master Iamfeld." He reached out his hand, looking curiously at the two islanders who were gritting their teeth and smiling at the same time. He took dwarf's hand and his left eyebrow twitched as Merk squeezed it. After whipping his watering eyes with a handkerchief, he gave the powerful dwarf a stoic nod.

"My thanks." Elizander flexed his fingers. "And so it is, though my mind tells me I am in a dream, my eyes and my … hand, tell me that this is indeed real." He turned to look at the monk. "I'm unsure if I appreciate the efforts of your organization, though there can be no doubt of its effectiveness."

Arief nodded. "It was a necessary thing, King Elizander. Humanity was not ready to remember those they'd forgotten. I remain unsure if we are ready even now, but that no longer matters."

"I cannot agree with your cynicism," Elizander replied. "I have faith that humanity could cope with this."

"The fact that ye say yer kin could "cope" with us, is proof that they couldn't, if ye'll pardon me sayin'." Merk shifted his feet, clearly uncomfortable in the middle of a human civilization without his human guise.

Dain stared at him for a moment then sighed. "Perhaps I have much to learn myself, before I can speak of the capacity of others." He smiled. "Given time, I think our two peoples can one day trade with each other again, as you've said we once did."

"We never stopped," Merk replied. "Ye just never knew it, is all."

Elizander drew back in shock.

Kenyatta elbowed Kita, who spoke up. "Ahem, King Elizander, if I may speak?" The king nodded, still eyeing the dwarf. "We've come here with information you must hear immediately."

"Then deliver it now," the king said, beckoning for them to be seated at the patio at a side entrance from the throne room. He listened quietly as each person took a turn when the tale came to their individual part. It was a couple hours in the telling and by the time they had finished, the sun was barely visible as it dipped below the western horizon.

Elizander went to his private balcony and paced the deck, hands clasped behind his back. "A bard would dream of delivering a story half as extraordinary as the one you've just told. And yet, I cannot deny the truth of it after my own experiences and that of my captain."

As if the mention of the captain caused him to appear, there was a heavy knock on the door a heartbeat before it opened to admit a large fuming man in burnished silver and green armor with a green cape fitted into the shoulders. He held his helm in the crook of his arm as he strode briskly forward and knelt before the king, ignoring the others.

"My lord. Might I ask what offense I have offered that would prompt you to forego my presence in what I have come to learn is an important meeting?" He glanced at the three warriors. "With armed visitors, I may add."

"Peace, Captain." Elizander approached the kneeling figure and placed a hand on his shoulder, bidding him to rise. There was a familiarity between them that spoke of a long friendship. "This is Captain Davros Naishere of the Ironshield." He gave the still unhappy captain a heavy pat on the shoulder.

"Please forgive my negligence, Captain. The situation was urgent and I felt safe in the presence of our ally, Arief of Dasha."

"Dasha?" Merk said, looking at the monk as though he had finally discovered a piece of a puzzle he had been missing. "That explains it! Yer one of them Dasha monks, then! No wonder ye caught me off me guard."

"I see our reputation precedes us," the monk replied.

"Don't know how I didn't add it up," Merk continued as though the monk hadn't spoken.

"Let us continue the discussion at a later time," Arief said.

Elizander noticed that Davros's features remained tight. The way he stared straight ahead, studiously not glancing at the newcomers, he could tell the man wanted to say more. "Speak freely, Captain. I have complete trust in Arief, and therefore, the visitors he's brought with him.

Davros hesitated. "As ... as your captain I must recommend you never act without my protection, my lord. The business of that night is still unfinished."

"You have my word," Elizander replied. "Which actually brings us to the purpose of our visitors, apparently." He turned back to the party, standing beside Arief. "What do you have for me?"

The warmth of the sun on her face and its light glowing through her closed eyelids drew Akemi out of oblivion. She cracked her eyes open, then squinted them closed again. She turned her head away from the sun and cracked her eyes open again.

"She finally rejoins the living."

Akemi immediately recognized the voice and the sarcasm. "Mmm. How long have I slept, Strider?"

"Three days."

She bolted upright, then regretted it when her head spun. She eased down onto her back again. Shinobu moved to her side. "Careful foolish woman."

"Where is Kenjiro?"

"On his way back here, no doubt. You have a devoted brother, Akemi. I had to pester him to leave your side for a visit to the baths. If the sun hadn't awoken you, his fierce odor would have."

"We look after each other," she said, easing herself upright again.

"I'm aware."

The door opened to admit Kenjiro. "I heard voices." He looked at Akemi, then glared at Shinobu. "I told you to send word if she awoke."

"Peace, my friend," Shinobu said. "She woke just now." He smirked. "Besides. I would think you'd wish to remove that odoriferous coating on your skin."

Kenjiro ignored the last comment and knelt beside Akemi. "How do you feel?"

Akemi pressed the butts of her hands against her eyes. "Lightheaded and hungry."

"We'll get you some food."

Akemi held up a hand. "I will walk to the kitchens to take my meal." She threw off the covers and the two men rose and turned their backs. "Such gentlemen," she teased, slipping into a simple flowered kimono that had been left folded in a chair at her bedside. "I doubt I'm possessed of anything you haven't seen before."

Shinobu and Kenjiro wore looks of enticement and horror respectively.

"I find it impossible and undesirable to envision my sister naked," Kenjiro said.

"I don't," Shinobu said, ever so softly.

"Mind the thin line you walk, Strider," Kenjiro warned. Shinobu snickered.

After securing her swords to her lower back, Akemi ran her hands over her kimono, satisfied. "Okay, my guardians. I'm decently presentable." The two men faced her again. Kenjiro nodded while Shinobu smiled appreciatively. Akemi rolled her eyes, though she did enjoy the attention from the handsome strider. "Shall we go?"

"After you," Shinobu said, holding the door open.

"You may leave the room first, strider," Kenjiro said darkly.

Shinobu sighed. "I only meant to be gentlemanly—"

"I know what you meant."

Shinobu opened his mouth to say more, but noticed that Kenjiro had rested his hand on the hilt of his sword. He left the room first.

"So," Akemi said as they strode down the corridor. "I presume a lot has happened during my slumber?"

"Oh yes," Shinobu said. "After you killed Qian, or what was left of him, the battle had already been decided."

"The warlord made an error," Kenjiro said. "By raising his fallen troops so quickly, he tipped his hand to his still living soldiers."

Akemi grinned. "He hadn't expected them to turn against him."

"Not so quickly, at least," Kenjiro replied. "I think the demon within did not understand that humans like walking corpses less than any living enemy. Once the men on both sides became aware of the new threat, they united." Kenjiro allowed a rare smile to cross his face. "And once they realized it was their own leader responsible for their fallen comrades rising from death, their allegiance to Warlord Qian shattered."

"And what of Qian's army now?"

Shinobu barked a laugh. "That is a tale best served at a campfire. After Hua's soldiers saw him for what he truly was when he battled you, to a man they dropped to their knees and lowered their heads. It was as though they were awaiting execution! Like him or not, the warlord knew how to instill discipline in his men."

Akemi frowned. "Please tell me Liu Xiang did not put them all to the sword."

"No," Kenjiro said. "Given that they were just soldiers obeying their leader, he offered them clemency, the opportunity to join his army and live as citizens of Shu Han."

"And here's the best part," Shinobu added. "There were three noteworthy men in that battle. Two of them known as the Twins of Qian. They rarely speak, but their martial skill is becoming legendary across Ba Guo. Even more impressive is that Guan Xi fought them by herself! I caught a glimpse of their fight." He shook his head. "That woman is amazing, and definitely the descendant of Guan Gong. She came away scarred and cut, but so did they, and one has a broken arm. I believe that had the circumstances not turned them into allies, she might have beaten them!"

They reached the kitchen and were ushered to a sitting area where they took seats upon beautiful handwoven pillows on the floor. A servant brought them tea, and a few moments later, hot soup with thick noodles and diced chicken were placed in front of them.

The aroma that wafted from the bowls was enough to send Akemi into a frenzy. She hadn't realized how hungry she was till that smell found her nostrils. Maintaining as much dignity as she could manage, she took to her bowl while Kenjiro and Shinobu continued their tale.

"As always," Kenjiro said, "there are heroes on both sides of a battle. The army of Qian is no exception. I would not have believed it if I had not seen it with my own eyes." He looked at Shinobu who smirked.

"You are versed in Ba Guo history. You will not believe who I fought on the field," Shinobu said.

Akemi finished her bowl and glanced several times at the one in front Shinobu. The strider laughed and slid it over to her. "I suppose it will take more than two bowls to satisfy a three-day fast."

She nodded her thanks and went straight into the dish. It took an effort not to shovel the noodles into her mouth by the fistful.

"This man, the third noteworthy warrior on the battlefield." Shinobu whistled through his teeth. He was easily the largest man I've ever seen, and even stronger than his size let on. He was also fast. Not faster than myself, you understand." The strider spread his hands in mock shyness. Kenjiro rolled his eyes and sipped his broth. "But surprisingly quick."

"Are you going to give a name," Akemi asked, her voice amplified by the bowl, "or shall I crawl into your lap and moon over your battle prowess?" Kenjiro snorted, nearly spilling the contents of his bowl.

"Siblings for sure," the strider said sourly. "No appreciation for the build-up."

"No appreciation for verbal dung," Kenjiro remarked. He took another sip.

Shinobu glared at the samurai, then shrugged. "Does the name Wei mean anything to you?"

"Wei?" Akemi tapped a slim finger to her cheek. "I can't say I ..." she trailed off as her face lit with recognition. "Surely you aren't referring to ..."

"Dian Wei," Shinobu confirmed. "Or rather, his descendant. The man looks like Dian Wei reincarnated. I swear to you, it was like battling the man himself! His parents even named him after his ancestor."

"You speak as if it was fun."

Shinobu snorted. "Fun? It was a near-death experience several times over. The man is dangerous. Twice he almost got a hold of me with one of those massive hands. I'm positive he could have crushed me, had he caught me."

"It seems that this region of Ba Guo is a treasure trove of descendants of legendary warriors." Akemi sat her bowl on the floor, her hunger finally sated. "Nothing is random. When the descendants of legendary warriors appear like this, there is a reason."

Shinobu arched an eyebrow at the siblings. "So says Akemi Musashi, daughter to Ryuenjiro Musashi, descendant of one of the most legendary samurai in our history. Who also, I should add, supposedly had no children."

Kenjiro frowned and glanced at Akemi, who looked equally caught off guard.

Shinobu laughed. "Come now. Did you truly believe I didn't recognize the distinct facial features," he nodded at Akemi, "the body stature," he then nodded at Kenjiro, "not to mention the unmatched obsession with your skills?"

"The only warrior who remains alive is the one who obsesses with improvement," Kenjiro countered.

"I can't think of a more typical reply from the descendant of Musashi," Shinobu replied. "Among my strider faction, we learn of our legendary warriors at a young age. Miyamoto Musashi, I took a shine to immediately."

"I wasn't sure when first we met a couple years ago, but the more time I spent with the two of you, the more certain I became."

"You remained silent about it all this time?" Akemi asked.

Shinobu shrugged. "You hadn't mentioned it, so why should I? I only say so now because we're discussing legendary warriors reborn." He stared at them. "I don't know which is more noteworthy, legends reborn, or the fact that most of them were recorded to have not sired children."

He spread his hands. "And here you are. Legendary warriors reborn and destined to follow in the footsteps of your ancestors as legends of this age. Perhaps this marks the beginning of a transition. Maybe the world has begun to evolve, or a new age cycle has begun. Who but the Gods know for certain?"

"I think we've strayed from our original subject," Akemi reminded.

"Of course." Shinobu rested his hands in his lap and went silent for a few moments. "No battle is without its own horrors, but the outcome of this one has shined favorably on Liu Xiang. He's greatly increased his force, and eliminated his most dangerous enemy."

"And," Kenjiro added, "he sent messengers from his army and Qian's to the warlord's city to inform them of the outcome. He is currently planning his visit alongside Empress Zhao Xiaoyu. They will go bearing a banner of peace, but they also want to give enough of a show of force to make any remaining loyalists in Qian's army think twice, should they consider action. A better outcome could not have happened."

"I am glad you approve, Kenjiro." The trio turned to see Zhuge Xiaoyin standing several paces away. "May I join you?"

The two men stood and Kenjiro indicated that she take a vacant pillow.

They sat in silence while Xiaoyin politely refused an offer for a bowl of noodles, but accepted a cup of tea. After a few sips, she smiled again. "I'm also pleased at the outcome. Though no battle is without tragic loss of life, the future looks positive."

She inclined her head to Akemi. "I've been told that your contribution to the battle was nothing short of legendary."

"Tales become more dramatized with each telling."

"True." Xiaoyin took another sip of tea. "But neither General Zhang Da, nor Emperor Liu Xiang are given to dramatics. Ba Guo has benefited from your presence here. All of you. I gather you've learned of the coming trip to Qian?"

"We were just getting to that," Shinobu replied. "Please, take up the story. Better that it comes directly from one better informed."

"As you may have surmised, Qian's ill-timed power move decided the battle against him. His forces have been willingly sided with Shu Han at least for now. In two days, we march alongside Empress Zhao Xiaoyu to the land of Qian with hopes of a peaceful conclusion to the matter."

She took another sip, staring into the hand-painted mug she held in her palms. "I've been trying to think of a way to relate the more macabre events of the battle. I doubt even the endorsement of Qian's own men will sway those who weren't there. Easier to believe those men had betrayed Qian and his son, rather than the possibility of the fallen rising again in death, inhabited by demons."

"Should things go smoothly, what will happen next?" Kenjiro offered her more tea, which she declined.

"All of Qian's land and holdings, his army and resources will be divided between Liu and Zhao."

"That is generous of Xiang," Akemi said, "considering he alone fought the battle."

"That isn't entirely correct. Xiang did fight the bulk of Qian's forces, but when Empress Zhao discovered that Qian Hua had detached a contingent of his men to watch and discourage her from entering the battle, she was incensed. By the time I'd arrived to warn her of just such a possibility, she had already been quietly marshaling her forces to strike at him in a vicious thrust from her walls.

Xiaoyin grinned. "She never got the chance. When word came that Hua's battle was taking a less favorable turn, their captain had decided to leave Zhao and aid his master. Remember, neither Qian nor his captain knew that Empress Zhao had gotten word of their plot.

So, once we received news that the captain was departing to aid Qian, Zhao waited until the full contingent was gone, then dispatched her forces and surprised him from the rear.

With my help, we were able to convince their captain that should they not surrender, we would offer no quarter. Those who might be able to escape would be run down and crushed between the forces of Zhao and Liu. I believe the captain hadn't thought Empress Zhao, a woman, had the nerve for such a thing." Xiaoyin chuckled. "The foolish words of Qian Hua, no doubt. In the end, they surrendered and are now held captive."

"What will you do with them?" Kenjiro asked.

"As a show of good faith, we will allow them to march with us back to Qian. Once there, they will be allowed to enter the city and rejoin with the rest of the Qian forces."

"Is that wise?" Shinobu asked. "You would allow an army to strengthen itself against you? It could end up a siege and this could give them the leverage they need."

Zhuge Xiaoyin rose, and the others followed suit. "It is a gamble, but the situation greatly favors us. Should it come to a siege, the combined forces of Zhao and Liu would crush it. But I don't believe it will come to that. The captain of the Qian forces will see the remainder of the attacking force sided with Xiang, and the secondary force released unharmed back into the city. Once the reports have been given and the tale told in full, I believe an agreement can be reached."

"It sounds like you have the situation well in hand," Akemi said. "And it sounds like our presence is no longer required."

"The emperor has asked that I extend to you an invitation to march with us to Qian. I believe he also wishes to offer each of you positions under his employ. He holds you three in near as high regard as he does the prowess of his sworn brother and sister, Zhang and Guan. And that is no small compliment."

"We are honored," Kenjiro said. "But our efforts do not stop here. We must leave to finish the business that brought the demon-ridden Qian to your gates to begin with."

The strategist smiled knowingly. "I believed as much. Will you visit upon Liu Xiang before you leave? He and a certain Zhang Da and Guan Xi would like to see you once more."

"Of course," Akemi said.

"How soon do you plan to leave?"

They looked at each other. "That's the interesting part," Akemi said. "The guardian of Takashaniel has been keeping a watch on parts of the world that have been touched by the spreading evil. Once we had resolved the issue here, he would send for our transport from these lands."

"The woman who brought you," Xiaoyin surmised.

"Hopefully they're aware that the battle is over and she'll be here soon," Akemi said. "Otherwise, we're stranded."

"The offer stands, now and later. Emperor Liu Xiang made it clear that should you wish to visit Ba Guo after your business is done, you have a home and friends in Shu Han, and by extension, Wuhan."

55

Malimokuru didn't know which were worse, the constant nagging of mosquitoes that buzzed his ear and tried to drink his blood, or the marshy swamp they were forced to trudge through.

Despite his grumblings, there had been little choice. It was either endure this hellish musty wetland and its bloodsucking denizens, or travel around through the trees. Malimokuru had even linked with Nyaka who had gone hunting in those woods. Through the goar cat he had learned that the ground inside the forest was little better, and was more or less a wooded version of what they traveled across now. They would have been delayed by more than half a day at the least. That was not the only thing that deterred the nature reader for the swampy woods.

"You seem thoughtful, friend Malimokuru," Ayanda said, sloshing beside him.

"I was thinking of a close brush with death I had with some friends when we traveled through a wooded marsh similar to that over there." He pointed toward the tree line.

"Ah, the hunter. *Inkosazana* told your story. You and only three other humans survived an attack in *The Craig,* not only by a full grown goar cat, but also a hunter. You and your friends must be a formidable team, *Umntwana Onomuntu.*"

"I suspect there was a little bit of luck mixed with that formidability," Malimokuru replied. "We had Nyaka with us too."

The amahle hunter nodded. "Even as young as she was at that time,

Umzingeli Unwabu are still very dangerous." He glanced at Nyaka, painstakingly high-stepping through the marsh alongside them. "You were very lucky to have her with you."

As the sun continued on its path across the sparsely clouded sky, steam rose from the heating swampland. The air became thick and heavy, clinging to the laboring group like a filmy blanket. They traveled as quickly as they could while keeping a careful eye on their surroundings. The twin demons could still be around and they were in an undesirable situation, sloshing across the mushy terrain.

The going was slow and the distance was long, but fortune held. A few hours past midday they finally reached the other side of the swamp and climbed onto higher, solid ground. At Darius's suggestion, they took only enough time to recuperate before setting out again.

"Tell me, nature reader," the drojan said. "Now that you've fought a demon; two, in fact. Do you believe you're prepared for what lies ahead?"

"Can't know for sure until I'm there," Malimokuru answered. "What I *can* say is that I'm still quite fond of living, so I plan on being as prepared as I can. I've fought demons before, though they were nothing like the two back at the valley. Even though I can't image anything worse than those two, I've lived long enough to know better."

Darius's responding chuckle made the air vibrate. "Wise."

Malimokuru took a closer look at him. Darius wore pants and a shirt made of material that was unfamiliar to him. The cloak that hung about his shoulders was also made of the same material. He remembered when Darius had leaped onto the back of the lava leech and tore into it, riding it down into a molten pool. He had thought it was the end of the drojan. Darius had not only surfaced unharmed, but with his clothes intact. Malimokuru could think of no materials, whether cloth or steel, that could withstand the immeasurable heat of lava.

"You have something on your mind?" Darius asked.

They entered a patch of woods and were greeted by the song of chirping insects and birds. Malimokuru used the beautiful sounds to distract himself from the exertion of the hike, and his heavy breathing as a result.

"Just random thoughts," Malimokuru huffed.

"I do not wish to pry into your privacy, but I cannot dispel my curiosity either. Might I ask what so occupies your thoughts, my friend?"

"Mmm."

"Your reluctance suggests me as the focal point," Darius ventured.

"You've got a bit of ego going on there, eh?"

"I am wrong?"

Malimokuru looked farther uphill. Sakhile had gone ahead to scout, and was just visible as he crouched atop a grassy knoll. "You're not wrong, but I feel uncomfortable speaking about it."

Darius looked at him with a hint of a smile. "Your kind are discovering a very different world that has existed around you for ages. If you had no questions in your mind, you would be a fool. I never mingle with the likes of fools."

"Fair enough." Malimokuru looked again at Darius's clothing.

Darius glanced down at himself and grinned. "You admire my physique?"

Malimokuru snorted. "Hardly. I was wondering how it is that your clothing is so durable as to withstand a lava bath."

"Ah, now we come to something interesting."

"Interesting?" Malimokuru waved a hand over the drojan. "You have an amazing seamstress you're going to tell me about?"

Darius chuckled. "No. But let me start with a question for you. Not many people know what a nature reader is, and what you do, correct?"

"Not many at all," Malimokuru agreed. "There aren't many of us on this side of the world. In Jamaica it was well-known what I am and what we do. The farther north and west you go, the less of a good idea it is for people to know."

Darius nodded. "I find that fact intriguing. Even during your Age of Technology, humans studied and used what you call magic."

"Yeah man. But the problem is that magic and technology don't mix too well."

Again Darius nodded. "No, they do not. The two are rather incompatible." They climbed the knoll where the scout waited. From their position, they could see that the land dropped off not far from where they stood, then stretched out in rolling hills. It reminded Malimokuru of the ocean; a rippling sea of trees, shrubbery, and boulders.

"I place us two more hours from our destination," Sakhile said, shielding his eyes while he read the sun's position.

"I will feel better arriving before night," Naiyala said.

Her meaning was hard to miss. No one wanted to risk the night catching them, especially so close to their destination.

"In my years upon this world," Darius continued, "I have witnessed many a laughable instance when humans have come in direct contact with magic and dismissed it. It is fascinating how your kind can be so forcefully oblivious to it."

"Not all my kind."

Darius nodded. "But the reason I asked you if many people know what you are and what you do is because many humans do not know anything beyond their own villages, but there are some who know much more. My clothes, as you call them, would be recognized by a group known as the Korahl. They live in the highest peaks in the deserts of Chem."

Malimokuru frowned. "Chem? How could anyone live in that oven-like heat? And I've never heard of a people called the Korahl."

"The dragon tribe," Darius continued. "We are known to the Korahl. Even the mighty Daunyarka are known to the Korahl. I would say that they are one of only a few groups of humans who truly understand magic, but one of even fewer who know its source."

"I think we're going off topic," Malimokuru said.

"My clothes are not what they appear to be," Darius clarified. "Because I have the blood of the Reds flowing through me, part of my nature is magical."

"So your clothes are magical, then?"

"What you look at is my skin made into the likeness of what you use as clothes."

Malimokuru swallowed a bit of bile. "So your saying that you're actually naked, but making yourself look like you're wearing clothes."

Darius laughed and shook his head. "Not naked, exactly, but think of it as the fur of an animal, or the scales of a dragon. Did mighty Khairon look naked to you? Does a bear look naked to you, though it wears no clothes? What you see is the appearance I give myself to blend in with your society. My true appearance would disturb you."

Malimokuru glanced at the amahle walking silently around them. "Have you seen them when they fight?" he said, jabbing a thumb over his shoulder."

Darius looked him square in the eye, and for just an instant, Malimokuru saw the seriousness in the normally easygoing Darius. "You would be very disturbed, nature reader."

Malimokuru believed him.

"Okay." He cleared his throat. "This source of magic you mentioned. What is it?"

"There are three types of magic. The third, is wild magic. Your Daunya Masters and Daunya Warriors harness this power in addition to the power of the Daunyans Themselves, who are the first source. The Daunyans, who created the world, are the ultimate source of everything there is, including magic. It takes a great deal of discipline and strength to wield the power of the Daunyans. This is why there are so few in the world, and fewer still Chosen."

"And the second source?"

Darius smiled. "The Daunyarka."

"Dragons?"

"Yes. But should you be so shocked? Think about it, my friend. Daunyarka, or dragons, as you call them, are the guardians of the Daunyans. They are Boraka's army, and the first creation."

Malimokuru rubbed his chin as he tried to digest it all. "So, three sources of magic, which means three sources to harness it from?" He stiffened with indignation at Darius's answering laughter.

"I apologize, my friend. It is not you that I laugh at, but the mental imagery of your question. How comical it would be to witness a human trying to harness magic from a dragon. I cannot imagine the outcome. No, friend. Though Daunyarka are a living source of magic, their power cannot be harnessed."

Malimokuru snapped his fingers. "So when humans built more and more cities and created advanced technology—"

"The farther away Daunyarka moved, and other magical beings followed them."

Malimokuru nodded in thought. "There is so much that is unknown. It's like I went to sleep and awoke on a different world entirely. Those foolish boys told me stories of their travels, but I wasn't sure how much was truth and how much was fanciful imagination. I think I know, now."

Darius patted the nature reader on the back. "If I may offer a bit of advice? Do not fall into the trap of trying to understand the mysterious. That was a preoccupation of humans during their technology age. That which is mysterious in this world is only revealed to those who live within it.

"A sword master would no sooner attempt to understand a cleric's skill any more than the cleric would attempt to understand the way of the sword. As the warrior trains, his skills are refined and new insights are revealed when he is ready. The same holds true for those who study the intangible."

"We have arrived, friends Malimokuru and Darius," Naiyala said. Malimokuru followed her gaze to see the top of a gleaming tower standing above the distant trees.

Amata Daunyana stared unblinking at the magnificent structure. "Even from here, I can feel it. I have been told the stories, but I hadn't imagined the power it contained. I look forward to experiencing it up close."

"You will experience it from within," a gentle voice said. A man dressed in a simple yet glowing blue robe stepped from behind a tree. The amahle tensed, but Amata signaled for them to relax.

All sense of decorum gone, Malimokuru squinted at the man. No, not a man at all, but something else. His skin looked like polished marble; gray, black, and white all blended together.

"I apologize for my abrupt arrival," he said. "But I thought it best to meet you here. My name is Iel. Welcome to Takashaniel."

* * *

Many miles away, Greash watched the little insects and the guardian of that blasted tower. He could see them perfectly despite the distance between himself and his quarry. He looked across the miles to his right, where Zkora was no doubt feeling the same frustration. That decrepit human with his four bodyguards would have been an easy kill in those marshes. But there was something about the new human traveling with them that gave Greash pause. It made no sense. It was just another human, but something about him compelled Greash to keep his distance.

Zkora had thought otherwise and had argued against waiting. Always the more rash of the two, he would have gone for them as soon as they'd left the human civilization. Greash's refusal to join him had stopped the other, and also left him seething. Once they'd reached the marshes, it would have been a perfect place to attack, but luck had conspired against them.

The marshes provided the perfect environment to hamper their prey, but it was also too close to that thrice cursed tower. Even from his position so far away, Greash could feel Takashaniel's power. Without Kabriza or the *tether*, they could only venture so close without being blasted back to the abyss. The demon bared its fangs in something resembling a smile. That was one little thing the guardian didn't know. That first battle was only possible because Kabriza had been close enough to the tower to allow the demon force to attack. What would Iel do this time?

Greash spread his wings and looked at the ruined left tip. If it had been a wound inflicted by an ordinary weapon, it would have healed long ago. But this was done with Daunyanic power, and would never heal. He narrowed his glowing red eyes at that amahle slave of the cursed Gods. He would take his time with her. She could only channel so much of her Gods' power, but it would not be enough to stop him. He would delight in her agony.

56

King Elizander Dain paced back and forth in his study, Davros, Milpheus, and—the more frequently present—Arief of Dasha stood watching. Their unusual visitors had shared a disturbing tale before he'd released them into the care of his staff. If they had arrived just a week earlier, he would have questioned their sanity and dismissed them out of hand. Or would he have?

That the short fellow was a dwarf and woman an elf—or partially an elf— was undeniable. "These demons conspire to turn Mairson and me against one another for the sole purpose of enjoying the carnage that would result from a war."

"There is more to it than that," Arief said. "Lower demons thrive on chaos and destruction, but these are more powerful and smarter demons. The one you encountered in the forest was more animalistic in nature, but still smarter than the smartest of its weaker kind."

"At a later time I will ask you to completely fill me in on the genealogy of hell," Elizander replied. "For the time being, however, we need to decide how to deal with this. Does anyone have suggestions?"

"Given the presence of our visitors," Milpheus offered, "and the fact that the dwarf fellow says there are more of his people outside our gates that stand ready, I believe the demon problem can take a secondary position to the issue of Lord Mairson."

"I agree," Davros said. "So long as this demon problem doesn't get any worse, we should concentrate on Mairson."

"We must not forget the ever-flicking forked tongue of a certain Holy Arbitrator," Arief added. "Though he would seem a small issue, given the circumstances, I assure you he is gaining momentum."

"Based solely on the fact that there have been no more attacks, and that his new position of power keeps it so. If our visitors are to be believed, these monsters will return. When that happens, allies of King Elizander will stand beside him."

"The public must bear witness to such a thing," Davros said.

"That could be arranged," Milpheus replied.

"I'll not have the citizenry brought to harm, or even the potential of it for the sake of politics," Dain said.

Milpheus stared at the floor, his thick stack of papers wrapped in his arms against his chest. "Your benevolence is duly noted, my lord, but unfortunately the people are who they are. The lack of faith by many have forced our hand. Dinman has been a growing problem since before the killings began.

"He's been using them to strengthen his case against not only Bishop Marquis, but yourself as well. My informants tell me that his following is still growing more rapidly by the day. He's not yet powerful enough to challenge the bishop outright but he is slowly eroding him, and by extension, you."

"It's a signal that the world has turned upside down when I must agree with your attendant yet again," Davros said. "This is war of a different type, but war nonetheless. And in war, there is the risk of casualties." He inclined his head before Elizander could argue. "Please allow me to finish, my lord."

Elizander stared at him for a few heartbeats, then nodded and resumed his pacing.

"I will do everything in my power to ensure there are as few casualties as possible when these things return," Davros continued. "I'll have men posted throughout New Dainland."

"They will be casualties as well, Captain Davros," Arief said in his quiet, even voice. "Their weapons are not properly infused to harm this enemy."

"Infused? What does that mean?"

"I have contacted the head of my order and with your leave, I can have five monks of Dasha patrolling New Dainland within a day."

Davros snorted. "What good would five monks do? Are you not aware of the size of New Dainland? And what if a large number of the things attack?"

"I assure you, Captain Davros, that five Dasha monks in one city even as large as New Dainland are equal to the task, unless a full army of demons descended upon us."

"Is that not a possibility?"

"No."

"So says the mysterious man in the hooded robe," Davros scoffed.

"Enough," Elizander said. "You didn't see him destroy that thing in the woods, Captain. I believe him."

Davros bristled at the comment, but nodded respectfully.

Elizander softened and walked over to place a hand on his friend's shoulder. "Had you been armed with the proper weapons, I've no doubt you would have slain our hellish foe. We are both lucky to be alive, and that luck has increased in the form of better understanding. We must be smart about it."

"If I may interrupt, my lord?" Milpheus said.

"What do you have, Milpheus?"

"A quandary."

"You're thinking of Lord Mairson."

Milpheus nodded. "I'm sure I need not verbalize the reaction we would receive should we simply reveal the truth of the irritants inhabiting out two lands."

"That would indeed be folly," Elizander agreed. He felt a weariness settle over him, as heavy as any armor he might wear.

"We have not received any correspondence from Mairson in days," Milpheus went on. "It could be that he's encountered the enemy for what they are and is having a similar conversation with those in his trust."

"Not likely," Arief said. Elizander had nearly forgotten the monk was there, so silent and still was he. "I have someone keeping watch, and the bishop of Mairland is as much in the know of our identity as is Bishop Marquis. If a demon had appeared in that city within the last several days I would have known."

"Perhaps your man was dispatched?" Davros suggested.

The hooded figure slowly turned his head to regard the captain. "Even more unlikely. Two demons like the one you encountered in the woods could not take her if they attacked at the same time. And if she had died I would know that also."

"Is ubiquity a trait of your Order?" Davros asked, the question laced with sarcasm.

"It would appear so to the secular," the monk replied. "But the answer to your question is no, I am not everywhere at once."

Seeing that the monk didn't intend to speak further, Davros let it go. "I suppose we're to simply trust in the mists of mystery to see us through this."

"You've more wisdom than you let on, Captain."

"Must everyone close to me quarrel?" Elizander said, looking at the three of them. "We are on the verge of crisis. I expect cohesiveness from you three, not arguing."

The room fell silent and Elizander continued his pacing. Once he realized they were watching him, he stopped. "Our visitors and the dwarf's people will remain outside the city, as is their want." He looked at Arief. "Should an attack happen, you will be up to the task, and if things are worse, you have the means to send for ... reinforcements. Am I correct?"

Arief nodded.

He turned to Milpheus. "And you are certain the public can bear witness to these monsters while keeping the risk to life at a minimum?"

"There is more than one way to approach it," Milpheus replied.

Elizander held up his hand. "No explanations for now. We will hold conference later. I've a nagging feeling that we need to act quickly." Finally he addressed Davros. "That leaves us with the issue of Mairson. He's already suspicious of me planting murderers in his city."

"He was never endowed with sharp wits, my lord."

Elizander repressed a chuckle. "Be that as it may, we must find a way to reach him. I'm finding all this difficult to digest and I, *we*, have been witness to it personally."

"So a similar scenario must play out in Mairland."

"Would that there was another way, I would gladly do it."

"I may have a way," Arief said. "But it is not without risk."

"Speak it," Elizander said.

"With the proper skill and ability, it's possible to contain a demon for a short time. This is more difficult than defeating one and sending them back to their dimension, but it can be done. Perhaps if we were to contain one here and one of my colleagues in Mairland can do the same, it will provide the proof necessary to reestablish the people's confidence here, and turn Mairson's gaze away from you at the same time. He need not even know of your knowledge about it."

Elizander shook his head in disgust. "I like none of this. It smacks of the political scheming I loathe."

"You've been left with little choice, my lord," Milpheus said.

"Of course I haven't. But it always starts small, and with good intentions. Before long, it becomes a system of deceit and games. You know this as well as I. You once tutored me in world history. Humanity nearly fell because of the games our rulers played using the people as pawns."

"And it is your distaste for it and your personal integrity that will disallow that reality to repeat. My lord, there will always be one who covets power, whether that power is yours or of their own design. The best we can do is move against them and hold fast to our principles."

"For centuries," Arief added, "the Order of Dasha has watched from the shadows and tried to guide humanity. What Milpheus speaks is truth. The simple fact that the demon realm exists at all is proof enough that we will always be tested. What is important is how each person rises to their own personal challenges."

"I hope no other ruler is confronted with this."

"It's already begun, King Elizander Dain. This is just one instance in many. The veil is lifting and humanity will once again see the world as it truly is."

"And how we react," Elizander said, "will determine our survival." The monk's silence was confirmation enough. "So be it. We will do what must be done."

Milpheus and Arief departed while Davros remained. They stood in silence for a while before the captain finally spoke. "I think you're doing the right thing."

Elizander nodded absently. "I wouldn't be doing this if I didn't believe it was the right thing to do, but my belief of what is the right action doesn't make it so."

"I believe you labor over this too deeply."

"How can I not, old friend? Look at what we plan to do. The best action would be to bring those dwarf people in and post them throughout the city along with Arief and one or two of his monks. If he is to be believed, there are no more than three to five of those things out there. They might even have the means to hunt the things down."

"We've been over this," Davros replied, picking his words carefully. "That soft-spined fool Dinman has been making aggressive efforts to under-mine you for weeks and more. If you hadn't taken the measure you had, and what you're about to, he would continue to gain momentum. There's no telling what we'd be dealing with."

Elizander ran a hand through his close-cropped hair. "On days like this, old friend, the weight of this mantle feels unbearably heavy."

Now it was Davros's turn to clamp a hand on his shoulder. He gave it a squeeze. "You are the only person in all of Winsor who could bear it, old friend." With that, the captain turned on his heel and left, gently closing the door behind him.

Brooding in the dim silence of his study, Elizander knew his childhood friend was right. Though he spoke the words, he would not wish to be anything other than what he was. Though the responsibilities of a king were heavy and trying, the ability to affect positive change and help to create a better life for his people made it worthwhile. With a resigned smile, he walked to the balcony and gazed out at the city below, and the people he hoped he could protect.

57

"You're sure you don't need another day or two before we leave?" Kenjiro asked. "Since the fight with Qian Hua and her subsequent fall into unconsciousness, Kenjiro had been like a mother hen pecking at her to stay put and not strain herself.

"I'm fine to travel, Brother," she replied in as patient a tone as she could manage. "Whatever residual maladies I might have would be more quickly mended at Takashaniel than here."

Kenjiro grunted. "That is true enough, I suppose."

"I think I need a little time to myself, Brother. We have much yet to do and I can feel the gathering darkness. I need time to center myself."

"The time comes soon," Kenjiro replied.

"It upon us. The gathering darkness is like nothing I've ever felt. I doubt we have more than a day or two before it begins."

Behind Kenjiro, Shinobu sat in a chair, a distant look in his eyes. Feeling Akemi's gaze on him, he smiled. "I suppose we should leave and give the lady her space." When he stood, Akemi grabbed his arm and looked to Kenjiro.

"I will see you shortly."

Kenjiro grumbled but complied. He stopped in the open doorway, staring at Akemi and the surprised Shinobu. He narrowed his eyes at the strider who shrugged helplessly.

Akemi shook her head and smiled. "I will see you soon, Brother." Kenjiro grunted again, then disappeared through the door.

"How may I be of service?" Shinobu asked innocently, watching from his seat as Akemi crossed the room. She knew he was trying not to let on how he watched her walk, the sway of her hips, the way her raven hair slid down her shoulders when she untied it.

She straddled him and sat in his lap, and rested her arms on his shoulders.

"Um. This may cause a certain reaction," he said as he stared into her light brown eyes. A few locks of her silky black hair fell over an eye, which he gently slid away.

She slid a hand down the side of his face, feeling the angular contours of his cheekbone, jaw, his neck. She slid her hand down the middle of his chest, feeling his body tense. She leaned toward him and he closed his eyes.

Just before their lips met, she tilted sideways until her lips brushed his ear. "Your sword will take your mind if you are not careful."

His eyes popped open. "How—"

She kissed him, gently at first, then with more urgency. She felt him sit more upright as he leaned into her, their passion growing more desperate until finally she pulled back, gasping. Shinobu's shoulders rose and fell as he also caught his breath.

Akemi followed his lowered gaze to see it lingering on her heaving chest. With a smirk, she leaned forward, burying his face in her cleavage as she stood and walked to the window.

She looked over her shoulder. "Care to join me?"

"I would if I could stand," Shinobu said.

She didn't respond, but continued to stare out at the land beyond. A few heartbeats later, she felt his arms slide around her waist. She leaned back against him and enjoyed his warmth. She felt his growing desire and let her head fall back, a questioning smile on her face.

"So tense."

"So cruel."

"I know." Akemi turned in his arms and slid her hand down his tensed abdomen. Her lips parted when she felt him shudder under her gentle touch.

Shinobu scooped her into his arms and crossed the room to place her gently on the bed. As slowly as his crumbling restraint would allow, he undressed her, exploring every curve and angle of her body as he revealed it.

Akemi closed her eyes as he explored her, lingering on the occasional pink scars on her otherwise smooth skin.

"Beautiful," he whispered.

"Imperfections," she replied.

"You no more believe that than I."

She lifted his tunic over his head and kissed every scar she found. He shuddered again as her hand explored ever downward. No longer able to contain their desire, they merged, their kisses deep and urgent. Their spirits expanded and joined as they made love. They felt the quick beat of each other's hearts, the intensity of each breath, the brightness of their spirits.

A warmth settled over their entwined bodies that startled them at first. The warmth intensified; not a warmth of heat, but of love that radiated, pulsated with each heartbeat. Spent, they collapsed beside each other and Akemi rolled onto her side and Shinobu draped his arm over her shoulder.

She lay awake with her eyes closed and sank into the warmth of Shinobu's body combined with the loving radiance that enveloped them like a cocoon.

Eventually she slipped into a lucid sleep. She heard a distant giggle not with her ears, but from deep inside. The sound was that of a girl between childhood and adulthood, yet there was power in it. She felt her spirit rise from her body and tether itself with that of Shinobu's. She felt his startled awareness as much as her own. A feeling of power and creation washed over them, through them, and then drifted away.

Before they had time to bask in the bliss, another overwhelming feeling of the beautiful unknown washed through them. Again it was instantaneous but lasting. The feelings came and went, again and again. The feelings of love, destruction, redemption, and balance. Finally, they felt their spirits join as one, and the raw bliss and aliveness they felt was like nothing they could fathom. Seven experiences that lasted but an instant and for an eternity at the same time.

Akemi opened her eyes and twisted around to see that Shinobu was also awake. They looked at each other and no words were needed. That they had been blessed by the Daunyans was no question. But as they lay there, bodies entangled, Akemi felt exhilaration and trepidation intermixed.

She had felt Shinobu to his core and knew his love for her, as she knew that he'd felt the same from her. She reveled in what they'd shared, but when she closed her eyes and felt the tiny spark that had ignited deep inside her, like the tiny flame of a candle, she knew both joy and fear. The Gods had touched their union and she knew that eventually, through her, the legacy of the Children of The Gene would continue.

58

A kemi opened the door just enough to peak her head out and ensure no one was in the hallway. She let out a sigh of relief before she could stop herself, then scowled. What was she, a child? She straightened her back with an air of defiance and opened the door. Why should she be nervous about her brother's reaction? She was a grown woman, after all! It was none of his business! Behind her, Shinobu placed a gentle hand on her shoulder.

"We should get going. We've lost an entire day."

"You regret?"

He chuckled, giving her shoulder a squeeze and then taking his hand away. "You know better than that."

"I imagine my brother will be annoyed. We were supposed to have left yesterday."

"He may surprise you."

Akemi cast him a doubtful look and stepped into the hall. After navigating the many twists and turns of the palace, they finally arrived at the gardens. To their surprise, not only was Kenjiro waiting on them, but Liu Xiang, Zhang Da, Guan Xi, and Zhuge Xiaoyin.

"I've come to understand that you cannot remain with us, but it gladdens my heart that you chose to remain a day longer."

Akemi dipped into a light warrior's curtsy while Shinobu executed a subtle bow.

"Your brother explained to me yesterday that you would need an extra day, which fortunately gave me the time to come and see you off personally."

"You are most kind, Emperor, Shinobu said."

"Nothing I can do will equal your contribution to Shu Han," Xiang said as an armed guard approached with Taliah in tow.

"Your timing is almost unsettling," Liu Xiang said, to which Taliah inclined her head. "It is a practiced skill, Emperor."

Liu Xiang raised a hand, and four servants approached, one standing in front of each of the visitors. "There is little I could think of to offer you as gifts for your service. You are already equipped with weapons no blacksmith could rival, and gifts of luxury would be of little value."

The servants bowed and presented folded silk garments to each of them. "Instead, I offer you gifts of comfort. I had my best tailors craft garments of silk unique to each of you."

"A beautiful gift of immeasurable value, Emperor Liu Xiang," Akemi said, holding the soft garment. "It will remind us of the kindness and strength of this land."

"And also," Liu Xiang replied, "to remind you that you have friends that await your visit again."

"Of that, there is no question," Kenjiro said. "Our thanks, Emperor."

"You are friends of Wuhan, and by extension, Shu Han," Xiang said formally. Wherever you travel in my province, you will be welcomed as my most esteemed friends."

Guan Xi stepped forward and surprised Akemi with a hug. "I am not normally given to this affectionate nonsense, but there are mostly men in my line of work. We hardly know one another but I feel a sisterly connection to you that I cannot explain."

"Yes," Akemi replied. "When this dark business is done, perhaps we may adventure together." She almost laughed at the other woman's girlish smile.

"I shall hold you to that, Akemi Miyamoto, Ninja Demon Huntress."

Liu Xiang came to Taliah, who'd been waiting aside while everyone said their goodbyes. "I've had even less time to know you, but I extend to you the same welcome as them, friend of Wuhan, Shu Han, and Ba Guo."

Taliah listened as Shinobu translated. "I am honored, Emperor. Thank you. If good fortune shines upon me, I will return."

"I've a feeling good fortune will see you through your trials. The stars do not lie."

Taliah smiled and bowed her head. "There is indeed much to be divined by studying the stars. None can predict the will of the Gods, but They have provided many guiding signs for those who know how to look."

They took their leave of the bustling and industrious city of Wuhan. "It isn't often a situation like that one ends in such a neat and tidy way," Shinobu remarked after they had crossed through the gates. "That Liu Xiang was able to bring Qian's forces into his own is in itself an amazing feat, but he thinks to move on to the land of Qian and convince what's left of the military there to stand down and join with himself and Empress Zhao."

Akemi untied her hair and let it fall to her shoulders, then ran her fingers through it. "Liu Xiang is very much a descendent of Liu Bei, who had great fortune on his side. I have a feeling he will accomplish his vision."

"He is a great and competent ruler," Kenjiro said. "And he's surrounded by equally competent and loyal friends."

"It's too bad we couldn't borrow a few of those competent friends," Shinobu replied. "We need all the help we can get."

"Without the Gene of the Daunyans," Akemi replied, "their extraordinary abilities would be wasted. Liu Xiang is a good fighter, and Zhang Da and Guan Xi even more so. But their abilities would be strained past the limits of normal human stamina."

Taliah nodded. "Without the Gene of the Daunyans, they would not have the necessary augmentation of their respective attributes. Besides," she pointed ahead. "I think there are others who wish to contribute."

Further up the trail, three monks were sitting in a patch of grass on the side of the road. Seeing the approaching group, they stood. Akemi recognized one of the figures as Shi Xing Long. As they approached, the three monks pressed their palms together and bowed, uttering the traditional greeting of their station.

"The Order of Shaolin wishes to aid your cause," Shi Xing Long stated, straight to the point. "This," he indicated the two younger men to his left, "is Shi Xiao Ren and Shi Xing Wu. We will accompany you to do battle against the darkness."

Taliah's brow creased with concern as Shinobu translated the monk's words. "I admit that not much of your Order is known to me, but our foe may be beyond your formidable abilities." Shinobu translated and the monk replied again, speaking quickly.

"He says that he is aware that the Gene of the Daunyans aids us, but his small sect within the Order of Shaolin has silently battled the darkness for centuries. Though they do not carry the Gene of the Daunyans, they are blessed to wield Their power."

Taliah was silent a moment. "It is not my place to permit or deny those who would fight with us so long as they are possessed of at least some of the tools to battle the abyss. If they wish to fight by our side, we would be honored to have them." The strider translated and the monks pressed their palms together and bowed again.

"I think we are far enough out of Wuhan that I may transport us. A warning, though. We must again travel through the upper levels of the abyss. The last time I passed through, I encountered … difficulty. There is no reason it won't happen again. Also," she indicated their weapons. "So long as your weapons are in some way connected to your bodies, they will remain in that dimension. The instant they disconnect from you, they will fall back into this realm, and be lost."

"Hold on to our weapons," Shinobu replied. "Got it."

As Taliah began weaving the space about them into a bubble-like substance, Kenjiro had a thought. "Why must we travel through the hells? Can we not skim through the heavens instead?"

"Two reasons," Taliah replied. "First is that the heavens exist on a much higher vibration than our physical bodies do. Without the proper training to contain them, our spirits would simply attune themselves to their native home and leave our physical vessels. The result would be our lifeless physical bodies falling back to this world while our true forms remained among the Daunyans."

Akemi arched an eyebrow. "I don't think I'd like that.

"You're wrong, Ninja." The air flexed and rippled, and soon they found themselves standing in a desolate valley of cracked black ground and twisted, rotted vegetation. "As soon as your spirit experiences the bliss of the heavens, the desire to stay would overwhelm you. You would not hesitate to remain. And that is the second reason. It takes years of training to have the discipline necessary to enter the realm of the Gods and not be enticed to remain."

The trio of monks calmly studied the new environment. Though they appeared calm, each had a white-knuckled grip on their weapons.

"You ready?" Taliah asked. Shi Xing Long caught her meaning and nodded. "There is a vortex not far from here. We shouldn't linger here any longer than necessary."

"No arguments here," Akemi said. "This world makes me …" she trailed off at the sight of two demons easily fifty feet tall approaching. A curse from her brother told her that he had seen them too.

"Mercy of the Gods," Taliah swore. "This again! Must we …" she stopped, puzzled by the sudden retreat of the two giants.

Kenjiro's face darkened. "Whatever made them flee, I don't want to see it."

"I agree," Taliah said. She remained still, searching about for the potential threat.

A shadow passed over the group, blotting out the dim light that seemed to just float in the sunless sky.

"What now?" Shinobu looked from the ground to the sky, and the blood drained from his face. "Oh no."

Though high in the sky, the winged creature's shadow enveloped the seven humans and a fair amount of space around them.

"They truly exist," Shinobu whispered. "Myth and lore made flesh."

"But here, in this world," Kenjiro responded gravely. "The sight of a dragon in the demon realm brings no joy to my heart."

"I nah welcome da sight of it were it in *our* world," Taliah said, her accent slipping through her nerves.

Kenjiro unconsciously rested a hand on the hilt of his sword. "Maybe it will pass us by if we don't move."

"And our thrice cursed luck lives strong," Shinobu growled as the dragon wheeled about and glided in an arc and descended so rapidly, the ground quaked when it landed before them.

The violent impact threw the party into the air left them sprawling on the ground. Quickly they regained their feet, readying what felt like laughably tiny weapons.

Glowing red orbs larger than a human body narrowed at them, revealing a malevolent intelligence that left no doubt about its intent. It looked from one human to the next, considering each of them. The right side of its narrow maw curled up into a snarl that revealed a fang as long as a tall human. Its smoky black spiked and curved plated scales shimmered, though there was little light to shine on them. Huge, corded muscles flexed underneath those razor-sharp scales as it shifted its weight.

For many nervous heartbeats no one moved, and each of the warriors

stole glances at their surroundings, trying to find a way to escape or some-
place to hide. It was useless, for they stood in the middle of a blasted and
barren valley.

"What now?" Shinobu whispered. "It's just staring at us."

"Everything we have ever heard about dragons suggests they are intelligent," Kenjiro said. "Even the ones in western lore. I see in its eyes a cat
toying with the mice it plans to eat."

"Optimistic," the strider remarked dryly.

"Realistic," the samurai countered.

"Let's test it out." Akemi took a small step to the left. As soon as she
moved, the dragon lifted a huge claw and slammed it into the ground beside
her. The thunderous impact launched her into the air. Akemi turned her body
in a somersault and landed in a crouch. She narrowed her eyes at the thick,
black claws as they sliced into the ground. Slowly, deliberately, the dragon
drug its claws back in front of it, tearing wide trenches that were at least a
dozen feet deep.

"Well, now we know." Akemi didn't dare move from where she'd
landed.

"We need to figure something out fast," Shinobu said. "The longer we're
here, the more likely we'll have demons on our backs."

Taliah stared into its large crimson eyes. "I doubt anything will bother us
so long as it's nearby."

"I guess that's something good."

"Hardly."

"Split up and run?" Shinobu suggested.

"It will stomp us into the ground before we gain any distance," Kenjiro
replied.

"We have to try something quick. How long will it sit there?"

"I have not lived this life to be eaten by anything; dragon or not." Taliah's
resonating voice crackled with power, filling the air itself.

The others backed away as the woman's braided hair unraveled itself and
drifted about her head, as though she were under water.

"If you understand me, dragon, find prey elsewhere." She took a step
forward and despite her infinitely smaller frame, Taliah's presence felt every
bit as large as the dragon's. "We are not for you to devour!"

At that moment, Akemi wondered which of them was more dangerous.

The dragon's scaled lips twitched and curled back to reveal rows of sharp
teeth and a set of red fangs at the top and bottom of its maw. It let out a
screeching roar that brought the warriors to their knees, hands pressed to their

ears. All except the Daunya Chosen. The dragon regarded her more carefully, then threw its head back and roared again, lifting its right claw.

Taliah's hands glowed with a bright white aura, and just as the claw descended on her, she brought her hands around in an arc from right to left and deflected the massive claw. The effort threw her aside, but it also caused the dragon to stumble. She recovered more quickly and launched a wave of searing bright light into the dragon's face, knocking the beast on its side. "WITH ME, NOW."

The group sprinted after her as the thrashing dragon recovered.

"There's a vortex not far ahead. I'll guide you, stay straight."

"Take the lead! Shinobu yelled over his shoulder." Just then he saw the dragon lift itself up and shake its head. It whipped its head around and glared hatefully at them. It was the most chilling gaze Shinobu had ever seen. Never had he known truer fear.

"I cannot," Taliah replied. "I have to keep it off of us!"

"You can't fight it by yourself!"

"Your concern is touching, strider. Look after yourselves so I don't have to."

The dragon came after them, tearing into the ground as it ran. The triple thud that it made as it loped behind them shook the ground. Beside Akemi, Taliah's hands started glowing again.

Akemi reached behind her back and gripped the hilt of *Onihakaisha*. Taliah made eye contact and shook her head, and Akemi released the blade.

The white aura spread from her hands to the rest of her body, then her eyes. She leaped into the air and hovered in place. In an instant the dragon was on her. With a swipe of her hands the white aura leapt from her body and slammed into the side of the dragon, sending it into a sideways tumble.

The beast recovered quickly and came at her again in a snarling rage. Taliah filled herself with the power of the Daunyans and brought up a shield just as the dragon rammed its spiked head into her.

Despite the strength of her shield, the raw power of the impact sent her flying.

All of this Akemi saw over her shoulder as she ran with the others. "All of you, SPEED UP!" She yelled. "I don't know if she's dead, but she's out of the fight."

They sprinted straight ahead, trusting to luck that they would find the vortex. The triple thud footfalls behind them told them that the dragon had resumed the chase and was rapidly closing the distance.

Kenjiro glanced over his shoulder and his eyes widened. "DIVE RIGHT!"

Though the monks of Shaolin did not understand his tongue, they saw the others and reacted, diving aside as a huge claw slammed into the ground where they'd been an instant earlier. Akemi landed in a roll and came to a spinning crouch. In one quick motion she drew her swords and slashed the nearest claw.

The attack had no effect, and she was forced to leap backwards as the dragon swept its claw outward, nearly disemboweling her. The warriors stood their ground while the faint blue-green swirl drifted mockingly close, behind a nearby outcropping. It may as well have been half a world away, for the dragon was far too close for them to reach it. Kenjiro stepped beside his sister and Shinobu came to her other side. The three monks stepped on either side of them all, readying their weapons.

"So it ends, Sister."

"So it seems," Akemi replied, not taking her eyes off of the snarling beast.

"I can think of no better friends to die beside," Shinobu said.

"Who said we were friends?" Kenjiro replied.

"Is that humor I hear coming from the ever-stoic samurai?"

Kenjiro smirked and drew his sword, and Akemi settled into a crouch.

Shinobu drew his sword from its sheath and feelings of excitement nearly overwhelmed him. *You're insane*, he told the weapon with his mind. Oddly, the only response he received was even more exhilaration.

The monks readied themselves as well, Shi Xing Long whipping two pair of nunchaku from his hips and whirling them around to finally tuck under his arms. The rounded ends of each of the hardwood sticks was fitted through the middle with a curved blade in the style of a scythe. Akemi couldn't help but admire the creative alteration.

Shi Xiao Ren leveled his double-ended spear at the dragon, and Shi Xing Wu held a long chain, handle in his left hand, the spinning chain that ended in a dart-blade on the other. Akemi had seen the weapon before. A whip dart, it was called.

The dragon lunged and snapped at the group. They scattered, some rolling aside, others somersaulting away. Shi Xing Wu leaped away and turned midair, launching the dart straight as an arrow.

It struck the dragon on the side of the head, bouncing off harmlessly. At the same time, Shi Xiao Ren spun his spear and struck the dragon across the neck several times with each revolution. Again, the masterful attack dealt no damage. Shi Xing Long and Kenjiro both had struck at the left claw in a frenzy before being forced to retreat. Akemi leapt backward, avoiding the snapping jaws by mere inches and slashed her swords down on its nose. The dragon recoiled, but she couldn't tell if it was from pain or irritation.

Shinobu had a bit more luck. Having been out of its sheath for a prolonged period of time, *Zaiku* had taken on its true form. Shinobu held the insubstantial sword at his side and snapped it forward and back, as one would a leather whip. The spectral sword scored a stinging blow to the side of the dragon's head. It let out a surprised screech and turned toward him, and Shinobu felt a fresh wave of fear as its blood-red gaze settled on him. *Looks like I got its attention.*

That is because there is no armor that can stop my bite, the sword said into his mind.

"Good to know. Let's just hope I can survive to put you to good use."

There will always be another, if you fall.

"Thanks for that." Shinobu backed away and the dragon stalked toward him. The other five warriors took advantage of its diverted attention and attacked. it ignored their efforts as if they were mere gnats buzzing around its feet. Shinobu held the waving blade out to his side, still backing away. The dragon lowered its head to his level and bared its teeth just as it snapped its claw out, quicker than one could see, and stamped the ground where he stood.

Where he'd been standing.

Shinobu had begun his training since he was able to walk. Speed and reflex were an unmatched traits of farstriders, and Shinobu was the most skilled of his clan.

He dove into a sideways roll and came upright. He spun and planted his feet, slashing at the huge claw with several horizontal and diagonal slashes before retreating again. The dragon recoiled, and this time it was clear that Shinobu's assault had hurt it. The beast roared and stomped the ground, whipping its tail around and nearly cleaving two of the monks of Shaolin in half. One of them ducked as the other leaped over the bladed tail.

It became a chaotic dance, as the six diminutive humans leapt and dove, scrambled and rolled in every direction to avoid one attack after another. Kenjiro managed to sheath his sword before he ducked the whipping tail. There was no time to counterattack as it was all any of them could do just to keep from being killed.

"We cannot win this fight!" Kenjiro shouted over the resounding crash of yet another claw pounding the ground.

"I thought we knew that already!" Shinobu replied.

Before they realized it, all six warriors were standing together again.

"Clever," Akemi remarked. Though it looked like a crazed frenzy, the dragon had actually herded them back together. It reared its head back, and the unmistakable sound of inhaling filled the air. Not waiting for death to come for them, the warriors lunged forward in hopes of attacking before it could loose its deadly breath. They weren't fast enough. The dragon thrust its head forward and breathed upon them. They skidded to a stop, flinching as they brought their weapons up reflexively.

Akemi opened her eyes when she realized she hadn't been incinerated. "How ..."

Waves of what could only be described as black fire flowed around them, and in the center of the blast was a glowing blue object. For longer than seemed possible, they waited in the safety of their invisible dome until the dragon's breath was finally spent.

The flames died away to reveal a very much alive Taliah. Though her legs wobbled, she managed to remain upright. She drew back a hand that was now glowing with a white aura tinged with red. She thrust her hand forward, and the built-up energy slammed into the dragon's chest. The force of the Daun-yanic power lifted the dragon off the ground and sent it crashing on its back into a nearby cluster of boulders.

Kenjiro and one of the monks rushed to Taliah's side as she sagged to the ground. "We need to keep going," she said. "I will recover." And to their surprise, she did grow stronger as she spoke. Without a word, they ran for the outcropping, and the vortex on the other side.

Akemi glanced over her shoulder. The dragon was rising, a bit slower this time, but it looked little more than dazed. It shook its head and took off after them again.

"What does it take to make it stay down?" she asked, more in frustration than curiosity.

"I've hit it several times with enough force to shatter a fifth hell demon to pieces," Taliah said. "I wish I could answer that question."

Akemi spared the Daunya Chosen a glance. It was the first time she'd seen the woman less than confident. They reached the outcropping but had to dive aside as a giant black claw came crashing down, smashing boulders into gravel. Pelted by rocks and dirt, the seven humans powered on, weaving between boulders and large rocks, hopping and diving as the enraged dragon tore after them, smashing and scattering boulders as though they were pebbles.

"What in all the hells did we do to so anger that thing?" Shinobu barely ducked in time to avoid a flying rock the size of his head.

"We failed to provide an easy meal?" Akemi offered. They came to a wall of boulders and her heart nearly stopped until she spied an opening large enough for only two of them to squeeze through at a time.

"Go!" Taliah said, and this time they didn't argue. Taliah called on the power of Boraka. She leaped into the air and turned to face the dragon. It was nearly on top of her as she glided backward and swung her arms over her head. She swung her arms in a downward arc, releasing the energy as she swung them up.

The blast slammed into the dragon's plated head and sent it and Taliah tumbling backward.

Kenjiro leapt and caught her in his arms, and he grunted under her weight when they fell.

Taliah nodded breathlessly in thanks and helped him up. They continued on, ignoring the bone-shaking roar of the enraged dragon.

One by one they crawled through the opening in the boulders and went sliding downhill out the other side. Taliah squeezed through last, and had barely begun her descent when the dragon burst through the wall in a shower of rocky debris. Huge, split boulders and rocks crashed down around them, showering the fleeing party with dirt and soil.

The dragon leapt into the air and glided downward to land at the bottom of the little valley between them and the swirling vortex.

The unmistakable sound of its inhalation filled their ears. As the dragon reared back, Shinobu gathered his feet underneath him and leaped forward. He drew *Zaiku*, and the sword must have sensed his urgency, for it was almost immediately in its ethereal form. He was almost in range when the dragon thrust its head forward, and he knew he was dead.

Black fire split around him, and through the roaring flames he heard Taliah. "Strike now, Strider!"

He struck. *Zaiku* came down, then up, slicing a vertical line across the dragon's face. Once, twice, a third time, he cut the dragon across the face before he finally landed.

The mighty spectral blade scored a thin scratch on the dragon's smoky gray scales. It flinched, looking as though it was in a similar pain as someone with a splinter or a cut finger. That split second of hesitation was all the group needed to half-slide half-run between the beast's legs. Seeing the vortex so near, they lowered their heads and sprinted for the swirling gateway. They were pelted again with dirt and rock as the dragon rounded on them and raked its tail across the ground. Again they heard the massive intake of breath just as they reached the vortex.

Taliah jumped and turned to face the assault just as the dragon loosed its breath on them. She crossed her arms, and when the black fire reached them, she whipped her arms outward, blasting the flames harmlessly to either side.

Finally, they were inside the vortex. Exhausted, Taliah landed inside the swirling energy and struggled to focus on their destination.

With all the strength left to her, she channeled the energy to the lands of Takashaniel. The dragon barreled toward them, roaring and spitting black flames. The world twisted and contorted like bubbling water.

Akemi looked from the nearly unconscious Taliah to the sky above. Black jaws of death swallowed the sky and closed around them.

60

Brother Dinman pinched the bridge of his nose and let out an exhausted sigh. He'd been giving multiple sermons a day and had been tirelessly building his congregation. Elizander and his lackeys had handed him the noose with which to hang themselves.

Fools. A part of him couldn't believe their stupidity, yet another part of him was still wary of some plot to displace or dispose of him. They couldn't simply throw him out, he knew. They wouldn't dare. That left the possibility of some plot to discredit him. Try as he might, though, Dinman could not figure out what that plot might be. There was no crime against preaching the word of Holy Jemanah, and they had given him even more power to do just that.

He pushed the thoughts from his mind. Whatever those idiots had planned for him, he would deal with them when the time came. Neither the king nor that decadent pig Marquis had the wit to plot against him, though they may try.

The monk lay down on a thickly packed bed of soft goose feathers. Such was a rare luxury, but one of his station should be afforded at least this much. He worked hard. He deserved it.

Dinman closed his eyes, thinking of how he would lead the flock with the firm hand neither Marquis nor Dain possessed. They would see the true way of leadership and bow with the others as he led the flock to prepare themselves for the return of Holy Jemanah.

The hour is nigh upon you, my child.

Brother Dinman's eyes popped open and he bolted upright. He looked around his spacious room as he tried to calm his pounding heart. "Who's there?"

It is your savior. Your King. Your salvation made flesh.

"If you are salvation made flesh, why can I not see you?"

It is because I have waited for the right time, my child. And that time is now. You, the Holy Arbitrator of the city of Winsor, have worked tirelessly to prepare the flock for my return.

"Your return? Now?" Dinman frowned. "Who are you. It is blasphemy to claim the identity of Holy Jemanah."

Of course it is, my child. But I am He. Is this such a surprise? None but the True King Himself knows when the return will happen. Is that not what you have preached? Have you not taught this with the expectation that I would one day return?

The monk was speechless. There was no one in the room, yet he could clearly hear the voice that seemed to speak inside his head. "I … you are Him? You are the savior, Holy Jemanah? How can this be possible?"

How could it not be possible? The calm and persuasive voice left no doubt to Dinman of who it was.

"I … had not thought Your coming would be so soon."

People do not believe great times will happen in their lifetime, child. But come I must, and come I shall. In this time. In your time.

"What do you require of me, my King?"

You have been a good and faithful servant. Your tireless work has not gone unnoticed, and shall be rewarded, my son.

Dinman dropped to his knees. "To live in service to Holy Jemanah is reward enough. How may this unworthy one serve you?"

There was a lengthy pause, and Dinman was beginning to doubt his sanity when the voice spoke again.

My coming has been foretold throughout time, and now I must come to save the flock from themselves. You, my faithful, tireless servant, will aid me in spreading the Word and reaching the people. As Holy Arbitrator you stand as a pillar of strength that connects this world to the next. You connect me to the people, my son. Dinman felt the pain of anticipation as he waited for Holy Jemanah to speak again.

I have returned to deliver the flock, good Brother Dinman, but to do this, I will need the aid of my most devout and loyal servant. I believe you are him.

"I am, my lord. I am that man!" Dinman licked his lips, his eyes going wide with hunger. Holy Jemanah had come to him! Had chosen him to do His bidding!

He would rise beyond any in the history of the Church of Jemanah! He would be revered for generations as the first Holy Arbitrator and the man who had walked beside Holy Jemanah to lead the flock! None would be held in higher regard than Brother Dinman. He would stand above Bishop Marquis and even King Elizander!

If you wish to walk beside me and lead the flock to its proper place, you have only to let it be so, my child. I will give you power beyond anything you could dream. All will scramble to satisfy your smallest whims. Open yourself to me, and together we will gather the people in our hands and deliver them. I choose you, my son, to deliver the people to me, and to lead the flock to eternal life. The time is now. Receive me, my son.

As the monk knelt to the floor, a tiny flicker of warning flared in the back of his mind. Brother Dinman frowned at himself. Doubt was blasphemy, and he would not fail such a crude test.

He pushed the feeling away in irritation and lowered his forehead to the floor. This was his chance. Holy Jemanah had come to him to lead the flock, and he would not let simple mortal trepidation hinder his aspirations. He straightened and let his head fall back, raising his hands toward the ceiling.

"I receive you, my Lord Father," the monk whispered. And then he felt it. A wave of blackness like nothing he could have imagined in his most wicked nightmares. The surge of darkness assaulted him, stabbed through him again and again, raking and tearing inside his body.

Dinman clenched his teeth. The pain was more than he could bear. He felt the wrongness of it, but he was helpless to stop it as he felt his soul being drowned by the tide of darkness that filled him.

He doubled over and gasped, one hand on the floor, the other reaching for something, anything to hold onto. The spike of fear Dinman felt blossomed into a dark blanket of hopeless panic that enveloped him. In that instant he felt the blackness grow more excited, as though it delighted in his dismay. He tried to fight it, tried to focus on the glory of Holy Jemanah, his savior.

For an instant, the darkness hesitated. Then, as though laughing hysterically, it rushed him again and pounded at his resolve. It scratched and hammered, whipped and flayed his soul. It pummeled him and forced Dinman to retreat deep into his subconscious until he was no more than a tiny speck, surrounded by darkness.

Brother Dinman rose and carefully arranged his robes. He must not be seen looking anything but his best, after all. He stretched his neck and arms, and arched his back. A smile slithered across his face and he walked to the nearest window and looked out, hands clasped behind his back.

The rolling hills and fields, the grassy mountains and tree-littered lands beyond. The people and animals. All would be brought to heel, then crushed under it. After he'd disposed of that fool bishop and the equally foolish king, he would step forth and tie the kingdom to him, and solidify his power. Dinman smiled, thinking of the many nations and distant lands that would bow before him. His future subjects. His future slaves.

He had been sent here to help fulfill a plan that had been long set in motion. He didn't care. The world was big enough to share, and his share would be large indeed. The *seaph* smiled. Kabriza could wait. This was his time, and this kingdom would be his to rule.

61

Seung awoke with a start, covered in a cold sweat. She'd felt it, but what was *it*? Something was wrong. She wished Yurin Kei Daunyana and Tinnoviel were here. Though she had no doubts about Kenyatta and Kita, and the dwarf seemed capable enough, she would have felt better if the other elves were here.

She quickly dressed, tied her hair into a ponytail, and went for the door. She peeked her head out into the hallway, but no one was about. Of course not. It was still in the small hours of morning, evidenced by the loud snoring of Merk Iamfeld in the room down the hall.

Seung chuckled to herself and wondered how any living thing could breathe so loudly. She rapped on the door and waited. After a few moments the door creaked open and a shirtless Kenyatta appeared. He slipped out and closed the door behind him.

Seung's eyes flicked up and down and a smile crept across her lips. Kenyatta frowned with a crinkled smile. "You wake me up just to stare?"

"If there was time, I'd like to do more than stare, love. There's something wrong."

"Yeah, man. It's all coming from the nasal passages of a certain Merk Iamfeld. I don't know how such a huge sound can come out of such a small thing."

"I'm serious," Seung said, all thoughts of flirting gone. "I had a dream that darkness was closing in on us, and when I woke, the feeling was still there. I still feel it now."

"Dreams can do that," Kenyatta said skeptically.

"No." Seung shook her head. "This is different. I can feel it, somehow; like a little bit of evil just slipped into the world, and it's close. That's the best I can explain."

A tiny line of concern creased Kenyatta's brow. "How close?"

"I don't know, but probably right here in New Dainland. Just get Merk to alert his people outside the city and get to the king's rooms as fast as you can. I'm going to rouse the captain."

"I hope you're right about this," Kenyatta said.

"If I'm not, the only harm done is to my pride." She turned away just as Kenyatta disappeared back inside the room.

Returning to her own room, Seung grabbed *Vyirayoi* and secured it to her back, then left again. She quickly passed through the tavern hall, ignoring the curious looks directed at her. Once outside, she hopped down the steps and hit the ground running.

As soon as she reached the captain's home, four guards moved to intercept her.

"Hold! What's your business?"

"I must speak with Captain Davros. This is urgent."

Seeing that she was one of the visitors the king had spoken with, the commanding officer sent a subordinate off to the captain's quarters. "What is this about?"

"Your king is in danger. We don't have the time to discuss this."

The guard gave her a suspicious look. "And yet you come running away from the king's palace with a weapon strapped to your back."

Seung looked over the guard's shoulder. It had been several minutes since that runner had left, and the captain's home wasn't far. "Something's wrong."

"I have the same feeling," the guard said, taking a step forward. "Remove your arms and—"

Seung lunged forward. When he brought his sword to bear, she slapped it aside and spun to the outside of his reach, slapping him in the back with an open palm that sent him stumbling forward and gave her a push as she sprinted toward Davros's quarters.

As she neared the house, she saw several bodies strewn on the grass, twisted and broken, stabbed and cut. The young guard that had been dispatched hadn't made it far past the gate before he'd been quietly cut down.

She continued past the grisly scene, feeling the Gene of the Daunyans suddenly burning hot within her. So, this was what it felt like. When she reached the gate, she leaped into a forward flip and tucked her body in tight.

She brought Vyirayoi to bear and snapped the halved weapon's shaft together.

The hidden attacker hadn't anticipated the maneuver and lunged out right under her. Seung landed beside him, *Vyirayoi* whirling. She deflected attacks that came from behind while blocking attacks that came from in front. She ducked and spun low, taking the legs from under one attacker, then swinging her double-bladed weapon high, beheading two more.

Her attackers were shrouded in the shadows of the pre-dawn darkness, but she knew them for what they were. She could feel the wrongness, as though the space around them was tainted. Was she too late and the captain was already dead? A sudden roar from inside the house renewed her hope.

A body crashed out of a window to lie still on the ground. The door flew open, snapping off the hinges to skip across the ground. The captain leapt from the doorway, crashing into the assassins who'd surrounded Seung, blasting three away with his initial attack, and cleaving another nearly in two with his broadsword.

His energy was contagious, and Seung whirled her weapon over her head, pressing her enemies back. By then, the rest of the guard had arrived only to stare at the spectacle of the two warriors cutting down their enemies. As abruptly as it had started, the fight was over. The two scraped and bruised warriors stood in the middle of the corpse-littered lawn.

Mouths agape, the guards stared as some of the corpses began to evaporate while others melted into the grass.

To her disgust, Seung saw that the grass where the bodies melted turned as black as the blood soaking into it. *The bodies are tainted. They're poisoning the earth.* She looked around until she saw the blazing wall sconces that lit the front gate.

"Captain, we must hurry! Your king is in danger!" To the guards she said, "take those torches and burn the bodies, they're poisoning the ground they died on."

"What?" the commanding guard said. She recognized him as the one who'd challenged her earlier. "Set fire to the bodies? Here?"

"Do as she says," Davros bellowed. "And see to it that my house doesn't burn down!"

"Yes, Captain!" the guards saluted.

Seung was already out the gate and headed back toward the palace with Davros right behind her. "What in all the hells is going on? I don't know why, but I woke from my sleep and barely avoided being skewered in my own bed!"

"I don't know either. I had a dream that I know was a warning. We knew there would be an attack, but this—"

"Is unexpected, yes."

The guards, seeing their captain running beside Seung, stepped aside and opened the gates.

"Alert the city guard," Davros called to them. "The king is under attack!"

They crossed the courtyard and bounded up the stairs. As they passed through the halls, the bodies of servants and guards lay slumped in the corners and against the walls. The closer they came to Elizander's chambers, the more numerous the bodies became. They rounded a corner and nearly trampled a fleeing Brother Tardein. His normally shrewd and disdainful expression was replaced with carefully concealed terror. Seung was impressed by the man's control given the circumstances.

"What happens, monk?" Davros demanded.

"Given the circumstances, I will allow your tone to pass."

"And if my king dies because of your nonsense, *you* will pass, through the gates of this city if you're lucky, from this world if not."

Seung placed a hand on the big captain's arm. "There is evil everywhere tonight, good monk. Please, what news have you?"

Tardein turned his perpetual sour look on her. "There is indeed evil about. Shadows are moving through the palace, slaughtering people with arms made of steel blades. Some who have died rise again and turn against the living. I doubt Holy Jemanah Himself has ever seen such terrors. It was only because I was in the kitchens having my nightly mug of tea that I went unnoticed in the attack."

"Where are they going?"

"I think you've already figured that part out, child," the monk said to her. "The last I saw was your friends were cutting a path through those horrors to get to King Elizander's private rooms."

At that moment, Merk Iamfeld came trotting up. "Paigra's preparin' to bring 'em all. Should be here soon."

The monk stared in disbelief at the dwarf. Merk, having done away with his human guise, stood resplendent in his sleeveless spellcaster's robes.

"By Holy Jemanah, what craziness has this night brought."

"Get to your abbey and warn as many as you can, monk," Davros said. He continued down the hall.

"One other thing, captain," Tardein called after them.

"What is it?" Davros replied.

"It pains me to say this, but at the center of the attack was Holy Arbitrator Dinman."

"Dinman?" Davros echoed in disbelief.

"And he was wielding some sort of power. I've never seen anything like this before. Whatever evil has set upon Winsor, Brother Dinman is at the center of it." With a sad expression that was uncustomary to the stern monk, he left.

"I would never have made Dinman out for this kind of thing," Davros said as they ran from one open hall to the next. "Ambitious and unlikable he may be, but I never would have placed him for this sort of action."

"I think yer monk is probably wrapped up in some kind of demon influence," Merk said as he huffed along beside them. "With the barrier weakening between this dimension and the others, it's easier for them to come causin' all sorts of trouble. Problem is, ye human folk're so danged susceptible."

They rounded a final corner and came to a wide-open hall. It swarmed with creatures like Tardein had described, as well as more of the walking corpses of palace attendants and guards as well.

"There must be at least thirty of the things!" Davros said. The doors to King Elizander Dain's rooms had been torn open, and the sound of fighting erupted from within.

Kenyatta and Kita darted past the doorway in a whirlwind of swords and staff as they felled enemy after enemy. Farther back in chamber, Elizander stood surrounded by his personal guard. They had formed a square around the King and battled fearlessly against the inhuman assailants. Sword in hand, Elizander stepped between two soldiers and took up the fight.

"Without the proper enchantments they can't kill those things," Seung said. "The best they can do is knock them down long enough for one of us to deal the mortal blow."

"That will have to be enough," Davros said. He swept his broadsword around and cleaved through sinew and bone as he cut down one former comrade after another. He gritted his teeth through the revulsion and heartache he felt with each stroke, for many of the twisted faces belonged to men who'd served under him. With every stroke that felled an enemy, either Seung was there to deal a final blow, or Merk set them aflame.

Seung wove her way through the mass of demons and former humans as though in a deadly dance. With every movement of her body, *Vyirayoi* was there to compliment her actions. A demon that looked to be no more than a shadow with swords for arms came for her, swinging one of its sword-arms in an arc for her head.

She leaned back and the tip of the sword passed in front of her face. At the same time she swept *Vyirayoi* in a horizontal arc and cut the demon in half at the waist. Seung turned while bent at the waist spinning her weapon over her back. Three more shadowy demons fell in pieces and began to evaporate.

Vyirayoi still spinning, Seung turned with the weapon's momentum placing one foot over the other. She spun the weapon high, then low, then high again. Most of her enemies died at once, but a few managed a weak parry. Those were either cut down by the nearby captain, or blasted away by the dwarven spellcaster.

Somewhere outside the palace, they heard an alarm sound. Seung could only hope the attack had not spread through the entire city. She managed a glance toward the doors and saw that Kenyatta and Kita had made their way to Elizander's side. Several of his personal guard had fallen, only to rise again in death.

The Gene burning hot within, her vision and senses more acute, Seung Yoon of Kyu Village, Kiluriel Sen'Mora of Yathienel, blasted away anything that came near, cut down any enemy she caught. With her heightened senses it felt as though her enemies were moving underwater. She could feel their movements, their intentions, their limitations. She was a Child of the Gene, born to destroy them.

Finally the trio reached the king and settled into a defensive formation around him.

"I am not a helpless babe!" Elizander said.

"Take care, my lord," Davros shouted over the noise of clashing steel. "Our weapons do nothing to stop them."

"So we've discovered, old friend. We've had to fight every human enemy twice, and these shadows are like nothing I've ever seen."

The right wall of the room exploded, and a hulking beast climbed over the rubble. Yellow flames danced atop its glowing red skin, and its yellow eyes dilated when spotted them.

"What in the name of Holy Jemanah?" one of the guards swore. They lifted their shields and began to back away. The demon spat a stream of molten saliva that burned the nearest guard into a liquid corpse.

"By the Gods! My lord, step back!" Davros moved in front of the king and held his broadsword before him.

"Both of you get back," Seung said, stepping in front of the captain. She and Kenyatta, Kita and Merk, spread out around the demon just as more shadow creatures stalked in from the hall.

"Seung!" Kita called. "You're closest to the door! Can you hold them?"

"Let's find out," she said, turning to face the coming fiends.

The fiery demon crouched and a set of wings thrust out of its back. They extended straight up and tore into the stone ceiling. A large piece of ceiling fell over two of Elizander's personal guards just as Merk Iamfeld launched a wave of blue energy into the demon. The fiend howled as steam rose from the sizzling wound.

It spat a molten stream at Merk, who deflected it with a wave of his hand. A nearby soldier shouted a war cry and impaled the flaming beast with his pike. The demon barely acknowledged the man. With a swat of its flaming claw it burned the unfortunate soldier to ashes.

The demon threw its head back and roared, and Seung thought the chamber would shake apart.

Kita ran in and thrust his rune-carved staff forward. Blue sparks exploded from the area of impact. For the first time the demon seemed affected. When it staggered away, Kita followed and pressed forward with a spinning blow to the side of its leg. As the demon's leg buckled, it swung its claw around to swat him away.

Kenyatta leaped over the ducking Kita and brought both swords down in a side-by-side overhead chop, severing the arm between wrist and elbow. The demon screeched and recoiled its maimed arm. Merk waved his blue-glowing hands in a circular pattern and swept them toward the monster in an underhand pitch. Another wave of blue energy swept over the demon.

The fiend had risen to its full height by then, and the blue wave hit it square in the chest. Its agonized wail was short lived as its chest froze, and the ice spread over its fiery body.

Kita leaped at frozen twelve-foot-tall beast. He turned in midair with his back to the monster and thrust his staff backward. The end of the staff struck into the frozen chest and the demon exploded into hundreds of shards of ice that bounced on the ground and began to evaporate.

"Dramatic," Kenyatta teased.

"You wish you could do it," Kita retorted as he whirled his staff and cracked a nearby shadow demon across the head.

"Yeah man," Kenyatta said. He leapt into the path of a shadow demon, stabbed it four times in the chest, then beheaded it. The fiend crumbled to the ground and broke apart into a black mist, returning to the abyss.

With a heavy sigh, Elizander sheathed his sword. "What a dark day this is."

"I wouldn't relax yet, King Elizander," Seung said.

"She speaks the truth," Davros agreed. "We encountered that tart monk, Tardein. He said that he saw Dinman at the center of all this."

"Dinman?" Elizander's eyes widened. "I wouldn't have expected this. Not even from him. Demons? Has he been behind this all along?"

"We don't know yet," Seung answered.

"He's not here," Davros said, "so my wager goes to the chapel for our answers."

"Then let's get there."

"That's the last place you need to be, my lord. You're the one he's after."

"I and Bishop Marquis are the two he is most likely after, and if these things found me here, they'll find me anywhere." A shadow passed over Elizander's scowling face. "Best to go and stand together."

"He's right," Kita said. "I'll feel better with him in our sight."

The ground shook. They crouched, everyone looking to each other and the ruined chamber.

"I don't want to know what did that," Elizander said.

The chamber rumbled again.

62

To their relief and surprise, they encountered no resistance on the way to the chapel. Bodies lay twisted and broken throughout the streets. No one had to speak their thoughts, as each of them wondered how long it would be before the corpses rose again. When they reached the abbey, they encountered a brown-clad monk, setting fire to a pile of bodies using nothing more than a motion with his hand.

"What news?" Elizander asked.

The Dasha monk turned to face them. "The man who was Brother Dinman battles Arief. Their struggle commences now." It was a woman's voice that came from within the dark cowl.

"And you aren't helping him?" Davros demanded.

"The twice dead must be burned, lest they contaminate the earth beneath them."

"Then we will go."

"The struggle between them is theirs alone. You cannot interfere."

"Spare me the honorable duel nonsense!" Davros spat. "We're not dealing with humans, here!"

They hurried down the corridor that was once aligned with intricately carved pillars as big around as a man's body. Various depictions were brought forth from the polished marble that now lay scattered and broken on the ground. A jet of fire streamed past an open doorway and the group sprinted toward it."

"STOP!" It was Merk who'd spoken. "There's a ward blocking the door. Ye canno' pass through it!"

"A *ward*?" Elizander turned his frown from the door to Merk and back. "Are you serious? This has passed far into the unbelievable! Demons and zombies, magic and wards. What remains of this fantastical nightmare? Fairies?"

Seung scowled at an unwelcome recollection of her first encounter with fairies. "You've no idea."

"I've never seen anything like this," Kita said from outside the door.

"Yeah man," Kenyatta agreed as he, too, watched in a mixture of awe and hesitation.

Against the far wall lay the motionless body of who they guessed to be Bishop Marquis. In the center of the room, two monks went at each other in a fury of fire and projectiles that promised death, or worse.

* * *

It was starting. Arief felt the signs; sensed the suffocating wrongness that crept through the air. The sickness and feeling of foulness that only a demon could produce. Arief stood on the roof of a building overlooking a large section of the city. He glanced in the distance and saw his protégé, Leianna, watching from another building.

It started with a scream, followed by another. Still as a statue, his eyes darted in every direction as he scanned the streets. Finally he spotted the disturbance. Unsurprisingly it was a kalistyi, or shadow demon, as some called them. They could appear anywhere a shadow was cast, and in the pre-dawn light, the city was full of them.

He ran across the roof and leaped to another, and another, making his way toward the stalking demons with no more than a whisper in the air to sound his passing. He looked to where Leianna had been standing and saw that she had already gone, no doubt finding another disturbance.

His targets were close. Once within range, he leapt from a low rooftop and landed on two kalistyi stalking side-by-side, taking each one down with a hand and foot to the back. As soon as he touched the demons, he sent waves of Daunyanic energy coursing through them.

In less than a few heartbeats the kalistyi were nothing more than a vapor that drifted into the air and disappeared into nothingness.

Screams erupted from all around as the sleeping city awoke to the assault of the abyss. Arief wondered why the attack came like this. It had been subtle, before; cunning. This outright attack would alert the whole city of their existence instead of pitting Winsor and Mairland against each other. Something had changed.

Like a whisper, Arief passed through the streets as stealthy as the demons he stalked. Every path he took, he saw dead citizens rising against the living. Now Arief understood. "A *seaph.*"

The Order of Dasha had been dealing with *seaphs* for ages, but despite his vast experience dispatching the things, Arief's sense of disgust at their nature never diminished.

Given his understanding of what it took to create a *seaph*, Arief's mind immediately settled upon Dinman. Elizander and his captain were good of heart, and the bishop was also a good man. None of them were likely to be tempted by the whisper of a demon in his ear. That left the ambitious Holy Arbitrator.

The king and bishop would need to be protected, but that left the issue of the people running in the streets to escape being cut down.

Arief dispatched a trio of kalistyi as he made his way toward the palace. He heard a foreign battle cry and to his relief, saw the band of dwarfs that had been camped outside the city, a spellcaster among them. They would be enough help to free Arief to reach the king.

Halfway to the palace, he changed his mind and turned toward the abbey. The king had three warriors carrying the Gene of the Daunyans inside them, and another dwarven spellcaster. Elizander would be well defended. The bishop, however, was vulnerable.

Arief cursed himself for not thinking of this sooner and sprinted through the streets toward the Church of Jemanah.

He reached the broken and burning abbey and was immediately assaulted by the stench of blood and charred bodies. Laughter echoed from within. Arief hurried toward the prayer auditorium to arrive just in time to see Brother Dinman dispatch the Bishop of Winsor.

With merely a swipe of Dinman's hand the poor bishop went spinning in the air to crash against the far wall.

Arief kept his eyes on the lavishly clad monk as he entered. Dinman looked him up and down with an amused expression. Arief circled the room, keeping Dinman in his line of sight until he reached the bishop. He crouched beside Marquis and felt his neck for a pulse. Dead.

His brown eyes narrowed as he silently studied the *seaph.* It was a newborn, he was certain. If Dinman had been a *seaph* before now, Arief would have sensed its presence. What he found disturbing was that it had become so powerful so quickly.

"You appear to be a monk, though I do not recognize your affiliation," the *seaph* that was Dinman said. It was the former monk's voice that spoke, but the underlying malevolence floated on his words like smoke in a breeze.

"I hope you have more at your disposal than your hands if you wish to battle me. Too long have I watched that fool and his child king guide this land to ruin. It is time for proper leadership to take its place. Through me this land will be remade in my vision." He tilted his head to regard Arief. "Nothing to say? Do you not understand my words?"

Arief remained silent. He had no words for this monk who had become a faithless creature of the abyss. He continued to study Dinman, or rather, the powerful aura wafting from him like a toxic cloud. This wasn't a weak fiend that inhabited the upper levels of the abyss. This was a creature from the third hell.

It was rare for a demon of this type to attempt a possession, as they emitted an aura so strong it would alert even the most oblivious potential host. Dinman must have been so obsessed with his goal that this demon had seen an opportunity.

"There's something more to you, monk." Dinman sniffed the air. "I can smell it. You have power, yes? You can join me. As my underling, we can attain great power throughout this land and rule as we see fit." The *seaph* spread his hands and offered the most wicked smile. "Who would stop us? All you need do is open yourself to the power that I can grant you."

In answer, Arief slowly pulled back his cowl. The smile on Dinman's face evaporated as he took in the tattooed head and glowing yellow eyes.

"A monk of Dasha!" the *seaph* hissed. He lifted his left hand and waved it toward the door. The air in front of the portal wavered and tiny red sparks danced in the air. The empty space of the open door was replaced with a red-tinged transparent barrier.

"My luck is good this day. Not only have I acquired a capable host, but here stands a single Dasha monk."

Arief started to gather the power of the Daunyans inside when a flash of green light sparked in front of Dinman and he disappeared. An instant later he reappeared in front of Arief and lashed out with clawed hands.

The sudden attack was a surprise, and Dinman almost caught him. Arief slapped the hand aside and backstepped. When Dinman lunged again, Arief snapped his right hand out and grabbed him by the wrist. With a twist, he forced Dinman to kneel, then snapped his knee up into the former monk's elbow. There was a loud crack, and Dinman's arm bent the wrong way.

The *seaph* grunted, and wrenched his arm away. He straightened and looked down at the disfigured limb, then lifted it and gave it a sideways jerk. The resounding pop filled the room.

Dinman tilted his head as if studying his hand and arm. He flexed his fingers, then smiled at Arief.

An instant later, he was on the move and standing in front of Arief again. He moved so quickly Arief barely registered the movement in time to react. He ducked and sidestepped punches, kicks, and raking claws.

To his surprise, Arief was forced on the defensive. Every monk of the Order of Dasha trained intensely in the martial arts beyond the level of even the most skilled brothers of the Church of Jemanah. Dinman's martial prowess exceeded anything he'd ever seen from the church.

Arief let go of these thoughts and let his training take over. While his body acted as if detached from his mind, Arief allowed the power of the Daunyans trickle into his body.

Every hand parry, every sidestep, every block and counter came to Arief as thoughtlessly as the next step, walking down the street. Despite Dinman's exceptional skill, to the Dasha monk, his movements seemed as though he was underwater.

Arief leaned aside to avoid a kick aimed at his face. He grabbed the ankle, stepped to the outside of his combatant's stance, and twisted. At the same time, he tucked the leg under his arm, held it sideways, and dropped to the ground.

There was a sickening crack, as though a tree had been felled. Arief spun away and stood. He circled Dinman as he struggled to stand on a leg broken at the knee.

"We've played enough." The *seaph* reached down and popped the joint back in place. Dinman grinned as a smoky black aura crept over his body.

Arief could see as well as feel power radiating from the former monk. *So it begins.*

Dinman leapt the fifteen-foot distance between them, arcing high into the air. Arief stood his ground and watched as the monk glided up, then down toward him. An instant before impact, the Dasha monk hopped aside in a sideways spin. He landed just as Dinman was pulling his fist out of the cracked marble floor.

He called upon the power of the Daunyans. A blue aura settled over his body and his yellow eyes glowed brighter.

"I see you, Dasha lap dog!" Insanity shown in Dinman's wide eyes.

Arief closed the distance between them, and feinted a right jab. When Dinman leaned out of reach, Arief drew his fist back, shifted his hips, and snapped a foot out sideways.

Dinman's head snapped back when Arief's foot connected with his chin. Already leaning backward, the *seaph* stumbled and Arief pressed forward. He threw a barrage of punches and stiff-handed chops that would have felled a horse. Stiffening his index and middle fingers, Arief thrust his hand toward Dinman's neck. A hair's breadth from his throat, Dinman snapped his hand up and caught Arief's wrist. Arief struggled to break free, but the grip was like an iron vise.

With a chilling grin, Dinman raised an open hand in front of Arief's face. "This will hurt before you die. A lot." His hand glowed, and a wave of black energy erupted from his palm.

Arief's reflexes saved him. At the instant the of the blast, he jerked his body aside, delivered a sideways kick to Dinman's ribcage, and twisted his wrist free.

Dinman to lurched sideways but he still dealt Arief a glancing blow with the demonic energy that sent him flying across the room. He hit the ground hard, but ignored the pain in his side and scrambled to his feet.

On pure instinct, Arief dove sideways. Once again he avoided death. Having leapt after him, Dinman was practically on top of him the moment Arief hit the ground.

Dinman shattered the stone floor, and Arief shielded his face against the shrapnel. He backpedaled away from the offensive flurry of the former monk. Where Arief would normally block a strike, the demon-augmented strength of Dinman forced him to avoid contact altogether.

"I'm impressed you've lasted this long," Dinman taunted.

Arief ducked a kick to his face and came up with an uppercut. Dinman retracted his foot and caught Arief's fist, then balled up his own fist and punched the Dasha monk in the ribs. The force of the punch launched Arief away, and he hit the floor and slid into the wall.

Arief got to his feet a bit slower this time. He was certain his ribs were cracked at best. If the power of the Daunyans hadn't been flowing through him, he would be dead.

Dinman sauntered across the prayer hall, an evil smirk painted on his features. Along the walls and at the altar, candles burned, making the images of the two men dance on the walls.

"I think this calls for something a little more appropriate, don't you think?" Dinman waved a hand and all of the candles went out. He then waved his left hand, and the candles re-lit, but instead of yellow flames, they were red.

Without another word, the *seaph* hurled a smoky black wave at the Dasha monk. Arief whipped his arm in an outward arc, throwing the evil fog aside. He gritted his teeth through the pain in his side and pushed away from the wall.

"Still some fight left, eh?" Dinman narrowed his eyes. "Let us finish this." The black aura around his body intensified. The blue aura around Arief did the same.

* * *

"My mind refuses to believe what my eyes show me," Davros said. "How could any of this be possible? They fight tirelessly and defy natural law."

All they could do was watch in amazed helplessness behind the transparent barrier as the two monks clashed.

"You know less of the laws of nature than you think, good captain," Seung responded. "I mean you no insult," she said when he frowned. "I just mean that there is so much more to this world than humanity realizes."

"I think that's changed, this night," Elizander Dain said, flinching away as a bright blast of energy shot past the doorway. "Is there nothing we can do to help?"

Davros snorted. "You would step in the middle of those two?" I think this barrier is protecting us more than them. And, even if we could get in there, I've no intention of letting *you* get near them, my lord."

"The lad's right," Merk Iamfeld said. "Ye'd only get blasted to cinders."

"Lad?" the captain said. "I haven't been a lad in over thirty years."

"Ye've lived less than a century, yer not much more'n a boy, pardon me fer sayin'."

Davros shook his head.

Elizander signaled for one of his surviving personal guard. "I need you to find First Attendant, Milpheus, and tell him that the struggle is here. He'll know what to do."

"My lord, I'm to protect—"

"Go, son," Davros said. "I'm capable of looking after our king."

"Yes, sir!" He saluted Davros, then executed a precise bow to Elizander. "Yes, my lord!"

"What are you thinking?" Davros asked as he watched the young soldier depart.

"The worst," Elizander said. He looked again to the embattled monks, flying across the room and hurling power at each other like nothing he'd ever seen. "And I pray for our great city."

63

B rit watched from his balcony as wave after wave of demons flooded through oval-shaped tears in space. He would have preferred to have Kabriza rip one large portal open, but it would have created too much instability in the space between this world and the world they skimmed across in order to reach the tower of balance.

Takashaniel. He smirked at the thought of the doomed tower. Whether it was in waves, or all at once, his force of quentranzi would finally tear down the troublesome structure. Once Takashaniel was destroyed, he would be free to feed on the energy of this world unchecked.

Brit smiled at the possibilities. The world was a practically limitless supply of energy to be fed on so long as he allowed it just enough time to replenish. In but a century, perhaps even less, he would be powerful enough to challenge the Daunyans, let alone any demon squatting in the abysmal realms.

When he thought about the meager force Iel had scrounged together against him, Brit almost laughed. A small handful of God-touched humans, Iel himself, his fragile student, and a clan of centaurs. Brit grinned. This shouldn't take long at all.

An overbearing sense of wrongness and poisonous energy filled the atmosphere, giving away the presence of a powerful demon.

"What is it, Kabriza?"

"What is what, my lord drek? What is the day, the hour, the year? What is our goal for the day? What is the state of affairs in the fifth hell? If you wish—"

"You know my meaning, animal." Brit shrugged off the sarcasm and didn't bother to look at the demon. Kabriza was annoying, but he knew better than to let the fiend know it strained his patience.

"Even a demon is possessed of some humor," Kabriza teased in his slow-speaking, rumbling voice. "But if lord sour mouth must know, we will reach Takashaniel in a few hours."

"Why so long? Are they not skimming in and out of this dimension to speed their travel?"

"There is something blocking us from skimming directly to the tower," Kabriza replied. "The first hundred of my force that stepped through my rift dissolved once they entered the vortex that went directly to our destination. A detour has become necessary for our little expedition. Through the realm of Neirvan."

Interesting. "What is the difference, since you're skimming in the first place?"

The demon responded with an animal-like snort. "You have no knowledge of the between realm."

"I appreciate that you are about to educate me."

"I'm sure you can find a book."

Brit ground his teeth. After what he was sure Kabriza found to be an amusing moment, the demon spoke again.

"Suffice it to say that any number of forces you send marching directly through that place are forces you deem unneeded."

"Why is this?"

"Perhaps after you have conquered this dimension, you might pay the guardian of Neirvan a visit. I'm sure you two would have an interesting time."

And then, the demon was gone. It was just as well. Conversations with Kabriza grew increasingly frustrating as time passed.

Still, he wondered about this realm called Neirvan, and who the guardian of it was. Perhaps after he had dealt with Iel and his precious tower, Brit might indeed pay the place a visit.

A thought for another time.

* * *

"W e're betraying our master."

Zshegaza rolled her eyes. "Don't be a fool. If we had returned to him defeated, what would he have done to us?"

Zreal watched the massive procession of demons filing into Kabriza's spatial tear. There had to be twice as many of the fiends than the first battle. Though it galled him to admit it, Zshegaza was right. In fact, she was quite often right, and reminded him of it just as often. "He would probably have ripped us apart for our failure."

"And yet you would have us rush back into his "loving" embrace."

"Do you truly believe he thinks us dead?" Zreal asked.

He already knew the answer to that, of course. Brit would not have believed he and Zshegaza had been dispatched so easily. The irony was that Zreal would have been killed, had Zshegaza not been there.

Not that he had any illusions about her, however. Zshegaza's loyalty was first and always to Zshegaza. All else was a convenience. "When he finishes with the Ilanyan and his tower, his thoughts may turn to us."

"Why would he think of us?" Zshegaza asked. "He'll have an entire world to play with. What value do we have against that?"

"Brit never forgets. He hasn't bothered with us because he's been busy with this." Zreal waved a long-fingered claw at the mass of twisted creatures below. "When he's finished this business, he may well come looking for us."

"My dear Zreal." Zshegaza patted him on the cheek. "You worry too much. Your prowess nearly rivals my own, yet you think as though you sit low on the food chain here."

Zreal almost laughed. Zshegaza thought much of herself. Dangerous though she was, he could bend her mind till it snapped before a confrontation ever came to blows. As for physical strength, she was certainly a threat. He let it go. "I'm concerned about a potential foe that could deliver a torturous death on us."

"I don't discount the danger," Zshegaza agreed," but it presumes his victory over the Ilanyan."

"How could he not succeed?" Zreal looked at her, then back at the horde. "This force is far larger than the first. I've no doubt he will become person-ally involved should things go ill. And let's not forget Kabriza."

Zshegaza waved a similarly clawed hand. "An impressive force, and the demon general is formidable, but Iel is not without his own hand to play. He is formidable. I don't doubt those five humans will fight beside him as well as the centaurs. If things become more personal between them, I'm sure Iel would bring the whole of Takashaniel's power to bear before he'll let it fall. And we haven't mentioned that our poor former master has absolutely no knowledge of this world's ... other inhabitants."

The Four.

"That has been his mistake from the beginning," Zreal replied. "His seclusion in his fortress blinds him."

Zshegaza nodded. "He is wholly ignorant of potentially powerful enemies." She grinned, revealing her sharp teeth. "Imagine the possibilities for us, should he fail! The world would be our playground, Zreal."

He snorted at that. "The moment I become boring to you, you would dispatch me and seek adventure alone."

Zshegaza placed her hand over her chest. "You wound me!"

"You wound my intelligence."

"You are the only other like me in this world, cousin. Even your insufferable caution is better than being alone."

Though he wouldn't admit it, Zreal grudgingly agreed. He and Zshegaza were not cousins by blood, but their two species were related. Often she wondered if Brit put the two of them together intending that each of their respective traits would balance each other. "You make both my hearts skip a beat."

She laughed. "Come. It's a long way to Takashaniel even by flight. I wouldn't miss this for anything. And if the battle tips in an unfavorable direction, perhaps a subtle push from a hidden player or two might move things to a more desirable outcome."

Zreal looked at her. "We do something like that, we better be sure the battle goes our way. If he were to—"

Zshegaza waved him off. "Yes, yes. If he finds out we're involved, he'll tear us apart, slowly. I've not lived this long by not knowing the odds. For now, we watch. If need be, we act."

Zreal shrugged and pointed southwest, toward Takashaniel. "Then let us witness the final conflict."

The three humans craned their necks to gaze up at the onyx skinned creatures towering over them. Shinobu stood a fraction taller than Kenjiro, a bit nearer to six feet than five. Still, his head did not reach the shoulder of the shortest of these people Iel introduced as amahle.

"So many hidden wonders," the strider said. "I never seen anything in human lore that describes you."

The one named Naiyala—the leader of the band of warriors and princess of their tribe—smiled. "Our peoples intermingled long ago, but the memory of humans can last little more than a few generations. Times changed, and we thought it best to withdraw and take knowledge of our existence with us."

Kenjiro frowned. "You would be wise to remain hidden from our kind longer, I think."

"Our friend here holds a more cynical outlook," Shinobu remarked.

"You feel differently?" the one named Ayanda asked.

Shinobu had to lean back to look up at the hunter who stood to nearly eight feet! How tall did these people grow? "Not necessarily. I think some of our peoples will be more accepting than others."

"I see no reason to take such unnecessary risks," Ayanda replied. "I'll not risk my survival trying to socialize with *abantu*."

"We should speak with Iel," Amata Daunyana said.

"Is something wrong?" Akemi asked.

"Very. But the wrongness is why we are here." Amata made straight for the tower.

"Purposeful, isn't she?" Shinobu remarked as they followed behind the Daunya Apprentice.

"That one has a power about her," Kenjiro said. "A good ally."

Akemi nodded. "As you say; a good ally." She scanned the surrounding fields and hills as they followed the amahle back to the tower. The one named Sakhile was out there somewhere, scouting the surrounding lands. It seemed risky to her for the scout to be out there alone, should the drek's demonic army appear.

The scout had smiled at her offer to join him, stating that he could blend with the surroundings better than she could. With their pitch-black skin Akemi couldn't imagine how that was possible, but she'd let it go.

The grounds were eerily silent and still, as though the entire world held its breath.

Finally, they reached Takashaniel and found Iel and Mira seated on floor cushions conversing with an old man whose name neither Akemi nor her brother or Shinobu found ease to pronounce. Also present were the four elves they had met earlier.

The three warriors had seen much in their lives, and Akemi had encountered more demons than she could count. Still, it was more than a small shock when they were introduced to people out of human myth. She didn't know which was more of a shock, the existence of elves, or these tall people whom human lore never spoke of.

As they approached, the others rose to their feet. The elves nodded in greeting, while the amahle inclined their heads and the three humans bowed respectfully. "How is Taliah?" Akemi asked Mira.

The other woman smiled. "She will be fine. It was mostly rest that she needed, though some healing was provided to her on a non-physical level. She's skimmed across the abysmal levels too frequently these past weeks. The confrontation with the dokara compounded the burden on her."

Akemi's mind shuddered at the thought of the dokara, or dark dragon. When they'd come crashing through the vortex right at the steps of the tower, Iel and Mira had hurried to attend to them. Once they were able to explain their narrow escape from the thing, Iel looked as though he were seeing the beast before his eyes, so horrified was he.

"There are only two dokara that I know exist in the Abyss," the Ilanyan had said, "and they both reside in the fifth hell. Why was one on the first?"

"I don't know," Kenjiro had blurted as they rose shakily to their feet, "but I don't ever want to see anything like it again." Akemi agreed wholeheartedly. That thing had been worse than any demon she'd ever fought.

Mira had said that not even a Daunya Chosen could kill a dokara, and that their survival was a miracle. No one disagreed.

Akemi blinked herself back to the present, noting that the three monks of Shaolin were not present. "They're training outside," Mira said when she asked.

"I'm not sure allowing them to come was a good idea," Akemi confided.

"It wasn't your decision to make, demon hunter," Mira replied. "They may not carry the Gene of the Daunyans, but they are capable warriors. There have always been demons finding a way into this dimension. Not everyone who battles them is a Child of the Gene."

"Oh?" the ninja took a seat on a cushion.

"You are not the only demon hunter, and certainly yours is not the only group who work to contain and expel the darkness when it pierces the veil."

Iel took on a distant look, as though he peered into a distant place none but him could see. "Our enemy is near."

"How do you know?" Shinobu asked.

"Unlike when the Chosen skims dimensions, demons rip a hole in the space around them and step through it. This violent action causes something akin to an irritant in the space of this dimension, and I can feel it."

"Why aren't they here yet?"

Iel frowned in thought. "The guardian of Neirvan must have something to say about a large force of demons passing through his realm."

Shinobu's frowned as he tried out the word. "What's a Neirvan?"

"It's the dimension that exists between this world and the demon realm, or hells, as you call them. I will explain more later, but there's not much time left. I fear the force that Brit has summoned is much bigger than the first, and more than he can manage."

Amata Daunyana and Yurin Kei Daunyana stood in a still, vacant-eyed stare similar to Iel's.

"The guardian of Neirvan has only just realized the demonic presence," Amata said.

"Can he do something to stop them?" Tinnoviel asked.

"He fights them even now, and has destroyed many," Yurin answered. "But he cannot stop them all. The *norghar* are not at his disposal and he cannot destroy them all alone."

Shinobu laughed. "What is all this? What is a *norghar*?"

"Think of a monster that is neither good nor evil," Malimokuru answered. A being that lives in a place that is both heaven and hell, yet is neither."

"Riddle time?" Shinobu replied.

"There isn't a good answer for what they are," the nature reader said. "They aren't evil, they aren't good. But they are very powerful and *very* dangerous."

"Maybe we should pay them a visit," the strider said. "If Taliah is strong enough, perhaps we could go to this Neirvan and enlist some of these *norghar* to help us."

"They can't simply enter this world. They must be summoned," Malimokuru replied. "And if you're not strong enough to—"

"The guardian of Neirvan has been pushed back," the two Daunya Apprentices said in unison. The demons are here.

* * *

A hole the size of a building ripped across the air and out of it clambered bodies twisted and hulking, sinuous and grotesque, short and elongated. Some, Akemi recognized as the same species she had banished or destroyed. Others she had never seen before.

On her lower back, *Onihakaisha* and *Onisekairu* quickened. She absently gripped their hilts as she watched the demons descend, tearing across the land toward them. From the corner of her eye she saw Kenjiro eyeing the swords.

"Do you think you can control them both in the midst of that?" He gestured at the steadily increasing number of fiends falling through portals.

Akemi nodded. "I will fight and they will feed. We have an understanding."

Kenjiro's brow creased with concern, but he nodded.

"By the Daunyans," Tinnoviel said. "Has the abyss been emptied to stand against us."

A glowing white slit appeared near Takashaniel, and out of it stepped a glowing creature like nothing Akemi had ever seen. Snaking tendrils writhed atop its elongated head, and it's tall, slender body radiated power that she could feel even from this distance. It hovered just above the ground, a white glowing weapon resembling a spear held in each hand.

Brilliant, glowing slits appeared across the field as the magical protectors of Takashaniel materialized before the demonic force.

An icy mist settled over the group, and a heartbeat later, the magical entity Siti, materialized before them. "Iel, Guardian of Takashaniel. We come to fight with you once again."

Iel bowed. "It is my honor to have you stand with us against this terrible evil once more."

"I have never witnessed anything like this." Tinnoviel Nai SaunyaLi moved to stand beside the samurai. "I'll not deny my hesitance in the presence of humans, but today, at this moment, we stand as brothers."

Kenjiro bowed in response.

"TinTin?" Tikena looked up at the Daunya Warrior, uncertainty in her voice.

Tinnoviel rested a hand on her shoulder. "Remember all you have learned. Remember why you fight. Remember Nuviel."

The young elf looked back to the advancing wave of demons and spun her hand-spears through her fingers. "Nuviel. This is for her."

"For our people," Immendiel added.

Kenjiro slid *Kenzo* from its sheath. "For our homes. For this world."

Akemi felt the Gene quickening inside her, like spark igniting into a fire that burned through her body. The colors of their surroundings became more vibrant and sharp, her body felt lighter, stronger.

The poisonous presence and wrongness of the advancing demons was a knife that pierced the core of Akemi's senses. Though she faced darkness and death, she'd never felt more alive. She looked to Kenjiro. Her brother emitted the same aura of power as herself. On her other side, Shinobu also radiated the power of the Daunyans. He slid his sword from its sheath, and the foreign etchings on the naked blade pulsated.

"Use your minds," Naiyala said. "Blend with the earth and take the rage when needed. It is time to wash the spears!" The amahle warriors thrust their weapons in the air and howled.

Akemi almost backed away from their tall allies. Kenjiro and Shinobu looked equally wary, as the hue of the amahles' skin began to shift. Naiyala and Amata blended with the ground, becoming nearly invisible, while Ayanda and Sakhile grew dark as midnight. The sight of their bared, elongated teeth contrasted with their onyx-colored skin sent a chill down Akemi's spine.

"They scare me more than the demons," Shinobu whispered.

Luckily such fearsome people fight beside us. Akemi drew *Onisekairu* and *Onihakaisha* from their sheaths. Hunger and anticipation emanated from the swords. *Patience.* She scolded.

The abysmal horde must have crossed a point of significance, for the waiting Rizanti exploded into action. So fast were the slender magical beings that they closed the great distance across the hilly battlefield in but a few heartbeats.

"Is that wise?" Malimokuru asked as the thirty magical fighters cut a vicious path through the center of the horde.

"It is their way," Siti replied in her echoing glacial voice. More magical creatures rose from the ground or materialized from the air and flew into the twisted army.

"Now is your time, friend Malimokuru," Amata Daunyana declared, stepping up to the nature reader. She became visible once again, but her hue wavered between all the colors of the spectrum. Malimokuru gave her a questioning look. Though it was Amata who spoke the words, it sounded as though they came from someone else.

"Upon this world you exist and learn, and the darkness will once again be banished by you, its creators. Through love and light We touch you with our power. Spirit, Creation, Love, The Mystical, Destruction, Redemption, and Balance.

Amata Daunyana placed her hand on Malimokuru's forehead. He gasped and his body trembled as waves of power flooded through him. If the amahle woman had not been holding his head, he would have fallen. His mouth fell open as his body convulsed.

The sands in his pouches streamed out and swirled around him. Then, to his fright, the sands swept into his mouth. He felt them flowing through him, yet there was no pain. He felt the sand clinging to his insides, assimilating into his body. Each of the characteristics of the different sands merged within him.

When Amata finally released him they both staggered away from each other. Amata caught herself and blinked in confusion at Malimokuru, who stumbled into Immendiel's arms.

Malimokuru looked down at his hands. He felt stronger, more alive. His body felt far younger than it had just moments before, and he could feel the forces of nature inside himself.

He took several deep breaths to calm himself and contain the overwhelming forces swirling inside him. Instinctively he knew that he no longer needed the sands as a tool. The sands were a part of him, now. When he looked at the others, every face showed the same reaction; shock.

"You are changed, friend Malimokuru," Naiyala breathed.

"Carza lives inside you now," Amata Daunyana declared, her voice filled with wonder.

Malimokuru looked around at the shocked expressions directed at him. "What is it?"

Akemi placed a hand on his shoulder. "We have no time to discuss this, but have a look." She held her shining swords together in front of his face, and to his shock, he barely recognized the face staring back at him.

Malimokuru touched the side of his face. His formerly dark brown skin was now a mix of brown and red, and his eyes had turned as gray as the clouds that darkened the sky. He looked down at his hands. They tingled with power! He closed his eyes and felt the power flow through him.

A distant shriek drew their attention to where three Rizanti were cutting down a demon the size of a mammoth. The four-legged misshapen creature went down in a tangle of legs, fur, and rising and falling oval blades.

"They will slow as the magic runs its course. It's time." Another rip tore into the air and another wave of demons came flooding out.

Shinobu shook his head. "So many."

"More come to our aid," Iel said.

As if they'd heard the Ilanyan's a words, a roar filled the air. They looked to the east where a clan of centaurs raced toward the demonic horde, weapons raised high. Most notable was the centaur at the front—easily twice the size of the others—holding a hammer with a shaft longer than the average height of a man. The clan crashed into the new wave of demons, and the sounds of fighting and the screams of the dying rent the air.

Without a word, Akemi took off toward the conflict.

"Abrupt," Shinobu remarked, then he ran after her, the rest of the warriors in tow.

* * *

A kemi, Kenjiro, and Shinobu quickly closed the distance between themselves and the demon mass. Despite their Daunya enhanced abilities, however, the amahle overtook them and leapt high into the air. The tall folk arced across the distance and crashed into the fiendish army from above.

Moments later, the three human warriors joined the battle. As Iel had said, the Rizanti were beginning to slow, yet they fought admirably, defeating two to three demons each. Akemi realized that if she and the others had joined the fight earlier, they would have been more hinderance than help.

A spiky-skinned rotund creature swung an arm riddled with jagged spikes at her head. She ducked and slashed its leading leg in the same motion. The fiend let out an agonized screech as *Onihakaisha* cut it across its torso. Akemi followed through, turning as she brought *Onisekairu* around in a horizontal arc. Black ichor spilled to the ground as the disemboweled monster melted away.

Before the fiend had fully dissolved back to the abyss, Akemi had leapt over it. She drove her hungry swords into the back of a winged green demon that was creeping behind an embattled centaur.

The demon's mouth fell agape in a silent scream as the swords fed on it. The centaur finally noticed the dying monster and kicked it in the midsection. The winged demon flew backward, and Akemi rode it till as it fell near another fiend that battled the unfriendly little elf. At the last moment, she leapt from her dissolving foe and glided toward the new enemy. *Onisekairu* drank the black mist that was the demon's soul even as Akemi beheaded Tikena's foe from behind.

She continued her turn and stabbed *Onihakaisha* into the headless body. Akemi had to focus not to be overwhelmed by the wild glee of the sword as it blew the fiend apart. Tikena offered a grudging nod and a snarl, then darted away.

* * *

Kenjiro ducked the spiked tail of a green-scaled creature, then severed the arm of a yellow pincer as it tried to snap him in half. He slashed downward across his first enemy, cutting a diagonal line from left shoulder to right leg. He moved with the momentum and stepped forward in a turn. He swung the sword in an overhead chop across the demon's chest.

Whatever resistance the abysmal creature could offer only delayed its demise for a moment. The samurai walked away from his dissolving foe and towards his remaining opponent.

It whipped its tail toward his midsection. Kenjiro stepped toward the appendage and cut it in half. The beast's scream turned into a gurgle when Kenjiro plunged his sword into its side. He tore the sword free and turned his back on the falling demon. More enemies converged.

* * *

Tinnoviel Nai SaunyaLi threw himself at his enemies, his large, curved weapon imbued with Daunyanic power tearing into them. Some came away with gaping wounds while others were simply blasted away.

To his left, the three human monks were surrounded by a score of twisted creatures. He started to make his way to them but found he wasn't needed.

The monks of Shaolin cut down their enemies with a speed and grace worthy of an elf.

Despite the allies of Takashaniel's dominance of the battlefield, the enemies kept coming. Was there no limit to how many demons Brit could bring through? He knocked a tall and skinny demon with flat plate-like discs for hands off balance and ran up its chest.

He jumped straight up as it stumbled, and as he descended behind it, stuck it on top of the head with an overhead chop. The resounding crack pierced the din of battle, and the demon collapsed and immediately began to dissolve back to the abyss.

Tinnoviel had a brief moment to survey the field. Things seemed well in hand at the moment, as the organic and magical allies cut through the demon forces. A stab of anxiety pierced Tinnoviel's stomach, however. Where was Kiluriel?

65

A chunk of wall exploded just above Arief's head. If the Dasha monk had been a split second slower to react, his head would have shared the fate of the wall. This demon that inhabited brother Dinman's body was proving to be troublesome.

Dinman launched another ball of glowing red energy at Arief, who dove aside, then rolled to his feet in a full run. Explosions crashed at his heels as he sprinted across the room. In the blink of an eye, he stopped and dove backward into a roll. As he'd predicted, Dinman had continued to blast in the direction he'd been running, trying to pace the speed of the Dasha monk and catch him ahead.

Arief jumped out of the roll and brought his knees up to his chest as another blast hit the wall beneath him. Gliding backward, the monk channeled the power of Boraka and sent a wave of destructive power hurtling toward the *seaph*.

Dinman threw himself aside in time to avoid the blast, but when he lifted his head, it was just in time to see another wave slam him into the ground.

The dazed monk climbed out of the small crater created by the blast, and Arief was on him. The Dasha monk grabbed Dinman and dragged him out of the hole, but Dinman slammed his hands on Arief's chest and filled him with hot energy.

Arief tried to grab Dinman's wrists, but his movements were suddenly too slow. More heat funneled into him, and Arief thought he might explode. A guttural sound rumbled from Dinman's throat and he blasted Arief across the room.

The Dasha monk crashed into the far wall and lay motionless in the hole until finally tumbling out to hit the floor. Dinman was there in an instant, hoisting him to his feet and slamming him into the damaged wall again. Bits of stone crumbled from the impact and dropped onto Arief's head, though he barely felt it. He sagged, held up only by his unnaturally strong adversary.

Dinman lifted him again and smiled as he tossed Arief over his shoulder.

The dazed Arief had just enough of his wits about him to keep rolling when he hit the ground. He felt the ground shake behind him. He climbed to his feet and saw Dinman on one knee, pulling his fist out of the broken marble floor where Arief had landed.

"How long must we play this game, Dasha monk? We both know you can't kill me." Dinman flew at him again and drove his elbow into Arief's midsection.

The air blasted from Arief's lungs and he dropped to his knees, gasping. The *seaph* brought his knee up, and slammed it into his forehead. The force of the blow lifted Arief off the ground, and he landed flat on his back. Dinman grabbed him by the front of his tunic and lifted him again.

Arief gritted his teeth and drove his fist into Dinman's midsection with all his strength. The *seaph* staggered back and doubled over. Arief hammered his fist in the back of Dinman's head, then lifted the sprawled *seaph* up over his head and slammed him back to the ground. He lifted him again, then swung him in a circle and let go.

The *seaph* flew across the room and crashed into the wall. Part of it collapsed and fell on top of the former monk. Despite being buried under a ton of stone Dinman struggled out of the rubble and tried to stand. Arief battered the demon-inhabited monk with a barrage of punches and kicks that had his enemy's body jerking in every direction.

Dinman snarled and struggled to rise through the blows. Now, they stood toe to toe, battling with hands and feet, waves of Daunyanic and demonic energy lancing and arcing through the air. Their limbs were a blur of movement that the eye could not follow.

Dinman struck Arief in the chest with a solid palm. On his way down, Arief snapped his foot up and connected it underneath Dinman's chin. He hit the floor, and the *seaph* was tumbled backwards. The force of that kick would have ended the life of a normal person. The thing that rose slowly to its feet and gave its neck a little crack, was no longer a person.

* * *

"By Holy Jemanah, do my eyes deceive me?" Davros stared openmouthed at the titanic struggle.

"I've seen some crazy things," Kita said, "but I wouldn't want to be in that room."

Kenyatta whistled through his teeth. "Yeah man."

"I can't believe that's Dinman in there, and that he killed Bishop Marquis." Elizander Dain shook his head. "I can't believe he's fallen so far."

Merk Iamfeld scratched his broad nose. "Might be yer monk fell, but what's in there now ain't him."

Seung pointed at Dinman. "I think he's planning to cheat."

The former monk put some distance between himself and Arief. He raised a hand above his head, fingers curled, and the shadows of the room lurched to life and converged on the Dasha monk.

"Oh no ye don't," Merk said. "Get ready lads and lass. We're not fer lettin' him fight all that alone."

Kenyatta, Kita, and Seung readied their weapons. Davros did the same, but Kita stopped him. "Stay by your king. Your weapon can do nothing against them."

Merk raised his hands and closed his eyes, moving his lips silently. A few moments passed, then the transparent green barrier faded. Merk nodded, and the three warriors leaped into the fray.

* * *

Arief took some satisfaction in the *seaph's* frustration at the interference.

As he stalked toward Dinman, a shadow demon came at him. He never took his eyes off of his adversary as he waved his hand and obliterated the kalistyi.

Twice more he was attacked and he dispatched his attackers. The former confident look on the *seaph's* face was replaced with uncertainty.

"Your friends only delay your fate," Dinman spat, but the words rang hollow. "Have you nothing to say? Are all the monks of Dasha dumb and mute?"

Arief continued his silent advance.

Dinman's tongue flicked across his lips like a nervous snake. "SPEAK."

Once Arief was within range, Dinman threw a one-two punch and he caught both fists. Power radiated from their bodies as each struggled to gain the upper hand. Bits of rock and sections of the ceiling dislodged and fell to the ground as the structure crumbled around them.

Scattered bits of debris lifted off the ground and drifted into the air. Sparks of electricity sizzled around them, between them. Arief gritted his teeth. The building energy between them could no longer be contained.

The resulting explosion blasted them away from each other. Despite the ringing in his ears, Arief was back on his feet the instant he hit the ground.

"This ends now," Dinman hissed. His body glowed with a poisonous black aura that was nearly overwhelming even from Arief's distance. It would have choked the life out of any living thing near him.

Arief drew on the power of the Daunyans. What remained of the chapel gradually broke apart and floated in the air. The ground between them split apart as though sliced by a knife. "Come, demon."

* * *

Dinman hurled a wave of black energy at his enemy. The troublesome Dasha monk brought his blue glowing hands upward in an inside-outside arc, blasting the wave apart. Two pulsating discs of pure Daunyanic energy formed in his hands and he hurled them at the *seaph*. Dinman ducked under one, then leaped over the other.

"Pathetic," he taunted, then realized his mistake.

While he was distracted with the disks, Arief had jumped across the distance between them. They landed at the same time, face to face.

Arief snapped his left arm out and caught one disc, then his right hand caught the other. With as much force as he could gather, Arief swung his arms out, then forward.

The thunderclap of the energy exploding before the *seaph* was the worst white-hot burn the demon had ever felt. The searing white light tore into the fiend, and as its body was being burned away, the demon realized that it was not descending back to its home in the fourth hell. *"NO!"*

The cursed human wasn't sending it back to its abysmal home, but into nonexistence. Oblivion! It opened its mouth in a shriek of defiance, but then it was gone; burned away into the light of the Daunyans, where no evil can exist.

The instant the demon in him was gone, Dinman came to full awareness. All of the memories of his life came flooding back to him. He saw the mistakes, and the dark paths he'd chosen. He saw every action that left a doorway open for the vile creature to take hold of him.

Dinman knew true despair, for there was no denying that it was the darkness in his own heart that had allowed the demon to take him. If tears were possible, they would have flowed freely from the place where his eyes would be, in his vaporizing body. He knew he was bound for the endless torture and misery of hell. It was in that moment, that Dinman felt regret. Not because he had been defeated, or that he was bound for the abyss and his ultimate doom, but because he had failed Holy Jemanah as one of His faithful servants. He had allowed his desire for power to corrupt his heart and cast his soul into shadow.

I have failed you, my lord, my Creator. I am sorry. He heard a sound like that of a young girl giggling. *Have I so angered you, my Lord Holy Jemanah that you mock my descent to hell?*

More giggling. *"No, silly. You tried too hard and made mistakes. And please, stop calling me Jemanah."*

The spirit that was Dinman waited in confused silence until a gentle white light settled over him. A woman appeared several yards in front of him, her features hidden by the brightness of the light. Another figure appeared behind her, this one tall and imposing, yet Dinman felt no threat.

"You will be cleansed in Balance, wayward child." The voice was so deep it made Dinman's spirit vibrate.

"And you will then be Redeemed," the childlike voice added, and in that moment, Dinman knew the whole truth of himself. This time, he saw his entire life from birth to death flash through his mind's eye. Now, he knew the truth about God, the Gods, The Seven.

With a profound sense of relief yet regret at the tasks he had failed to accomplish, and his subsequent temptation by the demon, he looked back at the monk who had defeated him, being helped to his feet by others. He looked at the death and destruction he'd caused, then finally at the lifeless body of Bishop Marquis.

"Do not be sad, Brother."

It was Marquis's voice! A blurry figure came into focus and Dinman saw the spirit of the man he'd murdered. "You turned from the light, but have chosen to turn toward it once more. Even after this life of yours has ended, you can make amends. The Daunyans do not turn away those who turn to Them. Come home, Brother Dinman."

"How?" the spirit of Brother Dinman asked. "I murdered you and turned from the light of the Gods. I have fallen."

"What is your desire, Brother?" the spirit of Marquis asked.

"To right my wrongs. To do penance for what I have done, all I have wrought. I deserve not salvation, but damnation." Dinman's spirit withdrew within itself, diminishing, its light fading. "I am not worthy ..."

"You are a child of the Gods, of the Daunyans, Brother," Marquis interrupted. "You succumbed to the very real temptations we all face. You stand in the light of The Seven now, not in judgement, not in punishment, but in transition. You have been brought back to balance ..."

Dinman felt a Godly power envelope him, and his diminished presence brightened and grew, once again.

"... and you are Redeemed," Marquis continued.

Dinman was soaring. He felt his very being bathed in the light of redemption, awash in the power of the love of Nakia, The Redeemer.

Now Dinman understood, and now he could turn fully to the light, fully toward his salvation and his redemption. He looked to the spirit of Bishop Marquis and saw forgiveness and kindness. "We can help our people, even from beyond their world."

"I will make amends," Dinman said. "I will right my wrongs."

"Yes, Brother," Marquis replied.

Side by side, the two monks moved toward the indistinct figures that stood before them—one a small girl, one a towering presence—and ascended into the light.

* * *

Kenyatta, Kita, and Seung stood amid the rubble of the destroyed prayer hall. The fearful faces of what must have been hundreds of people kept their distance, gaping at the aftermath of the struggle they had witnessed.

After the battle had ended, some had begun to curse the Holy Arbitrator's name, calling him the devil's lapdog. Surprisingly it was Arief who had defended him.

"You have witnessed the unbelievable this day," the monk said with the last of his fading strength. "Know that I saw your Arbitrator's spirit after his death, and he has been forgiven. He was lured into temptation by a demon that took over his body.

"Undeniably it was the darkness in his own heart that allowed the demon entry, but such darkness lives in us all. He succumbed to his darkness and has seen the truth, as have you."

Arief's protégé draped his arm over his shoulders and helped him out of the destroyed building. The crowd parted before them, giving the two Dasha monks a wide berth.

"I'm tired after just watching that," Kita remarked.

"You'd better not be too tired, man," Kenyatta said. "Our part in this has barely begun."

"Will you not remain a while?" King Elizander Dain asked. "Your presence would be a great asset as I try to not only understand all this, but help the people understand as well."

"I'm sorry, we cannot," Seung replied. "We're needed elsewhere."

The king was about to argue further, but stopped and stared in astonishment as the air a few feet away rippled as would a body of water after a stone had been cast into it. Kenyatta sighed with relief when Taliah stepped forward. He lunged at his sister and wrapped her in a bone-crushing hug.

As soon as he released her, Kita came forward with a more passionate greeting that caused the onlookers to discretely look away.

"All right, man," Kenyatta said in a mock grudging tone.

"Will there be no end to the wonders we witness this night?" the king said.

"You haven't seen the least of it, King Elizander Dain," Seung told him.

"We don't have time to linger," Taliah said. "The battle has begun." She turned to the king and inclined her head. "My apologies for my abruptness, but things are in motion. Should we survive this, I will return."

She turned to the others, looking the group over with satisfaction. "I see I was able to send you to Dakra after all. And once again, I must do something desperate. Passing through the abyss has become too dangerous and so I must skim the heavens instead."

She looked at each of them directly. "You will feel compelled to remain, careless and free of this world and its toils and strife. It is not your time for this, so you must resist that urge and stay with me. Remain focused on me no matter the temptation. Our time to live among the Daunyans will come, but now isn't that time. Focus on me, on our journey home, our home on *this* world."

The air began to bubble around them once again, and the dwarves, humans, and the elf girl were gone.

For a long while no one spoke, but just stared at the spot where the group had been standing. Davros let out a breath. "I'm not ashamed to say that in the past few weeks I've seen enough to have nightmares left over for my grandchildren."

"And speaking of children," the ever-efficient Milpheus said, "tonight's events have convinced me more than ever that it is time to find you a bride, my lord."

Elizander sighed. "Let us speak of it on the morrow, Milpheus. I think we've been through too much tonight." He turned and let his gaze fall over the remains of several destroyed buildings and the lifeless bodies of those caught in the middle of the unbelievable struggle that had befallen his beloved city. "Far too much."

66

The instant they arrived in the heavenly dimension, they were set upon by temptation. Seeing the signs and knowing what to expect, Taliah moved to the center of the group and spread her energy to encompass them all. "Do not heed the temptations you're feeling. You are glimpsing a tiny fraction of our true Home, but it is not for us to return, yet. We must live out the entirety of our lives before our return."

"What difference does it make?" Seung heard herself ask. She thought she might drown in the flood of love and knowledge flowing through her. So much knowledge! Where the abysmal plane was bleak and hopeless, a place filled with hate and malevolence, the heaven realms were the opposite and so much more!

Seung knew that all would be okay. Every toil, every problem and every challenge that she had ever faced or would ever face was so small in comparison with the perfection that surrounded her. When she looked at the others, she saw the same realization. "None of it truly matters."

"Everything matters," Taliah replied, willing them to move forward. She saw flickers of temptation even in the eyes of the dwarves. They were more resistant, however, though whether it was through sheer stubbornness or discipline, she couldn't say.

"We made a commitment just by coming to this life, at this time, on this world. If we falter now and abandon our friends who fight for Takashaniel, even now, we fail not only them, but the world.

"The lass has a point," Merk said. "We're right here, yet ain't one of us heard the call of Boraka to his halls." The dwarves straightened their backs and lifted their chins.

Kenyatta, Kita, and Seung looked at each other, then at her. The nodded in agreement, but there was still hesitancy, there.

As quickly as possible, Taliah led them across rolling hills of grass and flowers, trees that grew so large, if they all held hands they wouldn't have been able to reach half around them.

Kita closed his eyes, enjoying a gentle breeze. "The weather is perfect; not too warm or cold." He closed his eyes and let the sun warm his face. "Even if we did remain here, our loved ones would come when their time on the earth plane is done. Their struggles would be gone the moment they get here."

Taliah watched Kita's face. She'd seen it before. He wanted to surrender to the infinite bliss. A tiny seed of doubt crept into her mind. Had she made a mistake.

"You know what I dislike more than the thought of leaving here, though?" Kita closed his eyes and frowned. "Giving up."

"Yeah man." A grim tone crept into Kenyatta's voice. "It may be all right when they arrive, but we're not lettin' our friends endure a lifetime of torment to get here."

"I know what must be done." Seung held her fist over her heart and wrapped her other hand around it. "But, even the Gene of the Daunyans burning inside me is nothing compared to this."

"Stay focused on me," Taliah said. "Focus."

Seung focused her mind on the Daunya Chosen and her resolve strengthened. "Your sister is right," she told Kenyatta. "We don't deserve to stay here right now any more than those demons and that drek deserve our world." She took a deep breath. "I'll not abandon my home to demons."

"Aye lass," Merk reached up and gave her a pat on the shoulder. "That's the spirit."

"The vortex." Taliah pointed ahead. Bright yet soft white and blue light swirled out of the ground and into an infinite blue sky.

Kenyatta frowned. "Why is nobody around? We haven't seen a single soul since we got here."

"They know the temptation we feel," Taliah answered. "One of the greatest desires a person feels is the reunion with those who've left us to go Home. Still, whether here or on the earth plane, if you think of them, they will know."

Kenyatta thought of their grandpa, lost to them since they were children. *Would have been nice to see him again,* he thought.

"Only if you can handle it," a familiar voice said into his mind. Kenyatta went rigid. He heard the voice not with his ears, but with his mind. *"Grandpa?"*

"Who else would I be, ya knucklehead bwoy?"

Kenyatta's mouth fell open. He excitedly tapped Taliah on the shoulder.

Taliah frowned and shrugged away from him, giving him an up and down look. "Yeah man, yeah man," she said, fending him off. "I hear him too."

Grandpa's amusement came through clearly, and then a figure materialized. It was a young man about their age who felt much older and looked familiar, but Kenyatta didn't immediately recognize him. *"So, ya make me be an old man, then,"* Grandpa's voice said. The young man changed into the salt and pepper-haired old man Kenyatta lost when he was a small boy.

"Keep doin' whatcha doin' bwoy. Dem Gods put you and your sister in the world for a reason, and we're proud of you."

We? Kenyatta thought. And then he felt it. A wave of love that came from not one, but three individuals. Kenyatta saw their grandfather smiling.

"Mama and Papa." Taliah sounded like the little girl Kenyatta had known off-and-on since he was taken in by Kita's parents and she was sent to Ghana.

"We've watched tha both ah you, all these years." The voices of their parents were unfamiliar to their minds, but their souls leapt in recognition. *"We're proud of you and we look forward to seeing you again when it's time."*

"But you got a long time to go," Grandpa said. *"So gwan fight, gwan live, and never forget that we're always with you."*

Kenyatta and Taliah felt the presence of Grandpa and their parents receding as they reached the vortex.

"Had to wait so many years for that," Kenyatta said. "It was worth it."

"Yeah man," Taliah breathed.

"Who was that man?" Seung asked.

The question startled Kenyatta. He'd forgotten the others were even there. They'd seen Grandpa, but had remained respectfully quiet during a conversation they apparently couldn't hear. "My grandpa," was all he could bring himself to say, for the emotions were too strong at the moment.

"It's time," Taliah said. "You'll need to prepare yourselves. It will be a shock shifting from this plane back to earth. You will feel more dense and less alive than you do now, and all of this niceness will evaporate."

Kita chuckled. "I can't wait."

Felk slapped him on the back, causing his heart to skip a beat. "Just take it out on the demons, laddy."

"I can't promise that we won't enter directly in the middle of the fighting," Taliah said.

Kenyatta drew his sword and flipped the little latch on the hilt, separating it into its two parts.

Kita gripped his staff and the glowing blue runes pulsated.

Seung reached around her back and drew *Vyirayoi*, connecting the two parts of the shaft as one and snapping them into place.

The dwarves hefted axes and hammers, and a soft glow surrounded both Merk and Paigra.

Taliah took a deep breath. "Let's go."

D arius took his time descending the steps. The battle was on in full, and the defenders the Ilanyan had gathered were holding admirably. Though quentranzi were the most powerful and smartest demons of the fifth hell, they sacrificed a small bit of that power on the earth realm. Still, it was a sight to behold. The Ilanyan had summoned incredibly powerful earth magic to his side. Earth magic was wild and difficult to control, which was why only the most skilled elves, dwarves, and amahle used it.

Iel and his human student remained close to the tower with a small contingent of magical warriors beside them. Malimokuru was also there. Darius stopped and looked again at the nature reader. The old man was different. There was power that wasn't there before. Even his appearance was altered.

"Found a bit more power, my friend?" the drojan said, moving beside him.

"Hopefully it's enough."

"You look as though you mean to leap into the fray," Darius observed, noting Malimokuru's forward posture.

"I just might."

That surprised Darius. But what surprised him more was that he believed the old human could actually do some considerable damage to their enemy.

"Of course, I'll not tell you what to do, my friend," Iel said, placing a hand on Malimokuru's shoulder. "But the fight will inevitably reach us here."

"I know."

Iel studied Malimokuru. "You'd prefer to fight alongside your friends."

"Since I got wrapped up in this whole ordeal over a year ago, I've been able to help, but not like I feel I can now." He studied his hands seeing something they could not. "For the first time since I can remember, there's toughness in this old body. There's power."

"Then do what you must," Iel said.

Darius scanned the battlefield with narrowed eyes. "So many choices, hmm?"

When Malimokuru looked at him, Darius grinned. "Go where you will, my friend. I will see you on the battlefield." Darius bounded high and far into the air.

The air in his face lit a fire in Darius he hadn't felt in many years. As he descended on a mass of twisted demonic bodies, he felt a rush of excitement and bloodlust. His canine teeth elongated, a flash of red lit his eyes, and the air itself shuddered under the weight of his roar.

* * *

Darius hit a pit demon from above with enough explosive force to send all nearby flying away under a rain of rock, soil, and demon insides. He turned away from the evaporating remains to see a four-legged monstrosity stomping toward him, jaws agape, saliva dripping from red fangs stretching towards him.

His eyes widened above a slanted smile. The beast leaped at him, and he caught it by the throat. He let the beast writhe in his iron grip for several moments before finally snapping its neck. The demon fell limp, and he dropped the evaporating carcass. He immediately spun and drove his fist straight through the chest of a scaled monster that had crept up from behind.

"This is more fun than I've had in centuries."

* * *

Kenjiro kept a wary eye on his red ally as she tore the throat from a brutish creature and then drove her spear through its chest. *Our allies are just as fearsome as our enemies.*

He blocked a downward chop of a demon with blades for arms. Apparently kalistyi shadow demons weren't the only ones with blades for limbs. He muscled the blade over his head and down, then stomped his foot on the top of the blade. He whipped his sword around and down with his left hand and severed the arm.

The demon had barely staggered away when Kenjiro thrust his sword through its throat.

He sighed at the sight of yet another tear opening nearby. They had dispatched so many of the things, and when it seemed they were on the verge of gaining an advantage, another tear would appear. He swore in his native tongue and sprinted toward the new threat.

To his surprise, the elven ranger Immendiel appeared at his side. "We fight together."

Kenjiro responded with a grim nod, and side by side, they cut their enemies down.

* * *

Naiyala bathed in the inferno of the *rage* and met her hellish enemies with equal viciousness. She whirled her spear and thrust backward, impaling an enemy from behind. She then lifted the monster over her head and slammed it atop an advancing pit demon. Before the impaled fiend began to evaporate, she slung it aside to crash into a handful of smaller creatures nearby. She closed in on the recovering pit demon and drove her spear through its back.

She leapt over it and drove her spear into the back of another fiend that was pressing a centaur with wildly swinging claws and snapping jaws. The centaur nodded in thanks and, seeing Naiyala's warning look over his shoulder, leaned forward and kicked his hind legs out. He sent it tumbling into another demon battling Shinobu.

Without breaking his rhythm, the strider swept his ethereal sword downward and severed its head.

The amahle princess had a brief moment to take stock of her surroundings. The centaurs had lost one of their clan, and though most of the magical defenders were beginning to fade, they still had the battle well in hand. Across the field, Amata Daunyana jumped backward and swept her hand toward a cluster of pursuing demons. A single blinding spark of Daunyanic power blew them apart.

She landed in a crouch and spun in a circle, sweeping both her arms outward. Any fiend within a dozen foot radius of the apprentice was destroyed.

Naiyala started to take heart, but the moment faded when more demons leapt out of new tears.

* * *

Tinnoviel Nai SaunyaLi saw a new portal rip through the air not far away, and Immendiel and the human samurai rushing to meet it. The Daunya Warrior wondered if there was an end to this madness. They had dispatched countless enemies, yet there were always more to replace them.

Now, it seemed they were even more outnumbered than at the start. He ducked under a sweeping tail, then brought his weapon around and smashed the monster in the side of the torso. The demon flew aside and dissolved before it hit the ground.

Several yards away, Yurin Kei Daunyana wielded the power of the Daunyans ruthlessly. Her fierce purple eyes glowed wildly as she thrust out a hand, fingers curled. Blue fire erupted from her fingers and lanced through the four demons at once, sending them screaming back to the abyss. She crouched and crossed her forearms. A soft glow crept from her hands to her arms until her entire body was enveloped in the glow.

Amata Daunyana thrust her hands to the sky, then swung them out to her sides. Streams of Daunyanic energy shot from her body and blew apart a cluster of advancing fiends.

She gasped and dropped to a knee, trying to catch her breath. More demons approached, but Tinnoviel was there, leaping and slashing, blocking and countering. Many fiends fell before him, but there were always more. So many more.

"Get 'em, TinTin!" he heard a tiny voice call from behind. Anticipating the young elf's next move, Tinnoviel crouched. He felt tiny feet run up his back and Tikena Mojin glided over his head and right into the face of an advancing pit demon. It looked as if the little elf girl had gone into a frenzy on its head.

The pit demon fell on its back, reaching for the elusive little creature. She was too fast, and in short order the monster was dissolving back to the abyss. Together, Tinnoviel and Tikena battled the advancing monsters, buying Amata time to recover. His power and her speed complimented each other as though they were partners in a deadly dance.

Many fiends fell to their Daunya-blessed blades. More portals appeared.

472

T he battle drew too near the tower for Iel's comfort. He and Mira had entered the fray in an explosion of the guardian's natural abilities, and Mira's innate psionic power.

Malimokuru fought beside them, and his starling power surprised Iel. When before he wielded the sands from his pouch, now he called upon their power from within.

He spread his hands across the air, and everywhere he did, sparks of acidic sand grains attached themselves to nearby fiends and burned them to ashes. Two Zzrt stalked toward Malimokuru, tongues waving out of their wide, perpetually grinning maws.

"Afreetuminos!" A blazing wave of sand draped over the hulking beasts and lit them aflame.

Though the defenders were gaining ground, more tears were ripping across the air, and more demonic forces came through. It seemed endless, and powerful though he'd become, Malimokuru had not the same stamina as the Children of the Gene. Not even Iel and Mira, nor the amahle and the elves could fight on indefinitely.

Those that battled in the middle of the demon onslaught were surrounded and slowly being herded together. Before this new development, the defenders had begun to break apart the fiendish hoard from the middle. Now, though they lay mass devastation upon their enemies, reinforcements continued to appear.

A horn sounded in the distance. HAAAOOOOOOOOO! Iel ducked a

snapping pincer and thrust a wave of Boraka's destructive power through his enemy's torso.

He stole a glance in the direction of the horn. A force of warriors similar in size to the dwarves charged onto the battlefield. They rushed into the nearest cluster of fiends, swinging clubs, maces, and sometimes each other. Where these new allies struck, scores of demons fell.

"The brunts have come!" Mira shouted.

The brunts crashed into the side of the demonic horde as if taken by bloodlust, beating their way toward the encircled warriors.

It's still not enough, Iel thought. Though the brunts were careful not to allow themselves to be surrounded, there were still too many demons to fight, and more still appearing. Already, several of their number had fallen, as well as another centaur. "So be it," he said to himself. *We die together.*

A violent tremor shook the earth. Iel searched about for the source of the quakes. Around the side of the tower, the ground burst open and an enormous four-legged creature climbed out of the crater. Tiny tentacles waved about its red-brown body, and with every step it took toward Takashaniel, the ground shook.

To his alarm, Iel saw that Malimokuru was closest to the approaching behemoth. He hurled a cloud of acidic sands at the monster, and its skin lit with thousands of tiny sparks. Its screech pierced through the cacophony of battle and then it turned its malevolent gaze on the nature reader.

Malimokuru stood his ground and threw another blast into the charging monster. It screeched again but continued its charge. He attacked again, but the monster shook its head and kept coming. It was nearly on top of him when a bright blue blur crashed into the side of its head.

Nyaka was a whirlwind of claws and teeth and spiked tail. She savaged the monster up one side of its head and down the other. The monster staggered, then reared up and slammed its front paws back to the ground, causing another quake.

The goar cat lost its grip and hit the ground rolling. She sprang back to her feet and charged in toward the open jaws of the massive beast. Her color shifted and she nearly disappeared.

When the beast hesitated, having lost track of her, Malimokuru struck again. "Afreetuminos!" The terrible fire struck the monster's underbelly and this time, it curled in on itself and stumbled away.

It hadn't taken a full step in its retreat when blood and tentacles suddenly flew from the back of its neck. Nyaka appeared, claws and teeth rending flesh and muscle. It reared up on its hind legs and twisted its body, but the behemoth had no way of dislodging the troublesome goar cat.

Every time a tentacle reached for her, a whip of Nyaka's tail cut it apart. In moments, Nyaka had savaged the monster's neck so badly, it fell face first to the ground where it lay still. Nyaka climbed out of the gaping wound and shook some of the blood and gore from her body. She looked in Malimokuru's direction, then crouched and hissed.

Without thinking, the nature reader dropped to one knee and spun around, spraying a wall of sand. A smaller fiend, not much larger than himself was nearly on top of him. It fell away screaming as the sands burned it away. "Thanks, my friend," he called out to the goar cat. She regarded him for a moment, then bounded past him and into the mass of twisted, grotesque creatures that now blanketing the field.

* * *

U nlike the first time, the vortex that transported them also cleansed them inside and out, and a feeling of clarity and strength filled them. Kita felt Taliah in his mind. *Be ready.*

He felt his body grow denser as they came nearer to the earth plane. Then they heard the fighting; the dying. The world around them bubbled and shifted. The warriors finally returned to the earth plane, surrounded by chaos.

At Kita's side, Kenyatta drew his swords and cut a Zzrt nearly in two. Then he leaped ahead, stabbing a pit demon in the back, one, twice, thrice, a fourth, fifth, and sixth time. He leaped away as the demon fell on its back, dissolving.

Kita whirled his staff over his head and bashed the side of an oblivious fiend's head. It fell in a heap, and Kita brought the end of his staff crashing down on its abdomen. The runes blazed, and the monster burned to cinders.

"Boraka's hairy forearms!" Paigra cursed. "Did the whole durned abyss throw up on this place, then?" He clapped his hands together and sent a shockwave of Boraka's energy barreling through a cluster of fiends. By the time the suddenly airborne demons hit the ground, Merk muttered an incantation. Another, more violent Borakan shockwave flew at the demons and blasted them to nothingness.

"Let's get to work, boys!" Felk shouted. With him in the lead, the dwarves raised their axes and hammers and cut a violent path into the battle.

Seung danced with lethal grace through a sea of twisted evil. She ducked and spun *Vyirayoi* over her back horizontally. Having leapt at her from behind, the attacking demon had no way to stop or reverse course. The blade disemboweled it, but before it had a chance to verbalize its agony, she spun and lopped off its head.

She moved with the momentum heavy weapon, slicing and whirling, ducking and spinning. The blades of her magnificent weapon cut her enemies down one after another, and sometimes multiple at once.

Kenyatta knelt under the sweeping arm-blade of a kalistyi. In the same motion he swept one of his swords across its midsection, sending it back to the abyss. He hopped back to his feet and leapt into a forward flip, tucking his legs in close to his body.

Holding one blade in front of him in a forward grip and one behind him in a reverse grip, he tucked his arms in close as his body spun. Like a circular blade, he sliced up the front and down the back of a hulking green demon with vulture wings spread in anticipation of a kill. The fiend fell apart and Kenyatta launched himself into a mass of fiends even as it dissolved.

After a quick assessment of the field, Taliah realized the battle had taken a desperate turn. The magical defenders had all but faded away, and the brunts and centaurs were suffering more casualties.

One of the amahle warriors had taken injury, but was still in the fight. Then she saw Tinnoviel, cut in several places, also beginning to slow. Kenjiro stood defending a slowly recovering Immendiel, though he looked no less worse for wear.

"You will not win, drek," she said under her breath. The power of the Daunyans filled her, and she became a glowing light in a wave of darkness. Her light pierced the black canopy covering the sky, and blinded their abysmal enemies.

Taliah waved her right arm in an outward arc, and stopped it in front of her body, then thrust her index and middle finger together upward. Brilliant spears of light rained down on the demon horde. The spears stabbed into the ground like arrows feathering a battlefield.

Those demons who hadn't been skewered—and thus destroyed—shielded their eyes against the burning light. The light emitted from the spears widened until they became one huge cloud that encompassed the battlefield. The light exploded, and even the defenders were forced to look away. When the light faded, more than half the quentranzi force had been vaporized.

Taliah swayed on her feet. She was still recovering from her confrontation with the dokara, and this desperate move sapped what energy she'd recovered.

Several Zzrt saw her in a vulnerable state and charged. Iel and

Malimokuru reached her first. Though Zzrt demons were bullishly tough, the combined efforts of Malimokuru and Iel soon had them melting back to the abyss.

"Are you all right?" Iel asked as he and Malimokuru helped her up.

Taliah looked about the battlefield and felt a glimmer of hope. The tide had turned, and the defenders of Takashaniel were pushing the demonic forces back.

In his scrying mirror, Brit saw the catastrophe that had just befallen the bulk of his force. He'd seen the little female human speck, but hadn't taken her for much. He couldn't fathom how so much power could be channeled from a simple human. His red eyes narrowed.

"You have called and I will answer." He walked to his balcony to see that Kabriza had just transported the last of his quentranzi forces. The titans should be able to tip the battle back in his favor. He linked his mind with the scrying mirror and stepped through.

fter the last titan demon stepped through the tear, Kabriza looked up at the vacant balcony and narrowed its eyes.

G rimhammer brought his massive war hammer down onto the head of his enemy, and it immediately crumbled to the ground and burned away. The bruised and battered centaurs fought bravely, but the steady stream of demons were overwhelming them.

The arrival of the brunts had provided some relief, and then the appearance of that human woman had turned the tide. He didn't know who or what she was, but he was thankful for her arrival. The forces fighting for Takashaniel had begun to beat the demon invasion back, and the battle was moving steadily toward its conclusion.

Warsong moved up beside him. "The battle is all but won, Chief."

"Not so," Grimhammer replied. "The source of all this still has yet to make an appearance."

"Indeed," said a voice from behind.

Grimhammer and Warsong spun as one. As big as the centaur chief was, even he had to crane his neck to look up at the towering enemy before him.

Before he or Warsong could react, Brit slapped Grimhammer in the side of the head. The blow sent him tumbling away as though he were but a foal.

Grimhammer retained just enough consciousness to witness Warsong spin around and kick out. He hit the drek's midsection, then roared and spun to face Brit. He lowered his head, and barreled into the drek, but Brit merely growled in irritation and planted his feet. He wrapped his arms around Warsong's equine body and hurled him aside.

Another charging centaur thrust his spear at Brit's abdomen. He caught the spear and pulled the surprised centaur in. With little effort, he snapped the weapon, then reached out and grabbed his attacker by the throat and lifted him up. Brit bared his teeth, and the muscles in his arms bunched. He snapped the centaur's neck and hurled the lifeless body aside as though he were a sack of rice.

A group of fearless brunts charged in, clubs held high. He swept his hand in an arc, and the air between them sparked. Before they could stop, the four warriors crashed into the transparent wall and fell burning to ashes.

* * *

"He's come." Iel started toward the drek.

Mira fell in beside him. "We will fight him together—"

"You cannot, child." Before she could protest, Iel held up a hand. "He is too much for you, and he knows this. He would use you against me. I must fight him alone."

"What of the others?"

"If they can, they will stand with me. I need you to defend Takashaniel in my absence." He looked at her with pleading eyes. "Please."

She fought back tears as she nodded. "I will. But don't look at me this way. You look like you're walking to your death."

"Whether I am or not, you must be ready." The air around him shifted and he was gone.

* * *

"He finally shows himself," Amata Daunyana said.

The amahle and the elves, as well as the human warriors had come together and battered the demon force until few remained.

The magical being, Siti, finished the last of the demonic horde just as her sustaining energy began to fade. Within moments, she would return to the earth. "The Ilanyan has gone to meet him."

Yurin Kei Daunyana started toward them. "Then let's join with him and be done with this."

An earth-trembling growl stopped her mid step. Everyone froze and scanned their surroundings.

Tinnoviel tightened his grip on his weapon. "What now?"

"Me get a sinking feeling," Malimokuru said.

Just as the last words left his lips, a black portal taller than Takashaniel itself tore a hole in the air, and out stepped four of the largest monstrosities they had ever seen. Eleven sets of eyes rose to take in the sight of towering demons that stood taller than the tower they defended.

"Those are bigger than the one we fought before," Kita breathed.

"And there's four of them," Kenyatta said.

"Looks like our old friends have found us," Malimokuru said.

Some of the group wrenched their eyes from the approaching titans to see two twin demons gliding toward them.

Malimokuru swore under his breath. "Should have known they'd wait for something like this."

Naiyala's chest rose and fell as the rage crept over her. "This ends."

The elves and humans flinched away at the sound of her suddenly deep, growling voice. She craned her head back and let out a blood curdling sound that was half sigh, half hiss. The other three amahle responded in kind, and she, Ayanda, and Sakhile bared elongated fangs.

Fully taken by the rage, their skin shifted from onyx black to red, and the amahle warriors sped away to meet their enemy. Looking no less fierce, Amata Daunyana blended with the surroundings and bounded behind them.

Kita looked after the departing amahle and took a deep breath. "This is gonna be a tough one."

"Yes it will be," Taliah agreed. She pointed at Seung, Kita, Kenyatta, and the elves minus Yurin. "You must aid Iel. He needs you." She beckoned to Malimokuru and Yurin. "Stand with me." At Kenyatta's hesitant look, she waved him away. "We each play our part, Brother. Go and do what must be done, as I do the same."

"Watch yourself," Kenyatta said, an unusual look of concern on his face.

Kita stared at her, clearly not wanting to leave her side.

"Gwan bwoy! All of you!"

Tinnoviel put a hand on each of their shoulders. "Come, friends."

Taliah turned to the two who remained. "You ready?" The apprentice and nature reader spoke in unison.

"Yes."

"No."

They looked questioningly at Malimokuru, who shrugged. "You ask, and me tellin' the truth. I nah tink I'm ready for this, but I'm here and I'm not goin' anywhere."

"Ye got two more to add to yer number." Merk Iamfeld and his mentor, Paigra, came trotting up. "The boys'r handlin' the last o' them nasties. Figgered ye could use a couple more hands."

"Stubby hands," Yurin remarked under her breath, still watching the towering demons.

Merk glared at the elf. "Seems to me miss fairy sprinkles got her robes in a twist."

Taliah stifled a snort. "Seems to me we don't have time for this. Save your arguments for after this is done. If you survive, you can argue forever."

One of the titan demons turned toward them while the other two had started in on the tower. The earth trembled under their every step.

"Impossibly massive," Yurin breathed.

"Then let's chop 'em down," Paigra said.

"Yurin," Taliah said. "You are with Malimokuru. Take the one closest to Takashaniel. The tower will aid you the closer you are to it." She motioned to the others. "Paigra and Merk, you two take the one closest to us."

"You cyan't fight two of dem tings on your own," Malimokuru said.

"Worry about yourself," Taliah replied, and then she was away.

"Can you do this, human?" Yurin asked. Her tone was not derisive, but candid.

"I guess we'll see," Malimokuru replied.

B rit was about to crush the life out of the centaur leader when he felt the Ilanyan drawing close. He dropped the limp Grimhammer and turned in time to slap aside a sphere of light energy. He smiled. "Finally. I thought you would be cowering in your crumbling tower."

"As you have cowered in your dismal fortress all these years," Iel countered. "And, Takashaniel yet stands."

"Until you're dead. Let us finally settle this."

Brit focused a poisonous yellow-green light toward the Ilanyan. Iel chopped his hand down and cut through the stream. He chopped his hand back up and sent an arced blade of orange light toward the drek, who sidestepped it. They circled each other for several moments, studying the other.

"Do you really think you can kill me?" Brit taunted.

"We will know soon enough," Iel replied.

"Indeed."

Back and forth they went, hurling bolts of energy at each other. Powerful though Brit was, Iel matched him. He threw a bolt of dark light toward Iel, who slapped it apart. In that instant, three figures came gliding down over his shoulder. Two pounded him with the blue glowing power of Boraka.

The force of the unexpected attack threw Brit off balance. He recovered quickly, but the third arrival clamped his hands together and his body erupted with blue fire. The flames burst away from the new enemy and enveloped Brit.

Iel was startled by the arrival of the forgotten monks. He hadn't seen them since the battle had started and had hoped they hadn't met their demise. Despite their ragged appearance and obvious injuries, they fought on.

Brit's resounding growl drew Iel back to his enemy. Brit hurled spheres of dark, twisted earth energy at the newly arrived allies. The three monks separated, two jumping to either side and one jumping up and over the black ball of energy.

Iel saw Brit's face light in anticipation as Shi Xing Long descended on him. Brit snapped his hand up attempting to snatch the monk out of the air.

Shi Xing Long reflexes saved his life. He slapped the reaching hand with not a strong enough power to injure, but to spin himself safely aside. He called forth the power of The Destroyer, and delivered a flat-palmed strike into the drek's shoulder.

The maneuver caught Brit off guard and lifted him off his feet. He hit the ground hard, but slowly, deliberately, he rose, leveling his baleful gaze on the tiny human. Another powerful force hit him from another direction.

Stung and knocked off balance again, Brit recovered only to be hit again by a third assault. Iel hit with the force of Boraka. The Daunyanic assault sent him flying backward to crash into a tree.

Lying at the base of the broken tree, Brit shook his head and climbed to his feet. His eyes glowed with anger and hate, and he drew in a dangerous amount of earth energy, taking it into his body and twisting it to his will. The energy flooded into him as he drew in still more, channeling it and reshaping it to his desires.

When he could stand the strain no longer, he released the raw power from his body in the form of an expanding dome.

One of the monks was simply burned away. Iel and the remaining two monks skittered backwards, narrowly avoiding incineration long enough for the guardian to kneel and draw power from Takashaniel. He created a dome of his own; a protective shield against the lethal and poisoned power of the drek.

No sooner had Brit's aggression played itself out, two burning pains penetrated his back, and he felt two feet push off. He turned to see the human who had battled against his forces four years ago gliding away from him. He looked from this new threat, back to Iel and the remaining monks just as he was hit by an unfamiliar—yet hellishly painful—power.

* * *

Kita knew that the blow he'd landed had hurt when the drek stumbled over. Seeing an opening, he moved in and swung his staff into the leg, then spun in the opposite direction and hit the drek in the ribcage.

Brit staggered sideways just as Immendiel ran past. She dealt him a passing cut with her bark-made weapon that brought him to his knees.

Tikena and Seung darted past him in a crisscross, striking him across the face.

Brit grunted through the assault and forced his way up to a kneeling position. Tinnoviel slammed his shoulder into the drek's head. When the drek was knocked in the opposite direction, Iel blasted him with light energy again and sent him sprawling. The two monks summoned the power of Boraka and burned the drek with His fire.

Iel saw Brit crouching in on himself and his eyes widened. He felt the drek drawing on the power he'd leached from the earth. He shouted in defiance and pushed the energy away from his body.

The allies flew away; all except Iel, who'd crossed his arms and formed a barrier. He leaned into his defense even as his feet slid backwards. When the counterattack ended, Iel hurled a ball of orange energy at Brit.

The ball of energy fizzled out against Brit's quick defense just as Kenyatta descended on him. Brit rose and slapped him out of the air, then fired a bolt of his own twisted earth energy. The bolt whizzed through the air and sliced through Iel's defense. It hit Iel through the chest and the guardian flew away.

Kita couldn't allow himself to flinch at the terrible blow to their ally and friend. He spun his staff over his head and whipped it around for the drek's hip. The staff struck true, and Brit nearly collapsed.

Despite being dealt injury from every direction, the drek fended off the relentless assault. The defenders pressed the attack. This was their chance.

Kita gritted his teeth and set his staff spinning. He struck the drek in the head, the shoulder, he stabbed straight, punching the butt of the weapon into the drek's midsection. *Die, damn you!*

A dark portal ripped the space beside him, and Kabriza stepped through just as Kita was spinning around to deal a devastating blow to the head. The quentranzi general caught Kita's hand and held him aloft.

It seemed like time itself froze. Kabriza brought the struggling Kita closer to his face and inspected him as though he would a mouse. Kita pushed away the fear the hideous demon invoked, and struggled to get free. It had grabbed the hand holding his staff, and so Kita kicked it in the face.

Kabriza bared its fangs in an open-mouthed laugh. It lazily raised its other hand and lined its palm directly in front of Kita. "Die, human." Kabriza's hand glowed, and he hit Kita with a solid punch of demonic energy that sent him flying away.

"Kabriza," Brit said. "After we kill the rest—" The words died in his mouth when the demon general drove its clawed hand into his chest. Brit gasped, then coughed on a mouthful of blood. He looked up at Kabriza in disbelief.

The quentranzi general smiled at him, then yanked its claw out of his chest. It held Brit's heart aloft so that the drek could watch its final beats.

"There is someone who would like to meet you,"—Kabriza put his face right in front of Brit's—"*tether.*" The demon said the last word mockingly as he crushed the drek's heart in his hand, then dropped it on the ground like a bloody stone. Kabriza ripped open a portal behind Brit, then threw him into it.

* * *

Kenyatta saw his friend blasted away, his body in one direction and his staff in another. The confrontation between the drek and his demon general was largely lost on the islander as he stared in the direction his friend, his brother, had flown. When he turned his attention back to the demon, it had just thrown Brit through a portal. His hands tightened on the hilts of his swords until his knuckles had gone white. Slowly, purposefully, he stalked toward the monster.

* * *

Kabriza looked at the approaching human with amusement. The two humans behind it had started to approach as well. With a casual gesture, the demon whipped its claw outward. The resulting blast sent the little gnats flying and falling away.

Another human with a strange ethereal sword approached cautiously. Again, Kabriza sent a blast of abysmal power at the human.

He jumped impossibly high for a human; easily clearing the assault. Kabriza grinned, for it was just a feint. He punched the fragile animal, or tried to. The speed of the human surprised the quentranzi general.

A downward chop of that awful sword cut through Kabriza's fist, and what a burning agony resulted! The quentranzi recoiled even as it backhanded the cursed human away. He turned just in time to see the other human closing in.

* * *

White-hot rage burned inside Kenyatta. After the demon knocked Shinobu out of the fight, it turned its attention back to him.

That was a mistake.

Akemi came gliding down on the demon, driving both her swords into its back. It howled and spun in a circle, trying in vain to dislodge her. The ninja held on for a few heartbeats, then jumped away.

Even from his distance, Kenyatta saw the surprise on her face that the fiend had not been mortally wounded.

Good. Kenyatta wanted to utterly destroy this monster himself. Three bounding jumps had him on the quentranzi. His strokes were fast, his blows savage and strong. Only the marks on the demon's body indicated the stroke of Kenyatta's swords, for the warrior's hands and arms were a blur of unending cuts and slashes that had the demon general giving ground.

In the periphery of his mind, he sensed both anger and sadness from his sister. He pushed it away. He needed to focus on his hated enemy.

The demon general was surprisingly tolerant of his weapons. Every wound Kenyatta inflicted did minimal damage. It didn't matter. The Gene of the Daunyans, the adrenaline, and the rage that burned in him fueled his body. Every time Kabriza managed to block or avoid an attack, Kenyatta dealt it several blows from a different direction. Black blood spattered the ground from countless cuts and stabs.

Kabriza managed to fend Kenyatta off long enough to put some distance between them. "You fight well, though it is not enough to defeat me."

"I've as long as it takes," Kenyatta answered icily.

"I don't suspect you will survive that long."

"Then come."

* * *

Taliah saw Kita blasted away into the distance. It was such a powerful and terrible assault of black energy that she'd felt it from where she was. She sensed that he was alive, but he was fading in and out, as though his spirit was resisting the pull of returning Home. *Fight it, my love.*

A short distance away, Yurin grunted, and a bright gout of green and blue flame burned into one of the titan demons. Right on the heels of that attack, a shower of acidic sand flew onto it, the tiny granules burning holes wherever they touched demon flesh.

Paigra and Merk took a different approach. The Master Spellcaster and his protégé had combined their power and were beating the enormous monster back. Paigra slapped his hands together and sent a shockwave hurtling into the fiend.

Merk followed up with waves of Boraka's destructive power, hurling balls of blue fire like stones, one after another. The relentless dwarves struck the fiend in the chest and face repeatedly. Only its massive size helped it to stay upright. With a deafening screech, it stomped the ground. The resulting quake sent everyone sprawling. Deep trenches split the earth and snaked away from the impact.

Malimokuru barely managed to keep his feet under him. He dove aside to avoid being swallowed up by one of the rifts. H wisely scrambled to his feet and ran for his life as a huge green foot raised into the air again.

"Hurry human!" Yurin shouted. She hit the monster with the power of Boraka, but it was not enough. Seeing that he was not going to make it, Malimokuru called upon his abilities as a nature reader. He expanded his awareness and sensed a disturbed and angered presence beneath the trenches in the earth. Wasting not a moment, he reached out to that presence and beseeched it for aid to save the land from the tainted presence that had awakened it.

He was too late. He clamped his eyes shut as the foot came down, but a sudden explosion of earth sent him tumbling to safety.

Two massive arms burst out of the earth and grabbed hold of the titan demon's foot. The ground split further and a molten rocky creature climbed out, still holding the foot. With a deep, rumbling moan, the molten creature gave a great heave and toppled the gigantic quentranzi.

"You summoned an earth elemental!" Yurin said, half in disbelief and half in admiration. "How did you convince it to answer your call?"

"I don't know," Malimokuru said, "but we'll talk about it later."

The smaller earth elemental traded blows with the giant quentranzi, bits of fiery rock and black demon blood raining down when either took damage. The great fiend let out an ear-splitting screech and plunged its black talons into the elemental's chest. The molten rock creature moaned in agony and spat a gout of lava into the demon's face.

"It can't win," Yurin said. "We must help it. Elementals help to balance the forces of nature. Every one lost is a sad loss to the world."

"I've got one last thing left in me," Malimokuru said wearily. "I hope this works."

The world around him dropped away as he focused within. He sent his awareness through the veil and out of the earth plane. His presence pierced veil after veil until he was neither in the earth realm, the heavens or the hells, but in between. He felt the presence of the guardian, and the anger at the intrusion of his realm. At first, the spirit of Malimokuru recoiled, thinking he was the source of the anger. Then he realized that the anger was not directed at him, but another. The presence of the guardian focused on him.

"*I am Dreaph,*" the guardian of Neirvan declared. "*Why are you here?*"

"*I plead for your aid, noble guardian,*" Malimokuru replied.

"*I guard the realm between the realms, the world between the worlds. I do not take part in the conflicts of yours or any other. I am the keeper of thoughts and emotions, desires and fears, dreams and nightmares. I am Neirvan.*"

"*Your world will be threatened if mine falls,*"

Silence stretched for several moments and Malimokuru thought Dreaph might not answer.

"*No one dares attack Neirvan.*"

"*Demons exist for death and chaos, noble guardian. If they destroy my world, they would not stop here—*" At the mention of demons, the guardian spoke over Malimokuru, and he knew he'd touched the mark. Dreaph's only response was what Malimokuru had hoped against hope to receive.

"*Speak the words.*"

Malimokuru's spirit was pushed away and sent flying back to his body. He opened his physical eyes to see the Daunya Apprentice standing over him, sending blasts of Daunyanic power in a paltry attempt to aid the slowly faltering elemental.

"Did you decide to nap, nature reader?"

"Hardly," Malimokuru climbed to his feet on shaky legs. He stepped a few feet away from Yurin, who looked at him questioningly. He didn't know how he knew what words to say, but he did. Perhaps the guardian had telepathically infused them in his mind. Either way, Malimokuru knew the words and the cost, but he had to try.

"Exist between the heavens and the hells, the *lyrghis* plight. I call on you, Ifrit, and all your might!"

Yurin's mouth fell open. She shrank away from him. "You fool! You … you summon a *lyrghis*? You summon Ifrit?"

The words hadn't fully left her lips before the ground around them came alive.

"Get away!" Yurin shouted. She grabbed his arm and pulled him away as glowing lines appeared on the ground. They traced in every direction, connecting and forming glowing symbols. One by one, runes neither of them recognized came aglow as though by fire. Yellow light encircled the runes, and the ground exploded in a geyser of rock and earth.

A massive, horned beast shot into the air, spinning inside the explosion of rock and flame. It thrust its arms and leathery wings out at its sides and roared to the heavens. Flapping its great wings, it hovered for a few moments, watching the struggling giants before finally descending to the earth.

Shimmering black fur covered its muscled body, and it bristled as the great beast heaved, steam puffing from its nostrils. Atop its head sat a crown of antlers sharper than any blade. Its green eyes glowed in rage at the giant demon that still battled the earth elemental.

"This may have been a mistake," Malimokuru said softly.

"Pray it depletes the power that sustains it here, or it may turn on us."

Malimokuru took another step back. "You think it would do that?"

Yurin gaped at him. "You truly have no idea what you've done. If you have not the strength to restrain it, a *lyrghis* will turn on you if it feels that it has been manipulated, which is almost always the case!"

"But it fights the evil with us."

"You are naïve, human. *Lyrghis* are neither good nor evil. They are chaotic and dangerous."

The Ifrit stalked in and punched the demon in the side of the head. To their amazement, the punch lifted the massive quentranzi off its feet. Malimokuru thought the earth itself might break apart under the resulting quake of its impact. Before the fiend could rise, Ifrit grabbed it by the neck and hoisted it up. With an unearthly bellow, it slammed the monster down on its upraised knee. There was a sickening crack like the sound of a hundred trees being felled at once.

Ifrit lifted the demon again, drew back a clawed hand, and thrust it through the monster's abdomen. It pulled its bloody hand free and dropped the gigantic fiend. The *lyrghis* turned its back before the broken titan had fully evaporated back to the abyss.

It stalked past the recovering earth elemental and leapt on the back of the titan that Paigra and Merk were struggling against.

Little more than half the size of the demon giant, the Ifrit punctured the monster's back with its claws and held on as the fiend tried to dislodge it. Ifrit pounded its fist on the demon's head repeatedly as it turned to and fro. With a great bellow, the *lyrghis* opened its wolf-like maw wide and bit down on the titan's shoulder.

Black blood flowed freely from the wound as Ifrit hooked its muscled right arm around the demon's neck so that its right shoulder was against the back of the opposite shoulder of the fiend. Jamming its claws into the demon's back again to gain leverage, the *lyrghis* rammed its right knee into the quentranzi's back.

Ifrit repeatedly thrust its knee into its demon's back until it stopped resisting and bent backwards. Its feet back on the ground, Ifrit pulled on its head until the great demon fell on its back. The *lyrghis* grabbed its ankle and spun it round and round, then upwards, launching the gigantic demon high into the air.

The *lyrghis* spread its clawed hands wide and its body started to shake as orange light formed in the space between its clawed hands. The ball of light grew brighter and larger till it enveloped Ifrit's body, then shot into the air. The force of the blast threw the *lyrghis* backward and the impact lit the sky.

One moment the giant quentranzi was in the air, the next, the orange sphere collided with it and blew it apart.

Ifrit regained its feet and turned its fiery glare on Malimokuru, who felt as though he would shrivel under that gaze. It took an earth-shaking step toward him and, thinking quickly, the nature reader fell into himself and sent his thoughts to the approaching monster. As soon as he connected with the massive beast, he felt a mind so primal and so ancient and powerful he was nearly overwhelmed. It took every bit of his will just to remain sane in the presence of such a force.

Thank you, mighty Ifrit, for your aid. The demons who would have threatened your world have been destroyed by your powerful hand and we stand before you in gratitude.

It stopped its advance and regarded him curiously. He could feel the intellect there; the intelligence. For a few tense moments, the three faced each other, the towering *lyrghis* considering the two nervous creatures that were no larger than mice.

Finally, a cylindrical light erupted from the ground and encircled it. The Ifrit faded until it became transparent, then finally disappeared.

Malimokuru let out a breath he hadn't known he'd been holding. The exhaling sound beside him told him Yurin had done the same.

"Impressive," the Daunya Apprentice said. "But do not do that again."

"Trust me," Malimokuru replied. "I have no intention to."

* * *

Taliah tightened the grip of the glowing blue energy of Boraka's power entangling the two titans. Every time one of them flexed to break free, it nearly buckled her knees. They were huge and powerful, but she was smarter. After every flex, she gave just a little, then squeezed tighter when they tired, much like a giant constrictor snake.

To her surprise, the air beside her warped, and DaunyaSai appeared.

"The Lady Seiyun sends her regards, Chosen." His face darkened when he regarded the monstrous fiends before her. "Would you allow me to assist?"

"By all means." Taliah released one of the demons just as the Daunya Master hurled a solid sphere of Daunyanic power into its face. The fiend's head snapped back, and DaunyaSai rose into the air.

Fists aglow with the blue flames of Boraka, DaunyaSai punched the monster in the abdomen. The sight of the tiny glowing elf against the massive demon would have looked ridiculous but for the power of the impact. The resulting explosion of Daunyanic energy doubled the quentranzi over. It cried out in rage and brought its hand crashing down on the elf.

Yurin Kei Daunyana choked back a scream as she saw her mentor crushed into the earth by the massive hand. She shared the demon's surprise, however, when its hand was forcibly raised.

Glowing brightly with the aura of Oberon, DaunyaSai rose to his feet while holding the giant palm aloft. In a blinding flash, the aura surrounding DaunyaSai streamed into the demon's hand.

When the quentranzi recoiled, DaunyaSai lifted into the air again. With the power of Boraka once again surrounding his body, he balled his fist and swung a round house punch in the air.

Though his physical fists did not touch the demon, the power of the Destroyer pounded the giant. Once, twice, thrice, another, DaunyaSai rained blow after blow upon it. The giant stumbled away from each blow like a massive rag doll until it finally crashed to the ground.

DaunyaSai descended and knelt upon it. The power of Boraka filled his body again as he pressed his hand on the massive chest. The aura funneled from his body into the demon. Light filled its body from the inside, and holes burned through its skin where spears of The Destroyer's Daunyanic power escaped.

In a final screech of agony, the titan demon burned away, sent back to its abysmal home.

"Well done." Taliah raised her hand in front of the eye the titan she'd just felled. Blue flames roared to life from her hand and immolated the beast. In a heartbeat it was gone as if it had never been.

She started in the direction Kita had fallen when the sound of fighting drew her attention. On one end of the field, the amahle fought two twin demons. One of their number lay unmoving away from the fight, and she said a quick prayer to the Daunyans for his survival.

Naiyala and her band had dealt great injury to the winged fiends, however. One had lost a wing and the other was impaled and pinned to the ground.

"Our friends need our help," DaunyaSai said.

On the other end of the field, Kenjiro, Akemi, the elves, and the dwarves fought the demon general, Kabriza. The quentranzi was proving a match for them all, and even as she started in that direction, it dispatched four dwarves with one stroke of its hand, burning them to ash. The strider lay several yards away, and Iel was at his side, coughing blood.

The ninja demon hunter leaped and slashed the fiend in the back several times. Kabriza roared and spun on her, swiping at her head. She ducked and slashed its leg. The demon tore a space in the air and fell back into it, then came out of another tear behind her. It stabbed her from behind with a finger talon. Akemi screamed and dropped one of her swords as she fell to her knees.

Kenyatta was there, slashing at the beast, and as she neared, Taliah saw the deceptively calm expression on her brother's face. She felt a chill. Kenyatta had moved beyond rage and nearer to hate. She broke into a run and extended her hand. Blue flames shot from her hand and blew the demon off its feet.

* * *

Naiyala and her amahle warriors pummeled the twin demons with such ferocity, the demons could do no more than stagger under the onslaught. Sakhile lay on the ground, gone from this world to be with the Daunyans. Though she knew he was now in bliss, Naiyala had been enraged by the loss of one of her dearest friends.

One of the demons who had lost a wing feebly lunged for her throat. She caught its wrist and yanked it outward, forcing the demon to lean sideways and expose its chest. With a loud hiss, she stabbed her clawed hand into its midsection, drawing an agonized screech from the fiend.

With her hand still plunged into its midsection, Naiyala tucked its arm under hers and quickly lifted. The demon's wail followed behind resounding crack of breaking bone. She released its ruined arm and reached over her shoulder.

The demon's arm was already repairing itself as she drew her remaining enchanted spear. She looked into the demon's evil glowing orbs and thrust the spear through its chest. The demon's wail sped away from its dissolving body and echoed across the field.

Naiyala turned to where her remaining friends battled the second winged fiend. She started in that direction when a bolt of lightning struck the ground not far away. Then another, and another. Naiyala's eyes narrowed. She'd seen that before.

In a brilliant flash of light and electricity, a demon wrapped in wildly dancing electricity appeared before them. Naiyala bared her teeth at the new enemy.

A cry of pain broke through the confrontation and she saw that Ayanda had been impaled through the shoulder with his own spear. A dozen feet away, Amata was climbing to her feet, dazed. Naiyala looked back to the electrical fiend, then to her friends.

"Do not worry about the skelion," A baritone voice said.

Darius approached, leaving behind a trail of broken and evaporating fiends. "Help your friends."

Naiyala nodded and bounded away.

A shadow of a smile crossed Darius's face as he watched the skelion make its way toward the amahle and the winged demon. In one leap, Darius closed the distance and landed in front of the fiend.

The skelion flinched away but quickly recovered and lashed out. Darius felt a tremendous jolt of electricity course through the impact on his face and down his body. He staggered back a step, then looked at the demon again, almost laughing. "You'll have to do better than that."

The demon howled and punched him again, or tried to. The drojan had caught its arm and held it in an unbreakable grip. The energy around the skelion flared as it sent a pulse of electricity through Darius that would have burned an elephant to ashes. Darius smiled. "That tingle is bliss. My thanks."

The demon tried to yank its arm free, and this time he did laugh. "Part of my existence is an expression of nature, dark one. Your elemental weapons cannot hurt me."

With a mighty roar, the drojan pulled the demon toward him and punched his fist straight through its chest. He lifted the screaming demon by its arm and swung it over his head. Still holding on to the dazed demon's arm, he gave it a twist and snapped it out of the socket. The demon shrieked and thrashed, but a moment later was silenced when Darius flung it into the air.

Darius leapt after it and caught it around the waist. For a few heartbeats they continued to ascend, the demon trying to beat him off of it. Darius ignored the pounding fists and struck the fiend across the jaw.

As they fell back to the earth, Darius pounded the demon till it stopped resisting, then sank his elongated claws into its chest. Their speed increased, and as the ground rushed up to meet them, primal energy filled Darius's body. They hit the ground in a tremendous explosion, and in that instant, Darius released the built up energy.

The ground rippled away from the impact, sending rock and trees and chunks of earth flying. In the middle of crater, Darius straightened and looked at the place where the skelion had been. Nothing remained but a charred stain.

He jumped out of the crater and had a look around. The amahle had dispatched the remaining demon, and were tending to their fallen comrade.

Darius turned his attention to the quentranzi demon on the far side of the battlefield and his eyes narrowed. He admired the bravery of the humans and the Ilanyan, but doubted they could overcome such a powerful enemy.

He'd barely finished the thought when the fiend fell backward through a rip in the air. A moment later, a power so immense and so dark and terrible enveloped Darius and cast him aside with such terrible force that he was knocked into darkness.

* * *

495

Kabriza had been trying to find an opening in the tireless onslaught by the human speck when he felt the presence of a drojan near. The wretched hybrid spawn of the Daunyarka was a true threat that must be eliminated before he entered the fight. The quentranzi general had to be quick if he was to surprise this new enemy. Abruptly he tore a rip in the air and fell through, reappearing behind the meddlesome hybrid.

Before he could react, Kabriza summoned as much power as he could and sent it in a mass of black energy right into the drojan. He caught the hybrid by surprise and managed to knock him unconscious.

Kabriza would have liked to finish the job, but other enemies were advancing. He fell back through another tear in the air and reappeared behind the human with those stinging swords.

Before the insect could react, Kabriza drew back a clawed hand, intending to rip him apart when a searing blast of light energy burned into his side and sent him flying. He hit the ground in a roll and slid to a stop.

Kabriza slowly rose and gave his head a shake. The only thing that could channel such power from the accursed Daunyans was a Chosen.

Thinking fast, the quentranzi general fell through yet another rip in the air. He leapt out behind the human with the swords just as he was turning. Kabriza heard the human woman scream "Kenyatta!"

He opened another tear in the air and came out just as the bewildered human was turning. Kabriza's backhanded slap sent the human spinning away through the second tear.

Anticipating another attack, the demon stepped through another tear and came out in front of the woman. Before she could react, he stepped through yet another tear and came out behind her, then beside her. He appeared in front of her again, simultaneously opening another rip behind her and swatting her through it. Kabriza closed the portal and turned to the remaining humans, hunger burning in his eyes.

Sensing a powerful wave of energy approaching, the quentranzi general turned just in time to be hit in the face by a sphere of Boraka's destructive power. It hurt. A lot.

The demon general thought that perhaps the Chosen had somehow returned, then another blast rocked him on the side of the head, then the other side. Kabriza managed a glimpse of an elf hovering in front of him, raining painful blows of Daunyanic-powered punches on him.

Kabriza clenched his teeth. "Elf vermin." He released a black cloud from his body that enveloped the elf. When the cloud broke apart, the elf collapsed.

The quentranzi lifted the elf with one hand and hit him with a gout of black fire. After watching with amusement as the elf flew far away, Kabriza knelt and closed his eyes. An octagon traced its way through the ground and lit with glowing red runes. Kabriza grinned. It was time.

* * *

Brit was on hands and knees, coughing blood, but alive. He put a hand to his chest and felt the empty space where his heart had been. How was he still alive?

He balled his fist and punched the ground. More importantly, how could he get back to the earth plane and begin slowly dismembering that treacherous demon general. He stood and looked around.

This was some kind of twisted, macabre hall shrouded in a sickly mist where the bodies of humans as well as other creatures were depicted in scenes of endless torture.

On closer inspection he saw that they were not depictions at all, but actual squirming victims. No stranger to inflicting his own brand of cruelty, even Brit was disgusted by the sight. "Where in the abyss am I?"

"Is your question rhetorical or genuine?"

Brit turned on his heels and scanned the empty hall. The voice seemed to come from everywhere. "Who speaks? Come before me!"

The voice chuckled. "You have grown powerful over the centuries, drek. Any who could so easily dispatch one of mine and send it back here is worthy of praise." More chuckling. "But I believe your amassed power has clouded your judgment, which is why you are here."

"Where is here, and who are you?" Brit demanded.

The mist thinned to one side of the hall, revealing a throne of squirming creatures. Brit's mouth tightened. If he sat upon that throne his feet would barely dangle over the front. Then, realization dawned on him. He knew that throne. He'd seen it when scrying Zreal's visit to this very chamber but a few years ago. "Grala."

The resulting chuckle vibrated in Brit's hollowed chest.

"Do you know why you are here, mortal drek?" The mist thinned on the opposite side of the chamber to reveal the lord of the quentranzi. As tall as Brit was, Grala easily doubled his nine feet. Brit watched the quentranzi lord come to stand before him; uncomfortably close.

"I am here because of your general's betrayal," Brit said. "I am here, because he thinks to have sent me here to be dealt with by you. I am here—"

quicker than Brit could react, the demon lord's hand snapped out and caught his throat. It lifted him off the ground and brought him to eye level.

"You are here because without *you* as the tether in the earth plane, *I* can enter. You live still, simply because this world functions differently than in your dimension. But still, you can die."

Brit bent his arm and curled his fingers. He released a blast of twisted earth energy into the demon lord.

The attack served only to move Grala as much as a gentle shove to the shoulder.

A fresh wave of dread settled over Brit. He had channeled everything he had into that blast and it did nothing.

Grala's half-laugh half-growl reverberated through the throne room and vibrated through Brit's body. The demon lord continued to laugh, not louder, but stronger. The power behind the quiet laughter shook the room.

Brit thought his body would shake apart under the force of that laughter. For the first time in his life, the drek new fear. If he'd been prepared, Kabriza could have been dealt with, but not this. The demon lord would have been far beyond him on the earth plane, and this was its realm. Death could commence for an eternity here, and in that moment, Brit knew that he was powerless to stop whatever Grala decided to do to him.

Finally, mercifully, the laughter stopped. "Do you have no more to say, mortal drek? Do you have no words of warning, no threats or promises of merciless agony?"

Brit didn't respond, for what could he say? The concept of mercy was a pitiful thing to Brit, and wholly foreign to a demon. And, this wasn't just a demon, but the lord of the quentranzi. All he could do was wait.

"I have destroyed creatures far more durable than you, mortal drek. Your death would only stave my boredom for a few moments before I forget your existence. Perhaps I shall preserve you for later amusement. I will send you to death, rebirth, death, and torture. I will send you to fear and hate, freedom and imprisonment." He squeezed Brit's neck, and he felt and heard the pop of several bones in his neck. He hung limp and in silent agony.

Grala tilted its head at the helpless drek in mock sympathy. "The pain of a broken neck must be excruciating. Worry not, mortal drek. I will send you to be healed." A black portal opened beneath him. The last words Grala spoke had Brit wishing the demon lord had just destroyed him and been done with it.

"I will send you to the Mephisto."

Despite the numerous wounds she had inflicted on Kabriza, *Onisekairu* and *Onihakaisha* dealt far less damage than Akemi would have thought possible. The demon general was far more powerful than any fiend she'd ever fought.

It had easily dealt with Kenyatta and Taliah, knocking them through portals to who knew where. Shinobu was still down and she wasn't sure whether or not he still lived. A new elf she had never seen before had dealt the quentranzi general a might offense only to be defeated just as decisively.

Akemi studied the monster while it stalked toward Iel and Mira and at the same time created a gateway.

The guardian finally stood and faced the towering fiend, and Akemi was unsure if the Ilanyan could have defeated Kabriza if he had been at his best. The fight with Brit had weakened him considerably, and Mira would be no match for it. The thought of how easily it had eliminated the drek had been a shock.

Kabriza may have caught Brit off guard, but the mere fact that it had dealt such a mortal blow so quickly had caution at the forefront of her mind. Akemi stealthily circled around behind it.

"You do not look ready to fight me, guardian," the demon mocked. "Has your little scuffle with Brit weakened you? Should I allow you to strike the first blow?" It spread its long yellow arms. Even open to attack, the demon was intimidating. Jagged spikes littered its body as though it had bathed in broken knives.

"If you insist." Iel threw a ball of light energy into Kabriza. The fiend staggered back a step, then huffed. Its amusement was cut short, when a stone spear pierced its chest. It grunted, but still kept its feet.

A streaming cone of acidic sand blew into it from the side, and this time the demon showed pain.

Malimokuru stalked toward the demon, hand raised, face twisted in anger. "I don't know whatcha did wit me friends, but if ya wan war wit us, we're right here." The nature reader's eyes glowed as he sent wave after wave of acidic sand washing over Kabriza. Thousands of tiny burning dots sizzled on its body.

Two blue spheres of Boraka's power assaulted the demon, pounding it backward. "Get ye back where ye come from, stinkin' demon!" Paigra hurled another blue ball of fire at Kabriza just as Merk Iamfeld summoned up the power of Boraka.

Merk threw another ball of blue fire. Kabriza's horned head snapped back, and its head erupted in flames.

The quentranzi general straightened its head again and eyed the surrounding defenders with amusement. "Such a valiant effort."

Greash's anguished scream rent the air, and everyone—including Kabriza—looked to the distance where the amahle warriors punished Greash mercilessly. Zkora lay in ruins upon the ground, his remains already beginning to evaporate back to the fifth hell.

A spear pinned the thrashing Greash to the ground through the chest. One of the females walked casually to the squirming demon and held her palm over him. Blue fire erupted from her hand and burned Greash to cinders.

"And so I fight alone, for now," Kabriza said, and indeed it looked as though the fiend hardly cared about the demise of the demon twins.

Those last two words filled Akemi with a sense of dread. With Brit out of the way, was the fiend somehow bringing more of its kind to this world even as it fought? It was clearly plotting something that they wouldn't like.

Iel's body glowed with the power he drew from Takashaniel. Just as he was about to strike, the demon fell backwards into a portal.

Her instincts screamed at her, and Akemi sprinted toward Iel, but she wasn't fast enough.

Three long claws punched through the guardian's torso and the power he had been drawing dissipated.

Kabriza lifted the groaning guardian into the air and stepped back through another portal before the screaming Mira could react. It stepped back onto the field right in front of her.

With a casual laugh, the quentranzi hurled the limp body of Iel at Mira and knocked her unconscious just as Akemi reached them.

The demon heard Akemi's swift footfalls and spun just in time to see *Onihakaisha* slice it across the face. The demon general wailed in fury, swinging its arms in blindness while its face mended. The demon brought its hand away and looked in outrage at the black blood covering it and still dripping from the slowly closing wound.

Having glided past its head to deliver the blow, Akemi slid to a stop and sprinted back at the wounded demon. She slid underneath it and slashed its left leg. When it dropped, she whipped *Onisekairu* around to slash the kneeling demon across the chest.

Seung came running from behind and jumped into a forward flip, holding her double bladed weapon vertically and pressed against her body. Like a turning, bladed wheel, she sliced the quentranzi general from behind. The fiend arched its back while stumbling forward.

The amahle warriors were there. Ayanda descended on the demon from on high, his spear held in a two-handed grip over his head.

Impossible as it seemed, the quentranzi general mended itself enough to stand up and catch Ayanda in one hand. It squeezed, and the hunter's eyes rolled back in his head and he hung limp in the demon's grasp.

A wailing voice drew Kabriza's attention just as one of the female amahle drove a spear through its abdomen.

Kabriza dropped Ayanda to face the new threat when Amata Daunyana landed on its chest. She drove her nails into its face and unleashed Daunyanic fire.

They pounded the demon with godly power from every direction and for a moment, it looked as though they would prevail.

But this was the second most powerful quentranzi of the fifth hell. Kabriza roared and slammed its fists into ground. The resulting tremor sent rippling black waves of demonic power speeding away from the epicenter.

Merk was dealt a glancing blow from a flying boulder that sent him spinning to the ground, while Paigra took the full force of one of the unholy waves. The spellcaster was knocked into a backward summersault and to crashed into a nearby tree.

Amata Daunyana summoned a shield that protected her and Naiyala from most of the assault, but a direct collision with such power dashed it to pieces and sent them flying.

Malimokuru held on briefly before he, too, was overwhelmed.

Akemi stayed low to the ground, struggling to hold her footing and hopefully remain unnoticed while the frenzied demon played out its rage. A hand on her shoulder startled her, but instantly she recognized the familiar squeeze. Squinting through the assault, a stone-faced Shinobu crawled next to her and nodded.

Like a bolt shot from a crossbow, DaunyaSai flew straight into the evil tempest and stopped in front of Kabriza's face. The Daunya Master curled his body into a ball, then straightened with a roar that surely must have been heard the world over.

From the enraged Daunya Master grew a dome of blue-yellow light that lit the demon general aflame.

The demon general fell to its knees, but then its body glowed with a blackness that swallowed the light.

DaunyaSai lashed out with a punch across the demon's face just as an octagon traced across the ground and several red runes appeared inside it and started to glow. Akemi knew what that meant, and her heart shuddered in her chest.

* * *

Grala could feel the outrage and agony of the broken drek after he'd dropped him through the portal that would land him in the realm of the Mephisto. He smirked in amusement and even a bit of appreciation that despite his grievous wounds and desperate predicament, the drek still had a few curses and promises of revenge to offer before the portal closed.

That business finished, the demon lord felt the pull of his general. Only a *tether* of Kabriza's power was enough to grant Grala access to the earth plane. The quentranzi lord waited patiently. The portal appeared, and Grala stepped through.

* * *

Brit felt nothing when his limp body tumbled through the portal. Rage consumed him, most of it for the betrayal by Kabriza, the rest for Grala and himself for being caught off his guard. He knew the nature of demons, and had not expected loyalty. But in his arrogance, he had let his guard slip, and the demon had made him pay a heavy price.

His neck broken, he could only lay where he'd landed, eyes moved as he took in the new environment. Everything was red, from the hanging mist in the air, to the walls that seemed to be made of molten rock. Even the stalactites that hung from above looked like the red teeth of a great beast closing down on him.

A slender, robed figure strode through the mist and stopped in front of him. The ends of the black robes lay spread on the ground, concealing the feet of the tall pole-like figure. Suddenly, Brit found he could feel his body again, and he realized that his neck was mended. For a moment he lay unmoving while he decided what to do.

A whispering voice floated on the air. "Why do you remain on the ground, mortal drek?" The sound of it was enough to freeze his spine. "Stand."

Brit climbed to his feet. Though the figure was about his height, its body was no larger around than one of his arms.

A pair of smoldering green eyes bore into him like two slits between sharp mountain peaks that was the collar of its robe.

"You have a quite powerful enemy, mortal drek," the voice sighed through the air.

"Oh?" Brit's mind raced. There was a way out of this. He just needed to find it.

"Few are powerful enough to send you to me." It tilted its head. "And, you have the smell of Grala about you."

"And you are?"

"Your hopelessness personified."

"There is no quarrel between us." In response, Brit felt, more than heard, the quiet laughter.

"Should there be?"

"We could have a mutual interest."

"Truly?"

"Yes. We could share the earth realm, or any realm. There are endless possibilities in the other dimensions. You would never know boredom."

"And I am bored now?"

"Perhaps not. Consider my offer to be that of diversity. Why limit yourself to this realm when you may freely move about the earth dimension?"

There was silence for several moments while the two stared at each other. Finally, the figure spoke again. "Perhaps we may have a mutual interest. What is it you desire?"

Brit didn't hesitate. "The death of Kabriza and Grala. After, we can return to the earth plane. The cloaked figure seemed to think on that. "Your proposal sounds beneficial, but it cannot be done without a price."

"Name it."

"Soul-splitting anguish."
Red flames erupted inside Brit's skin. He screamed.
The Mephisto laughed.

72

The ninja demon hunter had seen enough portals linked to the abyss to know that whatever was coming through this one was more powerful than the demon general.

She sprinted at the demon's back. Impossible as it seemed, Yurin Kei Daunyana was back in the fight and had Kabriza on its heels. She couldn't last, however. Even as she raced toward the two, Akemi saw Yurin beginning to falter. If she could get there in time and take that thing's head off, the portal would fall apart.

She leaped at its back, and was repelled by a blast of energy so dark and evil, she felt as though she had been poisoned from the inside out. She tumbled to the ground, breathless and shaking.

Gradually she regained control over her body enough to stand. Shinobu had tried to attack from behind, and would have succeeded had Kabriza not gained the advantage over Yurin in that moment.

The demon overwhelmed Yurin with black abysmal flames, then hit the airborne strider with a backhanded slap that sent him straight to the ground, unconscious.

Akemi's mind went to Kenjiro, and she wondered where her brother was, and if he still lived. She groaned and lifted herself to her knees. Through the increased durability granted by the Gene of the Daunyans, her strength steadily returned.

Where was Kenjiro. She looked about, forcing herself to ignore the stab of fear in her heart for her brother.

Kabriza spotted her and started in her direction. Akemi rose and tightened her grip on her swords. This one was smart. It understood the weapons she wielded.

The demon general spread its arms in welcome. Akemi started toward the powerful fiend. She had dispatched hundreds of fiends from every hell. She was the demon hunter, and she would fight to her last breath.

With each step she took toward her enemy, Akemi realized she would fight alone. She summed her will and steadied her nerves. She scanned the area for any advantage, anything that could help in this fight.

And then she saw him.

* * *

The demon had done something to him after it had dispatched Kenyatta and his sister. It felt like the residue from its dark energy had wrapped around him like a blanket. It took all of his focus just to push the taint away.

Kenjiro closed his eyes and sank into the void of *mushin*; mind-no-mind. Gradually he pushed the taint back and kept it from destroying him. With a final thrust of his will, he pushed the taint out.

He pressed his hand to his head and gave it a shake, then looked to where his sister and the strider had fallen.

Kabriza and Akemi were stalking toward each other, the demon's arms spread in a mocking welcome, his sister's steps steady, her face determined.

The dead or unconscious bodies of his allies lay sprawled about the field, and he wondered how many of them were left. There was a grunt from not far away, and he saw Shinobu struggling to rise. Good.

Musashi, Kenjiro called from within his mind. *Ryuenjiro, my father. Fight with me.* Silent as death, the samurai sprinted toward the demon's back. Sword in both hands, tip pointed at the ground behind him, the samurai caught up to the fiend just as it and his sister reached each other.

Kenjiro brought his sword up in a diagonal slash, nearly severing one of its legs.

Surprised and wounded, the demon roared a curse and toppled over.

Akemi swept one of her swords at its throat, but amazingly, frustratingly, the fiend still managed to deflect her attack and hit her with a gout of black flames before it fell over.

Kenjiro wanted to go to his sister, but not yet. He needed to finish this. He stabbed the demon in the back and when it fell, he drove his sword into Kabriza's neck. "Return to hell."

"Go, yourself," Kabriza gurgled. Its hand snapped around Kenjiro's body and lit his insides afire. His focus shattered and he released the sword.

Kabriza climbed to its feet and with another strangled curse, ripped the Daunya-blessed blade from its throat. Just touching it burned the demon's hands and it dropped the weapon to clatter on the ground.

The angry demon tossed Kenjiro aside just as angry red flames spouted from the summoning octagon.

Grala ascended.

Kenjiro watched the demon kneel before the lord of the quentranzi and he felt his hope flicker. As big as the demon general was, the winged giant standing over it easily doubled Kabriza's size.

Consciousness threatened to flee him, and Kenjiro fell onto his back and stared up at the sky.

Grala looked over the surrounding lands. The bodies of human and dwarf, amahle and elf, centaur and brunt, lay scattered about the battlefield. The demon lord turned to regard its kneeling general. "Have you brought me here to boast of your prowess, Kabriza? There is nothing left."

"There is plenty left, my lord," Kabriza replied. "A world for you to do with as you please."

"Yes." Grala turned its hateful gaze on the glowing tower. "My rule of this world begins with the destruction of the Tower of Balance. The fool Gods have never been our equals. They cower in Their realm and commission weak mortals to build the symbol of Their fear."

Grala spread an arm to encompass the battlefield. "Not their Masters, their Warriors, or even their Chosen, can stop us. It is time for me to take ownership of this realm and when that is done, the Daunyans Themselves will know the power of Grala."

Tears fell from Akemi's eyes as she looked upon the still form of her brother, lying amid the bushes. She turned her gaze to Kabriza, and its much larger and more powerful master. If she must die, she would die inflicting immeasurable agony on them both.

Slowly, quietly, she got her feet under her. The pain in her shoulder screamed at her but she ignored it.

Not far to the side, Shinobu had finally recovered, though he still looked a bit shaky. They shared a nod and, quick and quiet, the two warriors charged the conversing fiends.

Shinobu went skidding past Grala, scoring six zigzagging slashes with his ethereal sword. The powerful weapon drew black blood and a grunt from the demon lord.

In the same instant, Akemi had scored several deep wounds on Kabriza. She turned to charge again only to see that both quentranzi had already healed. Akemi swore an oath and prepared herself for a fight they could not win.

A distant roar tore across the battlefield. Even the immensely powerful quentranzi couldn't withstand the power of the *spirit shout*. The shockwave rippled through them and brought them to their knees.

Tinnoviel Nai SaunyaLi ran straight for the abysmal monsters. "Haaaaaa-AAAAAAAA!" The ground shook as the Daunya Warrior's *spirit shout* ripped across the ground and collided with the two unholy beasts again, keeping them off balance as he brought his weapon around and dealt a heavy blow to the midsection of the nearer Kabriza.

The blue fire of Boraka engulfed the two demons, and Yurin Kei Daun-yana focused every ounce of her will into holding them.

More blue flames engulfed their enemies. Sweat rolled down the faces of Merk Iamfeld and Paigra Stormshield. Those two had survived after all.

Another gout of brilliant blue fire descended from heavens, the arcing cone of fire streaming from the statuesque Amata Daunyana. The demons were barely visible inside the dome of Daunyanic fire.

The allies backed away from the onslaught as the roar of the blue flames intensified, pushing the demons down into the ground.

Rumbling laughter shook the air, and Grala stood amidst the flames. Despite the channelers straining to their limits, the demon lord seemed unaffected by blue inferno raging around it. Grala tucked its wings in close to its body. Then, with flaring red eyes, thrust its wings out, and the flames broke apart.

The four channelers staggered back, disbelief painted on their features. Kabriza stood once again beside its powerful lord, glaring ravenously at the defenders.

DaunyaSai flew from the trees and crashed into Grala in a shower of bluish yellow light. The Daunya Master whipped a two-handed ball of energy around to smash into Kabriza.

DaunyaSai lowered to the ground, chest heaving from the exertion. Both fiends had been toppled, and for a moment, the onlookers dared to hope they might yet win the day. Their hopes melted away when first Grala, then Kabriza rose again. Though the quentranzi general was visibly weakened, the demon lord never stopped chuckling.

"Valiant effort," Grala said. "So much power from such small creatures. Your Gods should be proud. You have given me no small amount of fun." The demon lord and its general each raised a hand in the direction of the exhausted Daunya Master, and two funnels of evil black fire hurtled toward him.

DaunyaSai was barely able to summon enough strength to form a shield. It held only for a moment before he was blown away into the distance, and out of sight. "Now," Grala continued, "I will send you to your Gods, in bits, then pull you back and send you to the abyss—"

The air in front of the two demons warped, and in the blink of an eye, the Daunya Chosen was standing in front of them. Her long black hair floated in the air, though there was no breeze.

Kabriza looked down on her with a derisive snort. "Another angry human. Would you allow me to deal with this one, master?"

"This one for you, the rest for me," Grala consented.

Kabriza hurled black fire at Taliah. The flames crashed into her, wrapping around her body in a dark embrace of snapping black jaws and rending claws. Abruptly the waves broke apart and Kabriza looked in confusion at the unharmed woman. It hurled another blast that split apart when it reached her.

"Have you grown weak?" Grala teased. The demon lord didn't move, but the pitch-black force of its will crashed into Taliah.

She merely flinched.

"What—" the demon lord started to say, when the space to Taliah's side warped. Kenyatta stepped out of the portal. His locks, once shoulder length, were now twice as long. They floated gently in a breeze that was not there, like writhing snakes eager to strike. A goatee lined his once clean-shaven face.

A faint purple hue tinged his skin, and his eyes, once brown, now glowed with a chilling purple fierceness in his calm face.

Taliah's heart would have leapt in joy at the sight of the brother she'd thought lost to her, but not now. Not with all that had happened and the memory of what that demon general had done to Kita, her love.

"Two humans to fight," Grala said. Black flames formed around its body, and Kabriza followed suit. "Let us do battle, little mortals."

A pale blue-white light formed around Taliah's body, and her brown eyes paled until the light shone through them. The light intensified, matching that of the demons before her. The ground rumbled in protest of the massive amounts of power building between the three combatants. Rocks and chunks of earth broke apart and floated into the air.

Malimokuru crawled to his knees and took in the sight. His eyes widened in disbelief at the display of power. A whimper to his side drew his attention. Nyaka crouched beside him and looked as though she would rather be anywhere but where they were.

"I'm guessing if you're scared, I should be terrified," he said to the goar cat. As if in answer, he felt a wave of fear from her mind. He put a comforting hand on his companion. "There's nothing more we can do here. This is their fight.

73

Kenyatta saw Kabriza gathering its power and sprinted for the fiend. He dealt it a vicious cut that broke through its focus. The demon lashed out, but Kenyatta wasn't there.

With speed enhanced by the Gene of the Daunyans, Kenyatta was already on the move by the time Kabriza had recovered. He slashed the demon across the back, rolled between its legs when it turned, and slashed its back again.

Kabriza screamed in frustration and leapt back while turning to face him. Expecting the move, Kenyatta leapt forward in sync with the beast. He delivered a one-two stab to its abdomen, causing the demon to double over while still midair.

The demon general hit the ground in a heap. Stung and enraged, Kabriza stood and rounded on Kenyatta, who waited just a few feet away, still as a statue and silently staring.

Kenyatta saw confusion in the demon's face. The fiend launched balls of black fire at him and he burst into action, speeding ahead of the projectiles and making a right-hand arc around the demon general. Just as Kabriza had begun to track his movement, Kenyatta stopped and sprang forward.

Once again he caught his enemy off guard. Kenyatta's swords moved so quickly they were nearly invisible, his hands a blur of speed and precision. He cut and stabbed the demon in a dozen places before it realized he was there.

Every time Kabriza struck at him, he dealt a stab or deep gash to the attacking limb. And then he stopped.

Kabriza never took its glowing red orbs off of him as it straightened again. Trails of black blood ceased to flow as the wounds Kenyatta inflicted closed up. It grinned at him, no doubt thinking him overconfident. Kenyatta looked into its hateful eyes and thought of Kita. "I'm going to destroy you."

A small figure descending on it from the edge of its periphery drew Kabriza's attention. When it lifted its head to look to the sky, Kita slammed his rune-emblazoned staff down on Kabriza's head.

The force combined with the release of Daunyanic power drove the fiend down into the ground.

Kabriza's earsplitting screech filled the ruined battlefield. It climbed out of the mini crater and looked down to see one of its arched horns lying at his feet. Kabriza turned its baleful gaze on Kita and charged.

The site of Kita pulled Kenyatta out of his enraged trance. His best friend, his brother, stood on wobbly legs, staff pointed at the charging demon.

Kita raced toward the quentranzi, staff whirling. He spun the weapon and turned with the momentum, smashing the side of Kabriza's leg. It fell sideways, but caught itself with one hand.

Even as the reflexive action placed Kabriza's head closely enough in line with Kita's height, he was already spinning in the opposite direction. Kita swung the staff around and smashed it into Kabriza's head.

The demon fell onto its back and the shards of its remaining, shattered horn, rained down on its face. It tore the ground as it stood again, and hurled a wave of black fire toward Kita.

Kita ran toward his enemy and leaped over the abysmal fire. With all of his remaining strength, he brought his staff down on the demon's head with a crack and an explosion of light and sparks.

For the second time, the quentranzi was slammed into the ground by the force of the staff and its wielder. This time, Kabriza was slow to rise.

Kita took a wobbly step back, then another, and staggered. Kenyatta was there in an instant to brace him. Before he could speak, Kita pushed off of his friend and went at the rising demon, his staff a blur in his hands.

All Kenyatta could do was watch as Kita pummeled the demon in a shower of blue and white sparks. The glowing runes were all he could see of the rapidly spinning staff.

For the first time since it had arrived on the battlefield, Kabriza was hard-pressed to fend off its enemy. Every feeble attempt at a counter missed, and received a barrage of counterattacks before it could begin to react.

Kita smashed the side of its leg when it tried to rise. He whirled his staff around and smashed it in the side of the head and it had to put a clawed hand to the ground to stay upright. Kita spun his staff vertically and blasted the demon under the chin over and over, each impact snapping its head back until it fell back into a sitting position.

He raised his staff over his head, then staggered. He raised it again, but his adrenaline had played itself out. The staff fell from his grasp.

Kenyatta caught and lowered him gently to the ground, keeping an eye on the dazed quentranzi. "Rest, man." Kenyatta said. "You rest and I kill dis ting for you."

Kita looked at his brother with dimming eyes. "Yeah. You go handle it for me, Ken. I would ... say hurry up ... and go help Taliah ... but I know ... she can handle ... herself."

"Don't talk, just rest."

Kita smiled at him. "I think my fighting's done, Ken."

"Yeah man. No more."

"Tell Taliah I love her. And I love you, my brother."

"Quit talking like dat, man!" Kenyatta whispered. Kita's pained smile blurred as tears welled in his eyes. "Quit getting dramatic on me."

"Gotta ... say it now ... or I won't ... get the chance." Kita gasped, then smiled again. "You're ... gonna make ... a great ... uncle. It would've been fun."

A growl rumbled off to the side, and Kenyatta saw the dazed quentranzi give its head a shake.

Not far away, the earth quaked and split apart as the contest of wills between Taliah and Grala continued. The sky had darkened, and it seemed as though the world was hurtling toward its end.

"C'mon bwoy. Ya cyan't leave me like dis. Ya cyan't leave me sister."

"I cyan't make that decision for myself," Kita replied with in his playful imitation. He coughed specks of blood on his chest. His dimming eyes took in the surroundings as though he saw something Kenyatta could not.

"I can feel Them, Ken. I'm starting to see Them too." When he focused back on Kenyatta, he looked content. "Gotta go, my brother. You know what to tell Taliah."

Kenyatta nodded silently. "I love you, Brother."

Kita smiled. "Yeah man." He closed his eyes and one last breath left him.

Time seemed to stop as Kenyatta's childhood friend, the boy he'd grown into a man with, side-by-side, was gone.

He gently lowered Kita to the ground. Tears streamed freely down his cheeks. His shoulders trembled as he fought to control the sobs. The sound of shifting rock behind him drew Kenyatta's attention, and he turned toward the rising demon.

Kita had done tremendous damage to the demon. Kabriza struggled repeatedly to rise, only to stumble back down again. Even its normally healing body struggled to mend its wounds.

Kenyatta took his time, straightening and grabbing his swords. He looked down at his friend once more, then drew a deep breath and blew it out. He turned and faced the now upright Kabriza.

The field quaked and chunks of earth lifted away and split apart. Kenyatta stood amidst a catastrophe that may as well not exist. There was nothing, in that moment, but his enemy. For Kenyatta, only he and Kabriza existed.

"You," he hissed, "are *dead.*"

He saw what looked as close to concern as the demon was capable of as it struggled to remain standing while its wounds mended. "Don't worry," Kenyatta said darkly. "I won't attack until you are totally healed. You will know that you were beaten at your full strength. From behind, he heard Seung's pained voice.

"Don't let it heal, Kenyatta! Kill it now!" He ignored her. Ignored the protests of the others who had been severely injured by the demon general.

"Your weapons are not capable of destroying me in this world, little mortal," Kabriza said, standing tall once again. "You would have to follow me back to my world and defeat me there."

Kenyatta narrowed his eyes. "So I shall."

The demon laughed, then a portal ripped the air in front of it. It stepped through, and an instant later, it stepped out of another rip behind Kenyatta.

One moment Kenyatta was facing the space Kabriza had just occupied, the next, he spun and delivered a downward chop with his left-hand sword.

He'd burst into action so abruptly and so quickly that Kabriza hadn't the time to react. It had been thrusting its taloned claws for Kenyatta's back, but instead, lost it to a Daunya-blessed blade.

The severed claw hit the ground with a thud, and oh how the demon general howled.

Kenyatta's mind crossed into the void of *mushin.* His mind receded, his thoughts disappearing in the stasis of mind-no-mind.

Kabriza hurled a ball of demonic black fire at him. Kenyatta dove under the projectiles and sprang forward. He dealt the fiend a deep slash across its chest, then followed up with three stabs to the same wound.

The quentranzi's pained retort was like metal grinding on metal. Before it could fight back, however, Kenyatta retreated. Once again he stood before the demon, his baleful gaze boring into the evil red orbs of his abysmal enemy.

For a moment, they stared at each other, still and silent as the world came apart around them. Kabriza took a step forward and was met with seven stabs to the midsection and a spinning sideways slice to the side of its leg.

It happened so fast that the fiend hadn't even registered the movement. It happened again and again. The human might have been a statue until Kabriza made the slightest move.

Frustration overtook the fiend, and Kabriza raked its claws through the ground, sending chucks of earth flying at the immobile warrior.

Kenyatta dodged through the assault as if it happened in slow motion. Over, around, and under the debris, he made his way toward the waiting demon. Kabriza's maw widened in anticipation.

He leapt straight for the demon, and Kabriza snatched him out of the air. Its satisfaction lasted till the moment Kenyatta brought both his swords down in a crisscross, slicing off its remaining hand. Kabriza's responding shriek lasted only until Kenyatta leapt straight up cut it across the throat.

Staggering away from the lethal human while black blood flowed from its opened throat, Kabriza stole a quick, final glance at its master, then opened a portal back to the demon realm and fell through it.

Kenyatta saw the demon's relief evaporate the moment it spotted him flying through the portal after it. He drove one of his swords into its midsection, then the other.

The quentranzi general lost focus, and instead of appearing back in the fifth hell, they entered the first hell in a free fall. Kabriza went into a rage and slapped Kenyatta aside.

Kenyatta shrugged the pain away. Before he flew out of reach, he snapped his swords together as one, drove the blade into the demon's shoulder, and drew himself back in.

Having entered its home world, the quentranzi had fully healed, even growing back its hands and horns.

Kenyatta grabbed one of those upward arching horns, sliced it off again, and drove the tip through the demon's throat. Kabriza coughed and spat blood, then grabbed Kenyatta in one massive hand and squeezed.

Turning end over end in a dizzying spin, the combatants plummeted through the dark abysmal sky. They hit the ground of the first hell and broke through it as though busting through a wall of glass.

Kabriza crashed into a flock of bachatttas passing underneath. The winged minor demons squealed as some of their number were reduced to a spray of black blood and scattered wings.

Kenyatta stabbed the squeezing hand and Kabriza barked a curse and released him. He grabbed hold of a finger half the length of his body, and held on as the world spun around him.

It reached for him with its other hand, and at the last instant Kenyatta whipped his sword out in an arc, severing several fingers.

Kenyatta pulled himself in and over Kabriza's wrist, careful of the many sharp spikes that covered its body. He gritted his teeth to keep from growing dizzy as they turned and spun toward the ground.

As with the first hell, they burst through the ground of the second. Kenyatta held on as the demon fell end over end in an uncontrolled free fall. Whenever the quentranzi drew its hand in too close to its body, Kenyatta took the opportunity to take a slash at the nearest body part. The confused demon seemed not to know what part of its body the human was attached to.

Through the third and fourth hell they passed, fighting, spinning, and falling. Finally, the entered the fifth hell; the realm of the quentranzi.

Here, Kabriza was at its strongest. Fiery wings stabbed out of its back and stretched wide. The quentranzi general began to glide downward, and Kenyatta could feel its power growing. Still, the demon hadn't seemed to realize that he was holding on to one of the spikes on its arm. Once they were a safe distance from the ground, Kenyatta snarled and curled his body, wrapping his legs around the monster's wrist. He drew his sword back and brought it down, burying it just below the hand.

Kabriza shrieked and drew its hand in, but not before Kenyatta had taken a second swing, and lopped its hand off, again. The human and its lost appendage fell away, and Kabriza tucked its wings back and plummeted. The ground shattered beneath its feet, and the demon straightened and turned toward the recovering human.

"In my world, you are mine!"

"Den come war wit me! Come die wit me!"

The quentranzi general and the human warrior charged each other and met in a blinding clash of claws and swords, Daunyanic, and demonic power. Many brutal moments passed until they finally parted.

Kenyatta hunched forward, his shoulders heaving.

Kabriza similarly panted, staring in disbelief at the impossibly powerful human. It would have been plausible, had this had been a Daunya Chosen, or at least a Daunya Master. But a simple warrior, touched by the Daunyans should not be this powerful.

Kabriza's body burst into red fire. A sword of flame grew into its hand, and fire erupted from its grinning maw.

They combatants charged each other and met in a clash of demonic fire and Daunyanic steel.

Kenyatta avoided a swipe that would have cleaved his body in two, and countered with a diagonal slashed that missed when the demon lifted its foot and kicked Kenyatta away.

Dazed and tumbling, Kenyatta rolled back to his feet and shrugged off the pain in his smoldering body. He watched the approaching monster and tightened his grip on his swords.

They clashed again. Kenyatta beat the demon back, each stroke falling faster and harder. As the quentranzi general gave ground, Kenyatta stepped closer, always finding an opening, always scoring multiple hits in less than the span of a heartbeat.

With a great flap of its fiery, leathery wings, the demon leapt backward and landed out of reach. Kenyatta leapt after it. Shoulder leading, he glided right into the demon's chest with enough force to knock it to the ground.

He quickly moved away before he caught fire from its flaring body, then moved in again with a series of stabs before retreating once again.

Kabriza had barely found its feet when Kenyatta was there. Two opposing swipes of his swords sent part of the demon's leg falling away. It slapped its hand down to keep from falling, but the blur of Kenyatta's whirling swords took its arm.

The demon roared in anguish and the fires on its body winked out.

As soon as the flames disappeared, Kenyatta leapt on top of it. In less than the time it took Kabriza to thrash about, Kenyatta had cut its chest into a mass of crisscrossing gashes as deep as his arm.

His instincts screamed at him, and he knelt and whipped his sword in upward. Kabriza had been reaching for him with its remaining hand, and now it recoiled, black blood gushing from the wound.

Kenyatta completed the turn of his body while simultaneously reversing his grip on the sword. He drove the blade into its chest. The quentranzi's agonized cry rippled across the abyss. Flocks of bachatttas took wing, and even a nearby pair of the fearless Zzrt loped away.

Leaving his sword imbedded in the demon's chest, Kenyatta hopped to the ground and chopped his other sword down on its neck. His sword rose and fell, over and over, sprays of black blood spattering him.

When the demon stopped moving, Kenyatta hopped back on its chest, pulled his sword free, and leaped into the air. As his body turned, Kenyatta locked his two swords together as one. As he descended, he brought the weapon down for a final stroke, severing the head of Kabriza, the second most powerful demon of the abyss.

For a moment, there was silence. For the first time, Kenyatta was aware of other demons watching from the shadows. None made a move to challenge him, but only stared at the sight of the battered carcass of the quentranzi general. Tiny flecks of skin and scales began to crumble fall away from the body, then an explosion of dark light burst free and spiraled into the red tinted sky. The ground trembled and violent winds carried the evil onlookers away.

Kenyatta stood in the middle of the tempest, his long locks whipping about his head. He had entered the demon realm, knowing there was no way out. It mattered not. He had avenged his brother, and the second most powerful demon in the abyss was dead. Truly dead, for the death of a demon in its own realm meant true oblivion for the fiend.

He thought of Taliah, battling the lord of the quentranzi. She was a Daunya Chosen, and though Kenyatta feared for her survival because she was his little sister, he knew she alone could challenge the fiend and win. Perhaps after she dealt with the demon lord, Taliah would come for him.

Whether she did or not, the anger and hurt that he felt had so consumed him that he could spend his eternity here dispatching every fiend that caught his eye. The spiraling cone of evil energy expanded toward him, and he waited in stoic resolve. *So be it.*

"No, Child of the Gene," a voice spoke into his mind. A presence, like light and love made manifest, filled him. Kenyatta gritted his teeth, for it was almost overwhelming. He dropped to his knees, his sword clanging to the ground beside him. The presence was so powerful, so massive and limitless, that he felt insignificant before it. The voice spoke into his mind again, a mountain, no, the world itself, speaking to a creature smaller than an ant.

"Do not allow pain of loss to fill you with hate. Hate is the province of the abyss, child. We have created you for something greater. Do not choose hate."

Kenyatta's mind went to Kita, and the presence immediately wrapped around him like a blanket and filled him till he could bear it no longer.

Another voice came into his mind. *"You have fought for my creation, child. You have lived and died for it. You have endured enough to fill many lifetimes."*

"Then let it end here," Kenyatta said aloud. He could feel the presence disagree.

"You will return to your world and finish your life. There are some who

depend on you to return. Would you inflict the pain of loss on them, as you have experienced?"

His mind went to Seung and Taliah, and he knew the words to be true. He sensed approval, then two figures appeared in the swirling black tempest. One was a large, dark figure. Its presence was at the same time ominous and comforting. The second figure was the size of a human. Kenyatta moved closer, but they remained out of his reach, though they didn't move.

You will find Balance before your earth life is done, Child of the Gene. You will find Me, *before the end.* The black tempest broke apart, and glowing golden white light replaced it. Kenyatta continued to move toward the two figures, but they remained out of his reach. Another voice entered his mind.

Go home and live, Brother. Tell Taliah of my love and that I will never be far away. Take my staff to her. He will need it."

He? Kenyatta thought. "Kita? Kita! Kita, wait!" He moved faster. "I just want ... I need to talk ..." He took another step and stumbled on suddenly shaking ground.

Kenyatta looked around in bewilderment.

He was back in the earth realm.

74

The surrounding lands shuddered under the force of the contest of wills between Taliah, the Daunya Chosen, and quentranzi lord, Grala. The huge, winged fiend's eyes blazed as black demonic flames swirled around its body.

Despite facing a beast ten times her size, Taliah's presence was far larger. She stood filled with the power of The Seven. She lifted her glowing white eyes to the heavens, and when she spoke, her voice projected the seven Gods in unison.

"You have moved outside your province, lord of demons. You have distorted the balance of the worlds upon which your existence depends."

Black flames streamed away from the quentranzi's body to envelope Taliah. The waves broke apart before they touched her.

Grala drew in more power, sucking the black flames inside its body until its glow radiated with abysmal energy. The demon lord raised its hands, and a lance appeared in its grasp. Grala thrust the lance toward her.

Taliah caught the weapon and held it fast. The talons on Grala's feet dug into the ground as it struggled against the diminutive woman, the disbelief clear on its face.

She snapped off the tip of the lance and it crumbled in her hands. Grala threw its head back and bellowed at the heavens, then brandished a whip of black fire. The quentranzi lord drew back and snapped the whip at her.

The glowing white eyes in her expressionless face flared and then she was gone. The whip blasted the ground apart where she'd once stood. An instant later, Grala was looking into the glowing eyes of the woman now hovering in front of its face. It opened its mouth and a green ball of dark energy exploded from its throat. It collided with an invisible barrier in front of Taliah and fell apart.

With a great beat of its wings, Grala leaped away and brought its hands together, sending forth a spiraling cone of black and green fire at the Daunya Chosen. The fiery assault smashed into her, wrapping around her body and passed beyond.

Scattered about the scarred battlegrounds, the surviving defenders watched in fear and amazement at the titanic confrontation that each knew was so far beyond them. Taliah would defeat the demon lord, or the world would perish under the weight of that terrible power.

Grala roared and it seemed the world shuddered under the weight of terrible power it drew in. The ground ripped apart around the demon lord, and the sky darkened as pitch black clouds blanketed the sky. Black lightning bolts flicked out of the clouds like the forked tongue of a serpent.

Hundreds of the bolts struck the Chosen while the onlookers watched in helplessness, barely able to keep from being carried away in the violent storm.

"She cyan't survive dat!" Malimokuru shouted over the cacophony.

"She is a Chosen!" was all Tinnoviel said in response.

"You have broken the laws of balance and challenged the will of the Daunyans." Though it was Taliah's mouth that moved, it was the voices of The Seven that spoke.

"Born of the evil in the earth realm, evolved in the darkness of the abysmal realm, the hells are your domain. The higher realms are not for you to taint. The higher realms are not for you to subjugate. You have moved outside the province of your existence, lord of demons. And here, in the realm where you cannot exist, you will meet The Daunyans."

Abruptly, the demonic fires winked out. Taliah hovered untouched before the giant demon lord. She raised a hand and flipped it around, palm to the sky. Light flared from the woman's hand and washed over Grala. Like a weight many times its own the light pressed the demon general to the ground until it was kneeling.

Taliah looked down at the beast, expressionless as she spread her arms. Golden white light dissolved the black clouds and washed over the land.

Grala's eyes smoldered in hatred. Its hands sparked and two black disks appeared in them. From its kneeling position, Grala hurled the disks at the Daunya Chosen.

The disks stopped in front of the floating figure and some of the soft yellow light surrounding Taliah's body enveloped them. The now yellow disks flew back at Grala and embedded themselves in its chest. The demon lord's mouth fell agape in a silent scream of agony, then the yellow light poured into its mouth.

The agony of being flooded with the cleansing Daunyanic power overwhelmed the demon's sensibilities. Indeed, Grala was being burned from the inside out. From above, Taliah, the Daunyans, spoke again.

"I am Boraka." The transparent form of a dwarf, easily twice as large as Takashaniel, descended from the sky as he drew his axe. With a mighty swipe, his axe chopped down and passed through the demon lord as he disappeared. Grala's eyes widened, and his body convulsed.

"I am Oberon." An equally large, dark cloaked figure descended. His fingers curled and his hand shot forward and passed through the demon's chest. Grala gurgled, its body shaking uncontrollably. The Daunyan faded away.

"I am Nakiya." A figure—this one resembling a young female elf—descended and blew a kiss from her hand. A spear of crackling light shot through Grala's forehead and his head snapped back. The goddess's eyes narrowed above a slanted smile, and her appearance shattered in a shower of tiny glowing shards of light.

"I am Se'lir." A transparent female resembling an elf descended, chopping her hand through the demon's body before fading away.

"I am Quel'yar." A male elf-like figure descended and drove a weapon resembling that of Tinnoviel's in a downward chop through the fiend from the head down.

"I am Omalah." A male figure resembling an amahle appeared and drove a glowing spear of light through Grala's neck. The demon lord's eyes twitched as it stood paralyzed, back arched, mouth hanging open in silent anguish.

"I ... am Amayilah. Know the Daunyans." A final figure descended, this one resembling an amahle female. As she glided down to the demon lord, she swiped a cupped hand upward through the convulsing demon, and a trail of blinding light passed through it.

Taliah disappeared, then reappeared right in front of the agonized demon's face. *"You have met with Destruction, Balance, Redemption, Mystic, Love, Spirit, and Redemption."* She still spoke with words of The Seven joined as one inside of her.

The light enveloping Taliah's body intensified. *"Know oblivion."* She lifted her hand in front of Grala's face, and the light of The Destroyer surrounded her body and flowed to that hand. The light blasted into the lord of the quentranzi, widening until it fully enveloped its body.

Grala bared his fangs in denial as flecks of its blue-gray skin drifted from its body and dissolved. The blast intensified and in that moment, the lord of the quentranzi, the most powerful demon of the abyss, was obliterated in the light of the Daunyans.

Taliah descended back to the earth, swayed on her feet, then fell over.

Moments later, the others where around her.

"That was a mighty display there, lass," Paigra said, shaking his head. "Never would'a believed it if I ain't seen it with me own crusted eyes."

"We need to get her to the tower." Mira said, walking over. "Her strength will be restored more quickly, there."

Tinnoviel looked up at her. "The guardian?"

Mira closed her red-rimmed eyes and shook her head.

The Daunya Warrior sighed, rising. "This battle has been won at great cost."

A short distance away, Seung sat on the ground, weeping silently. Tikena limped over and draped a tiny arm over her shoulder. "Come. Let's get to the tower."

Seung looked up into her solemn face. It was the kindest she'd ever heard the little elf speak. "I'm fine," she lied.

Tikena rolled her eyes. "What do I care about that? I need help walking!"

Seung forced a smile in response to the kind attempt at humor, but she felt dead inside. Kenyatta, her love, was gone.

She stood and hoisted the little elf up on her back, slipping her hands under Tikena's knees after the elf girl wrapped her arms around Seung's neck.

"It hurts my tongue to say it, but he was a good warrior, for a human. He also must have been a good man, the way you lit up when he was around. It was nauseating."

"You're not helping," Seung said, trying to keep her voice from breaking.

"Sorry. You … chose well, Kiluriel. A good man and a good warrior."

"And also over there." Yurin pointed into the distance where a lone, ragged figure stood. Seung's eyes widened and she nearly dropped Tikena.

"Hey now! I take everything back!"

Seung gently lowered the grumbling Tikena, never taking her eyes off of him. His arms hung limp from the weight of the swords clasped in his hands.

"I'll be back, little sprite," she said absently, rising.

"Come, little one," Shinobu said, lifting the thunderstruck elf in his arms. "I've got enough strength to carry you."

"No, I'm fine," Tikena protested, holding her nose. "Stink! Human *stink!*" To the shock of all, however, she stopped protesting and finally allowed the strider to carry her.

Malimokuru helped Immendiel to her feet, and Amata, Ayanda, and Naiyala carried wounded dwarves over their shoulders.

Seung's steps came faster and faster until she was running. Tears flowed freely from her eyes as she neared Kenyatta. She skidded to a stop a few feet away.

He still hadn't seen her, but stared at the ground a few paces in front of his feet. A goatee that hadn't been there before was on his face, and his locks, once shoulder length, were now midway down his back.

Confused, Seung reached out a tentative hand, then drew back. She waited until he finally looked up into her eyes. The sorrow she saw in his eyes was so potent she felt it, herself. She wrapped him in a tight embrace.

His arms still hung limp, and his shoulders began to tremble as the sobs came.

Seung felt the thud of his swords hitting the ground a moment before his arms wrapped around her.

Seung buried her face into his chest. "I love you," she said, her voice muffled.

A few moments of silence followed, then she felt his hand stroke her disheveled, hair. He hugged her tighter and kissed the top of her head.

"Love you too."

Naiyala stood between Amata and Ayanda, her arms interlocked with her two remaining companions as they solemnly watched the ceremony. With them stood the surviving dwarves, brunts, centaurs, elves, and humans. All of the bodies of the fallen had been placed upon a large floating disc.

As the new Guardian of Takashaniel, Mira stood resplendent in the color-shifting robes of her station. She spoke words of honor and gratitude for the sacrifices of the survivors, and especially those who had given their lives.

As the ceremony drew to conclusion, Mira spoke the names of each of them. With each pronouncement, the body of the fallen warrior levitated from the disc and was enveloped in bright white light. The body disappeared and a beautiful mural appeared on the wall of the circular room depicting the warrior in glory.

With each name, Grimhammer and his clan stamped the butts of their weapons on the floor. The brunts pounded their fists to their chests in their fashion, while the dwarves wept openly.

Kenyatta held Taliah close, remaining strong for his grieving sister. On her other side, Seung held her hand. Kenyatta was barely able to watch as the body of the man he had been raised with as a brother was lifted into the air and disappeared into the light. The mural that honored him was nothing short of magnificent, and Taliah's sobs infected him and Seung.

Kenyatta forced himself to remember the words Kita told him, that he had shared with Taliah. "I will always be near." One day those words might be comforting, but not now.

Next and finally was Sakhile. The amahle said quiet prayers for the fallen tracker and wept silently.

Kenjiro, Akemi, and Shinobu watched in respectful silence. "They are with their ancestors now," the samurai said.

The ceremony had ended and all had begun to exit.

"A place we all must go," Akemi added.

"Not before we have lived our lives fully," Shinobu replied, and he found Akemi's hand and squeezed it. Kenjiro placed a hand on both their shoulders and gave them a squeeze. He turned and limped away.

Seeing the two still remaining, Mira came to join them. For a while she stood beside the couple, staring up at the depiction of her mentor and friend, Iel. "The Daunyans use Their servants hard," she said. "Still ..." She was quiet for a moment. "What is death to us is a rebirth to bliss for the fallen. The ultimate reward."

"Yet we who remain mourn them," Akemi said. "We grieve and live with the hole in our hearts for those who have gone to be with the Gods, who work us so mercilessly."

"Pain of loss is why we mourn," Mira replied. "It is not for the fallen that we cry, but our loss of them. Death is a harsh word to describe ascendance through the veil that lies between this world and our true Home."

Akemi stiffened. She thought of how she'd nearly lost her brother in that battle. Just the thought of it nearly broke her. She couldn't imagine the pain Kenyatta felt at losing Kita, who was in every way but birth, his brother. "I have fought the darkness for so many years, yet my life will one day end with more evil and toil and suffering in my wake while I return ... Home."

"You have battled darkness too long, demon hunter," Mira said. "One can only endure what you have for so long before the weight becomes unbearable."

"Yet bear it I must, and bear it I will." Akemi clenched her jaw, the grief held fast between her teeth. "For every demon I send back to the abyss, another finds its way to this world. What do I have to show for my life?"

Mira rested a hand on her shoulder. "If your life could be relived, would you walk a different path?"

Tears welled in Mira's eyes and overflowed, streaming down her upraised face. "When the pain is not so near, meditate and speak to the Daunyans. I promise you, they listen." She took a deep breath. "If you will excuse me, friends, I must be alone for a while." She bowed, offered a sad smile, and left.

"Death is a part of what we do," Shinobu said. "But for some reason, this has a deeper bite."

"Maybe because they've sacrificed for a world that may never know who they were and what they sacrificed for," Akemi replied.

"I don't care what the world knows," Shinobu said, drawing a surprised look from Akemi. "I think it's because they may never have fallen to a human enemy, but they fell to creatures that never should have entered this world in the first place."

Akemi couldn't disagree. "Yet it happens more often than you know, my love."

"Then what of this "mighty" tower we've given so much to protect? If it's supposed to maintain balance, why are demons even able to walk this world?"

"The evil inherent in those who live here," Akemi answered. "Remember what Iel said. Demons are the creations of the evil in this world. It was the Daunyans that guided enlightened hands to create Takashaniel to seal them away from us. But the evil of the abyss has its origins in this world, and so some of that evil can slip through. It is because of the Tower of Balance, that we are not overrun."

"Until someone powerful enough brings such a scenario about."

"The hands that crafted the tower are fallible."

"Then why not create it Themselves?"

Akemi could hear the barely contained anger in the strider's voice. She couldn't blame him. "That is not Their way. We have been given the freedom to manifest our will while upon this world. It is through us, that great deeds of good or evil happen."

"Then one day, perhaps, humans will evolve and the fight will end."

Akemi almost smirked at Shinobu's own disbelieving tone as he uttered those words. "That is … unlikely."

"There is always hope."

Akemi gave him a dubious look. "You've more optimism than I. The world has been nearly broken more than once."

"And yet here we stand in a world unbroken because of ours and their efforts." He indicated the murals.

"In vain?" the ninja asked.

"Perhaps, perhaps not."

"The Gods are cruel."

Shinobu half smiled, and there was an uncharacteristic sadness in his eyes. "Only by granting us choice."

S everal weeks passed before the defenders of Takashaniel began to take their leave. All had declined Taliah's offer of transport back to their homes, partly out of not wanting to cause her any more exertion, and partly not wanting to chance the lower realms again. Though the Chosen had insisted that with balance restored, she could skim the lower planes again with far less risk, all had insisted on making their own way home.

"Beggin' yer pardon, Chosen," Felk had said with a deep bow. "Me lads'r need'n a good travel to clear their heads and lift their spirits. I'm thinkin' a trip across these lands we ain't traveled so long might be a good idea. Might be time to think about comin' outta that mountain sometimes."

Taliah smiled as the gruff dwarf kissed her hand. "Tell King Shatter-hammer that I will pay him a visit in the near future."

"Ye got me word," Felk said.

"You're to get more visitors sooner than that, errr dwarf cousin," Grit said, crossing his arms over his barrel chest. Felk looked down at the shorter brunt, an older brother resisting the urge to muss his younger sibling's hair.

"Sure, Grit. Been too long since we seen the likes o' the brunts in our halls. Ye got only to come knockin' and the dwarves of Shatterhammer'r greetin' ye." They clasped forearms.

"It is time also for us to leave." Naiyala declared a short while later. "In place of the king and queen of my people, I name you friends of the desert amahle. May you always have love and abundance." Unsurprisingly, Malimokuru opted to accompany the tall folk back to their desert home.

"I've had enough fighting to last this lifetime and another," the nature reader said. "That is, should I be so foolish to come back for another round of livin'." Beside him, Nyaka rumbled contentedly in her chest.

"What will you do, Kiluriel?" Tinnoviel asked Seung as the elves prepared for their departure. "You have chosen a life with the human." He nodded his chin in the direction of Kenyatta, who was speaking with Taliah out of earshot.

"I don't know," she answered. "I must visit my village for a while, but I will not remain. Things inside of me have awoken that cannot tolerate the world of humans as I have before." She looked over her shoulder at her approaching love. "Yet can I return to Yathienel with a human companion? And," her heart shuddered at what came next. "Even if he is welcomed, or rather, tolerated, would he be willing to live there?"

Beside Tinnoviel, the battered DaunyaSai smiled. "I believe he would have a place among us. And as to his willingness," he winked at her. "I've seen his heart. He went to hell and came back, for his sister, but also for you. I know this. I've known the loss and hopelessness that he's felt, but his heart is with you, and by extension, Yathienel."

Tikena wrinkled her nose. "Just make him bathe first. Oh, that human stink!"

They shared a much-needed chuckle as Kenyatta reached them. "Why do I have a feelin' you all talkin' 'bout me?" Though he spoke in jest, his tone was flat and tired.

"We were just saying our goodbyes, my love."

"Yes, *my love*," Tikena mocked. "We must say goodbye."

"Goodbye, little friend," Kenyatta said, leaning down and kissing her on the cheek.

Tikena pressed her lips together, enduring the kiss. Then abruptly spun and started walking away. After a few steps she stopped and looked over her shoulder. The insinuation of a smile touched her face, and in a flash it was gone. "Take a bath!"

"Feisty little thing," Kenyatta said.

"You've no idea," Tinnoviel replied wearily. He clasped Kenyatta's forearm in a firm grip.

DaunyaSai placed a hand on Kenyatta's shoulder. "I speak for Seiyun, Queen of Yathienel. You and your brother are friends of the Elfinestraya of The Wood. May the stars bathe you in their glorious light." And with that, the elves took their leave.

"I still can't believe they're real," Akemi said as she, Shinobu, and Kenjiro came to stand beside Seung and Kenyatta.

"Which ones?" Kenjiro asked.

"All of them."

"The time to remember will come one day," Seung said, staring after her departing friends.

"Maybe soon," Shinobu said.

Seung looked doubtful. "Not for a while still, I think."

"And now we must go, friends," Kenjiro said. In the short time of their stay, Mira had been able to restore his leg to basic functionality, but his fighting days were over, she had told him. After he'd thought on it, he'd told Akemi that it was as it was supposed to be, and perhaps it was time to enjoy life. Akemi wondered what kind of uncle her brother would make.

"Will we ever see each other again?" Seung asked, hugging the three warriors from Japan.

"If fate allows," Akemi replied. "It would be a good thing."

Shi Xing Long bowed and spoke in his native tongue. "It has been an honor to fight beside such great warriors," Shinobu translated. "Know that you all have a place of honor not only among the Order of Shaolin, but also in the history of Ba Guo. Emperor Liu Xiang will have the events we relate to him recorded. Wuhan will know your stories. When the time is right, all of Ba Guo will know your stories."

The other surviving monk, Shi Xiao Ren looked at Kenyatta and spoke. Shinobu listened, then translated.

"Our friend here has a question that I must admit has been on my mind as well. What happened to you?" The strider indicated Kenyatta's goatee and longer locks.

"Time passes differently in the abyss, is the only explanation I can really give you." Kenyatta rubbed a hand over his mouth. "I spent a year trying not to get killed till I finally found my way back."

Amazed and horrified, the strider translated. All eyes fell on Kenyatta with amazement. "How did you endure such a place for so long?" Shinobu asked. "It seems impossible."

"The thought of killing Kabriza," Kenyatta said, and a shadow passed over his face before he brightened again, if barely. "It's done now, and I'm not ashamed to admit I don't ever want to see the likes of that place again."

"I hope that in time you will cleanse the darkness inside, my friend," Shinobu said.

"So, what now?" Kenyatta asked as they watched their companions depart.

Seung wrapped her arm around Kenyatta's waist and leaned against him. She closed her eyes and enjoyed the feeling of his strong, yet gentle arm draped around her. "Home?"

"It lies underwater," Kenyatta replied.

Hearing the thinly veiled grief in his voice broke Seung's heart. How would she have handled losing her homeland? How would she have handled losing Kim?

"You have more than one home," she said. "I must introduce you to my family in Kyu, then my family in The Wood."

"I don't think the latter is much interested in meeting me."

"I think they may surprise you. I think they may surprise themselves." She looked up at him. "But where to first?"

"Kita's family," Taliah said, joining them. "*Our* family. They deserve to know the truth of who he was and who we all are."

Seung could barely meet Taliah's brown eyes, so sad were they.

Taliah smiled at her. "And as Kenyatta and Kita are brothers, I think it's time for them to meet their new daughter-in-law, little sister."

Seung returned her smile, and Taliah laughed when the other woman wrapped her in a crushing hug. "I've always wished I had a sister."

"Well," Seung replied. "Someone has to work out his bad habits." She jabbed a thumb at Kenyatta, who recoiled as if struck.

"Now wait a minute—"

"Hush, Ken," Taliah said, steering Seung away. "Go for a walk or something. I need to talk with my new sister."

Kenyatta threw up his hands. "It's already started."

* * *

"Now *that* ... was unexpected." Zshegaza chuckled. "Of course, Brit was a fool for thinking he had as tight a leash on the quentranzi as he did. Still, what an amazing outcome!"

Zreal found the zitarian's excitement disconcerting. "What now?"

Zshegaza spread her hand out to indicate the surrounding lands. "It's a big world, Zreal. So much to do. So much Fun!"

"You'll get us killed."

She shook her head. "I'm not like your former master."

"*My* former master?"

"I merely worked for him till it was no longer convenient."

Zreal refrained from rolling his eyes.

"Come." Zshegaza turned her back on the distant tower.

Zreal didn't move. "Come where?"

She beckoned over her shoulder. "We're free to explore as we will. I would see as much of this world as we can!"

"Are we vagabonds, then?"

Zshegaza laughed. "We've been vagabonds for nearly four years, Zreal. But there is an uninhabited fortress sitting in a land that is no doubt already healing itself now that the leeching drek is gone."

That lifted Zreal's spirits a bit. "I like the idea of that fortress without him in it. I've never known comfort in that place."

Zshegaza grinned. "As I've told you. I think of everything. Trust me."

Zreal followed behind her, staring at the zitarian's winged back. If there was one thing he would never do, it was trust Zshegaza.

* * *

Darius watched from a distant mountain as one by one, the various groups of Takashaniel's defenders departed for their respective homes. In all his centuries of life, he had never known such adventure. Though it was difficult to feel the same sense of sadness and pain that the others felt at the loss of their comrades, he still was able to sympathize to a degree.

He blew a puff of crisp spring air that puffed in front of his face. "Where to now?" he asked himself. So many years he had lived either in solitude or occasionally among humans in one civilization or another. After knowing friendship for the first time in more years than he could remember, the drojan didn't want to return to a life of isolation. Not yet, anyway.

He thought of the elves and laughed at the absurdity of the notion. His mind went to the human nature reader and the amahle. Perhaps he would pay them a visit? As much as Darius tried to deny it to himself, he enjoyed the friendship of that human and the tall folk. He smiled and turned in the direction the nature reader and the amahle had gone.

So ends the Legend of Takashaniel

ACKNOWLEDGMENTS

A very special thank you to Cat Lee for helping with proofreading. I can't say enough how much I appreciate the work you do. A hundred times, thank you.

And a huge thank you to Flora Samuelson. You've been there with me since day one, and I cherish our friendship and your helping me to make Heroes of a Broken Age the best it can be.